ALL MY WORLDLY GOODS

She looked through the albums several times, the snatch of conversation overheard at the buffet table at Winterbrook echoing in her mind. *Like so many old English families, his has been crippled by taxes. There's a house falling into ruins, and the title.* She also remembered North referring to 'my crumbling old house' and his obligation to have a son to inherit the title, if little else.

As she pored over the pictures of Longwarden in the days when its owner had been a rich man, it seemed to Jane that, at one stroke, life had presented her with a compellingly attractive man, a project deserving of her immense financial resources and an escape from another two years of her aunt's supervision.

When she left the library she was in the grip of an idea which she knew most people would think crazy but which she felt made excellent sense. When they met in New York, she would ask North to marry her.

Anne Weale was a journalist before she became a novelist. In her twenties she was a staff reporter on the *Eastern Evening News*, *Western Daily Press* and *Yorkshire Evening Press*. For the past ten years she has lived in Spain, latterly in a cottage in Catalonia. High summer is spent in the Channel Islands, and every year she spends six weeks travelling outside Europe.

Her interests include antique furniture, Georgian architecture, interior decoration, food, English and foreign gardens, eventing and canvas embroidery. She is a member of the British Horse Society and the Royal Horticultural Society.

D1416525

ALL MY WORLDLY GOODS

Anne Weale

ARROW BOOKS

Arrow Books Limited
62–65 Chandos Place, London WC2N 4NW

An imprint of Century Hutchinson Limited

London   Melbourne   Sydney   Auckland
Johannesburg and agencies throughout
the world

First published in Great Britain by Century 1987
Arrow edition 1988

© Anne Weale 1987

Typeset by Rowland Phototypesetting Limited
Bury St Edmunds, Suffolk
Printed and bound in Great Britain by
Anchor Brendon Limited, Tiptree, Essex

ISBN 0 09 954630 2

This novel, written for women, owes
a great deal to three men:

To 'Chinese' Wilson whose book *A Naturalist in Western
China with Vasculum, Camera and Gun* introduced me to
an heroic breed, the plant hunters.

To another adventurer, my son, who at the age of
eighteen enlisted in the Spanish Foreign Legion.

And, above all, to his father who began his adventures
even younger, taking a schoolgirl's heart with him.

To Malcolm and David
with much love

This novel, written for women, owes
a great deal to three men:

To 'Chinese' Wilson whose book *A Naturalist in Western China with Vasculum, Camera and Gun* introduced me to an heroic breed, the plant hunters.

To another adventurer, my son, who at the age of eighteen enlisted in the Spanish Foreign Legion.

And, above all, to his father who began his adventures even younger, taking a schoolgirl's heart with him.

To Malcolm and David
with much love

PROLOGUE

A spring wedding in the private chapel of an historic English house.

An aroma of flowers . . . cedar panelling . . . French scent . . . mothballs. The last emanating from the Sunday-best suits of two old countrymen, seated in the front row of chairs, whose ruddy complexions indicated a lifetime out of doors in all weathers.

Dearly beloved, we are gathered together here in the sight of God, and in the face of this Congregation, to join together this man and this woman in holy Matrimony; which is an honourable estate, instituted of God in the time of man's innocency . . .

Beside the tall man on whose arm the bride had entered the chapel stood the youngest of the married women present. It was barely six months since her own wedding, but her mind was not, as it had been on that earlier day, fraught with apprehension and doubt.

Her imagination was winging into the future, looking ahead to a time in the twenty-first century when the embryo in her womb might be married here or, more likely, in the village church. The chapel, although spacious enough to accommodate a large staff of servants for morning prayers in days gone by, was not really suitable for a wedding other than the small informal one which was starting here now.

In the row behind her a woman was thinking with anguish of the man who would never be her husband. Because he was dead. Obliterated. Nothing left of him. Not even mouldering remains in a coffin. He had no grave. Only that

7

terrible place she tried not to think of, the scene of recurring nightmares. She had known it was a place of doom the day he had taken her there.

I shouldn't be here, she thought, staring blindly at the bridegroom's back. It would have been better to stay away. I shouldn't have come. This is unnecessary torture.

... for the mutual society, help and comfort, that the one ought to have of the other, both in prosperity and adversity ...

Someone else had her eyes on the groom, finding in his upright bearing a painful reminder of her lost happiness.

Where are you now, my love? If you knew how things were with me, would you come back? I should be glad you didn't stay. If you hadn't gone and the police had wondered what I wondered ...

But if there was no real evidence, only vague suspicions, and you were already abroad, they may have decided not to pursue it. Whatever happens to me, however much people stare and whisper and snigger, I can bear it better than what would have happened to you if you hadn't gone away ... if there *had* been some proof.

Will you ever come back here? I doubt it. I'll never see you again. Oh, God, how can I stand it? The rest of my life without you.

The bride stood with hands loosely clasped, listening intently to the vicar, waiting to make her vows. When the moment came she spoke in a clear sure voice, her face turned up to the man who had already promised to love, honour and cherish her.

They continued to gaze at each other while the best man produced the ring and the vicar blessed it.

The two wedding guests for whom that exchange of loving looks had the keenest poignancy gave no sign of their innermost feelings. Trained by the same elderly nanny to control their emotions in public, they watched with expressionless faces which belied the pain in their hearts.

PART ONE: Spring

MAY

On a sunny morning in late May, when throughout southern New England the dogwoods had put on their spring show of pink and white flowers, one hundred and eighty-three descendants of Jonathan Blakewell converged on Winterbrook Farm, a National Historic Landmark not far from Boston, Massachusetts, to celebrate the three hundredth anniversary of their ancestor's arrival in America.

Among those attending the reunion were Jane Graham, a quiet reserved girl who was heiress to fifty million dollars, and a tall sun-tanned man with a camera slung round his neck.

The first Jane knew of his presence was when, as she was waiting to hear the speech of welcome by Marcus Blakewell, someone standing behind her remarked, 'With that hair and that profile you have to be some relation to Flora Carlyon.'

It was the familiar name, not the reference to her looks, which made Jane turn around.

The speaker was a man whose accent had already revealed he was not an American. That he was a stranger to her wasn't surprising. Although almost everyone standing about on the sloping green lawn in front of the beautiful old house was related to everyone else by close or distant blood ties, many had not met each other before today.

Jane herself knew few people there. Her mother, born Rosalind Blakewell, had died when Jane was a small child. Her father had made his fortune outside the United States. It was only since his death, a year ago, that she had come to Boston to live under the wing of her formidable aunt Mrs Stanton Foster, née Julia Blakewell.

Now, as Jane turned to meet the blue gaze of the darkly-bronzed man looking down at her, his smile faded slightly; as if, upon seeing her full face, he were disappointed.

'Yes, I am,' she replied, in answer to his remark. 'Flora Carlyon was my great-grandmother.'

'And mine. Which makes us cousins. My name's North. How d'you do?' He held out a lean brown hand.

As his fingers closed over hers, her insides churned and she felt a deep throbbing wave of excitement; a spontaneous surge of powerful sexual attraction. It was startling and disturbing to react as strongly as this to a stranger, the more so because it was a long time since she had had any feelings of this kind.

After the abortive relationship with Charles Helford, there had been no more love affairs and since her father's death all her other emotions had been subordinated by grief. Until a few seconds ago. Suddenly she was alive again, her blood pulsing, her nerve-ends tingling.

The need to control and mask her response made her sound a little distant as she said, 'How do you do? I'm Jane Graham. My mother was a Blakewell. What brings you here today? Are you an English descendant of Jonathan Blakewell's father?'

The founder of the great American dynasty to which she belonged had come to the New World from Devon in England, and his sons and grandsons had ventured beyond Massachusetts to establish branches of the family all down the eastern seaboard as far as North Carolina.

Her cousin shook his head. 'No, my connection with the family is that way back in the twenties my Great-Aunt Rose married a Blakewell, and I know Marcus Blakewell who's organized this reunion. I'm here in a professional capacity.' He tapped the camera hanging against his flat midriff. 'I've been hired to take pictures of everyone and, later on, a group photograph.'

'One hundred and eighty-three people is a pretty large group. Can you fit us all in one picture?'

10

'I'll do my best.'

In the few moments since she had turned to him, his vivid blue eyes had been scanning her slender body in as close an appraisal of her points as if she were a thoroughbred filly.

Her study of him was more discreet, although she was aware of his powerful, broad-shouldered build. Facially he was the most striking man she had ever met. His head was elegantly set on a long strong neck and, with one exception, all his features were a gift to a portrait sculptor. However at some stage of his life the bridge of his nose had been broken, leaving it permanently misshapen. Without the injury he would have been impossibly handsome. With it, he was still very good-looking but of a somewhat raffish appearance which would not be approved of by Aunt Julia.

In any case his job would debar him from Aunt Julia's esteem. In her eyes a photographer was beyond the pale of eligibility. Within it were investment brokers, lawyers and diplomats. The late Stanton Foster had ended his career as an ambassador.

Julia had been strongly opposed to her younger sister's marriage to a man outside the charmed circle of old New England families and old money. That John Graham had subsequently made a fortune had not redeemed him in her eyes. He had remained an outsider. As the antipathy had been mutual, Jane had never understood why her father had appointed his sister-in-law to be one of the three trustees who had control of her inheritance until she was twenty-five years old, or until her marriage.

'When I knew her, our great-grandmother's hair was white. But this is how it must have been when she was young,' said her cousin. He lifted a thick tress of Jane's glossy hair and let it slip through his fingers. 'Like black silk.'

To be touched in this intimate way on so short an acquaintance was disconcerting. She wasn't sure whether to thank him for the compliment or to draw back, indicating that, although they were cousins, it was their first encounter.

11

Before she could make up her mind, he added, 'It's a pity your eyes are grey. Otherwise you're amazingly like her. At your age she was the most beautiful woman I've ever seen.'

'You couldn't have known her when she was my age.'

'There are portraits of her . . . dozens of portraits. Everyone wanted to paint her. Her eyes were dark brown, almost black, and she had the Mongolian epicanthus. A little fold of skin . . . just here.' Again he lifted his hand and touched, very lightly, with one fingertip, the inner corner of her eye.

Her long lashes fluttered. She blinked. Did he make a habit of touching people within minutes of meeting them? The English were supposed to be formal and stand-offish. Not this Englishman.

Jane had travelled in the East with her father. She would have understood what he meant by the epicanthus if he hadn't explained it. She said, 'Do you mean Flora Carlyon had some oriental blood?'

'More than some . . . her mother was Chinese.'

'I had no idea,' she said, astonished. 'How fascinating. I wonder why my Aunt Julia never mentioned it? She's told me all about the Blakewells but nothing about my English ancestors. In fact the only reason I know my maternal great-grandmother's name is because I have a book that belonged to her. It's bound in green leather stamped with some kind of crest. Inside the front cover it has Flora Carlyon's book-plate.'

'As the Blakewells are widely regarded as the quintessential White Anglo-Saxon Protestants, perhaps your aunt prefers to overlook the fact that she's one-eighth Chinese,' he said dryly.

Privately she thought this a very probable explanation of Mrs Foster's failure to mention her grandmother's mixed blood. But loyalty forbade her to agree with him.

In her way, Aunt Julia had been kind. The fact that she and her niece had nothing in common wasn't her fault. Mrs Foster was the product of her conventional WASP upbringing, and Jane – although nobody guessed it from her subdued manner – was as different from most of the daughters of the Boston Brahmins as a golden oriole from a flock of white fan-tailed doves.

She seemed to fit in only because for the first six months the pain of her loss had numbed all normal reactions; and because now, until she had decided what she wanted to do with her future, there was no point in antagonizing Aunt Julia.

'If you want to know more about your English forebears, you should read my sister's book,' he told her. 'Our great-grandfather was a distinguished botanist and explorer. A couple of years ago Allegra found a trunk full of his diaries which inspired her to write his life story. It's already been published in England with considerable success. The week after next it's coming out over here. She'll be in New York to launch it. You should meet each other.'

'I'd like that very much. Allegra . . . what a charming and unusual name. Has she written many books?'

'This is her first, but I think she'll write others. What do you do? At a guess, something to do with fashion.'

Again the blue eyes appraised her, evidently recognizing the understated chic of her black pants, black-checked white blazer and red silk shirt, all by Umberto Ginocchietti.

'I'm interested in fashion – yes. But not professionally. Unfortunately I haven't found *my* métier yet. While my father was alive I was busy doing things for him . . . entertaining and so on. He died last year. Since then I've been adjusting to the American way of life, which has been a new experience for me.'

'Where did you live before?'

'All over the world. I've lived just about everywhere but my own country.'

'You like travelling?'

She nodded. 'I love it. Does your job involve much travelling?'

'Buy next month's *National Geographic* and you'll see the photographs of my last trip . . . to Ulan Bator. Have you been there?'

'No, and I'm embarrassed to admit I don't know where it is.'

13

He laughed, showing excellent teeth and causing two deep grooves to form in the brown skin between his high cheekbones and his strongly marked angular jaw.

'Very few people do. It's the capital of Outer Mongolia. It took five months to get a visa and at the end of the trip half my film was confiscated. But I managed to smuggle some out. Not enough to pay my expenses, but it was an interesting trip. It's amazing how many Mongolian traditions have survived Soviet rule. The horsemen still ride saddles decorated with silver, and in the archery contests they still use the curly bows which go back to Ghengis Khan's time.'

Near them someone started to clap. They turned to see Marcus Blakewell and other leading members of the clan taking their places between the tall white Grecian columns which were one of the features of Winterbrook.

'See you later,' her cousin murmured.

The speech-making didn't take long and when it was over people began to drift in the direction of the large marquee where the buffet lunch was being served. Afterwards those who had never been to Winterbrook before would be able to explore the house and its extensive grounds. Some of the most important members of the family branches were staying there as guests of Marcus and his wife Alison. Others were being accommodated in Blakewell houses on Boston's Beacon Hill and in the suburb of Brookline, birthplace of President Kennedy and of The Country Club, the first and foremost of all American country clubs. Some Blakewells were putting up at the Ritz-Carlton Hotel or the Copley Plaza, the latter being where, tonight, the reunion ball was to be held.

Until now, Jane hadn't been looking forward to the ball. Her partner was one of the young men urged upon her by her aunt. He was pleasant enough, and probably not after her money, his parents being extremely rich. But he had no sense of humour and, she suspected, not much heart in him either. Also he was interested in politics. The last thing she saw herself as was a politician's wife.

However if her newly-met cousin was going to be at

14

the ball, it might turn out to be more fun than she had anticipated.

Presently, while she was helping herself to poached salmon and other delicious things from the buffet, she heard the two women next to her talking about him.

'Who's the good-looking photographer? Someone from *Town & Country*?'

'No, no . . . Marcus would never allow the press in, not even *T & C*. The photographs Carlyon is taking are strictly for private circulation.'

'Carlyon? Carlyon Blakewell? Which branch does he belong to?'

'Carlyon isn't his first name. It's his title. Lord Carlyon. But he drops the prefix for his work . . . you know, like Snowdon, Princess Margaret's ex. Or Lichfield who photographed the Prince of Wales's wedding. Carlyon was at school with Prince Charles, somebody told me. But weddings, even royal ones, aren't his forte. He photographs deserts and jungles and vanishing species.'

'What's he doing here if he doesn't like civilization?'

'Marcus persuaded him to come. He's related to Henry Blakewell's first wife, who was English.'

'Is he married?'

'No, but if you're thinking he might do for Martha, forget it.'

'Gay?'

'The reverse! An enthusiastic heterosexual, but not, according to Marcus, looking around for the future Lady Carlyon. He'll only do that when it's time to produce some heirs. Not that there's much to inherit. Like so many old English families, his has been crippled by taxes. There's a house falling into ruins and the title. Not much else. Talking of ruins, have you seen Alice? My God, how she's aged in five years . . .'

On the other side of the Atlantic, where England had also been enjoying a fine spring day and it was now late afternoon, the distant but aggressive roar of a powerful motorbike broke the stillness.

The sound – in a part of the countryside seldom disturbed by anything noisier than birdsong, the clop of hooves and the occasional drone of a far-off tractor – brought a slight puzzled frown to the face of the fair-haired girl riding an unusually large Arab chestnut along the narrow by-road called Ice Lane.

The lane took its name from an ice-house built in the eighteenth century to store blocks of ice from the lake in the great park surrounding Longwarden, country seat of the Earls of Carlyon, now hidden behind the high wall erected to enclose the park in the nineteenth century.

Ice Lane, which was four miles long and, although tarred, rarely saw much traffic, was a convenient place for Sarah Lomax to give Bedouin Star his roadwork in preparation for his next horse trials.

At school Sarah had been known to the staff as a daydreaming idler. An obedient girl with good manners, but an indifferent scholar with no hope of achieving academic distinction.

Must learn to concentrate . . . *Could do better if she paid more attention* . . . had been recurring comments on her end-of-term reports.

To Sarah every day away from Longwarden stables, where during her reluctant absence her best friends had been in the care of her father's groom, had been a day wasted. She hadn't needed a place at university or even a respectable number of O levels. Her future was already settled.

Daughter of a National Hunt jockey who had won the Grand Military Gold Cup at Sandown Park at the age of twenty-three, and niece of the eighth Lord Carlyon, a famous Master of Fox Hounds, she was a born horsewoman who had been put on a pony at eighteen months old. Her first rosette, in a leading-rein class, had been won before she was three.

In the saddle her mind never wandered from what she was doing. She knew how easily even a trained horse could be spooked by a piece of paper flying on a gust of wind or a dog bursting out of the bushes.

Her understanding of the nervous nature of horses and their tendency to panic when threatened by something alarming was the reason for her frowning reaction to the raucous sound of the motorbike. Was it coming along Ice Lane, or was that merely a trick of the breeze? Sarah hoped so.

One of the reasons why the lane was seldom used by cars or lorries was because it had very few gateways to form lay-bys where vehicles could pull off to give way to oncoming traffic. Or where a horse could be removed from the path of a motorbike.

Usually the youths of Longwarden village, whose meeting place was a corner of the public car park where most of them lounged on a low wall while the élite straddled motorbikes, never came along the quiet lane.

They revved their engines in the main street, causing muttered complaints among their elders, or roared along the new by-pass which had taken away the heaviest traffic and left the village comparatively peaceful.

Even before she was certain the bike was in the lane, and coming up fast behind them, she had begun to speak reassuringly to Bedouin.

Luckily one of the gateways was not too far ahead. But they barely had time to reach the grassy bay before the bike was upon them, its rider revving impatiently until, with a thunderous surge of power, he swept past, leaving Sarah with a fleeting impression of his helmet and the emblem on the back of his jacket.

Given a similar fright, Tartar Princess, the nervous mare known as Tatty, would have been hard to control. Fortunately Bedouin and Sarah enjoyed the mutual confidence that as long as they were together nothing bad could happen to either of them.

Beddo's curveting reaction to the passing of the strident machine might have alarmed a novice rider. Sarah knew he was merely demonstrating his displeasure at the loutish behaviour of the motorcyclist.

As he calmed down, she patted his neck and agreed with him.

'Stupid showing-off idiot! Someone should tell him he

17

could cause a serious accident tearing along narrow lanes as if they were motorways. If I see him again I shall tell him. But I probably won't get the chance. Don't think he's local. Good thing I was with you, lovie. Tatty or Berber would have been scared out of their wits.'

They re-entered the lane where the sour city-smell of petrol still hung on the warm still air.

By the time they reached the chained and padlocked gate which gave access to Longwarden park but was no longer used except by Sarah and her horses, she had forgotten the incident.

In the garden at Winterbrook, Jane Graham was pondering the reliability of the gossip she had overheard at the buffet table.

She hadn't realized that the man who had spoken to her before the speeches was one of the world's top photographers. Carlyon was a name she had seen many times, printed under wonderful, arresting photographs of endangered fauna and flora and primitive people living in the planet's dwindling number of wild places. However, she hadn't been aware that Carlyon was another of England's outstanding photographer-peers.

That he'd been at school with the Prince of Wales was probably also true. But the rest of what had been said about him could be merely gossip. On the other hand she had to admit that the way North Carlyon had looked at her when they met had suggested a somewhat predatory attitude to women. She hoped he was not a womanizer.

'Jane!'

Her aunt's imperious voice killed her hope of being able to find some secluded corner of the garden in which to eat her lunch in peace, an observer of the reunion rather than a participant.

'I've been looking everywhere for you. Why are you here by yourself instead of being sociable? You will never make friends if you won't talk to people,' Julia Foster admonished severely. She was a tall, large-bosomed woman with a florid complexion.

'I have been talking to someone,' Jane told her, smiling. 'Until the speeches began I was having an interesting tête-à-tête with an eligible man.'

Unaware that she was being teased, Mrs Foster mellowed a little. 'You were? I didn't see you. Who was it? Where is he now?'

They both took a glass of champagne from the tray being offered by one of the waiters.

'I expect he's been ambushed by someone with a daughter to get off her hands,' Jane answered, straight-faced.

'You shouldn't have let him get away. You seem to have very little idea how to hold a man's interest,' her aunt said impatiently. 'What was his name? Can you see him?'

They were standing not far from the line of people waiting to enter the lunch tent, with a view of the terrace and lawn where others were lingering to chat.

Jane looked for the tall rangy frame and dark head of the man from England.

'He seems to have disappeared. Run for cover maybe,' she said lightly. 'He isn't a Blakewell. His name is North Carlyon . . . Lord Carlyon.'

Her aunt's reaction was not what she had expected. Far from kindling the gleam of the huntress in Julia's light blue-grey eyes, the name brought a scowl to her face.

'That insufferable man!' she said sharply. 'What is he doing here?'

'Marcus asked him to take some pictures. I'm rather surprised he agreed. Ours isn't the kind of tribe he prefers to photograph. Do you know him? You've never mentioned him.'

'I haven't seen him for years – and I don't wish to meet him again. I'm amazed Marcus should invite him when he knows how badly he behaved. Have nothing more to do with him, Jane. He's a man without morals or scruples. He –' She broke off, catching sight of the couple approaching them. 'Katherine, my dear . . . James . . . how are you both? It must be four years since I saw you. This is my niece, Jane Graham . . . poor Rosalind's daughter.'

For the rest of the afternoon Jane was kept firmly under

her aunt's wing. From time to time she caught glimpses of North Carlyon taking pictures of small groups of beaming Blakewells. She wondered what he had done to incur her aunt's animosity and how Julia would react when he came to take a picture of them. But whether by chance or design, they were two people he missed out.

At four o'clock the historic fête came to an end when all the Blakewells and their offshoots crowded together, the children in the foreground, Winterbrook in the background, and Euphemia Blakewell, the nonagenarian doyenne of the family, seated in an antique cherrywood armchair immediately behind the cross-legged children.

For this picture North used a tripod and kept them waiting a short time while he asked for some rearrangements. The adroitness with which he picked out not only the important people, but also the self-important, suggested to Jane that he must be better acquainted with the Massachusetts Blakewells than he had let on. Either that or Marcus had briefed him carefully beforehand.

She herself, in spite of her mother's blood, felt rather an interloper. In character she took after her father. Physically, only her eyes were a legacy from her mother. Where she had come by the genes which had produced her black hair and fine ivory skin had, until today, been a mystery.

It's a pity your eyes are grey.

As she remembered the critical comment, the delicate curves of her lips twisted in a wry half-smile. Most of the men she had known would have found no fault with her looks if she had been flat-chested, cross-eyed and had ankles like an elephant's. With fifty million dollars one didn't have to be beautiful to excite heavy breathing.

Long ago her father had warned her that every privilege had its price; and therefore, as John Graham's daughter, she would only know if her husband loved her after years of marriage.

'Unless I marry a man who's much richer than you are – or change my name to Jane Doe and go and work for my living,' she had suggested.

'Pretending to be a poor girl might have worked in old

Hollywood movies, but it wouldn't work out in real life,' her father had answered. 'Living a lie never does. That's often why people get divorced ... because before they were married they put on an act and then found they couldn't keep it up. As Shakespeare put it: *To thine own self be true ... thou canst not then be false to any man.*'

She had been nineteen then, and her father a healthy, vigorous man in his forties with a charming French travelling companion whom Jane had hoped he might marry.

But, three years later, he was gone and Marie-Simone, generously provided for in his will, had returned to France.

Roused from her thoughts of the past by the realization that the people around her were beginning to disperse, Jane remembered North saying 'See you later', and wondered if, now that his professional duties were over, he would seek her out.

Not by nature a shy or diffident girl, she wouldn't have hesitated to seek him out but for the fact that her aunt had expressly forbidden further contact. Intrigued by the hint of scandal in her aunt's warning, Jane wondered how she could find out what he had done. Two people who would know were Marcus and Alison Blakewell, but they were both fully occupied with their rôles as chief host and hostess.

'Come along, Jane. You must have an hour on your bed if you're going to be dancing till the small hours,' her aunt ordered, bearing down on her.

Mrs Foster's household consisted of Sherwood, her late husband's English valet who was now her butler-cum-chauffeur, Mrs Lilian Sherwood, who had been her personal maid during her years as the wife of an ambassador, and Mrs McPeak, her American cook-housekeeper.

The Fosters had had four children; two sons and two daughters, all married now and living too far from Boston to have attended the reunion without considerable inconvenience. Jane had met both the sons and one of the daughters when they and their families had spent Christmas with their mother. The younger daughter, Susan, was in Australia and unlikely to return to America for several years.

As Sherwood drove the car home – a stately Rolls-Royce Silver Shadow which The Honourable Stanton Foster had bought in London and shipped home – the two women sat in the back and exchanged sporadic conversation about the excellent catering and Euphemia's increasing deafness.

The presence of Sherwood, who had spent the day helping the butler at Winterbrook to supervise the staff hired for the occasion, prevented Jane from indulging her acute curiosity about the nature of North Carlyon's insufferable behaviour. It was not until they were back in the house in Louisburg Square, having tea before going up to rest, that she asked, 'What did Lord Carlyon do to make you dislike him so much?'

Mrs Foster's high colour heightened. 'It's not a subject I wish to discuss,' she said shortly. 'Suffice it to say that he is *persona non grata* in this house and always will be.'

It irked Jane that her aunt refused to be frank with her. Accustomed to being treated as an equal by her father, she found it hard to accept Mrs Foster's old-fashioned attitudes.

'But not at Winterbrook apparently . . . and you say Marcus knows whatever it was that he did.'

Julia gave her an angry glance. 'Marcus may consider North's professional kudos outweighs his disgraceful past conduct. I do not. Both he and his sister Allegra are two thoroughly spoilt, selfish people who have caused untold pain and embarrassment. In fact, with a few exceptions, for generations that family has been known for its wasters and roués. North has run true to form. I suppose he said something flattering and you were impressed by his charm?'

'I was interested when he told me I looked like our common great-grandmother, and that she was half-Chinese. Did you know Flora Carlyon, Aunt Julia? Was she still alive when you lived in England?'

'Yes, she lived to a great age but we didn't have much contact with her. The only time she paid an extended visit to Boston was when she and Mother were both widows. I know Father never liked her.'

'Because of her Chinese strain?'

22

Mrs Foster ignored that. 'He found her a difficult mother-in-law. It has to be said that, although *The Times* in London gave her a flattering obituary, it would have been far more sensible had her husband married a well-bred English girl instead of introducing a foreigner into the family.'

'Am I like her . . . apart from my eyes?'

Her aunt looked frowningly at her. 'I hadn't realized it before but yes, I suppose you are. Mother wasn't and neither was Rosalind. But at least you have normal eyes. Hers were noticeably oriental.'

Knowing it would annoy her Jane said, 'Lord Carlyon told me it was a pity my eyes weren't like hers.'

Her aunt gave a snort of indignation. 'A nonsensical statement if ever I heard one. I hope you won't be so foolish as to let that man turn your head. He's a thoroughly unscrupulous bad lot who would seduce you as soon as look at you. I'm going up to nap until Lilian runs our baths for us.'

In the pretty green and white bedroom which had once been Susan Foster's room, Jane undressed and put on a robe. Then she sat down to take off her make-up.

The cosmetics she used were French, recommended to her by Marie-Simone who, when Jane was in her mid-teens, had taught her to care for her skin. The Frenchwoman had been in her late twenties then and already a successful sculptress. John Graham had seen her work in an exhibition and commissioned her to sculpt a head of his daughter. By the time the bust was completed, she had become his mistress and joined his ménage, much to the disapproval of the middle-aged virgin who was then his personal assistant.

Jane had never been jealous of Marie-Simone. She had understood that her father needed more than she could give him; and Marie-Simone had accepted that between the dynamic American entrepreneur and his teenage daughter there was an intellectual rapport it would be foolish to resent.

The three of them had lived together for seven years,

during which time Jane had superseded Miss Grant as her father's assistant. After his death, she had hoped Marie-Simone would stay with her.

But the Frenchwoman had said, 'No, I think it's better that you go to your mother's relations and see how you like America.'

'Why not come with me?'

'Because John has told me about Boston and how he wasn't accepted by your mother's family because he had no money then and wasn't *bien-élevé*. I don't think your aunt would approve of me. It's better to go by yourself. Also, if we stay together, we shall grieve for him longer and that isn't what he would want. There's a poem in one of your books . . . *Better by far you should forget and smile than that you should remember and be sad.*' And then she had turned her face away and, with a tremor in her voice, added, 'But I think he was never able to forget your mother. He was fond of me, but she was the one he loved.'

Poor Marie-Simone, thought Jane with a sigh, as she sat at her dressing table, missing their affectionate friendship and mutual interest in fashion, art and music.

There was no such warmth, no such sharing, between herself and Aunt Julia. Her aunt was a petty dictator – well-meaning but inflexibly diehard – to whom for a year she had surrendered her independence.

But not for much longer.

For some time the need to be free and more purposefully occupied had been stirring in her. There was nothing for her in Boston. She might have Blakewell blood in her but she would never be one of them. Her future lay somewhere else and any man who she was involved with would have to have more fire and steel in his nature than these inbred Preppy Bostonians her aunt considered ideal husbands.

The problem was that if she decided, for example, that she wanted to try living in New York for a year, Mrs Foster had the power of veto. She and her two co-trustees, one a banker, the other a lawyer, held the purse strings for two more years.

Meanwhile Jane had an allowance which was more than

24

adequate for her present needs but not sufficient to cover the expenses of living on her own in the style to which she was accustomed. Being a realist, she knew that having for years been cushioned by luxury – not nouveau-riche gold-faucet luxury but the much-harder-to-give-up luxury of space, quietude, fine views and beautiful objects – she wouldn't be happy living any other way.

The best she could hope for was to be allowed to share a place with two or three other girls – the daughters of Blakewells or one of the other great dynasties. That might have been fun a few years ago but not now, at twenty-three. She wouldn't mind sharing an apartment. But not with a gaggle of girls. With one kindred spirit – male.

The thought of taking a lover brought her mind back to North. As she crossed to the bed and lay down, and clasped her hands under her head, she wondered if it might be a good idea to let him make love to her, if he wanted to.

Memory took her back to a shadowy room in Bangkok where, with the sides of the old-fashioned tent of mosquito netting gently billowing in the breeze from the fan, Charles Helford had taught her to make love.

They had not been *in* love with each other. At nineteen, still a virgin and consumed with impatient curiosity, she had chosen Charles as the man least likely to botch her initiation. She had known him for several years, Thailand being a country where her father often spent time when on business in Asia. While Jane was in her early teens, Charles had had a beautiful, talented Thai girl living with him. But a year or two later she had died, leaving him desolate, uninterested in other women until the evening Jane had gone to his house and tacitly offered herself to him. Had he been completely sober, he wouldn't have taken her. But a few drinks had undermined his self-control and accentuated his loneliness. He had regretted the act immediately, but she hadn't. She was glad it had happened and grateful to him for being sensitive and skilful.

Against Charles's better judgement they had continued to meet and make love. Then her father had found out and angrily accused him of seducing her. Jane had cleared

Charles of that charge, explaining that it was she who had taken the initiative. While her father was digesting this confession, Charles had taken them both by surprise by announcing that he wanted to marry her.

This had angered John Graham even more. He had assumed his daughter must be in love with Charles but thought her too young for marriage, especially to a man fifteen years her senior.

Not wishing to wound her lover by admitting that she didn't want to marry him – for by this stage his attraction for her was beginning to wane and she had no desire to make Bangkok, where he ran a silk business, her permanent home – Jane had allowed John Graham to play the heavy father and break up the affair.

She would have been less biddable had she given her heart to Charles. But he hadn't been her true love, and since their parting there had been no one else. Casual sex didn't interest her. Although she had met men whose looks were attractive, none had charmed her in other ways. She wanted her second lover to be someone special, not necessarily a long-term partner but certainly someone she would remember with pleasure and affection, as she did Charles.

Was her English cousin that man? Superimposed on her memories of Charles's gentle love-making came erotic visions of how it would be if North were lying on the bed with her, loosening the sash of her robe and peeling it open to explore, with those long brown fingers and sensual lips, the parts of her body which tingled and throbbed with desire.

She had intended to go to the Blakewell ball in an under-stated pale-grey dinner dress and a discreet pearl choker.

But when she walked down the staircase, just as Sherwood was opening the front door to Howell Adams, it was not with the whisper of chiffon that her long skirts trailed on the stairs. She swept down rustling twenty metres of saffron-coloured silk taffeta, gold bracelets by Ilias Lalaounis gleaming on her slender wrists and dramatic

Byzantine-style earrings dangling brightly against her black hair.

'You look very lovely tonight, Jane,' Howell said dutifully, as soon as he saw her.

But as he took in the billowing skirt, the low-cut strapless top and the black satin sash which cinched her waist, it was startlement rather than approbation which she saw in his eyes. Tonight he was seeing a side of her which for a year had been under wraps. Clearly he wasn't sure that he liked it.

'Thank you, Howell.' As she reached the chequered marble floor of the hall she held out her hand to him.

In most of Europe she would have had her hand kissed or, at the very least, bowed over, and many sophisticated Americans would have reacted in the same way. When Howell shook her hand it confirmed her opinion that he wasn't a man with the instincts which made a good lover – or a good husband.

She turned to Sherwood. 'Has my aunt come down?'

'Yes, Miss Graham.' He moved across the hall to open the door of the living room for her.

As she smiled and thanked him she wondered what he thought of her dress. She had needed his wife's help to fasten it, and Lilian had said, 'It's a wonderful colour on you, Miss Jane. It brings out the gold in your skin and the black sash matches your hair. But I'm not sure Mrs Foster will like it as much as the grey.'

Jane was certain her aunt would hate it. Virginal white, shell pink and powder blue were the colours approved by Aunt Julia for unmarried girls. Not singing saffron yellow.

The living room had its original painted pine panelling, and most of the furnishings were museum-quality antiques. Mrs Foster was sitting in her favourite winged armchair with a glass of sherry on the tripod table beside it.

She was wearing a dignified dress of steel-blue brocade, probably made during her reign as an ambassador's wife, with a diamond bow brooch on her shoulder and triple string of pearls.

At the sight of her niece she stiffened, saying, in a tone

of displeased surprise, 'That's not the dress you showed me.'

'No, I changed my mind. This is a dress Father chose the last time we were in Paris. The bracelets are a souvenir of Athens.'

Perhaps it was Howell's presence which made Julia Foster decide not to express her opinion of the dress, although in the fifteen minutes before they set out for the ball she could not refrain from shooting several glacially disapproving glances at it.

Jane wasn't ruffled by the unspoken censure. Unlike the fête at Winterbrook, where the guest list had been restricted to members of the family, the ball was a larger affair at which friends of the Blakewells would be present. There would be any number of attractive girls attending it, and the way to catch North's attention was not with low-key good taste but with drop-dead Parisian glamour.

'I shall come home at midnight but I leave it to your discretion what time you bring Jane home, Howell,' said Mrs Foster while he was helping her into her sable coat. 'She has a key. It won't be necessary to disturb Sherwood.'

She was going to the hotel in her car, with Howell and Jane following behind in his Lancia.

'Maybe you should have gone with your aunt. There's not a lot of room in my car for a skirt as voluminous as that,' he said, watching her furl the billows of taffeta and the stiffened tulle underskirt which supported them. 'I hope it won't get too creased.'

'Don't worry, Howell. It will shake out. Okay, it's under control. You can close the door.'

The Copley Plaza Hotel had been a Boston landmark for almost three-quarters of a century. Tonight's function was being held in one of the hotel's large banqueting rooms which had been beautifully decorated with white and yellow spring flowers and garlands of greenery. The kind of extravaganzas – thousands of orchids, Tiffany favours, truffles sprinkled with gold leaf – seen at the celebrations of the newly rich were not indulged in by Blakewells.

The seating plan for the dinner before the dancing had

been carefully worked out by Alison Blakewell, Julia Foster and some other experienced hostesses. Before Howell found their places at one of the round lamp-lit tables, each seating ten, Jane knew she would be between Howell and Alison's youngest son, seventeen-year-old Peter Blakewell.

Where North would be sitting, if he were there, she had no idea. Not near her or her aunt, that was certain. She wondered if, later on, Marcus would ask her to dance, giving her an opportunity to ask him what the Englishman had done to deserve Aunt Julia's implacable enmity.

Although the festoons of foliage decorating the ballroom walls and the banks of flowers round the dais for the band were the work of professional florists, the table flowers had been done by a team of green-fingered Blakewell wives. Each table had an exquisite centrepiece of white and yellow tulips, white irises, gardenia, narcissi, white lilac and pale-yellow paeonies. Beside each place setting was a smaller posy, each one different. The one by Jane's place was composed of young hosta leaves, pale yellow with a green edge, white forget-me-nots, some of the trilliums called wood lilies, a white guelder-rose and some flowers from the pearl tree at Winterbrook.

'How clever of you to find a dress to go with the floral theme, Jane,' said Lucy Blakewell, one of Marcus's nieces, speaking across the unoccupied chair between them. 'I just love that strong vibrant yellow but with my skin I couldn't wear it. It looks stunning on you.'

'Thank you, Lucy.'

On Jane's left was a table of elderly people, while those at the table on her right were of her parents' generation, the women in their mid-forties, the men a little older. Watching them she felt a momentary pang for the mother she could barely remember and the father who had been the centre of her universe. She had no shortage of relations – half the people in the ballroom were her kinsmen – but the only person who was close to her was Marie-Simone, far away in Paris.

For the first six months after separating, they had written to each other frequently. Gradually Marie-Simone had taken longer to reply and her letters, when they came, were shorter. Although she hadn't mentioned anyone, Jane had begun to wonder if there was a new man in the French-woman's life and she wanted to break the tie with her last lover's daughter, or at least to loosen it.

As Jane's eyes wandered round the ballroom, pausing here and there to admire a dress, her gaze was suddenly arrested by a man in a white dinner jacket.

It had been said of the Blakewell men that they were as at ease in black tie as other Americans were in jeans. But of all the debonair men strolling across the polished dance floor or drawing out chairs for their women, none looked more innately distinguished than Lord Carlyon.

With Marcus's second son, Bunny, he was escorting Euphemia to her place at the table of honour for those who, fifty years ago, had been present at the ball to celebrate the 250th anniversary of Jonathan Blakewell's arrival.

Between the two tall strong men to whose muscular arms she was clinging with her small, claw-like, jewelled hands, she looked pitifully wizened and frail, almost all trace of her beauty ravaged by her great age.

'Isn't Euphemia a marvel,' Jane heard somebody say at the table to her left.

But it seemed to her, watching the two men taking short steps to match the old lady's unsteady shuffle, that it must make Euphemia's heart ache to remember how, at the time of the previous ball in the thirties, she had still been playing tennis and golf at The Country Club, a lovely woman in her prime with no inkling that forty years of widowhood lay ahead of her.

Jane switched her gaze to North, who was inclining his dark head to listen to Euphemia's soft babbling voice. His well-brushed hair had the sheen of a jackdaw's plumage in the light from the chandeliers. It was as black as her own hair, but not straight. Above his ears and behind them, and where it touched the collar of his dress shirt, it flicked upwards slightly. Where it sprang from a peak on his forehead it would, if not brushed strictly back, have curved forward towards his dark eyebrows. She had seen that happen at Winterbrook when a breeze had sprung up while he was bending over his camera, taking the group photograph. He had raked the unruly lock back with his fingers; the long brown fingers now loosely clenched as he gave Euphemia his arm and smiled down at her wrinkled face with its aureole of spun-sugar hair showing the outline of her scalp.

There were two wine glasses and a champagne flute as well as a glass already filled with iced water by each place. Now, as the last-comers entered the ballroom, the waiters began to fill the crystal flutes.

'Who should be sitting next to you?' Howell asked, looking at the still-empty chair between Jane and Lucy.

'Peter, but maybe he's doing some last-minute thing for his parents,' she answered, wondering where North would be seated.

She was listening to Howell telling her about his day when the vacant chair was drawn out and she glanced up to find North about to sit down next to her.

'Good evening, Jane.'

As he took in her smooth bare shoulders and the curves of her breasts exposed by the low décolletage, the look in his eyes made her heart thump with startled, delicious excitement.

'Good evening.' Quickly recovering her self-possession, she said, 'Lucy . . . have you met Lord Carlyon? North, this is Lucy Blakewell, one of Marcus's nieces.'

'How d'you do, Miss Blakewell.'

He shook hands with her and with the young man beside her who had risen to shake hands with him. Then Jane introduced Howell who also rose. When he and North were sitting down, Howell leaned forward to ask, 'Where's Peter? Isn't he here?'

'He's in my seat. I asked him to change places with me,' North replied pleasantly. 'I wanted to be next to Jane. We're long-lost cousins, you know, and as I'm leaving tomorrow this is my only opportunity to talk to her.'

'I see.' Howell's expression suggested that he wasn't sure he did see.

Briefly Jane explained her relationship with North. 'Where are you going tomorrow?' she asked.

'To 'Sconset on Nantucket Island. I've friends with a summer place there. They're going over early this year and I'm spending a few days with them before my sister arrives in New York. Have you been to Nantucket?'

She shook her head.

'It's an interesting island. If you've no unbreakable engagements, why don't you come with me? I'm sure you'd like Lee and Sheila and they'd be delighted to have you. They're extremely hospitable people.'

And perhaps used to you having a popsie in tow, she thought. For it wasn't a cousinly suggestion, of that she felt certain.

Evidently Howell had formed the same impression. He said, in his most pompous tone, 'I don't think it's quite Jane's style to arrive anywhere uninvited, and we have a date for the theatre early next week.'

It was a bluff which she was tempted to call by saying, 'You haven't mentioned it to me, Howell.' But although she was irritated by his possessive attitude, she couldn't quite bring herself to make him look foolish.

It was North who did that by asking, 'What are you going to see?' to which Howell had no ready reply.

'Er ... I've forgotten what it's called,' he muttered, reddening.

North gave him a mocking glance before turning to make some civil remarks to Lucy.

'I can speak for myself, Howell,' Jane said in a low tone.

'I know, but the nerve of the guy.' He cast a look of dislike at the Englishman's bronzed quarter profile. 'I don't care for the way he looks at you.'

In London, where it was one o'clock in the morning, the light was still on in Allegra Lomax's bedroom. She was going through her wardrobe choosing clothes to take to New York, the first stop on a coast-to-coast tour of America to promote her best-selling biography, *The Travels of an Edwardian Naturalist*.

She was by nature a night-owl who often stayed awake, reading, into the small hours. Tonight she was restless after dining with an old friend and half-regretting her refusal to allow him to share the silk-curtained Hepplewhite bed in which, at one time, a succession of lovers had slept with her.

That phase of her life was over. At twenty-eight she was not the dedicated sybarite she had been at twenty-six. In two years her life had changed in almost every aspect.

Bitchy paragraphs beginning *Vivacious red-haired Lady Allegra Lomax, until recently a close friend of international yachtsman* or *seen about town with National Hunt jockey* or *partner-in-fun of Cresta Run champion . . . has a new escort this month* no longer appeared regularly in the gossip columns, although the columnists and their stringers did their best to keep her reputation as a playgirl alive.

Padding around her cluttered bedroom, originally a maids' dormitory on the attic floor of the Carlyons' town house, now the last privately owned mansion in Park Lane, Allegra was conscious of sexual hunger aroused by several hours *à deux* with a personable man. But trying out new combinations of favourite garments was an effective distraction. Clothes were a passion with her, a passion more lasting and satisfying than any of her many love affairs.

> *Where's the man could ease a heart*
> *Like a satin gown?*

The cynical wit of Dorothy Parker summed up Allegra's experience.

One of the things she was debating taking to New York was a six-year-old gold-embroidered black suede jacket from Saint Laurent's couture collection. She still loved it as much as when she had snatched it off the rail in a second-hand shop near Sloane Square, the source of many of the designer labels in her crowded closets.

Although in the past twelve months she had suddenly become quite rich because of the runaway success in

England of her first book, for most of her life money had been in short supply.

Her father, the eighth Earl of Carlyon, had cared for nothing but hunting and racing, both extremely expensive pastimes which had rapidly depleted the fortune left by her great-grandmother. Her father had cut off her allowance, ostensibly as a punitive measure to bring her to heel, as he put it, but actually, as she well knew, because he needed every pound he could lay hands on to maintain his position as sole Master of the Carlyon Hunt.

The winter after the thunderous row about her disgracing herself and the family name by her outrageous behaviour at a May Ball, he had been killed while hunting. Her brother, his heir, hadn't been able to restore her allowance because as well as being left with their father's large over-draft, he had also had to pay enormous death duties.

So although the gossip columnists had always managed to make her sound spoilt and extravagant, the truth was that she had been a pioneer of the eighties vogue for recycled *haute couture* and antique clothes and had earned her living with a succession of jobs ranging from chalet girl to receptionist and travel courier. These the columnists chose to ignore, or to refer to in terms which suggested that, for a whim, she was taking the wage packet which rightfully belonged to a girl of inferior social class but higher moral character.

Allegra had treated the columnists' snide and near-libellous comments on her love life with the same indifference she had shown when reproved by mistresses at school or lectured by her parents. The only person whose good opinion *had* mattered to her had been her adored great-grandmother, known to the staff at Longwarden as 'Countess Flora' to distinguish her from her successor, Allegra's mother.

Fortunately Countess Flora had outlived the eighth Earl or undoubtedly he would have sold off the house in Park Lane to pay for his excesses. Later North had considered selling it, but instead he had had the main floors of Carlyon House converted into two luxurious flats now leased, at

34

astronomical rents, to an international consortium for the use of their highest executives. By this means he had been able to retain an increasingly valuable freehold, maintain the fabric of the building and provide a flat for his sister and pied-à-terre for himself. He was now the only person with whom, occasionally, Allegra could discuss her problems, although he was seldom in London for more than a brief flying visit.

North knew America well. For her this was the first trip across the Atlantic, in circumstances which would have been inconceivable a few years ago when no one had thought she had it in her to be good at anything but making love and looking decorative.

Pyjamas and dressing gowns to wear around town in the evening; now top designers are helping to bring nightwear out of the bedroom – Harpers & Queen had proclaimed in the autumn of 1984 after the publication of Allegra's book which had kept her away from the fleshpots for much more than a year.

Titian-haired, amethyst-eyed Lady Allegra Lomax wearing black silk pyjama legs under a claret silk dressing gown under a black velvet smoking jacket – all culled from the sumptuous Edwardian wardrobe of her great-grandfather, the plant-hunting seventh Lord Carlyon had been the caption under a full-page photograph in *Vogue* a month later. *The adventurous Earl and his beautiful half-Chinese wife, who took London society by storm when she made her début as a bride in 1903, are the subjects of a biography, based on diaries and letters discovered at Longwarden, the family seat, which Lady Allegra, sister of the present Earl, has written. It will be published next year by Brentwood & Dunbar.*

The announcement in *Vogue* had been part of a fanfare of publicity orchestrated by Brentwood & Dunbar's PR girl. Allegra had chosen to send her manuscript to a new firm of publishers because both the directors were women and she liked to support successful members of her sex. For the same reason her gynaecologist and her dentist were also women.

The first time she met Ellen Brentwood and Claudia

Dunbar, she learned they had launched their imprint when, after twelve years in publishing, they decided they didn't like working for large organizations and would be happier running a small, independent house. Ellen was married with children. Claudia had lived with a man since her middle twenties but, as they didn't want children, they saw no point in legalizing their relationship and incurring tax penalties.

While she was lunching with them at Inigo Jones, Allegra had been aware that her prospective publishers were trying to relate the image of her presented by Nigel Dempster and other columnists with the author of a book which, in spite of its romantic elements, was a serious, well-researched biography.

They had liked her book and she had liked them and been warmed by their enthusiasm for the story of her great-grandfather's travels and his gradual metamorphosis from a selfish, unscrupulous womanizer to a devoted husband who, as a very old man, had written letters to his wife which had made Allegra cry when she read them.

It was thought to be Countess Flora's oriental blood which had given her only son his dark chestnut hair, a colour previously unknown in the Carlyon family but said to be not uncommon among the offspring of a union between a European and an Asian. The colour had skipped a generation, reappearing move vividly when Allegra was born. From whose genes she had inherited the unusual colour of her eyes was a mystery.

Although she did sometimes dress in amethyst to match her eyes, most of Allegra's day clothes were in neutral colours. With her fiery hair, beige became subtle, not dull as it might be on a mousey-haired person. She loved black, white, navy and grey; the classic colours which never went out of fashion.

Her choice of clothes for New York was dictated by the need to look good on television and to stay soignée through a punishing schedule which might not allow any time for having clothes laundered or pressed.

With these governing factors in mind she continued

going through her cupboards, rejecting crushable garments and selecting Missoni knits, Jean Muir jersey dresses and a Zandra Rhodes ice-green top made with the special Rhodes seams which gave it the crinkly edges of a Webb's Wonder lettuce.

Most of the girls with whom Allegra had grown up would, in her present position, have felt entitled to splurge on a whole new wardrobe for a promotional trip such as the one arranged by her American publishers.

However although, theoretically, she was a free agent, without ties or responsibilities, she felt it would be unfair not to share the proceeds from the book with her brother and her cousin Sarah.

Any money she gave to North towards the upkeep of Longwarden was a drop in the ocean of his terrifying overheads. But contributions to Sarah's funds made a significant difference to her chances of gaining a place in the 1988 British Olympics equestrian team.

In any case, second-hand dressing had become a habit which Allegra saw no reason to change merely because she could afford to swan into Bond Street boutiques and Knightsbridge designer rooms and pay massive mark-ups on new clothes which sooner or later would be re-sold for much less in the shops she patronized.

Right at the back of the cupboard containing her evening clothes was an outfit by Caroline Charles which had once been a special favourite. Unwilling to remember the last time she had worn it, yet knowing it would be invaluable in America, she took the hanger from the cupboard and lifted the polythene bag protecting the thin printed silk of a dipahanous cover-up teamed with black jersey pants and a black top with shoestring straps.

Designed to be worn together, the three pieces could be split. Before she had put them away – feeling at the time that she never wanted to wear them again – she had teamed the pants with her Saint Laurent jacket and a gold lamé halter and, for a summer dance, worn the skimpy black top with a frou-frou of ruffled white cambric Victorian petticoats.

As she looked at them now, she was remembering the night she had thought up a third permutation and worn the transparent silk coat without the chemise underneath it and cinched by a wide gold kid belt wrapped twice round her narrow waist.

Why the hell not? You want to. I want to. And you've been to bed with plenty of other guys.

Even now, two years later, the memory of that accusation still made her smart with anger and humiliation.

Who was it – Tallulah Bankhead? – who had been quoted as saying, 'I'm not promiscuous. Promiscuity implies that attraction isn't necessary.'

In that sense, Allegra hadn't been promiscuous either. At the beginning of each affair she had always been wildly, irresistibly attracted to the men she gave herself to, longing to fall deeply, lastingly in love. It had just never happened.

She had never given a damn for what anyone thought of her numerous affairs. Not until the night she had worn the Caroline Charles with her breasts bare under the thin silk and her hair in the wild cloud of curls which had been the fashion that season.

What had hurt and enraged her was that the first man to accuse her point-blank of being an easy lay had also been the first man who had seemed to have a mind as engaging as his face and body. A combination she had almost despaired of ever finding.

At the anniversary banquet in Boston the guests were eating the first course, Savoy cabbage leaves stuffed with lobster, garnished with Beluga caviar and surrounded by a creamy fish sauce.

'I'm sure I've had this before,' North said to Jane. 'Yes . . . I have. I remember now. It's one of Seppi Renggli's inventions.' He saw that the name meant nothing to her. 'He's the chef at The Four Seasons restaurant in New York. I expect my sister will be wined and dined there, lucky girl. It's a favourite place with publishing people. You haven't been there, I gather?'

'I haven't been to New York yet, would you believe?'

'Then you've got a terrific experience ahead of you.'

'You like New York? I wouldn't have thought you were a city person.'

'I'm not. I shouldn't want to spend all my time in a city, but to live well you have to have contrast. A simple life in the country is best for the body and spirit, but the mind recharges its batteries in the theatres and galleries and museums of the big cities. You're only a hop from New York here. Why haven't you been?'

'My aunt detests New York and she's against my going there alone. In fact most Bostonians seem to feel that New York has nothing to offer which can't be found here.'

He leaned closer and said confidentially, 'Bostonians are some of the most parochial people in the world. You must have heard the old joke about the Bostonian who returned from a tour of the world and the first question everyone asked him was: "Did you meet anyone from Boston?" I like Boston myself. I was at Harvard for a time. But this city can't be compared with New York. Nowhere can. You must go. Why not go while my sister is there? I'm sure she'd be glad to have someone to go shopping with her.'

'Won't she be fully occupied promoting her book?'

'If I know Allegra, she'll find time to explore the best shops. Clothes are an addiction with her. When she's busy, I'll be around to introduce you to my favourite places.'

'It sounds fun but I'll have to think about it.'

His glance travelled beyond her to Howell. 'You're not engaged to him, are you?'

Jane shook her head. 'We're just friends . . . in the old-fashioned sense,' she tacked on as he raised a quizzical eyebrow.

'Not on his side, judging by the way his hackles rose when I asked you to come to Nantucket,' he said dryly.

'We have only just met,' she pointed out.

'But we are cousins.' His eyes smiled into hers.

His charm was as heady as champagne and she didn't mask her response to it. Her eyes shone. Her full lips curved.

'Distant cousins,' she answered.

The blue gaze shifted to her mouth. 'Kissing cousins perhaps?'

Before she could reply a waiter's arm came between them to replenish her wine glass and a moment later Howell turned to ask if she had seen a news item in that morning's *Boston Globe*. From then on, perhaps deliberately, he kept up a steady flow of conversation which lasted through the second course, lamb rib-eye cooked with fresh sorrel in puff pastry.

On the back of the souvenir menu was printed the long formal dinner of the thirties celebration with its alternate relevés and removes, the last remove being followed by the classic entrée and that being succeeded by salad, then cheese, then entremets followed by fruit.

The menu Alison had chosen was designed for the smaller appetites and trimmer figures of the eighties and, after the almond mocha torte, while coffee was being served, she and her husband led the dancing, followed by others from their table.

Jane had noticed Howell keeping watch for the dancing to begin. No sooner had Marcus and his wife stepped on to the floor than he rose and asked her to dance. As she put her napkin on the table, North pushed back his chair and stood up. Thanking Howell for pulling out her chair, she caught his look of alarm as, for an instant, he misread the taller man's intention. Of course North had only risen out of courtesy. But as she walked on to the dance floor and Howell took her in his arms, she couldn't help thinking that, had she come as North's partner, it wouldn't have occurred to him that another man might pre-empt his privilege.

The floor wasn't crowded as yet. In a gilded mirror on the wall she glimpsed a reflection: a girl with a bell of black hair above a bare ivory back dancing with a fair-haired man. Then Howell swung her round and she saw the pair in reverse with her own face above his shoulder and the golden gleam of her earrings.

'I shall have to dance with my cousin, Howell. It would

be rude not to as he has no partner. Anyway you'll have to dance with the other girls at our table, won't you?'

'I suppose so,' he agreed reluctantly. 'But not more than I have to. I only want to dance with you.'

'That's very complimentary, but I must say that I find North an interesting person and there's a lot more I want to ask him about his work as a photographer. Perhaps you haven't heard of him but he's very well-known.'

'Really? I assumed he spent his time hunting and shooting and whatever else English lords do with themselves.'

'Nowadays I think most of them work as hard as everyone else, if not harder. Marcus doesn't lead an idle life because he inherited Winterbrook. He's always busy.'

They had almost circled the floor. She glanced at their table and saw that now only three people remained there: North and a couple on the other side of the table. He had moved round to talk to them. Although facing the dance floor, he wasn't looking towards it. Jane felt a little disappointed. She would have liked to find him watching her. The thought of being in his arms sent a strange shudder through her.

Howell would have stayed on the floor when the tempo changed but she pointed out that their coffee might cool if they had the next dance. The others in their party had had the same thought and the table was soon complete again, with North in the chair next to hers.

With the coffee, brandy and liqueurs were being served, and dishes of hand-made chocolates and *marrons glacés*.

'North was also at Harvard, Howell,' said Jane, hoping this would be a point of rapport between the two men.

'Only for a year. Then my father died and I had to go home and take over the reins at Longwarden, which is an old house like Winterbrook but not in such good repair,' North said dryly.

He then picked up the cue she had intended for Howell by asking the younger man when he had been at Harvard. From the ensuing conversation it emerged that North was five years older than Howell, which made him thirty.

41

'Why did you come to Harvard rather than going to Oxford or Cambridge?' she asked him.

'It was part of a parental plot to break up a relationship they didn't approve of and start one which had their approval. Howell, may I have your permission to ask Jane to dance?'

He had chosen the moment when the band had begun to play one of Marie-Simone's and Jane's favourites – 'A Man and a Woman'. She had already recognized the opening bars, played at a very slow tempo.

There was a moment, at the edge of the dance floor, before he took her in his arms, when she knew with absolute conviction he was going to be her next lover; and there was no mistaking the desire in his narrowed blue eyes as he reached out his arms and drew her slowly against him.

Her high-heeled gold sandals made her almost as tall as Howell, but even on three-inch heels she couldn't see over the top of North's broad shoulder. As his arm tightened round her, she yielded to its firm pressure. He held her as close as if they were already lovers, his hard thighs in contact with hers as they swayed to the slow, sensuous rhythm.

She looked at her hand enfolded by his long fingers with their well-kept squarish nails. It was hidden from her now, but during dinner she had noticed that on the little finger of his left hand he wore an oval gold signet ring engraved with the same crest which was stamped on the cover of Flora Carlyon's book.

His other hand was making small stroking movements at the side of her waist, caressing her in time to the music. Locked together, they moved in an effortless unison she had never experienced before.

Every now and then he would vary the pace by spinning her across a clear space, making her saffron skirt swirl round his long black-clad legs.

The last notes of 'A Man and a Woman' merged with another of her favourites, 'Feelings'. As they went on dancing, she wondered if Howell was doing his social duty with one of the other girls, or if he was sitting glowering at

42

her and North. If Aunt Julia noticed them dancing, she would be fuming, that was for sure.

'If I delay my departure for Nantucket, will you have lunch with me tomorrow?' North asked, his voice deep and vibrant as he inclined his head to speak close to her ear.

She leaned back over his arm so that she could look into his face.

'I'd like that very much, North. But before I say yes will you answer a question?'

He smiled. 'If I know the answer.'

'I'm sure you must.' She hesitated, wondering if when she heard it she would wish she had held her tongue. 'This afternoon Aunt Julia warned me that, to quote her exact words, you were a thoroughly unscrupulous bad lot who'd seduce me as soon as look at me. Does she have any grounds for that charge?'

His smile faded. For the first time in their brief acquaintance she saw his features stiffen. Bereft of its lurking amusement, his face became hard and cynical.

'Yes,' he said, with a slight shrug. 'She does. The last time I was in Boston, I seduced one of her daughters.'

After North's casual admission, his hold on Jane slackened slightly as he waited for her reaction. He said nothing to vindicate himself.

It was the cold, hard look on his face as much as the nature of his offence which disturbed her.

'Was it Susan? – The younger daughter?'

'Yes. She was a freshman at Amherst College. A naïve virgin of whom I took unfair advantage.'

'If you were a freshman at Harvard you couldn't have been too much older.'

'Two years in age. A lot more than that in experience.'

'Well, it was a long time ago and by all accounts Susan is now happily married to an up and coming diplomat, so I expect she's forgotten about it even if her mother hasn't.'

'I'm surprised Mrs Foster was so restrained in her animadversions,' North said sardonically. 'In her eyes I'm not only a seducer but responsible for her daughter's attempted suicide. When I dropped Susan, she tried to kill herself.'

'Oh, my God! How dreadful,' Jane exclaimed, with a horrified expression. 'For you as well as for the Fosters.'

'For me?' he said, raising an eyebrow.

'Why yes; that's a terrible punishment to inflict on a young man, however badly he's behaved.'

'As far as I remember my only reaction was exasperation,' he said indifferently.

She said, 'I can't imagine any circumstances in which I'd commit suicide – certainly not because of an unhappy love affair. She wasn't pregnant, was she, and terrified of facing her parents?'

'No, she wasn't pregnant. I made certain of that.'

The music came to an end and with it that sequence of dances.

'That was one point in your favour,' Jane said, taking her hand from his shoulder.

For a few moments longer he kept his arm round her waist. 'I don't think your aunt and uncle saw it in that light. Now that I've answered your question, how about lunching with me tomorrow?' His blue eyes held a glint of challenge.

'I'd be delighted,' she said calmly. 'I don't think something that happened so many years ago has anything to do with me.'

Later in the evening, while she was dancing with Howell, Marcus Blakewell cut in.

'Are you enjoying yourself, Jane?'

'Immensely. Thank you for a wonderful evening, Marcus.'

'I should thank you for enhancing the occasion by being the outstanding belle which every ball needs,' he said gallantly. 'A little while ago I heard someone remark that they hadn't realized before what a beauty you are. Singularly unobservant of them! I saw it the first time we met. But tonight there's a special glow about you. Could the presence of an Englishman have anything to do with it?'

'It's possible,' she agreed, smiling. 'But if you're planning to reinforce Aunt Julia's warnings about him, you needn't bother. North himself has admitted that he deserves her dislike. He's told me what happened and made no excuses for himself. But you can't think too badly of him or you wouldn't have invited him here.'

'I like North. I always have. I think Julia and his fool of a mother were largely to blame for Susan's troubles. Lady Carlyon wanted to break up his affair with an older woman and Julia liked the idea of her daughter becoming a countess. But although I feel sure that the years you spent travelling with your father taught you to be a good judge of character, I'd like, if you'll allow me, to tell you some things about North which may help you to understand him. Having met him so recently, I'm sure you're reserving your final judgement?'

When she nodded, Marcus went on, 'North's reputation as a black sheep began when his father was asked to remove him from his public school which, as I'm sure you know, in England means a leading private school.'

She nodded. 'What had he done?'

'He had a fight with another boy. Had his own nose broken but almost killed his adversary, who was older than he. Why they fought was never found out. But the father – an important man and perhaps a more generous subscriber to the school's funds than Lord Carlyon – brought pressure to bear and North was expelled. After that he went to a crammer in London so that he could pass the examinations which would get him a place at university. When his parents found out about the involvement with the older woman, they insisted he come to Harvard – a bad move as matters turned out.'

'What sort of girl was Susan?'

'Pretty. Bright. Spoilt by her father. Not a girl who was tactful about turning down dates with young men who didn't interest her. My daughters thought her vain. However she got her comeuppance when she tangled with North. The overdose of pills was an attempt to bring him to heel. She made sure she would be discovered in time.'

'What a crazy thing to do,' Jane exclaimed. 'If her plans had gone wrong she might have died.'

'Yes, and she misjudged her man,' said Marcus. 'North isn't the type to submit to emotional blackmail. He knew she wasn't really heart-broken. He had been an attractive conquest for her to flaunt, and although *he* played down his background everyone knew who he was – Julia made sure of that. According to my younger daughter, there was a whole crop of girls who fancied themselves as the future Countess of Carlyon.'

'I can understand that,' she remarked. 'There's something very romantic about an old English title – or is North's one of the more recent ones?'

'No, it goes back three or four centuries. But there's not much substance to it now. His father died prematurely and when North was barely out of his teens he inherited more debts than assets. Talking about it last night, when I had some private conversation with him, he made no bones of the fact that, if he's going to keep Longwarden, he has to marry for money. That's why he's in America – to look for a rich wife.'

'Are there no rich girls in Britain?'

'I'm sure there are many, but he seems to have the idea that a transfusion of fresh blood would be good for his line.'

'Doesn't that rule me out? – If you had it in mind that he might cast an eye in my direction.'

'He's already done more than cast an eye. As soon as the fête was over he wanted to know all about you. Apparently you bear a striking resemblance to his great-grandmother . . . who was also your great-grandmother. I never met her – I wasn't in Boston during the years she spent here – but I know she was a stronger influence on North than his parents. He never got on with either of them.'

'Did his inquiries about me include questions about my financial status?' asked Jane.

'Yes, they did. Alison and I hedged on that one, but it won't take him long to find out that your father died a very rich man. He could guess that by the way you're dressed tonight.'

She was silent for a few moments. Then she said, 'At least North will be giving something in exchange for the money he wants to get his hands on – a historic house which, to me, is more tempting than his title. Some fortune hunters have nothing to offer.'

'I think Alison would tell you that a loving husband is worth more than a historic house,' said Marcus.

'Of course. I know that. But Alison wasn't in my position when you asked her to marry you. Had she been, only time would have proved that you loved her for herself, not her money. I can never be sure that it's me, not Father's funds, which is the big attraction.'

He looked thoughtfully at her. 'I think you underestimate yourself, Jane. You're a lovely girl and an intelligent one. There are many reasons, other than your father's fortune, why young men should fall in love with you – as I suspect Howell has.'

'Oh, I hope not! I didn't want that to happen. I could never marry him,' she answered positively.

'In my opinion you'd be wise not to marry anyone for a year or two. The fact that you don't need to earn your living doesn't preclude your making a career for yourself.'

'I know and I've been thinking about it for the past six months, but nothing really appeals to me. I guess by nature and training I'm cut out to be a home-maker. Marie-Simone wasn't. She was an artist first and last. I took care of the domestic details of our life. Aunt Julia treats me like a young girl, but in fact I'm quite an accomplished hostess and organizer.'

'It's unfortunate that you're under Julia's aegis. I believe you'd have been happier with us at Winterbrook. But I think your father's intention was to reinstate you with your mother's family.'

She nodded. 'That clause in Father's will was made long ago, when I was too young to take care of myself. For some reason he never altered it. I suppose it didn't seem important because he expected to live his full three score and ten, if not longer.'

Now, a year after the accident which had cut short John

Graham's life, she could speak of it unemotionally, even though there was still an inward pang.

'Yes . . . well, it can't be helped. It's not really that long before you'll be your own mistress.'

At this point the music stopped and he took her back to her table.

'More dire warnings?' asked North, who had evidently noticed Marcus talking to her on the dance floor.

She felt a white lie was justified. 'No, just Marcus demonstrating what a nice, considerate man he is by making sure I was having a good time. He and Alison have both been very kind to me.'

'Which reminds me I should dance with my hostess. As I can't call for you tomorrow without outraging Mrs Foster, shall we meet downtown? How about the bar here at noon?'

'That would be fine. I'll look forward to it.'

He rose to his feet and, obviously not intending to return, said goodnight to Howell.

The music and the buzz of voices had prevented the younger man from hearing North's arrangement with Jane.

'You're leaving this early?' he said, looking surprised but far from disappointed.

'I've arranged to borrow a dark-room. I want to develop the film I shot at Winterbrook today,' North explained.

He turned to say goodnight to Lucy Blakewell and her partner. The others from the table were dancing.

Finally he turned to Jane. He bent down and kissed her lightly, first on one cheek and then the other.

'*Au revoir, belle cousine.*'

Seen from the north, at first light on a still May morning, the great English country house called Longwarden appeared to be closed up, if not deserted. Several of the tall, many-paned windows were partially covered by the foliage of a vigorous oriental creeper. All had their internal shutters closed.

On the south side of the house where low spreading plants and lichens grew on a wide flagstoned terrace, every

48

ground-floor window was shuttered. Two on the first floor were not.

These were the windows near the corner of the east front where another pair of windows had their shutters folded away and their curtains open to show the linings and the faded, worn edges. One of the four windows was open, admitting ample fresh air to the bedroom of the present Countess of Carlyon who, like her seven predecessors, slept in a four-poster bed but, unlike the first five countesses, did not regard the night air as injurious to health.

While the early light brightened over the remaining acres of an estate which for two hundred years had expanded and then stayed in opulent equilibrium for more than a century before going into reverse during her time there, Lady Carlyon continued to sleep.

All that was to be seen of her was a long, thin shape under the bedclothes and a mass of thick mouse-brown hair beginning to go grey.

As the imminent sunrise brought her surroundings into sharper focus, it revealed that not only the curtains were in disrepair. The large, high-ceilinged room was furnished with a hotchpotch of chairs and tables from various periods of Longwarden's long history. These had aged well, gaining beauty as the years passed. But the carpet was threadbare, the wallpaper peeling away from the dusty cornice, and the once-white paint on the woodwork and the old-fashioned cast-iron radiators had become yellowed and chipped.

Having evolved, the room's décor lacked the cohesive stamp of a professional designer but reflected its occupant's interests. The landscapes and battle scenes adorning the walls of many country-house bedrooms here had been replaced by a collection of exquisitely fine and detailed botanical paintings by such masters as Dürer, Redouté and Turpin.

On one night table lay a copy of a book widely known as *Bean* and behind it were stacked the current catalogues of many well-known nurserymen. No great powers of detection were needed to deduce that the sleeping woman was keenly interested in gardening.

It was a quarter to seven when the gadget on the other night table began to perform the first of its functions which was to make tea for the Countess before waking her up.

Roused after eight hours' sound sleep, Penelope Carlyon was not immediately conscious that today was a special one. Her fiftieth birthday.

A widow for over ten years, she had slept alone for much longer. Although now, in middle age, she was strong and healthy, often working in her garden for nine or ten hours a day, in her youth she had lost two babies. The two she had carried to term had been difficult births.

After Allegra's birth, her gynaecologist had advised her not to try for another son. From then on she and her husband had slept apart, a circumstance of even greater relief to her than his death; although it hadn't been until he was killed in the hunting field that she had been able, finally, to put out of her mind the revulsion evoked on their wedding night.

As long as Edward was alive, she had never been able to forget what had happened on the twelfth of June, 1954, in Room 46 at the Hyde Park Hotel.

A stallion covering a nervous filly would have been less brutal than her heavy, clumsy, silent, slightly drunk bridegroom. From that night on she had loathed him and despised herself for allowing a domineering mother to chivvy her into a marriage which had been a disaster from within a few hours of the elaborate, expensive wedding.

But in those days, more than thirty years ago, marriage had seemed the right and proper destiny of every woman. Being tall, thin and shy, and knowing she wasn't attractive to the opposite sex, Pen had felt herself lucky to receive even one proposal.

With hindsight she could see that when Edward had asked her to marry him she should have said a firm no and set out to make a career for herself as a gardener. Today it would be easy for a girl with green fingers to do that.

Sitting up in bed, drinking a cup of tea made by the invaluable if unsightly machine, she faced the fact of being fifty without many pangs of regret.

50

. . . as the quick years pass and the body grows old around the still young heart . . .

The years had been passing more slowly when she had first read that line in Gertrude Jekyll's *A Gardener's Testament*, the original Country Life edition bought by Flora Carlyon for her husband in 1937. It was on Pen's night table now.

Nevertheless for a woman such as herself, a plain Jane with no beauty to mourn, middle age was a good time of life. That she was no longer fertile didn't depress her. To have done with the curse was a relief. She knew now that both physically and temperamentally she had been unfitted for motherhood. She had long been aware that her children found her a bore. She was not on their wave-length, nor they on hers.

Even so she understood the devotion most mothers felt towards their offspring. In her own case, maternal feelings of love, anxiety and pride were aroused not by her footloose son and difficult, headstrong, unaffectionate daughter, but by the trees, shrubs and plants whose welfare was the chief purpose of her existence.

Her tea finished, she climbed out of bed and, pulling an old kimono over her cheap chain-store nightgown, went to the open window.

The pale clear sky held the promise of a warm dry day. There were numerous tasks competing for her attention. This morning she had planned to tackle the suckers on the roses before they had time to weaken their parents.

It seemed a humdrum way to celebrate one's half-century, but what else did she want to do.

A leading French amateur gardener, the Vicomte de Noailles, had called a garden 'a shelter from the hardships of life'. That had certainly been true for her. Without the garden at Longwarden the hollowness of her marriage would have been unendurable. Always a taciturn man, except with his hunting cronies, for years Edward had scarcely spoken to her. When, in front of the staff, she had striven to keep up some sort of conversation, he had answered in monosyllables and grunts. In the end she had given up the effort. The servants of those days must have known they didn't sleep together and probably suspected, as she had, that his sexual needs were supplied by female members of the Carlyon Hunt.

Why Edward hadn't married a horsewoman was something which had baffled her until, in a fit of spleen, he had told her his reason for choosing her.

A movement in the garden caught her eye. It was Ashford walking away from the house with the old gun-dog, Ben, at his heels. It had been the spring of last year when Ashford had replaced Gisburn, their previous butler. Ashford was more of a general factotum, willing to turn his hand to anything. He had none of Gisburn's self-importance and stuffy pomposity.

Allegra had once called Gisburn a pain in the arse. While deploring the expression, and much else about her daughter's manners and morals, Pen had had to admit it summed up her own irritation when Gisburn had put on his aggrieved look.

Ashford never looked aggrieved. He seemed to accept from the first that theirs was an odd, unconventional household, run on a shoestring with a minimum of staff.

Before coming to Longwarden he had been in the service of a retired and reputedly eccentric general whose sister had provided him with a reference, his only reference. Before that, they gathered, he had been a batman and spent most of his life overseas.

Not content with one written encomium, North had been to see the late general's sister. 'There are still some valuable things we haven't been forced to sell yet, and this chap wouldn't be the first crook to write himself a glowing recommendation,' he had told Pen.

She had been present when the two applicants were interviewed. She had liked Mr Ashford on sight.

'I'm sure he's not a crook, North. I preferred him to the other man. *He* looked like a drinker.'

'So was Gisburn. Most butlers are,' North had answered, with a shrug. 'One thing in Ashford's favour is that, for a man of his age, he still looks in pretty good shape. Having an able-bodied man in the house is some protection for two women on their own.'

'How old is he, d'you think?'

'Middle fifties, but he could pass for late forties if he weren't grey.'

Now, as she looked down at Ashford from her bedroom window, it struck Pen that although in the past fourteen months he must have learnt everything there was to know about them, they still knew no more about him than he had volunteered at the interview.

Some weeks after his arrival, she had asked Mrs Armitage, their cook, how they were getting on with each other.

'Never grumpy like Mr Gisburn when the mood took him, but very reserved,' had been Mrs Armitage's opinion of the new butler. 'Not one to talk about himself. Not much of a talker at all.'

This had made Pen suppress a smile because Maisie Armitage, who had come to the house as sixteen-year-old Maisie Lotts, never stopped talking.

Undoubtedly she would have regaled Ashford with her own life history and everything she knew – which was a great deal – about the Carlyon family, past and present. Pen found it disturbing to realize that Ashford was probably privy to the dismal history of her marriage.

That he also had been married but was now a widower were the only details of his past which the cook had succeeded in eliciting.

Before Mrs Armitage had wormed the fact of his marriage out of him, Allegra, who was curious about what made people tick but rather less blatantly inquisitive than the cook, had speculated about his sexual inclinations.

'I don't think he's homosexual but I doubt if he's hetero either,' she had remarked to her brother.

'What makes you think that?' North had asked.

'The way he looks at me. Not a spark, not a flicker of interest. One can always tell.'

Pen had put in rather sharply, 'Don't you think you may

be overrating your attractiveness in expecting even our butler to succumb to your charms?'

It had been a horrid remark for a mother to make to her daughter and she had immediately regretted it. Somehow they always rubbed each other the wrong way.

She remembered Allegra's reply, delivered in the patronizing tone of a beautiful, self-confident woman who had had many lovers to one who had been a virgin when she married and was now too old and weather-beaten to merit a second glance from anyone.

'*You* may not have noticed it, Mother, but Ashford is a man as well as a butler. Twenty years ago he must have been quite a dasher. For his age, he's still not bad-looking.' She had paused. 'It might be amusing to see if I can raise a gleam in those rather nice dark brown eyes.'

Pen, knowing the outrageous behaviour of which her daughter was capable, had been horrified.

'Allegra, you are not to flirt with him. It would be most unbecoming. North, do make her see –'

'Don't panic, Mama.' Not for years, since they were tiny, had either of them called her the more affectionate Mummy. 'Allegra is only trying to get a rise out of you. Anyway I'm sure if she did give Ashford the come-on she'd be politely but firmly rebuffed – and made to feel foolish,' North added, with a glance at his sister. 'He strikes me as a man who can cope with every contingency, including importunate females trying to lure him into bed, which I daresay has happened before now.'

'I don't want him in my bed. Mother is the one who needs a man in her bed,' Allegra had answered. 'If you don't find a lover soon it will be too late,' she had told Pen, not for the first time. 'And who could be more convenient than Ashford? Old Lady Ingoldisthorpe had it off with her groom for years and never made any secret of it. Jolly good luck to her.'

Pen had been furious. Red in the face she had walked out of the room, hearing North say as she left it, 'You are a bitch to bait her, Ally.'

But he hadn't sounded more than mildly annoyed. He

thought Pen should hit back when Allegra teased her. He didn't understand that she couldn't. It wasn't in her nature to be aggressive. She loathed scenes and squabbles – and outspoken talk about sex.

All she wanted was to be left in peace with her two old gardeners, Mr Craskett and Mr Hazell, both in their seventies, to talk to during the day, and her tortoiseshell cat, William, and the radio for companionship late at night, after Sarah had gone back to the stables. A man was the last thing she needed.

But now on this fine May morning, still leaning out of her window, with Ashford a distant figure on the far side of the ha-ha, Pen saw how fast the years of her life had sped by, and how soon she would be an old woman.

With luck, an energetic old woman, still capable of kneeling to weed and bending to dig. Perhaps these later years might be enriched by grandchildren who would love her as much as her children had adored their great-grandmother, the legendary Flora Carlyon who, in spite of her kindness, years ago, to Edward's nervous fiancée, had made Pen doubly aware of her own lack of grace and charm.

It might be that, having made a hash of marriage – not wholly through her own fault – and a poor job of being a mother, she would make a success of being a grandmother. It would be nice to be loved just once in her life. Sarah, her niece, was fond of her, but affection fell short of love.

It was never having been the dearest person in the world to another human being which Pen found herself regretting. Loving and being loved: she had missed them both, she thought wistfully.

Lost in thought Pen watched her butler walking back from the obelisk without really seeing him.

It was not until he was inside the boundary of the ha-ha that her mind came back to the present and she thought how well he had adapted himself to life at Longwarden; doing things which weren't required of him but which were thoughtful and helpful, such as taking the elderly dog for a walk every morning and evening to help keep his weight under control.

He fitted in perfectly, thought Pen. Like Mrs Armitage and Sammy, Ashford was a treasure. They were lucky to have found him. But was he equally satisfied? It was hard to tell. Once or twice during the worst of last winter, she had noticed him looking out of the windows at the leafless trees and rain-sodden grass and wondered if he were longing for a drier climate.

She felt sure he would have no problem obtaining a post anywhere in the world, for a good deal more than they were paying him. But perhaps he liked the quiet here. And on spring mornings such as this nowhere could be more lovely than the park laid out by Humphry Repton in 1790 and the pleasure grounds full of plants brought back from China at the turn of the century by Caspar Carlyon who had also found his bride there.

Ashford was coming along the dew-spangled grass walk leading to the terrace below her window, his wellingtons leaving a trail of footprints. He was wearing corduroy trousers and a navy fisherman's jersey over a Tattersall-checked shirt. He looked more like an early-bird guest than the butler.

Perhaps he sensed he was being watched. Mounting the steps from the walk to the terrace, he glanced up and saw her leaning out of the window. For a moment they stared at each other. Pen was aware of a curious tightness in her chest.

A smile showed the sound natural teeth of the tall, greying man on the terrace.

'Good morning. A glorious morning.'

Suddenly conscious that her hair was tumbling about her shoulders instead of being pinned in the bun she had worn for the past ten years, Pen said, 'Good morning. Yes – glorious.'

She expected him to move on, but he didn't. He stood still, looking up until his intent dark gaze made her uneasy.

Colouring like a gauche girl, she said, 'I must dress. I'll be late,' and drew back out of sight.

Puzzling over why she should be flustered by merely exchanging good mornings with a man she met every day,

56

she went to her bathroom to brush her own excellent teeth. As a girl, her teeth and her skin had been her best features. Her teeth were still good. Her fine dry skin which for years she had neglected, working outside in all weathers without the protective creams Allegra had warned her were necessary, was beginning to be lined.

Before reaching for her toothbrush she studied herself in the mirror, wondering how old she looked to other people. When she had been Sarah's age, people of fifty had seemed to have one foot in the grave. To her two aged part-time gardeners, men in their fifties were still comparative youngsters. But how did her butler, only a few years her senior, see her?

Yesterday, if she had thought about it, she would have said that he didn't see her as a woman but only as a combination of asexual personae: the late Lord Carlyon's widow, the present Lord Carlyon's mother, Miss Sarah's aunt, a latterday Gertrude Jekyll whose devotion to her garden made her neglect her duties as Longwarden's chatelaine.

Now, after that strange piercing look, she felt that for the first time he had seen the person she really was, the inner self, the shy girl who couldn't believe that today she was fifty years old with a face beginning to wrinkle and a body which had borne two children but never experienced either desire or fulfilment.

She remembered Allegra saying '. . . *not a spark, not a flicker of interest . . . it might be amusing to see if I can raise a gleam in those rather nice dark brown eyes.*'

Was it possible that she, Pen, had raised that gleam a few moments ago?

With a shake of the head she took the top off the toothpaste and squeezed some on to her brush. Common sense told her she must have imagined it.

But she hadn't imagined her own reaction. The sensations she had felt when he looked up tallied precisely with those described by her fellow debs, years ago, when they were falling in and out of love and she was waiting for the lover who never came.

Oh lord! she thought. How absurd. I can't fall in love, not at my age – and especially not with my butler. Nothing could be more ludicrous. I must stop at once . . . control myself. If I don't, Allegra will spot it in a minute and bait me unmercifully.

While Lady Carlyon was dressing, her niece was busy in the stables, having been up for some time.

Until her eighteenth birthday, Sarah's room had been one of the thirty-eight bedrooms on the first floor at Long-warden. Then she had persuaded Aunt Pen to allow her to move to the room in the top of the triumphal arch which formed an impressive entrance to the stableyard.

From this eyrie, when her alarm clock woke her at six, she had only to descend a circular staircase, unlatch the door at the bottom and hurry across the large yard to the luxurious loose-boxes which, until World War One, had housed numerous hunters and carriage horses.

A number of the once-elegant carriages were gathering dust and cobwebs in the coach-house with some of the early motorcars which had superseded them.

Some of the horses of that time were commemorated by brass plaques engraved with their names above the saddle racks in the tackroom. Sarah was still using tack made long before World War Two and kept in immaculate condition by a dwindling retinue of grooms who had worked all their lives at Longwarden.

Only one remained, Sammy O'Brien. He was not a local man. Born in Ireland, the son of a stud groom, he had grown up with horses and horse-lore, eventually becoming a jockeys' valet. This was how he had met Sarah's father, Ranulf Lomax, who had at first shared Sammy's services with other steeplechase jockeys but later engaged him to be his personal attendant. Sammy had come to Longwarden and remained after Ranulf was killed when Sarah was five.

She could remember her father but had only the vaguest recollection of her mother who, within a week of being widowed, had walked out of the cottage they had occupied on the estate and had never been heard of since.

Fortunately Sarah's prowess on her second pony had endeared her to her uncle whose own children – much older than she – did not share his interests. A disagreeable husband and father who cared more for his horses than his closest relations, he had taken a fancy to his niece and would, had he lived, have been enormously proud of her first successes as an eventing competitor; successes which had already caused commentators to compare her to Lucinda Prior-Palmer, now Lucinda Green.

However in spite of the attention she had attracted Sarah was in no danger of having her head turned. Much as she admired all the riders who throughout her childhood and teens had been winning at Badminton, Burghley and other important British horse trials, it was the horses who were the champions in her eyes.

If she were ever to emulate Lucinda Green's list of triumphs, it would be because of Bedouin Star, a brilliant horse taking his intelligence and boldness from his Arab ancestry.

On the wall of her narrow room above the archway hung the words of a Bedouin legend which her cousin Allegra had had copied by a calligrapher, and framed, as a birthday present for her. Sarah knew them by heart.

Allah said to the South Wind, 'Become solid flesh, for I will make a new creature of thee, to the honour of my Holy One, and the abasement of mine enemies, and for a servant to them that are subject to me.'

And the South Wind said, 'Lord, do thou so.'

Then Allah took a handful of the South Wind and He breathed thereon, creating the horse and saying, 'Thy name shall be Arabian, and virtue bound into the hair of thy forelock, and plunder on thy back. I have preferred thee above all beasts of burden, inasmuch as I have made thy master thy friend. I have given thee the power of flight without wings, be it in onslaught or in retreat. I will set men on thy back that shall honour and praise Me and sing Hallelujah to My name.'

The legend hung on the wall behind the writing desk where, on the evenings she didn't spend in the house with her aunt, Sarah dealt with her paperwork – the entry forms and the bills. The worrying bills which every month seemed to go up so that very soon the allowance from North, and the money Allegra was giving her from the earnings from her book, wouldn't be enough to cover the outgoings.

Also, each week, there was one evening when she sat down to write a long letter to the man who was her secret love. It was almost two years since she had last seen him.

When Pen went down to breakfast her hair was secured in a bun at the back of her head, held there by large brown pins which during the day would emerge and have to be pushed back in place.

Although told by Allegra that the style didn't suit her, Pen found it by far the most practical of the various hairdos she had had since her schoolgirl pigtails. She could cut it as well as wash it, thereby saving the expense of six-weekly visits to London to have it cut at David & Josef in Berkeley Street, and also the need for weekly shampoos and sets in the market town twelve miles from Longwarden village.

Economies had become necessary when Edward, in financial difficulties, had reduced her allowance. Up to that time she had bought her few good clothes at Hardy Amies. Because her taste was conservative, her figure hadn't changed and she rarely went anywhere, most of them were still wearable and should last for many years yet.

To work in the garden she wore old trousers and sweaters or, in summer, blue jeans and shirts, sometimes North's cast-offs or, as today, pink cotton dungarees which when new had belonged to her daughter. At the beginning of the vogue for them, Allegra had worn the legs rolled above her ankles. On Pen's thinner legs they looked better rolled down.

Perhaps one of the reasons she had thought she liked Edward was because his height made it unnecessary for her to sag at the knees when she danced with him. Now the Princess of Wales had made tallness fashionable. In Pen's youth it had not been. Men had preferred to look down on women, and not only physically.

In summer breakfast was served in a small east-facing

60

room known as the Cabinet which received the sun early. When Pen arrived there she found Ashford had opened the french windows and moved the round table from its usual place in the centre of the room to a position closer to the open air.

Very often her niece was before her. Today she was not and Pen felt a certain awkwardness in being alone with her butler after the earlier encounter. She knew this was foolish and covered it by saying, 'What a good idea to put the table nearer the windows. In fact if this weather holds we might eat outside on the terrace. What was the forecast, Mr Ashford? Did you hear it?'

When she entered the room the butler had been bending to plug in the toaster, one of a number of gadgets of which Edward wouldn't have approved. He had been a stickler for traditional methods, even though toast sent from the kitchen wrapped in a napkin was never as hot and crisp as toast made at the table.

Nor would he have approved of her addressing a butler as Mr Ashford rather than by his surname alone. However although she had called their previous butler Gisburn, Pen had felt an instinctive reluctance to continue that patronizing usage with this man.

'The forecast is excellent, m'Lady. The weather is expected to be good for some days.'

Dressed now in well-pressed grey trousers, a black alpaca jacket, white shirt and charcoal tie, he drew out her chair.

'Thank you.'

As Pen sat down it struck her that when he had said good morning he had omitted the deferential m'Lady. Didn't that confirm her intuition that he had been seeing her with new eyes? Or had it been merely a slip of no significance whatever?

As she shook out her napkin she said, 'I wonder if you have time to give me a helping hand for about an hour this morning? Mr Hazell and Mr Craskett are growing too frail to help me put out the urns which were taken in for the winter. I don't want them straining themselves, but I can't quite manage alone.'

As she had known he would, he said, 'Certainly, m'Lady. What time do you wish to start the operation?'

'Not before about eleven. There are one or two things I want to tackle beforehand and I'm sure you have plenty to do.'

As she poured milk over her muesli she was appalled at the speed with which she had lapsed from her firm resolve in the bathroom. Less than half an hour ago she had been determined to quash this ridiculous attraction before it made a fool of her. Now here she was asking his help with a job which last year she had managed with Sarah's aid.

I must be going mad, she thought wildly. I didn't feel like this about him yesterday. Or did I? Secretly. Deep down.

It was North's light kisses on her cheeks, not Howell's embrace in the car when he brought her home, which Jane remembered when she woke up and saw her saffron dress hanging outside the closet and her gold ornaments glistening in the sunlight shining on the dressing table.

For the first time since her father's death she flung back the bedclothes and sat up feeling happy and excited. The day ahead seemed full of promise. Her world, which for a whole year had been out of kilter, was now, overnight, set to rights. The grey veil of sorrow had lifted and the future was bright and inviting.

In the shower she debated what to wear. If he planned to have lunch in style at the Café Plaza she would need a more elegant outfit than for drinks and sandwiches in Copley's, the bar. It would really be more fun to have a seafood salad in one of the lively young places in Quincy Market, part of the historic, beautifully restored Fanueil Hall Marketplace down by the waterfront, which always reminded her of Paris.

Maybe he didn't know about the market. The shops, cafés and food stalls might not have been there the last time he was in Boston.

Perhaps she should call him and suggest it. On second thought, no. Her bedroom didn't have an extension. Using

62

the telephone downstairs meant that her aunt might come in while she was talking to him.

There was sure to be a battle about him sooner or later, but she didn't want one *before* her lunch date. It wasn't her nature to be deceitful. She didn't intend to go on seeing him secretly, as she had Charles. But until they had spent a few hours together, she couldn't be sure that yesterday's instant attraction would stand up to the test of getting to know him. After a couple of hours *à deux*, she might find that he bored her. She didn't think so, but it was possible.

Small children were vainly chasing the tolerant squirrels, and the pedal-powered swan boats cruising slowly round the pond had had their spring coat of white paint, as she sauntered across the Public Garden.

'I thought you'd come this way.'

North rose from a bench, surprising her. Watching a swan boat, she hadn't noticed him sitting there.

'Oh . . . hello,' she said, smiling. 'Have you been here long?'

'Only a few minutes. I decided it was too nice a day to have lunch in the city. I've borrowed Alison's car and we're going into the country.'

He had left some things on the bench. A large envelope, a book – and a flower which he presented to her with a courtly inclination of his head. It was an apricot rosebud just beginning to unfold its delicate petals.

'Thank you . . . it's lovely. But I don't have a button-hole or a pin.'

'The shop provided a pin.'

He turned the lapel of his blazer and, taking a pin from the back of it, fastened the rosebud to her jacket.

'How did the developing go? Are you pleased with the results?' she asked as they strolled to where he had left the car.

'I have some of the prints with me.' He indicated the envelope. 'You can look through them on the way.'

'Where are we going?'

'Wait and see. What time did you get to bed?'

63

'Not very late. Before two. Howell has a heavy day today. He needed at least five hours' sleep.'

'Do you see a lot of him?'

'I'm going to see less from now on. Marcus thinks Howell has marriage in mind and, as I haven't, I don't want to hurt him.'

'You don't want to marry, or you don't want to marry Howell?' he asked, glancing down at her.

'I definitely don't want to marry Howell and I'm not in a hurry to marry anyone. Nor are you, presumably, as you're still a bachelor at thirty?'

She wondered how, in view of his admission to Marcus, he would answer. Half-expecting a flip reply, she was surprised when he said with apparent seriousness, 'My attitude to marriage is complicated by the fact that my work involves travelling to places where most women would be an encumbrance and wouldn't enjoy themselves either. At the same time I'm conscious that I'm the last of my line and owe it to my forebears to have sons to follow me.'

'There's no other male in your family who would be your heir if you died without a son?'

'No, there isn't. My father had a younger brother, but he was killed steeplechasing. He had only one child, Sarah. She lives at Longwarden with us.' The thought of Sarah made him smile. 'She's crazy about horses . . . spends all her time in the stables. Did you go through that phase in your teens?'

'I learnt to ride but it was never a craze with me. Why does Sarah live with you? What happened to her mother?'

'She didn't like living in the country, looking after a child, so she left. Allegra and I were both away at school, but the nanny we'd had as small children was still living near us. She came out of retirement to look after Sarah, although even then she spent most of her time in the stables.'

'How old is she now?'

'Nineteen – with no other thought in her head but to win next year's Badminton Horse Trials.'

They had arrived at the car. He unlocked the passenger

door for her before going round to the offside and swinging himself in beside her. Alison's car was a small imported one which she could tuck into parking spaces too short for a larger car. Jane had been inside it before and not found it cramped, but North's long legs and breadth of shoulder made it seem so today.

As they set off she opened the envelope and took out the prints. They weren't what she had expected. These had all been taken when people were unaware of being photographed. There was a shot of a woman critically appraising another woman's dress; a shot of a man laughing uproariously at his own joke while the people with him simulated amusement; an overweight teenage girl eating frosted cake and wistfully eyeing a boy who was talking to a slim girl; a woman who looked as if she were on her third or fourth face-lift in the act of repainting her thin lips.

'These are for your private album, presumably?' she said, looking at a brilliant picture of Euphemia's old bony hand stroking the floss-silk curls of a small child.

'Yes. Especially the last one.'

The last one was a picture of Jane which he must have taken a minute or two before speaking to her. It was a close-up of her profile. The breeze was lifting her hair, showing the pearl on the lobe of her small shapely ear. Of her face all that could be seen was the line of her forehead and cheek, the tip of her nose and an oblique view of the chin which people who had known her father recognized as a feminized form of John Graham's determined chin.

'And then I turned round and disappointed you,' she remarked.

He shot a smiling glance at her. 'I wasn't disappointed.'

'Yes, you were. You said so. You can't wriggle out of it now,' she said, teasing him. 'My eyes were a let-down. You were hoping for dark-brown almond eyes, not commonplace grey ones.'

As she had noticed yesterday, when he grinned it made a deep crease in his sun-burned cheek.

He said, 'Did that annoy you? Were you piqued by my less than total admiration? Is that why you agreed to have

65

lunch with me? To make me admit that your eyes are a very rare grey with the longest eyelashes I've ever seen?'

She laughed. 'You have a nice line in flattery, but I'd better warn you that you won't get away with feeding me compliments. I have an inelegantly hearty appetite.'

'I'm delighted to hear it,' he said. 'It bores me to take out girls, however stunning, who refuse to eat more than an omelette or a few lettuce leaves. Can you really keep that beautiful body in shape without counting calories?'

'As long as I exercise it. I jog round the common most mornings and two nights a week I go to an exercise class. My father took fitness seriously a long time before the present cult. He brought me up to believe that everyone should spend one hour a day protecting their health rather than relying on doctors to make them better when they got sick. Last winter I learned to skate on the pond at The Country Club. That was Alison's suggestion.'

'She's a nice woman, Alison. Not an ambitious old harpy like Julia Foster. Does she know you're lunching with me?'

'Not yet.' Ahead of them she could see the roofs of America's oldest university. 'Did you like being at Harvard? Apart from the complications with Susan, were you sorry to break off your time here?'

'Not really. My father's death in the hunting field meant that I could lead my life my way. Obviously you were very close to your father. I wasn't. Mine was obsessed by horses and it wasn't until after he died that we found out how much he'd lost betting on them. That he chose to spend most of his time in the saddle or at the races was okay by me as long as he didn't expect me to share his obsession – or interfere with my obsession. But he lumped photography with ballet dancing and hairdressing as jobs for homosexuals. Doing what I wanted to do was impossible while he was alive, so I wasn't sorry when he died. Does that shock you?'

'No, because I'm in a similar situation. I don't mean I wish Aunt Julia would die, but I do resent her power to ordain where and how I live for another two years. Not that I have any burning ambitions, but I should like to feel free,

66

which I don't at the moment. She's not my only trustee but she's the most influential one. The other two are elderly men who think because she and I are the same sex, she must know what's right for me.'

'I'd have thought, if you put your mind to it, you could persuade elderly men to agree to anything you wanted,' said North. 'You could me.'

She laughed. 'I doubt that very much – unless it was something which happened to suit your convenience.'

'I strike you as a selfish brute, hm?'

'Not selfish. Single-minded. Gifted people generally are. My father certainly was. He never did anything he didn't wish to. Marie-Simone, his companion, wanted to be his wife and have his child. He knew that but he ignored it because it wasn't what he wanted.'

'How did you feel about her?'

'I was very fond of her and still am. She taught me how to arrange myself, as the French say, which is more than a lot of mothers do for their daughters.'

North said, 'You were luckier than my sister. Our mother was neither tactful nor helpful during Allegra's teens. Their relationship was a running battle and still is.'

'Are you fond of your mother?'

'Not particularly. The person we loved was my great-grandmother. She was everything our parents were not: sympathetic, tolerant, loving. She was a darling.'

The warmth in his voice as he spoke of her counterbalanced the chilling indifference of his reference to the present Countess.

'Does your mother run the estate in your absence?' Jane asked.

'She works like a slave in the gardens but isn't much interested in the house. She's always urging me to marry someone who can take charge of that side. Unfortunately I'm not attracted by capable, bossy young women with large backsides and thick ankles!'

'I'm sure there must be lots of girls who combine capability with acceptable behinds and ankles. Perhaps you haven't looked hard enough.'

'I haven't looked at all,' he admitted. 'All the candidates so far have been produced by my mother. But I can't shelve my duty for ever.'

'Why not look for someone to love and hope that, for love of you, she'll make herself a competent chatelaine?' she suggested lightly.

'There aren't many of your sex who see things that way today. I don't blame them. But let's both forget our problems: your aunt and my crumbling old house.'

For some minutes they had been travelling fast along the Cambridge turnpike. Now they were approaching the historic town of Concord. Jane had been there on several occasions to visit the house where Louisa May Alcott had written *Little Women*, and also the one they had just passed, the home of Ralph Waldo Emerson. He and the Alcotts, and Thoreau and Nathaniel Hawthorne, were all buried in the Sleepy Hollow Cemetery.

Having assumed that North had reserved a table at the Colonial Inn, overlooking the green, she was surprised when they drove past it. A few minutes later, carrying the rug which he had produced, while he carried a picnic hamper and a cooler, she was crossing the wooden bridge spanning the quiet Concord River at the place where British Redcoats and colonial Minutemen had fired the first shots in the Revolutionary War. Soon she was sitting on the spread rug, watching North peel the foil from the neck of a bottle of champagne.

'This is some of the bubbly left over from yesterday's beanfeast,' he told her. 'So are the goodies in the hamper. This spring weather's too good to waste in a stuffy restaurant. It's going to be a hot afternoon. I'm going to take off my coat. How about you?'

He stood the bottle on the grass in a patch of shade and took off his blazer. His open-necked cotton shirt was almost as blue as his eyes and emphasized their vividness. She wondered if he were a vain man and wore blue shirts for that reason. Inevitably he must have flaws, like everyone else, but she hoped they weren't small-minded ones such as vanity, and that his motive for bringing her on a picnic

68

was a genuine preference for alfresco eating, not meanness.

North rolled up his shirt sleeves. His forearms were sinewy and lightly covered with the dark hairs she had noticed on his wrists while he was driving.

'I've been thinking about your trip to New York. Would it help if I asked Allegra to call you and suggest a meeting?' he asked.

Jane didn't tell him that Mrs Foster also disapproved of his sister. Having removed her own jacket, she slipped off her shoes in order to sit cross-legged, her pleated skirt fanned over her knees. Marie-Simone had taught her some yoga and it was more comfortable to sit on the rug in the lotus position than with her legs to one side.

She said, 'I'm sure your sister has enough on her mind without being involved in my arrangements. If I take a firm stand, I don't believe Aunt Julia will forbid a visit to New York. Up to now I haven't opposed her. It hasn't seemed worth it. But I'm not a meek person by nature.'

He was easing the cork very gently out of the bottle. It was a small point in his favour. Her father had taught her to disapprove of the ostentatious popping of champagne corks.

'Perhaps not, but your aunt can be quite ferocious when she's angry. Perhaps you've never seen her in a rage.'

She took the glass he was handing to her. 'Thank you. You said we should forget all our problems for a few hours and concentrate on enjoying all this' – with a gesture at the verdant greenery on all sides.

From the bridge a path wound across a meadow towards a handsome period house which she knew was called the Buttrick Mansion, having wandered round its gardens the previous autumn. North had brought her in a different direction to a grassy knoll from which they could see the placid surface of the river glistening in the sun.

Jane sipped the chilled wine. 'What could be nicer than drinking champagne in this setting?' she murmured appreciatively.

'I can suggest an improvement. How about eating smoked salmon and drinking champagne in this setting?' He began to unbuckle the straps of the hamper.

Presently he handed her a napkin, a fork and a plate heaped with appetizing delicacies including the promised smoked salmon, small flaky creamed chicken puffs, Russian salad, a stuffed tomato, black olives and country pâté.

'What else do you do with your time besides jogging, skating and fending off Howell and others?' he asked as they started to eat.

'I spend a lot of time in the Athenaeum. Have you been there?'

He nodded. 'What sort of books do you like?'

'History . . . poetry . . . travel. Right now I'm reading *News from Tartary*. It's about a journey made by an Englishman and a Swiss girl from Peking to Kashmir in 1935.'

He nodded. 'I've read it . . . more than once. Granny Flora gave it to me. I'd been brought up on her own traveller's tales and for one of my birthdays she gave me a copy. It was by far the most influential book I read as a schoolboy. Odd that you should be reading it now. You know that the author, Peter Fleming, was the brother of Ian, the creator of James Bond?'

'I didn't know that.'

'Peter Fleming married Celia Johnson, a very fine English actress. One of her best film parts was as the wife in Noel Coward's *Brief Encounter*. They're all three dead now, but I think *News from Tartary* will survive. It's a classic among travel books.'

'Do you think they were lovers as well as travelling companions . . . Peter and Kini, the Swiss girl? He says in the book that they neither fell in love nor got on each other's nerves; but it was a seven-month journey over more than three thousand miles of difficult, dangerous terrain . . . and he looks to have been very attractive.'

'One can't say the same of her,' North said dryly. 'The photograph of her plucking a duck makes her look more manly than womanly.'

'If she's still alive, she'll be almost eighty years old.'

Their discussion of the book lasted through the first part of their lunch. Jane felt encouraged by this small bond between them. It seemed a promising beginning.

She was glad he had brought some iced water as well as champagne. She knew that sparkling wine was more swiftly intoxicating than still wine and she wanted to keep her wits about her. After lunch he might try to make love to her. Where they were wasn't very secluded, but there were more private retreats not far away and no one had used the path from the bridge to the mansion since their own arrival. She wondered if this was where he had brought Susan Foster to make love to her on the warm spring grass.

'How did you discover this spot?' she asked.

'As one of my ancestors was killed in the Battle of Bunker Hill, I have a special interest in the War of Independence. This was where it all started,' he said, with a sweeping gesture at the meadows and woodland surrounding the bridge. 'It was a little earlier in the year – 19 April 1775. But it may have been a spring day like this when they started killing each other. You'd think that in two hundred years we'd have learned to stop killing.'

This led her to ask his opinion of the Irish situation and to like him all the more for the unbiased good sense of his views, the brevity with which he expressed them and, above all, the fact that he then asked her what she thought.

It was mid-afternoon and they had ranged over many subjects before there was a hiatus in the conversation. By this time North was stretched on his back with his hands clasped under his head and his eyes half shut against the bright light which, filtering through the branches overhead, burnished the angles of his darkly tanned face.

Jane was lying on her front, propped on her elbows, making a chain from buttercups and daisies picked from around the rug. In the lull, she thought it would be nice if she were the one on her back, with North leaning over her, kissing her.

She flicked a glance at his face, at the mouth which last night had brushed her cheeks and which now she wanted to feel pressed firmly over her lips. Merely thinking about it sent a thrust of excitement through her.

When, suddenly, using the muscles of his flat, hard

midriff, he rose into a sitting position, she tensed, her throat tightening with anticipation.

To her disappointment he said, 'I think it's time we made a move. Have you decided about coming to New York?'

She rolled over and sat up. 'Yes, I'd like to meet your sister. Aunt Julia may not approve, but –' She gave a slight shrug.

With another lithe movement he stood up and offered a hand to her.

'Is that your only reason?' he asked, retaining his grip on her hand after pulling her to her feet.

'No, it's time I had a break from Boston and found out for myself if New York is all it's cracked up to be.'

The blue eyes mocked her cool tone. He was sure – and how right he was! – that she wanted to meet *him* again. Well, she didn't mind his knowing that she was attracted to him. A moment ago, as he drew her to her feet, she had glimpsed the unmistakable evidence that he was equally strongly attracted to her.

'Would you like me to find out where my sister will be staying and make a reservation for you?' His hand was playing with her hand, his thumb in her palm, his fingertips feeling the fine bones from knuckle to wrist.

Gently but firmly she disengaged it. 'No, thanks. I'll take care of that.'

For a moment she thought he was going to take her in his arms. Why he chose not to kiss her then she couldn't guess. Certainly not from diffidence, she thought, as she helped to re-pack the hamper. North wasn't the kind of man who would feel any uncertainty about a girl's reaction to his kisses. He would take her enjoyment for granted, and with good reason. How could any warm-blooded unattached female fail to respond to the powerful sexual magnetism of this tall patrician?

The van from Longwarden Post Office which delivered letters and parcels to the farms and houses beyond the boundaries of the village didn't arrive at Longwarden until late in the morning. Usually Penelope Carlyon and her niece received their mail when they met for lunch.

In her incurious way Lady Carlyon seemed not to have noticed that every four or five weeks Sarah's post included a letter airmailed from abroad.

The outgoing mail, from long custom, was 'posted' in a mahogany letter box which had stood on a table in the main hall since early in the nineteenth century. This was no longer kept locked, to be opened only by the butler before its contents were dispatched to the village.

Nowadays the cleaning was done by a roster of part-time helpers who kept the principal rooms in reasonable order. Normally one of the afternoon cleaners would check the post box before going home and take with her any letters it contained.

However, because it would have caused talk in the village if the name and address on Sarah's airmail letters had been noticed, she preferred to post them herself. For fitness's sake she would bicycle there. To keep herself in good shape was as important as keeping the horses in condition.

After posting her weekly letter, and wishing she received more frequent replies, she pedalled towards a shop at the other end of the village to buy Polo mints for her four-legged beloveds.

It was Saturday afternoon, a time when most local men were watching sports programmes on TV. But some youths were smoking and chatting outside the fish and chip shop. The centre of the group, she noticed, was a young man with curly black hair who was sitting astride a large motor-bike. He was wearing black leathers and holding a bright-red crash helmet.

Sarah couldn't see whether the back of his jacket was plain or decorated, but she was almost sure he was the motorcyclist she and Beddo had encountered in Ice Lane recently.

The girl in charge of the sweet shop was Marilyn Brown whose mother worked at Longwarden. Marilyn was the same age as Sarah and they had known each other since childhood.

There was no one else in the shop. They chatted for a few minutes before Sarah said casually, 'Who's the new Hell's Angel? I don't think I've seen him before.'

The other girl looked out of the window.

'Oh, him,' she said, with a grimace. 'That's Tark Osgood, Mrs Barker's great-nephew. After she died, him and his mum came to live in her house. They're from London. She seems okay but he's a real nasty piece of work. Nobody likes him. Well, some of the boys are impressed by that Honda. But the girls can't stand him . . . not the nice girls,' she added primly. 'I hate him coming in here to buy cigarettes. Talk about personal remarks. I told him if he wasn't careful I'd report him to Sergeant Lacock. It just made him say something worse.' Her face reddened at the memory.

'Is there some snarling animal – a leopard, I think – on the back of his jacket?' asked Sarah.

Marilyn nodded.

As she paid for the large box of Polos the shopkeeper ordered specially for her, Sarah said, 'If he comes from London that explains why he didn't slow down when he saw me riding in Ice Lane the other day. I had better go over and tell him that not all horses are as imperturbable as London police horses.'

'He didn't make one of your horses bolt, did he?' asked Marilyn, looking concerned.

She herself was nervous of horses and had never understood how Miss Sarah had the courage to jump the high fences she had seen her go over on television. It wasn't as if she were tall like Lady Carlyon and Lady Allegra. Miss Sarah was only about five feet four and, until fairly recently, so skinny that but for the thick blonde pigtail hanging down her back, in riding breeches and thick navy fishermen's sweaters she could have been mistaken for an adolescent boy.

In the past two years she had changed and filled out a bit. Now, although she never wore any make-up and her hair was still braided from high on the crown of her head, she was really becoming quite pretty, thought Marilyn, admiring the other girl's deep blue eyes and her naturally red lips.

'I wouldn't say anything to him yourself, Miss Sarah,' she advised. 'He'll only tell you to get lost, and he won't put it politely neither.'

'I'm sure not,' said Sarah, lifting the box from the counter and tucking it under her arm.

This afternoon she was wearing jeans and a guernsey which had belonged to North when he was in his early teens. The tight faded jeans defined contours that were slender but unmistakably feminine; and her chest, which had once seemed destined to remain for ever flat, now made small but passable protrusions to the front of the guernsey.

'Don't say I didn't warn you,' said Marilyn anxiously.

Nothing would have induced her to confront a gang of disrespectful, sniggering youths, especially when they included that foul-mouthed, disgusting Tark Osgood.

Outside the shop Sarah put the box in the basket attached to the handlebars of the old-fashioned bicycle which she left propped against the kerb while she crossed the road.

At first they didn't notice her walking purposefully towards them. It was the one astride his expensive machine, the one with the air of being the leader of the group, who spotted her coming and paused before lighting the cigarette he had just placed between his lips. His stare made them all turn to look.

There were a few seconds when Sarah regretted her decision to tackle him here. A quick glance at the faces of his cohort showed one or two she had known by sight since their primary-school days. Most of them were newcomers, strangers. Greasy-haired, scruffy, generally unprepossessing, they were the rural equivalent of the youths who, in cities, hung around amusement arcades.

Tarquin Osgood had bold black eyes and a red bead on a gold ring adorning one ear. It gave him a gypsy-ish air.

The unlighted cigarette still dangling from full pink lips,

he gave Sarah an undressing look which might have thrilled other girls but only served to increase her antipathy towards him.

She managed a polite smile before introducing herself.

'Hello. I'm Sarah Lomax. May I have a few words with you, please? In private,' she added.

As she had expected, her voice was enough to provoke muttered parodies of her accent from one or two of the others, and sniggers from most of them. Only one boy didn't grin. The great-grandson of one of Lady Carlyon's gardeners, he shuffled his feet and looked uncomfortable.

Osgood took the cigarette from his mouth and flipped it at one of the others. 'Sure . . . why not?' he agreed, sliding forward on the saddle. 'Hop on and we'll go for a spin. I know a lot of private places.'

This was said with a meaning glance to which his audience reacted with appreciative guffaws.

'She ain't got no lid, Tarky,' said one. 'You don't want to let the fuzz see you with a bird on the back without no lid.'

'Lend her your lid then, Terry. We won't be gone more than an hour.'

There was another burst of sniggers as the one called Terry offered his helmet to Sarah.

'That isn't necessary, thank you,' she said composedly. 'What I want to discuss will only take a few minutes. We can talk by that bench over there.'

'He's done more than talk on that bench . . . int yer, Tarky?' said a wag in the background. 'That's where you fucked Sharon, innit?'

'Nah, 'e did 'er in the churchyard on that big old gravestone.'

Sarah, her fair skin flaming, had already turned away before the second remark, but she heard it and several that followed. Marilyn had been right. She shouldn't have attempted to talk to him here, surrounded by all the worst yobbos for miles around.

She was still heading for the bench, but about to change direction and return to her bicycle, when she heard a motorbike revving. A few moments later Tark had arrived at the bench.

By the time she joined him he had dismounted and propped up the heavy machine which had probably startled several old people and babies out of their afternoon naps.

Her blush hadn't quite died down.

He saw it, and said, 'Don't pay no attention to that lot. Have a fag.'

'No, thank you. I don't smoke.'

He shrugged. 'Suit yourself.'

As he lit a cigarette she noticed that his first two fingers were kipper-coloured and all his nails were lined with engine oil. But the shape of his hands wasn't ugly.

He sprawled on the slatted bench, slung one arm over the back and splayed his leather-clad legs, encased in boots up to the knee.

She wondered if he had really done what they claimed to a girl called Sharon either here or in the churchyard. If he had, she felt sorry for Sharon.

'What you want to talk about?' he asked, with a jerk of the head which she took to be an invitation to sit beside him.

She remained on her feet. 'I only wanted to warn you that if you come up behind a horse as fast and as close as you did to me and my horse in Ice Lane the other day, you risk causing a serious accident and possibly having your motorbike badly damaged. If, as I hear, you're from London, you may not –'

He interrupted her. 'If the horse int safe in traffic, it dint oughter be on the road.'

'He is safe,' she countered firmly. 'But you can't count on that; any more than you can count on other people driving or crossing roads safely. Whenever you have to pass horses, you should slow down and give them a wide berth. That lane where you passed me isn't used by much traffic, but of course you were not to know that. How long have you been in Longwarden?'

'Couple of months. It's not much of a place. Nothing to do,' he said moodily.

'How does your mother like it?'

'She's always fancied the country. She was born in a village. Not here. Somewhere near Portsmouth. Where d'you hear about us? Who said we was from London?'

'In a small village everyone hears when new people arrive,' she said vaguely.

'I int seen you before. Where d'you live?' he asked.

'A mile or two outside the village. I don't come in very often. I'm too busy looking after horses.'

'You work for his bleeding lordship, eh? How long you been there?'

Amused, she said, 'Two years, full time. Before that I used to be part time. What's your job?'

She hadn't intended to have a conversation with him but, close to, his face was more intelligent than she had expected. In a different setting, he could have passed for a Greek or Italian.

'There's nothing around here to suit me. I'm on the Social. Any jobs going up your place?'

'I don't think so – except perhaps gardening. My . . . Lady Carlyon is always short of help in the garden.'

He picked at his teeth with a thumbnail. 'Don't fancy gardening. What're they like to work for . . . Lady Whatsername and that lot? Expect you to work all hours for peanuts, do they?'

'They may have done years ago. They certainly don't nowadays. The person who works the hardest is Lady Carlyon herself. She's hardly ever *not* working. I don't think you'd want to put in the long hours she does,' Sarah said dryly.

'That's her bloody choice. She don't have to, not with the money they've got. Must be loaded to live in that place. I've been over the wall and had a look. Bloody great palace they've got there.'

'That doesn't make them rich. It's what keeps them bloody hard up,' she retorted, with wry humour. 'I don't think you understand the finances of large country houses. They're a constant expense, not an income.'

Seeing the sceptical gleam in his dark eyes, she thought,

What am I doing trying to explain to this lout things he will never understand?

Aloud, she said, 'I must go.'

'What's your hurry? You don't work Saturdays, do you?'

'I work every day. Horses don't stop eating or needing their stables mucked out on Saturdays and Sundays.'

'Seems a funny job for a girl, shovelling up horse shit.'

'That's only part of it. The rest is a lot of fun. Next time you meet a horse, try to remember to slow down, won't you? Goodbye.'

With a smile and a nod, she walked away.

In comparing Tark Osgood's looks with those of Greek and Italian waiters, Sarah had come close to something which Tark himself didn't know.

He was not the son of Ron Osgood, the bricklayer from whom his mother, Mavis Osgood, had separated when he was eight. He had been sired by a waiter from one of the Levante beach restaurants at Benidorm, a popular holiday resort on Spain's Costa Blanca.

Mavis had gone to Benidorm in the company of three other girls. She was already 'going' with Ron at the time and he hadn't approved of her having a holiday without him. But Mavis had heard of the pleasures of Benidorm from several of her workmates – the cheap shoes and other leather goods, the sun and the wine, the handsome sexy Spaniards – and was determined to taste them before she settled down with Ron.

It hadn't been her intention to do anything she shouldn't. But one night the wine went to her head and she let a waiter called Paco go all the way.

He was better-looking than Ron and it sounded ever so romantic when he murmured things to her in Spanish. But when he was lying on top of her, pumping up and down and panting, it wasn't any better than when Ron did it to her. As lovers, neither of them came anywhere near the heroes of the romantic novels which Mavis and her friends devoured while sunbathing on the beach.

At the end of the holiday she took home presents for her

family, including a fluorescent pink nylon fur donkey for her sister and a silver bottle of *Ponche* for Ron.

Two months later she told him she was pregnant. It must have happened the weekend after her holiday when, while the rest of his family were out for the evening, they opened the *Ponche*. It was more potent than Ron realized and made him less careful than usual.

Not that it mattered. They were going to get married anyway.

Although somewhat embarrassed when his wife's condition began to show rather sooner after the wedding than it should, Ron was pleased to discover that in Mavis he had chosen a wonderful little manager. The frequent new outfits she had worn when he first knew her had led him to fear she might make an expensive wife. It was a pleasant surprise to find she never overspent her housekeeping allowance, even with the extra expense of preparing for the baby. Every week, by careful housekeeping, she was able to afford to buy one or two items of babywear or nursery equipment. By the time the baby was due, it had a layette fit for a little prince.

Mavis decided, and Ron agreed, that if it were a boy they would call it Tarquin, if a girl, Jade. These were the names of the hero and heroine in one of her favourite books, *Tempest of Desire*.

When the baby was born it was bald and looked much like all other infants. It was some time before Ron began to wonder how his son came to have dark-brown eyes and thick black hair when no one in his or his wife's family had that colouring.

One day the ugly suspicion that he had been duped came into his mind and would not be dismissed. Something else worried him. He was beginning to realize that even the thriftiest housewife couldn't stretch her budget to encompass all the clothes, household goods and knick-knacks they owned.

But again, although strongly suspecting Mavis of habitual shoplifting, he said nothing to her. It was not her dishonesty that troubled him. He wasn't a rigorously honest man. The fear that she might be caught and her thefts reported in the local newspaper was what preyed on his mind and made him more and more irritable.

He began to pick on the boy. This infuriated Mavis and caused violent rows between them. She doted on Tarquin and, increasingly bored by her husband, had managed to convince herself that, if she could have stayed in Spain longer, Paco would have married her and they would now be the owners of their own restaurant.

By the time Ron started to drink she had worked out a number of ways to convert stolen goods into cash and had a nice nest-egg put by. They had their final row the night he dared to hit Tarquin for being cheeky to him.

A few days later, after an hour in the pub on the way back from work, Ron returned to find the house stripped of most of its contents. Neighbours had seen Mavis supervising the loading of a pantechnicon earlier in the day. Later she and her son had gone off in a taxi.

Ron was relieved to be rid of her and the spoilt little bastard she had foisted on him. He made no attempt to find out where they had gone.

Mavis had gone to London which she thought the best place to continue her activities as a bold and practised shoplifter.

At first there were difficulties. Without a husband or a job, she had no hope of a mortgage and, as all the London boroughs had long waiting lists for council flats, she had to live in furnished rooms and put most of her own things in storage. With no other means of support, she would have poured a sad tale into the ear of a social worker in the hope of some hand-outs from the state. But that might mean snoopers coming round. Mavis preferred to work as an office cleaner until she had made the contacts she needed to dispose of her easier source of income. Before long discreet inquiries at one of the local street markets put her in touch with the necessary outlet. Soon she was doing even better than she had before.

She and Tarquin were much happier on their own without Ron to bother them. Mavis had no need for a man in her life. Sex was something she could do without. She had her son to love and her taste for romance was satisfied by the paperback novels she stole every week from Woolworth's and then traded in at a swop shop.

The thought of being caught didn't worry her. In the huge metropolis of Greater London, few people noticed or cared what happened to their neighbours. At worst she could always move to another suburb. Her only anxiety was that, as he got older, Tarquin might get into trouble.

Mavis's mother was dead and she didn't keep in touch with her other relations except for an aunt whose marriage had taken her to another part of the country. At an apposite moment, when Mavis was seriously worried by the company Tarquin was keeping, her Auntie Grace died and left her a cottage at Longwarden. Tarquin didn't want to move but was persuaded by his mother's promise of the down payment on a Honda as soon as they were settled in the country.

On arrival in Longwarden village he was conscious of being an outsider in a more clannish place than the melting pot of south London. One or two girls gave him the eye when their regular boyfriends weren't watching. But in the pubs and at the village-hall disco on Saturday night, his attempts to mix in were not well received.

That changed once he had the Honda. At first he was happy just to ride around trying it out. One evening his mother asked him to go to the chip shop for their supper. Immediately he was surrounded by admiring, envious local lads. The girls, too, soon changed their tune. They all wanted to be the first to swing a leg over the pillion – even if the price of a ride was to have him mount them en route.

He had always been successful with girls. With the Honda and his new leathers, he couldn't go wrong. In his first two months in the village, he had made it with all the girls who were easy and several who were said not to be.

As the blonde bit called Sarah Something walked away from him, Tark wondered how long it would take to get

82

her on her back. He judged her to be the type who would play hard to get for a while; which would make a change from having them beg him for it.

He considered calling her back and suggesting they go to a disco of which, with the bike, he now had a wider choice. He already had a date, but it wouldn't bother him to drop her. Carol was pretty but dumb. This kid was pretty and bright. Made up and dressed up, she could be a knock-out, the kind of girl other guys wanted, the same way they wanted the Honda. He liked that: it made him feel good.

Then he changed his mind and decided he would play it cool too. Dropping his cigarette butt, he unpropped and straddled the bike and, with a loud roar of power, rode back to rejoin the others.

'What did she want to talk about?'

'Make a date with her, Tarky?'

'Mind your own effing business. It were private between her and me.'

'You know who she is, don't you?' asked the boy who had shuffled his feet.

'Yeah, she works up the big house. She told me. Asked if I'd like to work there,' Tark announced, preening.

'She don't work there. She lives there,' the boy said. 'Her dad and Lord Carlyon's dad was brothers. Her dad got killed in a horse race. Fell off and got it in the head. Suffin like that. Last time we seen her on telly, they said she was one of the best horse-riders in England. She might even get a gold medal at the Olympics.' Pleased with his superior knowledge and wanting to get back at Tark for calling attention to his acne, he added, 'The old bloke that works there is past it. I reckon she's looking for someone to muck out the horses and thought the job might suit you.'

There were muffled snickers.

Sensing that the pimple-faced runt had made him lose face, Tark said harshly, 'Why don't you piss off, Spotty, and play with kids your own age.'

But the brunt of his anger was directed at Sarah for not letting on who she was, for making a fool of him.

I'll fix her, he thought, enraged. I'll make her eat shit, little bitch.

The Athenaeum on Beacon Street is one of America's great independent libraries with three-quarters of a million volumes housed in an impressive building dating back to 1846. In the entrance to the building is a plaque: *Here remains a retreat for those who would enjoy the humanity of books.*

As one of the library's shareholders, Marcus Blakewell was entitled to four tickets a year for guests. Soon after her arrival in Boston he had given one to Jane. She had spent many happy hours in the Athenaeum's elegant rooms with their lofty ceilings, oriental rugs, antique chairs and tables, fresh flowers and marble busts of the many distinguished men of letters who had studied there.

On the day after the picnic with North, she consulted one of the librarians.

'I'm interested in an historic house in England called Longwarden. Do you think you might have some information about it?'

'I'm sure we'll have something, Miss Graham. Let me see what I can find for you.'

In a very short time Jane was seated in one of the bays with a leather-bound tome, *Country Seats*, open on the table in front of her.

Her first sight of North's ancestral home was a hand-tinted chromolithograph of Longwarden as it had been in Victorian days. Far larger and more splendid than Winterbrook, it had one feature in common with the Blakewell mansion, a columned portico. But the Greek-revival columns at Winterbrook were finished with white-painted stucco whereas those at Longwarden had been hewn from the same golden stone as the whole palatial façade.

She was reading the account of its history when the librarian reappeared and said, 'You're in luck, Miss Graham. It seems we have a great deal of material about Longwarden, including several photograph albums, which were left to the Athenaeum by Lady Rose Blakewell when she died in 1964. She was a famous needlewoman, you know, and she bequeathed us her collection of books about needlework and lace. It may be that her executors included the albums in her bequest by mistake. You would expect family photographs to have been left to her children, wouldn't you? However we have them here and they're cross-referenced in our catalogue as an outstanding photographic record of a strata of English society in the twenties.'

For the rest of the morning Jane pored over pictures of North's recent forebears, including his Great-Aunt Rose who had been her own grandmother.

Many of the photographs included a man remarkably like North except that his aquiline nose had not suffered an injury. This was clearly Rose's father, the husband of Flora Carlyon whose exotic beauty outshone all the other women depicted in the albums, and whom North had said Jane resembled.

She looked through the albums several times, the snatch of conversation overheard at the buffet table at Winterbrook echoing in her mind. *Like so many old English families, his has been crippled by taxes. There's a house falling into ruins and the title.* She also remembered North referring to 'my crumbling old house' and his obligation to have a son to inherit the title, if little else.

As she pored over the pictures of Longwarden in the days when its owner had been a rich man, it seemed to Jane that, at one stroke, life had presented her with a compellingly attractive man, a project deserving of her immense financial resources and an escape from another two years of her aunt's supervision.

When she left the library she was in the grip of an idea which she knew most people would think crazy but which she felt made excellent sense. When they met in New York, she would ask North to marry her.

The night before her flight to New York, Allegra had dinner with Mr Modbury. He was an unlikely companion for a young, beautiful woman.

A. C. Modbury, as he had signed himself, had been the

writer of one of her first and most treasured fan letters. As well as praising her book, his letter had offered a suggestion – which he hoped she would not think presumptuous – that, if she were ever to be stumped for a subject for a future biography, he knew of a notable figure who so far had been neglected by the military historians.

Field Marshal Sir Edward Blakeney was an extraordinary man whose career has been overlooked largely, I believe, because he had no descendants to keep his memory green, *he had written to her.* At one time I myself wondered if I could do justice to his eventful life. If, from the brief notes enclosed, you feel at some time in the future he might be a worthy subject for your own gifted pen, I should be honoured to hand over the more extensive notes I made at the time this idea was in my mind.

To which Allegra had replied, Not only was I delighted by your generous praise for my first book, but your suggestion about Sir Edward B. couldn't be more welcome. Ever since I finished writing *Travels,* I've been looking for another subject, until now without success. May I call on you to discuss possibilities?

At first he had been very nervous of her, even though she had played down her flamboyant looks by dressing as primly as possible in order not to disconcert a man whose letter had suggested he might be a retired schoolmaster or solicitor.

However their mutual interest in the field marshal had helped to break the ice and other meetings had followed as the timid elderly man and the reformed playgirl had discovered how much they had in common.

At the end of the evening she said, 'We must do this again, Mr Modbury. I've enjoyed it. I hope you have?'

'I have indeed . . . very much. I should be delighted to repeat the occasion, but I must confess it puzzles me that you have evenings to spare for an old fogey like myself. Your engagement diary should be full of young men's names.'

It was the most personal remark he had ever made to

her. She attributed his boldness to the two glasses of sherry they had each had before dinner and the bottle of wine they had shared at the table.

'When I was younger, it was,' she answered with a smiling shrug. 'But sooner or later they bored me. I can't imagine ever being bored in your company.'

He cleared his throat. 'Our acquaintance has certainly been a great pleasure to me, Lady Allegra.' The way he expressed himself was stiff but his tone and his swift glance were not.

'Our friendship,' she corrected him quietly.

'Our friendship.' He raised his glass. 'To the success of your book in America and a safe journey.'

Later they shared a taxi as far as Green Park Underground station where he climbed out and paid the fare to Park Lane. He then stood on the pavement while the cab drew away.

He was still there a minute later, when she looked back; an undistinguished figure carrying a mackintosh, yet one of the few people who mattered to her.

Knowing she would be too excited to sleep much tonight, she had not yet packed. Her final selection of clothes was still hanging in one of her cupboards. It included the Caroline Charles outfit which, in spite of its upsetting associations, she had decided to take. As she arranged it in a suitcase, her mind went back to the last time she had worn it.

It had been at a dinner party given by a London hostess to whom entertaining was an art form. Only people with something to contribute were invited to her parties. Allegra's contribution was her looks and her style. No one, two years ago, would have dreamed that she was to become a literary lioness.

The lion at that party had been Alessandro Risconti, the Italian painter who had sprung to prominence with his portraits of the Princess of Wales and the British Prime Minister.

Risconti's portrait of Margaret Thatcher had been compared with the famous portrait of Sir Winston Churchill by

Graham Sutherland which Churchill had so much disliked that he had ordered its destruction. How Mrs Thatcher felt about the Risconti portrait was not on record; but it was generally held to be a masterly summation of the qualities which had brought her to power and earned her the nickname of The Iron Lady.

In contrast to the formidable woman depicted in that unsparing portrait, his painting of Diana had been criticized for flattering her. Regardless of the critics' opinions, every beautiful woman who saw the second portrait wanted to be painted by him, the more so when television interviews revealed him as a prematurely grey-haired man in his middle thirties, not handsome but clearly extremely virile and with a charm as palpable as that of his royal sitter.

Allegra arrived at the party in a black velvet cloak, lined with Russian sable, which Flora Carlyon had worn to go to the theatre and opera at the beginning of the century.

She was curious to meet Risconti. Always honest with herself, she admitted to hoping that her unusual looks would prompt him to offer to paint her. She was not vain. She didn't consider herself a beauty. But she knew that, allied with her colouring, a broad forehead, the Carlyon nose and her cleft chin made her very striking and would continue to do so when she was no longer young.

Time would add to the first almost imperceptible lines beginning to appear round her eyes and would gradually extinguish the flames in her hair, but it couldn't alter the basic structure of her face.

Of the twenty-two people bidden to dine in the elegant house in Eaton Square, the star of the evening was the last to arrive. Even in the sophisticated mélange of talent, breeding and wealth assembled by their hostess there was a slight hiatus in the conversation as he entered the first-floor drawing room and kissed her outstretched hand.

It was a black-tie occasion. He must have been aware of it but had come dressed in black trousers, a black silk turtle-neck sweater and a blouson of thin and supple silver-grey kid, the same colour as his thick curly hair.

It was possible he didn't possess a dinner jacket but

he could have hired one, thought Allegra. Although she approved of men taking some interest in their appearance, she wasn't sure that she liked a man who deliberately flouted his hostess's wishes and dressed to dramatize his hair and his strange steel-grey eyes deep-set under straight black eyebrows.

As it was only a few minutes before dinner was due to be served, not many people were introduced to him beforehand.

Instead of having one long table in her large dining room, Sybille preferred four round tables, each with six chairs around it. Allegra was not at the same table as Risconti but she knew that before the pudding was served their hostess would ask all the men to leave their places and move in a clock-wise direction to the next table, thus ensuring that everyone present met at least half their fellow guests.

Seated between a producer of television documentaries and a neurosurgeon who spent his holidays skin diving, Allegra fulfilled her rôle as an ornamental good listener without any moments of boredom.

Seated at another table, the Italian artist was in profile to her. She was amused to observe that, evidently finding the dining room warmer than he had expected, he had taken off the blouson and slung it over the back of his chair as if he were in a waterfront bar or street café.

Sybille, being the kind of woman whose eyes never missed a detail and who could take in two other conversations while apparently listening intently to whoever was talking to her, would soon correct that when she noticed. Indeed, as Allegra watched, the offending garment was discreetly removed by her hostess's butler.

The black sweater the Italian was wearing outlined wide, powerful shoulders and a deep chest. There was no sign of flab round his middle. From the neck down he looked more like a young, fit stevedore than an artist.

In spite of her reservations about his clothes, from the moment he had entered the drawing room she had been aware of a pulsing excitement which had nothing to do with his leap to fame as an artist.

89

Only once, as far as she knew, did he glance at her. Suddenly, as she was noting the way his dense wire-wool curls sprang from his forehead and temples, he looked round and caught her eye. Only for two or three seconds, but she felt an odd sort of shock deep in her innermost being.

Perhaps it was only because his eyes were so unexpected under the heavy black brows in an olive-skinned face which, although closely shaven, showed a darker tinge where stubble would grow before morning. They should have been dark-brown eyes to go with the rest of his colouring and the typically Latin gestures he made all the time he was talking. Instead they were grey, the bright glinting grey of a sword-blade.

Later on, as she expected, Sybille tinkled a bell and made her usual request to the men to move.

As Risconti was the first man to move to the table where she was sitting, he had a choice of three chairs. The one nearest to his previous table was directly opposite hers. Instead of taking it, he came round and seated himself next to her.

Acknowledging the other women with a smiling inclination of the head, he then turned to her and said, 'I am Andro Risconti . . . and you?'

'Allegra Lomax. How do you do?'

Her manner was cool and formal, deliberately so because, inwardly, she found herself strangely nervous.

'In my language *allegro* means gay . . . in the old-fashioned sense.' He had almost no accent and obviously an idiomatic command of English. 'Was your first name well-chosen, Miss Lomax? Are you a light-hearted person? Or should I have said Mrs Lomax?'

She shook her head. 'I'm not married.'

'That doesn't mean you are unattached. Perhaps there is someone here with whom you are . . . very close? As an outsider in this milieu, it's easy for me to put my foot in it.' When she didn't answer immediately, he added, 'I'm unattached myself but I find it hard to believe that a lovely woman of your age has no claims on her. But perhaps, like me, you're wedded to your profession. Now let me guess what it might be. You're too tall to be a dancer. Perhaps you're a musician. No, you have beautiful hands. In my experience most musicians have ugly hands although they create beauty with them. That's an interesting ring. May I look at it more closely?'

He drew her left hand towards him to study the intaglio ring which, because it was made for a man, she was wearing on her second finger.

'This is your family crest?' he asked, looking at the device cut into the stone.

The loose clasp of his hand on her wrist made her blood beat faster. Could he feel her quickened pulse? Compared with her long slender hands, his were large and broad but well-shaped. Big, powerful hands more suited to the techniques of a sculptor than to wielding a brush was the thought that flashed through her mind. How skilled were those strong-boned fingers, now lightly locked round her wrist, in the techniques of love?

Her mouth was dry as she answered, 'No, it came from the Portobello Road . . . one of London's junk markets.'

'Ah, you like markets. So do I. Twenty years ago, when I was a student, there were more good things to be picked up. In those days I had no money and I couldn't buy much. Now most of the junk *is* junk. But still, if you have the eye for it, you can pick up a treasure sometimes. What do you collect besides rings?'

'Whatever appeals to me. Books more than anything.'

'What kind of books?'

His interest warmed her. So many people, women as well as men, talked endlessly about themselves but seemed to assume she had nothing to say, or nothing they wanted to hear. This man, whom she had expected to be more than usually full of himself, was watching her with an expression which suggested real interest in her reply.

'Biography . . . letters . . . poetry. Nothing of value – except to me. I'm not a serious collector. I'm what Shakespeare called "a snapper-up of unconsidered trifles". And you? What sort of treasures do you look for?'

'That's a very good expression. I haven't heard it before. I'm also a snapper-up of unconsidered trifles. I found one this morning. But first I had breakfast at one of the sidewalk cafés in South Molton Street. It amuses me to sit there for an hour, drinking coffee and watching the art students and the fashion people. Why have I never seen you going into Brown's? I'm sure you shop there.'

His eyes left her face and took in the diaphanous top and the soft flesh it veiled.

Like most European women of her generation Allegra had bared her bosom on Mediterranean beaches from the Greek islands to the French Riviera and the far south of Spain. In public and private, many men's eyes had admired her small russet-tipped breasts which still passed the pencil test. Why now, with this Italian, should she suddenly wish that tonight she had worn a body-stocking?

'I might – if I were rich. As it is, I go into Brown's merely to feast my eyes,' she said with a smile.

'I don't think this came from a chain store, nor these from Woolworth's,' said Risconti, indicating the Caroline Charles and her green drop earrings.

They were a legacy from her great-grandmother; part of the Carlyon emeralds, a fabulous *parure* of jewels including an emerald and diamond diadem which had once belonged to Catherine, Empress of all the Russias. Now the necklace was in Coutts' vaults, a bequest to North's future wife, as was a brooch for Sarah. The diadem and a pair of bracelets had been auctioned by Sotheby Parke Bernet at a sale of important jewels in Zürich in 1979. The diadem alone had fetched more than three quarters of a million pounds. It had enabled North to pay off his debt to the state.

'No, you don't look at all like a poor girl to me,' said Risconti, returning her smile.

Allegra shrugged. 'In England now there's a new class – *les nouveaux pauvres*. People who used to have money but don't any more. Shops like Brown's depend on the nouveaux riches. Arab petrocrats' wives and daughters . . . pop stars . . . soap-opera actresses.'

There was no resentment in her tone. She felt sorry for

North whose patrimony, partly because of their father's excesses, had become a worry and a burden. For herself, the life of an upper-class woman of her mother's and grandmother's generations would have been insufferably tedious.

'I'm one of the new rich,' said Risconti. 'Thirty years ago I was running around with bare feet in a village near Florence. If I hadn't been able to draw, I'd still be there . . . working in the vineyards or maybe driving a truck up and down the *autostrada* like my cousin Franco. Which reminds me, I still have to guess what it is that you do. Something to do with fashion perhaps? Not modelling because no model would eat this rich dessert. She would push it around her plate but she wouldn't swallow it. How is it you're very slim when you have such a hearty appetite?'

'My lunch was a carton of yogurt and I walk a lot. The nearest I've been to a fashion career is working at Harrod's when they take on extra staff for the summer sales and the Christmas rush. Instead of trying to guess my job, tell me about yours. Do I gather you're an artist?' She wanted to see his reaction to her pretence of not knowing who he was.

Risconti didn't look put out. He said equably, 'Yes, I was very lucky. Near the village where I was born there's a villa belonging to an Englishman. My mother cleaned the house for him. I won't bore you with the whole story. It's enough to say that the Englishman found I had a talent for drawing and became my patron, helping me to get a place at the Accademia di Belle Arti. Some of his house guests were artists who also helped me. My mother used to worry because they were all homosexuals and she was afraid of their motives for being kind to me.' He grinned. 'I didn't tell her she had nothing to fear because there was also an American lady living near us who, in matters of that nature, was a stronger influence than my patron and his friends.'

'And who taught you English, I presume?' said Allegra, having noticed and pondered his use of several American-isms.

'Yes. The Englishman spoke good Italian, but she wasn't very fluent and I knew it would help me later if I learnt to speak her language.'

Conscious that it was high time she turned to the man on her right, but unwilling to give up her present conversation, she asked, 'How old were you, and how old was she, when she took you under her wing?'

'I was thirteen. She was about your age.'

'I must say I can't imagine seducing a thirteen-year-old English boy. What with pimples and smelly socks, they couldn't be less attractive.'

'I didn't have pimples and she was lonely and bored, which I doubt if you are. She didn't seduce me. Seduction implies persuasion to commit a sin. My mother would have thought it sinful. I thought it a gift from the gods. Boys of that age don't need any persuasion to express their natural urges. Most of them don't have my luck.'

At this point the woman on his left made a determined effort to claim her share of his attention.

'Whose portrait are you painting at the moment, Signore Risconti?'

'I'm between two young and pretty duchesses. The woman I should like to paint is an English artist, a sculptor. Elisabeth Frink. Do you know her work?'

She didn't. Allegra did. Her last-but-one lover had been the director of a gallery specializing in contemporary art. She had learned a good deal about it during their three months together.

'Do you prefer paintings or sculptures?' she asked her neglected neighbour, feeling sure that this wasn't the end of her talk with Risconti.

If her instincts were right they were at the beginning of something very special. But then didn't she always feel this, each and every time? Even the foolish first time when, sixteen years old and driven by curiosity and chemistry, she had believed herself to be madly in love with an eighteen-year-old friend of North's.

Unlike Risconti, Tim hadn't had the benefit of tuition from an older woman. Nor did he seem to have gleaned any expertise from other sources. Later, when she could think about it dispassionately, Allegra had felt sorry for the girl he had married if he hadn't improved his performance by the time she went to bed with him.

Coffee and liqueurs were served at the tables. Most of Sybille's guests had occupations which obliged them to keep early hours on weekdays. Having more than usually comfortable dining chairs, she saw nothing to be gained by moving her guests to the drawing room for the last hour of the evening. A certain amount of place-changing usually occurred as some people left the room briefly, allowing her to bring together any guests who had not yet had a chance to meet and talk.

The man on Allegra's right was not unamusing and, having ignored him earlier, she gave him all her attention. She was laughing at his description of an incident involving his children's pet donkey when a hand fell lightly on her shoulder. She turned to find that Risconti had risen and was about to be led away by his hostess.

'May I take you home when we leave?'

Automatically she let a few seconds elapse before saying, 'Yes ... thank you.'

He smiled. She knew he hadn't been deceived by her hesitation. The attraction between them was too potent to be disguised by any artifice.

She realized then that within a few minutes of his arrival at the party she had known that here was her next lover. She suspected that, soon after making a beeline for the chair next to hers, he had known it as well.

Before midnight the party began to break up. Allegra saw Risconti looking at her. A silent message passed between them. A few minutes later she was in Sybille's bedroom, retouching her lips before retrieving her cloak from the furs and coats on the bed.

On Flora, the cloak had swept the ground. On Allegra it swung round her ankles. Barefoot, she was five feet nine which Risconti might top by an inch or an inch and a half. The low heels of her evening slippers would make them the same height. In high heels she would be taller. But she rarely wore high heels. She didn't like shoes which wouldn't allow her to match a man's comfortable stride.

Downstairs she found that in her absence Risconti had been talking to a politician who had once made a pass at her. She had turned him down pleasantly. Superficially they were still on good terms. But she had a feeling that some lingering rancour lurked under his affable manner.

'You're looking very fetching, as always, Allegra,' he said when she joined them.

'Thank you.' She disliked his caressing appraisal almost as much as she had disliked being touched by him. It made her wish more than before that she was less flimsily clad.

In contrast to the warmth of the house, the spring night felt chilly at first and Allegra was glad to be snugly enveloped in soft fur.

'Where do you live?' asked Risconti.

'At the top of Park Lane. It's not far. We could walk if you feel like some exercise?' She wanted time to decide whether to offer him a nightcap.

If she did, he would almost certainly take it as an invitation to spend the night with her and somehow she wasn't in a hurry to jump into bed with him. What she would like would be to stay up all night, talking, finding out more about the kind of person he was, if they could be friends as well as lovers.

As they began to walk to the end of the square he said, 'You're not Miss but Lady, I'm told. Why didn't you correct me?'

'I didn't think we'd be standing on ceremony for long. You don't mind if I call you Andro, do you? Is that what your family call you, or did someone else shorten your name?'

'My mother used Alessandro but it's too much of a mouthful outside Italy. Andro is better over here and in America.'

'Have you settled in England? Where do you live?' she asked him.

'I'm renting a flat in St George's Fields but I don't work there. It's too small. My studio's near Regent's Park.'

'Isn't that rather a nuisance . . . not being able to work where you live?'

'Yes, and I don't care for London as a place to live. I'd prefer to be in the country. I may look around for a house outside London. Or I may go to America. It depends how things go.'

'Have you spent much time in America?'

'When I was a student in Florence, I had an American friend who was also at the Accademia. After we'd completed our studies, Chuck's parents invited me to go back with him. They live on Long Island, not far from New York. I didn't realize till we got there how rich they were. Their house had twelve bedrooms which, to me, was a palace. There was also an apartment in New York which Chuck and I shared for a while. Then he fell in love with a girl, which made me *de trop*, so one day I went to the bus station and took myself on a tour of the rest of the States. I met a lot of interesting people and filled about fifty sketch books. It was a good year of my life – perhaps the best year.'

'I had a year like that . . . travelling through Europe. But I went with another person and after a while we began to irritate each other which spoiled things. Eventually we split up and I spent three months on my own which would have been fine except that men were a nuisance. I could never go anywhere without being pestered by someone.'

'It's better for girls to travel in pairs.' After a slight pause, he added, 'Or was your companion a man?'

She nodded. 'A friend of my brother whom you may have heard of. My brother, I mean. He's quite a well-known wildlife photographer. His name's North Carlyon. You may have seen some of his work in the Sunday colour supplements.'

'I've both seen and admired his work. He's an artist with the camera. So you're Lord Carlyon's sister. You told me you were unmarried. But you have been married? – If your surname is Lomax?'

'Lomax is our family name . . . the name our ancestors had before they managed to grab a title and land. My mother and brother are the only ones who use the name Carlyon. The rest of us are Lomaxes.'

'Are you a large family?'

'No . . . only my brother and me and our cousin Sarah who's much younger than we are. Have you many brothers and sisters?'

'Four half-brothers and three half-sisters who were grown up when I was born and didn't want to know about their bastard half-brother until I began to make money,' he told her sardonically.

'You mean you were illegitimate?'

Risconti nodded. 'My mother was forty when I was born. She'd been married at sixteen to a man chosen by her parents. She didn't dislike him and he was a good provider. Like all good Catholics they had more children than they could afford. Then World War Two started and her husband was killed. After the war nobody wanted to marry a widow, even though she was still a good-looking woman. There were men who wanted her – but not as a wife. As soon as she was visibly pregnant, the respectable women in the village refused to speak to her . . . including her own daughters.'

'Oh, God – how terrible for her,' Allegra exclaimed. 'And for you! Do you know who your father was?'

Again he nodded. 'Although he didn't acknowledge me as his son, he honoured his obligation to the extent of giving us money to live on for several years. Then he died but soon afterwards my mother was able to make a living working for the Englishman.'

'Where is she now? Not still there, being ostracized?'

'She's there . . . in a grave in the cemetery. She'd had a hard life and died at sixty while I was at the Accademia.'

'So now you're alone.'

'Alone but not lonely. For me, work is better company than a crowd of relations. Are you fond of yours?' he asked.

'I couldn't stand my father and I haven't much time for my mother. I'm very fond of my brother and cousin. Not that I see much of them. North spends most of his time overseas and Sarah lives in the country, obsessed by her horses. She's deeply involved in a rather esoteric sport called eventing. Probably you've never heard of it.'

'The only sport which interests me is skiing . . . both on snow and water. That I enjoy; but games played with balls and the English sports of hunting, shooting and fishing don't appeal to me. Horses are interesting to draw but I don't want to sit on their backs. You've ridden since you were a child, I suppose?'

'I was taught to ride. I never enjoyed it particularly. I have no affinity with horses. My cousin prefers them to people. Her father, who was my father's younger brother, was a jockey. Rather a good one until he was killed stee-plechasing. Horses are in Sarah's blood. My father was horse-mad, too, but neither my brother nor I take after him in that way. Or any way, thank God!'

'Why did you dislike your father? He's dead, I gather?'

'Yes . . . one of the frequent casualties in the hunting field. Every year at least one neck gets snapped. I disliked him because he was a bore and a bully. You're one of the few people who hasn't looked shocked when I've admitted to finding my parents a pain. Most people are such hypocrites,' she said scornfully.

'You should be glad they are. Otherwise you wouldn't be able to amuse yourself offending them with your out-spokenness.'

'It doesn't amuse me. Mealy-mouthed people annoy me.'

'Tonight it was the other women who were annoyed. None of them could have worn that pretty silk thing without underwear,' he said dryly. 'Don't tell me it didn't amuse you to make them envy the figure all the men were admiring?'

'That wasn't my object at all,' Allegra said, lifting her chin. 'I dress to please myself, not to make married men lecherous or their wives jealous.'

'I'd like to paint you as you're dressed tonight. Red hair . . . black velvet . . . fur . . . a glimpse of those Botticelli breasts through silk chiffon. It would be a study in textures as well as a portrait of a beautiful woman.'

'You're very flattering, but unfortunately I can't afford your fees.'

'You don't know what I charge.'

'Too much for my pocket.'

'Portraits of women are usually commissioned by a father, husband or lover.'

'All of whom I lack. But at least when I'm old I shall be able to say Risconti would have liked to paint me,' she answered with a smile.

'And did,' he said firmly. 'I shall do it for my own pleasure.'

'You can't be serious? You have a long queue of sitters willing and eager to pay your fees. Why should you paint me for nothing?'

'How do you know I'm a successful painter if until tonight you had never heard of me?' he asked mockingly.

Allegra chuckled. 'Well, of course I had really. I only wanted to see if you'd be piqued thinking I hadn't. But you weren't. You reacted admirably. Fame hasn't corrupted you yet.'

'I hope not. As far as I'm concerned it's merely a means to an end. Fame brings money and money brings freedom. When I have enough money to keep me in moderate comfort for the rest of my life, I shall stop painting people in the public eye and return to the subjects which interest me.'

'What are they?'

They had turned into Belgrave Square and were heading for Grosvenor Crescent. Passing under a street lamp, he gave her a thoughtful glance. 'Drop-outs ... drunks ... vagrants ... scavengers ... women who live on a park bench with all they possess in a couple of plastic carriers. Americans call them bag ladies. When you see them trudging the streets, talking to themselves because there's no one else to listen, don't you wonder what made them that way? I do. They fascinate me. With a few exceptions, I find the dregs of society more interesting than the *crème de la crème.*'

'Really? How odd,' said Allegra. 'I should have thought most of those people had brought their condition on themselves. I'm sure they'll willingly sit to you for the price of a bottle, but think of the stench in your studio. Most of them reek like old boots.'

'Perhaps I'm not as sensitive to the smell of unwashed flesh as you are,' said Risconti. 'In my village, thirty years ago, all the water was fetched from a well. It was very picturesque, my village, but Lady Allegra from Park Lane would have had to keep a handkerchief pressed to her aristocratic nose.'

He said it with a grin but his tone had a cutting edge which made her flash back, 'Don't kid yourself that you're closer to salvation because you were born a bastard in the backwoods of Italy and you think I was born to the soft life.'

'Not closer to salvation, but perhaps more in touch with the realities of most people's lives,' he said mildly.

'You may have been once. Are you now? – A fashionable portraitist, earning huge fees, with women like me fawning on you?'

'If this is what you call fawning, what are you like when you're angry?' he asked, amused.

She gave a reluctant laugh. 'Ferocious! My temperament matches my hair, or so I've been told. When did yours start to go grey? It's very striking.'

'It's the proof, if any were needed, that I'm my father's son. He and his father and grandfather all went grey early in life. It's a family characteristic. I pulled out my first grey hair when I was twenty.'

'So, if she hadn't already suspected, your father's wife must have known eventually that he'd been your mother's lover.'

'Not only my mother's. That, too, was a family characteristic. Our *principi* all spread their seed as freely as they could. There are prematurely grey heads all over the region they used to rule in the old days. In most houses *il principe*'s bastards were accepted. My mother was punished because she had kept her looks and other women resented that.'

Was he making it up? Had his father really been a prince, the hereditary ruler of that part of Tuscany? Or had he invented the story to add colour to his reputation?

101

She remembered the easy grace with which he had kissed Sybille's hand on arrival and departure. Perhaps it was true. Perhaps, on his father's side, he came from a line of overlords whose despotic powers had included the right to take any woman who caught their vagrant fancy.

'My mother had worked at the castle since before she was married. The servants knew everything about the family, as yours must know about you.'

'I look after myself. Do you think your mother could have been in love with *il principe*? Or did he threaten to sack her if she refused him?'

'I'd say no to both those suggestions. I'm told – never saw him myself – that he was a man of great charm. He would have got what he wanted by persuasion rather than coercion. As for her, she may have been unusual among her peers in missing her husband's attentions after he was killed. Looking at photographs of her taken when I was a child, I can see she had a voluptuous quality about her. She was not unlike Sophia Loren, even after having eight children. It may have been sex or it may have been pity which made her give herself to him. He'd lost his sight. Instead of being able to ride and play tennis and drive his Ferrari, he could only sit in a chair listening to the radio.'

'How did that happen?'

'During the war, I suppose. It had only been over for three years when I was conceived.'

Allegra did a quick sum. That made him about thirty-six, eight years older than herself.

She said, 'What about his legitimate children? Did you ever meet any of them?'

Risconti made a negative sound, then said, 'You've extracted my life history but I still don't know what you do. Or are you a lady of leisure?'

'It's an extinct species,' she answered. 'I work like everyone else, but not at anything special. I've had all kinds of jobs since I left school. You name it, I've probably done it. At the moment I'm working for a firm which supplies drivers-cum-guides to the wives of visiting tycoons and foreign politicians. My principle qualification, apart from being able to drive, is my title. American millionaires' wives seem to love being driven around by the sister of a genuine earl. The snag is they seem to think I'd be offended if they tipped me. How little they know!'

'If those earrings are emeralds and your address is Park Lane, you can't be too close to the breadline,' he remarked.

'Emerald earrings don't pay the bills and most of the house is occupied by other people. If it weren't, we should have to sell it.'

When they came to the Regency house which had been her great-grandfather's town house, the curtains were drawn but some chinks of light were showing from the first-floor windows of what had once been a drawing room with a bow-shaped balcony shaded by an iron canopy.

Usually Allegra entered by the front door but didn't go up the main staircase, which now served the two apartments below her own. Her quarters were reached by crossing the communal hall to a door leading to the back stairs.

At the gate in the railings protecting the small front garden, she said, 'It's not very late. Would you like a quick cup of coffee before you go on to your place?'

'Thank you . . . I should,' said Risconti.

'We'll go round the back way. There's something I'd like you to see.'

In Carlyon Mews, behind the house, the coach-houses had long since been converted into expensive cottages with bay trees outside the doors and security grilles on the windows.

Allegra unlocked the door leading into the garden at the rear of Carlyon House.

Here, seven years ago, Granny Flora had ended her long happy life under the flowering branches of the empress tree. This spring – after a long interval when the tree's buds, formed in the autumn, had failed to survive winter frosts – it was once again in blossom.

The flowers, which resembled foxgloves, gave off a delicious scent. Each day since they had bloomed Allegra had inhaled their fragrance and thought, with a sharp ache of loss, of the confidante she had lost and the wise counsel and warm affection she still missed.

'What a wonderful tree,' said Risconti. 'I've never seen one like it.'

'Most people haven't. It's an empress tree from China. My great-grandfather brought it back from his first plant-hunting expedition about ninety years ago. It doesn't blossom very often. You're lucky to see it in flower.'

She stepped from the brick-paved path on to the dewy grass, leading him closer to the moonlit tree.

'Smell the scent. Isn't it heavenly?'

Risconti reached up a hand to bring a flower close to his nostrils. He breathed in the delicate perfume. 'If you could bottle that you would make your fortune.' He let the branch swing back in place. 'May I come and see it by daylight?'

'Of course. If it's sunny tomorrow, why not come and have breakfast with me instead of in South Molton Street? I'm not working till the afternoon.'

'What a good idea,' he said quietly, and there was a note in his voice which sent a slow tremor through her.

They gazed at each other for a moment until, thinking that he was about to close the short space between them and take her in his arms, she said, with a catch in her voice, 'You . . . you haven't told me about the treasure you found after breakfast this morning.'

'It's still in my pocket. But you won't be able to see it clearly in this light. I'll show you when we're inside.'

The back entrance to Allegra's eyrie at the top of the house was by a door built to lead only to the back stairs. On each landing between the six flights a heavy mahogany door had once given access to the main part of the house. The connecting doors through which, for more than a century, footmen and housemaids, lady's maids and valets, had appeared and disappeared like the figures in a toy weather-house, were locked now; and the walls of the staircase had been changed from drab brown to deep red and hung with seascapes and sets of sporting prints borrowed from Longwarden.

Leading the way to her flat, Allegra was intensely

conscious of the man coming up behind her and of the violent attraction he exerted on her. But it was an attraction inhibited by a curious reluctance. Her body wanted to go to bed with him with all speed. Her mind and heart checked that impulse and counselled caution.

Immediately inside the door at the top of the stairs was a small lobby made, with mirrors, to seem like a tented corridor lined with ranks of life-size blackamoors. It was a dramatic illusion. There were only two statues, around one of whose gleaming black shoulders Allegra draped her long cloak.

Before shrugging out of his raincoat Risconti removed a fold of tissue paper from one of the pockets and transferred it to his trouser pocket.

The lobby led into a room where again the ceiling was tented and the walls hung with old Paisley shawls, some unearthed in the attics at Longwarden but many bought from junk shops and markets.

Watching the first comprehensive glance Risconti flashed round her eccentric living room, she said, 'Have a look round while I make the coffee. Or would you prefer a *tisane*? It's what I usually drink.'

'Then I'll join you.'

The kitchen was tiny, but in it she had prepared food for up to thirty people. As a child she had spent more time with the cook and the butler than with her parents.

While the kettle was boiling she slipped across to the bathroom to brush her hair and to spray it lightly with *Opium*.

Her cheeks, pale after a winter when lack of money for the air fare had prevented her from accepting an invitation to stay with friends in the Grenadines, tonight were tinged with faint colour whipped up by the brisk half-hour's walk. Her eyes sparkled with excitement because something new was afoot, something which might turn out to be the best yet, the best ever.

A few minutes later she carried a tray into the living room.

'Who was this beautiful woman?' he asked, turning from

the portrait of Flora Carlyon painted by Philip de Laszlo.

'My great-grandmother. Wasn't she stunning? Wouldn't you have loved to paint her?'

'Mm . . . she was very lovely . . . the golden skin . . . the dark eyes,' he murmured in agreement. 'But for my taste she looks a little too soft and gentle, a little lacking in the spirit which makes a woman exciting.'

'Oh, I'm sure she had plenty of spirit when she was a girl,' said Allegra. 'But by the time that was painted she'd had thirty years of being my great-grandfather's adored wife. You probably took her for a woman of my age. In fact she was almost fifty when she sat to de Laszlo.'

'Is that so? Remarkable. Although de Laszlo did have the reputation of flattering his female sitters.'

'I've also read that about you. Will you have a brandy with your *tisane*?'

'Thank you.' He came towards the divan where she was seated.

Her shoes had been wet from the grass. She had changed them and was sitting with one silk-slippered foot tucked beneath her.

'A false charge,' said Risconti. 'I never flatter. I shan't flatter you. There's no need to. You're at the peak of your looks. In five years' time they'll begin to deteriorate. Not much, but little by little. Your great-grandmother's oriental blood was what made her age more slowly. Asian women keep their looks better than Caucasians.'

She removed the sachets of camomile from the cups. 'Do you boost the morale of all your sitters by reminding them they won't look like their portraits for long?' she asked with an amused look.

Inwardly she was remembering something told her by Flora Carlyon: that the loss of youth and beauty only tormented women who were not loved. To those who were loved, none of time's ravages mattered.

'In general I let my sitters do most of the talking,' he answered, relaxing against the heaped cushions. 'This is an extraordinary room.'

'A lot of it is loot from the attics of my brother's house,'

106

she explained. 'The tenting was suggested by a friend who is a decorator. It was a quick way of disguising the dilapidated walls and dealing with the sloping ceilings formed by the roof pitches. This floor was where the maids slept ... with no heating and only rag rugs and cold linoleum underfoot. It must have been hell getting up on arctic winter mornings and having to break the thin ice in the water jugs on their washstands. I think of them, poor things, when I'm lying in a hot bath.'

'You feel sorry for them but not for today's underdogs,' he said, eyeing her with a sardonic expression.

Allegra handed him a cup. 'The difference being that many of those maids must have been intelligent girls who, given the opportunity, could have made something more of their lives. They were held back by being working class and female, two unalterable disadvantages which don't apply any more. Nobody with brains and gumption has to stay an underdog now. If you were a small boy today, your future wouldn't depend on luck and a private patron. The state would give you your chance. At least it would here and no doubt it's the same in Italy.'

This was not the kind of conversation she usually had with men late at night; and she wasn't accustomed to feeling that her looks were admired but her character and lifestyle were not. What did he think she should be doing? Devoting her life to the care of drop-outs?

'Anyway what are *you* doing to help the underdog?' she asked him.

Risconti smiled. '*Touché.* You're not easily put down, are you, Lady Allegra?'

His use of her title was mocking but not unfriendly.

'I thought you didn't like women who were soft and gentle. I'm certainly not. As you seem to have guessed, I'm a thoroughly selfish person dedicated to my own pleasures. I rather suspect you're the same. You may want to paint the underdogs but I doubt if you'd waste your time trying to rehabilitate them, or even donate a percentage of your fees to their welfare. Am I right?'

His broad shoulders moved in a shrug. 'My contribution

will be to make them noticed instead of ignored; to reveal them as human beings in spite of their degraded state. But you're right: I admit to being selfish. That's why I've never married. I don't wish to adjust my life to the needs of a wife and children. Artists, musicians and writers are better off living alone – or with someone who makes no permanent claims on them.'

A very clear statement of intent, Allegra thought wryly.

Risconti took from his pocket the fold of tissue paper. He handed it to her.

'I bought it in the antique market round the corner from South Molton Street. I expect you know the place I mean.'

'Yes – the Davies Street indoor market. I often browse there.'

She unfolded the wrapping. It contained a dealer's card and a wafer of ivory, about four centimetres square, with undulating edges and an incised design of concentric circles.

'I was looking for netsuke, which I collect, and I noticed that and asked what it was. Do you know?' he asked.

'I should think it's a thread winder for left-over lengths of sewing silk.'

'That's correct. How very clever of you.'

'What made you buy it? It really belongs in a collection of needlework tools.'

'I bought it because the dealer told me something interesting about it. If you look on the other side of her card, you'll see she's written a name on it.'

Allegra turned the card over. 'Holtzapfel? What does that signify?'

'It's the name of a lathe which was used in the eighteenth century by gentlemen of leisure who liked doing things with their hands. That winder would have been made for a wife or daughter's sewing box. I thought I might send it to the mother of my friend Chuck. She has always been busy with some needlework whenever I stayed there. That would interest her.'

'Why not send her several? I have lots of them, including some duplicates.'

Allegra rose and crossed the room to a table with baskets on it. Picking up a small shallow basket of woven grass, she came back to show him its contents: a collection of discs, squares and rectangles made of ivory, fragments of nacre, off-cuts of rosewood and many other materials.

'Have one of these mother-of-pearl snowflakes. They're the prettiest winders,' she said, picking one out for him.

'No, no – if you're a collector you must add this to yours,' he said, dropping the one he had bought into the basket. 'Please . . . I insist. You must have it. That must be why it caught my eye. Because it was intended to be my first present to you . . . a memento of our meeting.'

'What about Chuck's mother?'

'I'll find something else for her. This was meant to be yours. Don't you feel it was Destiny which brought us together tonight?'

He was flirting with her now, his grey eyes amorous, his magnetism almost as palpable as the warmth of a fire.

Allegra laughed. 'I thought it was Sybille . . . and if you hadn't left your first table before the two other men, we might barely have spoken to each other. Rather haphazard of Destiny, don't you think?'

'Not at all. She knew I had only to see you to make sure of getting to know you. If we'd passed in the street, I should have stopped you and spoken. We've been looking for each other, Allegra. I know it even if you don't. I knew it as soon as I saw you.'

As he spoke he had reached for her hands. Now he began to kiss them, the knuckles, the backs, the palms, his lips warm against her skin. She found herself quivering with eagerness to feel his kisses on her mouth. At the same time instinct warned her not to respond too eagerly to a man whose work brought him into contact with many desirable women.

Attempting to withdraw her hands, she said, rather breathlessly, 'Are you always as precipitate as this?'

He raised his head. His eyes were bright with desire. 'Always? No – never! This has never happened to me before. Do you think I make a habit of baring my soul to every woman I meet? Have you ever talked as intimately to a stranger as you have to me? We're not strangers, Allegra. We belong. It may sound like a line, but it's not. You feel it as strongly as I do.'

'I feel drawn to you,' she admitted. 'But it is only hours since we met.'

'Hours of talking as if we had known each other for days; and now it's time to stop talking and kiss,' he said firmly, taking her in his arms.

Locked in his powerful embrace, hypnotized by his burning gaze, she didn't protest as he pressed her back against the cushions. She could feel the strong beat of his heart and the rapid tattoo of her own as she waited, holding her breath, for his mouth to come down on hers. When it did, a shudder went through her and her lips softened and parted, all caution forgotten as their mouths fused in the kiss she wanted as much as he did.

But caution revived, some time later, when she felt him undoing her belt.

'No, Andro . . . not tonight.' Opening her eyes, she pushed his hand from the knot.

He had been kissing her neck. He stopped and looked at her, puzzled.

'Why not? You have your period?' he asked, with a disappointed expression.

'No . . . it isn't that. It's . . . too soon. I need more time.'

Her mind warring with her body which wanted desperately to let him continue making love to her, she made an attempt to free herself.

He wouldn't let her go. 'Time? For what? What more proof do you need? We're made for each other. You know it.' Tenderly, he traced the sweep of her eyebrow with his fingertip. 'You asked me to have breakfast with you. How shall we spend the night if not in each other's arms?'

'I didn't ask you to stay the night. I did make that clear,' she reminded him.

'You did . . . I remember. But that was then and this is now. Life is too short to waste one hour of it, darling. Especially *this* hour of our lives . . . our first time together.'

His hand slid down her throat and found the soft swell of her breast under the thin silk chiffon.

Resisting him, when every cell in her body was conspiring to make her surrender to the virile strength of his, was almost impossibly hard. She took hold of his wrist to remove his hand from her breast, at the same time trying to sit up.

'Let me go, Andro . . . please. I can't think straight like this.'

'Don't think – feel. Feel my heart beating like yours,' he murmured, still holding her breast, refusing to let her escape.

It developed into a tussle – Allegro exerting her strength to sit up, Risconti using his greater strength to keep her in a reclining position. For a bad ten seconds, as she struggled and squirmed to break free, she thought he was out of control and was going to force himself on her. As she began to panic, suddenly he let her go.

His olive skin flushed, his eyes angry, he sprang to his feet, striding away from the divan but only for a few paces before he spun round and said harshly, 'Why the hell not? You want to. I want to. And you've been to bed with plenty of other guys.'

The change in his manner shocked her. She flinched from his brutal tone. Yet she knew it was largely her fault. It was plain to see he had been strongly aroused. What man, in his present condition, wouldn't be equally furious?

She could guess who had said something to him which had prompted his scathing rider.

She said stiffly, 'You shouldn't believe all you hear – especially when your informant is a well-known lecher who probably slanders all uncooperative women if he gets a chance.'

He scowled at her. 'Are you saying that it isn't true? That you haven't had men?'

Allegra began to be angry. She had been aroused and then frightened and was now frustrated and keyed up.

'On the contrary – I've lost count,' she retorted recklessly. 'Although I daresay my score is no higher than yours.'

111

'Maybe not, but I'd like to know what makes me one of the few who hasn't made it with you.'

His contempt flicked her like a whip. Her temper reached boiling point.

'If you must know, your bloody arrogance in assuming you would,' she flared at him. 'Now I'd like to go to bed – alone. You know your way out. Goodnight.'

A few moments later she heard the outer door bang.

Why the hell not? You want to. I want to. And you've been to bed with plenty of other guys.

As she locked her suitcases, Allegra wondered where Risconti was now. She had never seen him again. She had never forgotten him.

For several days after their meeting, each time she returned to the flat and listened to the messages on her answering machine she had half-expected, half-hoped to hear his voice saying he regretted what had happened and could they meet again. However he hadn't made contact and although, knowing where he lived, she could probably have found out the number of the flat he was leasing, she hadn't done so.

A month or two later she had read that he'd gone to America. That was the last she had heard of him. Presumably he was still there. It seemed unlikely they would run into each other.

New York . . . Manhattan . . . Fifth Avenue . . . Central Park. The thought that very soon she would be there, in the world's most exciting city – and not merely as a tourist but as a celebrity to be met at the airport and given a VIP welcome – made her impatient for the adventure to begin.

She set out for Heathrow airport wearing black flannel pinstriped trousers and a white flannel double-breasted jacket, both by Saint Laurent, with a white silk wing-collar shirt by James Drew and a polka-dot pussy-cat bow, white spots on black. Apart from the floppy silk bow, all the pieces of her outfit had come from her usual hunting grounds. But nobody seeing her arrive at the Concorde check-in desks at Terminal 3 would have guessed she was wearing someone else's cast-offs. Especially as the suitcases, to which the clerk was attaching the distinctive embossed silver baggage tags with the airline's scarlet speedwing flash, has been made in the workshops of Louis Vuitton, the world's master luggage-maker. A long time ago, admittedly. They had been part of a set given to Rollo and Diana, her grandparents, as a wedding present. But early Vuitton had more cachet than new pieces.

Having chosen the morning flight which took off at ten-thirty, she checked in half an hour beforehand, a time of day when usually she hadn't much sparkle. Today was different. She was on a high of excitement with a swing in her step and a brightness in her eyes which turned several heads as she made her way to the Concorde passengers' lounge.

There her boarding pass was checked and the coat she had over her arm – a quilted black ciré jacket, also by Saint Laurent, the pink lining an arresting clash with her hair – was taken away to be hung up until the flight landed at Kennedy.

Very shortly boarding began, a leisurely, painless procedure with every passenger being shown to their assigned seat and helped to stow their belongings by the cabin staff.

Following a stewardess along the grey-carpeted aisle, Allegra found she had been allocated a window seat on the starboard side. The grey leather chairs were in pairs, with only twenty-five rows spaced to allow ample leg room. There was none of the struggle to cram coats into crowded lockers and shove flight bags underneath seats which typified ordinary air travel.

It seemed that the seat next to hers was going to remain empty until, shortly before take-off, a tall man was ushered to it.

He inclined his head to Allegra. 'Good morning.'

Allegra smiled at him. 'Good morning.'

His response was civil but reserved. She sensed he would have preferred to find himself next to a man or not to have a neighbour. He had no hand luggage other than a thick book. Having sat down and fastened his belt, he began to read. Out of the corner of her eye she noted the superior quality of his suit, the silk socks, the highly polished hand-made shoes. He looked to be about forty and emanated an aura of supreme power and influence.

Five minutes after take-off the passengers were served with bubbling golden Buck's Fizz and *bouchées* of lobster and caviar to keep them happy until breakfast arrived twenty minutes later.

Allegra enjoyed the fruit salad but declined the cooked course, eating a warm flaky croissant while her neighbour applied himself to grilled lambs' kidneys, mushrooms and buttered broccoli served on a white china plate narrowly rimmed with black and platinum.

'Some more coffee, Lady Allegra?' one of the steward-esses asked.

As her cup was replenished, Allegra was conscious of being studied by the man beside her. Whether it was her title or her unusual name which had caught his attention she had no way of knowing, although he didn't have the look of someone who would be impressed by her rank.

When the stewardess had moved away, he said, 'Is it by chance or design that you complement the new décor?'

'I didn't realize it was new. This is my first flight on Concorde.'

'All these interior fittings are less than a month old. The colours used to be blue and gold. Even the original mach-meters have been replaced by these computerized displays giving us more information.'

'I gather you are a regular passenger?'

He nodded. 'I should always fly Concorde if there were more scheduled services to more destinations.'

Why, when he spoke perfect English, did she have the feeling it hadn't been his first language? At no time had any of the cabin staff addressed him by name, she had noticed. Perhaps that was deliberate. He preferred to be incognito.

He began to talk, very knowledgeably, about the future of supersonic flight. The existing Concordes would reach the end of their commercial life soon after the turn of the century, he told her, and larger-capacity aircraft had already been designed.

Allegra tried to listen attentively but found both his face and the intensity of *his* attention very distracting. Most people, when they were chatting, looked away from the person they were speaking to at least half the time. This man didn't. He looked directly at her all the time. At such close quarters, it made it hard for her to concentrate on the possibility that the journey from London to Sydney could be reduced to sixty-seven minutes by a revolutionary dual-function rocket engine.

'That, at first, would be a military project with commercial possibilities,' he was saying. His eyes were the colour of honey with a dark ring round the outer edge of the iris. 'As far as Concorde is concerned, none of the international consortia are willing to finance development costs at the moment. So it looks very much as if the present fleet won't be replaced.'

'Really? What a shame. In that case I'm glad I've had the chance to fly on one now.'

And there the conversation ended. Instead of asking the purpose of her flight to New York, or explaining his own frequent journeys, he returned to his book. Allegra couldn't make out the title, only that it looked extremely abstruse. Footnotes on every page. But, it seemed, more interesting than talking to her.

After two hours in flight, the display showed Concorde was cruising at 1340 m.p.h., almost twice the speed of sound. They were more than halfway to New York where the time on arrival would be 9.30 a.m., giving Allegra ample time to reach her hotel and unpack before lunching with her American publishers.

Forty-five minutes before touch-down she rose to her feet. 'Would you excuse me, please?'

Book in hand, her neighbour stepped into the aisle to allow her to pass.

In the lavatory compartment she slipped off her rings

115

and put them in an inside pocket of her bag, a precaution learned after losing a favourite ring after leaving it on the rim of a public wash basin. Also in the pocket was the object which had become a kind of talisman: the ivory thread winder given to her by Alessandro Risconti.

At first a reminder of something she wanted to forget, its unpleasant associations had since been overlaid by the part it had played in leading her to the diaries and thereby to a career she had never dreamed was within her compass.

Risconti had claimed it was Destiny which had brought them together. She knew it had been merely Chance: one of a series of chances which, combined, had changed her life. If Risconti hadn't bought the winder ... if he hadn't given it to her, would she have spent a wet weekend at Longwarden poking about in the attics in search of a Holtzapfel lathe? And if she hadn't been looking for the lathe, would she, or anyone else, have discovered the trunk full of notebooks in which her great-grandfather had recorded his travels in the East?

Perhaps the luckiest chance of all had been that, of the many notebooks filled with his neat clear hand, the first once she had opened and skimmed had contained his account of meeting a half-Chinese girl of sixteen called Flora Jackson.

She knew by heart the first entry concerning the girl whose plight, poised between two worlds and *persona non grata* in both, had not moved the seventh Lord Carlyon to take pity on her.

Travelled about sixteen miles. Shot a mixed bag of pheasant grouse, hazel hen and Sifan partridge. Arrived at an RC mission run by an aged priest assisted by two Chinese nuns, one a deaf-mute. Also by Flora Jackson, the daughter of an Englishman who collected plants for Veitch and was killed in a landslide. The mother (Chinese) died earlier. Père d'Espinay wants me to take her with me. Had she been some years older, I might have agreed. She has the promise of beauty and will become somebody's concubine sooner or later. Not mine. I have no taste for unripe fruit and don't wish to be encumbered. The priest should have forseen the problems before he educated her.

But further on in the same notebook, the Earl had written
– *Returned to d'Espinay's mission to find him mortally wounded and the girl raped. Killed the brute who committed both crimes. The priest died soon after my arrival. It looks as if I have no choice but to take the girl to Shanghai. Damned nuisance but can't be avoided.*

In her book, based on the diaries, Allegra hadn't mentioned the rape. She felt sure that if her great-grandfather had ever envisaged his notebooks being read by his descendants, he would have destroyed that page and all other references of a personal nature. Discretion had been the watchword of the Edwardians. He would have been appalled at the details of Flora's ordeal being known to anyone but themselves.

At first, Allegra had found it difficult to believe that Flora Carlyon, as a young girl, had been a victim of rape; and that the man who later became her husband had killed her attacker.

That fact *was* revealed in the book because, as the old priest's death had made the rapist a murderer, there had been no reason to conceal the fact that, being in the wilds of China, far from law and order, her great-grandfather had taken it upon himself to administer summary justice and ensure that the man committed no more violent crimes.

From what she had been told about him, she felt sure the execution had not caused the seventh Earl to lose any sleep worrying about the rightness of his action. But Flora must have had nightmares for a long time afterwards.

When they had reached Shanghai she had suffered another ordeal, although the exact nature of it was a secret which had died with her.

Piecing together the story of their long, happy life together, and Flora's involvement in women's struggle for equality, had given Allegra intense satisfaction. She had spent innumerable hours poring over old newspapers and illustrated papers in search of references to her great-grandparents' public life. Knowing nothing, at the beginning, of the research techniques used by experienced biographers, gradually she had learnt how to do this particular form of detective work.

As she dried her hands and replaced her rings, she was thinking about her new book and wondering if she would be able to find out why Sir Edward Blakeney and his wife had had no children at a time when large families were the norm.

'I'm sorry to disturb you again,' she said on returning to her row.

The tall man was no longer reading. His book had been stowed away in the pocket of the seat in front .

'Not at all.' This time he smiled at her.

So now he wishes to talk again, she thought as she slipped into her place. Too late, my friend. Moved by one of the contrary impulses which once had been characteristic, she put on her head-set.

Three and a half hours after leaving Heathrow, Concorde's main wheels alighted smoothly on the runway at Kennedy. The last glimpse she had of her neighbour was of him striding away while the rest of the passengers collected their baggage.

As she watched him go she felt a momentary regret for the lost chance to discover who he was.

The 'jambuster' service from Kennedy to the helicopter pad in midtown Manhattan gave Allegra her first sight of the East River and the famous skyscraper skyline.

On landing she was met by her publishers' PR girl, Joni Carson, a perky blonde who seemed slightly awed by Allegra's *haute couture* chic and her title, but became more relaxed when Allegra stopped her using it.

'We've booked you in at the American Stanhope which is located right across from the Metropolitan Museum,' she explained as a car sped them uptown. 'We felt it was the most appropriate place for you to stay. The grandmother of the owner was an English duchess. You mention her in your book as a friend of your great-grandmother. The Duchess of Marlborough.'

'Have you actually read *Travels*?'

'But of course!' Joni looked shocked.

'It's only one of the dozens you must have to deal with. How long have you been with Laurel & Lincoln?'

In the next few minutes Allegra succeeded in finding out a good deal about the American girl and her career until Joni said, 'I shouldn't be talking about me. I'm here to explain the programme we've lined up for you.' She took a folder from her document case. 'That's your schedule until we fly to Chicago for the Phil Donahue show. I'm not sure how much you know about book promo in America?' She paused with her eyebrows lifted.

'Not very much.'

'Donahue has an audience of around eight million viewers every day except weekends. Eighty per cent of the viewers are women and women buy most of the books that are sold in this country. If a book and its author are considered suitable for his show they get a whole hour of attention and a lot of copies are going to be sold as a result.'

'That's marvellous! How clever of you to get *Travels* on the show, Joni.'

'It wasn't anything clever we did. It's what you did, Allegra, writing a book that really touches people's hearts and also being an unusually interesting personality.'

'I wouldn't say that. My great-grandparents were the interesting ones.'

'On the contrary, we at Laurel & Lincoln feel that your personal attributes are going to be a significant factor in making the book a major best-seller over here, as it has been in Britain,' Joni said seriously. 'Your aristocratic background and your looks and your style are going to have a big, big impact on the American public. Now I have some even better news for you.' She paused to give weight to what was to come.

Allegra clenched her teeth to stop herself grinning and strove to look suitably agog. It wasn't that she didn't appreciate the efforts these people were making on her behalf. She did. But she couldn't help feeling that if Joni and the American public knew the truth, that her ancestral home was slowly falling to bits and all her clothes were second-hand, they might be rather less impressed.

'As I've told you, Donahue has eight million viewers daily. But a once-a-week programme called *60 Minutes* on CBS has an audience of forty to fifty million – and they also want you,' Joni announced triumphantly. 'It's fairly unusual for them to do an in-depth interview with an author and it's very important you make the most of it. I know you've had television experience in Britain. We showed videos of two of your British interviews to the Donahue people because normally they like to pre-interview everyone going on the show to make sure they'll come over okay. You come over just fine but all the same, if I may, I'd like to brief you a little bit on how to handle interviewers here.'

'I wish you would. I need all the help I can get.'

'It's mainly a matter of sticking to the most important subject – the book,' said Joni. 'Some authors tend to get sidetracked on to other subjects. The more times you can mention the title, the better the chance that viewers or listeners will remember it when the programme is over. By the way, did you pack some evening things?'

'Yes, I did.'

'Good, because tomorrow night is a chance to wear your most drop-dead outfit.'

Concluding that drop-dead was American for what she would call stunning or knock-out, Allegra said, 'Oh, really? What's been laid on for tomorrow night?'

In the stables at Longwarden, Sarah was tacking-up Bedouin Star and feeling downcast because she had hoped for a letter from Nick today. It was over a month since the last one.

In her room there was an eighteenth-century workbox which no longer contained the sewing tools of its first owner and made a safe place to keep all the letters she had received from him during his long exile on the island of Fuerteventura, one of the Canary Islands off the north-west coast of Africa.

Everyone had heard of the French Foreign Legion. But

few people knew that Spain also recruited foreigners into her army and had more than one regiment of men known as *caballeros legionarios* – gentlemen legionnaires.

When Nick had left the house which had never been truly a home to him, no one knew where he had gone; not even Sarah. There had been many nights when she had cried herself to sleep, fearing that he might be huddled under a hedge, cold and hungry, with no money and nowhere to go. Had she known he was going to run away she would willingly have given him all the funds she could muster. But his flight had been unpremeditated. He had gone – as everyone could see by the bruise on Ted Rivington's face – because his foster father had tried once too often to give him a beating, and this time Nick had struck back.

The relief when at last Sarah received a postcard from Madrid was tempered by dismay. He wrote that he had enlisted in a service which, if it were anything like the French Foreign Legion as described in *Beau Geste* would, she thought, be almost as bad as going to prison for two years.

For that, she learned from his first letter, was the minimum period of enlistment. Two years! At the beginning it had seemed an eternity to her. But at last it was almost over. Soon she would see him again.

For years they had been like brother and sister. Then one day, not long before his disappearance, they had almost bumped into each other as she was entering the stables and he was coming out. She had lost her balance for a moment. He had grabbed her shoulders to steady her. It was all over in a few seconds, but it had made her wonder what it would be like to be hugged by Nick, kissed by him. Very soon she realized their long close friendship had, on her side, developed into love. She wanted to be with him all the time instead of saying goodnight after evening stables.

A few days later he had gone. Mr Rivington claimed to have thrown him out and Nick had never referred to the matter in his letters. Sarah and Sammy suspected that, after being goaded into an act of violence against the grim, violent

121

man who had been slapping and belting him all his life, Nick had walked out from choice.

He was the son of Mrs Rivington's younger sister and a soldier from the camp twelve miles away who had already been posted elsewhere by the time the village could see that, in a phrase still in use in Longwarden, he had 'got her into trouble'.

Not long before, Mary Rivington had had yet another miscarriage and had been advised by her doctor not to try again. This was known in the village because Mary was as friendly and talkative as Ted – the last gamekeeper to be retained on the Longwarden estate – was dour and tactiturn.

It was a mystery to everyone why, from among several boyfriends, she had picked Ted for her husband. When young he had been good-looking, but short-tempered even then. His unpleasant nature had grown more sour as he aged.

However at the time he had been sufficiently concerned by his wife's deep unhappiness over her failure to bring a baby to term to agree to her passionate desire to adopt her sister's child. But he had refused to make the adoption official or to give the baby his name. The infant was registered as Nicholas Dean, the surname being his mother's.

At first all went well. Mary Rivington adored him and her sister was free to resume her job as a hairdresser and, four years later, to marry a rep for a firm making salon equipment. Her marriage took her away from the area but she never had another baby because, before Nick was five, she was killed in a road accident. Consequently he had as few memories of his natural mother as Sarah had of her parents. The discovery that she was also an orphan had been the first bond between them.

By the time he started working in the stables after school and during the holidays, his foster mother was also dead. Nursing Nick and then Ted through influenza, Mary Rivington had refused to succumb to her own symptoms until she had collapsed. With the flu complicated by pleurisy, she had been gravely ill for five days and then died.

It was said by the village gossips that Mrs Rivington's death had turned Ted's brain. Dozens of people in the village had gone down with flu that winter, but because Nick had been the first in the family to catch it, Ted blamed him for bringing it home and considered him directly responsible for Mary's death.

From that time on, at the least provocation Ted would fly into rages. Many people, passing the lodge cottage beside Longwarden's main gateway where he lived, had heard him shouting at the boy and been shocked by the language he used and the venomous rage in his raised voice.

He made no effort to hide his detestation of Nick, habitually referring to him as an idle or lying little bastard. But when the headmistress of the village primary school began to suspect him of regularly thrashing the boy, he angrily denied her suggestion that his method of disciplining Nick might be excessive. And Nick, when questioned about the bruises which could not always be concealed, claimed they had been caused by falling from trees or fights with other boys. As no one had ever heard him crying out in pain, or begging not to be beaten, she had had to leave it at that.

Like Sarah, Nick had not enjoyed school and had usually been bottom of the class. Yet although his spelling and punctuation were still faulty, the thoughts expressed in his letters were those of an intelligent being with a sharply observant eye and ready sense of humour. Less than a year after his enlistment he had been sufficiently fluent in Spanish and a good enough soldier to be promoted to *cabo*, the equivalent of corporal.

She had hoped he would send her a snapshot of himself in uniform. But neither he nor his particular friend, an American ex-Marine, had a camera. She had no idea how much his two years in the Legion had changed him physically, and couldn't visualize the man whose return she awaited so eagerly. She thought of him as he had been the last time she saw him.

She spent hours wondering if, when they met and he

123

saw how much she had changed, he would realize, as she had already, that here was the person he wanted to be with for ever.

'Lady Allegra, may I introduce Paul Kovi, one of the two geniuses who preside here?'

Elliott Lincoln, grandson of one of the founders of America's most prestigious publishing corporation, had lunch at The Four Seasons restaurant several times a week, usually in the Bar Room Grill, an unofficial club for top people in banking, law, real estate, fashion and publishing.

Today, however, he was hosting a luncheon in the Pool Room, so named because eight of its tables surrounded a twenty-foot pool of carrara marble. Two days earlier his secretary had called the restaurant to tell them he wouldn't require his favourite table in the Grill today – like Betty Prashker, one of the most powerful women in American publishing, he preferred always to sit at the same table – and to reserve a table beside the pool where Paul Kovi and his partner Tom Margittai planned the seating with as much care as the wife of a US ambassador and her social secretary gave to the placement of guests at a formal banquet.

'It's always a pleasure to welcome one of Mr Lincoln's distinguished authors to The Four Seasons.' Paul Kovi, spruce in a brass-buttoned navy-blue blazer, kissed Allegra's hand with a panache which betrayed his Hungarian origins. The famous restaurateur had an audacious twinkle in his eye as he added, 'Particularly an author of such beauty and elegance.'

'Thank you, Mr Kovi. I consider myself very lucky to be having my first meal in America at the restaurant which I've been told is the quintessence of New York,' she replied sincerely.

As Elliott Lincoln and his colleagues paused for her to admire one of the restaurant's most famous features, a stage curtain created by Pablo Picasso for the Diaghilev and Massine ballet *Le Tricorne*, Allegra knew that few first-time authors received the VIP treatment which was being lavished on her.

Allegra had changed into an outfit by Valentino. Anyone who knew about clothes – and there were sure to be plenty of knowledgeable eyes at The Four Seasons – would recognize that it wasn't from the Italian designer's most recent collection. But they were unlikely to guess that Elliott Lincoln's guest of honour was not the first owner of the pleated silk skirt, in a grey herringbone print speckled with black and white, which swirled round her long legs as the publisher and his party were conducted to their table.

With the skirt went a black silk top with a low vee neckline and a scarf wound round her neck and flung over her shoulder. Over the hip-length top went a printed chiffon coat to match the skirt.

Few women would not have been flattered by the ineffable Valentino style of this ensemble, but it might have been designed for the chestnut gleams in Allegra's hair and the ivory tone of her skin. Having a neck to match her legs, she knew there was nothing sexier than a covered-up throat combined with a precisely-judged depth of décolletage. Naturally Valentino's judgement was impeccable. The vee showed enough of her bosom to be alluring but not enough to go beyond the limit of what was acceptable at midday.

'What would you like to drink, Allegra?' her host inquired when they were seated.

A fair man in his early forties with urbane manners, he gave her the feeling he was no mere figurehead at the top of the heap. She wondered if he were married or divorced and what he was like as a lover. Not that he attracted her, or not enough to overcome her reluctance to get involved with anyone with an influence on her newborn career.

'I'm somewhat of a purist myself,' he went on. 'I believe the only thing to drink before lunch is the excellent Williams & Humbert dry sack they have here. But don't let me influence you if you would prefer something else.'

'Sherry would be lovely.'

While he conferred with the others she took the

opportunity to look at the soaring room with its floor-to-ceiling windows of smoked glass draped with metal chains which, constantly moving, created the illusion of being inside a great waterfall.

When everyone had decided what to eat, their attention focused on her.

'How do you feel about the tour, Allegra?' she was asked by one of the three executive vice-presidents who, with Joni, made up the table. 'Did you do a similar tour when your book was published in Britain?'

'On a very much smaller scale. Nothing like the jam-packed schedule I'm going to undertake here. I hope I'm equal to it,' she said with a smile.

'I'm sure you will be, and Joni will be with you to see everything goes to plan,' said Elliott. 'Has she told you about the party at Le Club tomorrow?'

'I thought you'd want to tell Allegra about that,' put in his PR director.

'We felt a lot of influential people from all walks of life in this city would enjoy the opportunity to meet you before you become known to a wider public,' he explained. 'We drew up a list and arranged to hold a party at a private dining club. All but three invitations were accepted and the people who declined had prior engagements which they couldn't alter.'

'How exciting. Shall I know any of these important New Yorkers? By name, that is.'

'I feel sure you will, but the important thing is that tomorrow they'll be spreading the word about the new star name on our list. All of us at Laurel & Lincoln feel confident that *The Travels of an Edwardian Naturalist* is going to have an even bigger success here than it has in your country, Allegra. Isn't that so?' he appealed to his colleagues.

'I don't think there's any doubt of that, Elliott,' the most senior of the other men agreed emphatically. He turned to Allegra. 'Sometimes best-sellers aren't recognized as such right away. We understand that was the case with the British edition of *Travels*.'

'Yes, it had to be reprinted quickly when the first printing sold out much more rapidly than Brentwood & Dunbar expected.'

'Brentwood & Dunbar haven't been in this business as long as Laurel & Lincoln,' he said with a chuckle. 'I can assure you, Allegra, that everyone here recognized immediately that your book is a winner. I'm convinced that in a very short time *Travels* will be on all the major best-seller lists and stay there many, many weeks.'

'I hope so. Although I can't really see why Americans should lap it up as eagerly as English readers have. I always think of you as a tremendously vital, forward-looking nation, not as retrospective as we tend to be.'

He nodded. 'We are a nation of energetic, forward-looking people, but that doesn't mean we don't feel nostalgia for the slower pace of life in the past. Basically, *Travels* is a true-life Cinderella story in that Countess Flora was taken from extreme poverty and hardship to a world of extravagant luxury where her every whim was indulged by an immensely rich husband. It's a theme of very wide appeal, and the fact that both your great-grandparents were extremely charismatic personalities reinforces that appeal.'

Now the man on her right had something to say. She had memorized all their first names – Jack, Evan and Blair – but was confused about their surnames and exact status in the Laurel & Lincoln pecking order.

'And it helps that the writer of their story also has a lot of charisma,' he said, beaming at her. 'A great book won't fail to best-sell because the author lacks personality. There are top writers who refuse to take part in what Irving Wallace has called "the electronic circus". But in a television-oriented age, there's no doubt that someone like yourself who looks great and can express themselves fluently does have a definite edge.'

They continued to blandish her with compliments and encouragement throughout the delectable meal and, up to a point, Allegra enjoyed it. However by the time she and Blair were indulging in The Four Seasons' maple and bourbon soufflé, while the others restricted themselves to fresh strawberries and pink grapefruit sherbet, her appetite for praise had been sated. She found herself longing to be setting out up Park Avenue on her first exploration of the city.

Elliott had other ideas about how she should spend the remainder of the day.

When the lunch party finally broke up about three o'clock he said, 'Joni has arranged for a car to take you back to your hotel where I suggest you relax for the rest of the day. Your system still has to adjust to the five-hour time lag. It's been a very great pleasure to meet you, Allegra, and I'm sure a lot of New Yorkers are going to be waiting to share that pleasure at Scribner's tomorrow morning.'

As the Cadillac drew away he waved to her, flanked by the others, all of them smiling and waving.

Sitting in queenly isolation in the back of the enormous car as it glided north on Park Avenue, she wondered what they were saying about her among themselves. How sincere were their flattering remarks? Was she really on the brink of a huge success in America which would allow her to give more help to North and Sarah, as well as enjoying some extravagances on her own account?

She looked at her watch. It would be at least two hours before the shops closed, perhaps longer. If Elliott thought she could relax on her first afternoon in New York, he didn't know much about women.

Several hours later she was eating a peach from the presentation basket in her hotel room when the telephone rang and her brother's voice asked, 'How was your flight?'

'Terrific! The whole day has been terrific.' She told him about it. 'And now I'm about to have a bath and order a little something for supper and watch some American TV. How are things with you?'

'Pretty good. When are we going to be able to get together?'

'Tomorrow is out. In the morning there's a signing session. In the afternoon I'm doing interviews and tomorrow night there's a party for influential people at a place called Le Club. Do you know it?'

'Very well. In my wild youth I had some good times there.'

'Why don't you come and give me moral support? L and L wouldn't mind. I'm sure they'd be delighted.'

'Since when did you need moral support? You'll be in your element. Are you tied up the following night?'

'Let me check my schedule. It's been worked out like a royal tour. No . . . the night after tomorrow is free. Let me take you out to dinner.'

'Fine, but if you don't mind there's someone I'd like to bring along. A girl I met at the Blakewell tercentenary.'

'All right . . . if you must,' she added, having hoped to have him to herself.

'I think you'll like her. She's our cousin. Her mother was Julia Foster's younger sister. The one who made a "bad" marriage and died off early. Now the father is dead and this girl has been living with Julia for some months . . . a fate one wouldn't wish on anyone. She won't bore you. She's young but not witless.'

'How young? – And what's her name?'

'Early twenties . . . Jane Graham.'

They talked for a few minutes more. 'Good luck with the signing session,' he said before he rang off.

Jane flew to New York on an early shuttle and checked in at the Carlyle Hotel. The first thing she wanted to do was to walk down Fifth Avenue on this perfect bright windless morning when the city she had never seen seemed to bid her welcome.

She knew why her father had always discouraged her from accompanying him on his infrequent and brief visits to New York. He hadn't liked to be reminded of the first year of his marriage when he and her mother had lived in two rooms in a dilapidated brownstone in a seedy street on the West Side.

For him, their first year together had been marred by the knowledge that he was depriving Rosalind of the comforts she was used to. He couldn't bear to remember how pinched she had looked in the winter when their rooms

129

were inadequately heated; how exhausted in the humid heat of a Manhattan summer. All her life she had been the cosseted youngest child of a Boston banker. For love of John Graham she had cut herself off from her family, her friends and everything familiar. Before he was able to make it up to her, she had died in a polio epidemic in Venezuela, when Jane was too young to remember her clearly.

As she walked past the park which divided the now-fashionable East Side from the turn-of-the-century fashionable West Side, she wished she knew the address where her parents had lived and could go to look at the house where she had been conceived. If it hadn't been pulled down.

The first shop to make her linger at its windows was Tiffany's, where she admired the enticingly displayed jewels and bibelots without seeing anything she coveted. Next to it reared the sixty-eight bronze-glass storeys of the new Trump Tower. A stroll round the pink marble atrium with its eighty-foot waterfall left her disappointed. The branches of famous European shops seemed out of place in this glorified shopping mall. Obviously it was a showplace which would attract thousands of tourists even if they couldn't afford to buy there. But with its doormen arrayed in musical comedy versions of British Guardsmen's uniforms, complete with bearskin helmets, it didn't impress her.

She wondered if North had seen it and what he thought of the doormen. She must remember to ask him when they met. When they had talked on the telephone, he had suggested a breakfast date tomorrow. Today and tonight he had unbreakable engagements, he had told her regretfully. Although she was impatient to see him, she had claimed that shopping would keep her fully occupied until tomorrow evening. It seemed a long time away. But at least in New York there were plenty of ways to kill time.

The fine leather goods at Gucci she gave only a cursory inspection. Too many of them were spoiled for her by the status-seeker's letter G. She had an instinctive aversion to wearing anything with a designer's or maker's logo on it. Her father might have been a parvenu in the eyes of most of his Brahmin in-laws, but he had been a man of innate taste who had taught her that quality should advertise itself more subtly than with symbols.

Valentino's windows were more tempting. A black linen blazer reminded her of Marie-Simone and the weeks they had spent in Venice, staying at the Hotel Cipriani soon after it had re-opened after its winter closure and before the sightseers had begun to swarm in St Mark's Square.

Every day the Cipriani launch had sped them from the seclusion of the Guidecca to the city where every other house was a *palazzo*. It had been the happiest of times, the more so when her father had joined them. She remembered one crossing in the launch when he had sat between them, his arms round their shoulders, her black hair and Marie-Simone's blonde hair being whipped by the salty breeze like the launch's pennant at the stern. Both she and the Frenchwoman had bags containing delectable Missoni knits which John Graham had helped them to choose because he had been a man who was interested in everything.

She still had the sweater and the memory would stay with her for ever, but the comfort of loving and being loved had gone and it was hard to live without.

She walked on, past St Patrick's Cathedral, now dwarfed by its modern neighbours, and past Saks Fifth Avenue. She was looking out for Scribner's which North had told her was the most beautiful bookshop in New York or anywhere else he had been.

The shop was featuring a large display of *The Travels of an Edwardian Naturalist* by Allegra Lomax, with a notice saying that the author would be signing copies in the store from noon until two.

The book's dust jacket was a montage photograph of the man whom Jane now recognized as North's keen-eyed, eagle-nosed great-grandfather. It showed him in several guises: in the formal white-tie evening dress of his elegant era, seated outside a tent with a Chinese servant waiting on him, and as one of a large shooting party posed on the lawns at Longwarden.

In case North's hope of introducing them couldn't be

realized because of his sister's publishing commitments, Jane decided to come back at noon. She filled in the time by looking round Saks.

When she returned to Scribner's shortly before the signing session was due to begin, already a line had formed inside the store. Jane's first glimpse of the English girl was when she was about seventh in line from the table where North's sister was swiftly autographing the title page of each copy presented to her.

By the time she came near the table, Jane had already seen that Allegra was not like her brother in looks. Her hair was the colour of a chestnut when the green husk splits open. Her eyes were as striking as his but not the same deep-sea blue. Hers were the colour of lilac and her eyelids were painted to emphasize the unusual shade of her irises. She was wearing a close-fitting eastern jacket of dark-purple silk threaded with silver. Round her neck were many chains of silver and amethyst beads and her silver rings caught the light as she wrote her name. Most people were given only a smiling 'Hello'. With a few she had a brief conversation.

When Jane reached the table she received the contralto 'Hello' and the brilliant smile. But after scrawling her first name, the English girl stopped and looked up.

'Have we met before?' she asked uncertainly.

In spite of North's opening remark at the Winterbrook reunion, and the likeness she had seen for herself in the albums in the Athenaeum, Jane had not expected her resemblance to Flora Lomax to be recognizable by Allegra.

For a moment she considered introducing herself. Then mindful of the long line behind her, she only smiled and shook her head.

Having completed her signature, the other girl gave her another long searching glance. But she said no more and, having thanked her, Jane moved on to have the book wrapped.

The line-up was extending on to the sidewalk when she left the store. As she waited to cross the street she examined her impression of the sister of the man she planned to marry. Could they be friends as she and Marie-Simone had been friends? It seemed strange that Allegra wasn't married, a woman in her late twenties with a face of outstanding beauty and, at least as far as the waist, a figure to match.

Unlike her daughter who thrived there, Pen disliked London more and more as the years passed. But one London event which still drew her was the Royal Horticultural Society's Great Spring Show.

Popularly known as the Chelsea Show, and with a strong claim to being the world's finest flower exhibition, it was to Pen what Royal Ascot had been to her husband. Even though Members' Day had long lost its exclusiveness so that before mid-morning the enormous marquee, covering three and a half acres of the showground, was already unbearably crowded, she continued to go.

Often in past years she had taken her two old gardeners. However this year Bob Craskett's sister-in-law had died the week before the show and he had to accompany his wife to the funeral: and Henry begged to be excused on the ground that he found the long day in London was becoming too much for him.

Pen could have gone up by train the previous afternoon and slept at Carlyon House before taking a taxi to Chelsea to be at the gates when they opened at eight in the morning. However on the rare occasions when she had spent a night at the flat, she had felt she was being a nuisance. Even in her daughter's absence she wouldn't feel comfortable in the exotic surroundings Allegra had created for herself. She decided to stick to her custom of going up by car on the day, leaving Longwarden at half-past five.

The only worry was that her ancient car hadn't been running well lately and sooner or later was sure to let her down completely. A replacement was long overdue, but as long as the Ford continued to scrape through its MOT test she had been postponing the expense. Even second-hand cars weren't cheap any more and her resources were stretched to their limit already.

The night before the show, having dinner with her niece, she said, 'I do hope the car behaves itself tomorrow.'

'If you think it might not, why not borrow North's?' Sarah suggested. 'I don't suppose he'd mind.'

'I'm sure he would and it would be just my luck to have a biff in it. No, I'll go in mine and hope for the best,' said Pen as she helped herself to new potatoes from the dish her butler was holding for her.

He moved round the table to Sarah.

'If I might make a suggestion, m'Lady, would it relieve your mind if I drove up to London with you tomorrow? I could drive you in my car.'

As he always appeared to be deaf to their conversation, his mind concentrated wholly on the service of the meal, Pen was slightly startled to find that he did listen to them, and much more surprised by his offer. She had forgotten he had a car, and seemed to remember North thinking it must have been left to Ashford by his previous employer. She herself had never seen it. As far as she knew, he rarely if ever used his vehicle.

'That's a splendid idea,' said Sarah. 'It would be too bad if your big day at the show was spoiled by a breakdown, Aunt Pen.'

'It's a very kind suggestion, Mr Ashford, but I don't like to drag you out of bed at such an ungodly hour,' Pen said doubtfully. 'I usually set out at five-thirty because I'm not a fast driver.'

Edward had been very fast and a road-hog as well. Driving with him had petrified her. She wouldn't expect to be nervous as Ashford's passenger; she couldn't imagine him flashing, hooting and fuming – her husband's style on the road.

'I think six should be early enough if you haven't the problem of parking,' was Ashford's reply. 'I can leave the car in the underground park at Marble Arch and return for you when the show closes, or whatever time suits you.'

'What will you do with yourself?'

'There's always plenty to do in London, m'Lady.'

134

'In that case, thank you . . . I accept,' Pen said gratefully. She was guiltily aware that the journeys to and from Chelsea would now be as great a pleasure as the show itself.

'How very kind of Mr Ashford,' she said, when he had left the room.

'Well, yes – but it will be a free day out for him. Presumably you'll be paying for the petrol and parking?'

'Of course,' Pen agreed, deflated.

Was that why he'd offered to drive her? Not out of disinterested kindness, but to have a day out in London largely at her expense?

'You look sensational . . . but you know that. It was an inspired idea to wear one of Flora Carlyon's ball gowns tonight,' said Elliott Lincoln as he settled himself beside Allegra in the back of the Cadillac.

The party at Le Club wasn't over. But Elliott had decided his guest of honour had been on show for long enough and he was taking her back to her hotel.

'Thank you, Elliott. Actually this is the dress Flora wore for her first dinner party at Longwarden.'

All evening she had been receiving compliments about the dress of apricot silk which her great-grandmother had worn on the night in 1903 when, after some intensive coaching in correct behaviour, she had made her first appearance as the Countess of Carlyon.

With it, Allegra was wearing one of the most beautiful examples of art nouveau jewellery of the many René Lalique pieces Caspar Carlyon had given to his adored wife. This, too, had aroused great interest among her publisher's guests: an extraordinary piece, consisting of nine naked girls fashioned in gold on plaques ornamented with enamelled black swans and amethysts. Between the plaques were large matched opals in an ornate gold setting.

'Whatever it is, it's fabulous. Le Club has seen a lot of lovely women in the past twenty-five years, but none more beautiful than you look tonight, Allegra.'

She was beginning to wonder if it were entirely in her interest that he'd chosen to spirit her away from the assembly of famous and influential people he had induced to come to the party.

Henry and Nancy Kissinger . . . Pat and William F. Buckley Junior . . . Estée Lauder . . . Harold Evans and Tina Brown . . . Prince 'Aboodi' Ben Saud . . . Charles Ryskamp . . . Gunther Drechsler . . . the guest list seemed to have included people from every sphere of New York's cosmopolitan society.

'It's a night I shall never forget,' she said with a smile. 'You must have a great deal of power and influence, Elliott, to bring all those people together to meet a first-book author. Someone was telling me you're the natural successor to Alfred Knopf.'

Before tonight she hadn't known that, until his death two years earlier at the age of ninety-one, Alfred Knopf had been the most distinguished figure in American publishing.

'Whoever said that was flattering me far beyond my deserts,' Elliott said wryly. 'No one, as things are today, can equal Knopf's achievement. He and his first wife, Blanche, produced books that won twenty-one Pulitzer prizes and sixteen Nobels. I certainly agree with his dictum that it costs no more to produce a handsome book than an ugly one. I hope you've noticed that our edition of *Travels* is a superior piece of craftsmanship.'

He was too suave to say it was superior to the Brentwood & Dunbar edition, but she knew it was.

'I have indeed. It's a lovely book to handle. I'm very proud of it.'

'And we're proud to have you on our list, Allegra. I hope this is the beginning of a long and enjoyable association.'

It seemed to her that although in itself the remark was a pleasant platitude any publisher might address to any author, Elliott's look and his tone gave it a more personal meaning.

If he had a wife, surely she would have been at the party? Or her absence would have been explained.

'If you treat all your writers as royally as you have me, I should think they stay with you for ever,' she answered

136

lightly. 'Do you live in New York all the time, or have you a place in the country for weekends?'

'I used to commute from Connecticut but my former wife has that house now. In summer I rely on friends to offer me a respite from the heat of the city. The rest of the year living here suits me very well. I'm an urban being . . . as you are, I believe? You spend more of your time in London than at Longwarden, I think you said.'

'Yes, I do. Big cities may be unhealthy, but I find them stimulating.'

'If it weren't that I feel you must be tired – it's almost tomorrow morning in Britain now – I'd invite you to see my view of Manhattan by night. I've recently moved to a new apartment in Park Tower. When they were advertised as "pavilions in the sky" it was no exaggeration,' said Elliot. 'The view from my living room is really something to see.'

Ball in my court, thought Allegra. She had never had an American lover. She wondered if they were significantly different from European men. It might be interesting to find out.

'I'd love to see your view, Elliott . . .'

Jane was sitting up in bed, reading. North's sister's book had kept her engrossed all evening, and not only because she had a special interest in the great country house where Caspar and Flora Carlyon had lived and loved for more than half a century.

My darling girl,
Last night I slept under the stars and longed for your head on my shoulder, and the softness and scent of your hair close to my cheek.

You would have enjoyed today; and I should have enjoyed it more had you been beside me. I was climbing at an altitude of above five thousand feet and saw patches of brilliant pink which turned out to be *Viola cazorlensis* . . .

After reading some of the love letters the seventh Earl had written to his wife when she had been unable to go with him on a plant-hunting expedition to southern Spain, Jane paused to wonder if North would ever write as passionately and tenderly to her. It wasn't impossible. At the beginning, Caspar hadn't loved his bride. He had married her for convenience, falling in love with her later and remaining spellbound by her to the end of his days. He had been over seventy when these letters were written, yet they made it clear that he was still Flora's lover as well as her husband and friend.

Having skimmed the final chapter to see if North were mentioned in it, Jane already knew Caspar had died in his eighty-fifth year, not at Longwarden but on a houseboat on the Dal Lake in Kashmir, one of his and Flora's favourite places for a holiday.

She, seventeen when he met her, had survived him by twenty-two years, dying in her garden in London with his love letters close at hand. North had returned that day from a photographic expedition to the Himalayas. When he appeared in the garden where she had been having tea, she had mistaken her grandson for her long-dead husband. She had died in his arms, thinking herself reunited with her adored Caspar. The final seconds of her life had been moments of sublime joy.

Wanting to go on reading, but also wanting to wake up refreshed and clear-eyed on what promised to be the most crucial day of her life, Jane closed the book and put it on the night table. She turned out the light and lay down.

Part of her – the romantic streak inherited from her mother – yearned to experience the happiness Flora and Rosalind had known. At the same time, with the clear-eyed realism which was the dominant side of her character, she recognized the rarity of such marriages. Marry the life you want rather than the man you want. That down-to-earth maxim had been coined a long time ago, but it still made a lot of sense. With North she would have a life which suited her *and* an exciting lover. Whether that side of their relationship would dwindle or deepen, only time could tell.

Still wakeful, she turned on her side, wondering if North had the capacity to care deeply for a woman. His work told her much about him: that he had an artist's eye for beauty; that he cared about endangered species and the wanton destruction of the environment, and used his camera to make people share his concern; that he was an adventurous man, not desk-bound and fixed in his habits.

He probably had the defects of his qualities. Virtuosos, whatever their field, were usually single-minded to the point of sacrificing everything and everyone to their work. What Aunt Julia had called his selfishness might in fact be his creative force resisting the pressures and responsibilities which threatened to sap it.

The woman who married him would have to accept that his work came before his private life. A man who had waited five months for a visa to Outer Mongolia would be likely, when it finally came through, to fling some gear in a grip and be off on the first available flight – and to hell with the tickets for the opera or the anniversary dinner or whatever else he left behind.

But I shouldn't mind that, she thought. I might even go along, if he'd let me.

In the back of the Cadillac, Allegra was saying '. . . but you're right, I am flagging a little. It's been a long, exciting day. I think I should go to bed and hope to see your marvellous view some other time.'

'I guess you're right,' Elliott answered. 'Tomorrow is another busy day for you.'

At this point the car drew up outside her hotel and the driver jumped out to open the door for his passengers. Elliott stepped out first and turned to assist Allegra. She knew that in bending to step out she gave him a fuller view of her breasts in the low-cut bodice of the apricot dress. As she straightened and let down her train, she recognized desire in his eyes and knew he was regretting having to say goodnight to her.

Leaving the driver to await his return, he came inside the building with her and waited as she rustled into the elevator. As it carried her up to her floor, she wondered if it had been foolish to turn down the opportunity to spend the night, or part of it, in the arms of an agreeable man.

What a long time ago they seemed, all those years when she wouldn't have hesitated to respond to Elliott's gentle-manly pass. Life is short. Death is long. That had been her credo – once. Not any more.

Now what she craved as much as physical love was to have someone to talk to on nights like this when she needed time to wind down before she could sleep.

When, at ten minutes to six, Pen left her bedroom, she was wearing a Hardy Amies printed silk suit bought for a wedding when Allegra was still in her teens. A hat was no longer *de rigueur* on Members' Day, but from long habit she always wore one. It made her feel less self-conscious about her unfashionable hair when she met women who had come out with her, but who now looked much younger and smarter.

Ashford was waiting in the Great Hall when she walked down the staircase. He was looking extremely personable in a chalk-striped grey suit, with a mackintosh over his arm and a rolled umbrella in his hand.

'Good morning. I see you're playing safe,' she said, brandishing her own umbrella.

There was a folded plastic raincoat in her large sensible bag and, from long experience of Chelsea, she was wearing serviceable shoes which would not make her feet ache or let in water if it rained.

'Good morning. Yes, although at the moment it looks like being a fine day. Whether the sky is deceptive we shall hear on the early forecast.'

Pen took little interest in cars and knew by sight only a handful of the most distinctive makes. However it wasn't necessary for her to take a close look at the discreet badge on the bonnet to know which manufacturer had produced the recently-polished, claret-coloured car parked at the foot of the steps. Its lines were unmistakably those of a Jaguar.

'This is tremendous luxury compared with my ancient runabout,' she said as they fastened their seat-belts.

It surprised her that an elderly general should choose to drive, or be driven, in a powerful two-door coupé, but perhaps he had been a sporty old boy. The interior, with its leather upholstery and burr-elm-veneered dashboard, reminded her of Edward's Bentley Continental. But the man at her side with his aquiline profile, the skin at his jaw still stretched tautly over the bone, was very different from her husband whose features, never distinguished, had become gross before he was forty.

Many times during the journey her eyes were drawn to the thin strong fingers controlling the wheel and gear-stick with the same quiet efficiency he brought to everything she had seen him do.

Halfway there and making good time, he pulled the car into a lay-by and produced a flask of coffee and some of Mrs Armitage's shortbread.

'We have plenty of time for a ten-minute break,' he said. 'You may not find it too easy to get a cup of coffee there.'

'Have you been to the show, Mr Ashford?'

'No, never. I was speaking from experience of similar events. Is the Chelsea Show well provided with places to eat? Will you be able to get an acceptable lunch there?'

'I shall probably slip out for lunch. There's a pleasant little lunch place at the General Trading Company's shop near Sloane Square. If I get there before the main lunch hour I can have a light meal and look for a present for one of my godchildren.' She hesitated. 'If you've never been to the show, would it interest you to spend an hour there? My membership entitles me to two tickets, one of which is going begging this year.'

'I'd be most interested to see it.'

'In that case why not leave the car at Battersea Park and come with me on the mini-bus which runs from there to the showground? When you've seen as much as you want to, you can take the tube from Sloane Square to wherever you're intending to go.'

He said, 'I was thinking of having a look at the Summer

141

Exhibition at the Academy: something else I've missed up to now. Living at Longwarden has made me more interested in art than I used to be.'

As they were still in good time after leaving the car south of the river, they walked over Chelsea Bridge and arrived at the show by the Embankment entrance.

Inside the showground she said, 'If I may advise you, the best thing to do is to make straight for the marquee before it becomes overcrowded.'

Had she been on her own, once inside the vast earthy-smelling tent she would have made a beeline for the stands of her three favourite exhibitors: David Austin and Peter Beales, both growers of lovely old shrub and climbing roses, and Beth Chatto, a specialist in plants for dry or damp places from whose exhibit Pen had gleaned many ideas for effective plantings.

With Ashford's presence as a counter-attraction, she was torn between hurrying to see their stands before the aisles became thronged, and wanting to stay beside him. It was a novel experience for her to be out in public with a man at whom, in the short time since their arrival, she had already seen other women cast interested glances.

North had always attracted a great deal of feminine interest on the rare occasions when they went somewhere together. To have a good-looking son was gratifying, but it gave her a different pleasure from that which she felt now.

'A pale shadow of the one at Longwarden,' he remarked, when they passed the short laburnum walk at the centre of Notcutt's display.

This was not far from Beth Chatto's stand. Once there, the gardener in Pen overcame the middle-aged woman afflicted with what she knew to be adolescent feelings.

As she began to make notes, Ashford said, 'I'll leave you to concentrate, Lady Carlyon,' and was gone before she could reply.

With mingled regret and relief she watched him walking away. Every moment they spent together made her more foolishly vulnerable to the inevitable pain of loving him.

When the marquee filled to the point at which Pen began

to feel stirrings of claustrophobia, she slipped out by the nearest exit, which was close to the stand of Chatsworth Carpenters.

The shirt-sleeved, green-aproned figure of the Marquess of Hartington, only son of the Duke and Duchess of Devonshire, caught her eye. As she passed he was wrapping a black tray for a small white-haired woman with a plastic rain bonnet protecting her perm.

There was no sign of Deborah Devonshire whom Pen knew slightly, not well. Perhaps she would be there later. Chatsworth Carpenters had grown out of the Duchess's involvement in enlarging an inn on her husband's Yorkshire estate. Much of the furniture needed for the additional bedrooms had been made in the building yard at Chatsworth. From that initial project had grown the garden furniture business, all the seats, tubs and trellis pillars being solidly made and based on classical designs.

As she walked on Pen wondered if a more enterprising woman than herself could have instigated something similar at Longwarden, in the days before the maintenance staff had dwindled to one desperately overworked handyman.

She had sometimes toyed with the idea of emulating Priscilla Bacon, widow of a former Lord Lieutenant of Norfolk and the designer of the garden at Raveningham Hall, the house built by his forebears. Although a contemporary of Pen's mother, Lady Bacon still worked in what was now her son's garden, exporting snowdrops and daffodils and issuing a catalogue of uncommon plants and shrubs which she grew to sell.

However the grounds at Raveningham were much smaller than those at Longwarden. It was as much as Pen could manage to keep Pulbrook & Gould supplied with some of her own rarities.

She had looked at the gardens sponsored by *Woman's Own*, *Vogue* and other publications, and was thinking of having a coffee break, when ahead of her she saw Ashford. He was conversing with a man with a small grey moustache and a woman wearing a several-years-old Jaeger shirt dress which Pen remembered being tempted by.

143

As she walked towards them, Ashford glanced in her direction. And then something rather odd happened.

When the postman saw Sarah riding towards him along the wide verge bordering the main drive to Longwarden, he cut the best part of a mile off his delivery round by stopping, making a U turn and climbing out to wait for her to come up to him.

'Morning, miss. Just the one letter for you today.'

Her heart leaping with delight, Sarah dismounted and accepted the airmail envelope with the head of King Juan Carlos of Spain on the stamp. She smiled. 'Thank you very much.'

The postman climbed back in his van and drove back towards the lodge cottage, avoiding the worst of the ruts in a drive overdue for repair.

Sarah hitched Beddo to the railings between the verge and the parkland. The envelope felt bulkier than usual. She tore it open and drew out some folded graph paper, two sheets torn from a spiral notebook.

Dear Sarah, *Nick had written in green ballpoint*, Just back from two weeks on manouvers (*the spelling mistake brought a more tender smile to her lips*) in Lanzarote.

The object of the exersize was to chase some mili (national service) guys across a volcanic desert. Not being used to the heat, pretty soon they were totally knackered and it didn't take long to catch them. However the teniente (*she knew this meant his lieutenant*) decided we should cross the desert anyway. It's called Mal Pais (bad land) and the black rock looks something like Aero choc, some of it sharp and spikey and other parts smooth, like melted plastic. Quite an interesting trip, although I could have done without a 40 kilo haversack and a 12 kilo machine gun to carry. Also we had covered 27 kilometres the day before, partly in mountains, so were not exactly fresh . . .

Towards the end of the letter he wrote that his company had acquired a new *teniente*, the owner of a bull's pizzle.

Quite a nasty weapon in the hands of anyone who enjoys inflicting pain, as this guy seems to.

This news and Nick's comment troubled her. What if the new officer indulged his sadistic tendencies on the English *cabo* and, as he had once before, Nick lost his temper and hit back? What would happen to a legionnaire who struck a superior? Nick's contract was nearing its end, but a serious offence might make them postpone his discharge. She couldn't bear to think of him being subjected to the even harsher regime of the punishment block. His life was hard enough as it was.

The letter was signed *Love, Nick.* When Sarah wrote the word *Love* at the end of her letter to him, she meant it with all her heart, but she knew that above his name it probably signified no more than a brotherly affection.

Carefully folding the pages which a few days ago he had touched, she pressed them to her lips and kissed them.

The band of the Grenadier Guards had had their tea break and were playing the second half of their programme in the Ranelagh Gardens adjoining the showground when Pen collected her parcels from the left-luggage place and made her way to the Embankment entrance where she had arranged to meet Ashford at half-past five.

Tired now, she was looking forward to relaxing in the comfort of his car. She was still puzzled by his behaviour when he saw her approaching. And she had not been the only one to be mystified. The perplexed expressions on the faces of those people when he had suddenly made an excuse to cut short the conversation and leave them standing had been clearly visible to Pen. Then he had walked towards her but pretended not to have seen her until they were almost abreast.

Yet he had seen her: she was certain of it. It was seeing her coming which had made him desert that couple. If they had been merely casual acquaintances, normal behaviour on his part would have been to wait until she joined him. No introduction would have been necessary. Merely a greeting which indicated that he and she were, in a sense, at the show together.

That he had not behaved normally seemed to establish that they hadn't been strangers but rather old friends met by chance; friends who *would* have expected to be introduced.

Why he had wished to avoid that introduction was something which had been baffling her ever since.

He was at their rendezvous before her, having arrived in a taxi which was waiting to take them across the river to the car park.

'Ah . . . how nice to sit down,' she sighed, sinking into the corner behind the driver. 'Though I don't know why I should feel tired. I'm always on my feet and never normally weary at this time of day. Are you exhausted too?'

'I shan't be sorry to get back to quiet and fresh air,' he admitted. 'I think it's the constant drone of traffic and possibly the high level of carbon monoxide in the air which makes London tiring to country-dwellers.'

'It's the first time in years that I haven't met anyone I knew. That's very unusual. Did you come across any familiar faces?'

He was watching a river police launch skimming down Chelsea Reach. As his glance shifted to her face, she thought for an apprehensive moment he was going to lie to her.

'Yes, I did,' he said quietly.

That was all. No mention of who they were . . . how long it was since he'd seen them last . . . nothing but a bald answer to her question.

Pen flushed and looked away. Clearly she shouldn't have asked. What right had she to be curious about aspects of his life which were nothing to do with his job? Even so, acknowledging that she had none, she was hurt by the snub. It made her feel as if he had found her prying through the half-open door of his room which he had then closed in her face.

When he went on to inquire what she thought of the show in comparison with other years, embarrassment made her answer constrainedly. Motoring towards London that morning, she had thought that on the way back she might suggest stopping for a drink at one of several pleasant-looking country inns along their route. They might even have dinner out.

Now she felt that, were she to propose it, she might be rebuffed a second time.

'Lord Carlyon is in the lobby, Miss Graham.'

'Tell him I'll be down immediately, would you, please?'

She had been ready for half an hour and had passed the time reading Allegra's book. Without knowing where they were going to eat, it had been difficult to decide what to wear. She had settled for the dark-red silk shirt she had been wearing when North first saw her. It had a matching silk skirt which made it look like a dress, and a red cashmere jacket which she slipped on before leaving her room.

North was waiting for her to emerge from the elevator. 'Are you always ready on time?' he asked as they shook hands.

'Before time, as a rule. It's one of my hang-ups. I'm usually too early.'

'A good fault. I hate being kept waiting. Allegra is joining us at the restaurant. I hope you're not desperate to eat because the place I'm taking you to has two sittings. We're booked for the second one, at nine. I thought we'd have drinks here first.' He took her lightly by the elbow and moved in the direction of the bar.

'Did you have a good time in Nantucket?' she asked as they sat down.

'I did some sailing and a lot of walking. It's too early in the year to swim in the sea there. I did try it, but it was – Brr!' He gave a demonstrative shiver. 'Tell me what you've been doing? Have you had trouble with your aunt?'

'A little. Nothing I couldn't handle. I'd like a glass of white wine, please,' she added as the waiter approached.

North ordered a gin and tonic.

'And how did you handle it?' he asked.

'Aunt Julia was very annoyed when I told her I'd had lunch with you. I explained that you'd told me the reason for her dislike of you, and that I didn't want to upset her but I didn't feel it had anything to do with me – certainly not to the extent of preventing me from meeting your sister. She was furious with me for two days and then she began to calm down and to see that I wouldn't be bullied.'

'That was very resolute of you. Mrs Foster can be a dragon.'

'Yes, she can; and living with her, I'm in a difficult position. But I can be firm when it's necessary, and I'm glad I stood up to her. This is a wonderful city and I'm going to enjoy my few days here. By the way, I saw your sister yesterday. She signed a copy of her book for me and a long line of other people. I'm more than halfway through the book already. It's fascinating . . . and I'm sure I'd be equally riveted if the people in it were nothing to do with me. It's extraordinary how much you resemble Caspar Carlyon.'

'Except that he had a more presentable nose,' he said, rubbing his own with his forefinger.

'What happened to your nose?'

'It was punched when I was a schoolboy. Allegra tells me I look like an unsuccessful boxer, but I can't say it bothers me. I only see it when I'm shaving.'

'Allegra is your sister. I don't think other women would regard it as a disfigurement. You're still a very . . . personable man.'

He lifted a quizzical eyebrow. 'Are you flirting with me, Cousin Jane?'

She was prevented from replying by the return of the waiter bringing their drinks. When he had gone she picked up her glass and said, with deliberate coquetry, 'And why not?'

The light she had seen in his eyes before they danced at the ball reappeared in a burning blue stare which made her lower her own gaze.

'Why not indeed?' he said softly. 'Let's drink to that. To a closer connection between the two sides of the family.'

Jane smiled and sipped her wine. It wasn't difficult to guess what he had in mind.

'Oh . . . I've something interesting to tell you,' she said. 'I've discovered that my mother's mother – your Great-Aunt Rose – left all her books to the Athenaeum, including several albums of photographs taken at house parties at Longwarden in the twenties. I thought they might be of interest to you and your sister. But perhaps they are only duplicates of pictures you have at home.'

'I should think they are,' he agreed. 'The whole social history of Longwarden from Victorian times up to World War Two is recorded in scores of albums. My great-grandfather's mother, the sixth Countess, devoted her life to photography while her husband was chasing other women. Some years ago I raised some money for repairs by selling most of her work to the Museum of Modern Art here in New York. They were the pioneers in recognizing photography as a collectable art form.'

'What a pity to be forced to dispose of such an interesting facet of your family history, and particularly interesting to *you*,' she exclaimed sympathetically.

He shrugged. 'I couldn't have kept them even if I hadn't needed the money. Prints need to be kept in special conditions if they're to survive for posterity. Now they're available for study by many people instead of deteriorating at Longwarden.'

'Why did your great-great-grandfather spend his time chasing other women? Was their marriage arranged by their parents?'

'I believe so, but the Carlyons have always been a lecherous lot. Caspar reformed when he married, but my grandfather didn't. He had a very nice wife but he was a legendary womanizer. He was killed in the Anzio offensive in 1944. He was only thirty-nine so perhaps he was right to have grabbed everything life had to offer.'

'If a lot of affairs are preferable to one good marriage,' Jane replied.

He offered her a dish of nuts. Tonight he was wearing a navy-blue finely striped suit with a pink-and-white-striped cotton shirt and a pale-pink silk tie. A white-spotted navy silk handkerchief was loosely tucked in his breast pocket and an elegant half-inch of shirt cuff emerged from the sleeves of his coat. He was sitting with his long legs crossed and she had noticed and approved of the immaculate shine on his black tassel loafers.

'Probably not,' he agreed. 'But perhaps his marriage wasn't as good in private as it seemed in public.'

'And your parents? Were they happy together?'

'Not noticeably. Apart from meeting at meals, they didn't spend much time with each other. My father was reputed to have had one or two liaisons with women whose seat he admired, in and out of the saddle. If my mother knew about them, I doubt if it bothered her.'

'D'you expect to reform when you marry, or be like your father and grandfather?'

'That will depend on my wife.'

She was tempted to ask him then, but before she had quite mustered her courage a couple came and sat down at the table next to theirs and she couldn't propose to him with other people within earshot.

The restaurant he had chosen was in the part of Manhattan called Yorkville, on the chic, expensive Upper East Side. But it had an unpretentious façade with Mr and Mrs Foster's Place written over the entrance. Inside it was small and intimate. North had said it was popular with theatrical and television people, but they went there to enjoy the owner's cuisine, not to be recognized.

Allegra arrived about five minutes after they did. North rose and they greeted each other affectionately. As he turned to introduce Jane, his sister's eyes widened in surprise.

Before he could speak, she exclaimed, 'You're the girl who bought one of my books. I *knew* I'd seen you before. It's been nagging me ever since . . . when and where I had seen you. My God, how incredibly slow of me. You're almost the image of Flora.'

'But my eyes are different. I'm Jane Graham. Hello again,' Jane said, smiling and offering her hand.

Allegra sat down. 'I understand now why North was so insistent that I had to meet you. To be honest, I wasn't too keen. I've been meeting so many new people that I felt having dinner alone with him would be more relaxing than dining *à trois* with "a cousin from Boston" which is all he would say about you. Of course he's told you already how we both adored our great-grandmother. It really is the strangest sensation . . . looking at you and seeing Flora as she was in the early portraits but with, as you say, different eyes. Did you know who I was yesterday? Or had he been equally mysterious about me?'

'I knew you had written a book, but I didn't know you were going to be signing it in Scribner's. Is your wrist still aching? I should think it must be.'

While the two girls talked, North ordered the wine. Soon, all the tables being filled, the meal began with a small helping of grilled chicken livers served with hot herb-flavoured toast.

The second course was a hot quiche after which the tinkling of a bell caused a lull in the buzz of conversation. They looked round to see a smiling elderly woman, dressed in black and carrying a pink chiffon scarf, preparing to make an announcement.

This was Mrs Pearl Foster, the owner of the restaurant and its chef. What she had to announce was the evening's choice of soups which that night was Virginia peanut soup, purée of black bean with sour cream, fresh shrimp and corn chowder or cold apple soup.

'This is fun, North. How clever of you to find it,' said Allegra, glancing about the small dining room in which about thirty people were enjoying the delicious food. She turned to Jane. 'I've been given an introduction to a New York designer called Lisandro Sarasola. He's an Argentinian by birth and I'm told he makes wonderful leather belts and accessories and separates. Tomorrow morning I'm free so I'm going to visit his atelier and, I hope, spend some of the money I'm making from *Travels*. Would you like to come with me?'

'I'd be delighted,' said Jane, who had liked Allegra on sight and took to her more every minute.

After the soup came an unusually delicious salad followed by the main course which North had ordered in advance when he telephoned to reserve a table. He had chosen baked rainbow trout, stuffed with mushrooms and celery in rice, and sprinkled with macadamia nuts.

'What did you do before you wrote your book, Allegra?' she asked while they were eating the trout and drinking a very good white wine from California.

'I had dozens of jobs, and I mean that literally. If it hadn't been for finding the diaries I should still be a jill-of-all-trades. I was always envious of North for being sure what he wanted to do. I hadn't any ambitions. How about you?'

'Yes, I have an ambition, but it's a very unfashionable one. I'd like to marry and have children.'

'That's not what you told me last week,' said North.

'I said I wasn't in a hurry.'

'I'm certainly not,' said Allegra. 'In fact if I can make enough money to live in the way I want to, I doubt if I shall ever marry. I can't stand small children. I found that out when I was a nursery school helper. And in marriage it's always the woman who has to make all the adjustments. I don't want to arrange my life to suit someone else's convenience. I intend to be totally selfish.'

'As long as you can avoid falling in love.'

'I'm immune to love,' said Allegra. 'I've had almost as many love affairs as I've had jobs, and I always became just as bored with the men as I did with the jobs. When you boil it down, love is largely sexual attraction and once you've got that out of your system there's usually nothing much left.'

Jane was startled by this statement. North's sister did not have the air of a woman of wide experience and disillusioned outlook. She gave the impression of being a warm, caring personality.

Her smiles for the book-buyers that morning had not been artificial or blasé. The way she had kissed her brother, greeted Jane and said good evening to the waiter were all suggestive of someone who liked her fellow human beings.

152

Even the way she dressed contradicted her casual rejection of love as an important emotion. There wasn't a woman in the restaurant who looked as romantic as she did. She was even wearing a silver ring formed from the letters LOVE.

Noticing Jane glancing at it, Allegra said, 'This wasn't a present from a man. Sarah gave it to me. Has North told you about her?'

'A little. She wants to win the Badminton Horse Trials.'

'And will if determination has anything to do with it. She lives for her horses. Clothes . . . boyfriends . . . parties and dances mean nothing to Sarah. She's totally dedicated to bringing home the Whitbread Trophy. One of the nice things about making a lot of money from *Travels* is that now I can help with her running costs. Eventing is fearfully expensive. Most British riders have sponsors, including Mark Phillips, Princess Anne's husband.'

'Helping your cousin with her expenses doesn't sound "totally selfish",' Jane pointed out.

'Sarah is more than a cousin. She's our little sister,' said Allegra. 'And writing a cheque is no effort if one has the money. But you wouldn't catch me standing up to my ankles in mud waiting for her to come over the Normandy Bank.'

'The Normandy Bank is one of the hazards of the cross-country course,' North explained. 'I used to be dragged to Badminton when I was a small boy and my father was still hoping to make a horseman of me. Badminton is the Duke of Beaufort's estate and Father and the last Duke were cronies. In the early days Badminton was quite a small affair. Now, on cross-country days, they have two hundred thousand spectators and the Gloucestershire lanes get so jammed with traffic the police have to use a helicopter to unclog them.'

The repeated tinkling of the bell put an end to this conversation. This time, in her rich Southern drawl, Mrs Foster announced the desserts.

Allegra chose the lemon soufflé. Jane asked for the carob cheesecake and North had the black walnut pie. They all had a taste of each other's choice and agreed they were equally delicious.

When, after two cups of coffee, Allegra asked them to excuse her as she wanted an early night, North suggested that he and Jane should drop her at her hotel before going on somewhere to dance.

Jane had foreseen this possibility and decided that much as she would have liked to agree, she wouldn't.

'Perhaps we could do that tomorrow. Tonight I'm going to turn in with a good book. You can guess which one,' she said, smiling.

She was a little disappointed that he didn't try to make her change her mind but accepted her decision and arranged to call for her at eight the following evening.

'And I'll pick you up at nine-thirty, if that's all right?' said his sister.

'Heredity plays some odd tricks, doesn't it?' said Allegra when her brother returned to the taxi after escorting Jane to the lobby of her hotel. 'Who would have thought Flora's genes would jump two generations and reappear over here, among the American offshoots?'

North said, 'She even has Flora's hands. Did you notice that?'

'Yes, I did. I couldn't take my eyes off her. A lot of the uncanny likeness has to do with the shape of her head and the way it's poised on her neck. A swan's neck it used to be called when Flora was young. I remember her telling me that when I was fourteen or fifteen and depressed about my looks. My neck is my only resemblance to her. Jane's like her in a dozen ways ... but perhaps not at all in temperament. It's hard to judge on the strength of one meeting. Let's go somewhere for a nightcap. I'm not really tired. I was leaving the way clear for you to finish the evening alone with her, but she wasn't having it. I wonder why?'

'She told you. She wants to finish your book.' Her brother leaned forward to change his instructions to the driver.

In spite of his casual reply, Allegra suspected that it must have surprised if not piqued him when Jane had turned down his offer to take her dancing. His title and, for several years past, his increasing reputation as a brilliant photographer-adventurer, had put him in the position of being able to have any woman he wanted.

She had watched them fall over themselves to be next in his long line of conquests, but none had ever had a hope in hell of becoming the next Countess of Carlyon. As far as Allegra knew the only woman who had ever meant anything to him had been the much older actress with whom, as a very young man, he had had an affair which had enraged their father, shocked their mother and caused North to be banished to Harvard.

The scandal involving Susan Foster had been hushed up, but he had told Allegra about it. In those days they had been allies in a war with their parents. Now, more than a decade later, although still fond of each other, they no longer exchanged that sort of confidence.

He took her to the Rainbow Room on the sixty-fifth floor of the RCA Building. In the cocktail lounge there, they were able to get seats by the window. It was her first view of the island of Manhattan from a skyscraper. The panorama of scintillating lights took her breath away.

'This is a fabulous city. I wish I didn't have to rush off on the whistle-stop tour they've arranged for me. I shall enjoy it in some ways, but I shan't have time to see anything of the places on the itinerary,' she said.

'No, but afterwards you'll have the money to take a more leisurely look at the areas which particularly interest you,' he pointed out.

For a while they talked about the book and its impact on her life. Then he told her about his next project. Eventually, because she couldn't help being curious about his intentions towards their American cousin, she said, 'That was a delightful place we went to tonight. Where shall you take Jane tomorrow?'

'Probably to Windows on the World which is one hundred and seven floors up at the World Trade Center. There's also a place to dance there.'

She decided to risk being told to mind her own business. 'I like her. I really warmed to her. She and I could be friends – but not if you're going to do your love 'em and leave 'em thing with her.'

He didn't reply for some moments. She couldn't tell what he was thinking.

At length, he said, 'Do you think I could?'

She considered the question. 'She doesn't look like a pushover, but you do seem to have a lethal charm.'

'It's not my charm,' he answered dryly. 'It's Longwarden and the Carlyon emeralds which are the attraction.'

'Bullshit!' Allegra said crisply, having quickly added some Americanisms to her pithy vocabulary. 'That may have been true of one or two, but not all of them by a long shot. There was a woman in the restaurant who was giving you the eye all evening. She didn't know about Longwarden. She just thought you would be more fun in bed than the man she had in tow. Anyway, whether or not you *could* coax her into bed, I wish you wouldn't try,' she told him. 'If I do decide to take a holiday at the end of the tour, I might ask her if she'd like to join me. It could be lonely on my own, and men are less of a nuisance if there are two of you to brush them off. But I shan't really know if I like her as much as I think I do until we've spent the morning together. Usually I loathe shopping with other women so it could be a disaster. Perhaps I should leave a note for you. Either "Hands off" or "Good luck".'

North smiled. 'Not necessary. I have nothing in mind which will interfere with your friendship with her.'

'Really? That's unusual. Why not?'

'Because I'm going to marry her.'

In the act of swallowing some wine, Allegra gasped and had a choking fit. When she could speak, she said incredulously, 'But you've only just met her. Because she looks so much like Flora doesn't mean you *know* her, for God's sake.'

Her brother's face took on the closed look it wore whenever their mother read him a lecture on what he should or should not do.

'All right, so it's none of my business who, when or why you marry,' she went on hurriedly. 'But you can't expect me not to be startled when you suddenly announce your marriage . . . and as if it were *fait accompli*. When are you planning to break the news to her?'

'Perhaps tomorrow. I'll see.'

'You're serious, aren't you? You mean it. It doesn't even cross your mind that she might say no?'

'Why should she? She told us tonight that she wants to marry and have children.'

'Has it struck you that she might prefer a rich American to a penurious Englishman? Longwarden may look impressive, but without the money or the staff to keep the place up it isn't exactly comfortable, you know. As for the emeralds, they're gorgeous but you can't afford to buy her the designer dresses they need to set them off.'

'I can't, but she can,' he answered. 'Jane is heiress to fifty million dollars.'

'Oh,' said Allegra. 'I see.'

Suddenly she remembered being at a hunt ball which he also had attended and overhearing a girl say, 'North is a ruthless beast. Poor Caroline is still crazy about him, but he's finished with her and that's that. I pity anyone who falls for him.'

'But it must be fun while it lasts,' another girl had answered.

It was the first girl's indictment which echoed in Allegra's mind as she looked at her brother's face and recognized the hardness of his eyes when they weren't amused and the strong-willed jut of the chin below his wide, sexy mouth.

She hoped he was not going to be a ruthless beast to their cousin.

Jane finished reading the book a little before one o'clock in the morning.

She felt its basic appeal lay in the skilled evocation of a vanished age; the long golden afternoon before the dark night of World War One. A bibliography showed how much painstaking research had been necessary for her cousin to

157

re-create the luxurious life led by the seventh Earl and the rest of the English aristocracy at that period.

The book's second strength was the passionate and enduring love affair between him and the beautiful girl he had brought out of China. Illustrating their biography were many photographs covering his entire life and hers from the time of her presentation at the court of Edward VII and Queen Alexandra. The last photograph of Flora had been taken by her great-grandson on her ninety-second birthday. She had looked at least twenty years younger, a queenly figure in black chiffon with the Russian emerald diadem, referred to in the text, crowning her thick white hair.

Lying awake in the dark, Jane wondered what Flora Carlyon would have thought of a girl usurping the traditional masculine prerogative of proposing marriage. In Flora's youth it had not been unusual for American millionaires to arrange for their daughters to become duchesses and countesses, but the actual proposal would have been made by the man concerned, in the normal way. Even now, eighty years later, it was invariably the man who took the initiative, from the first kiss on to wherever it led.

Rehearsing her proposal to North she wondered if, when it came to the point, her courage would fail her.

'You had a very successful shopping binge this morning, I hear,' he said when they met the next evening. 'Is this part of it?'

He was looking at her airy chemise of palest buttermilk chiffon splashed with dark and pale grey zigzags, the hem and sleeves edged with beads.

'No, this is a Zandra Rhodes my father bought me in London three years ago. I wear favourite clothes a long time. But I did buy some new things this morning and we had a lot of fun,' she agreed.

She was carrying over her arm a short jacket of silver-grey silk with a white swan's-down lining. The silk matched her eyes, but she had coats in other colours and the lining fastened inside them, as light as thistledown yet as warm as chinchilla.

'Is this your wrap? It's a little chilly in the streets this evening.'

North took the jacket and held it while she slipped one arm into a sleeve and transferred her small grey suede evening purse to that hand. After he had lifted the coat into place his strong hands moved lightly over the curves of her shoulders and downwards to just above her elbows where they pressed more firmly for a moment before he released her.

A gesture of cousinly affection? The first light caress in a sequence ending in bed? The second motive seemed more likely.

It was the time of the evening when all over midtown Manhattan people were leaving hotels to go to the theatre or to the innumerable restaurants serving every kind of cuisine from nouvelle to soul food. They had to wait a few minutes before it was their turn to be ushered into a cab by the top-hatted doorman, his white-gloved hand ready to receive the tip North slipped into it.

Jane's filmy skirt rode above her knees as she settled herself on the back seat. She saw North looking at her legs. She was wearing pale Dior stockings and Italian sandals of entwined bronze and silver kid with narrow ties round her slender ankles.

'Did you like London?' he asked her.

'Very much. We were only there a few days. Allegra lives there, she tells me.'

'She has an apartment in what used to be the town house. The other apartments are leased to a consortium, which helps to defray the cost of keeping Longwarden watertight.' Switching away from that subject he asked, 'What did you do with yourself this afternoon?'

'I took a boat trip from Pier eighty-three. It went right around Manhattan, down the Hudson, past the Statue of Liberty, up the East River and back to the Hudson by the Harlem River. If you've never done it, you should. It's a great experience. It lasted three hours, so by the time I got back it was time to wash my hair and change.'

As he had within minutes of meeting her, he reached

out and touched her hair. But this time he wound a lock of it round his index finger.

'Do you wash your hair every day? It always looks as if you do.'

'Thank you. So do you, don't you?' She wondered how he would react if she reached up and slid her fingers through the thick dark hair at his nape.

'Yes, but it's easy for me. I just wash it in the shower, give it a rub with a towel and that's it. Girls' hair is more complicated.'

'Not mine. I have a little dryer and it takes maybe twenty minutes from start to finish. I only go to a hairdresser once a month to have it cut. I couldn't go three times a week the way some people do. What did you do with your day?'

'This morning I saw an exhibition at the International Center of Photography. Then I had a business lunch which lasted as long as your boat trip. Tomorrow I have a free day. If you're not doing anything special we could spend it together.'

'Well . . . that depends,' she said guardedly.

He was still playing with her hair. Now the tips of his fingers brushed the smooth curve of her cheek where it joined her neck.

'On what?' he asked.

'On something I want to discuss with you . . . over dinner,' she added, with a meaning glance at the back of the cab driver's head.

The vital statistics of the twin towers of the World Trade Center, the tallest buildings in the State of New York, had been listed by the commentator on Jane's boat trip as they passed the southern tip of Manhattan island. She could only remember they were more than a quarter of a mile high. Presently she found herself rising to the top of Tower One.

'Less than a minute,' said North, checking his watch as they stepped from the elevator.

There had been no sensation of swift motion as it sped them smoothly up to the restaurant.

This had a spectacular entrance of mirrors and semi-precious rocks leading to a multi-level dining room where every table had a view of the extraordinary vista of lesser skyscrapers, some of them floodlit, some lit from within.

'You might expect that, in a setting like this, the food would be mediocre if not uneatable,' he said when they had been shown to a table and presented with menus. 'In fact it's surprisingly good.'

Conscious that once they had made their choice he might ask her what she wanted to discuss, she was deliberately slow in making up her mind. However, to her surprise, he seemed to have forgotten her remark.

Distracted partly by the magical view and partly by her inner tension, she ate her meal with less than her usual enjoyment. When North asked if she would like a liqueur with her coffee, she asked for framboise, the fruit brandy made from crushed raspberries which Marie-Simone had liked to drink after dinner.

'Marcus tells me one of the reasons you're in America is to look for a rich wife,' she said casually.

North had been watching her with the relaxed, pleasant expression of a man whose appetite for food has been well served and who has reason to hope other pleasures are in store for him.

Her remark wiped that look off his face and replaced it with a furious scowl. It lasted only a second, but it gave her a glimpse of the side of his character which he normally concealed.

Swiftly masking his instinctive reaction, he said coolly, 'I may have said something to that effect but it wasn't intended to be taken seriously.'

'It wasn't? Oh . . . what a pity. I think it's a very sensible idea and I was going to suggest myself as a candidate.' She laid her hand on his wrist where it rested on the edge of the table. 'To spell it out unequivocally, I'm asking you to marry me, North.'

For some moments he showed no reaction at all. Anyone watching them might have thought they were gazing into each other's eyes with the wordless communication of lovers. In fact Jane couldn't read anything in his eyes.

Suddenly he covered her hand with his and smiled at her, shaking his head slightly as people do when told something amusing which stretches their credulity.

Having her hand sandwiched between his wrist and his palm sent a tingle of pleasure up her arm.

'Well . . . what do you think?' she persisted, returning his smile.

'I think it could be a good idea; certainly one worth discussing. When did it strike you?'

'After Marcus told me your plan to marry for money. I don't know whether you realize it, but I have a great deal of money – over fifty million dollars. I'm not in control of it yet, but as soon as I marry I shall be. *We* shall be, if you accept me. That should solve your problems at Longwarden.'

'Undoubtedly, but what do you stand to gain?'

'Many things. An attractive husband . . . a magnificent house . . . a congenial sister-in-law . . . children. With my father, I always lived in hotels or rented apartments. He had an aversion to putting down roots or acquiring personal possessions. We lived in the greatest possible comfort but, basically, we were nomads with no roots anywhere. I thought that perhaps in Boston, with my mother's family, I might feel a sense of belonging. But I never have. Then, last night, reading Allegra's book, it confirmed my feeling that Longwarden might be my place in the world. I've often envied Alison living at Winterbrook. There's something about an old family house in the country which appeals to me very much.'

She withdrew her hand from beneath his and picked up her demi-tasse.

North followed suit. She was aware of his searching glance on her face as, after drinking some coffee, she sipped the framboise.

'You haven't mentioned love,' he said. 'I thought that had top priority in most women's scheme of things.'

'It used to, I guess. Nowadays we're more realistic. You

heard Allegra's views last night. I'm largely in agreement with them, except that I don't share her dislike of children. As I missed having brothers and sisters, I want to have a large family. At least four children. Maybe more.'

'Allegra's views are based, as she told you, on extensive experience. Have you much experience?' he asked her.

'It's not only experience which makes people wary. You have only to read the papers, or to look around your own circle, to realize what a difficult relationship marriage is, and how often it fails. Also I believe certain people have a duty to look at marriage rationally rather than romantically. Your Prince Charles, for example. He was duty bound to choose a girl who was fit to be the future Queen of England. You also have a duty to your position. Not quite as crucial as his, perhaps, but still a serious responsibility to try to preserve a fine heritage. My duty is to my father; not to squander the fortune he built up. I must try to use it wisely and well.'

'I wonder if your father would consider that pumping money into a decaying house in England was a wise use of his fortune,' was North's dry comment.

'We might be able to arrest the decay and to arrange things in such a way that when your son inherits it won't be a burden upon him. I should expect that, while you were away on your travels, you would leave me with the authority to make any changes I felt necessary. My idea of marriage is a partnership of equals. I would share Father's money with you if you would share Longwarden with me.'

'It seems to me that instead of falling in love with a man, you've fallen in love with a house – and one you haven't seen yet, except in old photographs of the way it was years ago,' he said sardonically. 'Don't you think you ought to have a look at the reality before you commit yourself to a partnership with Longwarden's owner?'

'I don't think that's necessary. I'm sure Longwarden isn't so far gone in decay that it can't be restored. Perhaps revived is a better word because neither of us would want to live in the style of days gone by. A continual round of entertaining isn't my idea of heaven. I have my gregarious moods, but a lot of the time I like to be by myself. Playing hostess to all those house parties of the twenties and thirties wouldn't have suited me at all, even with a large staff of servants. Do you have any living-in staff at Longwarden now?'

'Only a butler and a cook. The cleaning is done by part-time helpers from the village. Most of the house has been closed up since my father's death. Part of one wing is all that's in use now; my mother's rooms, mine and the room Allegra sometimes uses at weekends. Sarah virtually lives in the stables and has slept there as well for the past year.'

'Are the rooms that are closed empty now? Or are they still furnished?'

'Furnished. I've had to sell some of the paintings but I've hung on to most of the best ones, and the furniture is still with us. Although whether it's being gorged on by woodworm under the dust-sheets I wouldn't like to say.'

'Oh, but that's terrible, North! You must marry me right away and let me get down to the task of opening up all those closed rooms and making them beautiful again. I admit it: I have fallen for Longwarden. But I also like you very much. You like me, too, don't you?'

'I think you're delightful,' said North. 'But I can't marry you right away because I'm leaving in two days. I'm committed to spending the next three months in Ladakh in the Himalayas and I shan't be back until late August. Even if we could organize a wedding in that short time, I think it would be better to wait. It will give us time to think things over.'

'If you already think it's a rotten idea, I'd rather you said so right now. Don't try to spare my feelings. I can take a straight no.'

'I'm sure you could. You're a redoubtable girl. But I'm not saying no . . . or even maybe,' he added, smiling. 'I'm suggesting we should be engaged.'

'Officially or privately?'

'I don't think a public announcement is necessary at this

stage. We can tell the people closest to us. The ring I'd like to give you is in a bank vault in London. Perhaps this will fit.'

He pulled off his signet ring and tried it on her engagement finger. It fitted perfectly.

'Would you dislike wearing that for the time being?'

'Not at all.'

North lifted her hand and brushed her knuckles with his lips. 'Let's go and dance in the piano bar. This may be a rational alliance, but I'd still like to hold you in my arms.'

In the softly-lit bar where a pianist was playing romantic music he ordered a bottle of champagne and then steered her on to the floor. As he had at the ball in Boston, he held her very close to him.

'I should warn you of one thing,' he said presently as they sat down at the table where a gold-foiled bottle was waiting in a bucket of ice. 'I have a deep-seated aversion to large, fashionable weddings of the kind your aunt will want to organize.'

A waiter came to open the bottle for them.

'I have my own ideas on that subject and they don't include weeks of preparation, hundreds of guests and total exhaustion by the wedding night,' said Jane, when the wine had been poured out. She gave him a radiant smile. 'Here's to the success of your trip and your safe return.'

'I think in my absence you should take a trip to England and see what you're letting yourself in for,' he suggested.

'No, I don't want to go to Longwarden until we're married. If I went there, and loved it and then we broke off the engagement, it would be doubly upsetting. I would rather not go until I'm your wife . . . the ninth Countess.'

His blue eyes narrowed. 'Is being a countess important to you?'

'I'll enjoy it. Why not? Won't you enjoy being able to buy a Ferrari if you want one?'

'I shan't expect you to keep me in expensive cars,' he replied rather curtly.

'But in the marriage service it says "with all my worldly

goods I thee endow". What I have will be yours and vice versa.'

They were sitting side by side on a banquette. She slipped her hand into his.

'I think, as far as everyone else is concerned, we should let them assume it was love at first sight, don't you agree? The cynics are going to say otherwise, but I see no reason to confirm their speculations.'

His long fingers closed over hers. Leaning closer, he said huskily, 'I don't have to pretend that I want you. Let's go somewhere more private, shall we? My place or yours?'

She was tempted to say, 'Whichever is closest.' The thought of spending the night with him was almost irresistible. But she knew if she did she would be aligning herself with all the other women in his life.

Steeling herself, she said calmly, 'I'm not going to sleep with you yet.'

He looked surprised, but more amused than put out. 'Why not?'

Again she avoided a direct answer. 'I once read that all the sensual pleasures are enhanced by doing without them for a while. Maybe you should try it. Shall I be able to write to you?'

He nodded, beginning to circle his thumb in the hollow of her palm, a subtly erotic caress which sent tremors flying along her nerves.

My God! How can I hold out when he looks at me and touches me this way? she thought, clinging to her resistance.

'Let's dance again.' He drew her to her feet and steered her back to the small floor.

She soon realized that dancing was a more effective way of weakening her will than verbal persuasion. Restricting their movements to the classic night-club shuffle, he made her even more conscious of how much she wanted him to make love to her.

He let go of her hand to put both arms round her. It didn't make them conspicuous. Other people were dancing that way. Bending his head to speak softly into her ear, he murmured, 'You see what you do to me? Three months is too long to wait. I want you now.'

She tried to make a space between them but he wouldn't let her.

She looked up at him, 'You're being unfair, North. This isn't an ordinary engagement. I'm not going to be hustled into bed against my better judgement.'

For a moment longer he kept her pressed tightly against him, his desire a tangible entity which she found both exciting and disturbing. Then his hold on her slackened. He drew a little away from her.

When he didn't make any remark she thought he was angry. He wasn't used to being told to behave himself. He wouldn't like it. Offended male pride added to physical frustration made an explosive combination. Yet how else could she have handled the situation when his superior strength had made it impossible for her to break the close body contact?

It wasn't long after this that the pianist took a break, to be replaced by a trio. As they walked back to their table she wondered which North would be – sulky or sarcastic.

He was neither. As they sat down he said, 'All right: if that's the way you want it. I don't know any beautiful, chaste girls. It takes a little getting used to.'

Relieved but not wholly convinced by his equable tone, she said, 'Tell me about this trip to the Himalayas. Where did you say you were going?'

'To Ladakh.' He spelt the name for her. 'It's a region like Tibet. Mountains . . . high plateaux . . . people who've not been exposed to much outside influence. The passes into Ladakh are snow-bound for most of the year. Summer is the only time to go.'

'It sounds like the back of beyond. I've always loved that expression . . . the back of beyond. Is it near where Peter Fleming ended his journey through Tartary?'

'He finished at Srinagar in Kashmir which is where we shall start. But he and Kini didn't cross the Ladakh Range. They circled it.'

Her curiosity about the expedition wasn't simulated to

take his mind off her. She was genuinely interested in the place and his reason for going there, which was to collaborate with a well-known travel writer on a book about it.

They didn't dance again. By the time he had told her all she wanted to know about Ladakh, they had finished the champagne.

He glanced at his watch. 'Shall we have a change of scene?'

He took her first to the River Café under the Brooklyn Bridge and from there to Maxwell's Plum, a famous singles bar, and finally to the Café Carlyle at her hotel, to hear Bobby Short playing and singing the imperishable hits of the Cole Porter era.

'What would you like to do tomorrow?' he asked when Jane said it was time to say goodnight.

'I'd like to spend some time in the Metropolitan Museum and then explore Central Park and the West Side. But if that would be boring for you, maybe we should spend the day separately and meet in the evening.'

'I enjoy ambling round a city. There's always something new to see. The museum opens at ten. If we get there early, we'll have maximum elbow room. I'll pick you up at nine-thirty. Make sure you wear comfortable shoes. We'll be doing a lot of walking.'

As they returned to the lobby he added, 'We'll say goodnight in the lift.'

The glinting glance which accompanied this statement made her insides clench.

The door of the elevator had barely closed before he took her in his arms. An instant later his mouth was on hers.

It was the most possessive first kiss she had ever experienced. All the other men who had kissed her had begun gently. North took her response for granted.

Usually it took a few seconds to reach her floor. Tonight it seemed to take longer.

When the lift stopped, he stopped kissing her. But only for the time it took to murmur, 'Wrong floor.'

Swept off balance by surging emotions, she was slow to

realize that, the way he was pressing the buttons, they were never going to arrive at her floor.

She managed to free her mouth. 'North ... what on earth will the clerk think when he sees the lift sign behaving like a jumping bean? You'll have me thrown out of this place,' she protested, but with laughter in her eyes.

'I've a comfortable bed you'll be very welcome to share.'

'No!' she said firmly, freeing an arm to press the correct button.

He used the remaining few moments to take her face between his hands and press a last kiss on her parted lips.

It was very nearly her undoing. Nothing in her life had called for a greater effort of willpower than, when the elevator reached her floor, to say, 'Thank you for a lovely evening. See you tomorrow. Goodnight,' and to step into the corridor.

Her room was close by. Halfway there, she heard him say softly, 'I might not come back from Ladakh.'

She didn't look round until she arrived at her door. He was standing on the threshold of the elevator, holding it open with his broad back, watching her.

'I'm sure you will, North. Goodnight.' She unlocked her door and went quickly inside.

In her bedroom she took off her jacket and looked at herself in the mirror; at the mouth which moments ago had been joined to his in the most sweetly sensuous fusion she had ever known.

Tonight she had managed – just! – to stick to her resolve. But tomorrow and the night after, her will would be tested again. Could she hold out against him when she wanted him so much?

In 1979 a Chicago developer, Charles H. Shaw, bought the air space above the new wing of New York's Museum of Modern Art for seventeen million dollars.

By 1984 forty-four floors of sumptuous apartments, crowned by a five-million-dollar, three-bedroom duplex penthouse with log-burning fireplaces and surrounded by a balcony, had risen to fill the space.

Unlike many less distinguished Manhattan apartment blocks, Museum Tower has no shops, no health club, no pool, no restaurant. An *embarras de richesses* of these facilities exists nearby. Delivery men are not allowed past the concierge. A condition of purchase is that owners may allow only three other people to use the apartments in their absence.

As well as high security and privacy, residents enjoy unmatched views of the city through their wide floor-to-ceiling windows. The floors are laid with blocks of teak in a herringbone pattern; the ceilings are nine feet above them.

The privileged people who live or stay in Museum Tower enjoy a standard of *grand luxe* not seen in New York since the thirties.

A few minutes before midnight, a man stepped out of the shower in one of the tower's smaller apartments. Swelling biceps under taut skin caught the light as he reached for a towel and rough-dried his hair and his feet before reaching for a white terry bathrobe.

In the living room, seen through a sixteen-feet-wide expanse of uncurtained glass, the city was still brightly lit. On the radio, which he had left on, a nationwide show which would go on until 5.30 a.m. was about to begin.

The man, who was on his way to bed, crossed the room to switch off the sound.

'Tonight my guest is from London, England. She's Lady Allegra Lomax . . .'

He changed his mind.

'. . . and she's come here to launch a book she's written. A book that's already been on the British best-seller charts for some time . . . am I right, Allegra?'

'Yes, Larry, it has. The book is called *The Travels of an Edwardian Naturalist* and it's been on two of our best-seller lists since it was published. The American edition came out this week and I'm keeping my fingers crossed that perhaps by next week it may be on some of your charts.'

'Now your title – *The Travels of an Edwardian Naturalist*

– doesn't sound too exciting, if you don't mind my saying so. Tell me, what does Edwardian mean?'

'It refers to the reign of Queen Victoria's son Edward, who was King of England from 1901 to 1910. Before and during his reign my great-grandfather was hunting for rare plants in Asia, particularly in China. He was also a secret agent for the British government so although the title might not sound it, the book is actually quite exciting. My American publishers Laurel & Lincoln, did suggest that a better title might be *The Chinese Countess*. Perhaps it sounds more intriguing but it isn't quite accurate. My great-grandmother was only half Chinese.'

'Allegra, before we get to your great-grandmother, I want to explain to listeners that you are a Lady with a capital L because your father was an earl. His title has now been inherited by your brother, the present Earl of Carlyon.'

'Yes, but the interesting thing about my brother isn't that he's an earl but that he's a marvellous photographer. Some of your listeners have probably seen his pictures of rare birds and animals . . .'

The man who was listening fixed himself a brandy and soda and took it to a deep armchair on a swivel base. Sitting down, he swung the chair to face the most exciting urban vista in the world, especially at night when the multi-coloured lights of Manhattan were as numerous as stars in a tropical sky.

Lady Allegra Lomax.

Listening to the cultured English voice and her soft, pleasant laughter when the interviewer made a quip, the listener remembered the subtle scent of her and those extraordinary irises, the colour of Tiffany's finest amethysts.

A beauty with all the hallmarks of wealth and breeding. Brains, too, it appeared. More than he would have given her credit for. In his mind's eye he saw the slightly long nose and strongly marked brows which made her a beauty rather than merely a pretty woman.

He remembered her swinging, from-the-hip thorough-bred walk, her long slender hands and, most clearly, the generous curves of her mouth. Like the creatures her

171

brother photographed, she was a *rara avis*; the kind of woman a man was unlikely to encounter more than once in a lifetime, if ever.

He had spent some hours in her company and, for a complex reason, had let slip his opportunity to know her.

'I'm talking to Lady Allegra Lomax from England who, a few days from now, may be visiting your city to sign copies of her best-selling book about the life-long love affair of her great-grandfather, Lord Carlyon, and the beautiful half-Chinese girl he rescued from a desperate situation in China in 1903.'

The interviewer was recapping after a commercial break. The programme was being heard in more than two hundred cities across America.

'But a few moments ago you were telling me that your great-grandfather was *not* in love with her when they were married in Shanghai, Allegra. What was the reason for their marriage?'

'I'm afraid at that point in his life my great-grandfather was like most men of his era. His attitude to women was summed up by an English poet. He regarded them as "*something better than his dog, a little dearer than his horse*". The only reason he married Flora was because he had to have a son to succeed him and because he felt she would be less of a nuisance than any of the debutantes whose ambitious mothers had for years been hoping to snare him as a son-in-law. Flora's father had also been a plant-hunter, but one who did it for a living, not an amateur like my great-grandfather. So she was accustomed to travelling in wild parts of the world where an English girl of that period would have been terrified. From Caspar's point of view she was an ideal wife for him. Also, as a bonus, he could see she was going to be beautiful when she was fully mature.'

'How old was she at that time?'

'Seventeen.'

'And he?'

'Thirty. Normally an intelligent man of thirty would find such a young girl boring. But Flora was exceptionally bright. She'd been educated like a boy by the French priest who adopted her after her father was killed. I don't think I should be telling you all this. Who's going to buy the book if they already know the story?'

'Okay, let's leave the book for a while and talk about the author. You've mentioned Edwardian men's attitude to women. Am I right in assuming you're a feminist, Allegra? Would your great-grandfather's attitude have bothered you?'

'If I'd lived in those days I'm sure it would. Although even then there were men who didn't treat women as chattels or toys. Later, when he'd come to love her, my great-grandfather gave Flora every freedom and supported her in her fight to improve other women's lives. She was an ardent feminist but never an aggressive one. She believed – as she said many times on public platforms and television and radio – the most useful thing women can do to make life easier for their daughters and granddaughters is to raise their sons not to be dependent on women for every meal and every clean shirt and made bed. I agree with that. When I read about some of the activities of the more extreme feminist groups, I wonder if they're bringing up their sons to be our equals as well as claiming equality for us.'

'That's an interesting idea that I'm sure many listeners will want to comment on later in the programme when we ask them to phone in. Is there a man in your life who has to do his own laundry, Allegra?'

'I'm not married, Larry. The most important man in my life at the moment is the subject of my next book and he died in the last century.'

The listener finished his drink. During the next commercial break he went to the kitchen and dropped a handful of ice into a tall glass before filling it with Perrier. There was a memo board on the wall beside the refrigerator. He wrote on it – *Travels of an Edwardian Naturalist. L & L.*

Two hours later, interspersed with other items, the interview was still in progress, going out to an unseen audience of night workers and insomniacs. The man in Museum Tower remained in his chair, held there by a compulsion to go on listening to the well-bred, self-possessed voice which conjured so clearly the face and form of its owner.

The longer he listened, the more strongly he felt that, having wasted his first chance, he must somehow contrive another.

When Jane returned to her room after her day out with North, she found a bunch of white violets in a posy vase on her dressing table.

Beside it was a florist's envelope containing a card on which was written – *Had we but world enough and time* . . .

He must have arranged for the violets to be sent to her first thing that morning. She knew the context of the phrase he had written: a poem by a seventeenth-century Englishman, Andrew Marvell. The next line was – *This coyness, lady, were no crime.* She couldn't remember the whole poem but it included a famous couplet.

> *The grave's a fine and private place,*
> *But none, I think, do there embrace.*

Picking up the vase and inhaling the delicate scent of the massed violets, she thought over the hours they had spent together. After looking at early American furniture, Tiffany stained-glass windows and some wonderful Impressionist paintings in the museum, they had crossed the park to the West Side, heading for a shop where North wanted to buy the makings of another picnic lunch.

Why he insisted on going to Zabar's in preference to any of the delicatessens they had passed along Columbus Avenue became clear when they arrived at the shop on Broadway at 80th Street.

Zabar's was an epicure's heaven selling an incredible selection of good things from all over Europe and beyond. The fragrance of newly baked breads, French and English cheeses, German and Italian sausages, combined in a delicious aroma as the busy assistants attended to customers buying smoked eel, Westphalian ham, home-made gefilte fish, Hungarian salami, Roquefort, herrings in cream sauce, baklava, Russian black bread, Oxford marmalade, caviar and many other delicacies.

If anything typified New York it was that extraordinary shop with its mingling of foods from so many different cultures.

They had left it laden with goodies to which, on the way back to the park, North had added a bottle of red wine and a bag of apples. He had with him a light canvas shoulder bag in which he carried his camera, various filters and a sweater. From it he had produced a corkscrew and a couple of glasses.

Although there was no escape from the muted drone of the traffic along Fifth Avenue on one side and Central Park West on the other, it was amazing how peaceful and rural it had seemed in their sunny green glade in the very heart of Manhattan.

Although soon she would have been wearing it for twenty-four hours, her hand wasn't yet accustomed to the weight and the feel of his signet ring. In the park today he had told her it had been his great-grandfather's ring. Flora had treasured it through the years of her widowhood and left it to North in her will, with some other cherished possessions, an antique watch and portrait miniatures bequeathed to her long ago by the French priest who had been her guardian in China.

While she was changing, Jane's telephone rang. It was Allegra, now on the first lap of her coast-to-coast tour.

'I've just been talking to North. He told me your news. I couldn't be more delighted.'

'It's sweet of you to say so. I wonder how your mother will take it?'

'She'll be even more pleased. She's been chivvying North to marry for years. Listen, if you're beginning to worry about sharing a house with your mother-in-law – don't. As long as you don't interfere with her beloved garden, she won't give a hoot what changes you make in the house. She'll be only too glad to shed that responsibility. In fact she may decide to move out. There's no dower house, as such, at Longwarden, but there are several buildings which could easily be converted into granny quarters. Even if she stays where she is, she won't make *your* life difficult.'

'North did mention that you and your mother didn't always see eye to eye,' Jane said cautiously.

'That's the understatement of the year. But our rows aren't as fierce as they used to be. Either she's becoming resigned to my errant ways or my threshold of irritation is rising. Anyway she'll welcome you with open arms.'

'I hope so. How's the tour going?'

'You won't believe it but I've done *eleven* interviews since I saw you, including being grilled by five journalists at lunch today. They kept me so busy answering questions I hardly ate a mouthful. Just as well. Tonight I'm being wined and dined at the best restaurant in town.' She laughed. 'I could get hooked on this celebrity life. I'll call you again in a few days. Where will you be? Are you going back to Boston as soon as North leaves? It's a shame he's committed to disappearing for the summer.'

'I may stay on here for a few days after he's gone. There's so much to see. I'd like to keep in touch with you, Allegra, but I realize you have a frantic schedule. If you aren't able to call me, I'll know you haven't had a minute.'

'There's always time for the things one really wants to do. It wouldn't surprise me if my mother invites you to stay at Longwarden. North says you don't want to do that but it's lovely there in summer . . . much better than sweltering in Boston with your dragon of an aunt.'

'She may be going to stay with one of her sons and I may be going to Cape Cod with other relations.'

They talked for a few more minutes before saying good-bye. Jane rang off with the heartening feeling that in her prospective sister-in-law she had found a new friend and an invaluable guide to the pitfalls and hazards of life among the English aristocracy.

Allegra ended the call with profound misgivings. She liked Jane and felt sure everyone at Longwarden would like her. But whether the gentle American girl could be happy with someone like North, who had never pleased anyone but himself, seemed highly doubtful.

North and Jane spent their last day together on a cruise up the Hudson River to West Point.

For some distance from where they embarked from Pier 41, the wide river, once the chief trading route between New York and Canada, was lined on both sides by busy wharves and docks. But in a surprisingly short time the docks and skyscrapers were left behind, giving place to forest-clad mountains, steep bluffs and small towns along the river's banks. Here and there the crags were surmounted by castles built in the nineteenth century as country retreats for rich city-dwellers.

'This reminds me of parts of Europe . . . it's not unlike the Rhine valley. I had no idea there were mountains and forests this close to Manhattan,' she said as they strolled the uncrowded weekday decks of one of the large modern vessels which had replaced the old side-wheel steamers.

The night before, when she had thanked North for the violets, she had made no reference to the message accompanying them. They had gone to the ballet and afterwards to Patsy's, a restaurant not far from the Lincoln Center, where they'd dined on large helpings of authentic southern Italian cooking.

The atmosphere in the restaurant had been busy and lively rather than intimate and romantic, and their conversation there and while walking back to the East Side had been general rather than personal.

Nevertheless she had been surprised when, instead of accompanying her into the elevator, he had said goodnight in the lobby.

Although, earlier, she had hoped he wouldn't repeat the previous night's kisses, going up to her floor by herself she had felt perversely disappointed at not being given the chance to resist him again.

Later, lying in bed, she had decided this was the way he wanted her to feel; that his fraternal goodnight had been a deliberate strategy to weaken her resistance to him on his final night in New York.

The turn-around point of the cruise was Poughkeepsie, giving the passengers who disembarked at West Point three hours to explore the campus of the Military Academy.

'As we shan't get back until seven, I thought we'd have dinner in SoHo, which won't involve changing,' said North while they were eating the picnic he had provided.

He was casually dressed in chinos and a Madras shirt. Having heard high temperatures forecast on the radio, Jane had put on a favourite Ralph Lauren top, a cotton-knit striped in broad bands of pale fondant colours, with a pair of white cotton pants. She had twisted a sea-green scarf and pulled it through the loops on the waistband. Her bare feet were cool and comfortable in glove-soft white leather loafers.

North also had bare ankles. His were as tanned as his neck and the top of his chest exposed by his open shirt collar and the sinewy forearms revealed by his rolled-up sleeves. She knew that before coming to Boston he had spent two weeks sailing with friends in the Caribbean. No doubt the whole of his body was the same burnished brown.

The thought of the long tanned thighs concealed by his khaki pants and the muscular torso inside the sun-faded shirt made her mind leap the long separation between now and their marriage in the autumn. But it wasn't the wedding which engaged her imagination.

She had been speaking the truth when she'd told him she didn't want an elaborate ceremony. It caused her no pang to forego the white dress and veil and be married quietly and informally. The public ritual seemed unimportant compared with the private beginning of their life as husband and wife. The night of the wedding, not the day, was what filled her with longing as she thought of his powerful bronzed body taking possession of hers.

'You've gone very quiet, Jane,' he said.

Taken off guard, she answered, 'I was thinking about our honeymoon . . . I mean where we might go,' she added quickly.

'After almost three months in the monasteries of Ladakh,

I shall probably be ready for a fairly high degree of creature comforts. Don't plan anything too away-from-it-all,' he said, smiling. 'If we're going to be married soon after I come back, you'll have to make the arrangements.'

'That's no problem. I'm used to organizing things. But we should discuss where to go. My idea of the perfect place may not be yours.'

'As long as the food is good and the bed comfortable, I shan't complain.'

The way he looked at her as he mentioned the bed they would share brought an apricot tinge to the creamy pallor of her cheeks.

She said, 'Have you any idea how much time you'll be able to spare?'

'As long as you like. I'll have stopped off in London to print all the Ladakh film before I come over here. I've no autumn commitments which can't be rearranged to suit our convenience. After Christmas I'm probably going to the Antarctic, but that isn't absolutely settled yet. Between early September and Christmas, I'm entirely at your disposal.'

By the time they returned on board, they had fixed a date for the wedding: 5 September.

As the vessel glided downriver to pick up the passengers who had got off at Bear Mountain, they sat on a secluded bench.

'Are you nervous about telling your aunt?' North asked.

'Not really. She and the other trustees have no power to interfere with my choice of a husband. I guess that's because my mother married in defiance of her family and my father didn't want me to be forced to the same expedient.'

'I doubt if old Julia's initial opposition will last long . . . no longer than it takes her to realize that the marriage will give her some kudos among her equally snobbish friends,' he said cynically. 'But I'm sorry I haven't the time to come and beard the lioness with you.'

The area of lower Manhattan known as SoHo, from its location south of Houston Street, had long replaced Greenwich Village as the hub of New York's artistic life. Hundreds of the city's artists, both established and up and coming, made their homes in the district around West Broadway, living in century-old buildings which had once been factories and warehouses and were now converted into spacious lofts with room for their tenants to work on massive sculptures and huge modern paintings.

Jane was unprepared for the sense of creative vitality which permeated the streets of SoHo with their plethora of galleries and craft shops. Here was the birthplace of most of the fashionable cults. Nowhere in New York was the street life more colourful and fascinating.

Many of the shops stayed open much later than those in midtown Manhattan. She and North spent a couple of hours strolling around, admiring the cast-iron palazzo-style exterior of the Haughwout Building, built in 1857, looking in avant-garde boutiques and listening to sidewalk musicians.

They ate at a Cuban restaurant near Bleecker Street, choosing red snapper poached in a green sauce of parsley, wine, garlic and lime juice, and finishing the meal with *coco quemado*, a tart filled with coconut and cinnamon and topped with whipped cream.

Afterwards, instead of taking a taxi back to her hotel, they headed for Sixth Avenue and walked uptown.

She knew that tonight he was not going to be satisfied with passionate kisses in the elevator. He would want to, would insist on staying with her; and even to herself she couldn't fully explain why, when her senses clamoured for a night in his arms, her intelligence still counselled 'Wait'.

'What time is your flight tomorrow?' she asked glancing up at him.

'Half-past eight, but I'm already packed and the helicopter service cuts the hassle out of getting to Kennedy.' After a slight pause, he added, 'I'll sleep on the flight.' Lifting their clasped hands, he gently bit the tip of her thumb, his eyes telling her that he didn't intend to do much sleeping before then.

Jane said nothing, knowing he would take her silence for tacit consent but unwilling to get into an argument now. It was better to wait until they returned to the hotel and then firmly reiterate what she had told him the night before last. Right now, with her whole arm tingling from the soft touch of his teeth, she wasn't at all sure her willpower was going to hold out. Yet some deep instinct warned her that falling into North's arms so short a time after meeting him would be a mistake.

They walked on in silence. Soon Central Park was in sight. From the corner of the park it was only a few blocks to her hotel. Outwardly calm, inwardly she was experiencing all the classic symptoms of intense nervous excitement.

Even when she entered the hotel lobby, she still wasn't sure whether this was the end of their last evening or the beginning of their first night together.

North took charge of the situation. A firm hand on the small of her back, he steered her towards the desk.

'Miss Graham's key, please.' He gave the number of her room.

The clerk selected the key. 'You have a visitor, Miss Graham. There's a gentleman waiting in the bar for you.' He glanced at a notepad. 'Mr Charles Helford.'

In her preoccupied state, for a fraction of time the name drew a blank in her mind. But only for an instant. As memories of afternoons of love in a fan-cooled room in Bangkok came flooding back, North said irritably, 'Who the devil is he? Not one of your trustees?'

Allegra had been having dinner at Les Nomades, a private bistro in Chicago run by Jovan Trboyevic who also owned the city's fashionable Le Perroquet restaurant.

The bistro was open only to members and their guests. Rumour had it that more than one famous person had been refused membership by the arbitrary Yugoslavian proprietor who had also been known to eject people from his public restaurant if they behaved in a way he considered annoying to his other patrons.

On the opposite side of the table was Martha, the super-efficient representative of a public relations company retained by Laurel & Lincoln to assist with the organization of their major promotions. Joni had had to go back to New

York overnight, leaving Allegra with the other woman. During a perfect bistro meal starting with an appetizer of home-cured salmon followed by a string-bean salad, with cassoulet as their main course, Martha had confessed that eating well in the evening had become the most important aspect of her private life.

'Food is better than sex, in my opinion,' she confided with a candour induced by a cocktail before they arrived, an aperitif before dinner, wine with it and now a liqueur with her coffee.

'For one thing it's always available, which the men in my life haven't been. If you once get involved with a married man – and in New York it's hard not to – you can count on being by yourself at times when other people are together: weekends, Christmas, Thanksgiving, even your birthday if it clashes with some family thing. How about you, Allegra? Do you have a nice guy waiting for you back in London?'

Allegra felt disinclined to reveal that for a long time now work had taken the place of men in her life. So far their evening together had been enjoyable. She didn't want it to deteriorate into a heart-to-heart between two lonely women having more luck with their careers than with their personal lives.

'I guess that was a stupid question,' Martha remarked. 'At your age, with your looks, you must still be picking and choosing. But I wouldn't leave it too late, if I were you. One day you're twenty-nine and the world's your oyster. Then, almost before you know it, you're out of your thirties and it's too late to have children.'

'I've never wanted children.'

'Nor did I – fifteen years ago. Now . . . I dunno. Would I be happier sitting home some place, watching my husband asleep in front of the TV and worrying what kind of trouble my teenage kids might be into? Maybe not. Uh-uh . . . positively not,' she decided, shaking her head.

But her laugh sounded forced and Allegra finished her coffee wishing she had not had this glimpse of the latent unhappiness behind the façade of a successful careerist.

*   *   *

182

'Charles isn't a trustee. He's an old friend,' said Jane. 'Come and meet him.' She turned in the direction of the bar.

Her last contact with Charles had been when he wrote a letter of condolence after her father's death. She had written to thank him for his sympathy but hadn't expected to hear from or see him again. That he should turn up in New York, tonight of all nights, was a very strange twist of fate.

He was sitting in a corner of the bar, reading a news magazine. As she approached he looked up and sprang to his feet. He was almost exactly as she remembered him, perhaps a little more haggard, with the first threads of grey in his brown hair and the yellowish tinge of the tropics in the colour of his skin. She was pleased to find that her nineteen-year-old judgement hadn't misled her into choosing a lover whose appearance now came as an unpleasant shock.

'Charles – what a surprise!' she exclaimed. 'What are you doing over here and how did you find me?' She gave him both hands and offered her cheek for a kiss. It seemed the natural thing to do.

'I came to find you. Your aunt told me you were staying here.'

The way he was looking at her, and keeping hold of her hands, made it unnecessary to ask why he had come to find her. Clearly he still cared for her. Why he had waited so long to seek her out, she couldn't imagine.

She said, 'This is my cousin from England . . . North Carlyon . . . Charles Helford. Charles runs a silk factory in Bangkok which is where my father and I met him, a long time ago.'

Making a poor job of masking the fact that both wished each other at blazes, the two men shook hands and exchanged clipped how d'you dos. Evidently realizing he would have to go through some motions of civility, North asked what Jane would like to drink.

In the following ten minutes most of the conversation was left to her. Somehow she managed to keep it going in spite of the mutual antipathy of her companions.

183

'I didn't know you had English connections, Jane,' said Charles.

Before she could answer, North put in quickly, 'Very close connections, Helford. It hasn't been announced yet but Jane and I are engaged. We're going to be married on September the fifth.'

Charles looked appalled. His shock was painful to watch and she felt very angry with North for breaking the news with what she felt sure was deliberate cruelty.

'I – I had no idea,' Charles stammered. 'When did this happen? Have you known each other long?'

'Not long. We met for the first time two weeks ago.' North reached for Jane's hand and grinned at her. 'It was love at first sight, wasn't it, sweetie?'

It wasn't until some time later, after Charles had excused himself to go to the men's room, that North relaxed the steely grip with which he had prevented her from wrenching her hand free earlier.

'That wasn't nice, North,' she said accusingly.

'Niceness has never been my chief characteristic. The man is an idiot. He should have made sure of you when he had you. He did have you at one time, I gather?'

'I don't think that's any of your business. I don't want to know about your previous relationships.'

'I'm sure you don't – and it's most unlikely any of them will reappear and fail to grasp they're *de trop* now. In his shoes, as soon as that had been made plain to me, I'd have pushed off. When he comes back, I'll make sure he does.'

'Don't you think that's up to me? Charles is my friend, not yours. I'm concerned about him. What *you* don't grasp is that he's already had one bad experience in his life. If he's come all this way to see me, the least I can do is to bear with him kindly. He's a sensitive, vulnerable man.'

'And I'm the man you're going to marry . . . and leaving town in the morning. Don't I have a claim to your kindness?' he asked, with a lift of one eyebrow.

'After September fifth you'll have first claim on my attention for the rest of our lives. Right now I think Charles

184

needs it more. If it *had* been love at first sight, that would be different,' she said levelly.

He gave her an enigmatic look before draining his glass. 'As you wish,' he said, with a shrug. 'In that case, I'll be off. Goodnight. Enjoy your tête-à-tête.'

When Charles returned she was alone, her lips still tingling from the one swift hard kiss North had pressed on her mouth before striding out of the bar.

'He has to be up early tomorrow. He asked me to say goodnight for him,' she replied in answer to Charles's question.

Looking relieved, he sat down. 'Jane . . . my dear girl . . . you can't be serious. Two weeks isn't long enough to know anyone well enough to marry them. Think what your father would say. You must know he wouldn't approve.'

'I'm twenty-three now, Charles. Old enough to make my own decisions.'

But, as he began to argue with her, she wasn't at all sure that choosing to be here with him instead of upstairs with North had been the right decision.

Laurel & Lincoln had spared no expense on Allegra's eight-city tour of America. All her flights were first class and there was always a large Cadillac waiting for her at the airport. Everywhere her accommodation was a suite at the best hotel with fruit, flowers and champagne awaiting her. In Los Angeles she stayed at the Beverly Wilshire, in Dallas at the Hyatt Regency, in San Francisco at the Fairmont.

Her whole attic-apartment in London would have fitted inside the sitting room of some of the suites she occupied, and many of the sixty interviews she gave took place in them. Each day, sometimes before breakfast, she was faced with a succession of press, television and radio journalists all asking much the same questions. It wasn't easy to repeat her answers time and time again without beginning to sound bored. Very soon she understood why only people with outsize egos actually enjoyed 'the electronic circus'.

The discovery that being fêted soon lost its initial excitement made her wonder, when she was tired, if her belief that *Travels* had transformed her life would turn out to be a false hope. She cheered herself up with the thought that, even if her taste of fame was quickly losing its savour, the enjoyment she had felt while actually at work on the book, and the security of earning large amounts of money, were not illusory rewards. They were real and would go on being real.

Joni and Martha were jubilant. Allegra's appearance on the Phil Donahue show had caused an immediate run on the book and the latest good news was that *People* magazine wanted to do a cover story on her.

Any mention of Phil Donahue reminded Allegra of another man with prematurely grey hair. She wondered if any of her publicity would catch the attention of Alessandro Risconti.

PART TWO: Summer

JUNE

The great park surrounding the gardens in which Penelope Carlyon had found a refuge from the humiliations of her marriage owed much of its beauty to Humphrey Repton.

This leading 'landskip' designer had been summoned to Longwarden at the end of the eighteenth century to produce one of his famous Red Books, a collection of watercolour drawings showing the grounds before and after his suggested improvements.

The next major influence on the park and the garden had been that of the fifth Lord Carlyon who had scandalized the neighbourhood by leaving orders that his remains were not to be placed in the family vault but buried in the garden, the spot to be marked only by a *Morus nigra.*

For decades the now-ancient tree had contributed delicious mulberries to summer afternoon teas and still, with the aid of stout props, marked the fifth Earl's unhallowed grave.

Aged ninety when he died in the 1880s, he had spent his last thirty years enthusiastically botanizing, an interest he had implanted in his grandson, the subject of Allegra's biography.

Between them these three men – Repton and the fifth and seventh Earls – had composed a garden as fine as any in England. With Lord Aberconway, Lionel de Rothschild and J. C. Williams of Caerhays Castle in Cornwall, Caspar Carlyon had been one of the four great amateur breeders of rhododendrons in the twentieth century. A few years after his marriage he had crossed two species to produce a group of hybrids, *Rhododendron carlyonii*, from which had come the beautiful apricot form called 'Flora Mary' after his wife.

However while North's great-grandfather had been a practical gardener, worthy of the Victoria Medal of Honour bestowed on him by the Royal Horticultural Society in 1925, he had also had unlimited means and, until World War Two, never fewer than fifteen gardeners.

When Edward succeeded to the title in 1957, the house and grounds had been in good order although run by a dwindling staff of ageing employees.

Pen had always preferred the country to the London life liked by her mother, whose idea of an enjoyable day was a morning spent shopping in Knightsbridge and an afternoon playing bridge and exchanging gossip. Lady Standish, a parson's daughter, had made an excellent marriage by catching the eldest son of the local squire, a baronet. She had been determined that her daughter should make an even better match and, having achieved that object in spite of Pen's many deficiencies, had coerced her easygoing husband into paying for one of the most lavish weddings of the postwar period.

A year later Sir Hugh had died, adding grief to Pen's other burdens, for by then she had recovered physically from the birth of North and was having to endure the resumption of sexual relations.

It had been the worst time of her life, yet it had never occurred to her that no one could force her to stay at Longwarden and submit to the nightly torture of her husband's repellent assaults on her tense, shrinking body.

Even if she hadn't promised to love, honour and obey Edward until death parted them, where could she have gone? Her mother's house was not a refuge. Lady Standish wasn't even sympathetic about the difficult birth which, never having had any problems with her own four pregnancies, she had seemed to consider Pen's fault.

The only person who had sympathized had been the Dowager Lady Carlyon. She had been wonderfully kind, perhaps suspecting the misery behind the stoic mask worn by her grandson's young wife.

During her pregnancy it had been necessary for Pen to rest a great deal, passing the time by reading and inexpertly knitting baby clothes. Safe from Edward's hateful attentions which had ceased as soon as she was pregnant, she had spent many hours in the garden at Longwarden, lying on a cushioned chaise longue which could be wheeled to sheltered corners.

North had been born at the beginning of November. The months before his arrival had been fine and warm, culminating in a glorious Indian summer in October. For six months, from early May, Pen had spent most days out of doors, her bruised spirit soothed by what Hugh Johnson, editor of *The Plantsman*, had once described as 'the timeless calm' of an ancient and lovingly tended garden.

From his quickening, her son had been a vigorous foetus, often keeping her awake at night with his restless movements. Sometimes, waking from an alfresco nap on her day-bed, she would find one perfect flower on the bamboo table beside her, put there by Mr Hazell, then the deputy head gardener and, to her, an old man, being at the time in his fifties.

She hadn't dreamed then that in thirty years' time she would be the head gardener – with Henry Hazell and Bob Craskett, both long past the official retirement age, working under her direction.

Pen had spent a lot of time wondering if she would love the child she was carrying. As long as it didn't take after its father, she felt she would.

The birth was a forceps delivery and the local doctor who attended her made a poor job of repairing the ragged tear in her perineum. She was sore for a long time afterwards, but it didn't stop Edward resuming conjugal relations as soon as the statutory six weeks' recovery period was at an end.

Sometimes, in later years, she wondered if her relationship with her children would have been better if she could have brought herself to nurse them. Most of the experts on child-rearing nowadays said it was an important factor in the establishment of a strong mother–child bond.

However the instant the infant had been put to her breast by an officious nurse whom Pen had greatly disliked, she had felt a great wave of revulsion, the small hungry mouth reminding her of the loathsome intimacies inflicted on her by her husband. With a shudder, she had thrust North away and pulled her nightgown together. When the nurse, a blood-sister of Lady Standish, had insisted she *must* let the baby suckle, Pen had become hysterical.

Fortunately Flora Carlyon who, since the death of the old Earl, had spent most of her time in America with her daughter, had returned to Longwarden for the birth of her great-grandchild. Although not usually an interfering matriarch, in this instance she had seen fit to take command of the situation.

The doctor had been graciously but firmly instructed to prescribe tablets which would dry up Pen's milk. The bossy nurse had been replaced by a mild, middle-aged nanny, trained in the days when many society women were impatient to recover their figures and resume the pleasures enjoyed before pregnancy intervened.

Edward, Pen knew, had been furious. Not, she felt sure, on account of his newborn son's welfare. Probably he had hoped that feeding the baby would improve a figure he regarded as lamentably lacking in womanly curves.

However although he shouted and swore at everyone else who displeased him, he hadn't dared to upbraid his grandmother. Flora was a woman of imperial mien when she chose to show it.

Although she never forgot that her own paternal grandparents had been servants, by the time North was born she had long forgotten her initial fears that she was an unsuitable wife for a man of her late husband's rank. For fifty years she had fulfilled her rôle as the mistress of a large household, a leading hostess and a woman of influence. She was more than capable of quelling her boorish grandson.

While North was still a bald scrap in a Shetland shawl, Flora had returned to Boston where her daughter, Lady

Rose Blakewell, was fighting cancer. After Rose's death, she had come back to England to find the baby grown into a small boy with a marked resemblance to the seventh Earl in his first years. Between the old lady and the small Viscount Hawksmere there had sprung up a strong affection, the feeling which should have existed between him and his mother.

Pen had two further pregnancies, both ending in miscarriages, before a daughter was delivered in a London clinic by the gynaecologist who had later released her from purgatory by advising her husband that it would be extremely unwise for her to have any more children.

'In that case there's not much bloody point in serving you any longer,' Edward had told her sourly. 'You lie there like a nun being raped and I don't bloody well enjoy it. I'll find a woman who likes it and you can do as you please.'

An ultimatum which, after he had slammed out of the room, had made Pen burst into tears of relief and thankfulness.

She was, as usual, busy in the garden when North came back to Longwarden to pack for his journey to Ladakh.

England had been having a dry spell. He found her watering some young rhododendrons.

'Hello, Mama. How are you?' He kissed her cheek.

'Hello, darling.' The endearment was standard among women of her age and class. 'I'm well. How are you? Was your trip to America successful?'

'Extremely successful. I've got some good news for you.'

She smiled at him. 'Oh, really . . . what?'

'I've met your future daughter-in-law. We're going to be married as soon as I get back from Ladakh.'

'North . . . are you serious?'

'Entirely. I thought you'd be pleased. It's what you've been wanting for years.'

'Yes . . . but so unexpected. Where did you meet her? How long have you known her?'

'We met at the Blakewells' tercentenary do.' He grinned at her. 'Love at first sight.'

'Really?' Pen looked at him doubtfully. To lose his heart so abruptly seemed unlike her philandering son.

'Her name is Jane Graham. She's my cousin . . . Great Aunt Rose's granddaughter. Both her parents are dead and she's living in Boston with Julia Foster.'

'An American . . . will she fit in here? They are so up to date,' Pen said anxiously.

'I think so – yes. She's very keen to settle down to keeping house and having children.'

'How old is she?'

'Twenty-three.'

'Rather young to be settling down.'

'She's mature for her age.'

'Well . . . I'm delighted, my dear . . . if you're both sure you'll suit each other,' said Pen, still taken aback. 'But surely you won't go to Ladakh now?'

'I have to go. I'm committed. Jane understands that. We're going to be married on September the fifth . . . very quietly . . . no fuss. She'll make all the arrangements. Then we'll have a honeymoon somewhere and afterwards come back here. You won't even have the bother of buying yourself a new hat. By the time you meet her, she'll be my wife, all set to take over the responsibilities which distract you from gardening. I'm sure you'll like her, Mama. She's the nice, intelligent, capable girl you've always wanted me to bring home. Allegra has met her. She likes her.'

'Oh, you saw Allegra over there? How was she getting on?'

'She was having a ball, as they say. It looks as if *Travels* is going to earn her a lot of dollars.'

'Good . . . how nice . . . I'm glad.' Pen's response was mechanical because she was still preoccupied by North's astonishing news. 'Have you a photograph of her . . . this girl . . . Jane?' she asked.

'Several. I'll show you later. I'm going in to sort out my kit.'

He returned to the house, leaving his mother to adjust to the idea of having an American daughter-in-law whom she was not to meet until the marriage was *fait accompli*.

She had arranged to have her tea break at four o'clock in the loggia by the fish pond. She and her butler arrived there at the same time.

Longing to talk to someone about North's bombshell, she said, 'Has my son told you his news, Mr Ashford? He is going to be married.'

'That's very good news, m'Lady.'

'Yes, isn't it.' She hesitated, then plunged on, 'The only thing is it's a case of love at first sight. They met for the first time last month, while he was in America. Do you believe in love at first sight, Mr Ashford?'

He looked at her gravely for a moment. She wondered if he thought it not only infra dig but, worse than that, disloyal of her to discuss North with him.

'I haven't given it much thought, m'Lady. But I should imagine that someone of his Lordship's age would be rather less likely to mistake glister for gold than a younger man.'

'Yes ... I'm sure you're right. I suppose I'm a little uneasy because, having been pushed – far too young – into a most incompatible relationship, I should hate to see either of my children repeat my mistake.'

Now she had really done it. Poor man, how embarrassing for him to have to cope with a revelation which no doubt didn't come as any surprise to him, but which he wouldn't have expected to hear from her lips.

Nothing seemed to ruffle the butler's imperturbability.

He said, 'Don't you think, m'Lady, that the children of unhappy relationships are less likely to rush into an ill-judged marriage, having had, as it were, an object lesson?'

'Yes, perhaps you're right. I hope so. You are very ... reassuring, Mr Ashford.'

For a moment she thought he was going to add something. When he spoke, it was only to say, 'The cake today is a new one ... a recipe from one of the women's magazines Mrs Armitage takes. *Woman's Weekly*, I believe. Rather appropriately, in the circumstances, it's an American cake ... carrot cake.'

'Do you mean it's made from carrots?' Pan asked, glancing at it.

'So I understand, m'Lady.'

'How extraordinary.' Emboldened by her failure to shock him so far, she ventured, 'Would you like to sample it with me, Mr Ashford?'

'Thank you, m'Lady, but I think I should see if his Lordship would like some refreshment. If you will excuse me . . .'

The flowers began to arrive on Allegra's first day back in England. First a bunch of white rosebuds, the next day a box of white lilac. By the end of the week she had a white cyclamen and a white azalea in the sitting room, a white hyacinth in her bathroom, a single white gardenia floating in a crystal bowl on one night table and white freesias on the other.

None of these offerings was accompanied by a card. She had no idea who had ordered them. Telephoning Moyses Stephens, she was told they were not at liberty to disclose the customer's identity without permission. There was nothing to do but to wait until the donor of the flowers chose to reveal himself.

The next week, instead of flowers, there were good things to eat and drink. On Monday a side of smoked salmon; on Tuesday a case of Ayala, the champagne loved by the Edwardians but now known only to a discerning few; on Wednesday a box of Lenôtre liqueur chocolates.

How much must this be costing him? thought Allegra when, on Thursday, she received a half-pound jar of fresh Royal Beluga caviar. The next day a Stilton arrived.

She had invited Ellen Brentwood and her husband and Claudia Dunbar and her partner Ben to dinner on Saturday night. They were intrigued when she told them how she had come by the goodies she was sharing with them.

'Surely you must have some idea who it might be?' said Ellen.

'No, not a clue. Unless this champagne is one. The fact that it's mentioned in *Travels* as being the Edwardians' favourite bubbly does suggest that he's read the book.'

'That doesn't exactly narrow the field,' said Claudia.

'Apart from all the people who've bought it, there are all those who've begged, borrowed or stolen it. A better clue is that anyone who woos with caviar has to be filthy rich. I wonder what he'll shower on you next week? Something to wear, such as diamonds, perhaps.'

'If he does, I shall take them back to the jewellers who supplied them,' said Allegra. 'I don't mind being lavished with flowers and champagne. In fact I've enjoyed it. But there is a limit. It's a slightly eerie feeling, receiving presents from an unknown person. It makes me feel I'm under surveillance.'

'I know what you mean,' agreed Ellen. 'It's the other end of the continuum from obscene telephone calls. Could your admirer be someone you met in America? The fact that all this began on your first day back points to that.'

'Possibly,' said Allegra. 'There were several proposals of marriage in that amazing deluge of fan mail which started while I was on tour and which Laurel & Lincoln are handling for me. But none of those crackpots would have known how to contact me here.'

'Never mind the crackpots,' said Ellen. 'What about the men at that fabulous party L and L laid on for you? Don't tell me you didn't dazzle at least one or two millionaires.'

'The only one who dazzled *me* was the director of the club, a giant of a man, with great charm, who was once a probation officer,' she told them.

Later, when her guests had gone and she was stacking the dishwasher, she wondered if it could be Elliott Lincoln who was behind this strange courtship.

Several times, while she was on tour, he had called her and had a long chat. At the end of the tour they had lunched *à deux* at Le Cirque, another top New York restaurant, and she had thought he would repeat his invitation to see the view from his apartment. But, perhaps because she had given him no encouragement, he hadn't done so.

Strangely, a man whose face kept coming to mind when she pondered the identity of her mysterious suitor was the one who had sat beside her on Concorde. But considering how little conversation they had had, it was absurd to imagine he had subsequently gone to the trouble of tracking her down and arranging this extraordinary courtship.

On Monday, her first thought on waking was to wonder what, if anything, *he* would choose to bestow on her this week.

Nothing arrived during the morning. In the afternoon she had an appointment at the Tower of London where, she had discovered, a portrait and other relics of Sir Edward Blakeney were housed in his regiment's museum.

The colonel in charge of the museum seemed surprised that the field marshal's biographer was a young woman, but he made her welcome and gave her some useful advice about possible sources of information.

On her way home she was preoccupied with thoughts of the book. It was a surprise and pleasure to find a parcel addressed to her on the table in the main entrance hall.

The shape and weight suggested a book. She hurried upstairs to unwrap it. It was an expensive book, a connoisseur's book on lacquer, from Hatchard's in Piccadilly, which gave Allegra some hope of discovering the identity of her mysterious admirer.

There had been a signing sesssion at Hatchard's when *Travels* was published. She felt she knew the managing director well enough to enlist his help.

The lead proved useless. The order for the book, and for others to follow it, had come from an organization which undertook every kind of commission from escorting unaccompanied children across London from station to station to tracking down rarities. Like the florists, they were not prepared to reveal their clients' names.

By the end of the third week Allegra was the possessor of six handsome additions to her bookshelves. The baffling thing was that she might have chosen them herself. How and when had he acquired this insight into her tastes?

When she discussed it with Claudia, who was on the way to becoming a close friend as well as her editorial adviser, her publisher said, 'He may have seen the feature *The World of Interiors* did on your flat. It was obvious from that where your interests lie. You know this is the kind of courtship which went out with floor-sweeping skirts. I'm in love with this guy already ... and I'm not the one he's after,' she added, laughing. 'Don't tell me your heart isn't warming to him, Allegra. How could it not when he takes this big interest in you?'

'For all I know he may be a small fat sheik who wants someone with my colour hair to fill the gap in his collection of women. Or it may be the person deputed to choose all three things who's the brains behind the campaign.'

'Mm ... yes, that's a possibility,' Claudia agreed. 'Anyway, sooner or later you're going to find out. If you're going mad with curiosity, he must be equally curious to find out how you're reacting. I can't see him keeping you or himself on tenterhooks for too much longer. My worry is that he's taking your mind off your work.'

'Don't worry: I shan't neglect Edward,' Allegra assured her.

On Monday the presents stopped.

When Allegra returned from a day researching in the Public Record Office, she found nothing had been delivered. All the way home from Kew she had been wondering what delightful surprise would be waiting for her. The disappointment was acute.

Upstairs in the flat, where the cyclamen and azalea were still flowering, she kicked off her shoes and padded through to the kitchen to pour out a glass of white wine before settling herself in the chair by her answering machine.

> *'How do I love thee? Let me count the ways.*
> *I love thee to the depth and breadth and height*
> *My soul can reach ...'*

As a man's voice spoke the lovely, familiar lines of Elizabeth Barrett Browning's sonnet, Allegra's heart leapt with excitement. So this week she was to be wooed with romantic poetry. Was this his voice? She thought not. It sounded like that of an actor speaking the sonnet as only a trained voice could.

197

The next night the voice recited a love poem by John Donne and, on Wednesday, Meredith's 'Love in the Valley'.

> '... *She whom I love is hard to catch and conquer,*
> *Hard, but O the glory of the winning were she won!*'

I *am* won, Allegra thought dreamily, when it was over. Claudia was right. How could anyone resist this man?

The poems continued till Sunday. On Monday she worked at home, reading contemporary memoirs which might throw light on Edward Blakeney's career, and waiting to find out what *he* had cooked up for this week.

After lunch the caretaker rang up.

'There's a packing case just arrived for you, Lady Allegra. Is it convenient for the van driver and his mate to bring it up right away?'

'Yes, by all means. Thank you, Stanley.'

A few minutes later, escorted by Stanley, the delivery men came up the stairs carrying a large wooden box secured with metal tapes.

One side of the box was made to unfasten easily, releasing a burst of plastic foam packing material. Inside this was something swathed in protective sheeting.

'It looks like a statue,' said Allegra.

'If you can lift it out, lads, we can take the crate and the packing out of her Ladyship's way,' Stanley instructed.

She waited until they had gone before she snipped the stitches holding the dustsheet securely wrapped round a life-sized figure. When, loosening the folds, she unveiled it, she gave a gasp of delight. His white teeth bared in a grin, his projecting left elbow and right hand protected by thin foam bandages, the statue revealed himself as a superb eighteenth-century Venetian blackamoor.

Even in her exotic room with its piles of rich cushions and colourful kelims, he was an arresting sight, his glistening black body dressed in exquisitely painted gold brocade and green silk. His turban was crimson and gold, with a fringed crimson shawl loosely draped round his hips over striped knee-length trousers.

For the second time in ten days, Allegra feasted her eyes on him. The first time she'd seen him he had been on show at one of the major events of the London season, the Grosvenor House Antiques Fair, a ten-day exhibition and sale of choice antiques which had ended on Saturday. Her heart had leapt at the sight of him because although he was sure to be wildly expensive, now she could afford such extravagances. When she had asked the price, the man in charge of the stand had told her the blackamoor wasn't for sale. He had been bought before the fair opened by someone who had agreed to allow the dealers to exhibit him.

It had been a sharp disappointment. She had bought herself a very pretty pair of Georgian paste shoe buckles, but they hadn't appeased her longing for the handsome blackamoor.

She stepped forward to take off the bandaging. In his extended right hand the figure was gripping a chalice. Tucked inside it she found a small sealed envelope with her name written on it.

Hurrying to her desk for a paper opener, her fingers trembling with excitement, she knew that in a few moments she was going to find out who *he* was.

Made clumsy by agitation, at first she couldn't fit the point of the blade into the unsealed gap at the edge of the flap. Having managed to slit the envelope, she drew out the paper inside it and read the message.

Sarah was in the tackroom, reassembling a saddle she had been cleaning, when she heard someone enter the yard. It wasn't Sammy O'Brien. He had been off colour all day. She had made him go to bed, intending to call a doctor if he didn't feel better in the morning.

In any case Sammy was a small man with a soft tread. The footsteps she could hear approaching were heavy, striking the paving with a sound suggestive of heavy boots. Army boots.

Sarah's head jerked up as she listened to the measured stride. Nick? Could it be Nick? Could he have been discharged sooner than he expected? Or deliberately misled her about his release date in order to take her by surprise?

She began to shake at the thought that in a few moments the long waiting time might be over and, if she ran into his arms, she might at last feel them close round her and receive her first kiss.

'Anyone about?'

The voice raised in loud inquiry wasn't Nick Dean's.

Her surge of excitement deflated, she left what she was doing and went to the door.

The man in the yard had his back turned towards the tackroom when she first saw him. Then he swung round.

Sarah and Tarquin Osgood stared at each other; she with acute disappointment that he wasn't a bronzed legionnaire, and he with a scowl which lightened at the sight of her slender figure displayed, more fully than when he had seen her before, in a pair of breeches and a close-fitting cotton sweater.

'Oh . . . it's you,' she said. 'What brings you here?'

'I came to see you.'

He had meant to tell her she was a toffee-nosed cunt who couldn't make him look a fool and get away with it. But when he saw the soft fringe of silky blonde hair curling over her forehead, and the large deep-blue eyes looking sad, as if something had upset her, suddenly he didn't want to snarl at her.

'I went to the front first. Some old bloke came to the door . . . said you'd be in the stables,' he said, coming closer.

As he spoke, the door from the yard into the scullery end of the kitchen block opened. With his usual upright bearing, the butler came across the yard.

Without glancing at her companion, he said, 'Is everything in order, Miss Sarah?'

'Yes, thank you, Mr Ashford. This is Tark Osgood. He and his mother have come to live in the village in Mrs Barker's house. Mrs Barker was one of our helpers several years ago.'

'I see. Perhaps, Osgood, you would be good enough to leave with rather less noise than you arrived. Lady Carlyon has a migraine – a severe headache. If you would do your best not to disturb her, it would be greatly appreciated.'

The butler spoke with quiet courtesy but the gaze resting now on Tark had a steely gleam which somehow conveyed the impression that if the young man ignored the request he would regret it.

'I'm sure Tark will be as quiet as he can. Where did you leave your motorbike?' Sarah asked.

'Round the front.'

He had left it propped on the gravelled sweep at the foot of the wide flight of steps which added dignity to the imposing entrance. From the sweep to the stable arch there was another stretch of drive, but Tark had chosen to leave his bike where it was and to walk round the side of the house to have a quick squint in the windows of the ground floor. His intention had been frustrated by the internal shutters securing the many-paned windows.

Looking for ways to get in, he had seen none. But neither had there been any sign of burglar alarms and the place must be full of stuff worth nicking.

'He don't look much like a butler,' he said when Ashford had left them.

Sarah guessed that Tark expected a butler to wear a tail-coat and to have a silver salver permanently balanced on one palm.

In fact there were a number of ways in which Ashford was not like a butler, but they had nothing to do with his clothes which were the same as those worn by most modern menservants. All the members of the family had been puzzled by certain things which set him apart from the general run of his colleagues.

He did not, like some of his confrères, have two personae: one voice and manner for the family side of the baize door and another for the staff side. He was always the same: quiet, efficient and impenetrably reserved. It was typical of him to have come from the other end of the house to check that the unusual visitor was in fact known to Sarah. North said he felt a lot easier about being away from Longwarden now that Ashford was there to protect his mother.

Sarah said, 'Have you changed your mind about working for Lady Carlyon?'

Tark shook his head. 'I'll get something fixed up some time. I'm not in no hurry. Why didn't you tell me who you was? You let me think you worked here.'

'I do. I don't get paid for it but I work just as hard as if I did – harder, actually. At the moment I'm cleaning some tack. You'd better come into the tackroom so that I can "whistle and ride", as Sammy calls talking and working.'

'Who's Sammy?'

'An Irishman who knows more about horses than anyone I've ever met. He worked for my father years ago and now he helps me run the stables.'

He followed her inside the building, glancing without much interest at the bridle hooks suspended from the ceiling, the saddle racks and saddle horses and the chests used for storage.

Tark lit a cigarette and watched her small, practised hands replacing the irons on the stirrup leathers. Most of the girls he mixed with had long painted nails and wore rings and bracelets and earrings. Her nails were short and unvarnished and she wore no ornaments. He would have expected her to have a fancy gold watch but the one strapped to her wrist was a man's watch.

Yet in spite of her plaited hair and lack of adornments, she was a very feminine girl. Her fine skin had a velvety bloom and she had small delicate ears and a long slender neck. She didn't look strong enough to control a large horse.

'Do you ever fall off?' he asked her.

She looked up and smiled, making dimples appear in her cheeks. 'Sometimes. I try not to. But it's an occupational hazard which I don't think about any more than you probably think about crashing your bike. Now that *would* scare me – being a pillion passenger with someone else in control.'

'You'd like it. Give it a try. I'll run you as far as the gates and back. It won't take five minutes,' he urged her.

Sarah shook her head. 'I'd rather not, thanks. As soon as I've finished in here it'll be time for evening stables.

That's what we call making the horses comfortable for the night.'

'I don't mind giving a hand.'

'Thank you, but I can manage – and the boxes are no-smoking zones,' she added, seeing him flick some more ash on the floor. She hadn't got over the disappointment of thinking Nick was back and finding it was only this rather cocky ton-up boy. 'You said you came to see me. What about?'

Tark was an experienced chatter-up of birds. Although this one was different from any he had known before, he could see no reason why she shouldn't react like the others. He had never yet failed to pull any bird he fancied.

He gave her a sexy look. 'Does there have to be a special reason?'

Sarah's devotion to her horses would have made it impossible for her to have the same kind of social life as most of her contemporaries even if she had been interested in dating. Because of Nick, she wasn't. From time to time in the hunting field and at horse trials she met young men who were attracted to her. But her own indifference was clear and they soon got the message. Never having needed to brush off unwanted admirers, at first she couldn't believe Tark was one. Yet how else could one interpret that look and a question he must have gleaned from some third-rate TV soap opera?

When she neither giggled nor made a pert retort, it occurred to him for the first time that she might already have a steady boyfriend. Not that that was any deterrent.

'You got a bloke?' he asked her.

Although they spoke the same language their phraseology was so different that it took her a second or two to grasp what the blunt question meant. She wished she could answer yes so that he would lose interest in her. But it wasn't true yet and might never be. She couldn't be sure that Nick would fall in love with her.

Apart from coming to see her and Sammy, his two friends, Nick had no reason to stay for long. He wouldn't want his old job back. It had been forced on him by his

203

foster father. Nick had become a good groom but he didn't share her feelings about horses. They were animals, not friends, to him. He was quiet, patient, gentle but firm with them because that was what horses needed. But he didn't love them as she did.

'I'm not engaged,' she said, hoping Tark would conclude an engagement was in the offing.

She had never thought of herself as a snob and was rather shocked to discover that, deep down, she was affronted by his gall in thinking he could attract her. She could see that his flashy good looks and that Hell's Angel leather outfit would bowl over the girls in the village. But didn't he realize that between them and her there was an impassable gulf?

Later, after he had gone and she was refilling Bedouin's water buckets and haynet, she wondered why she could dream of being married to Nick, although he was one of the village boys, but be horrified at the thought of even one date with Tark.

The reason, she realized, had nothing to do with their backgrounds and everything to do with their personalities. Tark was an arrogant show-off who fancied himself as a leader because his expensive motorbike gave him kudos in the eyes of a fairly moronic bunch of teenage youths.

Nick had somehow survived a pitiably miserable upbringing without becoming brutalized. North had once told her that boys who were beaten at their public schools often developed an urge to beat other people. She knew that when Nick had first come to work in the stables, Sammy had watched him closely for the first sign of careless, cruel handling of the delicate creatures who could so easily be lamed by a jab with a hoof pick, or made permanently head-shy by being roughly groomed.

But Nick had never been rough with the horses. She had a sharp mental picture of his long thin hand patting the neck of a horse he was riding. Like the puppies of large breeds of dog, he had shown before adolescence the signs of being a tall man; as tall or taller than the six-foot keeper who had terrorized his boyhood.

Later, before going to bed, she made a last check on the

horses before climbing the stairs to her room high above the archway.

While she was unplaiting her hair, Tark was adding to the smoke in the bar of the Longwarden Arms. He was watching a game of darts but thinking about Sarah, and about the vast house with room after room of valuable bits and pieces.

Pen had suffered from migraine since she was adolescent, but hadn't had one for a long time. The first sign was seeing moving patterns of small dots at the edges of her vision. Then would come the appalling headache which might last for an hour or several. Finally she would be sick and begin to feel better.

These debilitating headaches, for which the only relief, if it could be called that, was to lie in a darkened room, had always followed a period of emotional stress or worry.

Every migraine could be linked to a mood of impotent rebellion against her dictatorial mother, an angry tirade from her husband, or some upsetting incident in the lives of her children.

The sudden recurrence of an ailment she thought had left her was, she knew, when it was over, connected to North's announcement of his engagement to the American girl who, as his photographs of her showed, bore an extraordinary resemblance to the young Flora Carlyon.

Pen had suggested inviting her to Longwarden.

'I don't think it's fair to marry her without letting her see what she's taking on here, North,' she had told him. 'As your wife, she's going to have a great many worries and responsibilities. Have you been honest and told her how hard-up we are?'

'She knows that, Mama. I've laid all the facts on the line for her. Don't worry: Jane can cope. She's the daughter of a very shrewd man who started with nothing and ended as the president of an international company. You won't have heard of him, but everyone in Wall Street and the City has. There's a lot of her father in Jane. What you might regard as a problem, she'll sort out with no trouble at all.'

'If her father was as successful as that, she must have money?'

'She has means of her own – yes. She won't be dependent on me for her dress allowance as you were with Father.'

Thinking over the conversation later, Pen had come to the conclusion that the only child of a man known to financiers on both sides of the Atlantic must have very considerable private means. Was that the real reason why North was marrying her?

Before she had plucked up the courage to ask him, and to warn him how fatal it was to marry for anything but a strong desire to make the other person happy, he had gone.

When the migraine had passed off she made herself a pot of weak tea and ate a couple of Jacob's water biscuits from the tin by her bed. She had come to her room an hour before dinner, her last act before the headache blinded her being to speak to her cook on the house telephone. Mrs Armitage knew about her migraines. She would have passed the word to Ashford.

After a migraine, depending what time it came on, often Pen would sleep for the rest of the day and through the night.

However on this occasion she woke up at half-past eleven and couldn't get back to sleep. At fifteen minutes past midnight, after counting seventy-five sheep had failed to work, she decided some fresh air might help.

Unbeknown to her household, she had often strolled in the garden on warm summer nights. The familiar paths and vistas took on a new character at night as hedges and trees cast deep shadows and a moon-glade shimmered on the surface of the lake.

Tonight, with galoshes to keep her shoes dry, and Allegra's school blazer, taken from a peg in the cloak-room, over a pair of cotton pyjamas which North had outgrown years before and Pen had added to her assortment of night things, she returned to the garden with the added pleasure of being, for a change, free to wander about it at leisure.

By day there was seldom time to spend more than a few

odd moments admiring the results of her labours. Always there was some task urgently demanding her attention. At night that pressure was missing. She could amble as idly as her predecessors with their retinues of gardeners and garden boys.

In a little more than two months, my reign, such as it's been, will be over, she thought, still finding it hard to believe that her son had at last decided to give up his freedom.

Will this girl he's going to marry want to put in a swimming pool? I hope not. They are such an eyesore; that horrid bright blue which clashes with everything natural. There's nowhere to put a pool without spoiling some lovely spot which has taken years to perfect. But I mustn't oppose her in anything. That would be fatal. I must try to emulate Flora who was always so marvellously tactful and generous with me. It's a very difficult thing to be a good mother-in-law. I've been such a failure at everything else. Can I make a success of this?

The moonlit glory of the long laburnum walk made her pause before entering the tunnel formed by tall hoops of metal round which the trees had been trained so that the racemose flowers formed a canopy above the path, golden by day, silver-gilt at this hour.

On either side of the paving, Pen had replaced the original planting with borders of large-leaved hostas. The far end of the walk framed a sundial on which were inscribed the words *Horas non numero sed serenas*.

Walking towards it, Pen remembered the first time she had been taken round the garden by Edward's daunting grandfather.

'You know what it means, I presume?' he had asked.

Her brain paralysed by nervousness of the old Earl, she had stammered, 'I'm afraid I don't.'

He had made a sound indicative of disapproval. Then his wife, who had been strolling a few paces behind them with Edward, and who must have heard the question and Pen's apologetic reply, had said, 'It means *I only tell of sunny hours*, Penelope. Have you heard Hilaire Belloc's joke about sundials? I am a sundial and I make a botch of what is done far better by a watch.'

Flora had laughed, her dark-brown eyes dancing with amusement. And the merry look on her face had transformed her husband's expression from thinly-veiled boredom with his grandson's timid, tongue-tied fiancée to unmistakable pleasure in looking at his wife.

On a very hot day, she had looked cool and lovely in a pale melon-green cotton shirt dress. She had smelt deliciously of scent as she linked her arm lightly with Pen's.

'Did you have Belloc's *Cautionary Tales* read to you as a child? I know most of them by heart. But the lines of his I like best are, *From quiet homes and first beginning, Out to the undiscovered ends, There's nothing worth the wear of winning, But laughter and the love of friends.* That's so true . . . so wise. Laughter and love *are* the only important things in life.'

She had given Pen the impression that she knew Edward wasn't the man of her dreams. Whether there had been a warning in Flora's remarks was something Pen had never found out. She had never told the Dowager Countess that her marriage was a misery, and Flora had never intimated that she knew it.

From the sundial Pen turned in the opposite direction from the way they had walked on that long-ago summer afternoon. In those days the gardens had had a large number of splendid herbaceous beds which she had since had to replace with a less laborious form of planting. Many changes had become necesssary and she wondered what Caspar Carlyon would think if he saw them.

As she came round the end of a yew hedge, the sight of a dark-haired figure sitting with his back to her made her draw in a startled breath.

For an instant it seemed that her thoughts of the old Earl had somehow conjured his spectre at one of his favourite spots. From the seat, through a *claire-voie*, was perhaps the best of all the views of the lake and the park.

Almost immediately she realized that the man on the seat was no apparition but a flesh and blood being who shared the seventh Earl's habit of keeping his spine straight and his shoulders pulled back.

Although he had not heard her coming, as she stared at the back of his head some instinct seemed to alert him to the presence of someone nearby. He looked over his other shoulder and then in her direction.

As Pen, who had been standing still, moved forward, he rose to his feet.

'Is anything wrong, m'Lady?'

In the clapboard cottage on Cape Cod which was Marcus and Alison Blakewell's summer retreat, Jane was curled on the windowseat in her bedroom, re-reading her future mother-in-law's letter.

My dear Jane, *Lady Carlyon had written*,
The news that North is to bring home a bride in the autumn is a great joy to everyone here, especially to me. He tells me you have read Allegra's book. So you will know that the last time a girl from abroad took over the reins at Longwarden, it was one of the happiest periods in the history of this ancient house.

I feel sure, from my son's glowing description, that you are as beautiful and kind as your great-grandmother, Flora Carlyon, whom I knew and remember with the warmest affection.

If you should change your mind about coming to stay with us while North is away, please don't hesitate to propose yourself. Sarah and I would be delighted to welcome you to your future home. Do think it over. We look forward so much to meeting you.
She had signed herself simply – Penelope.

It could hardly be a nicer letter, thought Jane as she folded the single sheet of die-stamped ivory writing paper covered with the Countess's small, neat, fountain-pen handwriting.

But what, if anything, was to be read between the lines?

* * *

'No, nothing's wrong, Mr Ashford. Like you, I'm enjoying this beautiful summer night, said Pen.'

'I see. I'm glad you're better.'

'I don't often take to my bed, but with migraine one has no choice. For a time one literally can't see.'

'So I understand. Most unpleasant. I hope you weren't disturbed by our noisy visitor. A youth from the village came roaring up on a motorbike to see Miss Sarah.'

'I heard the noise and wondered who it was. Do sit down again, Mr Ashford. If you don't mind, I'll join you. This is one of the nicest places in the garden, isn't it?'

'A superb vantage point,' he agreed. 'But I'm sure you'd rather have it to yourself.'

When he started to move away, she stopped him. 'No, don't go. Four people could share this seat without being crowded. It came from a château which was being pulled down at the time my son's great-grandparents were motoring through France on the way to do their *Travels with a Donkey* walk. Have you read that book, Mr Ashford?'

As she spoke she sat on the seat which, although made of stone, wasn't cold. In hot summers it seemed to retain the heat of the day long after sunset.

'More than once. I imagine when the seventh Lord Carlyon did the walk, it wasn't much changed from the way Stevenson described it. That it remains unchanged still seems rather doubtful. There may be pylons marching across that countryside, or some other twentieth-century excrescence. I was thinking just before you joined me that not many people nowadays enjoy the luxury of a view with nothing unsightly to mar it.'

He waved a hand at the *claire-voie*. 'Some time ago his Lordship gave me permission to look at the Longwarden Red Book. It was interesting to see how closely this view still matches Repton's painting of the scene as it would be when the new trees had grown to maturity.'

What a knowledgeable man he was, thought Pen, admiring the dark silk dressing gown he was wearing over plain pyjamas. Had Gisburn known about the Red Book? She was inclined to doubt it.

'Do you often come here at night, Mr Ashford?' she asked.

'No, as a rule I go to bed early and stay there until my alarm goes. But tonight I couldn't sleep.' To her dismay, he stood up. 'If you mean to spend some time here, m'Lady, I think I should fetch you a rug. As you missed dinner tonight, would you like me to make you some sandwiches?'

'No, no . . . I shouldn't dream of letting you wait on me at this hour. But you're right: I do feel hungry. I'll go and forage in the pantry and find myself some cake or something.'

Reluctantly, she rose to her feet. She had hoped to continue their midnight chat for some time yet.

They walked back to the house together. When they were near it he said, 'The best thing for you to have would be an omelette. After studying Mrs Armitage's technique, I've become quite adept. Shall I demonstrate my expertise for you?'

'An omelette does sound awfully good. If you're sure you don't mind . . .'

'It will be a pleasure. I'll bring it up to your sitting room.'

'That's an unnecessary bother. I'll eat it in the kitchen. Do you know the story of one of the Mitford sisters whose ignorance of cooking was so complete that when her cook left a dish to be put in the oven at a certain time, Nancy Mitford put it in the oven but didn't realize ovens have to be turned on? I'm not quite as bad as that, but I'm ashamed to admit that if I attempted an omelette it would probably be a disaster.'

He laughed. 'You have other skills. Anyone who can clip yews into obelisks could quickly master the art of making an omelette if they had to.'

The original kitchen, a vast stone-flagged room with enormous black ovens and hobs, and dozens of worn copper pans used for cooking for the gargantuan appetites of former times, was no longer in use. After World War Two one of the larger stillrooms had been equipped as a modern kitchen.

'This is perfection,' said Pen after her first mouthful of

the omelette he set before her a short time later. 'Perhaps you missed your vocation and should have been a master chef, a latter-day Escoffier directing operations at the Ritz or the Savoy.'

Ashford smiled. In repose, his face was austere – one which seen behind the desk in a headmaster's study would make unruly boys quake. When he smiled, the austerity vanished. He looked younger and less reserved.

'I'm not sure I should have liked that, but the idea of managing a large hotel is quite appealing.' He shrugged. 'Too late now, I'm afraid. Not that I'm not well content with my present lot,' he added.

She had urged him to sit down and share the tea she had made in Mrs Armitage's brown earthenware pot. He had poured out a cup for himself but he hadn't joined her at the table. He was leaning against the dresser, rather in the attitude of a man on a shooting-stick. In artificial light she could see his dressing gown *was* silk, patterned with groups of navy dots on a dark burgundy background. His pyjamas were pale grey poplin, the collar piped with a thin rim of navy. She liked the way the grey hair at his temples flicked upwards, as crisp and neat as a Scots terrier's coat.

All too soon the omelette was finished. As she didn't really want anything else to eat, there was no reason for her to linger, keeping her butler out of the bed to which by now he was doubtlessly ready to return.

'Thank you, Mr Ashford. Cooking at this hour of night would *not* be approved of by your union – if you had one,' she said, with a smile.

'Nor would the hours you put in, m'Lady. Fortunately everyone here from his Lordship to Sammy has the good fortune to derive what I believe is called job satisfaction from their work.'

'The reason why my dear old pair, Henry and Bob, don't want to retire isn't because they need the little I pay them. They can manage comfortably on their pensions. But they've always enjoyed working here and taken a pride in their skills. Conditions weren't at all good when they were young men, but I don't think they'd have used striking as

212

a way to get higher wages and shorter hours, any more than a mother would stop attending to her children to wring a few pounds more housekeeping money out of a difficult husband. Gardeners and farmers and mothers can't stop working for one week, let alone weeks on end. If anyone works longer and harder than the average housewife with young children, I can't think who it can be. When one compares her conditions even fifty years ago with her conditions today, the improvement's remarkable.'

He said, 'I agree . . . up to a point. But it has to be said that conditions for wives are, to a great extent, dependent on their husbands' pay packets. Of course it's also true that some women have the ability to make a low wage go further than it would with another woman's management. If, for example, you lived in one of the council houses, it would obviously win the prize for the best-kept garden every year, and have a surplus of produce to sell to the greengrocer.'

'It might also have the grubbiest net curtains and the least clean windows,' she answered with a laugh. 'I think I was cut out to be a bread-winner, not a housewife. But when I was a girl the demarcation lines beween the sexes were more rigid than they are now. It was all right to take a Constance Spry course in flower arrangement but one wouldn't have been encouraged to apprentice oneself to a market gardener. Although I suppose I could have done it. Elizabeth Garrett Anderson managed to become a doctor.'

Out of the corner of her eye, Pen saw that the kitchen clock was showing half-past one. She knew he rose at six, which meant he would have only a little more than four hours' sleep tonight.

'I have a theory,' he said, 'that most of the women who made holes in the barriers, as it were, weren't necessarily strong-willed or career-minded from the outset. I think many of them found they were not going to marry, for one reason or another, and the life of an unmarried woman was then so extraordinarily restricted that boredom alone spurred them to their achievements.'

'My feminist daughter would say it was unusual for a man, other than a psychologist, to have any theories about

213

women,' Pen answered. 'She feels that women spend a large part of their lives pondering on men and their ways, but that your sex hardly ever bothers to think seriously about us.'

Not wanting to curtail their talk but also concerned not to deprive him of sleep, she brought the conversation to an end.

'We must go to bed, Mr Ashford, or neither of us will be fit for our labours tomorrow. Thank you again for the omelette. I've enjoyed our talk. Goodnight.'

As she dressed to go out to dinner on Wednesday evening, the unsigned note she had opened on Monday afternoon lay on Allegra's dressing table:

I hope you are free to dine with me on Wednesday. A car will fetch you at 7.45 p.m.

How many times since first reading them had she scanned those two short sentences? Of course he had known that, if she *had* had an engagement tonight, she would have broken it to meet him. What woman wouldn't?

All day she had struggled to concentrate on Edward only to find her thoughts wandering to the question of what to wear. A man who had taken such pains deserved to have his eyes ravished. The decision would have been easier had she known where they were dining.

In the end she had decided only one thing in her wardrobe was worthy of such an occasion. The Fortuny dress.

Mariano Fortuny y Madrazo had been born in Spain in 1871 but had spent a great deal of his life in Venice. A man of many parts, he had been a sculptor, engraver, architect, inventor, photographer, stage designer and creator of some of the most beautiful dresses ever made. Greta Garbo, Peggy Guggenheim, Gloria Vanderbilt, Eleanora Duse and Sarah Bernhardt were only a few of the women whose clothes had included Fortuny's pleated silk dresses.

The one Allegra owned, a clinging sheath of copper silk edged with purple silk, was more than seventy years old. It had been bought by Flora Carlyon on a visit to Venice before World War One.

There was a magic about the copper dress which even the Zandra Rhodes and Gina Fratini designs in her cupboards didn't have. A faint, faint scent of Françoise Coty's *L'Origan*, a perfume no longer made, still lingered on the shimmering silk, more tantalizingly erotic than any of the current perfumes, most of them made from chemicals rather than the essence of flowers.

Flora Carlyon, who had worn the Fortuny perhaps half a dozen times over a period of thirty years, had had shoes to match all her dresses made by Perugia, one of the great shoemakers of her day. Unfortunately none of them fitted Allegra, but she had once scraped together enough money for a pair by Manolo Blahnik, the half-Czech, half-Spanish designer who lived in England and who had shod, among others, Bianca Jagger, Jerry Hall and Lauren Bacall, women who could afford to cull the world for their clothes.

It took her two hours to prepare herself for her mysterious assignation. By twenty minutes to eight she was ready and waiting in the hall, her hair and shoulders veiled by a shawl of hand-made black lace, a *mantilla española* bought in Madrid by her great-grandfather on his way back from botanizing in the mountains of the Sierra Nevada. It must have taken the lace-maker months to compose the gossamer threads into their exquisite pattern.

The envelope bag in Allegra's hand had been given to Flora by another man who had loved her. Allegra had known him as Major-General Sir Harry Cromer MC, an old man with a walrus moustache who had to be pushed about in a wheelchair.

When her great-grandmother had met him, at a ball in 1903, he had been Captain Cromer of the Royal Horse Guards, a young man with curly fair hair and a bad reputation with women. At first he had made improper advances to Flora, even though brides were not 'fair game'. Later he had fallen deeply and lastingly in love with her. In his old age, when she was a widow, it had pleased him to give her extravagant birthday and Christmas presents, usually from Cartier or Asprey.

He had chosen the bag at Cartier for her eightieth

birthday. It was made from a fragment of eighteenth-century needlework surrounded by suede. With the perfection of detail characteristic of Cartier, it was fastened by a suede loop and a bead of carved coral.

Surveying her reflection in the huge gilded looking glass which reflected the graceful sweep of the curving staircase, Allegra remembered her great-grandmother's one and only love affair; a love which had never petered out in boredom or disillusionment like all her own amours.

This man she was meeting tonight: would he be a disappointment?

In the garden of the house on Cape Cod, Jane was sunbathing and preparing herself for the new life ahead of her.

During her travels with her father she had made a point of studying the language and customs of the countries where John Graham had business interests. Now she was setting herself to learn all she could about the British way of life, particularly in the strata of society she would be joining as North's wife.

She knew from Allegra's book that, in Lady Carlyon's phrase, the last time a man of the family had married 'a girl from abroad', she had received intensive coaching in English upper-class behaviour before appearing in public as the Countess of Carlyon.

In some ways Jane was better prepared to fill her new rôle than Flora had been; in others she felt as inadequate as Caspar's bride had at first. However she had two months in which to devour every book she could lay hands on which might give her some helpful insights into what would be expected of her. Luckily she knew how to ride, which seemed to be one useful asset for English country life.

Presently, rising from her sunbed, she dropped her straw hat on the grass and walked round the pool to the shower where a douche of cold water on her warm skin made her gasp. The weather had been so hot that without a series of sprinklers flinging shining veils of water over it, the grass would have dried out and scorched.

In a minimal French bikini of tangerine cotton, Jane

dived into the pool and began her afternoon stint of fifty lengths, changing her stroke at the end of every tenth lap.

As she swam she thought about North, who was now on the other side of the world in a remote mountain kingdom between Pakistan and Tibet. She wondered if he had written to her yet.

After he had walked out of the bar at her hotel in New York, and Charles had tried to dissuade her from marrying him, she had spent a restless night and, somewhat against her better judgement, had put through an early call to North's hotel.

His tone, during their short conversation, had been polite but preoccupied. She had sensed that his professional persona had already taken over and he didn't want to be bothered with personal matters, not even a last-minute talk with his future wife.

Later that day she had lunched with Charles who had again done his best to make her see reason, as he put it. Although at first he had claimed that finding her had been his primary reason for crossing the Pacific, later he had admitted it was also a business trip. Since their parting, his factory had expanded. Helped by a gifted designer he had discovered, Charles had built up a connection with a number of top-of-the-market retail outlets in Europe and was poised to break into the American market.

'I'll see you again before I go back to Bangkok,' he had said when they parted. 'By then you'll have had time to think things over.'

He had called her long distance several times. Any time now she expected him to reappear, determined to break up a relationship which he disapproved of as strongly as her father had once deplored Charles's connection with her.

The immaculately polished black Rolls-Royce glided with stately slowness along Piccadilly, or so it seemed to Allegra who, with her first royalty cheque, had bought herself a silver Limited Edition Mini 25 produced to commemorate the silver jubilee of Sir Alec Issigoni's famous little car.

The possession of a Rolls-Royce suggested that her host

was an older man. She hoped that, after more than four weeks of increasing pleasure in his wooing, she wasn't about to experience a horrible anticlimax.

The sun gleamed on the Flying Lady on top of the car's distinctive radiator. There had been a Rolls-Royce at Longwarden when Allegra was a child. She remembered being told the story behind the slender figure and her windswept draperies. The model for the mascot had been Eleanor Thornton, the mistress of Lord Montagu of Beaulieu, a pioneer motorist. In World War One, after fourteen years together, they had been torpedoed on a liner heading for Port Said. He had survived. She had been one of the three hundred passengers lost. But as long as Rolls-Royces were made, her graceful shape was immortal.

When the car swept up the slope of St James's, she felt certain they were heading for the Ritz Hotel.

The doorman on duty at the Arlington Street entrance touched the brim of his silk hat as he opened the door for her.

'Good evening.' She stepped on to the pavement.

Mounting the steps to the revolving door, she felt herself tensing with nerves and took a deep breath to calm them.

There was no need to announce herself to the hall porter. He said, 'Good evening, your Ladyship,' and signalled the waiting page to show her the way.

The last time she had dined at the Ritz it had been in the restaurant overlooking the park, one of the most beautiful rooms in London. However the page took her to the lift and she knew one of the private suites was her destination.

Outside the door of the Somerset Suite the page pressed the bell, gave her a funny little bow and returned the way he had come.

Waiting for the door to open, Allegra felt an impulse to turn tail. What if one look was enough to dash any hope that she could respond to her host's strange anonymous courtship in the way he wished? What if his romantic nature was housed in a body which repelled her?

The door opened.

They looked at each other, in silence, for what seemed a long time.

'Won't you come in?' He stood aside, indicating with his hand that she should pass through the lobby to a sitting room radiant with the last golden glow of the summer evening.

Allegra obeyed the gesture and found herself in a room with a grey and pink carpet and pale-pink curtains and sofas. There seemed to be flowers on every table, and champagne was on ice in readiness for her arrival, but she was far too unnerved to take in any other details.

She heard the outer door close and then the sitting room door. She turned, outwardly calm, inwardly knocked sideways.

'I saw you on television while you were in America,' said Risconti. 'You've haunted me for two years. Seeing you on the screen confirmed what I already knew . . . I was never going to have peace until I'd asked your forgiveness. Can you forgive me, Allegra? Can you forget the first time and let this be our beginning?'

For some moments she didn't speak but stood motionless, gazing at him, the copper silk of her dress burnished by the sunset light which caught the red gleams in her hair through the meshes of the *mantilla*.

Finally she shook her head. 'No,' she said, in a low voice. 'No, I can't ever forget that night.'

Alone in her first-floor sitting room, but for William curled on her lap, Pen was absently stroking his fur while thinking about her son and his future wife.

For long she had hoped he would marry a sensible, energetic girl who would care for the house as she herself cared for the garden. It was possible that a young woman with the right background to give her an understanding of the problems, and the driving force needed for such a formidable undertaking, could save Longwarden from falling into dereliction. As far as Pen could see the only way to do that was to open it to the public. To put it to rights and maintain it as a private house, impossibly vast sums of money would be needed. Hundreds of thousands of pounds. Even millions.

If, at the beginning of the century, Caspar Carlyon had been as hard-up as North, instead of exceedingly rich, he would have looked for an heiress to repair the family fortunes. That he hadn't loved her would have been less important than the preservation of his heritage. In those days few aristocrats married for love.

Nevertheless the domestic history of the family had included some extremely happy marriages, such as Flora's, as well as several miserable alliances, notably her own.

Edward's father, Rollo, whose posthumous VC for outstanding bravery in action in World War Two was displayed in the library, had contrived to combine a happy marriage with a succession of affairs. Whether Diana, his beautiful, delicate wife, had known about his infidelities was uncertain. Perhaps, living in the country with her children, she had been unaware of Rollo's activities in London. Or perhaps, knowing she had his heart, she hadn't cared if the insatiable sex-drive, a characteristic of the men of his family, had driven him into other women's beds while she was pregnant or convalescing from difficult births.

Thinking about North's forebears, Pen wondered if, when he was married, her son would be like his father and grandfather, or if he would emulate his great-grandfather who, although he had had a bad reputation when single, was said never to have looked at another woman after his marriage to Flora.

Pen wanted her children to be happy – happier than she had been. But it seemed unlikely, for both had shown early signs of having an inconstant nature.

She began to ponder the changes his marriage would make to her own life. Longwarden was a huge house, with many staircases, in which it would be easy for her to have her own self-contained quarters and not intrude on North and his wife.

Nevertheless she thought it would be advisable for her not to live under their roof. There were several lodges and cottages, and also the dairies. They had not been in use for their original purpose even in Flora's time when the home farm had supplied Longwarden with the copious quantities of milk, cream, butter and fresh eggs needed to feed the large indoor staff and the many guests and their servants who came for Fridays-to-Mondays, as weekends had been called in those days.

The dairies might make a very nice granny cottage – if we can scrape up the money to put in a kitchen and bathroom, thought Pen. Tomorrow I'll have a look at them.

And I'll ask Mr Ashford to come with me and advise me, was her pleasurable afterthought.

Someone pressed the bell of the Somerset Suite at the Ritz. Allegra heard a key turning in the lock of the outer door, followed by a knock on the inner door and a man's voice saying, 'Room Service, sir,' before it opened and a waiter appeared with a cloth-covered trolley.

'Good evening, madam. Good evening, sir.'

While he busied himself with the preparations for their dinner she and Risconti made small talk and she strove to get a grip on herself after the shock of finding that he was her mysterious admirer.

As they sat in chairs placed on either side of a low table by a window overlooking Green Park, she knew he never took his eyes off her. Allegra didn't look at him. She watched the waiter going deftly about his work or studied the bubbles in her glass of champagne.

As soon as the waiter had gone, Risconti said, 'I couldn't leave America until last night, but when I saw you on television I knew I must find some way to bring us together again. I wanted to get in touch with you at once, but that would have been a bad move. I gave it a great deal of thought.'

'Obviously,' she said coolly.

Ignoring her tone, he went on, 'When I read your book, it told me as much about you as about your great-grandparents. I knew I'd been wrong about you . . . wrong in thinking you'd rejected me because I had told you I was the bastard son of a village cleaning woman.'

She gave him a startled glance. 'That had absolutely nothing to do with it.'

'I know . . . I know . . . it was crass of me. But when you've grown up being shunned by your own relations, it makes you quick to suspect the same attitudes in other people. Also I'd been conditioned to think badly of aristocrats.'

He paused to shrug his broad shoulders. Tonight, in contrast to his informal appearance at Sybille's dinner party, he was wearing a white dinner jacket with a dark-red carnation on the lapel.

'Inside my worldly exterior there were – and perhaps still are – a lot of narrow-minded Italian peasant ideas about women and how they should behave. I was a stupid fellow two years ago, but I think I've improved a little since then.'

Allegra wondered how he would react if she told him she wasn't hungry and didn't wish to dine with him. But the annoyance she had felt at first, at being put in the impossible position of being charmed and intrigued by a man who had humiliated her, had already died down. Nevertheless she was still wary of him. What did he want from her this time?

As she joined him at the table she said, 'You must know I can't possibly accept the last thing you sent me . . . the blackamoor.'

'I haven't seen it yet. I merely gave instructions for the finest possible blackamoor to be found for you. I hope it's a good example.'

'Magnificent – but far, far outside the bounds of acceptable presents. But I'm sure the people who supplied him will take him back.'

Risconti pushed in her chair and moved round the table to his place. 'I don't think the rules of conventional behaviour apply to us, but let's not discuss that right now.'

It was early when he sent her home in the hired Rolls-Royce. When he kissed her hand, at the door of the waiting car, it was the first time he had touched her.

Still holding her fingers in his, regardless of the doorman

standing beside them, he said, 'You're more beautiful than ever. That's a wonderful dress. You must wear it when you sit to me. I can't rest till I've painted you, Allegra. I know it will be my masterpiece. I've painted some beautiful women since I left England, but none with hair like yours ... skin like yours ... eyes like yours.' He released her hand and bowed, as if to a queen. '*Arrivederci.*'

She rode home in great confusion of mind and heart. Apart from his saying he wanted to paint her, they had no arrangement to meet again.

Now that the evening was over she began to regret her coolness towards him. The truth was that once she had recovered from the shock of seeing him again, the magnetism he had exerted on her *chez* Sybille had revived. She wanted him as much as she had then, but it seemed that this time Risconti was determined not to rush his fences.

In her room above the stable arch, Sarah was crying.

She hadn't felt such despair since Nick's disappearance. Now, just when she was expecting him back from the interminable months of his Legion contract, he had written to tell her he wasn't coming.

This time he had written on cheap lined paper bearing the emblem of his regiment, the Tercio Sahariano Don Juan de Austria.

Dear Sarah, *she read for the umpteenth time,*
I've decided to spend the summer looking round the mainland. I haven't been able to save much of my pay, such as it is, but now that I speak pretty good Spanish it shouldn't be hard to earn a few *mil* when I need to. I want to have a look at Sevilla, Toledo etc. Hitch-hiking shouldn't be difficult. Most drivers aren't too keen on giving lifts to hippies etc – *Nick's letters were always peppered with et cetera* – but a clean-looking ex-*legionario* shouldn't have any problems. I reckon it will take at least a couple of months to see all the places on my list, so don't expect to see me before September, maybe later.

That was bad enough. The second paragraph was worse.

I've been thinking about doing a stint in the French Foreign Legion. There are people here who've been in it. They say the training is better, the equipment more up to date etc. Or I may re-join this lot. If I sign up again within six months, I can keep my present giddy rank of *cabo*.

I'll keep in touch by postcard. *Hasta luego*. Nick.

It was the shortest letter he had ever written to her; and, in a way, more upsetting than the one from Madrid announcing his enlistment. Because this letter showed the tenuousness of the bond between them. He had been glad to have someone to write to him but clearly he wasn't impatient to see her again.

The possibility that he might not return at all, but sign on in the French Legion or re-enlist in the Spanish Legion, filled her with anguish.

He had never been out of her thoughts for a single day. Now, for two months or longer, she couldn't even write to him. All she could hope for was an occasional postcard.

As she re-read the casual last line, fresh tears filled Sarah's eyes and overflowed down her cheeks. A tearing sob burst from her chest.

'Oh Nick, come back ... *please* come back ...' she whispered aloud.

Shortly before midnight Allegra's telephone rang.

'Hello?'

'I wanted to be sure you'd got back safely.'

'Did you think the driver might have abducted me?'

'Nothing is impossible when a woman is as lovely as you are.'

'If you were worried about it, why didn't you bring me home?'

'I'm not superhuman. It was hard enough to say good-night here. There ...' He left the possibilities to her imagination.

When she made no comment he said, 'By American time

224

it's still early. I shan't feel tired for some hours yet. Can we talk for a while?'

'I never go to bed before one or two. If you want to come over . . .'

'Are you sure?'

'I'm sure.'

'I'll be there in ten minutes.'

'I'll be waiting downstairs to let you in.'

As it turned out she wasn't in the hall when a taxi drew up outside Carlyon House.

She had been frantically busy putting clean sheets on the bed and preparing herself. When the bell rang she was only just ready, wrapped in a robe of pale grey crushed velvet and freshly scented with *Mystère*.

Barefoot, she raced down the carpeted staircase, her mules in her hand until at the bottom she paused to put them on.

Breathless, her heart beating fast, she opened the tall heavy door. Risconti entered.

The main light in the hall was a Regency chandelier of ormolu and crystal which had been wired for electricity when the house was converted. But Allegra had switched on only one crystal sconce. By its subdued light they searched each other's face for a moment.

Then Risconti stepped forward and took her gently in his arms. The first touch of his mouth on hers was tender, even tentative, as if he were still not quite certain of her response. She sensed that he felt, as she did, that for all their experience they were entering an unknown territory where everything would be different from other times with other people.

When she slipped her arms round his neck, he began to hold her more firmly, his natural assurance reasserting itself as their bodies moulded together and her lips softened and parted.

When their first kiss came to an end he surprised her by picking her up.

'Which way?'

The door to the back stairs was out of sight behind the wide graceful sweep of the main staircase.

'That way.'

As he paused for her to switch off the hall light, she murmured, 'It's a long way up to my flat and I'm not a featherweight.'

A big grin she had never seen spread over his face. 'Tonight I could carry you to the top of the Empire State Building.'

JULY

After breakfast, when Sarah had returned to the stables, Pen continued to read *The Times* until the butler came to clear the table.

'Mr Ashford, I'd like your advice on a project I have in mind,' she told him, folding the newspaper.

'Certainly, m'Lady.'

'We shall need the keys to the dairies. If you can find them, and it doesn't conflict with any arrangements you've already made for this morning, perhaps we could meet there at ten. You'd better wear your boiler suit. They're sure to be very dusty and cobwebby. As far as I know, they haven't been entered for years. Goodness knows what we shall find there.'

'Very good, m'Lady. Ten o'clock at the dairies.'

Pen wondered what he would think if he knew how much she was looking forward to spending some time alone with him. Would he be amazed and embarrassed?

Not once, since the morning of her birthday, had he given the smallest indication that he had any interest in her other than as his employer.

Shortly before ten o'clock, after an hour's work on the roses, she tidied her hair before walking round to the dairies.

Ashford was already there, waiting to unlock the door with one of several large keys attached to a metal loop. He wasn't wearing his boiler suit as she had suggested, but had on a pair of pale khaki cotton trousers and a blue cotton shirt which, in spite of its frayed collar, had the look of having come from a Jermyn Street shirtmaker rather than a chain store.

Perhaps it had been given to him by his previous employer, the general. But in that case would it have fitted his shoulders so perfectly? she wondered, studying his back as he started to try the keys.

If it hadn't been for the flecks of grey in his hair, he could, when seen from behind, have passed for a much younger man. Unlike most men in their fifties, he had no bulge of soft flesh above the brown leather belt slotted through the loops of his trousers.

When, having found the right key, he had to exert some strength to make the door swing on its rusty hinges, the taut cloth across his shoulders showed powerful muscles in play as he pushed it inwards.

'There are probably mice living in here, if not rats. Shall I go in first?' he suggested.

'Yes, do.'

The tales of Beatrix Potter being among her earliest memories, Pen felt kindly towards mice. She wondered what were the first books he had read, or had read to him. How could she be in love with a man about whom she knew so little?

Yet why not? What did details matter? She had known a great deal about Edward, but none of the important things. His bad temper had surfaced only after they were married.

If her butler had had a bad temper he wouldn't have shown it to her. But in fourteen months it would have been seen by the cook and the cleaners. No one could hide their true nature for as long as that, and Maisie Armitage, who had a sharp eye for other people's failings, had nothing but good to say about him. Indeed Pen had a suspicion that Mrs Armitage also had a soft spot for him.

He may like her better than he does me, she thought

with a pang. She's very plump, but men like a cosy armful. She's a wonderful cook and I've never done any cooking. Although they didn't have children, she and Fred Armitage always seemed very happy and loving with each other. She may have liked sex and miss it. Some women do. They're not all frigid as I was. But was that my fault or Edward's? How shall I ever know, unless . . . ?

The idea which came into her mind, of what it might be like if her butler made love to her, made her blush and bend her head in case he should look round and divine the nature of her thoughts.

They had entered a narrow hall which seemed out of keeping with the size and style of the rather grand entrance to the building. Like the main house, the dairies had been designed by Sir John Vanbrugh, the architect of Blenheim Palace, Castle Howard and several other historic English houses.

Ashford opened one of the inner doors and led the way into a room stacked with old-fashioned tea chests, heavy brown and beige stoneware jars and other obsolete containers.

'It smells musty but there seems no sign of damp,' he said, looking at the walls and ceiling.

'That's good because I'm wondering if I might live here – when my son is married,' Pen added. When he glanced at her, she went on, 'I know there's room for a self-contained flat in the house. Half a dozen flats, for that matter. But I think it might be nicer for my future daughter-in-law not to have me quite so close at hand.'

At first he said nothing. Then, smiling at her, he said, 'I think Lord Carlyon's bride is going to be exceptionally lucky in her mother-in-law . . . if I may so, m'Lady.'

It was such a delightful compliment that Pen's spirits soared. For a few moments he had forgotten their stations and spoken as a man to a woman – a woman he liked.

'Thank you, Mr Ashford. I certainly want to do my best to help her to settle down happily. She will be coming to live in another country, and in a house sadly lacking in all the comforts and conveniences which most Americans are used to.'

'She may feel that the beauty of Longwarden more than compensates for its deficiencies. Not many people live in such fine surroundings. I am conscious of that every day,' he said quietly.

As he spoke he had put his hands in his pockets, a posture which reinforced her feeling that he had again forgotten the barrier between them.

Anxious not to remind him, she said, 'It's a great mistake to ascribe one's own preferences to other people. That was brought home to me recently by an article by Doctor Germaine Greer, the feminist writer. I don't know whether you've heard of her?'

'I've read some of her views but none of her books,' he answered.

'Twenty years ago, when she was working on the thesis for her PhD, she lived in Calabria, one of the poorest parts of Italy. Something she learned there was that the village women, with their large families, weren't envious of her for being free and independent. They liked the way they lived and the prestige of being mothers. More recently she invited the housekeeper at her villa in Tuscany to use the house occasionally if her own house became overcrowded with children and grandchildren. The woman looked at her amazed. She didn't want to get away from her family. She didn't want peace and quiet.'

He nodded. 'And in old age she won't be left to live by herself, or put in a so-called "home". Not many people are lonely in societies we regard as backward. But a great many are in our culture.'

This gave her a cue to the question she had long wanted to ask him.

'Are you lonely here, Mr Ashford? I have sometimes wondered if you might be with no other men to talk to apart from Sammy – who only talks about horses.'

After a thoughtful pause he said, 'I think anyone who has been happily married and loses their partner must be lonely wherever they are. It takes a long time to get used to being single again. But it's eight years since my wife died and I've adjusted to it now. So the answer is – no, I'm not lonely. I should be sorry to leave Longwarden . . . although I realize Lord Carlyon may wish to reorganize the household after his marriage,' he added.

'Perhaps – but whatever happens I'm sure he won't want you to leave. Unless you prefer not to be in a house with small children about.'

'Not at all. I have none myself, but I don't dislike them. At least not when they're well-behaved,' he added, with the sudden smile which creased the lines round his eyes.

'I agree with that,' she said, smiling back. 'My children became rather trying in adolescence, but as little things they were never in the least objectionable. If ever they did behave badly, they were very soon brought to order by Nanny. Even I stood in awe of her. She was a real martinet, although wonderfully kind when they were ill or deserving of sympathy.'

'I've heard several stories about her from Mrs Armitage. She and your previous butler were not on the best of terms, I gather?'

'That's an understatement. It was open warfare between them. They both regarded themselves as the chief of staff, you see. One had to be frightfully careful not to say anything which one of them could use as ammunition against the other. I sometimes put my foot in it. I hadn't Flora Carlyon's gift for diplomacy.'

'Perhaps not then, when you were younger. Tact is an art we acquire with experience,' he answered. 'You are very much liked in the village, you know, Lady Carlyon.'

'Am I?' she said in surprise.

'I've often been told of your kindness to people in trouble. Even in a welfare state there's a need for someone to turn to when people can't cope on their own. The general feeling seems to be that, in the event of trouble, you are more likely to listen and give good advice than the vicar or either of the doctors.'

'Really? I didn't know that,' Pen said, astonished and gratified.

Often, while in the village, she had lent a patient ear to the problems of various inhabitants, letting them pour out their worries and trying to make helpful comments. When she heard of illness or misfortune, she did what she could, even if it were only to spend half an hour sitting by the hospital bedside of an elderly person with no one else to visit them. But this seemed to her no more than any reasonably caring person would do in the circumstances. She had never thought of herself as being a wise counsellor, or indeed of being wise at all.

'Most doctors, here and elsewhere, have so many patients nowadays they just don't have time to listen to people,' she said. 'I don't think I can be much help. The village has expanded so much in the last twenty years that at least half the people who live there now are strangers to me.'

'You may not know them, but most of them know who you are, and that you are kind and concerned,' he told her, with such a warm look that she felt her heart swell with pleasure.

But a moment later the mood of informal friendliness – of a conversation between equals – was lost when he said, much more briskly, 'Shall we look on the other side of the hall, or would you prefer to continue on this side, m'Lady?' – with a nod at the door leading to an adjoining room.

When they had seen all there was to see, and he was re-locking the main door, Pen said, 'I believe those two poky rooms and the hall between them were originally one large room which could quite easily be restored to its original size. What do you think?'

'The height of the ceilings seems to support that theory.' He came to where she was standing. Together they surveyed the façade. 'Those urns on the roof don't look too secure,' he remarked. 'I'll get Bob to make sure they're safe.' Bob was Longwarden's overworked handyman. 'If he can't find the time, I'll take a look at them myself.'

'Thank you. How lucky we are to have someone who doesn't insist on sticking to demarcation lines. Gisburn used to get very huffy if my son ever asked him to do anything outside his province.'

The glance he gave her was guarded. She had an uncomfortable feeling he might think it infra dig for her to have made a critical remark about his predecessor.

'I'm sure, when safety was involved, he would have stretched a point.' He glanced at his watch. 'Where would you like coffee served this morning, m'Lady?'

Feeling mildly reproved, if not snubbed, Pen remembered her plan for the day.

'I'll be hedge-clipping in the walk to Pallas Athene,' she said, referring to one of the many fine lead and stone statues which ornamented the garden. 'Would you bring it there, please.'

It was almost midday when Risconti showed signs of waking up.

Wrapped in a large bath towel, Allegra was sitting at the foot of the bed, leaning against one of the carved posts, when he began to stir. For some minutes she had been quietly eating yogurt, all she ever had for breakfast, while feasting her eyes on her sleeping lover, longing for him to wake up and repeat the caresses which, in the early hours of the morning, had transformed her ideas about making love.

Sex is not a three-letter word for love. A line from a book she had read while on tour in America had stuck in her mind.

It summed up the difference between past and present. With Risconti she had experienced a new dimension of pleasure because their feelings for each other had already stood the test of a two-year separation and went deeper, much deeper than any previous attraction.

He was lying on his side. When he opened his eyes and saw the empty space beside him, a slight frown contracted his eyebrows.

'Good morning. Did you sleep well?' Allegra asked softly.

He smiled. 'Good morning.' He rolled on to his back and stretched. 'I've never slept better. Why are you up so early?'

'It isn't early for me. It only feels early to you because you haven't adjusted to London time yet. What would you like for breakfast? I'm afraid there's not much of a choice.

Eggs or eggs or eggs. I wasn't expecting an overnight guest.'

'We'll go out to breakfast. If you haven't had them before, I'll introduce you to hot pastrami sandwiches at the Widow Applebaum's. But first I must take a shower.'

He flung back the clothes to swing himself off the bed. The hair on his body was still black. He was built like a gladiator. Seeing him stripped, it no longer surprised her that he had arrived at the top of her staircase last night without showing any sign of being relieved to set her down. Yet in spite of the swelling biceps and powerful chest and back muscles which showed as he sprang from the bed, there had been nothing brutal or clumsy in the way he had taken her. His touch, when he opened her robe and found her naked beneath it, had been as controlled and sure as his use of a paint brush.

He pressed his mouth to the bare silky curve of her shoulder.

'Do you think the Ritz may be worrying about you?' she asked. 'They must have discovered by now that your bed there hasn't been slept in.'

'They know I had dinner with a beautiful woman. Some time after she left, I left. The conclusion is obvious, don't you think?' He planted a row of kisses along the top of her shoulder and began to nuzzle her neck.

'I suppose so . . . and now it's gone twelve you'll have to pay for another night there,' said Allegra, whose thoughts, more often than not, were still those of someone who couldn't afford to waste money.

'It doesn't matter. I'll keep the suite until I've found an apartment.'

'You don't need an apartment, darling. You can share mine . . . unless you'd rather not.'

'I'd like that very much . . . but is there room for me here?'

She twisted round to embrace him. With her cheek pressed to his, she murmured, 'I'm tired of living alone. From now on I want to share my life. Perhaps this flat is too small. But let's try it for a while.'

Risconti was loosening the bath towel.

'There are many things I want to try with you, *bellissima*,' he told her huskily.

Pen returned to the house for lunch to find a letter from Massachusetts awaiting her.

She had been expecting a reply from Jane and had spent some time wondering what sort of letter the girl would write. Her future daughter-in-law had written on acceptable paper, in ink, in a well-formed hand.

Dear Lady Carlyon,
Thank you very much for your kind and welcoming letter. I will do my best to live up to your expectations but, like my great-grandmother when she first arrived in England, I will be in an unfamiliar environment and will have to rely on your patience and understanding to help me through my first year as North's wife.
The letter continued on a second sheet of paper and was signed Very sincerely – Jane.

It was a letter which encouraged her to hope the gap between their outlooks might not be too great. Nevertheless it seemed odd and slightly perturbing that she had politely but unequivocally turned down Pen's invitation to come to Longwarden before North's return.

Lying in Risconti's arms after they had made love again, Allegra murmured, 'You certainly know how to go about long-distance wooing. In my whole life I've never had as many wonderful presents as you've sent me in the past month, especially that final mad extravagance – the blackamoor. I couldn't understand how someone I didn't know could be so attuned to my tastes. The flowers . . . the books . . . everything was perfect for me. It's an amazing experience to be showered with presents by a stranger who seems to know one inside out.'

'You didn't guess who had sent them?'

'How could I? I didn't know what to think – except that whoever it was must be a remarkable man.' She paused.

234

'The poems were the master stroke, Andro. Did you choose those yourself?'

He nodded, a smile in his eyes. Very quietly, he said, 'She whom I love is hard to catch and conquer . . . but O the glory of the winning were she won!'

To hear it said in his deep, slightly accented voice moved her almost to tears.

She said, 'Last night you asked me if I could forgive you . . . forget the first time. That night changed my life. Rather than forgiving you, I should thank you. I'm not the same person I was then. The whore has become a nun. Can you believe that?'

He winced at the 'whore'.

'You were never that,' he said abruptly. 'I was a fool to listen to a malicious innuendo. Also you were the first woman who had ever refused me . . . and the first one I really wanted. All the others had been . . . diversions. Not affairs of the heart. It made me angry to think of other men making love to you. I wanted you to be mine and mine only.'

She wound her arms round his neck. 'I am . . . yours and only yours.'

Later, she showed him the parts of the flat he hadn't seen.

'This second bedroom and bathroom are occasionally used by my brother when he's passing through London,' she explained. 'But now that he's found a rich wife he can afford to stay at the Connaught or Brown's. It's a pity there isn't a room you could use as a studio.'

By the time they had strolled to the Widow Applebaum's Bagel and Deli Academy in South Molton Street, most of the people in the surrounding shops and offices had finished their lunch breaks and one of the tables outside the café was free.

'You say your brother has found a rich wife,' said Risconti, while they were eating a late brunch in the sun. 'Do you mean he has married for money, or are her riches incidental?'

'I'm afraid not. She happens to be a stunner as well as

an heiress, but I think it's her money which is the main attraction. I hope it works out, for both their sakes.' She explained when and where she had met Jane.

'Hm . . . a tricky situation . . . the woman holding the purse strings,' he said, with a shake of the head. 'I shouldn't like it.'

'That's one of the reactionary attitudes you told me you were trying to change. Why should it always be men who have the most money?'

He shrugged. 'Maybe it doesn't make sense but I know I wouldn't feel comfortable with you paying my bills.'

'Jane won't have to do that. North makes a reasonable living. It's just not enough to cover the enormous overheads at Longwarden. She won't be supporting him – only the house.'

'Well, as you say, maybe it will work out, but I'm glad it's not that way with us,' he said doggedly. 'I guess you've earned a lot of money from your book but I've done pretty well too. After painting the Princess of Wales, I can name my price in the States.' He drained his cup of coffee. 'Whether I can do that here, on a long-term basis, is uncertain. This is a very small country. Would you like some more coffee or shall we go round the corner and browse in the antiques market?'

'Yes, let's do that,' she said eagerly.

Today of all days she didn't want to concern herself with other people's problems or the implications of Risconti's remark about his prospects in England. She didn't want to think of anything but being together, being happy.

'You're mad,' Charles Helford said angrily. 'If it doesn't end in a divorce, it will bring you nothing but unhappiness. I've made some inquiries about him. He won't be faithful to you for five minutes, Jane. You can't marry someone like that. I won't let you.'

She didn't make the obvious retort. They were walking along a beach near the Blakewells' summer place. Soon it would be time to drive back to the cottage to join Marcus and Alison, down for the weekend, for lunch. Meantime she had resigned herself to bearing patiently with Charles's impassioned arguments against her marriage.

He wasn't the only one who thought she was out of her mind. Julia Foster had been so incensed when her niece broke the news to her that Jane feared she might have a seizure. Even Marcus and Alison had done their best to persuade her to postpone the wedding until she and North had spent more time together.

'Listen to me, will you?' Suddenly Charles lost his temper. Grabbing her by the shoulders, he swung her to face him. 'You loved me once. I've never stopped loving you. I let you go because . . . well, you know the reasons. Now you're older and I'm more successful, there's nothing to stand between us. I love you, Jane. We can be happy together. You'll never be happy with him. All you'll have is a title and a bloody great ruin of a house which will soak up money like a sponge. You'll have to spend millions on it.'

'I have millions, Charles,' she said evenly. 'And Longwarden isn't a ruin. It's been neglected, that's all.'

'How do you know what it's like?' he demanded, almost shouting at her. 'You haven't been there.'

He gave her an exasperated shake and the next instant pulled her close and began to kiss her.

At first she submitted, expecting him to stop when he felt her passive resistance and realized there was no spark left to rekindle. But Charles was not to be put off. Determined to make her respond, he kept his mouth glued to hers until, in sudden revulsion, she used all her strength to break free and backed away, wiping his unwelcome kiss from her lips.

'*Never* do that again, Charles,' she said in a low shaking voice. 'It's over between us. It's been over for years. I belong to North now. I've given him my promise – and my heart. He's the only man I want to kiss me from now on.'

He looked, for an instant, as if he would like to strangle her. Impotent rage and frustration darkened his haggard face.

'Then you're a fool,' he said furiously. 'He'll squander your father's money and make your life merry hell. For God's sake, Jane . . . come to your senses before it's too late.'

She looked at him without speaking, wishing he would go away. As she had already told him, for her the past was the past and he had no place in her future. She wanted him to accept that and leave her in peace.

He seemed to sense what she was thinking. His shoulders sagged in defeat.

'Perhaps your father could have made you see reason, but obviously no one else can.'

'No, they can't,' she agreed, and began to walk back to the car.

Charles followed, morose and silent. It wasn't until they were parked in the yard at the cottage that he spoke again.

'Just remember – when it goes wrong – that I'll still be waiting,' he told her. 'I'll always be waiting.'

Sarah was out on her black mare, Tartar Princess, the next time she saw Tark Osgood.

Tatty was a mare who, before and during her oestrous periods, could be very difficult to handle. That afternoon when, in Ice Lane, at the spot where Tark had roared past Bedouin Star, she caught sight of a strange machine propped on the grass and a man seated on the gate, it wouldn't have been surprising if Tatty had started suspiciously.

Instead she behaved impeccably, coming to a halt as if she were doing a dressage test. When Tartar Princess was in the mood, her manners matched her name.

'Hi,' said Tark.

'Good afternoon.'

Sarah's manner was formal because she didn't want to stop and talk to him.

When he walked over to them and produced several lumps of sugar, he made it impossible for them to move on without being rude. Although Tatty accepted his offering graciously, keeping her head turned towards him and inspecting him with both large dark eyes while she enjoyed the sugar, Sarah's blue gaze was less friendly. She didn't like the idea of Tark lying in wait for her, as obviously he had.

'This int the horse you was riding the last time, is it?' he asked, attempting to stroke the mare's nose.

This was something Tatty objected to. She threw up her head, making him take a hasty step back.

'Tatty, behave,' Sarah scolded. To him she said, 'I should have warned you. Some horses don't like being touched there. They prefer to be rubbed under the chin.' She leaned forward to demonstrate.

Seeing that he was embarrassed by his involuntary recoil, she went on in a more friendly tone, 'No, you're right, this isn't the same horse. The other was Bedouin Star and this is Tartar Princess.'

She patted the mare's sleek neck, trying to put Tark at ease. Instinct told her that, being the macho type, he would feel humiliated at having shown nervousness in front of her, although his reaction had been normal for someone unaccustomed to horses.

She was not to know that the caressing gesture had, in his own vernacular, turned him on. She glanced at her watch. 'We'd better be moving. Thanks for the sugar. Goodbye.'

Obeying the pressure of Sarah's seat and legs, the black mare stepped briskly forward, leaving Tark by the side of the lane, his eyes on the shapely lines of buttock and thigh revealed by the girl's tight breeches.

He was annoyed with her for cutting the conversation short. He had hoped she would tie up the horse and sit on the gate where he had been waiting for her for over an hour.

Her voice, her manner, everything about her was novel to him, and challenging. He wondered what he could do to change her indifference to interest. Or was she only pretending not to be interested? He wasn't sure.

But one thing he did know for certain; one day he would have her where he wanted her, not sitting on the back of a horse but lying on the grass with her arms round his neck while he pulled off those clinging white breeches.

Allegra opened her eyes and found Risconti leaning over her with such an anxious expression that she said at once, 'What's the matter?'

Even before she asked the look of alarm had given place to relief.

'For a moment I thought . . . no, lie still. I think you should rest for a while. I wish you'd warned me. I knew it happened to some women, but I didn't know you were one of them. You scared me.'

Baffled, she said, 'What are you talking about?'

Now he looked puzzled. 'You don't know what just happened? You don't feel at all . . . strange?'

'Strange? No, not a bit. You're the one who's acting strangely. What should I have warned you? That I snore? I didn't realize I did.'

'You blacked out . . . fainted,' he told her. 'You gave a tremendous shudder and then I felt you go limp and realized you were unconscious. What the French call *le petit mort*. For a few seconds I thought you were really dead. *Dio!* What a fright you gave me.'

'*Le petit mort?*' she said blankly. 'Andro, you must have dreamt it. You've been asleep . . . we both have.'

He shook his head. 'It's true, I assure you. You were out cold. Not sleeping. Unconscious.'

'I can't believe it,' she said. 'Did I really pass out? How extraordinary. It must be the way you make love.'

She traced his mouth with her fingertip. Already, only a few hours since he had shaved with one of her disposable razors, his strong dark beard had begun to shadow and roughen the surrounding skin. The rasp of his hard stubbled cheeks between the soft smoothness of her thighs was one of the things she remembered from a confusion of pleasures. No one had ever made love to her as fully and generously; with words as well as actions. Going to bed with Alessandro Risconti made every previous experience seem an inferior imitation of this, the real thing, the nonpareil.

'It was the first time? It never happened before?' he asked.

'Never . . . only with you.'

Presently he insisted she must sleep while he telephoned the Ritz to arrange for his belongings to be packed and sent round by taxi. When he had drawn the curtains and closed the door quietly behind him, Allegra gave a deep sigh and lay, wrapped in contentment, reliving the hours since his arrival.

Waking an hour later she found the curtains open to the westering sun and Risconti seated by the bed, completing a sketch of her face and one up-flung arm. Having no drawing things with him, he had sent a taxi to procure the materials he wanted, sticks of sanguine and grey Ingres paper, from the nearest artists' supplier.

'How extravagant . . . sending taxis here, there and everywhere,' she said.

'I didn't want to leave you.'

I hope you never will, she thought. But she didn't say it. Sweeping off the covers, she stretched her long legs. 'Would you like to draw the rest of me?'

'If you'll be warm enough.' But it wasn't with an artist's detachment that he was surveying her bare flesh.

'Perfectly. How shall I pose?' She raised herself on one elbow. 'Perhaps you'd better arrange me as you want me.' Her eyes teased and beckoned.

As she came to the end of another long day's work in the garden, Pen was still thinking over her conversation with Ashford at the dairies that morning.

The way he had spoken of his wife made it clear he had loved her deeply – and suffered deeply after her premature death.

I wonder what she was like? thought Pen when, her labours over, she was lying in the bath, up to her neck in warm water.

Because Ashford was still good-looking and must have been even more so when he was younger, she visualized his wife as having been a very pretty woman. The conviction that he had been married to someone lovely and charming made her feel she must be mistaken in thinking she might attract him.

Yet there were moments when he seemed to look at her so warmly, and had said such nice things. *You are very much liked in the village . . . most of them know who you are, and that you are kind and concerned.*

When she stood up to dry herself she could see her reflection in the mirror. Protected by clothing from the elements which had weathered her face, the skin on her body was still smooth and youthful. From the neck down she hadn't changed much except that she now had a little more bosom than she'd had at nineteen.

When she had dressed, Pen rummaged in the drawers of her dressing table. She was hunting for one of the lipsticks she rarely remembered to use unless she was going out to dinner or to a wedding.

She found one called Crystal Coral by Elizabeth Arden and rubbed it lightly on her lips, nervous of making too obvious an attempt to improve herself. Her motive worried her. There could be no harm in caring for someone unknown to them. But to try to evoke a response by making oneself more attractive might be wrong – *must* be wrong – when there could be no future in it.

It was all very well for Allegra to express approval of Lady Ingoldisthorpe's liaison with her groom, but Pen knew that Allegra and North would take a very different attitude if their own prim and proper mother were to kick over the traces.

What she had forgotten was that it was the butler's night off. Dinner was served by Mrs Armitage. Neither she nor Sarah seemed to notice the discreet touch of lipstick.

That night Pen made up her mind that she must be stern with herself. If she thought about it sensibly, nothing he had said or done gave grounds for believing he had any special interest in her. From now on she must be more disciplined and not let her mind harbour daydreams with no hope of realization.

All next day she made a strong effort not to think about

him and, when she saw him at meals, not to look at him more than was necessary. When he brought her coffee at eleven, and tea at four, she said, 'Thank you, Mr Ashford', and didn't stop working until he had gone away.

After dinner she went upstairs to her private sitting room to continue writing to distant relations to tell them of North's engagement.

She had finished one letter and was beginning another when there was a knock at the door.

'Come in.' She turned in her chair.

Ashford paused on the threshold. 'I'm sorry to have disturbed you, m'Lady. I can see you're busy at the moment. What I came to tell you will keep till tomorrow.' He started to leave.

'No, wait – don't go. I'm only writing a letter . . . nothing important.'

She could see he was carrying a portfolio. 'What have you got there?'

For a moment longer he hesitated. Then, to her secret joy, he came into the room, closing the door behind him.

There was a table in the centre of Pen's sitting room which had only a bowl of roses on it. Ashford moved the bowl to one side to make room for the large portfolio.

Untying the tapes, he said, 'I thought you might like to see these plans of the dairies. They show you were right in thinking the main block was one large room.' He spread out a number of sheets of architectural drawings. 'These are the elevations and this is the ground plan.'

Pen bent over the drawings. 'How fascinating. Where did you come across them?'

'If you remember, at the beginning of last winter I asked your permission to spend some time in the library when it wasn't in use. In fact I spent most of my afternoon off-duty hours there. I've always been careful to replace everything as I found it and to handle things carefully.'

She glanced up at him. 'I'm quite sure you are the last person to do any damage, Mr Ashford. We used to have an archivist, you know. But he died and my husband felt it was an unnecessary expense to replace him. Old Mr

Bramber had been a professional librarian. He worked here for fifteen years after retiring to the village. I remember he was most shocked to find the books here had never been "shelfmarked". Now they're all numbered in pencil, on the first fly-leaf, to show where they belong.'

'I've noticed that, and discovered the catalogue. Without it I shouldn't have been able to lay my hands on these plans. Look' – he drew her attention to another drawing – 'this is captioned *The Menageries*. If they were, in fact, ever built, they must have been where the dairies are now.'

'I've never heard any mention of wild animals being kept here.'

'I believe, at the time this was drawn, a menagerie wasn't a small zoo. It seems to have been a place where people went to eat and drink dairy products.' He smiled at her. 'My historical knowledge has improved a great deal since I've been here. Living in a house with a long past, one can't help becoming interested.'

Pen could feel, as her eyes met his, her willpower slipping away.

Surprising herself, she said, 'I was just going to have a nightcap . . . a little whisky. Will you join me?'

It was hard to read his expression, but she thought she detected surprise and a flicker of uncertainty in the dark gaze bent upon her.

In the pause before he replied, she held her breath. Was he going to refuse, making her feel a fool?

He gave a slight bow. 'Thank you.'

Masking her relief, she gestured towards the two arm-chairs flanking the open window.

'Do sit down.'

Although small by comparison with the other rooms, the sitting room was considerably larger than those in most modern houses, with a view of the garden and, in summer, the added pleasure of the scent of Léontine Gervais, a yellow rose climbing up the wall by the window. After dark, when the weather was hot, she could sit there enjoying the fragrance of night-scented stocks planted close to the house for that purpose.

'How do you like your whisky, Mr Ashford? I can't offer you ice; only soda or ordinary water.'

'Soda for me, please.'

He remained on his feet while she busied herself at the side table bearing the drinks tray. Less well-stocked than the one in the library, it held only a bottle of sherry and one of whisky. Pen was not much of a drinker.

Did it make him uncomfortable to stand by while she waited on him? she wondered. But a sidelong glance showed him to be looking at one of her favourite paintings, a watercolour of an old boat-house on a lake surrounded by rhododendrons in bloom.

'That's by Theresa Sylvester Stannard,' she told him. 'She specialized in paintings of gardens. It was given to me by my husband's grandmother so I shall take it with me if I move to the dairies. Most of the other pictures in here belong to the house.' She handed him his glass. 'There would be no problem furnishing the dairies. The attics are stuffed with unwanted tables and chairs.'

She sat down and sipped her drink, hoping she looked and sounded more composed than she felt. It was absurd for a woman of her age to feel rather wicked at entertaining a man at a not very late hour of night in an upstairs sitting room, yet she did. She couldn't help it. And she felt sure if people knew, eyebrows *would* be raised.

But I don't care. I don't give a damn what anyone thinks – as long as he doesn't think less of me, Pen told herself, searching his face for some sign of what he might be thinking.

'Some of them possibly finer than pieces in use on these floors,' was Ashford's response to her reference to the crowded attics. 'I'm not expert on furniture, but I've noticed several handsome things when I've been in the attics.'

He seemed completely relaxed; sitting well back in the chair, his legs crossed, his drink on the table at his elbow, his whole posture indicative of a man at ease.

She had noticed before how quickly and deeply he had tanned since the beginning of the hot spell.

She said, 'Judging by your colour, you aren't spending your free time in the library at present.'

'No, since the fine weather started I've been going up to the roof to enjoy the sun for an hour or so every day. The roof offers greater privacy than the garden. I like to expose as much of myself as possible and I feel it might undermine my professional dignity to be seen lying about in bathing trunks by the cleaning team,' he said, with the grin which dispelled the somewhat austere cast of his features in repose.

She laughed. 'It would certainly have undermined Gisburn's dignity. I imagine he would have looked like the great white whale. He became very stout in the years before he retired. You look very fit, Mr Ashford.'

'I try to resist Mrs Armitage's efforts to over-feed me, and not to indulge in too much of this,' he said, picking up his glass. 'You mentioned that you had no ice, Lady Carlyon. If you'd like to have ice on hand in the evening, I can easily remedy the deficiency.'

'Oh, no, thank you – I don't like my drinks on the rocks,' said Pen. 'I expect my new daughter-in-law will. Americans regard ice as one of the basic necessities, don't they?'

'I believe so.'

'Where are your roots, Mr Ashford? Where were you born?'

'I don't really have any roots. I was born in the Middle East where my father was working at the time. My mother died when I was five and I was sent back to England and shuttled about among relations.'

'Oh dear, how miserable for you.'

'I don't think it bothered me, and it was quite a good preparation for the postings of life in the service. When my wife was alive, we intended to put down some roots when I left the army. After she died, the plans we had made were no longer practicable. When I had finished my service I looked for something to occupy me in civilian life.' A glint of amusement replaced the sombre expression with which he had spoken of his wife. 'I didn't expect to change to domestic service but I find it suits me very well – at least

246

in this household. I'm not sure I'd pass muster with more exacting employers.'

'I don't know why not,' said Pen. 'You are quite as efficient as Gisburn who had been a butler for years, and a footman before that. It wasn't his own choice, of course. It was arranged for him by his parents as was usual at the time he left school.' Letting fall her usual reserve, she added, 'Most people of my age also had their lives more or less ordained for them. I often wish I'd been born a generation later. I should either have become a garden designer or had a small nursery specializing in all the lovely old roses which have been superseded by modern monstrosities with no scent and fluorescent colours. It makes one weep to see them in so many gardens. If only more people realized –'

She broke off and gave an apologetic laugh. 'I'm afraid that's a subject on which I become very boring to people who don't share my passion.'

'Not boring to me,' he assured her. He looked at the bowl of pale full-blown damask roses on the table beside Pen's chair. 'I can see that those roses, for instance, are far more attractive in form and colour than the gaudy variety grown in most public parks.'

'Yes, but those have the advantage of flowering for longer periods. Although as Lucy Boston, who used to own Hemingford Grey, once said, non-stop flowering can be as boring as non-stop talking.'

He laughed. 'Is Hemingford Grey near here?'

'Unfortunately not. It's a medieval manor on the banks of the Ouse in Huntingdonshire. The Norman solar is supposed to be the oldest lived-in part of a house in the whole of England. Mrs Boston was an expert on roses – my kind of roses. She also wrote books for children. A delightful person, by the sound of her. I wish I could have met her. Are there people like that in your life? – Whom you wish you could meet in person?'

He thought for a moment. 'There are several historical figures. The Iron Duke has always been rather a hero of mine, and also one of his generals, Lord Napier, who had

247

to have an arm amputated after the siege of Badajoz and carried on the next day as if it had been a mere flesh wound. Incredible stamina! I'd like to meet him in the next world – if there is one,' he added.

She wondered, not for the first time, if he could have been an officer himself.

If he had held a commission, what was he doing as a butler? He had spoken of finishing his service which must mean he received a pension. Surely an officer's pension would allow him to live in comfort without being reduced to taking orders after a lifetime of giving them?

On the other hand, the fact that his voice and manner seemed those of a well-bred person wasn't necessarily significant. Gisburn, so they had heard, had more than once been mistaken for Edward by newcomers to the village. It could be that Ashford's polish had been acquired the same way: by long association with senior officers. Yet his cultured accent sounded natural.

'Your general – the one you worked for before coming here – was he an interesting man?' she asked.

'He had been, when he was younger. For the last two years of his life he was partially paralysed by a stroke. The worst thing was losing the power to speak coherently. He could understand what was said to him, but his answers were usually too slurred to be comprehensible. It was an undeservedly miserable end for a fine man.'

Pen nodded. 'I was thankful my husband was killed outright rather than being left a cripple as he could have been after taking a bad fall. There can't be anything more dreadful for a person with no intellectual resources than to be deprived of their physical pleasures. Without hunting and racing, his life would have been an endless desert of boredom.'

He said, 'I imagine Miss Sarah owes a good deal of her present success to the late Lord Carlyon's encouragement when she was small.'

'Yes, in a way, and he would have been enormously pleased that she's doing so well. But according to Sammy my niece inherits her hands and seat from her father who was a much better horseman than her uncle. You don't ride, I believe?'

He shook his head.

'I thought not. I did learn to ride as a girl but I was always nervous, which makes a horse nervous as well, so I was glad to give it up. If you ask Sammy, who saw me ride, he'll tell you how hopeless I was. A sack of potatoes in the saddle. Actually my brother-in-law used to say the same of my husband.'

'But surely a Master of Fox Hounds –?'

'Must ride well? Not necessarily. I believe there are quite a lot of people who have hunted since they were children, and who don't know the meaning of fear, who are actually rather bad riders. Sammy was a wonderful horseman when he was younger. He's getting old, I'm afraid. I suspect the eventing season is far too much for him, but he won't admit it. He knows Sarah would be lost without him.'

For half an hour, perhaps longer, their talk ranged at random over a variety of topics. Pen drank her whisky in small sips, making it last as long as possible.

She had given him a larger measure. When his glass was empty, she said, 'Will you have another?'

'Thank you, but – no. I've delayed you too long already. You have your letter to finish and I have to check that everywhere is secure.' He rose to his feet. 'Goodnight, Lady Carlyon.'

'Goodnight, Mr Ashford.'

His empty glass in his hand, he bowed and walked out of the room, noiselessly closing the door.

Pen remained where she was, absently swirling the last half-inch of her drink and thinking how pleasant it was to sit quietly chatting with someone of her own age whose views seemed to coincide with her own.

If only they could spend every evening together, she thought longingly. Not always talking. Sometimes reading, or perhaps listening to music in companionable silence. Did he like music? There were still so many, many things she wanted to find out about him.

* * *

Although doubtful that all her letters would reach him, Jane had written to North every week since his departure.

Her first communication from him was a postcard from Delhi where he had been spending a night before flying on the next morning. Two weeks later came a letter written in flight to Srinagar.

I'm told Ladakh used to be called Kha-Chum-Pa, Land of the Snow, *he had written*. The present name means Land of the High Mountain Passes. I was planning to fly to Leh, the capital, but on the advice of a man I met in Delhi have changed my mind and shall do the last lap by bus. It's a two-day trip and pretty hair-raising by the sound of it. There are drops of as much as three thousand feet along parts of the road and the drivers have been known to fortify themselves with gin. (Some of the passengers fortify themselves with opium!) But I don't suffer from vertigo and the views are said to be incomparable.

Jane felt sure it hadn't been his intention to worry her. Clearly the thought that one day a bus might topple off the precipitous road up the Kashmir valley didn't bother him; and at one time she wouldn't have thought of that dire possibility. However, her father's fatal car accident had destroyed for ever her belief that disasters happened to other people. The thought of North entrusting his safety to a gin-happy Kashmiri driver caused her considerable anxiety.

She comforted herself with the thought that if there had been an accident and North had not reached Ladakh, it would surely have been reported that a busload of people, including a well-known British photographer, had crashed to their deaths.

Or would it? People on ramshackle buses weren't 'processed' like travellers by air. How would anyone know who had been on the bus until a search party was sent to recover the remains, and that could take days or weeks. Even if the bodies were found, identification could be difficult.

250

Gruesome thoughts of this nature troubled her days and nights as she waited for a second letter to allay her unease.

Sarah was longing for a postcard from Nick, but the summer was a busy time in the calendar of eventing and a succession of horse trials in different parts of the country left her little time to brood.

In an era when the craft of farriery was in dangerous decline, she was singularly lucky to have the services of an expert blacksmith who, with his wife, had also become a close friend.

Rob and Emily Wareham belonged to the late-twentieth-century species of young men and women who refused to conform to the patterns of their parents and grandparents if they found them uncongenial.

Rob, the son of a QC, had been educated at Stowe and encouraged to look for his career among the professions. An intelligent boy but one who liked using his hands better than taxing his brains, he had discovered that although hunting was still going strong in spite of the outcries of the opponents of field sports, and riding as a pastime had spread through all classes of society, blacksmiths were a diminishing band of craftsmen.

In his last year at school he decided – and his parents failed to dissuade him – that the work of a blacksmith satisfied his criteria for a rewarding life.

He would be performing an ancient, satisfying skill. He would be a useful member of society. And although he would never be rich, he would make a steady living for himself and his dependants.

A snag had been pointed out by his mother.

'It won't be easy to find a girl who wants to be a blacksmith's wife, Rob. Most girls want a career of their own, darling, and there aren't very many which would mesh conveniently with farriery.'

'Oh, I wouldn't say that, Ma. There are lots of girls in the horse world. Almost all the showjumping and eventing grooms are girls.'

Mrs Wareham, not horsey herself, was not eager to have

a horsey daughter-in-law. However too many of her friends had children who were a grave worry to them for her to be seriously upset by her son's unconventional choice of career. Nevertheless she did hope that when it came to marriage he would not pick a girl with whom it would be a tremendous effort for her to be friendly.

The young were so idealistic. They thought background didn't matter and pooh-poohed their parents' standards as snobbish and old-hat. In Mrs Wareham's opinion a mésalliance was still a mésalliance. Marriage was difficult enough without the extra adjustments which had to be made by people from different *milieux*.

To her subsequent relief, the girl her son chose to marry was the youngest of the three daughters of a surgeon and his gynaecologist wife. The two elder girls were careerists. One had followed her parents into medicine. The other was in academic publishing. But Emily's ambition was to have a cottage in the country, with an electric kiln, where she could combine throwing pots with organic vegetable gardening and bringing up babies.

She and Rob seemed ideally matched, although his mother did wonder if a vegetarian diet would be sustaining enough for a husband whose work involved wielding a nine-pound sledge hammer. However Rob said cheerfully that his bride-to-be had no objection to his grilling a steak for himself when the nut cutlets palled; and in fact Emily's nourishing bean soups, her home-made bread and yogurt, and the home-grown steamed vegetables which were the mainstay of their diet kept them both in flourishing health.

The young Warehams had come to Longwarden village soon after Nick's disappearance. By then Rob had five years' experience and he quickly established himself as a better smith than the old man whose forge he took over.

Instead of buying ready-made shoes, he turned his own from new iron, or occasionally followed the practice of regimental blacksmiths by hammering one and a half old shoes into one new one.

Because of his background, many of his customers in the hunting fraternity invited him and his wife to dinner. On these occasions Rob ate what everyone else was having and Emily resigned herself to be given, almost without exception, grapefruit or avocado followed by a cheese omelette.

When Rob first came to the village, Sammy and Sarah kept a close watch on his work to be sure he knew what he was doing. Soon reassured that there was no danger of his damaging her horses' feet, which could happen from over-lowering or too much rasping, Sarah would often leave the forge and spend some time in the cottage, chatting to Emily and admiring their baby son, Matthew.

Emily was one of the few people to whom Sarah talked about Nick, although not to the extent of confiding how she felt about him.

With more taste than money, Emily had transformed the cottage into a charming and comfortable home. On the roof a wild-goose weather-vane, wrought by Rob, showed which way the wind was blowing. Drinking coffee from a hand-thrown mug in the Laura-Ashley-papered parlour, or in the green shade of the vine when the weather was hot, Sarah had often dreamed of sharing a similar cottage with Nick.

In her mind she planned for him to take Sammy's place and let the old groom retire, or at least work less hard than at present. If that didn't appeal to Nick, and she had little hope that it would, perhaps there was some kind of craft training he could take.

Everything hinged on whether he fell in love with her.

'You look worried, Sarah. Trouble with the horses?' asked Emily, one morning when they were having elevenses together.

'No, they're all fine . . . at the moment . . . touch wood.' Sarah gave a small sigh. 'It's the usual thing . . . lack of money. Sammy works for his board and lodging and his glass of Guinness. I have a tiny income from the money my father left me plus an allowance from North and Allegra. But they barely cover expenses. Any day now they won't.'

Emily nodded sympathetically. 'It's a pity the prize money for eventing isn't better. That would be a help. What about a sponsor? Most of the top riders seem to have one. Virginia Holgate . . . the Greens . . . Mark Phillips.'

Sarah nodded. 'But as soon as one is sponsored, everything changes. The whole operation has to become much more businesslike. More horses, more helpers, more appearances. I would much rather not be under that kind of pressure if I can possibly avoid it.'

Especially with Nick coming back, was her unspoken thought.

'Even if I wanted a sponsor, I might not be able to find one,' she went on. 'There are so many riders looking for a sponsor.'

'But not many riders who've been as successful as you have,' Emily pointed out. 'You're in a class of your own, Sarah.'

'Beddo is in a class of his own,' the younger girl corrected her. 'As long as I'm on his back, I can't go wrong. He's a brilliant horse who has got me out of trouble far more often than I've helped him.'

'So you've said before, but I think you underestimate yourself. Sammy told Rob you're one of the very rare riders who can get the best out of any horse.'

'You shouldn't take Sammy too seriously. He's hopelessly partisan,' Sarah said with a grin. Her expression changed. 'I'm worried about him, Emily. He hasn't been feeling well lately but I can't persuade him to go to the doctor or to take life more easily.'

Emily said, 'It does seem unfair that showjumpers can make a comfortable living, if they do well, while most eventers are always hard-pressed for money. Have you ever thought of changing streams?'

Sarah shook her head. 'Showjumping has never appealed to me as much as eventing. There's a more cut-throat kind of competitive spirit in showjumping – probably because of the better prize money. In eventing we're pitting ourselves against the course more than against each other. I prefer that friendlier feeling.'

'What makes you think Sammy isn't well?'

'He's doing his best to hide it but he looks tired and he's much more subdued than he used to be. I think he's worried about his health but afraid to go for an overhaul. Do you think Rob might be able to influence him?'

'I shouldn't think so, if you can't. But I'll tell him what you've told me and see what he suggests. Oh, my God! That wretched –'

The rest of her exclamation was lost in a blast of sound from outside.

When she could make herself heard again, Emily said crossly, 'That frightful noise is perpetrated by a youth who's new to the village and seems to have nothing to do but batter our eardrums. He's become the idol of the other boys but is heartily disliked by the rest of us.'

'Tark Osgood. I've met him,' said Sarah.

She told Emily about her encounters with him.

'What incredible cheek: to roar up to Longwarden on that infernal machine and ask you to go out with him. What did Sammy have to say about that?'

'Nothing. He wasn't around at the time. Mr Ashford looked rather disapproving.'

'I can imagine he might. Sarah, is there anything about him – Mr Ashford I mean – that strikes you as odd? Not having known many butlers, I'm not a judge.'

'I haven't either,' said Sarah. 'What seems odd about him to you?'

'His taste in books is unexpected. We were in the library at the same time the other day and two books he'd requested were waiting for him. I happened to notice the titles. One was *Soviet Land Power in the 1980s* and the other was *Military Strategy in Transition*. There's no reason why a butler shouldn't be interested in military strategy, I suppose, but I'd have been less surprised if he'd taken out a couple of thrillers. Do you know where he worked before he came to Longwarden?'

'If I did, I've forgotten,' said Sarah. 'After Gisburn retired, Aunt Pen didn't want to replace him. But North insisted we must have a man in the house when he was away. He engaged Mr Ashford and I like him much better than Gisburn. Mr Ashford is much more flexible, but he's also extremely reserved. Unnaturally so, according to Mrs Armitage. She can never get him to tell her anything about himself.'

'It's rather unusual for someone never to mention any personal details,' Emily said. 'Most people pour out far more than one wants to hear – the most amazing revelations that I'd only confide to my nearest and dearest.'

'Rather as I've just been doing,' Sarah said ruefully. 'Not "telling all" exactly, but confiding my worries about Sammy and money. You have a sympathetic face, Emily.'

Her friend laughed and rose to investigate sounds from the Moses basket where her infant son had been napping.

Watching her as she bent lovingly over him, Sarah wondered briefly if her own mother had ever regretted leaving her, and if they would meet again some day. Such thoughts were rare and didn't stay in her mind long.

When a short time later she drove the horse-box back to Longwarden, the sight of Ted Rivington's cottage turned her thoughts to Nick.

Where was he now?

Sightseeing in Granada? Lying on a beach on the Costa del Sol, chatting up a pretty tourist? Riding through the sierras like Penelope Chetwode in *Two Middle-aged Ladies in Andalusia*? Exploring the backwoods of Spain on horseback, staying at small *posadas* or sharing a sleeping bag in the open was Sarah's idea of a perfect honeymoon.

Please, *please* let there be a card from him today was her prayer as she drove into the yard.

Black and white cows grazed on the lush summer grass of the pastures beyond the smoothly mown lawns where men in dinner jackets unpacked Fortnum & Mason hampers and opened coolers containing green foil-topped bottles.

Diamond brooches and earrings glittered in the last rays of the sun. Women in chiffon and silk from Bellville Sassoon and Hardy Amies and girls in ankle-length Laura Ashley cottons strolled in the garden before dining indoors or settled themselves on camp stools to dine in the open air.

It was the beginning of the seventy-five-minute interval at Glyndebourne; and the eight hundred fortunate people who had managed to obtain tickets for a revival of *Le Nozze di Figaro* at the world-famous opera house in the grounds of a Tudor manor in an unspoilt corner of Sussex were having their pleasure in the music enhanced by a perfect summer evening.

'Shall I confess something to you?' Risconti asked as they unpacked the picnic basket he had placed between them on the rug. 'I'm a little ashamed to admit it but this is my first opera.'

'That's wonderful, Ándro,' Allegro exclaimed, looking up in surprise and delight. 'I wanted to give you an unforgettable experience, but I felt sure you must have seen *Figaro* at least once and possibly several times. The seats we have tonight were miraculous luck. I really had almost no hope of getting us in at short notice. Glyndebourne is always booked out . . . and you can see why. It's not only the glorious setting but the operas are always superbly costumed and most of the soloists become international stars. As a matter of fact I've only been here twice . . . the first time rather unwillingly.'

'Why unwillingly?' he asked, as they began their supper with cold lobster and artichoke hearts filled with lemon mayonnaise.

'I thought it would bore me . . . like Shakespeare and string quartets. To my surprise I liked it. The second time I came on the train which perhaps is what we should have done. It's part of the Glyndebourne experience to arrive at Victoria Station in evening dress in the middle of the afternoon.'

They had come in her silver Mini, driving along country lanes and through picturesque Downland villages to park the car in a field among the Rolls-Royces and Jaguars of other opera-goers. Risconti hadn't known where he was coming.

'Why is it here, in the country, this opera house?' he asked.

Allegra sipped her champagne. 'It was the brainchild of the man who owned the house in the thirties. He was very rich, rather eccentric and mad about Wagner. In 1931, when he was forty-three and still a bachelor, a young soprano from Canada came here to sing for his guests in the Organ Room which is where people have to wait if they arrive late for the first act. John Christie fell in love with her. Soon after they married he decided to build a small theatre on what was then the kitchen garden. She persuaded him to make it an opera house, much smaller than it is now. Only three hundred seats. They enlarged it later.'

They had just closed and fastened the basket when the bell rang, summoning them back to the auditorium.

During Susanna's final aria, one of the most beautiful and moving outpourings of love in all opera, Risconti reached for Allegra's hand. They exchanged a glance. She knew he felt, as she did, that the music expressed their own feelings.

Since his first night at Carlyon House they had been immeasurably happy, savouring each day from the time they woke up together to the last tender kiss before they murmured goodnight and slept in each other's arms.

No thought of the future had intruded on the perfection of *now*. Like all new lovers, they had lived 'the world forgetting, by the world forgot'. It had been their honeymoon, their time of grace between their separate pasts and inseparable future.

In the sense that it was real while it lasted, it was not a fool's paradise. But although to a large extent Risconti was his own master and Allegra had become a person whose working life was ordered by self-imposed disciplines, both had commitments which couldn't be ignored for ever.

As she drove back to London by the motorway she was still unaware that, while she had been in heaven, the great dilemma confronting the women of sophisticated cultures in the closing quarter of the twentieth century had been lying in wait for her to re-enter the everyday world.

She had only a few hours left before the most intractable problem of her life would start to tear her apart.

AUGUST

In Pen's mind July and August were the lily months. There had been lilies at Longwarden when she came to the house, notably *Lilium regale*, the flower introduced to Europe by 'Chinese' Wilson, a contemporary of Caspar Carlyon for whom he had signed a copy of his finest book, *Lilies of Eastern Asia*.

One of Pen's favourite lilies bloomed in August and September; *Lilium henryi*, discovered by Augustine Henry in central China almost a century ago. The recurved apricot flowers with their red spots had to be planted in shade to preserve the delicacy of their colour. It was to their reappearance that she looked forward as the new month began, and also to the waterlilies and sweet peas. The latter she grew in abundance to cut for the house where, lavishly bunched in white cachepots, they looked like crowds of pastel butterflies and added their elusive sweetness to the scents of the lilies in pots which filled the rooms in high summer.

Pen sometimes wondered how people who were not gardeners managed to get through their lives without having flowers to look forward to. She knew she would be lost if ever she had to give up gardening. Condemned to live in a city, without even a windowbox, she would be like a lily with its bulb dried out and its roots trimmed. She wouldn't survive.

At the same time she was aware that her well-being was no longer dependent only on being able to garden. Nor was contentment the highest state she aspired to. Happiness, once as remote as another planet, was now an imaginable condition.

The worst thing, now, which could happen to her was not to find the lilies blighted by botrytis, or to see signs of the dreaded honey fungus. The worst thing would be for Ashford to give notice. Without his presence in her life there would be an emptiness, a sense of something missing. She would not go to bed looking forward to seeing him at breakfast, or begin her day's work with the pleasant expectation of at least four more encounters during the day.

'This is from my New York dealer,' said Risconti when he had finished reading that morning's post. 'Good news and bad news. The good is that he's lined up an interesting commission for me. The Metropolitan Museum wants a portrait of Diana Vreeland. Have you heard of her?'

'Silly question, darling. Everyone interested in clothes has heard of her. She was on *Harper's Bazaar* and then editor of American *Vogue* for years. Since then she's organized marvellous exhibitions for the costume section of the Metropolitan. If I'd had the money, I'd have flown over to see them. She's a woman I've always longed to meet.'

'Now's your chance. You can keep her amused while I paint her. The snag is it has to be soon. She's in her eighties and although she will probably live for years yet, one can't bank on it. Sigmund wants me to get back immediately. I was hoping to have the summer free, but he sees it as a very important commission and he's probably right. He says here . . . where is it? . . . oh, yes . . . *Truman Capote described her as "some extraordinary parrot – a wild thing that's flung itself out of the jungle and talks in some amazing language".'*

Allegra jumped up from the breakfast table and rushed to her bookshelves.

'I have her memoirs here somewhere. They were published a couple of years ago. You must read them. They're riveting. She's had an amazing life. She really has had it all.'

Seizing a book wrapped in a scarlet jacket, she brought it to him.

'Look, here's a photograph of her I clipped from *The Tatler*. It was taken at the hunt ball to launch her Man and the Horse exhibition. The man with her – grey-haired like you but not as good looking – is Ralph Lauren, the American designer. The caption says he gave three hundred and fifty thousand dollars to help stage the exhibits which ranged from medieval armour to Jackie O's riding chaps. Isn't Vreeland stunning in that black gaucho outfit with the pink satin cummerbund? And look . . . the front endpapers of her book show ten early portraits of her. Don't you love the Augustus John pencil sketch?'

'She has a fine forehead and hairline . . . then and now,' said Risconti. 'It's lucky you have this book. I can read it on the way over. It's always a help to know as much as possible about one's sitter.'

As Allegra leaned over his shoulder to look at the striking features of the doyenne of American fashion, the ruffled front of her summery white cotton peignoir loosened to show the inner curves of her breasts.

Risconti turned his head and planted a kiss between them. Then he hooked an arm round her and drew her down on to his lap.

'I'd much rather stay here in England until September. The summer is better here. New York gets intolerably hot, although Sigmund suggests it may be possible to work on the portrait somewhere with a better climate. Can you be ready to leave by the weekend, my lovely?'

'Yes, but I shall have to come back the following weekend. I can't take more than a month off work, Andro.'

'No, I understand that. You'll have to spend time working too. We can't spend the rest of our lives in happy idleness. Luckily your work is portable. A writer can work anywhere. I only wish I could.'

'Some writers can. Biographers can't, I'm afraid. They're tied to the country their subject lived in, or where the main sources are. Before you arrived to distract me' – she gave him a loving smile – 'I was spending a lot of my time in the Public Record Office. Before long I have to go north. Edward was born and educated in Newcastle. I need to visit his school.'

Up to now she hadn't talked much about the new book she had started. *Travels* had been a secret until she had finished it. Her instinct was not to discuss this one either, except with Ellen and Claudia. She didn't feel that Risconti was likely to be much interested in a long-dead British field marshal. There was so much else to talk about.

'How long is this book going to take you?' he asked, beginning to look perturbed.

'I'm committed to finishing it by September next year. Which isn't as long as it sounds. There's so much research involved. I suppose, at the back of my mind, I assumed you would come back to Europe and, if we couldn't always be together, we would be a lot of the time.'

'A lot of the time isn't enough. I want you with me *all* the time; if not every hour of the day, certainly every night. I'm serious about you, Allegra. Haven't I made that clear?'

'Yes . . . and I'm serious, too. I love you very much, Andro. More . . . much more than I used to dream of loving a man.' She slid her arms round his neck and kissed him softly on the mouth.

As he always did when she kissed him, however lightly, he responded with flattering ardour. It was barely two hours since they had made love on waking. Now, as they kissed, she felt his hunger reviving, as was her own. A few minutes later he carried her back to the bedroom.

'Allegra . . . will you marry me?'

He murmured the words in her ear as they lay, their bodies still fused, resting after the storm of passion. 'Will you be my wife . . . the mother of my children?'

It wasn't her first proposal. Other men before him had wanted her for their own. But she hadn't wanted them; by the time they committed themselves, she had begun to be bored.

Risconti would never bore her. She had no doubts about that. Neither in bed nor out of it. If he had asked her yesterday she would have said yes without hesitation, without thinking. Today, since hearing his wish to cross the Atlantic during the coming weekend, she had begun to grasp the size of the problem confronting two people who loved each other but whose careers were in conflict.

He lifted his head from the pillow and looked into her eyes.

'Why don't you answer? Don't you want to be my wife?'

'The first time we met you told me you didn't want to adjust your life to the needs of a wife and children . . . that artists were better off living alone, or with someone who made no demands on them.'

'Perhaps I believed it at the time. I don't any more. Be as demanding as you please, my beautiful love.'

Gently stroking the broad span of his powerful back, she said, 'I don't want to make any demands on you . . . only to give you pleasure and make your life richer and fuller than it would be without me. But that isn't going to be easy, darling. I have to be here. You have to be there. How are we to get over that? You can't . . . mustn't give up the portrait of Mrs Vreeland, and I can't give up my book.'

Risconti withdrew from her arms and rolled on to his back, stretching an arm for the box of tissues on the night table. The first one he took from the box, he laid over the tangle of damp curls between her still parted thighs.

Attending to himself, he said, 'No, of course you can't give it up . . . but could it perhaps be postponed for a few months? After the Vreeland portrait, and another commission already fixed for the autumn, maybe I can come back to Europe. When a man and woman have careers of equal importance, they have to compromise. I can only suggest you give me the rest of this year and I'll do my best to arrange next year to suit you. That's a fair arrangement, don't you think? Surely it can't make much difference if your book comes out a few months later than planned?'

She closed her legs and swung them over the side of the bed. Usually, after making love in the daytime, they dozed for a little or lay idly chatting. Love, even more than wine, clouded the brain and made it difficult to grapple with anything serious.

After making love twice – and with Andro it was never less than totally satisfying – she felt fit only for another shower and another pot of coffee. Not for tackling perhaps the most important issue of her life.

'Not to me perhaps,' she said in answer to his suggestion. 'But I'm not sure how Claudia and Ellen would feel. Publishers have fairly rigid schedules. They have to. Book production is such an involved process. I'll have to talk to them. As I've only just started, perhaps they can shuffle the schedule.'

Sarah returned from riding Berber in a one-day event to find a postcard from Spain awaiting her.

She read the handwriting before looking at the picture. Undated and signed only with one initial, the message was – *It's great to be a civilian again. I've been offered a job as a bouncer in a* discoteca. *Think I'll give it a whirl. Have been learning to windsurf.* Estupendo! *May buy a board and sell it when I move on. Cheaper than renting.* Hasta luego. *N.*

The picture on the other side was of a picturesque street in the old part of Marbella. She looked at it through a blur of tears, her pleasure in Berber's success ruined by this deflating news. Love was supposed to be an unselfish emotion. But the postcard depressed and worried her. In the disco and on the beaches, girls from all parts of Europe would be looking for a holiday romance. She was terrified he would fall for one of them.

'No,' said Claudia. 'No, I'm not going to agree to this, Allegra.'

They were having a sandwich lunch in her office. Ellen had been absent all week, nursing a sick child during the day and doing as much work as she could after her husband came home in the evening. Claudia was trying to ease the burden on her and consequently could spare only an hour to discuss the dilemma confronting their best-selling author.

Allegra was taken aback. She had anticipated that Claudia, a more fervent feminist than her partner, would not be too sympathetic. But she hadn't expected her request for a deferment of her deadline to be met with adamant rejection.

'I'm not going to aid and abet you in making your career as a writer take second place to your love life,' Claudia reiterated firmly. 'It may be that Alessandro Risconti is the great love of your life and you'll be together for ever. But, as Lauren Bacall once told an interviewer, *work* is what life is about. How right she was! Going to bed with a wonderful lover is great. Even going for a walk with a man you love is one of life's treats. I'm not knocking any of that. But the fact is that most intelligent women get *most* of their happiness doing some interesting work and achieving success in their chosen field. At the moment you're in the first flush of a marvellous affair with an exceptional man, so you're not thinking straight. Believe me, if you start out giving his work precedence, that's the way it will continue and later on you'll regret it.'

She took a large bite from her sandwich and continued to gaze steadily and seriously at Allegra, who said, 'I've nothing to lose by my book being slightly delayed. Andro stands to lose an important commission. Diana Vreeland is one of the most remarkable women in the world today. Not to jump at the chance to paint her would be like Graham Sutherland turning down the opportunity to do his brilliant portrait of Helena Rubenstein.'

'On the contrary you have plenty to lose. Time and momentum,' said Claudia. 'If you break off now, you may never recover the enthusiasm you feel at present for this book. If you go swanning off to America and let your work lapse for months, you may never get back to it.'

When Allegra didn't reply, she went on, 'If you want an example of what happens to women who start off on the wrong footing, you've only to look at Ellen. I have no objection to parents taking time off when their children are ill. But it's time we stopped thinking this is something mothers do but fathers don't because *their* work is sacrosanct. As you know, Ellen's husband is a lawyer. He can take days off as easily as she can, and work at home in the evenings. The equitable arrangement is for them to take turn and turn about. But no: that would upset his old-fashioned senior partners. Or that's his excuse. I think it's more likely he doesn't want to do a full stint in the sickroom and try to keep up with his work at night, when he's

265

tired. The most annoying thing about it isn't that Ellen is exhausting herself, but that her sons are growing up with the idea that Mummy's job isn't half as important as Daddy's. Never mind that it's Mummy's income which allows Daddy to send them to the bastion of male prejudices where he was educated,' she finished grimly.

Fundamentally, Allegra agreed with her. She had never had time for women who undervalued themselves. However she couldn't see a parallel between Ellen's situation and her own.

'Andro has promised that he'll make things easy for me next year,' she reminded her publisher.

'Hmm ... but what if some equally tempting commissions crop up for next year? The fact is that you are already involved in an important project. That should give you priority,' said Claudia.

'But I couldn't be comfortable knowing I'd caused him to miss the Vreeland portrait. Be honest: could you in my place?'

'Possibly not,' the other woman conceded. 'In that case the sensible course is for you both to get on with your career commitments and accept that, at least this year, you won't be able to be together as much as you'd like. Isn't this great love affair worth the expense of flitting across the Atlantic for weekends of unalloyed bliss?'

Claudia was right. It was the only rational solution, Allegra decided, on her way back to Park Lane.

If she went to America with Andro, much of the time she would be at a loose end, frustrated because her work was in suspension. It was no way to begin a lasting relationship.

But would loving her, which had already changed his mind about marrying, make Andro able to see the logic of Claudia's suggestion?

To Sarah's relief, as the time approached for the most taxing test of her partnership with Bedouin Star, Sammy seemed to recover both his energy and his good humour. Whatever had ailed him, it appeared to have passed off, leaving him none the worse.

Neither she nor the ageing Irishman had any doubt in their minds that Beddo was sure to distinguish himself at the horse trials at Burghley in September.

A good placing at Burghley, a better one at Badminton next spring and thereafter a place in the British equestrian team for the next Olympic Games: that was Sarah's cherished hope for him.

Indeed it had been her daydream since the first time she saw him, a leggy shape veiled by the membrane of his dam's water-bag.

In the early hours of an April morning, an Arab mare, Bedouin Sunset, lay down in a large foaling box in the stables at Longwarden.

It was the second time she had done this and the man and the child who were watching exchanged glances. Eleven months ago Sammy O'Brien had taken the mare to be served by Tuareg, a champion Arab stallion. Now, as she began to strain, they knew it would not be long before she dropped Tuareg's foal.

In the eighth Earl's lifetime, Sammy would have been under instructions to send for the vet as soon as foaling was imminent. Now that North was the owner of Longwarden, the stud-groom had carte blanche to do as he thought fit in matters pertaining to the horses, most of them soon to be sold at Tattersalls' bloodstock sales.

Furthermore the chestnut brood mare, known in the stables as Sunny, had belonged to the late Earl's younger brother and was now the property of his daughter. She had begged North to let her be present when Sunny foaled and he had agreed.

As the mare had foaled many times without complications, and he had his own ideas about the handling of normal births, Sammy had decided not to call the vet from his bed.

'She'll have a bit of a struggle,' he had warned Sarah beforehand. 'But she knows what's she doing, to be sure, and we'll not interfere. I don't hold with trying to hurry things.'

Sarah had seen kittens and puppies born and had long wished to see a foal's birth. Her blue eyes sparkling with interest and excitement, she watched the mare heaving and straining on her bed of long wheat straw. Sometimes she rested before resuming the convulsive efforts to rid her body of its burden.

Had she been on her own with the mare, Sarah might have been alarmed. But with Sammy beside her she knew there was nothing to worry about.

Mindful of his warning to remain absolutely quiet, she stifled a gasp of delight as two front legs appeared, one slightly in advance of the other. The legs were followed by a nose and when the whole of the foal's head.

But it was the shoulders, she knew, which sometimes caused difficulty. Holding her breath, her small fists clenched in suspense, she watched Sunny give a series of shuddering heaves until, all at once, both shoulders slid into view and moments later the birth was complete.

It was at this point that Sammy stepped quietly into the box and bent to open the thin slimy membrane. Rapt with wonder and joy, Sarah saw him free the nostrils of a bedrenched little creature who instantly won her heart.

The vet would have cut the umbilical cord but Sammy believed in letting it rupture naturally. He signalled to Sarah to help him move the foal round to the mare's head so that she could nuzzle its back and lick its wet coat while he applied iodine to the stump of the now broken cord.

The mare, exhausted and sweating, lay quietly recovering from her efforts; but even before the man and the child had withdrawn from the box the foal was trying to stand.

It was large and long-legged and its efforts were as unsuccessful as Sarah's first attempts to ride a bicycle. Watching it rolling about, sometimes half-rising before collapsing again, in vain attempts to coordinate all four legs, she longed to rush in and help it.

But Sammy's hand on her shoulder reminded her that he had said it was good for a foal to struggle. It toned up its muscles. Only when the new arrival got himself hopelessly stuck in a corner of the box did the groom give her a tap which meant she could go to its aid.

As, gently, she helped it away from the corner, Sarah's heart swelled with love. Every summer for as far back as she could remember there had been foals and yearlings kicking up their heels in the meadows at Longwarden. But this foal was special. She felt it in her bones.

Within half an hour of his birth, the foal had mastered the knack of getting to his feet and was standing unsteadily on his spindly legs. By this time the mare was also up and Sammy gave her a drink and a bran mash.

Soon the foal was ready for his first meal. After some uncertain searching he found the right place and began greedily sucking the colostrum which Sarah knew was vital to his well-being.

Her next contribution to his welfare was to hold him steady, one arm round his breast and the other round his quarters, while Sammy examined his rectum and gave him an enema.

He was still too small and unsteady to resist her embrace and showed curiosity rather than nervousness, turning his head to see what was happening. His soft muzzle brushed her cheek as she knelt, holding him carefully in her arms, knowing he was going to be the best and dearest of all her four-legged friends.

The next time she held him like that he did resist her. He was three days old and about to have his first outing in a sunny paddock. He would have followed his dam, but it was Sammy's belief that a foal's training should begin very early in life. While he held the watching mare, Sarah took hold of the foal who immediately struggled to free himself.

For a minute or two he tried every means he knew to escape her enfolding arms while she held him as gently as she could without letting him go. As soon as he realized it was useless, he gave up his frantic plunges. He had learned, and wouldn't forget, his first lesson: that human beings were his masters and he must obey and trust them, especially the soft-voiced girl murmuring lovingly to him.

Had he been born some years earlier, Bedouin Star

would have had a short childhood. It was almost certain Sarah's uncle would have raced him until he was four and then had him put to stud.

She and Sammy had other plans for the colt and they weren't going to risk his soundness by working him too hard too young. Although as an Arab he was less subject to the defects affecting other breeds, they wanted to give him the maximum time to mature. For that reason he wasn't gelded until he was three and, as much as Sarah longed to ride him, she didn't break him to the saddle until he was four and she was fifteen.

The following year she took him cub-hunting and rode him in a few shows. Fawn as a foal, he had become a dark chestnut with only slightly less brilliance to his glossy coat than had he remained an entire. Near the crest of his neck was the mark called the Prophet's Thumbmark – a sign, so Arabs believed, of an exceptional horse.

Although at 15.2 hands high he was slightly larger than was usual for his breed, he was smaller than most of the horses competing in horse trials. However, records of past championships showed that many different types of horses had excelled at eventing. Sarah was determined to prove that, although it had never been done before, it wasn't impossible for an Arab to emulate them. At the Olympic Games in Rome in 1960, a thoroughbred gelding called Salad Days, with nothing in his conformation to suggest that he was outstanding, had shown himself to be brilliant. Stamina and a natural prowess at jumping had made him one of the never-to-be-forgotten names in eventing history. Bedouin Star, she felt sure, had the same qualities.

Even the late Lord Carlyon, a breeder of thoroughbreds, had been willing to concede that all the light-horse breeds owed the best of their blood to the Arab; and Sarah's young Arab exemplified all that was best in the so-called Drinkers of the Wind. There was plenty of fire in his temperament but it was blended with intelligence and gentleness. His large eyes always looked kindly on the two people who cared for him.

When three years of careful grounding culminated in

first place in the Novice National Championships, Sammy shared Sarah's belief that they had a gold-medal horse in the making.

But it wasn't until he was eight that she entered him for the trials at Burghley, a contest in which his abilities, and her own, would be matched against some of the finest horses and riders in the world.

When Risconti was told Claudia wasn't prepared to put back the deadline, he didn't say any of the things Allegra had dreaded.

'In that case it looks as if we'll have to resign ourselves to being separated most of the time for the next few months,' he said, and she was inexpressibly relieved.

Deep down, she had had the fear he might put her to the test of choosing between him and Edward. Forced to make such a decision, she wouldn't have hesitated. There were other books to be written; only one Andro. But it would have been a cruel thing to do. Deep in her heart she could not have forgiven him if he had imposed such a choice on her.

Perhaps it had been a failure of trust on her part to fear that he might. But life hadn't made her trusting. It would take more than a few weeks of loving and being loved to dispel the lingering dread that something would happen to spoil this incredible new happiness.

After much discussion, they decided that rather than flying to America with him at the weekend, it would be better for her to go over later in the month.

The night before his departure they slept hardly at all.

'This is how people must have felt in World War Two on the last night of a leave,' she murmured, at one stage of that long wakeful night in his arms.

'Except that they didn't know when, if ever, they'd next see each other. We do. In two weeks' time,' Risconti reminded her comfortingly.

'Even without a war on, bad things happen to people. You might have an accident . . . be mugged . . . anything. Oh, darling, you will take care of yourself? If anything

271

happened to you, it would finish me, too.' Her eyes filled with tears.

'My foolish love,' he said tenderly, 'I am much more careful about crossing streets than you are, and were you mugged in New York? No – and neither are most of the millions of people who live there. You are not to worry about me, and I'll try not to worry about you stepping into the street without looking because your mind's on your book. But please be a little more careful than when you're with me, okay?'

He wouldn't allow her to go to the airport with him.

'I like to be met but not to be seen off. We'll say goodbye here. Then you can go straight to your desk and apply your mind to the other man in your life, this rather boring chap Edward.'

'If he were boring, I shouldn't be writing about him. He was old when that portrait was painted,' she said, with a glance at the photograph on her desk.

It had come from the archives of the National Portrait Gallery where pictures of most people of note in British history and of many lesser-known figures were to be found. It showed her subject as a white-whiskered old man, but still of commanding mien, in the years when he had been Governor of the Royal Hospital in Chelsea.

'When Edward was young he was as dashing as you are – possibly more so,' Allegra told him with a smile.

She was determined to send him off with a bright face. There would be no tears in her eyes however much it might be raining in her heart.

'Goodbye, darling. See you soon,' was her cheerful farewell from the landing as Risconti ran down the staircase.

It was while her mind was reviewing all the happy, laughing, tender, passionate moments they had shared since that unforgettable second meeting at the Ritz that she realized the matter of their marriage was still undecided.

Having asked her once *Will you marry me?* Risconti hadn't repeated the question.

Had he been waiting for her to return to the subject?

Had he changed his mind? Had his proposal, made while they were one flesh, been an impulse which, when his blood had cooled, he had thought better of?

While Risconti was flying to New York, Jane was crossing the Atlantic in the opposite direction.

It was Alison Blakewell, a subscriber to Sotheby's catalogues of portrait miniatures, who had received notification that the famous firm of fine-art auctioneers were collaborating with the Duke of Buccleuch and Queensberry to put on a series of courses to study his forebears' magnificent collections of furniture and paintings. Seeing that Jane was finding it hard to bear with patience the various pressures on her, Alison had suggested that enrolling for one of the Buccleuch Studies, as the courses were called, would not only help to pass the waiting time but be a useful preparation for her future as mistress of Longwarden.

Jane had jumped at the idea. Charles was still in America, pestering her with calls and letters, not accepting the situation with a good grace as she had hoped. A trip to Europe seemed the best way to avoid another unwelcome visit from him.

In a different way, her aunt was also being difficult. Her snobbishness had overcome her wrath. She had decided to be magnanimous and now was bent on organizing a traditional wedding. Although Jane was in no danger of succumbing to Aunt Julia's urgings, she did find the summer dragging as she waited in vain for news from Ladakh. Perhaps the fault lay with the mail service from that country rather than with her prospective husband. But, given the unusual nature of their relationship and the manner of their parting, she couldn't help feeling uneasy at hearing nothing more from him. Perhaps he was having second thoughts.

Far away from where he was thought to be, North was taking cover while a patrolling Russian helicopter strafed the mountainside in Afghanistan where he was travelling with a group of Mujahideen rebels.

His assignment in Ladakh had been completed in two

weeks. He had then flown to Peshawar to join an expedition taking arms across one of the most difficult passes between Pakistan and Afghanistan.

Whether he would get back to Peshawar with the stills he had taken intact – whether he would get out alive – seemed, at this moment, in doubt. Bearded, dressed like an Afghani freedom fighter, he lay under a projecting rock waiting for the chopper to finish raking the barren, boulder-strewn terrain where he and the rest of the group had hurriedly scattered on hearing the whirr of its blades.

Although not officially attributed to him, some of the most remarkable photographs to come out of the Afghanistan war had been his. Each time he crossed the border on another foray there was always the chance he would be killed, either by the Russians, the bandits who preyed on the caravans, or a rival group of Mujahideen. There was also a good deal of illness among the foreign adventurers who penetrated the country. Food was scarce in areas where the Russians razed the crops of suspected Mujahideen sympathizers. Germs were plentiful.

The chopper began another sweep. Watching the spurts of dust and splintered rock made by the bullets, North could see that this time they would come even closer. He could only lie still and hope the rock would protect him.

He wondered how Jane would react if she had to be told she wasn't going to be a countess. Or if he got back alive, but not in one piece.

Jane's arrival in London, for the first time without her father, made her sad. Several times, during a lonely evening at the Connaught Hotel where she had often stayed with him, she tried Marie-Simone's number in Paris. There was no reply.

The next morning she flew to Scotland where she would be staying at an hotel not far from Bowhill, one of the Duke's three treasure houses. During the short flight north she decided to take off North's signet ring and keep it in her bag. It was possible someone on the course might notice or even recognize the crest and be curious about her

274

possession of it. For the time being she felt it was prudent to keep quiet about her engagement.

'Tea time, m'Lady.'

Intent on her work, Pen hadn't noticed Ashford approaching. She was busy giving the yews their once a year clip, standing on the simple modern scaffolding system which had been a present from North to replace the stepladders and trestles used previously.

There being nowhere at hand for her to sit, other than on the grass, Ashford had brought a side-folding canvas chair.

Because at this time of year wasps could be a nuisance, he brought her tea in a covered basket rather than on a tray.

'Don't go for a moment, Mr Ashford,' she said when he would have left her. It was a very hot day and she was wearing a dark green celluloid eyeshade, a relic of prewar tennis parties. She pulled it off. 'I think it's time we began to make some preparations for my son's return ... with his bride. I don't know yet when that will be. Possibly not for some time ... depending on the length of their honeymoon.'

To her surprise he replied, 'The arrangements are already in hand, m'Lady. Before he left for Ladakh, his Lordship gave me instructions to prepare the rooms used by the seventh Earl and Countess. They're being aired every day and thoroughly cleaned. But his orders were not to change the appointments in any way. I gather he thought it would interest his future wife to see the rooms as they are. He was quite specific on that point.'

'Oh ... I see. He didn't tell me. Not that it matters as long as you know what he wants. It's years since I've been in those rooms. Are they in reasonable order?'

'Surprisingly good considering they haven't been used for nearly thirty years. I understand from Mrs Armitage that when the seventh Countess stayed here as a widow she preferred to use one of the visitors' rooms?'

'Yes, that's perfectly true. She did. My daughter's book

275

doesn't deal with that part of her life. It ends, as you know, with Caspar Carlyon's death. The years after that were very difficult for her. She showed a brave face to the world, but she was seventy-one when he died and they had been happily married for over fifty years.'

There was a pause in which she wondered if, thoughtlessly, she had reminded him of his marriage. In some ways her own long loneliness had become more acute since the evening he had come in to her sitting room and given her a taste of the companionship she had never shared with her husband.

He said, 'Perhaps when you've finished the yews and have slightly more time to spare you would come and inspect the rooms, m'Lady. I had intended to ask you when you had less on your mind.'

'Oh, dear . . . do I seem very harassed?'

'Not at all, but I'm sure it must tire you. It seems very hard work to me . . . work for a man,' he added frowning. 'I wish you would allow me to help you with the straightforward clipping.'

'It's kind of you to offer, Mr Ashford, but you have enough on your plate. I'm quite tough, you know. Hard work never killed anyone.'

'Perhaps not . . . but if I may say so, I think you work *too* hard at times. You've had hardly any days off since I've been at Longwarden, and no proper holiday.'

His concern was immeasurably warming. Smiling, she said, 'I've never gone in for holidays. In a way, because I enjoy my work, my life is all holiday. But perhaps I shall go away this autumn to let Jane – my daughter-in-law – find her feet here. I might take myself on a tour of other people's gardens. What sort of holidays appeal to you, Mr Ashford? Where did you go last winter?'

'To Venice,' he said. 'Where there were very few other tourists and the weather was surprisingly pleasant. If it's convenient, I'd like to take next year's holiday at about the same time.'

'I can't imagine why it shouldn't be. But what about your third week? You haven't had that yet.'

'I don't really feel the need for a third week's holiday, m'Lady. Like you, I enjoy my work and no one could ask for more delightful surroundings.' His gesture embraced the garden and the park beyond it.

'If you don't want to take a whole week off, why not take it in single days?' Pen suggested. On a reckless impulse, she added, 'I've been thinking of going to see the new gardens designed by Sir Geoffrey Jellicoe for Sutton Place. They're supposed to be the most ambitious scheme to be laid out in Britain for over a hundred years. Would it interest you to come with me?'

Allegra was missing Risconti. Physically. Mentally. Every which way.

That he missed her equally badly and had already spent a fortune on transatlantic telephone chats was some comfort. But last night, after his call, she had lain awake for hours, wanting him; not only to make love to her but to be there when she fell asleep and when she woke up.

Claudia had said an intelligent woman derived most of her happiness from her work. Perhaps that was true: if, while she was working, she knew at the end of the day she would be having dinner with the man in her life. In the light of recent experience, it seemed to Allegra that however well the day's work had gone, it didn't bring much satisfaction if the evening was going to be solitary and lonely.

For a long time she had enjoyed solitude and, with a good book to read, had never felt seriously lonely. Now she felt lonely most of the time – lonely and increasingly troubled because although Risconti had said many loving things to her on the telephone, they had not included a second proposal of marriage.

And marriage, the life-long bond she had once regarded as an impossible commitment, was suddenly something Allegra wanted very much.

Watching Ashford walk briskly away, Pen cursed the device in his pocket which had bleeped at precisely the wrong moment.

In general the bleeper was a useful innovation, enabling the rest of the staff to locate him quickly wherever he was in the house or garden. On this occasion the summons couldn't have come at a more inopportune moment.

After a marked hesitation, he had been on the point of replying to her invitation to go with her to Sutton Place. She couldn't be certain but she thought he would have said yes.

Instead the wretched bleeper had started its pip-pip-pip and all he had said was, 'Would you excuse me, m'Lady? I'd better go and find out who wants me.'

Which meant she wouldn't see him again until he returned for the tea basket. By then he would have thought it over and might decide to say nothing, unless she raised the subject again. Which she wouldn't have the courage to do a second time.

And yet . . . and yet she felt sure there had been a moment when he had wanted to accept. She had read the uncertainty in his eyes; the conflict between his innermost wishes and his sense of decorum. Or had she imagined it because she wanted to believe he was drawn to her as strongly as she to him?

Having finished her tea, she climbed the scaffolding and returned to her task. Still thinking of the visit to Sutton Place reminded her that long ago, in the thirties, Sir Geoffrey Jellicoe had worked with another great garden designer, the late Russell Page who had designed beautiful gardens all over Europe. It was he who had written, she remembered, that a garden should be for 'convenience and delight'. It struck Pen that this was also the purpose of marriage.

Convenience and delight.

The phrase lingered in her mind as she waited for Ashford to come back; thinking how convenient and delightful it would be if they could both set up house in the dairies. She couldn't imagine anything she would like more than to change from being the Countess of Carlyon to Mrs P. J. Ashford.

When it wasn't the butler but one of the cleaners who

came to retrieve the tea things, her spirits sank. Had she embarrassed him to the extent that he was avoiding her?

'We've had a bit of an emergency, m'Lady,' said Mrs Beccles, a dumpy little woman who lived next to the butcher's shop. 'Mrs Poole came over queer. Really poorly she looked . . . and dizzy. Mr Ashford had to drive her home.'

'Oh, dear, I'm sorry to hear that.'

Pen was also glad it wasn't embarrassment which accounted for Ashford's absence. She would have been disappointed in him if it had been. She had thought him able to cope with any eventuality – even the difficult one of being invited out by his employer's mother.

In Scotland Jane was enjoying herself. She and the other members of the study group dined together each evening after a day of lectures on Scottish history and architecture, interspersed with visits to other great Scottish houses within easy reach of Bowhill.

The group was small enough for its members to get to know each other. She wasn't the only person there on her own, although she was by far the youngest – and the prettiest, so an elderly gallant had informed her. The majority of the group were wealthy middle-aged art buffs of the same nationality as herself.

One evening, while changing for dinner, she finally made up her mind to telephone Lady Carlyon. She had something in mind which involved conferring with the Countess, and also because she wanted to be sure her future mother-in-law was not going to be hurt by being excluded from the wedding. North had claimed that she would be relieved rather than offended, but Jane had the feeling North's judgement was always coloured by his own wishes. It might be that Lady Carlyon was in fact deeply wounded by their eccentric plans. Of course she might also be hurt if she discovered Jane was in Britain. But the chances were she wouldn't inquire into her whereabouts but take it for granted that they were on opposite sides of the Atlantic.

Her mouth a little dry, her heart beating faster than

usual, Jane sat on the edge of her bed and dialled North's home number.

For the second time in twenty minutes Allegra dialled Longwarden. The number was still engaged. She wondered who could be having such a long conversation. Neither her mother nor her cousin had friends to whom they talked at length.

When, eventually, she got through, it was Ashford's clipped voice which answered.

Knowing he would recognize her voice, she said, 'Would you tell my mother I'm coming down for a few days, please, Ashford. It's unbearably stuffy in London and they say it's going to get hotter. I'll be there early tomorrow.'

'Very good, Lady Allegra. Do you wish to speak to her Ladyship? She is in the house at the moment.'

'No, no . . . I haven't any interesting news and I don't suppose she has. I'll see her tomorrow. Goodbye.' Allegra rang off.

Pen had taken the unexpected call from Jane in her bedroom. On her way downstairs to have supper with Sarah, she was conscious of being both relieved and disturbed by it.

Jane's telephone manner had been as agreeable as her letters. She had seemed quite touchingly anxious about Pen's reaction to not being present at the wedding. Clearly she wasn't the sort of egotistical, over-confident girl who would ride roughshod over her new relations' sensibilities.

But later on in their long and expensive conversation she had put forward such an extraordinary suggestion that, although obliged to agree to it, now Pen felt increasingly worried that this marriage of North's was not the love match he claimed.

She arrived at the library at the same time as Ashford. As he quickened his steps in order to open the door for her, he said, 'Lady Allegra will be arriving tomorrow, m'Lady. She says London is very unpleasant in these high temperatures.'

280

'I'm sure it must be,' Pen agreed rather vaguely. Her daughter's erratic visits had never occasioned eager anticipation.

While Ashford was pouring a glass of sherry for her, she told him the gist of her conversation with Jane.

Placing the glass on a small tray, he brought it to where she was sitting. For the moment she had forgotten the unanswered question put to him in the yew walk. Although it had been much in her mind, it had been driven out by Jane's telephone call.

It came back in a flash when he said to her quietly, 'In that case, m'Lady, it will be out of the question for me to take extra days off as you very kindly suggested the other afternoon.'

Sarah walked in wearing a blue cotton sundress in place of the tee-shirt and breeches she had appeared in at breakfast.

'Phew! What a sweltering day. Aren't you boiled in a coat, Mr Ashford?'

As he always did in the evening, he was wearing a collar and tie and a well-pressed dark jacket.

'My activities are rather less strenuous than yours, Miss Sarah.' Unexpectedly, he added, 'When I was serving in Malaya, as it was known then, Other Ranks not only wore boots but also hose-tops and puttees. They did tend to feel the heat.'

It was rare for him to refer to his time in the army.

'What are hose-tops?' asked Sarah.

'They were tubes of thick khaki wool, worn underneath the puttees, with the tops turned over like stockings. May I get you something to drink? Pineapple juice tonight perhaps?'

'Yes, please, that would be lovely. I thought puttees went out aeons ago.'

A slight smile touched Ashford's mouth. 'My time in Malaya was aeons ago, Miss Sarah. I'm speaking of the early fifties.'

He went out of the room to fetch the tall glass of fruit juice she had every night before dinner.

Sarah saw that Aunt Pen had missed the butler's dry joke and was looking rather down in the mouth. Perhaps she was starting to worry about the prolonged dry weather.

But it wasn't the welfare of her plants which caused Pen to sip her sherry with a faint frown contracting her eyebrows. It was the realization that Ashford's comment on what she had told him had been an adroit rejection of her invitation to visit Sutton Place with her.

It was clever of him to refuse in such a diplomatic way, but it didn't lessen the hurt. How absurd for a woman of her age to feel like bursting into tears.

Concorde, with Jane on board, was due to touch down at Kennedy in five minutes' time when a steward came to her seat.

'You're being met at the airport, Miss Graham.'

Jane was surprised. 'Who's meeting me?'

'We haven't been told that. I imagine whoever it is thought there might be a risk of missing you if you weren't expecting to be met.'

'I guess so. Thank you.' Jane's smile masked an upsurge of alarm.

Who was waiting for her at the airport? Marcus and Alison? Bearers of news about North? Bad news?

Was this why there'd been no letters? Because he was dead?

I might not come back from Ladakh.

She remembered the quiet statement in the hotel corridor on the night she had asked him to marry her; and how, in her innermost self, the primitive woman inside the civilized one, she had wished he hadn't said it. Remarks like that were tempting Fate.

She sat through the landing outwardly calm and relaxed, inwardly stiff with fear that, although Concorde would touch down with its usual smoothness, her hopes and plans for the future were about to crash.

The formalities, speeded up for Concorde's privileged passengers, seemed this time to take forever.

Then, as she braced herself for the sight of the

Blakewells' unsmiling, anxious faces, she saw who it was who was waiting for her.

North himself.

Jane had heard of distraught parents reacting with violent anger when a lost child was restored to them. For a few seconds the sight of the tall blue-eyed man waiting for her evoked the same rage in her. How dared he put her through those moments of anxiety, the thoughtless ape. She wanted to throw something at him ... wipe the big grin off his face. With an effort she calmed down, greeting him with a smiling, 'This is a surprise. What are you doing here?'

'I flew in yesterday. How was Scotland?'

Without waiting for her answer and regardless of the people around them, he took her in his arms and kissed her.

Even in public the strong, possessive embrace made her heart beat wildly. She emerged from it trying not to show his effect on her.

Releasing her, he said, 'I called you as soon as I landed, only to find out from Alison that if I'd rung up from London we could have met there last night. Instead of which I've had to kick my heels waiting for you to catch up with me. Never mind: you're here and looking marvellous.'

'Thank you. You're looking good too. We don't have much time to spare if we're catching the shuttle. Let's get ourselves on it, shall we, before I ask about Ladakh?'

On the short flight to Boston, she took him to task for not writing.

'I did write a couple of times but the mails in that part of the world are very erratic,' was his impenitent answer. 'Can we expedite the wedding arrangements? Is there going to be a problem rearranging our honeymoon dates? Where are we going?'

'It's to be a surprise ... but I don't think there'll be any difficulty in putting everything forward. Now that you've had time to think about it, you've no worries that, marrying in haste, you may repent at leisure?' she asked him.

'None at all ... have you?'

'No, I believe it will work for us . . . although next time you go away I shan't write unless you do. I can't believe there weren't times when you could have dashed off a few lines.'

'Were you worried about me?' he asked.

'We were all a bit concerned. Ladakh sounds the kind of place where it's not unusual for people to fall over precipices or die of strange fevers. But maybe it's not the way I imagine it. What's it really like?'

'Later I'll show you some pictures. At the moment I'd rather hear what you've been doing in Scotland. Some kind of course, Alison said.'

Jane explained where she'd been. 'While I was there I telephoned your mother. Did you see her while you were in England?'

'There wasn't time. I spent a night at the flat with Allegra. She gave me a parcel for you. I don't know what's in it. She's having a big affair with Alessandro Risconti. Have you heard of him?'

'Of course. He lives in America. I suppose she met him while she was over here. Is he going to do a portrait of her?'

'He already has. He seems to be as obsessed with her as she is with him. The flat is littered with sketches of her.'

'Did you like him, North?'

'He wasn't there. He has an important commission over here and Allegra is tied to London by the research for her new book. It may not last long anyway,' he said with a shrug. 'My sister's notoriously fickle. At one stage she was having affairs at the rate of two or three a year.'

'You know the old joke – before you find the handsome prince you have to kiss a lot of toads,' Jane said lightly. 'Your sister's a very special person. Maybe she finally met the special man she deserves.'

'Possibly. Whatever comes of it, I hope they'll stay on good terms long enough for him to paint you.' He reached for her left hand on which, before leaving London, she had replaced his signet ring. 'You won't have to wear this for much longer. I've brought you a proper engagement ring. As soon as we're alone I'll show it to you.'

He lifted her hand to his lips. She felt his teeth nibbling gently on the knuckle of her first finger and saw the glint in his eyes. It gave her the same sensation as if the aircraft had hit a pocket of turbulence.

They were met at the airport by Marcus who told them that he and Alison had a dinner engagement that night.

'But I won't apologize for deserting you. After all this time apart, I'm sure you'll be delighted to have a long tête-à-tête,' he said. 'By the way, a letter from Ladakh turned up in this morning's mail.'

'You see?' North said, 'I did write . . . but I should have sent it by carrier pigeon.'

Later she read the letter while she was running her bath. It began *My dear Jane* and ended *Yours ever, North* and, in between, was a concise account of his first week in Ladakh. It made no pretence of being a love letter. It might have been a letter from a brother to his sister.

After her bath she put on fresh underwear and sat down to re-do her face for the evening. She had finished her eyes when someone knocked on the door. Thinking it would be Alison, looking in to say goodbye, she called, 'Come in.'

It was North, with two parcels. Seeing her in a bra and briefs did not deter him from entering.

'Allegra's present . . . and also a Trifle from Delhi,' he said, putting the parcels on the dressing table. Clearly he intended to stay while she opened the parcels.

'How exciting.' She stood up and walked barefoot towards the adjoining bathroom where, behind the door, hung a cotton robe.

She didn't glance at him as she returned, wrapping it round her. She guessed he would be amused by her modesty. Little did he know the immodest longings he aroused in her.

She opened his present first, the allusion to a Trifle from Delhi not being lost on her. Only the week before, in one of the houses they had been taken to see, she had noticed an enamelled snuff box with *A Trifle from Edinburgh* on the lid. It was a message often to be seen on small objects in British antique shops.

North's trifle was a silk sari, the brilliant golden-green colour of a dragonfly's body and as sheer as its wings. A wide border of glistening gold threads ran along one edge. As Jane opened the folds, a faint scent was released, instantly evoking the Eastern bazaars she had explored with her father. For an instant the memory of him clouded her pleasure.

'It's lovely, North . . . such a gorgeous colour. I adore it.'

'I thought you could have it made up into a dress. Or, if you fancy wearing it as a sari, I got them to show me how it goes. I'll show you. You'll have to take off that dressing gown. Indian women don't wear much underneath saris . . . only a short-sleeved top which leaves their lower ribs bare.'

'I know. I have been to India . . . and I know how to fix it. One night, when we're on our honeymoon, I'll put it on for you. I have a gold lamé top that will be perfect with it. Thank you very much, North. It was nice of you to find time to shop for me.'

While he resumed his seat, the quizzical lift of one eyebrow showing that he knew where she thought a demonstration of sari-draping might lead, she put the silk carefully aside and turned her attention to the second parcel.

It was small. What it contained was even smaller – a tiny reddish-brown frog, carved from carnelian, which sat on the palm of her hand and seemed to fix bright beady eyes on her.

'Good lord!' North exclaimed in surprise. 'I never thought she'd give that away. She must like you very much . . . and why not?' he added, moving with one lithe spring from the windowseat to the end of the dressing stool and putting his arm round her.

On the card accompanying her present, his sister had written – *Something old. He's brought me my heart's desire. I've asked him to do the same for you. From your soon-to-be sister-in-law, with love. A.*

286

'Is he her lucky piece?' Jane asked.

'It's a button – Egyptian, I think – which Flora gave her when she was about ten. Allegra has always regarded it as a talisman. Whether or not you like the thing, you can take it as a very forthcoming gesture on her part. And my sister isn't noted for being nice to other women,' he added dryly.

'Don't call him "it". You'll offend him,' she reproved, half-seriously. 'I wonder what his name is. I'm sure he has one if she's had him that long. Why don't I call her and find out?'

'Why don't you kiss me?' he murmured, turning her face up to his and bending his head.

The frog clutched in her hand, she yielded to his embrace which quickly exceeded his ardent kiss at the airport.

There, he had been wearing a jacket. Now only a thin layer of cotton covered his broad chest and shoulders and the strong arms which held her a willing prisoner. The power of his body thrilled her as he crushed her against him. She felt his desire to possess her in the growing urgency of his lips and hands.

She wanted him, too, with a startling intensity of longing which made her unable to resist when the fingers caressing her throat slid downwards to open her robe and touch the soft flesh of her breasts through the flimsy lace.

Another tap on the door brought her down to earth. She struggled to break free. Reluctantly North released her, swallowing an angry expletive.

With unsteady hands, Jane closed her robe. 'Who is it?'

'Alison. Are you decent? May I come in?'

Jane rose from the stool. 'Yes . . . come in.' As the door opened she said, 'North has brought me a wonderful sari . . . and look at this from Allegra. Isn't he a darling?' She opened her hand to show the frog.

'How cute.' Coming closer, Alison plucked it from Jane's palm to look at it more closely.

She showed no surprise at North's presence, but Jane had the feeling she knew she had interrupted an intimate moment. The passion they had generated seemed to quiver in the air, disturbing the usual serenity of the bower-like room with its pale walls and rose-patterned chintzes.

Forced to rise to his feet when Alison came in, now North said, somewhat curtly, 'I'll leave you to change, Jane,' and made a swift exit.

After admiring the sari, Alison said, 'I'm sorry I burst in on you. Tactless of me. Not that *you* looked discomposed,' she added with a twinkle. 'But for a second there, those blue, blue eyes of your fiancé's did bear some resemblance to a death-ray.'

Jane laughed and a faint blush suffused her late-summer tan. 'I expect he was embarrassed, thinking you wouldn't like him to be in here.'

'Do I seem that old-fashioned? I assure you I'm not. You're not teenagers who need to be kept an eye on for their own good. If you want to spend the night together, that's your business,' her hostess said candidly. 'But as far as this evening goes, you might remind North that Swanage and Mrs Swanage are both rather strait-laced and Milly would be really shocked if she came to turn down the bed and found it occupied.'

Jane's colour deepened. 'There's no question of that happening, Alison. We'll be on our honeymoon soon. I'm sure we can both wait that long.'

'Waiting for anything at all seems out of fashion these days,' Alison said dryly. 'They say pre-marital sex cuts down the number of incompatible marriages. But you know I think any good marriage is based on friendship, not sex. If the friendship is there, everything else works out fine . . . sooner or later.' She patted Jane's cheek and left her.

As Jane put on a cool cotton dress and brushed her black hair, she wondered if North intended to come to her room tonight. Although, a short time earlier, she had been quivering with longing to feel his strong hands on her body, now her blood had cooled. She knew that it hadn't been her, and only her, he had wanted. All he had felt was the sexual desire any virile man, deprived of sex for some time, would feel for any passable girl.

The thought that in London, or on the trip to Ladakh, he might have felt free to amuse himself with other women troubled her. She remembered Charles's warning that North wouldn't be faithful to her and she knew that, if he were not, she wouldn't be able to accept it.

It was not until after dinner, served by the Blakewells' butler, that North produced a worn leather ring box.

They were about to have coffee in the cane-furnished, fern-filled garden room. North had been up to his room to fetch a large folder of photographic prints. Before showing them to her, he produced the box from his pocket.

'You may not care for this, in which case there are several others for you to choose from when we go to England,' he told her. 'But for the time being this is better than my signet ring.'

He reached for her hand and removed his own ring, replacing it with the one from the box.

Jane had never seen another like it. The gold shank was formed from three entwined mermaids, their raised arms supporting a cloudy dark greyish-blue stone she recognized as a star sapphire.

'But I love it! It's beautiful, North,' she exclaimed, genuinely enchanted.

'It was made by René Lalique, the famous French jeweller, and bought by my great-grandfather when he took Flora on her first visit to Paris in 1903. She preferred it to the diamond ring which was her official engagement ring. Lalique became her favourite jeweller.'

She turned her hand this way and that to examine the design more closely. The mermaids' bodies were burnished. Their breasts and hips glistened in contrast to the matt finish given to their sinuous golden-scaled tails.

'Are there any matches about?' she asked, knowing it would take a bright light held close above the sapphire to reveal the star in its depths.

'You know what the stone is, I gather?' he said, producing a match-book.

'I saw some star sapphires in Sri Lanka when my father was buying a present for Marie-Simone. She didn't like them. I did. To me they're mysterious and magical.'

He struck a match and a twelve-pointed star blazed into life in the misty depths of the cabochon.

'But none of those we were shown was as beautiful as this,' Jane added. 'Nor in as lovely a setting.'

'I'm glad you like it.' He placed her hand across his palm. 'It's strange to see it on a young hand. Your hands are exactly like Flora's in the bone structure and the shape of the nails.'

'Don't make the mistake of thinking that, because I look something like her, I *am* like her, will you, North? From what I've learned about Flora from reading Allegra's book, there's not much resemblance between us, except in some physical details. We're not the same kind of woman. Your great-grandfather was almost a god to her.'

'And I could never be that to you . . . hm?' he asked with a quizzical glint.

'You wouldn't want to be, would you? A wife who was desolate every time you went away would be a drag on you, surely?'

'In the case of my great-grandparents the idolization was mutual. He never went anywhere without her, apart from one trip to southern Spain when she wasn't able to go with him.'

'And then he wrote to her every day and cut the trip short because it was no fun without her,' said Jane, remembering the letters Allegra had quoted in her book.

'But he and Flora never travelled without numerous servants to take care of their creature comforts,' she went on. 'And they left their little boy in the care of a nanny until he was sent away to school. I hope to have more than one child and I don't want to be an absentee mother, or have my children go to boarding school from age eight. I know it was customary then, but I think it's wrong to send children as young as that away from home. This is something we haven't had a chance to discuss . . . one of a lot of important things we haven't talked out.'

'Too late now,' he said dryly. 'We'll have to take it on trust that we're both reasonable people who, if we can't reach agreement on every subject, can at least arrive at a mutually satisfactory compromise. My own experience of boarding school is that I was happier there than at home where I didn't get on with my parents. I know most Americans disapprove of the system, but it has its advantages. Anyway we've several years in which to argue about it. First make your baby, as Mrs Beeton might have said had she been a paediatrician instead of a housewifery expert.'

He still had hold of her hand and now he raised it to his lips and lightly kissed the inside of her wrist where a blue vein showed through the delicate translucent skin.

'Are you looking forward to that? To making a baby with me?'

The intent, faintly mocking scrutiny with which he awaited her answer revived the colour raised by Alison earlier.

She disengaged her hand to attend to pouring out the coffee. Not wishing him to know just how much she was looking forward to it, she said, in a matter-of-fact tone, 'Naturally I'm hoping that side of our relationship will be good. I've always thought it most unfair that a man's pleasure is more or less guaranteed but a woman's isn't.'

He stretched a long arm to run a finger down the line of her spine. 'D'you doubt my ability to make you share my pleasure?'

She didn't but, deliberately, she said, 'Isn't making love like listening to music? Not everyone likes Mozart . . . or Diana Ross . . . or whatever. The way you make love may have pleased other women but not be the right way for me.'

She wondered if he would be irked by her seeming to have less than total confidence in his prowess as a lover. But he surprised her by laughing, and saying, 'Then I'll have to discover the right way . . . or you'll have to learn to like my way. That's one aspect of marriage which I don't think is going to present any problems.'

And then, as she might have known he would, he shifted to sit close beside her, slipping both arms round her waist and murmuring into her ear, 'Why not find out . . . tonight? The others aren't going to be back for two or three hours yet.'

'North . . . you'll make me spill the coffee.' She tried to sound cool and unflustered, although her pulses were racing.

Gently, he stroked her breasts. 'You know you want to.'

'I *don't* want to upset Alison. She asked me, just before dinner, not to do anything that would shock Swanage or Milly. If we were to go upstairs now, they would guess what was going on and it would make me feel tacky.'

He stopped caressing her. As he shifted to his previous position on the adjoining squab, she knew by the set of his jaw that he was annoyed; and offended by the implication that he would have led her into tacky behaviour.

'You were going to show me your photographs,' she reminded him.

If, then, he had shown himself sulky, she might have reconsidered their precipitate marriage, at least to the extent of prolonging the engagement. However North accepted the rebuff good-humouredly.

In the months ahead, there were to be times when she felt it would have been better if he hadn't.

It was early, scarcely first light, when Jane woke up on her wedding day.

For a while she lay drowsily watching the view from her window coming into sharper focus, and listening to the chorus of birdsong from the trees and shrubs in the garden. Then, becoming more fully awake, she began to think about the momentous day ahead of her.

Her thoughts were not those of a bride serenely convinced that today was the beginning of a blissful future. Even brides who knew themselves to be loved felt eleventh-hour misgivings, so it wasn't surprising she should feel something like panic beginning to knot her insides.

After a while she got out of bed and, taking the photograph of her father from the dressing table, went to curl herself on the windowseat, seeking comfort and reassurance in the face of the man she still missed very deeply.

John Graham would never have made himself rich had he been afraid to take chances. But would he approve of her using the whole of his fortune to buy herself a husband, who without her lavish dowry, wouldn't have chosen her?

She thought of the numerous heiresses who had found only fugitive happiness with the men they had chosen – or, in earlier decades, had had chosen for them, notably Flora Carlyon's contemporary the Duchess of Marlborough, born Consuelo Vanderbilt. The most famous of those 'poor little rich girls' had been Barbara Hutton, the Woolworth heiress.

But I *will* be happy, thought Jane with renewed resolution. I will put as much thought and energy into being a perfect wife as some women put into a career. There will be nothing North wants that I won't give him – including the freedom to take off whenever he wants.

After placing her father's photograph in the half-packed case on the luggage stand, she sat down to compose a letter of thanks to Marcus and Alison for their many kindnesses to her, particularly in allowing her to be married at Winterbrook. Not that this arrangement had gone down well with Aunt Julia. It had made her furious again; but not so furious that she had refused to attend the wedding.

The hairdresser had been and gone. Alison had helped her to dress, fastening the simple short dress of cloudy white silk chiffon and carefully placing the unadorned circlet of stiffened silk which held the shoulder-length veil on Jane's glossy hair.

Now she was alone for a few minutes, standing before the long glass, gazing at her reflection, thinking of another wedding which had taken place in Shanghai eighty-two years ago.

Flora was married in an unbecoming dress made for her by a Chinese tailor in Hankow under the supervision of Mrs Hunter, the missionary's wife who had at first ostracized her in the belief that she was a girl of easy virtue, Allegra had written in her book.

Her wedding hat was the plain straw terai, with the puggaree *replaced by a length of white ribbon. However as she had not grown up with the expectation of wearing white lace and orange blossom, she was not disappointed. To the clergyman who married them*

*and the few witnesses to the ceremony, they must have seemed
an ill-assorted couple: the tall self-assured Englishman and the
waif-like girl of seventeen with her mixed blood apparent in her
straight, jet-black hair and the shape of her eyelids. No one, seeing
her that day, would have guessed what the future held for her.*

What does it hold for me? Jane wondered with a flutter
of last-minute nerves.

Jane had taken for granted that when her wedding day
came it would be her father who gave her away. Much as
she liked him, it gave her a piercing sense of loss to see
Marcus waiting for her at the foot of the curving staircase.

'You look enchanting, my dear,' he said, smiling, offering
his arm. 'North is a very lucky man.'

'Thank you,' she said, in a low voice. She placed her left
hand on his forearm. Earlier Alison had reminded her
about putting the Lalique mermaids on her other hand.

A recording of a favourite piece by Chopin had been her
idiosyncratic choice of music to begin the ceremony. It had
been playing as she came down the staircase and was timed
to finish as she took her place beside North.

Apart from the minister, only nine people were assembled
in the Blakewells' elegant drawing room. Mrs Stanton
Foster and Jane's two other trustees. Alison and her eldest
son Carter who had been at Harvard with North and
was acting as his best man. Carter's pretty wife Barbara.
Swanage and Mrs Swanage. Milly, maid at Winterbrook
for thirty years.

Aware that everyone was looking at her as she entered
on Marcus's arm, Jane kept her eyes downcast as they
crossed the long flower-filled room. She herself was not
carrying flowers, none of her favourites being in bloom at
this season.

Only when Marcus halted did she look up, through the
veil, to meet North's eyes. His expression was curiously
stern, making her wonder if he had spent the morning beset
by belated uncertainty.

Lifting her veil with both hands and folding it back, she
smiled at him before turning her gaze on the minister.

*   *   *

'Jane? Jane . . . where are you?'

Nineteen hours later she was woken by her husband's voice calling her.

A few moments later the door burst open and he found her. 'What the devil are you doing in here?' he demanded with a baffled expression.

'I was sleeping . . . till you woke me. Good morning. Did they just call you?'

He nodded. 'Ten minutes ago. I assumed you were in the bathroom till I knocked and got no answer.'

As their next flight left Kennedy at a quarter past eleven, they had arranged to be called at eight, not an unduly early rising in view of the time they had gone to bed.

Jane was now in the suite's second bedroom, lying in a twin bed. It had not been turned down the night before like the king-size bed in which North had spent the whole night.

She had slipped quietly out of that bed a little after midnight; padding soundlessly across the close-carpeted sitting room to a bedroom on the far side which, but for her specific instructions, would have had its door locked. Exploring the suite after their arrival late the previous afternoon, North hadn't even tried that door, concluding correctly that it led to a room which converted their honeymoon suite into a family one.

Before removing its cover and climbing into the twin bed, she had opened the ivory silk curtains to spend a few moments gazing at the lights of New York. Now, on this last day of August, sunlight flooded through the windows, but double glazing and air conditioning created a more temperate climate than the weather outside.

North approached the bed. He was naked, reminding her of Michelangelo's huge statue, *David*, in Florence. The sight of his muscular torso and long brown legs, and the memory of last night's loving, sent a spasm of excitement shooting through her. Under the bedclothes she was naked herself, as yet having had no chance to put on the exquisite nightdress she had bought for her wedding night.

'Don't tell me I snore so loudly you had to take refuge

in here. I wasn't aware that I snored at all,' he said, standing with feet apart and his fists on his hips by the side of the bed: a magnificent male in a state of semi-arousal.

She wanted to throw off the bedclothes, hold out her arms and quickly be made one flesh.

But she forced herself to say calmly, 'You don't . . . or not to my knowledge. But I'm not used to sharing a bed, or even a room, and I don't particularly want to. I thought it was customary in England for people to have separate bedrooms, if they had enough space to indulge in personal privacy?' she added, on an inflexion of faint surprise. 'We shall have our own rooms at Longwarden surely?'

He looked taken aback. As well he might, she thought, repressing a chuckle at his expression. Who, in her right mind, would prefer to sleep alone rather than snuggled up close to this gorgeous hunk of man-power?

'We can, I suppose. But it isn't usual for people to sleep apart on their honeymoon,' he said dryly.

'This isn't an ordinary honeymoon, is it?' she said reasonably. 'Naturally I'll come into your bed whenever you want. I'm not trying to avoid sleeping with you in that sense. But as far as real sleeping goes, I believe it's better for people to have complete freedom of movement. People who share a bed all night may not realize they're disturbing each other, but I'm sure they do. Aren't we supposed to change position about twenty times during the night? How can anyone do that *without* disturbing their bed-partner? What woke me last night was the weight of your arm on my waist. It's surprising how heavy an arm is when it's completely relaxed. Fortunately you were sleeping very soundly and I managed to slip out of bed without waking you.'

'I'm relieved to hear you'll come back whenever I want you. How about right now?'

Without waiting for her assent, he took hold of the bedclothes, threw them aside and scooped her warm bare body into his arms. As he strode out of the room and across the sitting room to the other bedroom, she slid both arms round his neck, feeling a primitive thrill at the ease with which he could carry her.

296

'Could I have a quick shower first?'

'No, you couldn't,' he said firmly. 'I don't want you washed and powdered and deodorized. You had a bath last night. You're fine the way you are.'

'At least let me brush my teeth.'

'Okay, we'll both do that.' He swung in the direction of the bathroom, setting her down on the threshold.

The bathroom had two oval basins sunk in a marble counter with a wall of looking glass behind it. As they squeezed toothpaste on to their brushes, she felt no shyness. After last night it seemed the most natural thing in the world for them both to be nude.

'You were very nice to me last night. Thank you, North,' she said, smiling at his reflection.

He shot up an eyebrow. 'Weren't you expecting me to be nice to you?'

'Of course . . . but it's a long time since I made love. It could have hurt if you had been . . . less considerate.'

He gave a slight bow. 'One strives to please.' He eyed her for some moments longer. It was her face not her body which held his attention. 'You're a strange girl.'

'Why? Because I haven't had many lovers? It's not so long since most brides hadn't had any.'

'I didn't mean only that. You seem to have your own ideas on most things.'

'It's the way I was raised . . . to be an individual . . . not a herd-person, as Dad used to say.' She began to brush her teeth.

Later she put her arms round him from behind and kissed him between the shoulder-blades, enjoying the pleasant taste and scent of his brown skin.

'Last night you were in charge. Now it's my turn,' she murmured, pressing her breasts against his back.

She couldn't see over his shoulder to watch his reaction in the mirror but, seconds later, as her hand slid down from his chest and across his flat belly, she felt it. Her fingers curled round him, tentative at first but rapidly becoming more confident.

* * *

Jane opened her eyes when North said, 'Time we made a move, sweetie.' He lifted himself off her. 'I'm going for a shower.'

She stretched. 'Call me when you've finished.'

After he had disappeared into the bathroom she lay staring at the ceiling, remembering Marie-Simone saying, apropos the divorce of one of John Graham's executives, 'The best way to hold a man is in your arms.'

Jane smiled to herself. Some of the things she had done had obviously surprised North. Perhaps because she was relatively inexperienced he had expected her to be timid. He might even have thought her under-sexed.

She wondered how soon she would become pregnant. She had considered consulting a gynaecologist about birth control but had decided against it, even though she wasn't sure that starting a baby right away was a good idea. There would be so much to learn in her new rôle as Countess of Carlyon. Maybe it would have been wiser to prevent conception until she had found her feet at Longwarden.

On the other hand if she got pregnant right away North would be flattered by the proof of his virility, and even more pleased if she gave him an heir.

'What a gargantuan breakfast,' she said when she joined him in the sitting room and saw what he had ordered for himself.

He had risen to draw out her chair. 'It's the logical time of day to tuck into something solid. I couldn't get through the morning on half a grapefruit and one boiled egg,' which was what he had ordered for her.

As he sat down he added, 'You don't need to watch your weight. I think you're a little too slim. Some more flesh here and there would be an improvement.'

'Oh . . . d'you think so?' she said, surprised and deflated. It was on the tip of her tongue to say, 'Okay, I'll try to gain a little.' Then she remembered it wasn't part of her strategy to indulge his every whim, like a woman in love. Indeed she was inclined to think that, even with love on both sides, it could be unwise to put all a man's wishes ahead of one's own.

She said pleasantly, 'I'm happy with my shape. Voluptuous curves may look great in the bedroom but they don't do anything for clothes. Or for health.'

It wasn't until they arrived at the airport that he discovered they were flying to Europe on Concorde.

As they sat in the departure lounge she said, 'I hope you won't be disappointed that I haven't picked a romantic resort. I've heard it can be a mistake to spend a honeymoon where there's nothing to do but relax.'

'Don't tell me we're going to join a guided tour for culture vultures?'

'No, no . . . nothing like that. But it will be a little different from the conventional honeymoon.'

'With a bride who wants separate bedrooms, that shouldn't surprise me,' he said dryly. 'Come on: tell me the worst.'

'As you haven't been there much this year, and I'm longing to see it, I've arranged for us to go to Longwarden.'

PART THREE: Autumn

SEPTEMBER

As North hadn't flown on Concorde before, Jane insisted he must have the window seat from which to see the curvature of the earth and the inky wastes of infinity.

He had received her announcement of their destination with surprise and perhaps some disapproval. A few moments later they had been called for boarding.

When lunch was served and he still hadn't said what he thought of her plan, she approached the subject by saying, 'I hope I can make your mother like me. She sounded a little bit stiff when I talked to her. Although she seemed quite sincere about not minding missing the wedding.'

'Mama prefers plants to people. You shouldn't worry if she keeps you at arm's length. She has no intimates,' he said with a shrug.

'Are you disappointed we're going there? Would you rather have gone to an hotel?'

'No, I don't mind going home . . . if you're impatient to inspect your domain.'

There was no mistaking the sardonic tone of this rider, and she wasn't happy about his use of the word 'your'.

Choosing to ignore the slight sting in his reply, she said, 'I'd like you to be the one to show me around.'

When the meal was over he spent the rest of the flight listening to a programme on his head-set. She did the same. No one would guess I was a bride, she thought rather forlornly. She began to wonder if she had made a mistake in by-passing the conventional honeymoon on which, for two or three weeks, they could have ignored the fundamental basis of their marriage and concentrated on the physical rapport between them.

Instead of heading for the uncertain weather of England, they could at this moment be unpacking their cases somewhere in the Caribbean, an aquamarine sea within yards of their private terrace, and dancing under the stars as a prelude to their second night together.

The more she thought about it, the more she regretted skipping that kind of honeymoon in favour of her present arrangements, although they had seemed a better idea until today.

Allegra was working when the telephone rang. Frowning at the interruption, she reached for the receiver. 'Hello?'

'I have a call for Lady Allegra Lomax.' The voice was female and American.

'Speaking.'

'Hold the line, please.'

Expecting the next voice to be her lover's, Allegra leaned back in her chair, work forgotten, a smile of anticipation curving her mouth.

'Good afternoon, Allegra. This is Elliott Lincoln. How are you?'

'Oh . . . Elliott.' She had almost forgotten him. Her smile faded. 'Hello. I'm very well, thanks. How are you?'

'I'm fine. I'm coming to Europe for the Frankfurt Book Fair and I'm hoping you're going to have dinner with me while I'm in England. The Fair opens October ninth. I'll be in London from the previous Friday. Do you happen to be free that evening by any chance?'

'I'll check my diary. That's Friday the fourth, isn't it? Yes, I'm free that evening.'

'You are? Terrific. My luck's in. I'm looking forward very much to seeing you again. I'm going to be staying in an apartment in the same building as Le Gavroche, the Roux brothers' restaurant. How would it be if you came to the apartment for drinks around seven and I'll make a reservation for dinner at eight? If you don't mind, I'd like

302

to ask a couple of publishing people to join us for the drinks but I'll make sure they leave early.'

'I'll look forward to it.'

The great wrought-iron gates, supported by tall brick piers topped with a pair of lichen-blotched stone urns, were standing open when they arrived at the main entrance to the Longwarden estate.

As the sleek black Daimler she had ordered to meet them swung off the quiet country road and entered the park, Jane had a glimpse of a somewhat neglected-looking lodge house in need of a coat of paint and clean curtains.

'I feel almost as nervous as Flora when she arrived,' she said to North.

In *Travels*, Allegra had recounted her great-grandmother's reminiscences of the unforgettable day when she had arrived at Longwarden, unprepared for the palatial size of her husband's house and only partially prepared for her role as the seventh Countess.

'There's no need for you to be nervous. There won't be any rows of indoor and outdoor staff lined up to receive you,' her husband said dryly. 'Even my mother and Sarah may not show up if they're busy.'

The long drive which, eighty-two years ago, had been lined with tenants and cottagers waiting to catch a glimpse of the bride his Lordship had brought all the way from China, passed through a stand of trees which screened the house until almost the last moment.

Suddenly it loomed in front of them, a palace of golden stone designed by Vanbrugh to replace the original house built in 1598. But today, as North had just told her, there were no ranks of black-clad maids and liveried footmen waiting to watch their new mistress step from the car.

As, with his unfailing good manners, North sprang out to help her alight, she saw that the only person there to greet them was a middle-aged man whose dark suit, white shirt and sombre tie proclaimed him as Ashford, the butler.

Of Lady Carlyon and her niece there was no sign; and as it was now seven o'clock, local time, an hour when most

303

people had finished their work or were at least taking a break, Jane couldn't help feeling that for her mother-in-law not to be there was somewhat ominous.

Pen was making a pot of tea in the small, old-fashioned kitchen at the back of Henry Hazell's cottage.

The old man had been taken ill shortly before it was time for him to bicycle home. One of the village's group of doctors had been called and, after examining the gardener, had driven him home with Pen in attendance to keep an eye on him until Sarah brought his widowed sister from her home on the other side of the county.

To Pen, accustomed to large rooms with lofty ceilings, the cottage seemed tiny, a doll's house. Although he looked after himself, the place was as neat and clean as he always was in his person.

He and his wife had been childless and she had been dead thirty years. Consequently the interior of 4, Fern Villas, a row of small brick-built houses with three rooms up and three down, lacked most of the facilities now standard in the other village houses.

There was no television in the lace-curtained front room with its German velour three-piece suite, elaborate overmantel and multitude of ornaments. Not that it would have been there if Henry had owned a TV. The chair where he spent winter evenings was beside the fire in the middle room where there was a dining table covered with a fringed chenille cloth.

However when his wife had become a semi-invalid he had had the small back bedroom converted into a bathroom, so now that he was ill he wouldn't have to come downstairs or use a chamber pot.

Wondering how she would manage without him, Pen hoped the doctor was right in his provisional opinion of the cause of Henry's collapse. Even if tests supported his diagnosis and the condition could be controlled with medicine, it seemed unlikely the old man would ever be fit enough to return to work.

I should have noticed he wasn't well, she thought guiltily.

This hasn't come on suddenly. He must have been feeling off colour for some time.

When she carried the tea tray up the steep narrow stairs to a landing and quietly entered his bedroom, she found Mr Hazell asleep. Above the head of the bed hung a print of *The Light of the World*. On the bedside table was the Bible she knew he read every night before he slept.

Careful not to disturb him, she filled one cup with tea and sat down in the Lloyd Loom chair by the window. The clock on the narrow ledge above the small black-leaded grate showed twenty minutes past seven. Pen wondered if North and her daughter-in-law had arrived at Longwarden yet. She wished she didn't have the strain of meeting the American girl to face later on this evening. She had always had difficulty making small talk to strangers and in her present worried frame of mind it would be harder than usual to appear gracious and welcoming.

When North showed her the bathroom next to the bedroom which had remained unoccupied since Flora Carlyon had last slept there, Jane was enchanted to find that each wall was painted with a Chinese landscape framed by painted curtains held back by painted silk cords. The effect was of standing in a hill-top pavilion with four views of ancient Cathay.

'What a charming idea,' she exclaimed.

'My great-grandfather had it done as a surprise for her birthday while they were away on a trip,' said North, standing with folded arms in the doorway.

'He must have loved her very much to have dreamed up such a romantic surprise.'

'I imagine he did . . . and he wasn't the only one. The afternoon she died she was having tea with an ancient retired general who had never married because of her.'

'I haven't seen a portrait of her yet, except for the reproduction of the portrait by Sargent in your sister's book.'

'There's one in the bedroom next door. Come and look.'

He led the way through an ante-room with a fine view of the park which connected Flora's pastel bedroom with a more masculine room, the walls oak-panelled, the bed a heavy four-poster. Clearly this had been where the seventh Earl had slept, or where he was supposed to have slept. But if his love for his wife had been the ardent emotion portrayed in Allegra's biography of him, Caspar Carlyon had probably spent most of his nights sharing Flora's pretty French bed.

'The portrait in here is by Philip de Laszlo,' said North.

The painting hanging over the chimneypiece showed Flora with a cloud of silvery tulle veiling her blue-black hair and bare golden shoulders. Her beautiful oriental eyes seemed to look directly into those of her great-grandson's foreign bride with a gentle, sympathetic expression which made Jane wish the Chinese Countess were still alive to advise her how best to adapt to this new and unfamiliar environment.

'She was lovely. I wish I'd known her,' she said, in a low voice.

As she studied the details of the portrait, the delicate wings of Flora's eyebrows and the sweetness of her un-painted mouth, she became aware that North was locking the door leading to the ante-room. He then locked the bedroom's main door.

'Why are you locking us in?'

'To make sure we aren't disturbed. If Sarah gets back shortly it may not occur to her that people who were married yesterday may not want her bursting in on them. Being impatient to meet you, she'll assume you are equally eager.'

As he spoke, he shrugged off his coat and swiftly loosened his tie. Casting both on the nearest chair, he came purpose-fully towards her.

She had travelled in a silk tweed blazer over a tie-neck shirt and fine wool pleated skirt. Clothes chosen to make a good first impression on his mother.

He slid his hands under her jacket. She felt the warmth of his palms through the silk of her shirt.

'I want you,' he told her huskily, before his mouth came

306

down on hers in a long sensuous kiss which demanded immediate surrender.

She responded at once, the movements of his lips and hands sending shivers of desire through her. She was about to put her arms round his neck when she changed the action, pulling her blazer from her shoulders and letting the sleeves slide down her arms. The jacket fell to the floor.

Without interrupting the kiss, North kept one hand spread on her back and used the other to untie the bow at her neck and unfasten her buttons. She was wearing one of the sexy wisps of silk and lace she had bought for her trousseau. Her small breasts were still as firm as they had been when she was eighteen. When she put on a bra it wasn't for uplift but for the same reason she sometimes wore stockings and a garter belt instead of pantyhose. It made her feel feminine, a sensation she enjoyed. Now she was married, pretty underwear was gift-wrapping.

His hand searched the band of her skirt till he found the centre-back zipper and pulled the tag. The skirt fell around her feet, soon to be followed by the shirt. Next he found the clip of her bra and that also was discarded, his cupped palms replacing the silk, his thumbs drawing light spirals round the smooth outer edges of the brown rosettes she thought might be too large in proportion to the size of her breasts. One day she would ask him, but not yet. For the moment it was still amazing that he was doing these things to her, making her tremble, making her soft and moist, ready to receive him.

'*Would you care to sin on a tiger-skin? Or would you prefer to err on some other fur?*' he murmured, close to her ear.

It had to be some kind of joke but she was too bemused to ask. 'Wherever you say,' she said dreamily, lost in the pleasure of touching, delving her fingers into his thick dark hair.

He took her, not on the bed, but on the floor; on what, she discovered later, was the skin of a Bengal tiger. The tiger's head had been stuffed. The long teeth showed in a snarl. The yellow glass eyes glared angrily.

'Poor thing! Who shot him?' she asked, when she discovered what they had been lying on.

'My great-great-grandfather. There are tigers all over the house. It's easy to forget where they are and trip over the damn things,' said North. 'That one will have to be moved if I'm going to use this room. Either that or decapitated.'

Languid from love, she sat up and stroked the broad head. The ears were showing signs of decay. It must be a century or more since the great beast had been shot.

'You can't do that to him. Why not have him so that his head is out of the way . . . under a chair maybe.' She climbed to her feet. 'I'm going to have my first tub in that beautiful bathroom.'

'No, you're not. We're going to share the amazing contraption which was the last word in modernity in 1899,' he told her as he sprang up.

His great-grandfather's bathroom was as different from Flora's as the two bedrooms. The very long, very deep bath was boxed in with polished mahogany and had solid brass taps, one marked Rain.

'That's supplied from a tank on the roof. According to Allegra and Sarah it's better than mains water for washing your hair,' he told her.

The 'amazing contraption' was a separate glass shower cabinet which looked as if, at the touch of a button, it might blast off into space. It had almost as many pipes and control-wheels as a ship's boiler room, and there was more than enough space inside for two people to shower without being crowded.

'This hasn't been used for a long time but I expect Ashford's made sure it's working,' said North, closing the door and turning to study the controls, their various functions being written in black lettering on white enamel discs in the centre of each wheel.

'Brace yourself.'

A second after his warning, Jane found herself engulfed in a deluge of icy water, coming not only from above but from every direction. Probably it wasn't as cold as it felt to her love-warmed body, but she couldn't repress a shriek.

'Turn it off!' she yelled through the freezing onslaught.

'I can't.' But he was laughing.

'You brute. You did it on purpose.' Half-blinded by the force of the torrent, she tried to see which of the wheels would stop the flood.

North pulled her into his arms and held her captive. Within a few moments the agony was over. The water began to feel less cold.

Holding her pinioned with one arm, he turned off the overhead jets and changed the temperature of the water coming out lower down to warm. Using an oval bar of transparent amber soap, he began to lather her back.

She could barely remember the last time someone had washed her. It was a nice feeling; being systematically lathered all over. He was very thorough, making her hold on to his back for balance while he picked up each foot in turn and soaped between her toes. When he came to the top of her thighs, she pressed them together, trying to resist his questing fingers.

'Are you hurting?' he asked, with a glance of concern.

She shook her head.

'You're sure?' he persisted.

Jane nodded. She believed in the precept attributed to the daughter-in-law of Pythagoras that, in going to bed with a man, a woman should take off her modesty with her skirt and put it on again with her petticoat. When North's mouth was on hers, and she knew his own blood was hot, she could accept his caresses without any inhibitions. But now his need had been satisfied by the passionate coupling on the tiger-skin and somehow that made a difference.

His knee nudged between her thighs, his soapy hand stroked her gently. Reluctantly she submitted, unwilling, in this area of their lives, to deny him anything he wanted or chose to do to her.

Almost at once she discovered that although his desire had been damped down for the time being, hers was quick to revive. Soon his experienced touch was sending ripples of pleasure down the insides of her thighs.

309

She closed her eyes, feeling the jets of warm water from the pipes behind her cascading against her back and legs. With a sigh, she relaxed against his supporting arm, her hands resting lightly on his shoulders until, as the lovely sensation grew stronger and stronger, her fingers tightened and clung.

He seemed to know just when to stop, leaving her poised on the brink of the ultimate bliss; and each time he started again the pleasure was more overwhelming, making her gasp and tremble. Finally he didn't stop, driving her on to a piercing implosion of feeling which made her shudder and cry out.

'That's the third time today ... I'm exhausted,' she murmured feebly, when it was over and she was leaning against him, feeling almost too weak to stand unsupported.

He turned her face up to his. 'You can do better than that. Tomorrow we'll say we're jet-lagged and spend the day seeing how much better.'

There was amusement in his eyes. She felt a sudden revulsion and withdrew herself from his arms.

'I must dry my hair. Would you turn off the water so that I can get out, please?'

He did as she asked, opening the door of the cabinet for her but remaining inside to wash himself while she stepped on to the rug-sized bath mat and took one of several white towels hanging in readiness on an old-fashioned mahogany towel horse.

Having rough-towelled her hair, Jane made the towel into a turban and used another to dry the rest of her. Then she went back to the bedroom, picked up her scattered clothing and returned to Flora's room where her luggage was waiting to be unpacked.

North's last remark in the shower had upset her. He had made making love sound like a form of exercise, with records to be equalled or surpassed. She didn't want to spend tomorrow in bed with him having a succession of soulless orgasms. But she knew this was partly because her sexuality was temporarily exhausted. By tomorrow her hungry senses would again be clamouring for fulfilment and he would have only to touch her to turn her on.

As she unpacked her overnight case and hung up a dress to wear for dinner, she noticed details there hadn't been time to see earlier. Such as the old-fashioned black daffodil telephone beside the four-poster bed.

The foot-posts were reeded and carved with running ribbon ties. Pushed close to them was a large sofa, covered and cushioned with the same flowery chintz as the bed's canopy and curtains. There were also a gilded day-bed, several elegant French bergères and a number of tables, some massed with silver-framed photographs and others with collections of objects.

Of the many pictures on the walls, the most arresting was a painting of a man and a girl riding on a white horse by the side of a river. On the far bank stood a city of onion-domed roofs and strange spires. She recognized the artist's distinctive technique. It was by Wassily Kandinsky whose work she had seen in the Städtische Galerie in Munich, with Marie-Simone, while her father was there on business.

It was a romantic painting which seemed to take its inspiration from some ancient fairy tale of lovers united after many misadventures. Perhaps Flora Carlyon had liked it because it symbolized her own love story.

North walked in, wrapped in a towel. 'It's occurred to me that you won't be able to use your dryer unless you have an adaptor to fit English socket outlets. If not I'll have to try to find Sarah's dryer for you.'

'Thanks, but I do have an adaptor. Don't forget I'm as used to changing countries as you are.'

'So you are.' He looked round the room. 'You'll want to have this redecorated. Colefax & Fowler are the firm most people use – those who can afford them. Or there's David Mlinaric who advises the National Trust, or Allegra's chum, Julian Fleetwood. Talk to her, if you want advice.'

'When I was in Scotland,' said Jane, 'people were discussing the changes Barbara Cartland's daughter had made at Althorp since she married the Princess of Wales's father. Some people there thought she had spoiled it, but several

311

others disagreed. As it's open to the public, I'd like to go and see it for myself. Is it far from here?'

'A couple of hours' drive, I suppose.'

He returned to his own room, leaving her to wonder if it had been a gaffe to suggest paying to look round someone else's country seat. But since Althorp was, as far as she knew, the only great English house to have undergone major refurbishments in recent years, she felt it might offer some object lessons.

They had been told by the butler why Lady Carlyon and his cousin had been absent when they arrived.

North hadn't closed either of the connecting doors. When she had finished drying her hair, she could hear him speaking to someone. A few moments later she heard him call, from the ante-room, 'Jane, are you decent? May I bring Sarah in?'

'Please do,' she called back.

He re-entered with his arm round his young cousin's shoulders. She was dressed in navy-blue breeches and an old navy sweater. The dark colour emphasized her fairness. Long sun-streaked blonde hair was fastened at the nape of her neck. Her eyes were the same deep blue as North's but their expression was different. He looked at the world either enigmatically or with slightly cynical amusement. Sarah's gaze was open and trusting.

'I'm terribly sorry we weren't here when you arrived,' she said, stepping quickly forward so that his arm fell to his side. 'I've been longing to meet you. Welcome to Longwarden.'

Jane rose to shake hands. 'Thank you very much, Sarah. I've been longing to meet you, too. I hear you're an outstanding rider. I'm hoping you'll help me improve. I haven't been on horseback for some time.'

'We can ride together . . . after Burghley.'

'Burghley?' Jane queried.

'The horse trials at Burghley in Lincolnshire, the week after next. It's the big autumn three-day event. I expect you've heard of the trials at Badminton in the spring. They're the most famous, but Burghley runs a close second.

312

This will be the first time I've competed there – that's if nothing disastrous happens in the meantime.' She touched the nearest piece of wood.

'How exciting. May we come and watch you?' asked Jane.

Before his cousin could answer, North cut in firmly, 'No, we'll have a much better view of the proceedings on television, particularly the cross-country course.'

Jane felt the girl might be disappointed by this somewhat casual attitude to an occasion which clearly meant a great deal to her.

But Sarah nodded, saying, 'Yes, you will – and besides it would be impossible to find anywhere to stay at this late date. All the hotels for miles around are booked up long in advance. If I get a ducking at the Trout Hatchery' – she crossed fingers on both hands – 'you'll see it best on TV.'

When her niece had returned from her errand with the news that Henry's sister was unable to look after him, being herself laid low with sciatica, Pen's immediate reaction had been guilty relief. It gave her a cast-iron excuse to remain where she was and postpone the critical first encounter with her American daughter-in-law until the following day.

When Sarah had gone on to say she had also called on the old man's niece who *was* able to come over and nurse him, but not until later that evening, Pen had felt there was still a good possibility she wouldn't be able to go home until after the honeymooners had gone to bed.

Sarah had been eager to meet Jane. But her future relationship with the American girl was not in any way hazardous.

Pen was in the cramped cottage kitchen, washing up the tea things in the white earthenware sink with its scrubbed wooden draining board, when she was startled to see Ashford passing the window.

With alarming memories of several recent air disasters suddenly in mind, she didn't wait to dry her hands before opening the thumb-latched door.

'Is anything wrong?'

'Nothing, m'Lady. His Lordship's flight was on time. He

arrived about an hour ago. I thought you might like me to stay with Mr Hazell till his niece arrives. His Lordship says he and her Ladyship will only require a light supper because of the time lag.'

'I'm sure they must be tired from the long flight so I shouldn't think they'll be late going to bed. It's good of you to offer to stay in my place, Mr Ashford, but I'd rather not leave poor old Henry until I can explain to his niece what happened and what the doctor thinks may be wrong with him. I'm sure my son and my daughter-in-law will understand the situation. You did give her my apologies for not being there when she arrived?'

'Of course . . . and her first concern was whether they could do anything to help. If you will permit me to say so, his Lordship's bride has what the Spanish would call a very *simpática* manner, m'Lady.'

'Has she?' Did he guess she was jittery about meeting the girl? Had he really taken to Jane? Or was he trying to be reassuring? She said, 'When you get back, do repeat how sorry I am and say I look forward to meeting her tomorrow.'

'Certainly, m'Lady. I took the precaution of bringing down a packed supper and also your reading spectacles and the new issue of *The Garden*.'

'Oh, now that is *most* thoughtful and kind,' she exclaimed. 'Without my specs I couldn't even read Henry's Bible.'

Ashford said, 'I'll fetch the things from the car. I brought yours for you to drive back in. It seems to be running quite well.'

He disappeared down the short path which led to a low wooden gate opening on to a communal back way. This passed behind the whole row of cottages, separating them from their back gardens, some well-kept like Henry Hazell's and others neglected and untidy, a great vexation to the old man lying asleep in the room upstairs.

Pen had finished the washing up when the butler reappeared with a hamper and an open basket. As well as the monthly journal of the Royal Horticultural Society, he had brought two books, and *The Times* which she never had time to read thoroughly at breakfast.

After washing his hands at the sink he spread a crisp check cotton picnic cloth, last used at a Fourth of June when North was at Eton, over Henry Hazell's chenille cloth.

'I'll just slip upstairs and make sure he's still sleeping,' said Pen.

Undressed to his stockinette underwear and helped into bed by the doctor, the old man lay with his arms outside the bedclothes, his hands and wrists knotted with veins, his thick fingers looking clumsy unless one had seen them, as she had, tenderly handling frail seedlings.

Returning downstairs, she said, 'I've left the door open a little in case he wakes up and calls.'

Ashford said, 'I think it might be advisable for me to stay here with you. If Mr Hazell wakes up, he may need some help which he wouldn't like to ask you for.'

Pen had many inhibitions but they didn't include embarrassment about the body's most basic functions.

'Yes, he may,' she agreed.

There were footsteps outside. They looked out of the window to see one of the two district nurses coming up the path.

'Good evening, Lady Carlyon. I've just popped in to see how he's doing,' she said when Pen opened the door.

Nurse Bagley was a solidly-built, muscular woman in her forties. Her husband, a fireman, had died fighting a factory blaze in Manchester. Now she lived for her work, attending to patients for much longer hours than were required of her. She had a brisk manner but Pen had been told that, when the occasion demanded it, she could be wonderfully sympathetic and supportive.

For someone with ample hips and calves like a racing cyclist's, she went up the stairs with a light tread.

She came down a short time later. 'Fast asleep so I didn't disturb him.'

Seeing the nurse eyeing the supper table, Pen said, 'Would you like a cup of tea or something to eat, Nurse

315

Bagley? Knowing my cook, she'll have sent down far more for my supper than one person could possibly eat. What's in that dish, Mr Ashford?'

'It's Mrs Armitage's cold grouse mousse, m'Lady,' he told her, lifting the lid.

'I wouldn't say no to a mouthful on one of those biscuits,' the nurse admitted.

'Yes, do try it. You'll find it delicious.' Pen dipped a knife in the mousse, spreading a generous dollop on one of the wholemeal biscuits which made a crunchy contrast to the smoothness of the rich mousse.

'Mm . . . it's good,' said Nurse Bagley, munching with gusto.

'Then sit down and have some more with this nice green salad,' Pen suggested.

'No, no, thanks – I won't stop now. I've a couple more calls to make before I call it a day . . . and a casserole waiting in the oven when I get home.' She wiped the crumbs from her lips with a tissue. 'I'll look in again in the morning. Goodnight.'

'If Nurse Bagley won't share this feast, I insist that you do, Mr Ashford,' said Pen when they were alone. 'There's more than enough for the two of us and you need your supper as much as I do. Lay another place for yourself and we'll both enjoy the mousse. I expect Mrs Armitage thought it would make an interesting starter for my daughter-in-law's first meal in England.'

He drew out the chair he had placed for her. 'I believe that was her idea – with baked trout for the main course and his Lordship's favourite treacle tart for the pudding. But in view of his instructions the trout is being kept for tomorrow.'

'I thought he loathed aeroplane food and never ate it,' said Pen.

'I understand the food on Concorde is considerably superior to the meals served on ordinary flights. His Lordship has just shared the experience which Lady Allegra enjoyed in May.'

'Oh, I see . . . how exciting.'

But not as exciting as this — our first meal together, thought Pen. How strange that a day of worrying first about Jane and then about Henry should culminate in such an unlooked-for treat.

'I'm slipping . . . I forgot the wine. It's still in the car. Excuse me,' he said, rising.

While he fetched it, she found a pair of wine glasses in the sideboard in Henry's front room and was rinsing them under the tap when Ashford re-entered the kitchen, carrying a cool box.

'This is not from his Lordship's cellar. It's a wine I sometimes buy for my own consumption which I thought you might like to try,' he explained.

While he opened it, Pen said with amusement, 'I'm trying to imagine Gisburn buying wine out of his own pocket when he had my son's cellar at his disposal. It's most unprofessional behaviour.' Ashford smiled but his glance was guarded. The wine was Spanish, she noticed, and potent enough to make her wary of drinking more than one glass.

'You used a Spanish word earlier to describe my daughter-in-law, and you like Spanish wine. Have you been to Spain often?' she asked.

'I used to go there at one time. I haven't recently. Some Spanish wines are much better than most people realize. Did the doctor give an opinion about Mr Hazell's condition?'

'He thinks it may be Ménière's syndrome, which causes attacks of vertigo. It's not unusual among people of Henry's age, apparently. Doctor Dunster says it's controllable. But probably Henry won't be able to go on working; a great blow to him as well as to me. I depend on my two dear old men and gardening has been Henry's life. I'm afraid if he's forced to take life quietly, the boredom will finish him off.'

There were noises from above.

'It sounds as if he's trying to get out of bed. Would you see what he's up to?' she asked.

'Of course.' He went swiftly upstairs.

She couldn't hear what was being said but she could

distinguish the high-pitched quaver of her gardener and the deeper, more resonant timbre of Ashford's voice.

Listening, she knew he hadn't wanted to talk about Spain. It was another of the mysterious areas of his life she was not permitted to penetrate. He was like a wood which could only be entered a short way before one came to a gate clearly marked NO ADMITTANCE – KEEP OUT.

And each time she came to that barrier, the more keenly she longed to know what lay beyond it.

Sarah had dined with the honeymooners but immediately afterwards had taken herself off, saying she had chores in the stables.

In fact she was sitting in her room over the archway, wishing Nick had come back to Longwarden in time to go with her to Burghley. He could have kept an eye on Sammy, who of late had become either forgetful or careless and whose breath often smelt of whisky early in the day.

He had always drunk a good deal, but it hadn't affected his work or his temper. She was worried about him and wanted to ask North's advice, but not on the second night of his honeymoon.

By now they were probably in bed, making love. Although if she hadn't known it, she would never have guessed yesterday had been their wedding day. They hadn't behaved like newly-married people. Rob and Emily were more demonstrative than North and Jane, which was strange because she was so lovely to look at that Sarah had found it difficult not to stare.

Allegra had told them Jane was a beauty and she was; but, more than that, she was nice. When Mrs Armitage had served dinner because Ashford was out, Jane had said all the right things to her. Then, while they were eating, she had asked Sarah about the horses, not just to be polite but as if she were really, really interested.

Jane possessed numerous watches, two of them inherited from her mother. At intervals during her growing up years John Graham had given his daughter watches; inexpensive fun watches at first, graduating to a more valuable one for her sixteenth birthday and a Vacheron Constantin when she was eighteen.

In spite of possessing a watch for every occasion, during her unannounced engagement she had bought herself another watch – for the specific purpose of reminding her that, for the time being, she must appear not to wish to sleep with her husband. Instead of making a sound, the watch's alarm was a pulse felt only by its wearer.

She had wondered if North, always sharply observant of details, might think it strange for her to wear a watch in bed. Since their wedding she had discovered he wore his own watch at all times, except in the shower.

On her first night at Longwarden the new watch didn't serve its purpose. Even after making long love, neither of them was ready to sleep. Midnight in England was early evening in New England. As she had found on her visit to Scotland, for the first few nights it was hard to get to sleep and harder still to get out of bed at 2 a.m. by one's body-clock.

They had made love in North's massive bed which, like an American king-size, gave its occupants ample space to sprawl.

But when at last North rolled away and would have turned out the light, saying, 'I suppose we'd better try to sleep,' Jane sat up.

'I know I can't sleep yet, North. I'm going back to my room to read a while. I'll see you at breakfast. Goodnight.'

She slid quickly off the high bed and went to retrieve her robe from the polar-bear skin by the fire. He had begun making love to her on the thick white rug – 'Time to err on another fur' – but later had picked her up and carried her to the cool smoothness of lavender-scented linen sheets.

The fire, unreplenished, had begun to die down as Jane wrapped her robe around her and put the brass spark-guard in place before turning towards the ante-room.

She didn't look at her bridegroom, who hadn't spoken, until she was at the door. Then she glanced quickly over her shoulder, smiled and repeated, 'Goodnight.'

319

North was propped on one long brown arm, watching her.

'Goodnight,' he answered.

What he was thinking it was impossible to tell.

The watch-pulse roused her from a deep sleep at seven. Although she longed to ignore it and slide back into oblivion, she forced herself to wake up.

This, even more than yesterday, was the beginning of her new life. She didn't want to waste a minute of her first full day at Longwarden. Her new domain, as North had rather sourly called it.

She began by taking a tub in Flora's delectable bathroom. The hot water was slightly rusty but it *was* hot and there was a big cast-iron radiator to heat the room later in the year.

At the moment, according to Sarah, England was enjoying an Indian summer. Heat was needed only in the evening and at present log fires sufficed. It would be some time, Jane had gathered, before central heating was considered necessary by the members of her new family.

Wherever Jane went in the world, a sapphire-blue glass jar with a silvery lid and an old-fashioned label always went with her. It contained a white cream, *Secret de Bonne Femme*, to which she had been introduced long ago by Marie-Simone. Made by Guerlain, the Paris perfumers, but never advertised, it was a favourite beauty aid among discriminating Frenchwomen.

Having protected her skin, but not bothering with other cosmetics, she dressed in a shirt and jeans and pulled on a cream cashmere sweater.

Quietly leaving her room, she set out on her first exploration of the great hundred-roomed house of which, for the rest of her life, she would be the mistress.

'What's she like? – The American girl?' asked Sammy, arriving for work while Sarah was quartering Tatty.

He was late, as he often was now, but she didn't say so. 'She's lovely, Sammy. You'll like her. You'll meet her today.'

320

'You think she'll fit in here, do you?' He sounded doubtful.

'I'm sure of it. She's the kind of person who would fit in anywhere . . . and she can ride and likes horses.'

'She may not ride well enough to be any help to us,' he said morosely, stumping off towards Berber's box.

'Oh dear, he's in one of his cross moods,' she murmured to the mare when the old groom was out of earshot. 'I hope he doesn't glower at Jane when she comes to meet you. I do wish Nick would come back. It will be awful if Sammy can't cope at Burghley. I'm not sure he's fit to go . . . but who else is there?'

'*Oh!*'

Jane recoiled with a gasp as the door she was passing opened and someone stepped out.

She had thought there was no one else about; or not in this part of the house. For an instant she didn't recognize the butler, dressed as he was in an open-necked shirt and a sweater.

'I'm sorry. I'm afraid I startled you, m'Lady,' he apologized.

'Yes . . . you did. Didn't I startle you?' she asked, recovering herself and smiling at him.

'Lady Carlyon is quite often about at this hour, but I didn't expect to see your Ladyship down yet. I'm going round opening the shutters but if you would like to have breakfast they can wait until later.'

'No, no – I'm not at all hungry,' she assured him. 'It's the middle of the night where I come from. I shan't want anything to eat until at least noon, so I may as well hold out till lunch. But if you could spare a few minutes I would like to be shown the way out . . . to the garden, I mean. It's such a beautiful morning I thought I'd take a walk outside.'

Ashford, as North addressed him, glanced down at her feet which were shod in tan leather loafers.

'By all means . . . but if I may advise you, it would be wise to wear a pair of galoshes or wellingtons from the

321

cloakroom. There's a heavy dew on the grass. You don't want to get your feet wet.'

It struck her that Ashford might know the answer to a question she had been meaning to ask North, but had so far forgotten whenever they were together.

Accompanying the butler along a wide passage spread with many oriental rugs, most of them threadbare she noticed, she said, 'I expect you know I'm a great-granddaughter of the "Chinese" Countess. I have a book that belonged to her with her book-plate in it and some words in Latin – *Dum vivimus, vivamus*. I assume that's the family motto. Do you happen to know what it means?'

'It means "While we live, let us live . . . to the full",' he informed her.

After a short pause she said, 'If Americans had family mottoes, my father would have liked that. He lived every minute to its fullest. I think it's a very good motto. I'll do my best to live up to it.'

'I'm sure you will have no difficulty in doing so, Lady Carlyon. Americans are renowned for their vitality and energy. I think it is very possible you will give the motto new meaning. You may be sure that I and the rest of the staff here will all do our utmost to support you.'

'What a nice thing to say, Mr Ashford. Thank you.' She had decided that to use his last name alone sounded too imperious. 'Thank you very much. As a newcomer here, and a foreigner, I shall certainly need all the help and guidance I can get. Now tell me: where is the silver staircase I read about in Lady Allegra's book? I know there's more than one staircase here, but the silver one sounds the most beautiful.'

'In fact you have seen it,' he told her. 'It's the staircase in the Great Hall. The original wrought-iron rail was replaced by a copy of a silver one at Versailles when the sixth Earl was making improvements in honour of Queen Victoria's son, later King Edward VII, who often visited Longwarden. The reason you wouldn't have recognized it as the silver staircase is that it's badly tarnished. While your great-grandmother lived here, there was a large-enough staff to cope with the constant polishing the staircase required to keep it bright. That would be impossible now. The team of cleaners we have here is fully extended already.'

'What a shame,' she exclaimed. 'You're right. I had no idea the stairs I used yesterday were the ones with the banisters copied from Madame de Pompadour's Petit Trianon. I didn't even notice them. I was busy looking at the paintings. This morning I found another staircase to come down. Quite a grand one by most people's standards, but here merely back stairs, I guess.'

'If you turned left outside your bedroom, I expect you came down what is known as the billiard-room staircase. It has a large portrait of the fourth Earl at the foot of it, and a pair of life-size marble dogs.' He opened a door for her. 'This cloakroom leads to the terrace. You'll find a variety of boots here.'

Jane entered a wide stone-flagged passage with another door at the far end and two more doors leading off on each side. Between all these doors, on shelves, pegs and in open lockers, was arranged an amazing assortment of headgear, clothing and footwear for outdoor pursuits. There was even, she noticed, an Australian bush hat with corks dangling from the wide brim. Who had brought that here? Her husband?

She was thinking of North and regretting that, unlike most brides on the second morning of their marriage, she wasn't sleeping in his arms, as she stepped outside into the warming air of a perfect fall morning.

Autumn, she corrected herself. Not as spectacular a season as the New England fall when the maple trees blazed like flames, a sight she had seen for the first time last year. But there was beauty here of a quieter, more mellow kind; beauty which caught at her heart, confirming that the balm for unhappiness she had found at Winterbrook had been only a foretaste of the strong sense of homecoming she was experiencing here.

As she crossed the worn stones of the terrace with their tiny creeping plants and mosses, and set foot on the dew-sparkling grass, she had a strange sense of *déjà vu*, as

323

if she had been here before, in another time, another life.

She knew that couldn't be so. People had only one life: which was why it was vital to live it according to North's family motto. The rational explanation of her feeling was that it wasn't the first time she had seen this garden.

The hours she had spent poring over Lady Rose's albums in the Athenaeum had made her extremely familiar with the view from the terrace and other aspects of the garden. Now, although subtly changed by the passage of sixty years, it wasn't surprisi⋯ ⋯se gardens seemed known to her.

Pen walked round the corner of the east and south fronts and came to an abrupt standstill.

A girl was standing on the lawn, a puff of breeze lifting a swathe of her glossy black hair.

Surely this couldn't be Jane? Not at this hour of the morning. They would be in bed for hours yet. Pen's mind shied away from the thought of her son and his bride in bed. Not that North resembled his father, either in looks or character. But for her the word honeymoon was indivisibly linked with the horrors of her own.

Unaware that she was being watched, the girl turned to look in a different direction. As she turned, she lifted her hand to push the Asian-dark hair behind her left ear, exposing a profile which told Pen instantly that this was indeed her daughter-in-law.

Although she had been prepared by North's photographs of her for Jane to resemble Flora, the astonishing beauty of her face still came as a shock. Here, in modern dress, was Flora as Caspar had known her when she was young. No wonder his cold heart had melted.

But why was Jane out so early? And on her own? There was no sign of North.

Winging back to the first morning of her own marriage, memory showed Pen a vision of herself creeping out of Room 46 at the Hyde Park Hotel and walking across the park to the bridge over the Serpentine. She remembered leaning on the parapet, wondering if she could drown herself before some interfering bystander fished her out,

giving the next day's *Daily Mirror* the banner headline
EARL'S BRIDE ATTEMPTS SUICIDE AFTER WEDDING NIGHT.

Desperate as she had felt, she hadn't been desperate
enough to risk making a botch of killing herself. In the end
she had walked slowly back to find Edward nursing a
hangover, annoyed that she hadn't been there to ply him
with Alka Seltzer as soon as he woke up.

She forgot her own worries and thought only of a young
girl, a long way from home, who might be shy and senstive,
as Flora had been when she first came to England.

The soft swish of footsteps on wet grass penetrated Jane's
reverie. She glanced round, surprised to see that North's
'fool of a mother' – who else could it be? – was quite
different from the image conjured by her children's somewhat disparaging references to her.

For a middle-aged woman, Lady Carlyon had a curiously
young look. Not the spuriously youthful appearance
achieved by American women dedicated to fending off age.
Clearly the woman approaching knew nothing of beautici-
ans' skills or even of simple cosmetics. Everything about
her proclaimed her as a person who spent no time on her
appearance.

She looked, thought Jane, like a nun – or would were
she not wearing pants. There was something unworldly
about her. At first sight she didn't look like a mother, or a
widow, or a countess; but like someone who had spent her
life in an enclosed order, tending the convent's garden.

When Pen was a few yards from her, the girl turned full
face to her and at once the illusion was dispelled. Jane
wasn't Flora's double, nor did she show any sign of being
in a troubled state of mind. Even before she smiled, her
long-lashed grey eyes held no hint of unhappiness. She
gave the impression of being an outstanding natural beauty
whose looks had given her the confidence to sail through
any situation, even the testing moment of meeting her
mother-in-law.

With a smile which showed perfect teeth, she came to

325

meet Pen who had checked when she saw the girl full-face.

'Good morning, Lady Carlyon. Isn't it a wonderful morning? As you can guess I'm Jane Graham.' Realizing her slip, she laughed. 'Or rather I *was* Jane Graham. I guess after having that name for twenty-three years, it will take me a while to get used to my new one.' She offered her hand.

Faced with that blithe self-confidence, Pen's compassionate impulse towards her evaporated. Her own innate shyness took over, making her manner formal as she answered, 'How do you do? Yes, it's a nice morning now, but the forecast is rain. I see you've had the good sense to borrow some boots. The dew is always very heavy at this time of year.'

Not a nun, a mother superior, thought Jane, quelled by this clipped response to a greeting which inward nervousness had made over-bright. Not normally lacking in social poise, she felt her self-possession slipping. Even when complimenting her for good sense, Lady Carlyon managed to convey that it wasn't good form to borrow things without permission.

Jane said, 'Yes, so your butler warned me. He suggested I borrow the boots. Are they yours? I hope you don't mind?'

'I have no idea whose they are,' was Lady Carlyon's vague reply. 'I'm sorry I wasn't here when you arrived yesterday. Is this your first visit to England?'

She spoke as if to a guest who was paying them a visit and would soon return whence she came. Maybe that was what she wished would happen, thought Jane.

'No, I've been to England several times. How was your gardener when you last saw him?' she asked.

'Very poorly, I'm afraid. He was sleeping when I left, but earlier on he woke up and was dreadfully sick and dizzy, poor old man. He's thought to be suffering from Ménière's disease. It may be called something else in America.'

'I don't know. I've never heard of it. Can it be cured?'

'In some cases, yes, I believe so. But perhaps not in

someone elderly. However I don't want to bore you with medical details. You came over on Concorde, I hear. What an interesting experience. It's been one of North's ambitions for years.'

Is that so? He didn't tell me that, thought Jane. Maybe the kick was spoiled for him because I paid for the tickets.

She had known that a man had to have a strong sense of his personal worth, unflawed by any feelings of inadequacy, to take in his stride the fact that his wife had more money, whether earned or inherited.

She had thought he was that kind of man. Maybe she had been wrong. Maybe it was going to irk him every time she paid for something he wanted but couldn't afford out of his own pocket.

I hope not, she thought uneasily. I hope that's not going to be *another* problem. Because I've got one with his mother – that's obvious. She's being very polite, in her stiff way, but inside she's hating me. The very last thing she wanted was an American daughter-in-law.

At lunch the next day, North said, 'May we take two of your nags for a hack round the park this afternoon, Sarah?'

Jane thought his cousin looked doubtful and deduced that she didn't like others riding her horses. It was a natural reaction. They were not ordinary mounts, kept for anyone's use. Jane had met them the day before and been impressed, especially by Bedouin Star with his intelligent eyes and gentle manners.

This morning, while North was taking her to see the long-disused brew-house, laundry and sawmill, they had stopped to watch Sarah riding him. Jane had never seen a horse and rider who looked better together: the handsome chestnut with a white star on his forehead and an Arab's distinctive way of carrying his long silky tail, and the slender girl on his back with her thick braid hanging between her shoulder-blades. Jane had suggested to North that it would make a marvellous picture if he photographed them on a gallop, with Sarah's blonde hair flying loose like the Arab's mane.

'Yes, if I could get her to gallop without a hat on. Riding is a high-risk sport and Sarah's very safety conscious. She won't let you ride without a hat. If you haven't got one, you'll have to buy one before she'll mount you,' he had answered.

As it happened her riding kit did include a hat. But before Sarah could answer his question, Jane said quickly, 'Couldn't we walk, North? The exercise would be good for us.'

'It's a long tramp on foot if you want to see everything,' he said.

He raised an eyebrow at his cousin who said, 'If you ride Tatty, Jane can have Berber. He's a very sensible horse who will give you a comfortable ride if you're a bit out of practice,' she told Jane. 'He was the horse I rode when I started eventing at sixteen, a year before Beddo was ready.'

'Will your mare be large enough for North?'

'Oh yes, no problem. He's tall but he isn't heavy. Uncle Edward weighed more than two hundred pounds and needed very big horses, but North is much lighter. What do you weigh?' Sarah asked him.

'Just under twelve stone . . . a hundred and sixty-seven pounds.'

'For six foot two that's not much. Mark Phillips is two inches shorter and he weighs a hundred and sixty-one,' said Sarah.

The conversation reminded Jane of how North had looked last night, strolling into her bedroom while she was brushing her hair, wearing only a towel wrapped round his long lean flanks, his body all bone and muscle under his sleek brown skin.

They had made love in her bed. She had known that if, later, she asked him to leave, he would refuse. So she hadn't said anything and before he turned out the light North had looked down at her flushed, excited face with an expression suggesting he felt there would be no more nonsense about sleeping apart.

This morning he had woken in her bed – alone. Woken by her alarm watch, she had slept in his. She wasn't about

328

to give up keeping him guessing at this early stage of the game.

But now, sitting at the lunch table, thinking about his broad shoulders looming over her and his warm mouth exploring her throat, suddenly she found herself wanting him with a disturbing urgency. Should she plead time-lag fatigue and suggest postponing the ride in favour of an afternoon nap?

'She's a good-looking girl, right enough,' said Sammy as he and Sarah stood outside the arch, watching the two on horseback move off. 'And not a bad rider either, by the look of it. Although that's not to say she's up to going hunting with you.'

'I'd rather have you with me, Sammy.'

They had been going to meets together since the days when her mount was a tough little Exmoor pony who could keep going all day and also had the ability to break out of almost any enclosure if he put his mind to it.

'That may be, but I'm getting on, girl . . . getting old. Not that I'd mind coming a cropper and breaking my neck like your uncle. It's a better way to go out than some.'

He turned back into the yard and she watched him go with a frown, knowing that if she told him again that he should see a doctor, he would bite her head off.

I must talk to North about him . . . soon, she thought, lingering to watch the two horses walking down to the main drive. North was, as always, bare-headed, but Jane had come to the stables wearing a riding hat and looking very well turned out in a grey-brown tweed hacking jacket and buff breeches over jodhpur boots. She had spent a few minutes talking to Berber before mounting him and adjusting her stirrups.

She seemed to have nice light hands and a relaxed seat. Sarah would have liked to go with them and observe her more closely, but she knew they would prefer to be alone. In any case she had no time to spare. When she wasn't exercising the horses, she had her own exercise programme to carry out. It was no use bringing Beddo to peak condition if her own condition didn't match it. When they set out for Lincolnshire, she had to be at the very top of her form to stand any chance of being placed, let alone winning the coveted Rémy Martin Challenge Trophy.

The park surrounding Longwarden was larger than Jane had realized, encompassing several woods and various buildings and monuments ranging from an eighteenth-century bath-house to a cenotaph erected after World War One to commemorate nineteen Longwarden men who had made 'the supreme sacrifice'.

Following the 1939–45 hostilities only one name had been added, that of North's grandfather who, as a thirty-nine-year-old colonel, had won a posthumous VC in the Italian campaign.

'If he had got through the war, very likely he would still be alive. My father would never have inherited and let the place go to pieces, and my responsibility for it might still be several years ahead,' said North.

'That sounds as if you're already regretting your lost bachelor status,' Jane said, her tone lighter than her thoughts.

'Hardly, when I now have a beautiful wife to warm my bed – if never for long,' he added with a sardonic smile.

Most of the open grass of the neglected parkland was too rabbit-holed and mole-hillocked to allow safe cantering, particularly with Tatty who was also entered for Burghley. In Sarah's place, Jane wouldn't have allowed anyone to borrow her second horse shortly before an important contest. But it might be that her financial dependence on North had made the girl feel obliged to permit it. Jane wondered if any of them realized they now had a millionairess – and that was the reason why North had married her – in their midst.

She hadn't missed the nervous glance given her by Lady Carlyon during lunch when Jane had made an oblique reference to the absence of a swimming pool at Longwarden. It was something that would have to be remedied before next summer. Swimming was one of her pleasures.

330

There had been few times in her life when she hadn't had access to a large pool. But none of the improvements she had in mind was so urgent it needed to be put in hand at once. The first essential was to make friends with these people. Sweeping changes, introduced too soon, would only alienate them.

'This was my favourite wood as a small boy,' North told her as they approached another large stand of trees, mainly green and copper beeches.

Near the fringe of the wood he dismounted and hitched the mare to a small tree.

'Is it all right to leave the horses standing?' she asked doubtfully.

'It won't hurt them to graze for twenty minutes.'

The horses secured, he took Jane by the hand and led her towards the wood, his quick stride forcing her to jog to keep pace with him.

The interior of the wood wasn't dark like the gloomy depths of a coniferous forest. Here, sunlight filtered through gaps in the canopy of branches, striping the springy leaf-mould underfoot. In shady places velvety emerald mosses grew on the exposed roots of the great grey-trunked beeches, whose arching branches reminded her of the ancient stone vaulting in medieval cathedrals. No sounds from the modern world penetrated the stillness. This was a place apart . . . a magic place.

They came to a halt in a clearing where one massive tree stood alone, encircled by bracken.

Putting her thought into words, North said, '*Enter these enchanted woods, you who dare . . .*'

They were still holding hands. She looked up at him. 'Is that part of a poem?'

He nodded. '"The Woods of Westermain" by George Meredith. He was in vogue when Flora first came to England. Nobody reads his stuff now. I only know that one line. She brought me here one afternoon when I was six or seven . . . in hot water with my father as usual. It seemed like a forest to me then. For a long time I really believed these woods were enchanted. A year or two later, I came back from prep school one summer to find she'd had a tree-house built for me.'

He tilted his head to point out a covered platform built in a fork high above them.

'How did you get up there?'

'There used to be a thick rope. Someone's removed it. I had to learn to shin up it before I could use the tree-house. It was two weeks before I could make it. That was the idea, of course. The Edwardians were great believers in character-building.'

'And muscle-building!' was her comment. 'That's a long rope-climb. You must have improved your biceps as well as your character by the time you got up there.'

'Would you like to feel my biceps?'

He pulled her into his arms, his mouth stopping her from replying to the teasing invitation.

Instantly, the desire she had felt during lunch, and managed to repress, flared up as he pressed her tightly against his hard body, kissing her as hungrily as if it were weeks rather than hours since their last close physical contact.

It wasn't until he walked her backwards into a thick drift of dry leaves, and then released her to strip off his army-green sweater, that she realized he meant to make love to her here and now.

'North, we can't . . . not here,' she protested.

'Why not? I want you . . . now.'

Again his mouth silenced hers while his hands pushed her unbuttoned jacket off her shoulders and down her arms.

'The horses . . .' she murmured feebly, as he spread it beside his sweater over the mattress of leaves.

'. . . can wait. Get undressed.' He unbuttoned the cuffs of his shirt before beginning on the front buttons, his blue eyes narrowed and brilliant, demanding her obedience.

She undid one button and paused. 'What if someone came by?'

'No one will. Have you forgotten your promise?'

'What promise?'

332

'You said you'd never refuse me.'

Her throat tightened as he bared his tanned chest and shoulders. As with the horses, every movement he made tightened or relaxed the muscles underlying his taut brown skin.

'I said I'd come to your bed whenever you wanted,' she answered, her breathing quickening.

'Isn't this bed good enough for you?'

Was it her imagination, or was there an element of anger in this sudden urgent lust for her? She trembled, her civilized self a little afraid of him in this mood, but a primitive part of her excited.

North pulled off his boots and socks. The second action reminded Jane of being told by Marie-Simone that a man who understood women never made love with his socks on.

Her fingers clumsy, she tugged her shirt out of her waistband and fumbled with the rest of the buttons. His hands were steady but impatient as he ripped the tongue of his belt from its buckle. Released from the tightness of his breeches, his erection sprang free, mesmerizing her with its powerful symmetry.

Barefoot in last year's leaves, as naked as Adam, he crossed the few feet between them, pushing her hands aside to undress her more quickly. When she was almost nude, her breeches pushed down to her thighs, he tumbled her roughly on to their rustling bed to remove her boots and tug the breeches down over her feet.

She shivered. At first the air felt cool on her exposed flesh. But his arms and body were warm and his mouth soon made her oblivious to any physical sensation except the pulsing excitement generated by his fierce kisses.

She thought he would take her quickly, even brutally; there was something fierce and primeval in the way he pinioned her wrists and held her spread-eagled while his mouth roamed her throat and breasts, making her arch with pleasure.

But when he pushed her legs apart and thrust himself rapidly inside her, there was no brute force on his part and no resistance on hers. Their bodies fitted as perfectly as a sword and its scabbard; and she locked her slim legs round his hips, wanting to make him her prisoner just as she was his willing captive.

Somewhere a horse whinnied. Jane's eyelids fluttered open. She looked up, through layers of green leaves, to chinks of blue sky far above.

She had not been asleep but at peace; so deeply at peace as to be in a state of trance from which she returned to reality slowly and with reluctance. It was a few moments before the sound which had roused her registered fully.

'North – the horses!' she exclaimed in alarm.

The whinny must have registered with him at the same moment. She felt his slack muscles brace. Seconds later he was on his feet, reaching for his clothes, dressing as hurriedly as he had undressed.

'It's probably nothing . . . don't panic,' he told her.

He was gone before she was half dressed.

She was making her way out of the wood when she heard him call, 'You can come out. There's nobody here but us chickens.'

Emerging from the green gloaming into full sunlight, she wondered if from their passionate coupling in the wood would come their first child; conceived at the foot of the tree where, in years to come, a rope would be put up for him to climb to his private eyrie. She rather hoped it might be so, but she didn't share her thoughts with North.

'Your hair's full of bits of leaf. Come here and I'll pick them out.'

When he finished, she wanted to seize his hand and kiss it and hold it to her cheek. But she said only a polite, 'Thank you,' and put on her hat.

As they rode in the direction of the house she was conscious that, having just been through the most intensely sensual experience a man and woman could share, emotionally they were still strangers.

And perhaps always would be.

*   *   *

In the year 1520, near the village of Stamford in Lincoln-shire, a child was christened William Cecil. By the age of sixteen he was a lecturer at Cambridge University. At twenty-three he was a Member of Parliament; at twenty-seven Secretary of State.

After a temporary set-back when he was imprisoned in the Tower of London for three months, he was released, given the first of his titles and made a privy councillor. The highest peaks of his career were still ahead of him. He became the most influential adviser to Queen Elizabeth I. It was she, never lavish with honours, who, when he was fifty-one, raised him to the peerage as Lord Burghley. The following year he became her Lord High Treasurer.

Naturally the custodian of England's coffers didn't fail to feather his own nest. Burghley House, the great Tudor mansion appropriate to his power and genius, and to playing host to a queen and her large retinue, took many years to build. It wasn't completed until 1589 when William was nearly seventy.

For almost four hundred years its distinctive spiked cupolas and tall paired chimneys have dominated the land-scape near Stamford. It was said that, during World War Two, Hitler's chief aide, Hermann Goering gave the Luft-waffe orders not to bomb Burghley because he intended to make it his country house after the German invasion of England.

The invasion never happened. Burghley remained in the hands of William's descendant, the Marquess of Exeter, who presently opened his doors to the public.

The visitors, most of whom lived in small suburban houses and bungalows, gazed in awe and admiration at the painted walls and ceiling of the Heaven Room, the exquisitely carved dead bird with a fly on its neck in the Green Damask Room, the original hangings of the bed where Elizabeth I had slept, and the portrait of her in a great lace ruff with a pearl on her forehead.

While the house was attracting large numbers of English and overseas sightseers, the park surrounding it was becom-ing well known as the setting for the most important three-day event of the autumn, an occasion rivalled only by the spring horse trials under the aegis of the Duke of Beaufort at Badminton.

The year Princess Anne won an individual gold medal in the European Championships at Burghley, she and the Queen and Prince Philip stayed at Burghley House during the contest. Sarah's uncle had been on friendly terms with Lord Exeter and, had they both been alive, no doubt he and Sarah also would have been invited to stay at Burghley. Instead she had a room at the George, an old coaching inn in Stamford.

With Sarah at the wheel of the horse-box, she and Sammy set out early from Longwarden, arriving at Burghley on a golden September afternoon. She helped him to settle the horses in their temporary quarters before walking the mile back to Stamford for a bath and rest.

Every year, at the time of the horse trials, all the rooms at the hotel were booked for competitors, most of whom she had met at other events. While she was asking for her key, and again on her way up the stairs, she was greeted by people she knew. But although there was no question of her feeling an odd girl out, as she relaxed in the bath she was conscious of something, or rather of *someone* missing. In a quiet interval before she was fully engaged by the problems of this year's course, her thoughts were of Nick.

With four cans of beer and two packets of crisps within reach, Tark lit a cigarette and settled down to watch the television coverage of a sporting event he had never seen or indeed heard of until recently. For several days past, talk in the pub had made him aware that Sarah Lomax was riding in an important competition which would be shown on TV. He had decided to be one of the many people in the village who would be watching her performance rather than football this afternoon.

'The Horse Trials sponsored by Rémy Martin here at Burghley this weekend are attracting at least a quarter of a million visitors,' the commentator began, as the screen showed a crowd of people standing behind a rope barrier, watching a rider approach a formidable fence.

If he gets over that he'll be lucky, thought Tark, impressed by its height.

'Not only is this the twenty-fifth event since the trials here were started by the late Marquess of Exeter in 1961, but it's also the European Three-Day Event Championships with twelve nations competing and teams from eleven countries,' the commentator continued, as horse and rider jumped the fence without mishap.

'In 1961 there were only twenty starters. This year there are fifty-nine, an indication of how this exciting sport has grown in popularity, both with riders and with the huge crowds who come to see them compete.

'The first winner, twenty-five years ago, was Anneli Drummond-Hay riding Merely-a-Monarch. This year's favourite is Virginia Holgate on Priceless. Last year she became the first rider ever to win at Burghley two years in succession, so it will be interesting to see if she can pull off a hat-trick riding as a member of the British team.

'At the end of yesterday's dressage, two individual riders were in the lead. Willie Huizing, from Holland, on Chico rode a beautiful test in spite of very blustery conditions, with a score of forty-six point eight. But the outstanding performer was Bedouin Star, ridden by nineteen-year-old Sarah Lomax, who had to contend with a violently flapping piece of canvas on one of the grandstands.'

Tark, who had no interest in past events and didn't know the meaning of dressage, was beginning to be bored until the mention of Sarah regained his attention.

'There was talk of an objection on behalf of the riders who rode their tests before the canvas was removed,' the commentator continued. 'But it didn't appear to bother Miss Lomax's Arab gelding. For once the three judges, from Poland, Switzerland and Britain, were in agreement. They all placed Miss Lomax first with only thirty-one penalties.

'Some people have expressed surprise that the Dutch selectors didn't include Huizing in their team. But dressage is his speciality and he may not maintain his advantage in today's speed and endurance phase. What is perhaps more surprising is that Sarah Lomax wasn't picked for the British team. She's been riding brilliantly all season, but of course she lacks the experience of the three ladies who were chosen. Lorna Clarke, the Scottish eventer, had her first big success here back in 1967. Lucinda Green's triumphs are too well known to need repeating; and having won this year's Badminton and the National and Scottish Championships, Miss Holgate was an obvious choice. It may be that Ian Stark beat Miss Lomax into the fourth place because the selectors wanted to avoid an all-female team.

'There are quite a number of people – some of them influential – who continue to doubt, in spite of all the evidence to the contrary, that eventing is suitable for women. They were not allowed to take part in Olympic three-day events until as recently as 1964, and there's still a strong school of thought that eventing is a fighting sport, demanding characteristics which are unbecoming in the fair sex.'

This was over Tark's head. 'Jesus, what a load of crap!'

'This year's course has been designed by Philip Herbert and, as in previous years, some new obstacles have been introduced and many fences offer a choice of approach. This gives riders a chance to gain time by choosing the difficult route. Altogether there are twenty-seven jumps and the four-mile course has to be ridden in twelve minutes . . . so every second counts.'

Tark stuffed a handful of crisps into his mouth. He tried to work out the speed they would have to ride in miles per hour but after a brief mental effort gave up the attempt.

'But if you think that's a tough test,' the voice went on, 'bear in mind that, before the cross-country, the competitors have already tackled the roads and tracks phase, followed by the steeplechase course on the fairways of the golf course. The total distance they have to cover today is thirteen miles with a time allowance of about one hour and twenty minutes. I think you'll agree that's a gruelling test for both horses and riders, one which not all of them will complete.'

The scene on the screen had changed. A different camera was focusing on a male rider going over a jump the commentator said was Lambert's Sofa, named after a fifty-two-stone man who had died at Stamford in 1809. Tark heard the rider's name but it didn't mean anything to him. Only one of the contestants was of interest to him.

He had to wait a long time before he saw her, at first without recognition. In their jockey-style chin-strapped crash skulls, the horsewomen looked much alike.

'. . . and now here comes Sarah Lomax on Bedouin Star after riding clear in the steeplechase with no penalties to add to yesterday's excellent score.'

As the slim figure bounced smoothly over a jump, Tark started to pay more attention. When she came into close-up at the next obstacle he could see that she didn't look tired or anxious as some of the others had. She was concentrating, but she was also enjoying herself.

He wondered why the horse had bandages round its ankles and covers over its front hooves. Next time he saw her, he'd ask her. That could be the way to get through to her: to put on a show of being keen to know about horses.

'Oh, beautifully jumped! This girl really knows her stuff. She gets everything right . . . every time. She's always going with the horse, which is very important, and you'll notice she never comes in to the jumps at a gallop but keeps at a nice bouncy canter with plenty of what riders call impulsion. She's approaching the Double Coffin now. The ground drops after the stockade and then there are a couple of ditches and a steep bank before the second fence. As we've already seen, a couple of riders have had a problem getting out here, but I don't think it's going to bother Bedouin Star.'

At this point, to Tark's annoyance, the programme's producer decided the viewers would be more interested in another rider taking a ducking at the Trout Hatchery where a large crowd behind the palisade had already enjoyed the spectacle of several riders getting drenched.

By the time Sarah came on the screen again she was

halfway round the course, nearing the Waterloo Rails where two horses had fallen and five had refused.

'A good time on the cross-country is not a matter of going flat out between fences but of not wasting time at the jumps,' said the commentator. 'Now let's see how she handles the Rails which have a very big drop on the other side. Over she goes . . . feet rammed home in the stirrups . . . ready to hold him on landing if he should peck. But he's nice and straight and lands well and off they go to the next one . . .'

The doorbell rang. Tark swore, heaved himself off the couch and went into the narrow hall.

Two spruce young men in conservative suits stood outside the front door. He recognized them as evangelists.

Before they could open their mouths, he said savagely, 'Piss off!' and slammed the door in their faces.

The cameras were still with Sarah, following a seemingly effortless progress which made the commentator almost lyrical in praise of her.

'Even the infamous Trout Hatchery holds no terrors for this pair. We haven't seen riding of this calibre in a girl of this age since Lucinda Green – Lucinda Prior-Palmer as she was then – won at Badminton for the first time in 1973. Sarah Lomax makes it look easy, doesn't she? Getting towards the end now. With time in hand will she play safe at the next jump or take the time-saving way? As I thought, she's going straight through . . . and over they go, very smoothly . . . and on to the next . . . Oh! . . . Oh, I say, what bad luck . . .'

Tark sat up with a jerk, spilling beer on his jeans, flinching as Sarah hit the ground.

'Christ! She's broken her bleeding neck.'

Because he didn't have a television in his room, Maisie Armitage had invited Mr Ashford to watch the horse trials on the large colour set in her sitting room.

As Sarah fell, the cook gasped, her hand to her mouth. For a moment she stared in horror at the picture of Sarah, now a tumbled heap on the ground.

340

'Oh, my God – just like her Dad!' she groaned, with a shudder. She flopped back in her chair, her eyes shut. 'I can't bear to look.'

In the library, nobody spoke. They were stunned by the unexpectedness of what had happened. It seemed unbelievable that after going so well over the most difficult jumps, Sarah had come to grief for no apparent reason. In the interminable seconds after her fall, the same apprehensive silence had fallen at the scene. Even the commentator was momentarily speechless.

Deeply shocked, Jane acted instinctively. Only the night before, North had told her the tragic way in which Sarah's father, Ranulf Lomax, had died on the race course at Aintree, riding as an amateur jockey in the Grand National. This must be an agonizing sight for Lady Carlyon.

Jane moved to sit close beside her and wrap both hands round the clenched hands on the older woman's lap. It was a comforting gesture she wouldn't have dared to make in any less heart-stopping circumstances. But she knew from her own experience what it was like not to know if someone you loved had been fatally injured, and her reaction was spontaneous.

The commentator recovered his wits. 'We don't know what happened there yet, but clearly something went wrong and Miss Lomax fell and is either winded or knocked out. The most appalling bad luck when she was going round so well. Now she's moving . . . she's getting up . . . obviously dazed but perhaps not seriously hurt . . . and just look at this, Bedouin Star is coming back for her. He went galloping on when she came off, but here he is on his way back. Well, that really is something to see . . . a quite remarkable example of equine intelligence and the rapport between this young rider and a horse she has bred and trained herself. Now Miss Lomax is on her feet, looking rather unsteady, and Bedouin Star is standing as still as a rock, waiting for her to remount. Is she fit to carry on? Yes, she is. A steward is giving her a leg-up, which is allowed after a fall. Ah, now we can see what caused that fall. Her reins have broken. Which means, I'm afraid, that she'll have to retire. Those of you who are horse-trials enthusiasts will remember the same thing happened to Captain Mark Phillips at Badminton some years ago. If my memory is correct, it was 1977 and he was riding Persian Holiday, with a very good chance of winning, but his reins snapped and that was that. In his case it happened a few fences into the cross-country –'

He broke off, again lost for words as the screen showed Sarah, now in the saddle, hurriedly looping the useless reins before grasping the Arab's long mane and urging him forward.

'Is she going to try and carry on without reins? Surely not. Yes, she is . . . she jolly well is. My goodness, this girl has got pluck. All these riders have courage. That goes without saying. But I've never seen anyone attempt a feat of this order.'

Still clasping her mother-in-law's hands, Jane looked across at her husband. 'Is it possible?' she asked him.

He shrugged, his eyes fixed on the screen. 'God knows? I suppose it depends on Beddo. She can hang on if he can get himself over the last two jumps.'

Lady Carlyon unclenched her fingers, not to remove them from Jane's hold but to return it. 'She used often to ride bare-back and without reins as a child. But after that fall I think it's terribly dangerous,' she added anxiously. 'She may be slightly concussed and not realize how dangerous it is.'

Gripping each other's hands, sharing the mounting tension as Bedouin Star's flying hooves carried him nearer and nearer to the penultimate obstacle, they watched the screen, dreading the sight of Sarah hurtling from the saddle a second time.

The fence was not one which, at a lesser event, would have attracted many spectators. Burghley's huge attendance meant that every obstacle had its crowd of onlookers.

A loud cheer went up as the horse sprang over the jump and galloped on, his energy undiminished, his rider still firmly astride him.

'Well done, Beddo. Good girl, Sarah.' North was leaning forward in his chair, his blue eyes blazing approval. 'By God, I believe she's going to make it in spite of falling,' he said excitedly.

Moments later Sarah and Beddo soared over the last jump and, to even louder cheers, galloped flat out to the finish.

It wasn't until the triumphant moment was over and the cameras had started to track the progress of another contestant that Jane and her mother-in-law let go of each other's hands, both giving sighs of relief. They also realized simultaneously that, in a few moments of stress, their relationship had advanced to a point which, but for Sarah's fall, they might not have reached for weeks or even months.

As they exchanged smiles, Jane realized also that Lady Carlyon's austere manner was a mask to conceal her real nature. Suddenly Jane was reminded of girls she had known at the various schools she had attended; timid, uncertain girls, usually neither pretty nor clever and with a family background which, if over-privileged in some ways, had deprived them of all sense of worth. Girls who were pathetically grateful for any friendliness shown them by their more assured contemporaries.

Could it be that this middle-aged peeress, mother of two of the most self-confident people Jane had ever met, was herself an intensely shy person with a very insecure sense of her own value?

'She can't have broken anything or she'd never have got over those last two jumps,' said North. 'But apart from the penalties for falling, being a mass of bruises won't help her in the showjumping tomorrow.'

'How many penalties will they give her?' asked Jane.

Her question was answered by the commentator: 'We've just heard that Sarah Lomax and Bedouin Star are still in the lead. Her fall was outside the penalty zone and, as you saw on your screens a few minutes ago, they were well within the time limit. Her very quick recovery from that nasty tumble and Bedouin Star's amazing performance over

343

the last two jumps mean that if they do well tomorrow they stand a good chance of winning the Individual Gold Medal.

'The last time something like this happened in a European Championship was in 1977 when Lucinda Green came off Mrs Straker's horse, George, during the steeplechase. Like Sarah Lomax today, she was *outside* the penalty zone and *inside* the time limit, and she and George went on to take the individual European title as well as helping Britain to take the team title. If Miss Lomax does maintain her lead, I think one can say with confidence that although she wasn't included in the team representing Britain here at Burghley this weekend, all other things being equal she will have made sure of a place in the 1988 Olympics team.'

'Which is her big ambition, isn't it?' said Jane. 'I think we should have some champagne, North, to drink to Sarah and Beddo . . . and to steady our nerves after that horrible moment.'

A quiet voice behind her said, 'I thought you might wish to reserve the champagne for tomorrow, your Lordship. Some Rémy Martin seemed the appropriate restorative after the excitement of Miss Sarah's performance across country.'

Unnoticed, the soft-footed butler had entered the library with three glasses of cognac on a tray. He looked inquiringly at North, who grinned and said, 'Perfect timing, Ashford. The very thing we need to pick us up after those tense few moments . . . in fact only seconds, I suppose, but they seemed a long time.'

Ashford offered the tray to the elder Lady Carlyon who said, 'You must have some brandy too, Mr Ashford . . . and Mrs Armitage. I'm sure your nerves were quite as frazzled as ours by that ghastly moment when Sarah fell.'

'Thank you, m'Lady. As you say, it was very alarming. I daresay before the programme ends we shall see an interview with Miss Sarah which will relieve your mind.'

He was right. About ten minutes later, while some of the less promising riders were going round the course, Sarah appeared. Her eyes were incandescent with happiness, and her forehead and temples were a mass of damply curling tendrils, making her look even younger than her years.

'How are you feeling, Sarah?' the interviewer asked. 'You must be pleased to have completed the course without penalties, but you took a heavy fall which, if it broke no bones, must have been extremely painful.'

Without any trace of camera shyness she said, with a laugh, 'I used to fall off regularly when I was younger, but not so much recently. There's nothing wrong with me that a hot bath won't cure. But I feel terribly embarrassed at falling off in public in that stupid way. Nobody ought to crash off because a rein breaks. But somehow I did and, if it hadn't been for my fantastic horse, we should be out of the running. I've always known he was brilliant, but he really saved my bacon today. I gave him a big hug afterwards, but I don't think he's very pleased with me for making an exhibition of myself and spoiling his time.'

'You trained Bedouin Star yourself, I believe?'

'Yes, but with the advice of a marvellous horseman, Sammy O'Brien, who taught me to ride and helps me look after the horses. As Sammy and I both checked all the tack beforehand, it's a bit of a mystery how the reins could have snapped. But all's well that ends well.'

'However it happened, your recovery and the way you and Bedouin Star completed the course gave everyone a big thrill, and we wish you the best of luck in the final phase of the trials tomorrow.'

'Thank you . . . thank you very much.'

For a few seconds longer the camera held her in close-up, no hint that she might be more severely bruised than she made out showing in her flushed, cheerful face.

That night, in the Longwarden Arms, much of the conversation was about Sarah's performance at Burghley. Pride in a local girl's achievement and admiration for her courage were the theme of most of the discussions. But not everyone was jubilant.

'I wouldn't mind having a quid for every ten quid that

lot spend on them horses,' said Sidney Coker, who habitually spent his evenings on a stool at the public bar before weaving home to easily the worst-kept of the Rural District Council's houses where seventeen-stone Maureen Coker and their five children would have had their fish and chip supper and left some chips to keep warm in the oven for him.

Overhearing this remark Eddie Melchett said, 'You'd be a rich man if you had, Sid.' He winked at the others round the bar.

Eddie also lived 'up the estate' as Longwarden people called the first rows of public housing to be built in the village. But his wife kept the windows shining and the net curtains spotless and his garden was in good order with flowers at the front and vegetables at the back. He came into the pub for a beer most lunch-times and for two hours on Saturday night. His other evenings were spent with his family.

Sidney glanced over his shoulder. 'They do say there's many a true word spoken in jest and I reckon you're right there, Eddie,' he answered sourly. 'Times int changed that much since my dad's old father slogged his guts out up at Mill Farm, with nothing to show at the end of forty years' hard but a clock for him and a china tea set for his missus. Them up at the House don't own the farms no more, but they're still a bloody sight better off than any of us.'

'You don't do too bad, Sid,' Eddie said dryly.

Sidney, an unskilled labourer, was out of work as often as in work. However, by taking full advantage of every provision by the state for people in need, he managed never to go short of his booze and his fags, and whatever other comforts they lacked his family was never deprived of a large colour television.

In the lounge bar, which the brewers had refurnished with a red and orange fitted carpet and Jacobean-style tables and chairs with hunting-scene cretonne squabs in keeping with the genuine beams and inglenook, Mrs Ashman and her friend Mrs Bailey, both part-time helpers at Longwarden, were sipping shandies before going to the Saturday-night bingo session at the village hall.

'She'll be black and blue tomorrow,' said Mrs Bailey. 'I thought she'd have to retire after a bad fall like that.'

Mrs Ashman nodded. 'So did I. It's a wonder she didn't break something. It can't be good for her, Connie. She'll pay for it later, I'm sure.'

'Oh, yes, she'll pay for it later, but at her age they don't think of that,' agreed Mrs Bailey. 'They say she takes after her grandfather. The one who was given the VC after he was killed in the last war. Not in looks because he was dark. Well, he would be of course, his mother being a Chinese. Miss Sarah looks like *her* mother, so I've been told.' She pursed her lips. 'How any woman could be so heartless as to leave her child with other people is beyond my understanding. She must have been as hard as nails.'

Mrs Ashman took a small embroidered handkerchief out of her handbag and wiped the edges of her lips. 'Miss Sarah may have her looks but she don't have her mother's nature. She's a lovely girl, I think. Nicer than Lady Allegra who's more off-hand and impatient. I must say you'd never guess they had Chinese blood in them, would you? Not to look at the present generation.'

After a decade of dusting Lomax possessions and flicking a feather duster round the frames of Lomax family portraits, Mrs Bailey prided herself on her knowledge of their history, which she was inclined to show off to helpers recruited more recently.

'The seventh Countess wasn't a full-blooded Chinese. Her father was English,' she explained. 'She was the one who turned the house into a hospital for shell-shock cases in the first war. And it was her who sold some of her jewellery to pay for the old people's cottages and their community centre. There's one old man there, Mr Nudd, who can remember the day she arrived as a bride. Ninteen hundred and three that was, and he remembers it as clear as yesterday. He often tells people about it . . . how they unharnessed the horses from the bridal carriage and it was pulled up the drive by some of the farm workers. Mr Nudd's getting on for a hundred. He was about seventeen then. He threw her a bunch of primroses and she never forgot that. The last time she came to see him, she reminded him about the primroses. According to him, she was the most beautiful lady he ever saw in his whole life, and *we* know that from the paintings of her.'

'Yes ... and the lovely clothes she wore,' agreed Mrs Ashman, who had often admired the Edwardian ball gowns and jewels worn by Flora Carlyon when she sat to the many artists who had immortalized her beauty. 'Mind you, I shouldn't have cared to live in those days,' she went on. 'Think what they went through, having babies, poor souls. And the number of children dying from scarlet fever and diphtheria was terrible. People can say what they like about the good old days: I think we're better off now.'

'In some ways we are,' said Mrs Bailey. 'Not in every way. Take young people now ... that lot who've just come in.' She nodded her head at a group at the far end of the lounge. 'Did you ever see such a sight as that Sharon Cook?'

Mrs Ashman looked disapprovingly at a brassy blonde in a black plastic mini skirt who clearly was not wearing a bra under her tight purple top. She turned to her friend. 'Shall we be going now, my dear?'

As they were leaving the lounge, the blonde said, 'Hello, Mrs Bailey.'

Mrs Bailey exposed her dentures in a brief artificial smile. 'Good evening, Sharon.'

'Who's that old cow?' asked Tark, as they went out of the door.

Sharon giggled. 'She heard you. She lives up our road in the house with a lot of little g-nomes in the garden. She works at Longwarden, cleaning.'

'You ever been up there? Inside the house?' Tark asked her.

She shook her head. 'The girl what lives there won a horse race today. It was on the News on TV. She beat some quite famous riders.'

'Yeah, I saw it. It weren't a horse race. They all rode

348

round the course separate, seeing who could do the best time. It were on for a couple of hours.'

'I thought you was doing a job for your mum this afternoon. That's what you said when I wanted to go into town.' Sharon's tone was aggrieved.

He shrugged. 'The job didn't take as long as I thought it would. If you wanted to go shopping that bad, you could have gone on the bus like Mum.'

'I wanted to go with you,' she said peevishly. 'You are a rotten sod, Tark. You never do anything I want.'

'Stick that in your gob and stop moaning.' He flipped a cigarette at her. 'What you want to drink?'

'I'll have a Tequila Sunrise,' she said, choosing the most expensive drink she could think of in retaliation.

He might be a pig in some ways, but at least he wasn't a mean pig. By the time they left the pub he had bought her three drinks, two packets of nuts and some gum.

Their next stop was the fish and chip shop. Sharon enjoyed her supper. As much as the chicken and chips, she relished the feeling of being the best-looking girl out with the best-looking boy. With his thick black tangle of curls and his sexy dark eyes, Tark was much more exciting than any of the local boys. She just wished he would be a bit nicer, a bit more loving.

Maybe her mother was right. Her mother said there were two kinds of men in the world: good-looking bastards and fellows who would never do anything bad except bore you to death. Her mother's advice was to have a good time for a few years and then find a bloke what would worship the ground she walked on, never mind how boring he was.

Stuffing hot chips into his mouth, Tark was thinking about the old bag who had spoken to Sharon in the pub. She had given him an idea. He mulled it over for a few minutes until, hearing a girl standing near them complaining that she was cold, his thoughts turned to the problem of where to fuck Sharon as the autumn nights became chillier.

That was the one disadvantage with a motorbike. It didn't have a weatherproof back seat.

He had already spent some time cruising around the countryside looking for a barn or a shed, or even an empty cottage, where he could take birds when it was raining or cold. There had been nowhere suitable.

As he finished the chips and wiped a hand over his mouth, he suddenly remembered noticing a couple of buildings a long way from the house the evening he'd gone to see Sarah and got the brush-off.

There had also been a building, he recalled, not far from the spot where he'd climbed the wall to see what lay behind it. Tomorrow he'd take another look.

Tonight they'd go to their usual place. If Sharon whined about it, like she had last time, she'd find herself walking home. That'd learn her.

On Sunday evening, after trying the number several times, Allegra got through to the George and asked to speak to her cousin.

'Sarah? It's Allegra. Congratulations! I couldn't be more proud of you. Sammy must be in seventh heaven, isn't he?'

'Yes, he is pleased ... but rather whacked, poor old dear. The grooms have all the work and none of the kudos, you know. How nice of you to ring up.'

'Were you crocked by that fall? When you were talking on TV, I wondered if you were making light of it. Was today's jumping agony?'

'No, no – not at all. But I was a bit stiff last night. One of the maids here very kindly rubbed my back with the special stuff Sammy used to put on Daddy after a fall. This morning I was as good as new. I wish you could have seen my darling gold medallist jumping today. He *soared* over everything, bless him.'

'He's certainly a terrific horse, but don't give him all the credit. He couldn't have done it without you on his back. Have you seen the papers? They're comparing you with Lucinda Green and calling you "the new golden girl of eventing".'

'That's typical journalese,' Sarah said dryly. 'I've got a long way to go to be in Lucinda's class. She can make any horse a winner . . . Be Fair, Wide Awake, Killaire, George . . . Regal Realm. I'm all right while I'm riding Beddo, but I haven't done anything spectacular with Tatty.'

'You will. Give it time,' said Allegra. 'People like you always get to the top of their tree. It's the dedication that does it. You eat, sleep and breathe eventing. But I do feel you ought to try to fit in *some* social life this winter. What's next on your agenda?'

'We're going to the Audi trials at Chatsworth next month and then we'll be taking it easy until it's time to start training for Badminton.'

'Is there any chance of your spending a few days with me between now and Chatsworth?'

'I'd like to, Allegra, but I don't think I can. It puts such a load on Sammy when I'm away and he isn't too fit at the moment.'

'What's the matter with him?'

'Nothing that he will admit to. Perhaps it's only that he's getting older and it's been a pretty tough season. We've been travelling and competing almost non-stop since April.'

'You need someone younger than Sammy . . . a full-time girl groom,' said Allegra. 'Especially if, as it says in one of the papers, you're sure to be picked to ride in the next Olympics.'

'That's nonsense,' Sarah declared. 'Nobody is ever *sure* to be picked for any team. Look what happened to Mark Phillips in 1976. He was on the selectors' short-list for Montreal, but he wasn't picked for the team. He went there as the reserve rider. If that could happen to him, there's nothing sure about my chances.'

'But at least a strong probability; and you can't get to the top with a groom who can't cope on his own when you want a few days off. Sammy ought to go into semi-retirement. Now that North's married, he can. All the money worries are over, thanks to Jane's millions. You can have as many horses and grooms as you want.'

'Jane's millions?' Sarah said blankly.

'Didn't you know? She's the heiress to a vast fortune made by her father.'

351

'No, I had no idea. But anyway I couldn't sponge on Jane.'

'You wouldn't be sponging. She and North have endowed each other with all their worldly goods. That makes him a very rich man who can easily afford to subsidize your eventing career. But I reserve the right to give you a pair of Maxwell's boots,' said Allegra. 'That's why I want you in London – to have the first fitting. Even if they're ordered now, they won't be ready until next year's hunting begins. They can only make about seven hundred pairs a year, they tell me. Hence the delay.'

'But Maxwell's boots cost the earth,' Sarah protested.

'Yes, but I can afford it and they last for ever if they're treed. One of the joys of earning all this money is being able to give people lovely extravagant prezzies. What are you doing this evening?'

'Having a quiet celebration dinner with Sammy. We're heading for home early tomorrow.'

'It sounds a rather flat ending to your day of triumph.'

'Not really. The hotel is still full of Burghley people. There'll be quite a party atmosphere.'

When Allegra replaced the receiver after her call to Stamford, it was with a guilty feeling that, instead of ringing up to congratulate Sarah, she should have made the effort to be there and watch her competing. It was rather a shame the poor kid had had none of her family present.

Her cousin's astonished reaction on being told about Jane's fortune made Allegra wonder if she should have held her tongue. But as, in New York, North had made no bones about his motive in marrying Jane, Allegra had expected him to be equally frank with their mother and cousin.

A short time later she telephoned Longwarden, feeling an obligation to discuss Sarah's win with her mother. Her call was answered by North. Having explained his presence, he said, 'We're having a small celebration tomorrow night. Not a large party. Sarah's friends the Warehams are coming, and the Dunster girl. Can you join us?'

'Unfortunately not. I'm going to Heathrow to meet Andro.'

'Bring him with you. I'd like to talk to him about doing a portrait of Jane.'

'Not this time, North. At the moment we have so little time together. We like to spend it by ourselves. I'm sure Sarah will understand. Is Jane there? May I have a word with her?'

After talking to her new sister-in-law she had a brief conversation with her mother, who sounded uncharacteristically animated. They had been celebrating already, Allegra gathered.

Later she had a call from Risconti.

'I'm sorry, *cara*, I can't make it tomorrow. Something has come up . . . but I'll be with you as soon as possible.'

'Oh, Andro – no!' she exclaimed. 'What happened? Why can't you come?'

'I'll explain when I see you . . . perhaps late next week or possibly the week after. How are you? Are you well?'

'I'm always well . . . but I miss you.'

'And I you . . .'

But somehow he didn't sound as profoundly disappointed as she felt. The call left her vaguely disturbed. In New York single women outnumbered the available men by something like ten to one, which was why so many had to settle for affairs with other women's husbands. Could it be that she had a rival? Someone who was *there*, not far away in London, researching, when he wanted a woman, not only to share his bed but all the other pleasures of that most exciting of cities.

OCTOBER

Apart from the Princess of Wales, Margaret Thatcher and the Collins sisters, Joan and Jackie, the only other Englishwoman who could be considered a household name in America was the flamboyant octogenarian novelist, Barbara Cartland. In Britain, Jane had discovered, an equally public and controversial figure was her daughter Raine, Countess Spencer, the Princess's stepmother.

Setting out in her new right-hand-drive car to visit Althorp, Jane wondered why, when neither of them knew her or had been there, North and Lady Carlyon seemed to disapprove of Lady Spencer and the changes she had made at Althorp, home of her husband's family since 1508.

Perhaps it was because, from all she had heard and read of them, the Countess and her mother had exceptional energy and a great deal of panache, qualities admired in America but thought rather suspect in England which, in spite of having Mrs Thatcher at the helm, seemed to be a firmly patriarchal society.

The changes made at Althorp under the direction of the present Countess were said to be the greatest single work of restoration by a private family in the twentieth century. In North's opinion, based on hearsay, the house had been ruined by over-restoration.

If a British-born countess, who had started her public life as the Debutante of the Year way back in the late forties, and whose first husband had also been a peer, could be the subject of criticism, Jane knew her own position to be even more exposed to disapproval.

Therefore to see for herself precisely what Raine Spencer *had* done at Althorp – rather than what she was rumoured to have done – and to form her own opinion of the refurbishing, seemed an essential preliminary to starting a similar programme at Longwarden.

On arrival, she followed some other visitors through a gift shop and refreshment room in part of the large stable block. From there a wide path led to the house and round it to the side entrance used by the public. The gardens struck her as bare, with large expanses of grass and none of the alluring glimpses which beckoned the newcomer to Longwarden to explore the walks and shrubberies.

Inside the house she discovered that visitors were not

allowed to wander round at their leisure. Here, groups were led by a guide as in the châteaux of France.

The group Jane joined was too large for her to catch everything the guide was saying or to see all the features being described. Rather than crowding closer, as some people did, she drew back, waiting until the group moved on to have a clear view over the barrier across the entrance to the dining room with its deep-blue velvet-hung walls and long rows of re-covered chairs.

As she was turning away to rejoin the group, a tall man in a cherry-red sweater emerged from a side door. She recognized him as Earl Spencer who, at that time recovering from an illness, she had last seen on television, escorting his daughter to the altar.

Looking now in much improved health, he nodded and smiled at her. 'Are you one of our overseas visitors?'

She smiled back. 'Yes, I'm American.'

After a few words with her, he spoke to some other people who were also lagging behind the main party and who were visibly thrilled to be engaged in conversation by the owner of Althorp.

Although it held a wonderful collection of pictures and other treasures, including a fine array of rare porcelains in glass cabinets in the China Corridor, as a house Jane didn't like Althorp and was glad it was not to this mansion that North had brought her.

When the tour was over – and not all the rooms detailed in the guide book were shown – she returned to the stable block where there was also a wine shop, she noticed.

She was sitting at a table in the refreshment room when she recognized a woman coming from the gift shop as Lady Spencer. A painting of her was among the family portraits lining the galleries on either side of the main staircase.

Jane visualized English peeresses as women who, like her mother-in-law, might perhaps cut a dash for a ball or some special occasion but who, at home in the daytime, wore understated or even shabby country clothes.

This concept didn't apply to the present mistress of Althorp. She was dressed to the hilt in a green dress and jacket with a matching pillbox-style hat set on the back of her immaculate coiffure. High heels, lacquered nails, pearls at her throat, gold at her wrists and plenty of make-up to accentuate her flawless pink and white complexion, combined to give the impression she might be on her way to a gala luncheon in nearby Northampton.

However it was soon apparent that in fact the Countess was 'on duty'. Jane watched her adjust some flowers, confer with one of her staff and smile graciously at a party of four elderly women who were openly goggling at her.

Trying not to stare, but fascinated by this unexpected close-up of someone who had accomplished the task now confronting her, Jane watched as she paused to chat to them. There was something more American than English in Raine Spencer's bandbox grooming and air of efficiency and drive.

For her to modernize Althorp, it had been necessary to sell a pair of gold ice pails and various other family treasures. Jane could afford to spend far more than the million pounds the restoration here was said to have cost. Even so she had no intention of pouring money into Longwarden without first trying to find ways to make the house self-supporting.

All the way home she thought about it, regretting that she hadn't introduced herself to Lady Spencer, who might have been prepared to discuss the economics of opening a house to the public. At Althorp the public's interest had been stimulated by the connection with the glamorous Princess of Wales. Longwarden's only advantage in the historic house stakes was that it had been the home of the charismatic Chinese Countess, and the background to the love story described in Allegra's best-seller.

When North had shown Jane the sawmill, the brewhouse and the laundry, it had made her realize how, until comparatively recently, all the great houses of England had been self-sufficient communities. Her intuitive feeling was that the future of Longwarden lay in reviving that state of independence, but in a new form.

* * *

The hall porter at 47 Park Street announced Allegra's arrival by telephone and ushered her into the lift. Elliott was waiting to meet her when she stepped out on the third floor.

'Allegra . . . it's great to see you.' He sandwiched her hand between his. 'The others are here. You may know them.'

An hour later, leaving her to cast an interested eye over the details of the sumptuous Mlinaric-decorated sitting room of his apartment, he escorted his other drinks guests back to the lift.

Returning a few minutes later he said, 'Let me refresh your drink.'

She glanced at her watch. 'Is there time?' It was a few minutes past eight.

'This is a service apartment. We can dine up here on the same food they serve in the restaurant. As I'm going to be seeing and talking to many, many people at Frankfurt next week, I thought tonight it would be pleasant to dine as quietly as possible.' Sensing her reaction, he added, 'Are you disappointed? Would you have preferred to see and be seen in that very attractive outfit?'

She was wearing a shoulder-padded Saint Laurent jumpsuit of navy silk crêpe with a soft leather sash knotted at the front and Tibetan silver earrings.

'No, it's not that . . .' She decided to be frank. 'It's merely that my life has changed since we met in New York. I was free then. Now I'm not.'

'I see. Well, I have to admit that's a disappointment. I was hoping . . .' He shrugged his shoulders. 'You're concerned that the man in your life mightn't like you dining alone with me, is that it?'

'Should I like it if I knew he was dining *à deux* with an attractive compatriot of yours?' she asked lightly. 'He's in America at present. If he'd been here I should have invited you to dine with us. I think you'd find him interesting. He's Alessandro Risconti, the portrait painter. Have you heard of him?'

'I certainly have. Last month at an editorial meeting one of our people suggested him as a subject for a biography.'

'Have you made any approach to him? He hasn't mentioned it when we've talked on the telephone.'

'Yes, but he turned it down. The idea was to have him give a series of interviews to one of our authors who does in-depth studies of interesting people. Excuse me one moment.' He moved to the telephone and she heard him asking to be put through to Le Gavroche.

A few moments later, he said, 'They don't have a table. Would you like me to try another restaurant?'

'No, no . . . don't bother. Let's dine here. After all you are one of my publishers. What reason did Andro give for turning down your suggestion?'

'That he didn't have the time. Do you think maybe you can persuade him to change his mind? Obviously, in the circumstances, you're the ideal person to write about him.'

'I don't know . . . but in any case I shouldn't be able to do it until I've finished my present book.'

'That's something I want to discuss with you, Allegra. We're not entirely happy about your present project. From the information we have on it, it wouldn't appear to have a strong appeal to an American audience and it would be a pity to disappoint readers who will be expecting you to repeat the sucess of your first book. Now I know you have a contract with Brentwood & Dunbar, but the book about Field Marshal Blakeney hasn't been announced to the trade yet and it could be postponed while you write something more saleable. In no way do I want to belittle your British publishers. But they aren't one of the major imprints and they have less experience than we do of sustaining an author's initial success. You don't want – and certainly we don't – your second book to be an anticlimax.'

Throughout the delicious meal Elliott concentrated on persuading her to put aside her present subject in favour, if she could persuade him to agree to it, of a book about her lover.

'Anyone who starts out with nothing and makes it to the

top of the tree has sure-fire appeal to Americans,' he told her. 'I've read through a stack of tear sheets of interviews he's given and it seems he came from a very deprived Italian background.'

'Yes, but even if he's mentioned that to interviewers, he may not want it revealed in every detail. I'll have to discuss it with him . . . and with Ellen and Claudia.'

'Naturally,' he agreed. 'But do bear in mind, won't you, that while *Travels* was extremely successful in Britain, its sales here were small compared with those of the Laurel & Lincoln edition. Your American sales should be your predominant concern.'

In fact her predominant concern was that, by postponing the Blakeney book and starting one about Andro, she could put an end to their separations. They could be together all the time.

Satisfied that he had convinced her of the wisdom of his views, Elliott didn't say anything of a personal nature until he was walking her home.

Then he said, 'I was very much attracted to you when you came to New York in the spring. I thought at the time it might be mutual, but perhaps I was flattering myself.'

'Not at all,' said Allegra. 'I imagine a great many women have been attracted to you, Elliott . . . as I was. But while you, I imagine, aren't keen on a serious involvement, I'm at the stage of wanting something more than a passing affair, however enjoyable.'

'I must admit I don't see myself remarrying. Is that what you and Risconti have in mind?'

'I can't speak for him. It's what I have in mind. After sowing whole fields of wild oats, I suddenly find myself wanting to emulate my great-grandmother and cleave to one man for the rest of my life,' she admitted, smiling.

'I'm sure any man you set your heart on would find it hard to resist you,' he answered gallantly. 'Beauty . . . brains . . . breeding . . . you have all three. My wife had the first and the last, but not a great deal of intelligence. Like many people, we married too young, on the strength of physical attraction. You're wise to have waited until you know who

359

you are and what kind of person you need to complement you. Has Risconti been married?'

She shook her head. 'And may not marry me. Please treat what I've told you as confidential, will you, Elliott?'

'Of course.'

A few moments later they arrived at Carlyon House. Earlier, discussing books, she had mentioned an author she liked with whom he wasn't familiar.

He said, 'May I borrow that book you were telling me about? I could read it tonight and have it sent back to you tomorrow.'

With some men she had known she would have suspected that, regardless of Risconti's place in her life, the book was an excuse to come up and try an unwelcome pass. Elliott was far too civilized to behave like that.

Because he was interested in the things in her sitting room, he was still there half an hour later when someone pressed the buzzer.

'It must be the caretaker,' she said. 'Though I can't imagine what he wants at this hour.'

'I must be leaving,' said Elliott, following her to the door. 'It's been good talking with you, Allegra. I hope you'll take my advice.'

'If I can change Andro's mind.'

Allegra opened her front door.

Her face lit with joy. '*Andro!*'

Her astonished delight was not reflected in Risconti's face.

'I thought I'd surprise you,' he said. His gaze flicked coldly over Elliott and back to her. 'I see I have.'

In the small, bare bedroom of his cottage, where the remaining inch of whiskey in the tumbler on the bedside table gleamed in the light from the reading lamp, Sammy O'Brien lay on his narrow bed, grey-faced and sweating, exhausted by the worst bout of pain since it started.

Thanks be to God the season was over for them now. At least he was free of the worry of being taken ill at a time when it would be the ruination of the dear child's chances of winning. The worst of it was that he wouldn't be around to see her ride in the Olympics. The pain was attacking more often, like a hell-fire in his guts, each time worse than the last.

It was the same evil disease that had carried off his mother and Uncle Eamon. He didn't need a doctor to tell him what was the matter with him. He had known all along, half-expected it. The only thing a doctor could do for him – but they never would – was to give him a bottle of pills to do him in quickly.

To be sure there were plenty of ways of putting an end to yourself; but some of them took time and others weren't a nice sight for the person who found you, in his case most likely herself. After taking care of the child since she was in her cradle, he wasn't about to give her nightmares from finding him with his head blown off or his throat cut. He would have to do it away from here, where it would be a stranger who found him.

After wiping the sweat from his face with a corner of the sheet, he stretched out his hand for the tumbler and gulped down the whiskey.

Tomorrow he'd speak to his Lordship, tell him the time had come for old Sammy to be put out to grass.

It was his belief young Lady C had brought money to the marriage. Hadn't Mr Ashford been told to engage more cleaners, and hadn't she bought a new car? Sure a new groom's wages weren't much to pay for the honour and glory Sarah was bringing to the family. It was the least they could do for her. An advertisement in next week's *Horse and Hound* would bring in plenty of applications if it gave a good hint who was advertising. He'd help Sarah pick out a good girl, and then it would only remain to do the deed on himself.

Risconti picked up his travel bag. Allegra had the impression he was so angry at finding a man with her that he was going to turn round and go down the stairs and she might never see him again.

Suddenly he looked very Italian, with all the fierce macho

361

pride and jealousy of his forebears showing in his furious eyes and the grim set of his mouth.

Before she could tell him not to behave like a fool, Elliott said smoothly, 'Mr Risconti, this is an unexpected pleasure. I'm Allegra's American publisher . . . Elliott Lincoln. If I had known you two were friends, I would have introduced myself in New York.'

He offered his hand.

For a moment Risconti ignored the gesture, his manner still stiff with suspicion. Then he replaced the bag on the floor and shook hands, but without any of his normal cordiality on meeting a stranger.

'You'll be tired after your flight so this isn't the moment for us to get acquainted,' Elliott continued pleasantly. 'But if you should still be in England when I finish my business at Frankfurt, it would give me great pleasure to have you both dine with me. I can easily stop over in London on my way back. I'll call you about that, Allegra. Goodnight. Goodnight, Mr Risconti.'

He moved past him and ran down the stairs.

Leaving Risconti to close the door, Allegra walked rapidly back to the sitting room, trying to contain her temper. Her pleasure at his unexpected return had been quenched by his reaction on finding a man with her. She felt he had made her look foolish in front of someone whose opinion was important to her professionally. He might have had the good manners to keep his suspicions to himself until they were alone, she thought furiously. That caustic 'I see I have' had made it humiliatingly plain how little he trusted her.

She flung herself on to the divan and gave him a smouldering stare as he entered the room. He didn't see it. Without glancing at her, he went directly to the bedroom. Part of her mind registered that he looked more than usually fatigued by the long flight but she wasn't in the mood to urge him to soak in the bath while she fetched him a drink and unpacked for him. Needing to vent her feelings, she jumped up and followed him.

'If you're going to make a habit of coming back without

362

notice, I should warn you I shall probably be spending more time at Longwarden now my sister-in-law is there,' she told him coldly.

Risconti threw her a glance she couldn't interpret. 'I came back on impulse.'

'How long are you here for?'

He shrugged. 'I don't know. Maybe it was a mistake to come.'

'What is that supposed to mean?'

Another shrug. 'You look as if you wish I hadn't.'

'You can hardly expect me to be pleased when, without knowing who my visitor was, you imply that you've caught us practically *in flagrante delicto.*'

'I thought publishers took their authors out to lunch when they wanted to talk to them.'

'Or breakfast or tea or dinner . . . whichever happens to be convenient. Elliott and I had dinner together and then he walked back with me to borrow a book I'd mentioned to him. It couldn't have been a more decorous evening – until you arrived and tainted it with your all too obvious suspicions.'

Risconti was shedding his clothes, tossing them around with his customary disregard for tidiness. In her present mood, his careless disrobing brought Allegra's simmering indignation near boiling point.

'Okay, I misunderstood. But what would you have thought if you'd arrived in New York and found a good-looking woman in my apartment this late?'

'If she were fully dressed and on the point of leaving, I'd wait to be introduced before I started looking daggers. If you love people, you trust them,' she retorted, but with a twinge of conscience about the thoughts she had had when he'd cancelled his visit last month.

By now he was stripped to the waist and barefoot. After the lonely nights without him curled snugly round her, the sight of his powerful olive-skinned torso made her anger dissolve into unwilling desire. She wanted him to spring at her, murmuring passionate apologies between kisses which demonstrated how much he had missed her.

363

Risconti unzipped his pants and stepped out of them. 'I've been in transit ten hours. Excuse me: I'll go take a shower.'

Allegra stood listening to the sound of the water running. Each previous time he had come back, within minutes of entering the flat he had been in bed with her, making love with the same famished urgency as her need for him.

This time he didn't want her. Upset as she was by his behaviour at the door, she still longed to be in his arms. But, as his body had shown, he felt no hunger for her.

Dashed and alarmed by her first experience of physical rejection, she began to gather up his clothes.

When a car drove into the stableyard, Sarah looked out of the loose-box where she was working to see Inspector Wallace of the RSPCA opening the driver's door.

'Congratulations, Miss Lomax. The wife and I watched you on television. It was thrilling, there's no other word,' he told her as they shook hands.

'Thank you, Inspector – but there's the person you should be congratulating.' She pointed to Beddo who was watching them from his box.

The inspector walked over to talk to the Burghley champion. His visits to Longwarden stables were not official inspections. He knew from long experience that the animals there were as well kept as any in England.

After spending some time admiring them, he accepted the offer of a cup of tea in the room next to the tackroom.

'I've a bit of a problem on my hands,' he said as Sarah filled the brown teapot. 'There's a pony a few miles from here which is in a condition you can't begin to imagine. He's been starved for weeks, by the look of him. We shall be prosecuting the owner for causing unnecessary suffering, but before that I have to decide what's to be done with the poor devil. I was called to see him by an old lady who paid the owner a hundred pounds for him yesterday. She has nowhere to put him, or any knowledge of horses – beyond recognizing cruelty when she sees it. Most people would have him put out of his misery. I thought I'd speak to you first. It's hard to tell, the state he's in, but I think he's an Austrian Haflinger.'

Sarah opened a tin of biscuits. There were few breeds which were unknown to her and many, such as the wavy-maned Lusitanos of Portugal and the Furiosos of Hungary, she would like to own.

'Haflingers. They're the chestnuts with flaxen manes and some Arab blood in them, aren't they?'

The inspector nodded. 'They're very strong, sound mountain ponies which normally live to a great age. That's one of the reasons I don't want to have him put down if he can be saved. But I must be honest with you, Miss Lomax. Even with care and attention he may not survive what he's been through, and I know you're a busy young lady. Perhaps too busy to take him on.'

Sarah knew that she was; at the same time the thought of a pony from the Austrian mountains, bred to live as long as forty years but dying from neglect in England, was too much for her tender heart.

Less than an hour later she was standing in a field looking at the most pathetic creature she had ever seen. The filthy, bedraggled Haflinger was no more than skin and bone. With his drooping head and dull eyes he looked certain to die within days.

Her gaze blurred by tears of rage at the perpetrator of this incredible cruelty, Sarah turned to the inspector.

'I don't think there's very much hope, but I'll do what I can.'

She had brought the small horse-box with her. Between them, with considerable difficulty, they managed to get the weak, listless pony inside it.

Sammy was crossing the yard when they returned. When they let down the ramp and he saw what they had brought back with them, he was furious.

'Are you out of your mind, Sarah Lomax? Can't you see that poor creature is dying . . . and covered with lice . . . and no doubt riddled with worms. Don't expect me to nurse him, my girl. Fool you are to let the inspector wheedle you into taking pity on a bag of bones only fit for the knacker's yard.'

'The inspector didn't wheedle me into anything, Sammy. He told me there wasn't much hope, which I can see for myself. But I won't have it on my conscience that I didn't even try to save him. All I'll ask you to do for him is to ring up Daniel and ask him to call as soon as possible.'

Daniel Langden was the son of and successor to the vet who had looked after her uncle's hunters and hounds. By the time he arrived the pony had managed a few sips of water but had failed to be tempted by a small feed of soft meadow hay soaked in hot water.

At the end of his examination, Daniel shook his head. 'I'm afraid you've taken on a hopeless case, Sarah. His heart doesn't seem to be damaged, something of a miracle considering his appalling condition. But I'm sure he's seriously anaemic. If you can get him to eat, there's a high risk of colic which, in his state, would finish him off.'

Determinedly cheerful in the face of the difficult and perhaps futile task she had accepted, she said, 'At least he hasn't got mange, which is something to be thankful for.'

Mange, a notifiable disease, was much harder to cure.

Before he left, Daniel gave the pony an injection to boost his appetite and promised to return in the morning.

To isolate the pony from the other horses in case he was carrying an infection, she had put him in the unused stable which had two rows of stalls facing each other across an aisle.

That night she slept in the opposite stall on a camp bed, woken at two-hour intervals by a low-pitched buzzer.

In the morning the pony was too weak to get up. He looked like a bag of bones flung down on his wheat-straw bed.

When Sarah came back after brushing her teeth and washing, she was surprised to find Mr Ashford in the stable. Obviously he had heard her talking about the pony during her rather rushed evening meal.

'Good morning, Miss Sarah. I thought you might like

tea and biscuits after your night on duty.' He indicated a vacuum flask.

'How kind of you. Thank you. He looks pretty hopeless, doesn't he?'

'He's in a bad way,' he agreed. 'But he's young and with your good nursing I expect he'll pull round.'

The confidence in his tone revived her determination, which had been at a low ebb after a broken night's sleep. A cup of hot tea and some food gave another boost to her morale. When Sammy appeared and gave it as his opinion that the pony was as good as dead, she refused to accept his grim verdict.

Nevertheless it was a relief when Daniel arrived before breakfast and decided to try an intravenous injection of calcium and glucose.

After the shot, helped by the butler, they managed to help the pony to stagger to his feet. But he looked as if the effort of standing was almost too much for him.

It was the butler who suggested he should be supported by slings until he was eating enough to give him some strength.

'That's a good idea if you and Sammy can organize it, Sarah,' agreed Daniel.

'Mr O'Brien will be busy attending to the other horses. I can make the necessary arrangements, Miss Sarah,' Ashford volunteered.

Surprised, but pleased to accept any help that was offered, she agreed to leave it to him.

More help arrived soon after breakfast when Jane came to the stables in a Madras shirt and jeans and offered her services.

By midday, under Ashford's directions, a stout frame had been erected over the stall and a block and tackle discovered in one of the store rooms. The slings were supplied by Inspector Wallace.

When the family, including Sarah, met for lunch, North took advantage of the butler's absence from the dining room to say, 'Ashford seems in his element taking an organizing part in Sarah's rescue operation.'

'That reminds me, while you were away, North, he expressed some concern about your father's guns,' said Pen. 'He said the Purdeys would normally be sent for cleaning once a year and even when not being used they ought to have some attention. He suggested that, if you were never likely to use them, they might be sold and the money spent on something useful. Afterwards he seemed rather embarrassed at having made the suggestion, but I thought it extremely sensible.'

'So do I,' North agreed. 'I don't know why I didn't think of getting rid of them myself. Even second-hand Purdeys must be worth quite a bit and I'm certainly never going to use them. Shooting bores the pants off me.'

'What kind of guns are these Purdeys?' asked Jane.

'They're bespoke shotguns specially made to fit their owners,' North told her. 'My father was given a pair for his twenty-fifth birthday. They cost a lot of money then. Today, I believe, they're about twenty thousand dollars each. Only very rich men can afford them, and' – a grin flashed across his face – 'the top brass in the Kremlin. Khrushchev had four, so I've heard, and Kosygin and Brezhnev one each. A splendid example of the fact that some comrades are more equal than others.'

After a thoughtful pause, he added, 'So Ashford knows something about guns. I wonder if he shoots himself? I must ask him.'

'I don't think I should if I were you,' said his mother. 'He seems not to like being asked questions and I've noticed he's very adroit at avoiding them. In any case we have no right to pry into his private life.'

'Does he have one?' said Jane. 'He seems to be around all the time. Does he have any off-duty periods?'

'Butlers have always worked long hours,' said North. 'They're supposed to have two hours off during the day, and a day and a half off each week, plus three weeks' holiday a year. But this isn't a typical household, or it hasn't been since my father died. What time off does Ashford have, Mama?'

'I really don't know,' she said vaguely. 'I leave it to him

o arrange his own time-table. In the summer, when it didn't get dark until late, he spent quite a lot of evenings working in the garden. I found his help very useful.' She glanced round the table. Everyone had finished eating. Would you ring for him, please?'

North rose and tugged a long bell-pull, a signal that they were ready for the next course.

A few minutes later the subject of their conversation came quietly through the service door and began to clear away the first course. When he came to where Sarah was sitting, she glanced up and smiled at him.

The butler, his own face impassive, seemed not to notice.

The pony's recovery was slow, the danger of colic a constant worry to Sarah throughout his first week in her care.

He had to be wormed three times to clear the red worms from his droppings. The last worming triggered the dreaded colic.

By the end of the following week, Sarah was visibly worn out Daniel had cured the colic and the pony was making some progress. What puzzled and hurt her was that the only person who gave her no encouragement was Sammy. He continued to be disapproving and his sour, pessimistic attitude upset her more than she showed.

For ten days she slept in the stable in case the colic recurred. She had christened the pony Chestnut from the colour his staring coat would be when he was well again.

Although she had never seen any rats scuttling about the unused stables, she felt more comfortable sleeping on the low camp bed with Sally, an elderly Labrador from the same litter as Ben, on an old rug beside her.

On the tenth night of her vigil she was woken up in the small hours not by the buzzer but by a low growl from Sally. Tired as she was, Sarah was not sleeping deeply. The growl alerted her at once. For some moments she lay very still, holding her breath to listen for a repetition of the sound which had made the friendly bitch give that deep-throated hostile rumble.

It was a clear night. The moon was shining in broad bars of light through the high Sheringham windows at the back of each stall. The one above Sarah was open. Her ears could just catch faint sounds from the paved yard outside.

Stealthy footsteps? Who would be there at this hour?

Again the Labrador growled. Sarah stretched out her arm to grasp the bitch by her collar. She didn't want Sally rushing out to investigate, barking her head off and frightening the still-sick pony.

At the same time she was rather frightened herself. Whoever was in the yard had no right to be there. Suddenly, the rest of the household seemed very far away. Even Sammy's quarters were too far to be within earshot if she yelled for help.

Moving as silently as possible and still keeping hold of the bitch, she threw aside her covers and sat up to put on her shoes.

She had just slipped her feet inside them when the unbolted side of the tall double doors gave the squeak she had been intending to deal with for days. Not much of a squeak in the daytime, at night it sounded much louder, making her smother a gasp, her body stiffening with tension.

The dog sensed her apprehension and gave a louder growl but was prevented from barking by Sarah grabbing her muzzle and also pulling on her collar in the hope of keeping her silent.

If whoever had opened the door was looking for a way to break into the house, he would see by the brilliant moonlight the blank wall at the far end and, with luck, go away, giving her a chance to slip out by the small door beyond the end stall.

Holding tight to the quivering, straining Labrador, she prayed for him to go away.

Allegra had woken up parched, a consequence of neglecting to end a vinous evening with water and vitamin C.

Having repaired the omission, she slipped quietly back into bed without disturbing Risconti.

They were on good terms again, making love every day

like honeymooners. Yet things were not *quite* as they had been before. Even though she couldn't define it, her intuition recognized a difference. She didn't think it had anything to do with their row on the night of his return. That had been resolved the following morning when, waking refreshed and vigorous, Risconti had apologized for being boorish and taken her with an enthusiasm which had made nonsense of her misgivings.

So why, now, did she have this awareness that all wasn't right between them? That while they had been apart something had happened which he was keeping from her because to know it would hurt her?

Jane also was awake.

Yesterday afternoon, to her disappointment, she had felt a familiar dull ache low down in her body, and had come up to the bathroom to find the box of tampons she had thought she might not need again until late next summer.

Last night, at bedtime, when North had come into her room and started kissing her shoulders while she was taking off her make-up, she had had to say to him, 'I'm sorry . . . I'm out of action for a few days.'

If he had been displeased, for either reason, he hadn't shown it. He had been unexpectedly solicitous.

'Does it make you feel off colour? Is there anything you'd like? Paracetamol . . . whisky and lemon . . . whatever?'

'Thank you, but no . . . I feel fine.'

'Must be a bore, being a female.'

'There are compensations.'

'Are there?' He sounded doubtful. 'Well, if you're sure there's nothing, I'll say goodnight.' He had kissed her on the cheek and left her.

For a couple of hours she had slept with her usual soundness. Then some noise in the night, perhaps the creaking of a joist, had roused her. Since then she had lain awake, wondering and worrying why not one of the myriad spermatozoa which had entered her body since that first night in New York had succeeded in its quest.

If, in spite of her apparently perfect health, there was

371

some fault in her reproductive system which would make conception a problem, even an impossibility, how would it affect her marriage?

The moments while Sarah clutched Sally and waited for the intruder to come into the stable or go away seemed the longest of her life.

A dozen thoughts – all terrifying – flashed through her mind. One well-aimed kick could put the old Labrador out of action, leaving Sarah with no defence against a man whose criminal inclinations might include rape.

The lights went on.

Sarah blinked, half-expecting the illumination to be momentary. Why should a burglar put lights on? Surely he ought to have a torch?

The lights remained on. Scarcely audible footsteps came slowly in her direction, as if whoever was there was peering into each stall.

Unable to bear the suspense she decided to risk setting Sally on him, hoping that, taken by surprise, he would give her enough time to make a bolt through the far door. Once in the yard she had a chance to out-run him. Staying where she was, she was helpless.

Springing up, she released the Labrador. 'Seize him, Sally! Go seize him.'

Barking loudly, the bitch rushed one way while Sarah fled in the other, with only a glimpse of the man she had hoped to startle.

Tall. Powerful. Young. Darkly tanned. Shorn like a Victorian convict.

Her eyes registered the impressions but, with her mind fixed on flight, they made no impact. Until, louder than the barking, she heard the shout, 'Sarah . . . Sarah, come back here.'

Her name, bellowed in the stentorian roar of the parade ground, made her skid to a halt by the last stall. She looked over her shoulder, her blue eyes widening incredulously.

'Nick!' she whispered.

*　　*　　*

'Quiet, Sally . . . sit, Sally . . . *sit!*'

Like Sarah, reassured by the use of her name and by the familiar commands given by a remembered voice, the old bitch quietened and sat down.

'Good girl, Sally . . . good girl.' For a moment he bent to pat her. Then he straightened and looked at the girl, still standing in paralysed surprise, at the far end of the stable. 'What are you doing down here at this time of night? You gave me the hell of a start.'

'I gave *you* a start!' The tension dissolved in laughter. 'You almost scared me to death. I thought . . . oh, but never mind that. You're here . . . you're home.'

Almost as fast as she had fled from him, now she dashed in the opposite direction, her face alight.

Nick strode to meet her, arms spreading. He scooped her up in a bear-hug, swinging her round in a circle before setting her back on her feet and giving her two hearty kisses, one on each cheek.

'Hey! What happened to you?' he asked, grinning down at her. 'You're not Skinny Lizzy any more.'

'What happened to *you*? I know they shaved your head in the training camp, but you didn't say you still had a Yul Brynner haircut – or very nearly.'

She leaned back, the better to view the half inch of dark brown stubble.

He ran a palm over his scalp. 'I find it more comfortable like this, especially during the hot months.'

'It's wonderful to have you back. I've missed you terribly, Nick. There's no one else I can talk to in quite the same way.'

He had put his hand back on her waist with his other one, and hers had slipped down from his shoulders and were resting on his chest.

'I missed you, too,' he said warmly, giving her a squeeze. 'It was great to have someone to write to me.'

For an instant there was an expression in his greeny-brown eyes which made her heart jump with excitement. Could it be that absence *had* made him fonder of her? That he now felt the same way as she did?

But the next thing he said was, 'You haven't explained what you're doing here. I was looking for somewhere to get my head down till morning.'

'I'm on night duty with a sick horse. I hope all this noise hasn't upset him. I'd better look.' Reluctantly, she disengaged herself.

Chestnut seemed undisturbed by the commotion. When she started to explain the cause of his condition, Nick interrupted her.

'Is there anything to eat around here? I had some food on the ferry first thing this morning – yesterday morning, that is. But I haven't eaten since and I'm pretty hungry.'

Almost twenty-four hours without food. Sarah was horrified. 'You must be starving. We'd better go into the house and I'll cook you a meal.'

'Bread and cheese will do. Anything.'

At the door he turned off the lights. With a full moon in the clear sky, the yard was as bright as day. Sarah unlocked the door leading into the house and, followed by Sally, they entered the warren of passages leading to the modern kitchen.

Here Sarah looked into the large refrigerator. A few minutes later Nick was seated at the table, hungrily wolfing a leg of cold roast chicken while she beat the eggs for an omelette.

'How come you haven't eaten since yesterday morning?' she asked.

'Ran out of money,' he said with a shrug of broad shoulders. 'The pay in the Legion didn't allow me to save much. The little I had scraped together soon went when I got to the mainland. There's high unemployment in Spain. Odd jobs aren't easy to come by. Anyway I'd had enough of Spain for a while. I went to Marseilles with the idea of signing on in the French Foreign Legion for a year or two. But with them it's a five-year contract and that's a hell of a long commitment. I decided to think it over and come back here while I did.'

The news that he had considered enlisting in another army, and indeed would have done so had the contract been

374

shorter, demolished her secret hope that their two-year correspondence had forged a bond which would blossom into love when he came back.

Hiding her disappointment, she said, 'I'm very glad you did. I should have hated not seeing you for another five years. Two have seemed a long time to me. Haven't they to you?'

'In some ways, yes. The first month or two seemed for ever. But since I was made up to *cabo*, with some power and influence, the time has gone a lot faster.'

While he was eating the omelette she made toast and a pot of tea.

'If you eat too much on an empty stomach, you may get colic,' she warned.

Nick laughed. 'Not a chance. Anyone who can stomach a lump of cold pork fat for breakfast, which is what we were given quite often, develops a cast-iron digestion.'

Presently, while he buttered the toast and cut off a large piece of Cheddar, she was able to study his altered appearance. It wasn't only his hair and his tan that made the difference. He had gone away a green youth, full grown in height but still a teenager.

Now he was grown up. Although only twenty years old, he had acquired the mature air of a man who had been through a hard time and survived it, toughened and tempered.

'Tomorrow I'll fix up a job,' he said between mouthfuls.

'That may be no easier in England than it was in Spain,' she said doubtfully. 'Unless you're willing to come back here for a bit. We could do with you, Nick.'

She could tell the suggestion wasn't welcome. He said, 'I wanted to look you up, Sarah, but there's no one else I want to see here. I don't plan to stick around.' He paused. 'Maybe I'll give you a hand, for my board and lodging, just for a few days.'

As he finished speaking, the door opened. They looked round to see the butler standing on the threshold, looking unexpectedly elegant in a silk dressing gown over navy-blue pyjamas.

He glanced briefly at Sarah and then, frowning slightly, at Nick.

Whereupon something odd happened. Nick jumped up in a hurry, his chair grating on the floor. He stood with his shoulders pulled back, his arms at his sides, his whole posture at attention.

'This is Nick Dean. He used to work here,' said Sarah.

The butler came into the kitchen. His neatly brushed greying dark hair suggested that whatever had brought him downstairs at this hour, he hadn't left his room in a hurry.

'And is now in the services, I gather?' he said, staring at the young man.

'Yessir. That is I was, sir.'

'Army?'

'Spanish Foreign Legion, sir.'

The butler looked surprised and interested. 'How did that come about?'

'Went to Madrid and enlisted, sir.'

'Enterprising.'

The succinct commendation brought a pleased look to Nick's tanned face.

'Thank you, sir.'

Guessing that he thought he was being addressed by a distinguished guest, Sarah felt it was time to say, 'This is Mr Ashford who has replaced Mr Gisburn, Nick.'

For a second or two it was obvious he couldn't remember the previous butler. When the name did ring a bell, he looked surprised and disconcerted.

Mr Ashford offered his hand. 'By the look of you, you've been stationed somewhere pretty warm,' he said with one of his rare smiles.

Nick relaxed his stance and gripped the older man's hand. 'I've spent two years in the Canaries.'

'Don't let me interrupt your meal. Where are you sleeping?'

'He can have my room in the arch as I'm not using it,' said Sarah.

'No, I can't,' Nick objected. 'I'm filthy after three days in transit. I'll doss down in the tackroom or somewhere.'

376

'If you feel dirty, have a shower. There's one in the arch
. . . and a lavatory. You might just as well be comfortable.'
She turned to the butler. 'Would you like a cup of tea, Mr
Ashford?'

'As I'm down here, yes. I'll take it to my room. Goodnight,
Dean. Goodnight, Miss Sarah.'

'Not much like old Gisburn, is he?' said Nick. 'When he
first came in, I thought he was somebody staying here . . . a
brass hat of some kind.'

'So I gathered when you jumped to attention. Would you
like some more toast, or an apple?'

'An apple would be great. Fruit is something I've missed.
And the kind of nosh Mrs Armitage used to dish up when
I worked here.'

The clothes Nick was wearing looked like things he
had had before leaving England. A navy anorak, slung on
the back of his chair. A khaki-green combat sweater
with cotton-reinforced shoulders. A check shirt. Blue
jeans.

Perhaps he hadn't grown taller, but he looked it because
of the upright way he carried himself now. There was also
a lot more muscle cladding the lanky bone structure. He
wasn't a giant like North, but he wasn't much under six
feet and looked impressively fit, even after travelling a long
way in tiring conditions.

They both munched their way through apples and drank
second cups of tea. Sarah glanced at her watch and saw it
would soon be time to try to coax Chestnut to take another
small feed.

'My bed is made up but the sheets haven't been slept
in,' she said as she led the way up the spiral staircase to
her eyrie. 'There's lashings of hot water for the shower that
North had put in for me. You can sleep undisturbed up
here for as long as you like. Round the clock, if you want
to.'

Nick dumped his kitbag on the fitted sisal matting which
covered the floor. He looked round the sanctum she had
made for herself.

It could be seen at a glance that the room belonged to a

horsewoman. Several fine paintings of horses, borrowed from the house, adorned the pale terracotta walls. Trophies were grouped on shelves. In a recess protected by a pane of glass hung the silks her father had worn when riding his elder brother's 'chasers. Most of the books in the room had to do with horses. They included a complete set of Dick Francis first editions and, lying on a table beside the comfortable armchair, a copy of Henry Wynmalen's classic *Equitation*.

But it wasn't a totally horsey room. The romantic, feminine side of Sarah's nature was shown by some soft-focus postcards of lovers at sunrise and sunset which were pinned to a cork-board; and by the pretty dressing gown of white broderie anglaise threaded with primrose ribbons which hung on a hook on the door to the shower.

As she was tidy by nature, it was only necessary to remove a bra and briefs left to dry on a plastic hanger hooked over the shower head, and to whip the cover off the bed, for the place to be ready for his occupation.

'I'll see you some time tomorrow. Sleep well. It's marvellous to have you back.' She wished she had the courage to reach up and brush a light kiss on his cheek.

He had already begun to unpack his kitbag. His answering, 'Thanks, Sarah. G'night,' was somewhat abstracted.

As she returned to the stable, she was very happy to have him safely returned to her.

But for how long?

A few moments after waking at her usual early hour, Sarah realized that in the excitement of Nick's return she had forgotten to bring her toothbrush and hairbrush, and a change of underwear and shirt, down from her room.

She wondered if she could fetch them without disturbing him. The yard had a lavatory with a handbasin for Sammy's use. She could wash in there.

When, having crept up the staircase, she opened the door of the archway room, Nick was lying face down on the bed with his head turned away from her. One sinewy forearm dangled loosely over the edge of the mattress. The bedclothes were bunched round his waist, exposing his broad nut-brown back.

Softly closing the door behind her, and pausing to study his sleeping form, she was struck by the incongruity of his muscular, tough male body and the pale-blue butterfly-printed sheets and pillowcase.

She trod stealthily closer. The brown skin overlying the muscles had the silky sheen of a well-groomed bright bay's coat. It invited her touch, but to do that would be sure to wake him. She moved on towards the inner room.

As he was soundly asleep, she felt she might as well wash in her customary place. Her main toilet took place at night, after evening stables. Having put on the clean underwear she had stuffed in a drawer by the basin the night before, from long habit she washed out the garments she had taken off. Then she stepped back into her jeans and pulled up the zipper, only to realize that her clean shirt was in a drawer in her bed-sitter.

Nick had rolled on his back when she re-entered the larger room. Round his mouth and halfway up his cheeks, his skin was darkened by twenty-four hours' growth of beard. A tuft of dark hair showed under his outstretched right arm but his chest was as smooth as his back, the nipples dark brown, his ribcage clearly outlined by each slow expansion of his lungs.

Moving quietly to a chest of drawers, she bent to slide open the second one, choosing a Ralph Lauren shirt from the American designer's shop in Bond Street where Allegra had taken her one day when Sarah had been in London to have her teeth checked.

'Good morning.'

Nick's voice from behind her made her jump 'Oh . . . good morning. Did I wake you?'

He shook his head, watching her under half-closed eyelids.

Suddenly conscious that the cups of her bra were made of transparent white nylon through which he could see her pink nipples as clearly as she could see his, she held the still-folded shirt to her chest.

'I'll be gone in a minute and then you can get back to sleep.'

He raised his left arm to peer at his watch.

'I've had enough sleep for the time being. I'm getting up.' About to throw back the bedclothes, he checked. 'I'm used to sleeping in the raw. Turn your back for a couple of minutes while I put on my trousers, will you?'

She was only too glad to obey and quickly to shrug on the shirt and fasten the front.

Her head was inside her sweater when she heard him say, 'Okay, I'm decent.'

Sarah's head emerged from the neck of the elbow-patched guernsey and she tugged out her still unbrushed plait.

'I'll help you muck out,' said Nick. 'Not doing any work for a while, I'm getting out of shape.'

But there wasn't an ounce of spare flesh round his lean supple waist. He looked in great shape to her.

'I'll have a quick shave and come down.'

'There's no rush. I haven't done my hair yet.' She pulled the elastic band from the end of her plait and began to loosen the thick strands.

Nick disappeared into the bathroom where he had left a cheap wet-pack on the window ledge.

Sarah picked up her black bristle brush but it stayed unused as she looked at the rumpled bed where his strong brown body had been lying. On impulse she put down the brush and went to pick up the pillow. She held it to her face. It seemed subtly, delectably imbued with the clean male scent of his body. She inhaled, held her breath, and expelled a long tremulous sigh.

Usually her first morning thoughts were of Beddo and Tatty waiting to have their boxes opened and to be checked for injuries in the first routine of the day. But overnight her world had changed, now she thought only of Nick.

In the back of her mind there had lurked the tiniest doubt that he might not be as she remembered him; or that she might have changed, outgrown her youthful love for him.

In fact he was better than she remembered: all the good things about him unaltered and the rough edges smoothed by two years of harsh discipline in an alien environment.

It was Sammy who suggested that Nick should ride with Sarah that morning.

'I'll keep an eye on the pony,' he told her.

'Sammy's aged a lot, hasn't he? He's beginning to look an old man,' said Nick as they rode out of the yard. 'I expect I notice it more than you do, not having seen him for two years.'

'It's been a long gruelling season for him,' she answered, confiding her worries about Sammy's health.

Earlier Sammy had told Nick about Burghley. Now he had all that muscle on him, he really needed a bigger horse than Beddo, thought Sarah, glancing sideways at her two favourite people – the graceful Arab with the handsome head and lively action typical of his breed, and the sunburned man on his back whose eyes were scanning the pastures on either side of the long drive.

'I'd forgotten how green England is,' he remarked.

The statement rekindled her hope that he might, after all, decide to remain at Longwarden.

'From the way you described it, Fuerteventura sounded a most desolate island; nothing much there but desert. Didn't you hate it at first? Didn't you regret enlisting?'

'Yes, I did for a bit,' he agreed. 'When I was a *recluta* in the training camp at Tefia, being knocked about whenever I did something wrong, I felt I'd jumped out of the frying pan into the fire.' His brows drew into a slight frown. 'Are we going past the lodge? I don't want to run into Ted.'

His expression would have indicated to anyone that he had no time for his foster father, but his tone wasn't infused with bitterness.

She had the feeling that all the bottled-up hostility and resentment which he must have felt as an unloved, ill-treated boy had somehow been healed during his time in the Legion.

She said, 'No, we're turning off here' – indicating a gate in the railings of the meadow on their right.

Nick opened it for her. Presently, riding abreast again, he went on, 'As I was saying, for the first month I often wished I could get the hell out of it. Once I picked up some of the language it wasn't so bad.'

'You must speak it perfectly now.'

'In a fashion. I wasn't mixing with educated Spaniards. Most *legionarios* have limited vocabularies that include a lot of words *you* wouldn't use if you were Spanish. At that level I'm fluent.'

'Perhaps you could get a job as a courier, looking after British tourists in Spain,' she suggested. But it wasn't a rôle she could see him in.

'Possibly, if I wanted to,' said Nick. 'But I don't. I want to go on being a soldier. I could join the British Army, but sooner or later that means being sent to Northern Ireland. I shouldn't have minded seeing action in the Falklands, but Ireland is like Vietnam. It's a meaningless waste of lives . . . a war kept going by religious fanatics and crackpots.'

Sarah nodded agreement. This was Sammy's view, too. He came from the west of Ireland, far away from the strife in Belfast, and he was a peaceable man who detested violence and saw the futility of it.

Nick was wearing an old pair of breeches, left behind when he went away, with boots he had brought back from Spain. The morning being mild, he had nothing on his top half but an olive-green Legion shirt.

'What happened to the rest of your uniform? Did you have to hand it in?'

'No, it's in my kitbag.'

'You must put it on and let me take some snaps of you. When you're old and telling your grandchildren about the Legion, you'll regret having no photos to show them how you looked in uniform.'

And I want some for myself, she thought.

Nick laughed. 'Okay, I'll dig it out and press it some time. When we get back, remind me I've got some things for you, will you?'

'What sort of things?'

'You'll just have to wait and see, won't you, Sarah Georgiana Millicent.'

It had been a long time since, to tease her, he had used all her Christian names.

Nick's only name was Nicholas. All he knew of his father was that he had been a soldier. He didn't even know if Nicholas had been his father's name. Whatever Mary Rivington could have told him about her sister's lover was lost, and Sarah felt certain he would never ask Ted for information, if indeed his foster father could or would have given him any.

Her own situation was the reverse of his. She had grown up surrounded by portraits, photographs and other mementoes of her father and his relations. It was her mother who was a mysterious person.

Althea Lomax, née Morris, had been the daughter of a country parson. She had trained for the stage at the Webber-Douglas School of Drama and had been in her first West End part when Ranulf Lomax had made a point of getting to know her.

Nanny Lomax – whose real name had been Miss Florence Howard – the kind disciplinarian in charge of the nursery when Edward and Ranulf were small, had still been living at Longwarden when Sarah's mother had deserted her.

Nanny was dead now. In her last years, when her eyesight had failed, Sarah had often read *The Times* social columns to her, and *Jennifer's Diary* in *Harpers & Queen* which recorded the doings of people she had nursed or known as children.

'A pretty flibbertigibbet – that was young Mrs Ranulf,' Nanny had murmured once, speaking more to herself than to the girl beside her. Then she had peered at Sarah, as though through a misty window. 'You're not as pretty as she was. She was very pretty . . . and very vain and selfish. They say she went to America . . . to Hollywood. I don't know if it's true. If it is, it's a good thing she left you with us. Goodness knows how you would have turned out if you'd been brought up by her.'

'How about a little more rev?' Nick suggested.

She nodded and shortened her reins. The two horses started to trot and, presently, to canter across the smooth sheep-shorn turf which, in this part of the park, had not yet deteriorated into a maze of molehills and rabbit holes as it had in most other areas.

It would have been easy to jump the low railings on the far side of the meadow. But Sarah was mindful that Nick hadn't been on horseback for two years and wasn't wearing a hat.

The park offered many routes through woodland and over open ground. This morning they went in the direction of a gazebo where, in the early years of their friendship, they had sometimes taken elevenses to eat sitting on the stone steps while their ponies cropped the grass.

When they reached it, there were signs that someone else had been there. A twisted beer can, several cigarette ends and a crumpled tissue lay on the grass.

'I wonder who left all this mess?' she said, with a frown.

Nick slipped his feet out of the stirrups and swung himself off Beddo's back. Keeping hold of the reins, he picked up the empty can and used it as a receptacle for the butts.

'Nick, look! Someone's been inside,' Sarah exclaimed as she noticed that the door to the basement part of the gazebo had been broken open.

A moment later she had dropped lightly to the ground and was looping Tatty's reins through one of the rusty tethering rings which had probably hung from the wall since the eighteenth century. While Nick did the same with the gelding's reins, she pushed open the door and looked into the dim interior.

Whatever its original purpose had been, the lower section of the building was now disused and empty. But several more butts on the floor showed that whoever had forced the door had spent more than a few minutes there.

'How odd,' she murmured perplexedly. 'Who'd want to spend time in here?'

Nick followed her in and bent to pick up a butt. He

showed it to her, the tip smeared with dark plum-red lipstick.

'Probably someone from the village looking for somewhere private to spend time with a girl.'

'Oh . . . I hadn't thought of that. It's not my idea of a trysting place,' she said with a slight grimace.

'Nor mine, but at this time of year it's cold and damp in the woods at night.'

'But it's quite a long way from the –'

Sarah broke off, remembering the blush-making sally by one of Tark Osgood's toadies the day she had first spoken to him.

The gazebo was not a long way from the village by motorbike. Had he brought a girl here and . . . done that to her where they were standing? On the floor? In this cobwebby place? How unutterably sordid.

Nick saw her disgusted expression and wished he had kept his mouth shut. She might look more grown up, but he guessed it was largely skin-deep. She was still devoted to her horses, with no time to spare for boyfriends. Her letters had made that clear.

'We need something to carry this junk in,' he said, referring to the first can and two others found inside. 'In the absence of a plastic bag, may I borrow your scarf?'

A pink cotton square was knotted round her long neck. As she took it off, Nick crushed the soft aluminium cans between his powerful brown hands. He then used the kerchief to make a bundle he could attach to his saddle.

Outside he gave her a leg up and they continued their ride. 'How do you like your cousin's new wife? More importantly, perhaps, how does your aunt like her?' Nick asked.

He had long been privy to the fact that between Lady Carlyon and Allegra there was little love lost.

'Jane's very nice. We both like her. You'll meet her at lunch. I asked Mr Ashford not to let on who my guest was. I want you to be a surprise.' A thought struck her. 'Actually North is the person to take some pictures of you in uniform. Silly of me not to think of it.'

Nick was frowning. 'I can't have lunch with them, Sarah.'

'Why not? He and Aunt Pen will be fascinated to hear what you've been doing for the past two years.'

'I should think they've forgotten my existence,' Nick said dryly. 'I was a groom here, remember? My conversations with Lady Carlyon were limited to a few polite orders on her side and "Yes, m'Lady" or "No, m'Lady" on mine.'

'That was then. This is now,' she said firmly. 'Now you are ex-Cabo Caballero Legionario Nick Dean of the Tercio de Don Juan de Austria; one of the select band of Englishmen to have served in the Spanish Foreign Legion. That makes you a very unusual, interesting man.'

'There's nothing "select" about any of the Brits or Americans who've been in the Legion,' he replied. 'The Yank I was friendly with was AWOL from the Marines, and the only other Brit I came across admitted to having a prison record. Tough troops, maybe, but not exactly knights of chivalry.'

She said cheerfully, 'The French Foreign Legion was full of bad lots and sadists when Beau Geste joined it, but he wasn't one of them.'

'He came from an upper-crust family and that was only a story anyway. I'm the foster son of your cousin's gamekeeper and this is real life. I'll have lunch with Sammy,' Nick said decisively.

Sarah saw that he meant what he said. Her heart sank. This was an unforeseen obstacle. She had thought that, some time in the future, her family might be opposed to her marrying outside their circle. She hadn't expected to encounter inverted snobbishness from Nick. She didn't know how to deal with it.

After a long pause she said, 'As you've never got on with your foster father, and you don't know who your real father was, I thought you meant to make your own way in the world; starting from scratch the day you left here.'

'I did and I do. But Longwarden isn't the world. It's where I grew up. Around here I'll always be Sally Dean's bastard,' Nick said quietly. 'I shouldn't feel comfortable having lunch with Lady Carlyon, and although she'd try not to show it she wouldn't feel comfortable either.'

Sarah gave him a cool blue glance. 'I don't know about my aunt, but I know my great-grandmother wouldn't have had much in common with you,' she said with deliberate disdain. 'She wasn't only a nobody when she came here, she was a half-Chinese nobody. My great-grandfather married her in Shanghai without telling her who he was. When she found out she was a countess, it was a terrible shock. But she was the sort of person who was never daunted by *anything*. I thought you were like that. Evidently not. You'd rather embarrass me than risk being embarrassed yourself.'

Nick's lips compressed. He said shortly, 'It's not a question of that, and I don't believe all that stuff about your great-grandmother. I remember her. She may have been half-Chinese, but I expect her father was a mandarin or whatever they call their nobs.'

'It was her mother who was Chinese. Her father was the son of a keeper and a cook. It's all in Allegra's book about her. Read it if you don't believe me.'

Nick had seen the last Dowager Countess of Carlyon on only a few occasions. She had been very old when she died. Several times in Nick's teens, when Gisburn had seconded him to fill the log baskets, he had seen portraits painted in her youth. She had been the most beautiful and also the most aristocratic-looking girl he had ever seen, far more like a countess to look at than his Lordship's mother. It was hard to believe that the dark-eyed beauty of the portraits could have been a gamekeeper's granddaughter.

'What did the new butler say when you told him you'd asked me to lunch?' he inquired.

'He said, "Very good, Miss Sarah." What else would you expect him to say?'

'I bet if he finds out from Sammy or Mrs Armitage what I used to do here, he won't think it's good. He won't like having to wait on someone who used to be at the bottom of the pecking order.'

'Mr Ashford seemed very interested in you. He asked

me how old you were now and how long you'd been away. But he didn't ask what your work here was. What he *did* say was that you must have a lot of backbone. Which, at the time, I agreed with,' she added pointedly.

He gave her a considering look. 'You're determined to make me feel a lily-livered cur if I don't come to lunch, aren't you?'

The term was from an Edwardian boys' book Sarah had found on the shelves in the schoolroom. It had provided them with various archaic expressions to include in their private language.

'Yes, you dee-dash-dee scoundrel!' she retorted instantly.

They began to laugh.

'Okay, you win,' he conceded. 'But don't say I didn't warn you if it turns out to be pretty sticky.'

The presents he unearthed from his kitbag before lunch were a black headscarf printed with emblems of different regiments and an enamelled badge which was part of the Legion uniform but could be worn as a brooch.

'I'm sorry the scarf is nylon. They didn't have silk,' he said apologetically, watching her shake out the folds.

'It's a lovely scarf, Nick. Thank you.' Again she longed for the courage to reach up and press a kiss on his sun-burnt cheek.

As she had forecast, her family were extremely interested when, in introducing him to Jane, she told them how Nick had spent his time away from Longwarden.

North and his mother wanted to know about the fauna and flora on Fuerteventura. Jane revealed that she could speak passable Spanish. All three of them were at pains to put their unexpected guest at ease.

For his part, it wasn't long before Nick relaxed the somewhat stiff manner in which he shook hands and answered the first of their questions.

'So what are your plans now, Nick?' asked North towards the end of the meal.

'I'm not sure what I'm going to do, sir. If I go back into

the Legion within twelve months of my discharge, I can get my rank back – such as it was,' he added with a grin. 'I wouldn't mind that if I could be sure of being stationed near Madrid. But I don't particularly want to be posted to Ronda, the garrison in the south of Spain.'

Feeling he had talked about himself too much already, and having been told by Sarah about North's trip to Ladakh, he began to question the Earl about his recent journey.

In the presence of her family, Sarah was careful not to let her eyes linger too long on Nick's face. She didn't want them to guess how she felt about him, not yet. Not till she knew how he felt about her.

It was while they were having coffee in the library that Jane said, 'Where do your parents live, Nick? In the village or outside it?'

'My parents are dead, Lady Carlyon. I used to live at the lodge but I shan't go back there.' He turned to North. 'If it's all right with you, sir, I'd prefer to sleep in the stables as long as I'm here. I don't suppose it will be for more than a week.'

Before her cousin could reply, Sarah intervened. 'Nick can use my room, as he did last night. When I feel it's all right to leave Chestnut, I can either go back to my old room or use one of the visitors' rooms.'

She thought North looked slightly doubtful about this arrangement, but he said only, 'Yes, very well.'

'There . . . you see?' Sarah said, smiling, when she and Nick were on their way back to the stables. 'What did I tell you? What was sticky about that?'

'Nothing. They were very nice to me,' he admitted.

'Of course. Why not?' she said happily. 'If I like you, why shouldn't they?'

She would have been rather less sanguine had she known what was being said by the three people still in the library.

'That's an interesting young man,' said Jane to her mother-in-law as she refilled their coffee cups.

'But not so interesting that I want to see him at dinner tonight and at lunch and dinner tomorrow,' her husband said shortly. 'In addition to lending him her room, is Sarah proposing to inflict him on us at meals?'

'North, that's unkind. Inflict? He isn't a bore,' Jane protested. 'I found him a very nice person. I'm sorry I made a gaffe, asking him about his parents,' she said, turning to his mother. 'What did he mean by saying he used to live at the lodge but wouldn't go back there?'

'Nick is the illegitimate son of Ted Rivington's dead wife's sister,' her husband explained to her. 'Rivington is reputed to have beaten him . . . knocked him about. A couple of years ago, Nick disappeared and Rivington was seen to have a black eye. The consensus of opinion in the village was that Ted had taken his belt off once too often.'

'And you still employ him?' said Jane, shocked. 'A man who would beat up a young boy?'

'It couldn't be proved that he did. There were no other relations to give the boy a home. It was a difficult situation. I only hope we aren't about to have another one on our hands,' he added, frowning.

'In what way?'

North's long fingers drummed a tattoo on the arm of his chair, a mannerism she was beginning to recognize as a sign that something displeased him.

'He's not a bad-looking chap now. Quite presentable in fact. It's not impossible Sarah could take a shine to him.'

It was on the tip of Jane's tongue to say she thought it a foregone conclusion if Nick were returning for good. In her eyes he was more than presentable. His rugged soldierly appearance combined with a quiet modest manner was, she felt, extremely engaging.

'Would that be bad?' she inquired, aware that many of North's and his mother's values were different from her own and that she had to tread carefully.

'Not if he behaves himself, but I'm not sure one can rely on that.'

'He's only here a short time. I don't think you have to worry. Sarah's heart is given to her horses. It will take a very special person to supersede Bedouin Star,' said Jane.

'If they've more or less grown up together, he's probably like a brother to her. Don't you think so, Penelope?'

Lady Carlyon had not been attending to their conversation. When addressed directly, she came out of her thoughts with a start.

'I'm sorry. I was miles away.'

'We were discussing the undesirable aspects of Nick Dean's reappearance,' her son informed her, with the touch of impatience he showed whenever she was caught wool-gathering.

His own mind was always alert to what was going on around him, Jane was learning. Even when he appeared to be deep in a book, he would sometimes look up and make a pertinent comment on other people's conversation. She had seen him notice the military brooch pinned to Sarah's shirt, clearly a present from Nick. Most men wouldn't have spotted a detail of that sort, but North's vivid eyes were keenly observant of minutiae.

'What undesirable aspects?' his mother asked blankly.

'North is afraid Sarah might fall for Nick.'

'I'm sure she wouldn't be so foolish.' Lady Carlyon dismissed the idea with a positive shake of the head. 'I must get on. I'll see you at tea.'

'Considering Allegra has committed every kind of foolishness, I don't know why Mama thinks Sarah is immune to folly,' said North as the door closed behind her.

'Why would it be so terrible if Sarah did have a romance with Nick? Most girls her age do have boyfriends. After all she is nineteen.'

When he didn't answer at once, and gave her the feeling it was a question she shouldn't have asked, she went on, 'Because he used to be a groom here? Is that your objection to him?'

'Basically, yes. You think that's snobbish, I suppose?'

'Isn't it?'

'Not at all. I don't look down on Nick. I admire his guts and initiative. But if he couldn't ride a horse he and Sarah would have nothing in common.'

'Neither had your great-grandparents. Yet they seem to

have been the best-matched and happiest couple in your family's history.'

North said, 'You're putting too much emphasis on the fact that my great-grandmother was half-Chinese and had a cook and a keeper among her antecedents. It's more important to remember that she'd been educated to a much higher level than most women of her period, and she was the daughter of a botanist which made her sympathetic to my grandfather's interests. In practical terms, she was an ideal wife for him. If Sarah wants to be happy, she'll have to choose a husband who can afford to support her horses as well as her.'

'I guess you're right,' she agreed. 'But you can't keep her under wraps until she's ready to marry. Just for dating, I can't see anything wrong with Nick.'

'He's young. He's in peak condition. He's been stuck for two years on an island where probably the only girls who mix with legionnaires are prostitutes. If he patronized the brothels down there, he may have picked up a disease. If he didn't, he must be as frustrated as hell. A twenty-year-old man who's bursting for some sex and a nineteen-year-old girl as inexperienced as Sarah make a dangerous combination. I'm responsible for her and it's up to me to keep an eye on her. From now on if someone has to sleep with the pony, it'll have to be Sammy or Nick. I want Sarah here in the house.'

Jane was rather amused by this sudden demonstration of an old-fashioned paterfamilias attitude.

'Aren't you being a bit over-alarmist? Someone as attractive as he is doesn't have to go around seducing girls like Sarah. If he was eighteen when he left here, I'd expect him to have several girlfriends waiting to welcome him back.'

'Perhaps. I don't know,' said her husband. 'But I remember what I was like at his age, so I'm inclined to keep a close eye on her while he's around.'

Tark had spent the lunch hour in the pub. Returning to the cottage and finding his mother not back from her midweek shopping trip, he crossed the street to the village

392

self-service shop and acquired a pork pie, two Mars bars and *Playgirl* magazine.

He was sitting at the kitchen table, chewing the pie with his mouth open and studying the full frontal nude centre-fold, when his mother came in by the back door.

'Sorry I'm late, love. I missed the twelve o'clock bus and there weren't another till one-fifteen. It's a rotten service,' she complained, dumping a handful of plastic carriers on a chair.

He looked up. 'I thought you'd been done.'

It was meant as a joke but Mavis wasn't amused. Her plump face, already flushed from hurrying, turned a deeper pink. Any direct reference to her method of shopping embarrassed her. She had been very upset the first time he let on he knew.

She said sharply, 'Don't be cheeky,' and turned to put on the kettle for a cup of tea.

Tark scoured his mouth with his tongue and eyed the bags, recognizing the bright green ones as being from Marks & Spencer, the source of most of her clothes.

'Got anything for me?' he asked.

She shook her head, still annoyed with him. 'It's time you was working, Tarquin. People is starting to talk. I've had several remarks passed lately about you not doing nothing.'

'Oh, yeah? What you tell 'em? To mind their own sodding business?'

She spun round, her eyes bright with anger. 'Don't you use no bad language to me. As long as you live in my house, you'll keep a clean tongue in your head.'

'Okay, okay, Mum . . . calm down. Don't get yourself in a sweat.'

He had noticed that when she was worked up, and sometimes when she wasn't, she would break out in great beads of moisture. It was happening now, as he watched her, making her go to her handbag for a tissue to mop her hot face.

Mavis sat down at the table, dabbing her forehead and

upper lip. She was 'on the change', and twice already that morning had been overcome by a hot flush. They were always worse on her shopping days.

'Sharon says they're looking for help up the big house,' her son remarked, while she was sipping her tea and sampling one of Marks & Spencer's new lines in biscuits. 'Part-time cleaners they want. No scrubbing nor nothing heavy. Dusting the family heirlooms and that.' He unwrapped the second Mars bar. 'I've heard they've got so much stuff, they can't keep track of all what they have got. That's the sort of job would suit you, Mum. You've always said you liked dusting.'

This was true. It gave her great satisfaction to keep her house nice, her crowded cupboards in order. Luckily the cottage had plenty of storage space for the reserve supplies she was accumulating. One thing she could never resist was a pretty tea towel. Tights were another weakness. She must have at least thirty pairs upstairs in a box in the wardrobe.

She finished eating the biscuit, thinking over what he had said. The main reason she didn't like Tarquin making remarks like the one when she first came in was because, at the back of her mind, she was always a little uneasy in case one day, after a few drinks, he might let slip something incriminating. In her line of business it paid to be very discreet.

The trouble with Tarquin, although it pained her to admit it, was his looks were better than his brains. He was as handsome as his father, and several inches taller than Paco Lopez. But he wasn't a bright boy.

'If you mean what I think you mean, you must be dafter than I took you for,' she said irritably. 'If I went up there as a cleaner and something went missing, who'd be the first person suspected? Anyway that sort of stuff, silver and such-like, isn't easy to get rid of.'

'That weren't the idea,' he said, scowling, annoyed by her tone.

His mother could make him feel small. He remembered the rows between her and his father and how she had always come off best, lashing his dad with her tongue until he did what she wanted or withdrew to the pub.

She never lashed Tark like that. If she tried it, he'd belt her – he told himself. Deep down, he wasn't so sure. If he belted her, even if she'd asked for it, she might decide to ditch him the way she'd walked out on his dad. Without her, life would be harder. He'd have to find somewhere to live and a bird to look after him, and he might have to stick at a job instead of, as now, being able to tell the boss to get stuffed if he got bored after a few weeks.

'What was the idea then?' asked Mavis.

'No one wouldn't suspect you if the place was done over at night . . . an outside job. I've got contacts in London who'd pay good money for the right information,' he told her grandly.

'How much money? What kind of information?' she asked.

'The money'd depend on the job. It'd be a cut, like. What they'd want to know is how to get in, quiet and easy, and where the best stuff's kept. You wouldn't have to do nothing. Keep your eyes peeled, that's all. There's no risk in that.'

She thought for a bit. 'I don't know as I want to work there. I've got enough to do now. Who are these people in London? How do you know you'd get your cut?'

'That's my worry, Mum. The less you know about it the better. I shouldn't let on where I got the info neither. No names, no pack drill. Right?'

'I'll have to think about it. Where d'you hear there was a job going?'

'Sharon told me. She lives near someone what works there.'

Money, especially easy money, was always welcome. At the same time Mavis had certain scruples and there were three aspects of Tarquin's suggestion that troubled her. Her strongest objection was to her son's involvement with criminals. Was he equal to dealing with them?

Mavis had never regarded her own acts as criminal. She didn't take things from small shopkeepers, only from the big stores which, making profits by the million, could well afford to supply her modest needs.

Nicking, or being instrumental in the nicking of stuff from private owners, was another matter. The boards of directors of chain stores and supermarkets were faceless rich men who were fair game. Towards royalty and the aristocracy her feelings were warmer. She liked the Queen and the Queen Mum, and she idolized Princess Di. She had sent her a wedding present – picked up in Harrods which she knew was Di's favourite store – and been thrilled to see it among the hundreds of presents on show to the public after the wedding.

About Lord Carlyon and his family she didn't know much, except that he'd recently married an American, and the girl who'd won some big prize for riding not long ago was his cousin and lived at the big house.

'If you think about it too long, someone else'll get the job,' said Tark.

Mavis watched him light a cigarette. Although she tried not to think about it, there were times when his future worried her. He hadn't turned out as she'd hoped. Sometimes she wondered if she ought to go back to Benidorm and find out how Paco had done for himself. But even if he had prospered, he'd be sure to be married. In which case he wouldn't welcome the sudden appearance of an unknown son, however unquestionable the resemblance between them.

Putting aside past and future, she brought her mind back to the present and the subject under discussion. Even if she didn't go along with Tarquin's scheme, it might be interesting to get an insider's view of a stately home. She might make friends with the other cleaners. Up to now, apart from a few words about the weather while she was waiting for the bus, she had had very little to do with the local people.

'All right then, I'll give it a try,' she said, on a decisive impulse. 'But I'm making no promises, mind. If it's not to my liking, I won't stay.'

* * *

The Haflinger pony had just completed his first walk round the yard when the butler brought a message for Sarah. Mrs Wareham had telephoned and would like Sarah to ring back as soon as it was convenient.

'Thank you, Mr Ashford. I'll call her back now. Take Chestnut inside, would you, Sammy?' Handing over the leading rope, she headed for her room.

As the Irishman led the pony back to his stall, Nick turned in the direction of the archway which, from inside the yard, framed a prospect of autumnal woods and the stream which fed Longwarden lake.

He was standing with folded arms, admiring the view and waiting for Sarah to return, when a voice said, '*Es una vista hermosa.*'

The language, spoken with many accents, with which he had lived for two years, took Nick by surprise. In an instant it conjured a vision of the barracks at Puerto del Rosario and the men who were still serving there. A pang of intense nostalgia for those crude surroundings, and the rough camaraderie of the friends who had signed their names on the back of his certificate of service, overcame him. In his case, the sudden yearning experienced by all ex-servicemen was made doubly potent by the fact that for most of his life he had felt an unwanted outsider. The Legion had been like the family he had never had.

A sudden lump in his throat made a nod of agreement his only immediate acknowledgement of the butler's remark that it was a beautiful view.

The older man said, in English, 'My Spanish, such as it was, is pretty rusty these days. It's a long time since I've used it.'

Nick recovered his voice. 'Have you worked in Spain?'

'No: I've spent . . . holidays there. At one time I thought of retiring there. Not to Marbella or Benidorm, but to a quiet place further inland, out of the way of the tourists. I liked the sierras, the climate and the Spanish people. But it's several years since I was there. It may have changed a great deal.'

397

A few minutes later Sarah came out and saw Ashford and Nick in conversation outside the archway.

As they stood side by side, with their backs to her, she was struck by the similarity of their straight-shouldered upright bearing.

They turned and came back through the arch.

She said, 'I'll be out tonight, Mr Ashford. I'm bidden to supper with the Warehams. You're invited as well, Nick.'

As the butler went away, she said, 'You and Mr Ashford seem to have hit it off. Usually he's not very communicative.'

'We were talking about the army as a career. He's a nice bloke. I like him.'

When their guests had departed, not staying late because they were all early risers, Rob and Emily washed up the coffee cups.

The rest of the dishes had been done by the two girls earlier while Rob and Nick remained in the sitting room, talking. The men had volunteered to help but had been urged to relax because Sarah had wanted – as her hostess was aware – to test Emily's reaction to Nick.

Now, in her turn, Emily was curious to know what her husband thought of him.

'He seems a nice chap,' said Rob. 'You liked him, didn't you?'

'Very much, but that's only my personal reaction. I think Sarah's family are going to be a bit fussed when they realize she's madly in love with him. What I couldn't make out was how he feels about her. Did you get any clues?'

'I didn't even realize she was keen about him. What makes you think so? Has she said so?'

'Rob, she's suddenly lit up like a Christmas tree. Of course she's in love with him, dope. How could you miss it?'

'I hope you're wrong. By the sound of it, he's not going to be around long.'

'Yes – poor Sarah. Not that I see any future for them. By her family's standards he must be as ineligible as they come. No money. Working-class background. No education to speak of.'

'They're both far too young to be thinking of settling down anyway,' said Rob.

'I know, but I have the feeling it's no mere calf love for Sarah. I suspect she's loved him a long time, and it's not something she'll grow out of, any more than she's outgrown horses, the way most girls do sooner or later. Horses are necessary for her, and so is Nick, even if he doesn't know it. She'll be heartbroken if he signs on for another long spell abroad.'

The following evening Sarah was again absent when her family assembled for dinner.

Forestalling his employer's inquiry, Ashford said, 'Miss Sarah asked me to tell you that she and Mr Dean are dining with Mr O'Brien tonight, m'Lord.'

The next day, when the evening meal was a cold one because it was Mrs Armitage's day off, Sarah mentioned to Jane that she and Nick would have their supper on trays in the archway room.

Jane passed this message to North when they were alone for a few minutes before being joined by his mother.

Seeing that he disapproved, she said, 'It's a little awkward for Sarah, North. She must realize that you and your mother don't want Nick here every night, but she can't leave an old friend on furlough to eat on his own.'

'He has O'Brien for company.'

'Sammy is off sick today. He cooked them a curry last night – it's his specialty – and it seems to have upset his stomach. If he isn't better tomorrow, Sarah's having your doctor to check him over. He hasn't been well for a while now. But Chestnut is doing fine, which is good news. As he isn't strong enough yet to go down to the forge, the blacksmith is coming here to trim his feet. Sarah says he and his wife are two of her closest friends. Have you met them?'

He nodded. 'The Warehams are a nice couple. Farriery is one of the old country crafts which are having a revival.

At one time we thought the village smithy was in danger of closing down when Tiny Bossom began to get a bit past it. Years ago, there was a blacksmith here. The village smith dealt with the Shires and the other working horses, and the chap here made shoes for the hunters. But that stopped with World War Two.'

Life at Longwarden in past decades fascinated Jane. She would have liked to draw out her mother-in-law's reminiscences. However from the beginning of their acquaintance her intuition had told her that Penelope preferred the forward view. Lady Carlyon spoke of the distant past, but avoided any reference to the years of her marriage.

Jane had thought this might be because she was still mourning her husband. North had killed that illusion.

'They were always civil to each other, but they didn't get on,' he had told her.

They were always civil to each other. What an epitaph for a marriage, Jane had thought, wondering if, in time, the same would apply to her marriage.

After supper, Sarah and Nick went to look at the horses. He was going to attend to Chestnut during the small hours to give Sarah her first unbroken night's sleep since the pony's arrival.

After their round of the stables, they returned to the archway room where Nick resumed his study of the Jobs Offered columns in the local morning and evening newspapers.

She picked up yesterday's *Times*. Most people read a paper from front to back. Sarah and Sammy began at the back with the news, if any, of eventing, followed by the racing columns.

She had been reading for a few minutes when she made a distressful sound which caused Nick to look up and ask, 'What's the matter?'

She gave him an anguished glance. 'Something awful happened the day before yesterday. Sammy probably heard it on the radio but he didn't tell me. One of the best two-mile 'chasers in England had to be put down on the race course. He had a clear twenty-length lead but he slipped after clearing the last fence. He got to his feet but his off-hind fetlock was shattered and they had to . . .' Her voice unsteady, she broke off.

'God, what a lousy thing to happen,' Nick said sympathetically.

'He was only a seven-year-old. It says' – her voice quavered again – 'it says *His Jockey, who had ridden him to win fourteen of his eighteen races, returned to the weighing room in tears.*'

Not greatly to Nick's surprise, because he had known her when younger to weep for dead cats and dogs, Sarah's eyes brimmed.

As she fumbled vainly for a hanky, he plucked two or three tissues from a box within his arm's reach and crossed the room to the sofa where she was sitting.

Putting the tissues into her hands he sat beside her and, with an arm around her shoulders, said, 'That's why Sammy didn't tell you. He knew it would only upset you.'

Sarah's feelings had been stirred by her capacity to visualize Beddo or Tatty with a shattered fetlock. But Nick's closeness also had an effect. Her sorrow became tinged with joy at having his arm round her.

Instinctively she relaxed against him for comfort while she dried her eyes and blew her nose.

'I'm sorry,' she murmured shakily.

His arm tightened slightly. Suddenly she had the feeling that, if she stayed very still, he might turn her face up and kiss her.

She was holding her breath, her heart beginning to thump, when North walked in.

Not having heard North's footsteps mounting the staircase, the two young people side by side on the sofa were startled when the door opened, but neither of them was in a hurry to move. When Nick withdrew his arm from Sarah's shoulders and rose to his feet, it was without haste or embarrassment.

Seeing the spiky wetness of his cousin's eyelashes and the crumpled tissues in her hand, North said quietly, 'What's upset you?'

It was Nick who answered. 'She's just read the news about the steeplechaser which had to be put down on the course the day before yesterday.'

'I see,' was North's only comment. He also knew that his cousin, although resolutely stiff of lip when she hurt herself, was easily reduced to tears when animals died or were injured.

Looking at the room he hadn't been in for some time, his glance passed from Nick's kitbag to an olive-green uniform jacket with scarlet braid on the sleeves which hung outside Sarah's clothes cupboard.

'Is that your walking-out uniform?'

'Yes, sir.'

North moved closer to examine the insignia; red and gold enamel badges on the collar, a regimental flash on the shoulder and a brass belt buckle embossed with a crossbow, musket and halberd.

'Very smart,' he said. 'What's this badge?' – touching a small one attached by a piece of leather to the button of the right breast pocket.

'That's the *pepito* . . . the emblem of my battalion, sir.'

'The cap is the best part.' Sarah jumped up and seized it from the top of a chest. 'Look, North – isn't it dashing?'

She perched it on her blonde hair; a green cap to match the jacket, trimmed with thin scarlet braid and a scarlet silk tassel which dangled down over one eyebrow. A black patent-leather chin-strap, fastened to small brass buttons on either side, rested on the crest of the cap.

'Will you do me a favour?' she asked. 'Will you take some photographs of Nick wearing his uniform?'

'I don't think that's quite Lord Carlyon's line, Sarah,' Nick said quickly, looking embarrassed.

'On the contrary, I'd be delighted,' North told him pleasantly. He glanced at his watch. 'It's getting late for you people who rise at cock-crow. Shall we walk back together, Sarah?'

She nodded. 'I don't suppose there will be any emergencies while Nick's here and I'm in the house. But, just in case, I've shown him the room I'm sleeping in. He'd never been upstairs before.' She turned to Nick. 'Perhaps you should have written down the directions. All those corridors on the first floor can be confusing until you're used to them.'

'Don't worry, if I need you, I'll find you,' he assured her. 'Goodnight. Goodnight, sir.'

As he met her cousin's eyes, he thought he knew why the Earl had walked the considerable distance from the far end of the house to look in on them.

The next day Rob arrived to trim Chestnut's feet. Although still far from a full recovery, the pony was no longer the listless, hollow-flanked wreck he had been. His mouth and nostrils were regaining a healthier colour and he was beginning to take an interest in his surroundings.

'He'll look a lot better when we can give him a bath, but that won't be for some time yet,' Sarah told Jane, as she stood by his head while Rob went to work on the neglected feet.

Presently they asked him if he knew of any horses which might suit Jane, and continued discussing this subject when the job was done and he accepted the offer of a cup of tea.

It was a sunny afternoon. They drank the tea sitting on the bench outside the tackroom. Sarah was pleased to see that the other two seemed to have taken to each other. Jane had already invited Rob to use her first name, and suggested that he and his wife should come to dinner the following week.

Sammy and Nick were out with the other horses. As the stable clock struck the hour, the sound of hooves made the three on the bench look expectantly towards the archway.

To their astonished consternation, they saw that Nick, mounted on Beddo, was also holding the mare's reins. Sammy was in the saddle but doubled up over her withers.

'Give a hand here, will you, Rob?' Nick called on a note of urgency.

Rob hurried forward to help, the two girls hard on his heels.

It was fortunate someone of his big, strong build was there. Sammy seemed to know where he was and took his feet out of the stirrups, but he was incapable of dismounting. With a warning cry, he collapsed sideways. If Rob hadn't caught him, he would have fallen on the bricks.

'Well, that seems to solve my job problem, at least until Sammy is fit again,' said Nick several hours later, when the doctor had been and gone.

Sarah's face, which since four o'clock had been clouded with anxiety, took on a more cheerful aspect.

'If you would stand in for him, Nick, it would be an enormous help,' she said gratefully. 'Four horses, one of them an invalid, are rather a lot for me to handle on my own.'

If he hadn't offered to take Sammy's place, she wouldn't have suggested it. Now he had volunteered, she could accept, with relief, an arrangement which seemed almost a gift from the gods. Not that she liked the idea of having her heart's desire realized at the cost of Sammy's well-being. But if he had to be ill, it was wonderful luck to have someone on hand who wouldn't need to be watched and supervised. Someone the horses already knew and trusted.

'I just pray it is only gallstones as Doctor Reid seems to think,' she went on. 'Horribly painful, but nothing to panic about. Obviously Sammy believed these bad bouts of pain he's been having were a symptom of something much worse. I think he's still worried, poor dear, and will be until the provisional diagnosis is confirmed.'

When medical tests supported Doctor Reid's diagnosis, the Irishman was advised to have an operation. On learning that, under the National Health Service, a considerable delay was probable, Jane insisted the groom must have private treatment.

'He's had months of worry already, poor old man. Sarah

says he's terrified of hospitals. Let's help get it over quickly for him,' she said persuasively to North.

He agreed and it was arranged for Sammy to be admitted to a private clinic almost immediately.

On the day Sarah drove him there, Nick was busy in the stables when North came to see him.

After some general conversation, he said, 'We're fortunate to have you to fill the breach while Sammy's laid up. But I gather you're not inclined to come back to work here permanently?'

'No, sir,' Nick agreed.

Even though he was now on the Longwarden payroll again, he didn't intend to revert to addressing North as 'm'Lord'.

'I don't see much future in being a groom,' he went on. 'I see myself as a soldier. But I haven't yet made up my mind whether to go back in the Legion or try another army.'

'So Sarah tells me,' said North, watching him carefully picking out one of Bedouin's feet. 'But you have agreed to stay on until Sammy is fit to resume work or until a new groom has been found, I understand?'

'Yes, sir, I'll stay here till Christmas or New Year.' He moved the skep used to catch the dirt out of the way and let the horse put his foot down. As he straightened, he added, 'By then it'll be time to start training for Badminton. I think Sarah should find a girl groom to help her with that. Even if he gets over this operation all right, Sammy's past handling the kind of season she's likely to have next year.'

North nodded. 'I think you're right. On her present form she shouldn't have any trouble getting a good girl to work for her. What time are you expecting her back?'

'She said about five. There's a spare bed in Sammy's cottage I'm going to use so that she can have the archway room back.'

'I don't see much point in that arrangement,' said North. 'Sammy will be convalescent for some time but he won't be in hospital long. He won't like sharing the cottage. He prefers to be on his own. It's best if you stay where you are. Sarah can move her clothes out to give you more room for your kit. She won't mind using her old room for the short time you'll be here.'

Nick looked him straight in the eyes. 'Are you worried about her being up there with me around?'

The blunt question showed him to be more acute than North had realized.

'Not worried, no,' he answered. 'I think you're a decent chap. You and Sarah have known each other since you were children. You've been friends for years and that friendship has been good for both of you. But now that you're grown up – although Sarah is young for her age in many ways – there are factors to be considered which didn't exist before. I'd like to feel you were aware of the pitfalls and would do your best to avoid them.'

Nick's level stare didn't waver. After gazing at North for some moments, he said, 'I don't think I see any pitfalls, sir. Perhaps you'd better explain them.'

North had no objection to putting the matter more plainly. He had set out to be tactful, but frankness suited him better.

'It's clear that Sarah is very much impressed by your service in Spain's Foreign Legion. As indeed we all are. But in her case it's close to hero-worship. No' – as Nick would have spoken – 'let me finish, please. Sarah has been too involved in eventing to have time for anything else. Late nights at parties and discos aren't compatible with early-morning stables. As a result she has little experience, if any, of dealing with the opposite sex. Therefore it's up to you, Nick, to avoid letting her hero-worship develop into a serious crush on you. She's growing up a charming girl and you may feel attracted to her. But quite apart from the fact that you're both far too young for any serious relationship, you are set on a career as a soldier which will probably take you abroad again. Meanwhile you and Sarah are going to be working together every day for several months. I'd like to have your assurance that, as the older and more worldly-wise of the two of you, you'll behave with the discretion the situation requires.'

Nick's face, as North finished speaking, showed no reaction. After a moment he picked up the stable rubber and used it to dust a speck from the Arab's gleaming quarters.

Looking at the horse, not at North, he said, 'Sarah and Sammy were my closest friends until I joined the Legion. She was like a kid sister to me. Getting letters from her helped a lot at times when it was rough going. I wouldn't do anything to hurt her.'

'I'm sure you wouldn't – not intentionally. But life is rather like the cross-country phase of a horse trial. It's a help to "walk the course" beforehand by thinking of possible problems and ways to avoid them. Forewarned is forearmed, as they say.'

North gave him a friendly clap on the shoulder and went on his way.

Sarah drove home from the clinic, after seeing Sammy settled, in an optimistic mood.

Confident that he was in the hands of excellent nurses and a first-rate surgeon, she felt sure the operation would relieve him of the long unspoken fear of cancer he had admitted to her on the outward journey.

Often in pain, and continually worried that he was suffering from what, like many of his generation, he regarded as an inevitably terminal disease, it was not surprising he had been morose and short-tempered.

Relieved of her worries about him – although naturally she would feel happier when the operation had been successfully accomplished – she was free to enjoy the prospect of the weeks ahead, working with Nick.

Remembering her cousin's invitation, after Burghley, to visit her in London, Sarah pondered asking Allegra's advice on how to improve her looks. Her present hairstyle was practical but it had the disadvantage of leaving her thick hair crinkled when it was unplaited. Perhaps there was some other style which would be as easy to manage but more adaptable.

It was also high time that she started using more make-up

– perhaps not during the day when she was busy in the stables, but certainly in the evening.

She arrived back at Longwarden looking forward to an evening alone with Nick.

Her first surprise was to find he had changed his mind about moving into Sammy's spare room. He said, if she didn't object, he would rather stay in the archway room.

She was only too happy to surrender her eyrie to him. But his next announcement came as an unexpected blow.

He said, 'D'you think I could have a fiver from my first week's wages? I thought I'd go down to the pub for an hour or two this evening.'

'Of course,' she said brightly, masking her disappointment.

It wasn't only that she minded his tiring of her company so quickly; but she knew that time spent in pubs would do nothing to enhance her family's estimation of him.

When a tall young man with cropped hair and a darkly tanned face walked into the lounge of the Longwarden Arms that evening, he caused a momentary hiatus in the low buzz of conversation.

Apart from a couple of reps staying for bed and breakfast, everyone present was local. None of them recognized the newcomer as Ted Rivington's foster son who had disappeared two years before.

Aware that he was the cynosure of considerable curiosity, Nick approached the bar.

'A half of lager, please.'

'Turned chilly this evening,' the landlord said as he served him.

Nick nodded and put a one-pound note on the counter.

'You've been enjoying better weather, by the looks of you,' said the landlord.

'Yes.' Nick's expression was pleasant but his tone was uncommunicative.

The publican took the hint and resumed a conversation with the reps at the far end of the bar.

'Hello, Nick. Where've you sprung from?'

A heavily made-up girl with a wispy peroxide-streaked hairdo slid on to the stool beside him and put her arms on the bar.

He looked at her, trying to discern what she might have been like two years ago without the punk-influenced hair and the overdone pink eye make-up.

'You don't remember me, do you?' She wasn't offended. 'I'm Sharon Cook.'

The name rang a faint bell. It didn't help him to remember what she had looked like then. What she looked like now was a tart. Did she think he might be a customer?

'Hello. How are you?' he said politely.

'I'm fine. You look pretty good. When d'you get back?'

'A few days ago.'

'Staying with your dad, are you?'

'If you mean Ted Rivington – no.' He picked up his glass, hoping she would take his failure to offer her a drink as the brush-off. She was less attractive to him than the dusky-skinned, dark-eyed girls of the Playa Blanca brothels to whom he had sometimes chatted during a spell of military police duty.

Neither they, nor the girls of the village during his teens, had tempted him to risk a dose of the clap. His introduction to sex had come at the age of sixteen when an Australian artist had rented a cottage on the outskirts of Longwarden and engaged him first to mow the grass on his day off and later to model for her. She had said he had interesting bones, but it was his flesh she had been more intersted in. For two months she had taught him to make love and then she had gone back to London, leaving him a signed drawing of his head but no address.

His next woman had been the bored thirty-five-year-old wife of a scientist in his fifties who had come to Fuerteventura to study microscopic worms. He had met them in a café in Puerto del Rosario, the island's chief town and port. Later he and the wife had met again, several times. She had given him her address but he wasn't planning to look her up. He knew it was hypocritical when he had been a party to her deception of her husband, but privately he had despised her for staying, out of habit or laziness, with a man she didn't love.

He had seen her looking down her nose at a pretty half-Arab whore talking and laughing in a bar with a couple of *legionarios*; but it seemed to him that her life with her elderly husband was another form of prostitution.

In his second year in the Legion, he had spent a leave on the more touristy island of Tenerife where he met a couple of English secretaries looking for a holiday romance. He could have had either of them; not by virtue of his looks or charm, he recognized with rueful amusement, but because they were thrilled by his uniform.

He wouldn't have minded having both of them, one in the afternoons, and the other in the evenings. But they were conventional girls from a somewhat higher social stratum than the one he belonged to by birth. They would have been shocked if he had suggested that arrangement.

A bird in the hand being better than two in the bush, he had settled for the one called Jacky. She and her friend were staying in one of the package-tour tower blocks. He had a room in a cheap but clean *hostal* where the proprietor emerged from his quarters only when summoned by the buzzer on the desk in the small ground-floor lobby.

There had been no difficulty in taking Jacky up to his room for active *siestas* in the dim light admitted by the chinks in the plastic *persianas*. At first she had been reluctant to allow some of the caresses taught him by the uninhibited Australian. At the end of her holiday, she had spent the last night with him and waved a tearful goodbye from the coach taking her to the airport.

There had been no one else since then. No acceptable opportunity offered itself; and his need was never stronger than his instinctive aversion to girls like the one sitting next to him, waiting to be asked, 'What's yours?'

'You're ever so brown. Have you been abroad?' she asked.

He nodded.

'Been working for the Arabs, have you?'

She had heard there was good money to be earned

wherever it was the Arabs had their oil wells. Somewhere uncomfortably hot where people caught drinking were flogged and thieves had their hands cut off was all she knew about it.

'No,' said Nick. 'What are you doing these days, Sharon?'

'I'm on the check-out up the supermarket. It's dead boring but what else is there?' she said with a shrug. As the publican came towards them, she said, 'I'll have a vodka and tonic, Stan.'

When she picked up her drink, Nick noticed that where the dark varnish was chipped her long nails were not very clean.

In his mind's eye he saw Sarah's nails. She did a lot of dirty jobs around the stables, but when she had finished she scrubbed her small capable hands and she always smelt clean and fresh. The night he had put his arm round her, when she was upset about the steeplechaser, he'd caught the faint scent of shampoo from her thick, silky, streaky blonde hair.

Strangely, he hadn't known then that he was powerfully attracted to her. Even though she had changed in his absence, it had taken some time to recognize that she had grown into the girl he had hoped to find some day. The girl he would eventually marry.

In fact that knowledge hadn't hit him until Lord Carlyon was warning him off. Inwardly he had been angry that her cousin didn't trust him with her.

Later, when she returned from taking Sammy to the clinic, Nick had realized he could no longer trust himself. He had wanted to put his arms round her and hold her close, to kiss her.

In the light of such a discovery, it had been essential to get away and think things out: hence his presence in the pub. However it was impossible to think with Sharon Cook at his elbow.

Nick's feelings about women were influenced by amorphous early memories of a loving voice, a comfortable lap, a protective feminine presence. She had not left him by choice. She had been taken away. In spite of evidence to the contrary, he still tended to think of all females as gentler, more vulnerable beings than men, and to treat them with the good manners he had learned more from Sarah's example than from the precepts of his teachers or Rivington's brutal strictures.

The street door opened, admitting a group of young people none of whom Nick recognized, except that the first one in looked surprisingly Spanish.

Sharon spoke to him. 'I was here early. I've been talking to Nick Dean who used to live round here. This is Tark Osgood. He's new here.'

The custom of shaking hands, not usual among the young in the village but a common habit, even among teenagers, in Spain, made Nick extend his hand to the dark-eyed *chico* with the black leathers and the swagger.

Tark took it but looked surprised. The nod which would have been his only acknowledgement of the introduction was more hostile than friendly. He moved to the other side of Sharon and stared at Nick while she reeled off the names of the others.

Not liking the look of any of them, he said a general 'Hello' and finished his lager. 'I've got to be going. Goodnight, Sharon. Goodnight.' He made for the door.

As he pushed it open, he heard someone behind him mutter, 'Toffee-nosed bleeder. Who does he think he is then?'

In summer he could have found a dozen places in which to be alone with his thoughts. At this time of year there was nowhere. He would have to walk about.

The encounter with Sharon, reminding him of his origins, was doubly depressing coming a short time after his discovery of his love for Sarah.

While he had been in the Legion, where many of the other legionnaires had backgrounds far more disreputable than his own, he had forgotten the feeling dinned into him by Ted Rivington, of being an unwanted bastard, a predestined misfit. The Legion had given him confidence and a sense of achievement. He had not only survived an experience which would have made nervous wrecks of most

412

youths with respectable backgrounds; for the most part he had enjoyed it.

He wished now he hadn't come back. What was there for him here but the pain of loving a girl who could never be his?

Mavis Osgood's first day as a cleaner at Longwarden was spent under the wing of Mrs Bailey who, by virtue of her long service, regarded herself as second in command to Mr Ashford.

Connie Bailey was not sure she approved of Mrs Osgood being given the vacancy. Mrs Osgood did have local connections, being the niece of the late Mrs Barker, but she was also the mother of that Darky or Sparky or whatever his name was. The tales Connie had heard about *him*, and the row he made with his motorbike, made her doubtful that his mother could be the type of person the rest of the cleaning team would welcome.

When Mavis arrived for work neatly dressed, with a plain blue nylon coverall to wear over her dress, and a pair of indoor shoes to be kept in the cleaners' cloakroom, she made a favourable first impression.

From nine till eleven, under Mrs Bailey's supervision, she vacuumed and dusted the ground-floor rooms used by the family. The exertion combined with a nervous awareness of being under critical surveillance brought on one of her turns. She suddenly felt boiling hot, with perspiration bursting from every pore.

Mrs Bailey's sharp eyes didn't miss the flush which suffused her face or the beads of moisture she tried unobtrusively to blot. Her magisterial manner at once became more benign for, as she was wont to tell anyone who would listen, no one would ever know what she had suffered 'on the change'.

At eleven they had a short coffee break in the kitchen where Mavis was introduced to Mrs Armitage and the two cleaners dealing with the bedrooms. Then she and Mrs Bailey returned to finish the library and Mrs Bailey regaled her with her complete gynaecological history beginning with her first confinement and ending with her hysterectomy.

'How d'you get on?' asked Tark, when his mother came home.

'I was on the go every minute. I'll be glad to sit down,' she said wearily.

As they sat at the kitchen table eating cold pork pie, kept-hot chips and pickled beetroot, Mavis described her morning at Longwarden.

'With that Mrs Bailey on my back all the time, I didn't get much of a chance to have a look round. I think she was showing me the ropes. Next time I'll be on my own.'

'You must have seen something,' said Tark. 'You can't clean a place with your eyes shut.'

'Of course I saw something – but not nothing to interest those people in London. I was quite surprised how shabby the place was. They haven't no nice fitted carpets. Mind you, some of their squares would do a whole house this size. But there's more Persian rugs than anything and half of them are worn out. They're devils to hoover. Every thread of the fringe has to lie straight to satisfy that Mrs B. She's a proper fuss-pot, that woman.'

'What about silver?' said Tark. 'And clocks. They're good stuff to nick.'

'I didn't see nothing like that. It's not like an ordinary house where you've only got a few rooms. They've got dozens . . . hundreds, I reckon. Maybe all the best stuff is kept where I haven't been yet. You can't expect me to see it all, my first day.'

She sounded worried and pettish. It had taken a lot of persuasion to get her to apply for the job. He couldn't force her to keep it. Some soft soap was needed.

'That's okay. There's no rush. Take your time, Mum. I thought you might be a bit knackered. I got you a treat. A big box of After Eights.'

She couldn't resist chocolate mints. 'Oh, Tarquin, you do waste money. I brought two of them back from town the last time I went. Never mind, it's the thought that counts. You're a good boy, when you've a mind.'

'I'll make you a cup of tea,' he said with a smirk.

He had paid for the things Mavis had asked him to get from Longwarden's mini-market. But he hadn't paid for the mints or his cigarettes. Not with Sharon on the till.

NOVEMBER

In North's father's time, the Carlyon Hunt had ranked with the Heythrop and the Beaufort as one of the three most exclusive and famous hunts in England.

Many of his heir's financial problems stemmed from the fact that the eighth Earl had been a Master of the old school – a sometimes tyrannical despot who had financed the Hunt from his own pocket and stamped it with his personality.

Sarah had been foxhunting in winter for as long as she could remember. Were it not for hunting, she knew, foxes would have been exterminated long ago. That, combined with the benefits to the horses, helped her to overcome her aversion to the times when a fox was killed. Fortunately for her peace of mind there were many days when the fox outwitted hounds or went safely to ground.

On a misty morning in November, both immaculately turned out in black coats, pale breeches, silk stocks and velvet caps, she and Jane set out to hack the four miles to a meet at the manor house belonging to one of the Joint Masters who had succeeded her uncle.

'I wish you were coming with us,' she said, looking down at Nick before they rode out of the yard which now housed Jane's newly-bought hunter.

In spite of Sarah's persuasions, Nick had refused to go with them, saying he would feel out of place. She had argued but failed to budge him. He seemed stubbornly determined to stick to his rôle as groom, even though he was doing the job as a favour.

'Take care.' With his crooked half-smile, he stepped back to watch them move off.

'I can't think why he's so obstinate. He would have enjoyed it,' said Sarah, looking downcast.

Jane said nothing, suspecting that Nick's refusal had to do with what North had said to him and later mentioned to her. She had felt that North was being old-fashioned and, for someone of his age, amazingly reactionary. However, conscious of being a newcomer who needed to feel her way carefully among people who spoke more or less the same language but had many dissimilarities from Americans, she had said nothing at the time. After all she didn't know Nick. Perhaps North had been wise to warn him off. Sarah *was* unsophisticated for a girl of nineteen.

It took them about an hour to arrive at the meet. They said good morning to the Master whom Jane had already met at one of the several dinner parties to which they had been invited as soon as news of North's marriage got about the county. She had expected him to be in scarlet but his coat was bottle green as were those of the hunt servants.

While the Master's wife and manservant and other helpers offered trays of sherry and port, and the hunt secretary collected the caps in his leather pouch, several people Jane had met at dinners said, 'Good morning, Lady Carlyon.'

She was conscious that many people present, not merely those she had met, would be watching to see how she acquitted herself. She was glad of Sarah's supportive presence.

Soon the pack of foxhounds arrived, thirty couples carrying their sterns like banners, following the professional huntsman and accompanied by whippers-in.

At ten o'clock they moved off, eager hounds crowding behind the huntsman on the way to the first covert, a thicket of trees between the grounds of the manor and open country. Here the field had to wait.

Excited and nervous at taking part for the first time in this most traditional and colourful of all English country pursuits, Jane sat quietly on her bay gelding, admiring the mahogany-topped boots of the men in white breeches and

416

the subdued tweed hacking jackets worn by the children. Sarah told her the jackets were called ratcatchers.

As hounds spread among the trees, all busily sniffing the ground, she hoped she wouldn't disgrace herself by falling off. North, uninterested himself, had not been too keen on her hunting. Having made up her mind to ride at least once with the Carlyon, she had ignored his disapproval. Now, when at any moment hounds might pick up the scent, she hoped she wouldn't regret it. She was a little afraid of hurting herself, but more alarmed at the thought of becoming a laughing-stock.

'I hear Carlyon's Yankee bride came a cropper at the first fence.'

She could imagine the guffaws and giggles that information would provoke as it filtered through the rarefied strata of society into which she had married.

The pack began to give tongue. On the other side of the copse a whipper-in gave a halloa as he saw the fox breaking cover. The huntsman blew Gone Away and, led by the Master, a field of a hundred riders on mounts of all sizes and colours thundered towards the first fence, a hedge which looked formidably high compared with the jumps she had practised over.

Peking, the hunter Sarah had advised her to buy, was an experienced ten-year-old, which was just as well because it was wholly his expertise which got them over the hedge in creditable style.

Once over the first one, Jane gained confidence. Soon she was enjoying herself, not attempting to keep up with the neck-or-nothing riders, and letting Peking dictate the pace of their approach to fences, but enjoying the gallops between them and the ease with which he cleared them.

This exhilarating run in full cry didn't last long. The pack lost the scent and checked. She saw the huntsman dismount and start making a cast to recover it. As Peking obeyed her signals to slow down, she gave him a grateful pat.

Sarah had warned her not to buy him unless she took to him. She had, and now that he had helped her through her first run she felt they had begun a partnership which could last the whole season – unless she started a baby.

It was during the wait that she noticed a man in a blue coat with scarlet cuffs whom she didn't remember seeing at the meet. She could see only the back of his head on which he was wearing a hunting cap. This was puzzling because she had thought the only men who wore caps were the Master and the hunt servants, or farmers who had this privilege because it was their land which provided the Hunt with its country.

She was about to ask Sarah, who was nearby, for enlightenment, when the man turned his head. With an indrawn breath of surprise, she recognized one of the world's best-known profiles.

Almost as if he felt her staring at him, he glanced over his shoulder, turned his horse and rode towards them.

'Congratulations, Miss Lomax. I wasn't able to watch it, but I hear you put up a marvellous performance at Burghley.'

Sarah gave him the glowing smile which produced her engaging dimples.

'Thank you, Your Royal Highness.'

He looked at Bedouin Star. 'And this is your partner in that splendid achievement?'

'Yes, Sir.'

They chatted for a few moments until Sarah said, 'May I present my cousin's wife, Sir?'

Jane had been sitting transfixed by this unexpected encounter. As the Prince of Wales turned to look at her, she wondered wildly how she was supposed to behave on being presented to the heir to the throne of Britain.

Prince Charles had a friendly, interested gaze which, had he not been who he was, would have relaxed the shyest person. Normally Jane wasn't shy, but as their eyes met she was stricken by total paralysis.

'Is this your first experience of hunting on this side of the Atlantic, Lady Carlyon?' he asked, in the voice which charmed everyone who heard it.

She collected her scattered wits and followed Sarah's

example, saying, 'Yes, Your Royal Highness ... here or anywhere. I have never hunted before.'

'In that case I hope we have a good day's sport and you enjoy it,' he answered pleasantly.

'Thank you, Sir.'

'I believe the last Countess of Carlyon to ride with the Carlyon was the subject of your sister-in-law's recent biography,' he went on. 'My wife has read it and tells me it's a fascinating story.'

At this point hounds began running and Jane had no chance to reply.

It was much later in the day, while she and Sarah were returning to Longwarden at a steady hound-jog, that she said, 'Won't Allegra be thrilled to hear that Princess Diana has enjoyed *Travels*?'

'Yes, but she'll have to keep that to herself. It was the sort of remark he'd expect to be strictly sub rosa.'

'Don't worry: I shouldn't dream of spreading it around,' Jane said quickly. 'I can't believe I've met him. Does he often hunt with the Carlyon?'

'More often with the Beaufort and the Quorn. He loves hunting but it upsets the anti-blood-sports brigade which is why he avoids the meet and turns up at the first draw.'

'I was surprised he knew I was an American.'

'Oh, the royals are always well-briefed even when they're not on duty.'

For the last mile home they dismounted and led the horses. Nick met them as they entered the yard. 'Good day?' he asked.

Jane said, 'Terrific! But I think Sarah would have enjoyed it more if she hadn't had to keep an eye on me.'

'Not at all. I enjoyed having you there,' Sarah assured her. 'Go and soak in a nice bath, Jane. You've been in the saddle a long time today.'

Jane was feeling rather exhausted. It was the aftermath of excitement as much as physical fatigue.

As she handed Peking over to Nick, she said, 'Yes, a long lazy tub sounds great ... and maybe a glass of my special sherry to drink while I'm in it.'

'You go ahead. I'll be in shortly.'

Sarah had two reasons for wanting to attend to Beddo herself. He had been carrying her for hours and deserved to have her make a fuss of him. And she wanted to be near Nick more than she wanted a bath.

Jane went into the house. She was longing to see her husband and tell him about the day. She thought that what she would like after her bath would be to have an hour's nap, waking up refreshed to spend the evening alone with North, with a light supper *à deux* instead of dining downstairs with his mother and Sarah.

But until they could find more staff to relieve the burden on Ashford that sort of thing was impossible. They had to eat with the others, which ruled out any intimate conversation. In some ways, in this great house they had less privacy than newly-weds living in a walk-up apartment in a poor part of New York, she thought, with a sigh.

She met North coming down the Grand Staircase as she was going up.

'Enjoy yourself?' he inquired.

She gave an emphatic nod. 'It was tremendous fun. Are you busy? Could you help me with my boots?'

When North opened the door and she walked into her room, she exclaimed with pleasure in seeing the guarded fire burning in the hearth. Outside the mistiness of the early morning was beginning to close in again, shrouding the trees in pale vapour and giving the park a somewhat desolate appearance. The fire was cosy and welcoming.

'Did you light it for me?' she asked, touched by his thoughtfulness.

He shook his head. 'It must have been Ashford's idea.'

'What a nice one.' As she moved towards it, a glint of rich colour caught her eye. It came from the liquid in a cut-glass decanter on the table conveniently placed at the elbow of the comfortable wing chair close to the fire. 'That man has a genius for anticipating people's needs. Look, he's put out the sherry he ordered for me.' There were two glasses on the tray, she noticed. 'Will you try a glass, North?'

'No, I only like very dry sherry. Let's get your boots off.'

420

The boots disposed of, he poured out a glass of sherry for her. Because sherry was the customary drink before meals at Longwarden, Jane had tried to acquire a taste for the straw-pale, extra-dry sherry he preferred.

The butler must have detected that she found it more penance than pleasure. One evening he had asked if she would care to try a different sort. This she had found delicious. It turned out to be a wine Ashford had tried in Spain after finding a reference to it in an out-of-print book about the city of Cádiz. He had the book in his quarters and had later given it to her, the relevant passage marked in the margin in pencil. It had read like poetry.

Sherry is a supercivilized wine which must be delicately smelt, and held up to the light, so that it glows, before beginning to sip it gently and slowly, as if it were a flower, a jewel or some precious essence. In the twilight of the cellars the wine seems to burn like fire. The jerez fino is a topaz; the amontillado has orange veins running through it like gold leaf; the jerez oloroso is a ruby; and the sherry called Pedro Ximenez negro the colour of a black cherry, like an amethyst.

On the fly-leaf of the book, written in a clear, well-formed hand, had been the butler's full name. *Piers Ashford.*

Remembering the writer's instructions, when North handed her the glass she thanked him and held it up to admire the amethyst colour by firelight.

She took a small sip of the wine before saying, 'You'll never guess who I met today.'

'Someone you knew in America?'

'No ... somebody British ... with German connections,' she added, to give him a clue. 'Connections all over Europe, I guess.'

North shook his head. 'No idea.'

'Does this help?' She bobbed a curtsey.

'Princess Michael?' he suggested, the tall Austrian-born princess being a well-known horsewoman.

'Uh-uh. His Royal Highness the Prince of Wales, no less. How about that? Does it count as a début even though I wasn't able to curtsey to him?'

She laughed, her whole face alight with the thrill of

meeting a man who, besides being a future king, personified by his personal achievements that rare combination of daring and responsibility which was many women's *beau idéal* of masculinity.

To her surprise, this announcement was received by North with none of the amused interest she had expected to be his reaction. Instead he looked almost annoyed.

'So you've met Prince Charles,' he said curtly. 'What more can life have to offer? If I were you, I'd have a bath and a rest. I'll see you later.'

With a nod, he walked out of the room.

The unequivocal set-down left Jane stunned and hurt. What had she said to deserve that sarcastic rejoinder – *What more can life have to offer?*

Perhaps to North it seemed vulgar to be elated by meeting royalty. Perhaps it wasn't the well-bred behaviour of a gentlewoman, she thought glumly.

Upset, all her pleasure quenched, she ran a bath and undressed. Lying in the warm, scented water, sipping sherry and looking at the murals of old Cathay, she thought about the almond-eyed Countess for whom they had been painted.

Had Flora ever displeased her husband when she was trying to adapt to her position as his wife?

In the stables, Sarah was filling a small haynet while Bedouin ate warm bran mash out of a bucket. When he had finished the mash she gave him the net as an aperitif to his corn feed.

As she wiped him over before a more thorough rub-down, she thought that although she liked Jane – indeed was already quite fond of her – it would have been a better day had Nick been in Jane's place.

Somehow having him here wasn't working out as she'd hoped. They were hardly ever alone together, except when they were both occupied with stable chores.

In the evening he often went out, having discovered that various classes were in progress at the secondary modern school. He was taking Tai Kwondo on Monday nights,

French for beginners on Thursdays and First Aid on Fridays. Last Wednesday he had gone to the theatre in the nearest town with Mr Ashford.

When Beddo was comfortable, she gave him his oats and went to see how Nick was getting on with Jane's horse. He was feeling Peking's face and neck for embedded thorns.

'You look bushed, Sarah. Go and rest.'

'I'm not very tired. Let's have a cup of tea. How was your day?'

'Quiet. I took Tatty out and gave Chestnut his exercise.' After a pause, he added. 'I ran into Ted.'

She had been wondering when this would happen: his first encounter with his foster father.

Although he lived and worked on Longwarden land, Ted was no longer North's employee. He worked for a syndicate which paid her cousin for the right to breed birds on the estate and shoot them over it. Therefore Ted seldom came near the house now and, although she passed the lodge regularly, Sarah caught only an occasional glimpse of him.

'What did he say? What did you say?'

'He ignored me so I said nothing,' Nick answered with a shrug.

They left Peking to enjoy his supper.

'Pull my boots off for me, would you?' she said when the kettle was on.

She sat down on a sturdy bench. He straddled her outstretched leg and took a firm grip on the foot of the boot while she put the sole of the other against his backside and pushed. With the first boot off, she changed legs and this time it was her stockinged foot which made contact with his hard buttock.

Nick placed the boots neatly together. 'I'll clean them up for you later. There's no need for you to trek back again after you've eaten. I'll put the horses to bed.'

'But I'd rather come back and help. You forget I've been riding all summer. I'm not whacked by a few hours' hunting. Anyway I feel rather in the way at that end of the house. If

Aunt Pen turns in early, as she often does, the others want to be alone. I'd rather be talking to you – unless *you* want to be alone?'

He didn't say 'Don't be silly' or 'Of course not, idiot' or anything to allay her mounting doubts that he liked her as well as he once had.

He said, 'There's a good film on TV. If you don't want to watch it with the others, I'll carry your portable in and you can watch it in your room.'

'Then you won't be able to see it.'

'I'll be busy cleaning the tack.'

'Oh, leave the tack till tomorrow and we'll do it together. Let's both watch the film in your room.'

'No, I'd rather get the tack done.' He turned away to deal with the boiling kettle.

She looked at his back through a sudden shimmer of tears. Short of telling her outright, he had made it unmistakably clear he didn't want her around during his free time.

It was Allegra who mooted the fancy-dress ball.

She had come down for the weekend, bringing her Italian artist who was over in England now for several months.

The subject came up at tea on Sunday afternoon. Shortly before half-past four the butler had spread an old-fashioned white linen cloth bordered with snowflake-patterned crochet over a large round table. On this he had set the equipment for making tea: a copper kettle suspended over a spirit burner, two caddies, a teapot, milk jug and sugar bowl with the mellow patina distinguishing very old silver, an extra teapot for those who preferred China tea, and cups and saucers of translucent gold-rimmed porcelain from a service which had been a wedding present to North's great-great-grandmother.

On Jane's first Sunday at Longwarden she had been surprised by the substantial nature of the food served at tea time. Small sandwiches and fancy cakes had no part in the ritual. A large fruit cake with almonds on top was always served, sometimes accompanied by a meltingly light sponge dusted with icing sugar and generously filled with home-made raspberry jam and Devonshire cream, or by an orange or ginger cake.

But before the cakes came the hot things: potato scones, crumpets, muffins, Sally Lunns, toasted soda bread, all to be spread with butter or cream cheese to which could be added greengage or apricot jam, lemon curd, bramble jelly or honey on the comb.

Jane's particular favourite from Mrs Armitage's reper-toire of traditional tea-time goodies was the delicious dark Irish fruit bread called barm brack.

She was enjoying a thick slice when suddenly Allegra said, 'Before this year ends we should do something to celebrate all the major events in our lives which have happened in the last twelve months – North's marriage to Jane, Sarah's win at Burghley and my book going to number one on the *New York Times* best-seller list. I think we should give a dance.'

North wasn't present when she made this suggestion. In spite of a lowering sky and the threat of rain, he and Risconti had gone for a tramp with the dogs and not yet returned. Only the four women were present.

'That's a great idea, Allegra,' Jane agreed enthusiasti-cally. 'What do you think, Penelope?'

'It's entirely up to you, my dear. Even a small dance involves a great deal of organization,' Lady Carlyon warned her.

'Nonsense, Mother,' Allegra said briskly. 'Everything can be handled by professionals. All you and Jane have to do is decide whom to ask. If Sarah invites some eventing people and I ask some publishing people, we should get a more interesting mixture than the usual country-house jump-up. What about the week before Christmas when everyone's in a festive mood?'

Soon afterwards the men joined them. Jane was afraid North might veto the plan. She was relieved when he didn't.

'As you know the ropes and Jane doesn't, she'll need you to help her tie up the basic arrangements,' he told his sister.

'I did handle some quite large-scale entertaining for my father,' Jane pointed out.

He nodded. 'But you don't know the best people to approach in this country.'

'In my opinion,' said Allegra, 'Liz Shakerley's Party Planners are the *only* caterers to have. I'll ring her up first thing tomorrow. In the season we shouldn't have a hope, but at this time of year she may be able to fit us in. For the decorations I think we should try to get Ken Turner. He's expensive but brilliant,' she told her sister-in-law. 'When Andrew Wyeth had an exhibition at the Royal Academy, Ken Turner's topiary trees and hydrangea fountains were stunning. However booked up he is, I don't think he'll be able to resist the chance to decorate this house for a Christmas ball.'

'Now hang on a minute, Allegra,' her brother said quickly. 'We're talking about a dance, not a ball.'

'What is the difference?' asked Jane.

'Several hundred people,' he said dryly. 'A ball is usually well over five hundred. I assumed we were talking about a couple of hundred.'

At this point the butler came in with some freshly made hot eggy bread for his employer.

North said, 'We're thinking of putting on a dance, Ashford. Does the prospect fill you with dread?'

'Not at all, m'Lord – although I have to admit I have little or no experience of such occasions. But I shall be happy to perform whatever duties are required of me.'

'I'm quite sure you will prove a tower of strength, Mr Ashford,' said Lady Carlyon.

After tea Allegra produced paper and pencils and made them start work on their guest lists. Presently she had another brain wave.

'Wouldn't it be more fun if we made it a fancy-dress dance? There are trunks full of clothes in the attics. You could wear one of Flora's wonderful Edwardian ball dresses, Jane. With a little alteration at the waist they should fit you perfectly. Every dress she ever wore – and she adored clothes – is still up there, with the shoes and the

426

fans and the silk flowers she sometimes wore in her hair instead of jewels.' Her glance went to the mermaid ring on Jane's left hand. 'Apart from the art nouveau pieces Great-grandfather gave her, she gave most of the family jewels to Father when he started getting into debt. The one I regret is the Carlyon diadem which she's wearing in the Sargent portrait in the drawing room.'

Even though Risconti had left the room to return to the sculpture gallery, where there was a fine collection of marbles brought back from Italy two centuries earlier, and only the family was present, Jane sensed that her mother-in-law disliked the reference to her late husband's debts.

Confirming this intuition, Lady Carlyon said stiffly, 'It was most unlikely the diadem would ever have been worn again.'

Allegra reacted to the veiled reproof with one of her negligent shrugs.

'I should have loved to wear it. I expect Jane would, too. Rather than selling off heirlooms, it should have occurred to Father that financing the Hunt single-handedly was pure self-indulgence. Are we agreed on fancy dress? Let's take a vote. What do you think, Sarah?'

Sarah had realized at once that a fancy-dress dance offered Nick the chance to wear his Foreign Legion uniform and impress everyone with his soldierly looks and his enterprise. It would also allow her to appear in something infinitely more glamorous than her one and only dance frock, a demure white spotted voile from Laura Ashley which was fresh and pretty but not designed to shake Nick out of his present indifference.

Perhaps no dress could, but it was worth a try. She had once gone rummaging in the attics with Allegra and remembered seeing a glittering twenties dress of silver-spangled azure chiffon. In that she might stand a chance of making Nick look twice at her.

'I'm all in favour,' she answered.

'Jane?'

Jane nodded. 'I second that.'

'Mother?'

'I have no objection, but I think you should give men the option of wearing a dinner jacket or hunt evening dress if they prefer to. Most men dislike dressing up.'

'It's news to me,' said Allegra.

'It depends,' said North. 'I don't mind putting on kit from the twentieth century. I draw the line at powdered wigs and lace ruffles.'

'Why not make that the theme?' Jane suggested. 'Fancy dress – post nineteen hundred.'

'Would you mind staying on for a few days so that I can help Jane get this dance launched?' Allegra asked Risconti when he came to her room that night.

He had been given a bedroom on the same corridor. He used its bathroom and wardrobe but slept with her; the first man to share her bed at Longwarden.

'I also have a reason for staying. This afternoon your brother asked me to paint your sister-in-law. While you and she are planning the dance, I'll be making some preliminary sketches. In fact it might be a good idea to stay here until the portrait's finished. It would be more convenient for her to sit to me here, and I feel like some time in the country. Could you stand your mother's society for as long as it would take me to paint Jane . . . possibly a month?'

Allegra was startled; although no more surprised than when he had not only agreed to let her write his biography but, a few days later, had announced the cancellation of all commitments in America.

Instantly seeing how a day-by-day diary of the portrait's progress would add interest to the book, she said, 'That's a marvellous plan, darling. As for Mother . . . we don't have to live *en famille* all the time. We can turn the bedroom next door into a sitting room where we can be by ourselves. You'll also need to set up a studio. Must it face north? All the rooms on that side of the house are appallingly cold. Not that North has to worry about heating bills any more. Does he know your fee for a portrait?'

'That wasn't discussed.'

'It isn't important. Presumably Jane will be paying.'

'There will be no fee,' Risconti said abruptly. 'It will be a privilege for me to have my work hung in a house where all the finest portraitists are represented.'

His reply made Allegra feel he thought her remark rather vulgar. It was a new experience for her to care for anyone's good opinion as much as she cared for his. She couldn't bear him to think badly of her, even in small ways.

Perhaps she had misinterpreted his tone and expression. The next moment he drew her into his arms.

'I shall paint you again while we're here. None of the things I have done of you has satisfied me. De Laszlo, whose work I admire more than any other, said a successful portrait must reveal the sitter's soul and all the potentialities of character and temperament.' He gazed deeply into her eyes. 'I think it could take me a lifetime to do that with you.'

Happiness welled up inside her. She said impulsively, 'Darling, a long time ago you asked me to marry you and perhaps I hurt you by hesitating. I've regretted it ever since. If you asked me again, I shouldn't hesitate a second. There's nothing in the world I want more than to be your wife.'

Risconti's body betrayed his reaction before his face did. She felt him tense and become unnaturally still. She knew in a flash she had said the wrong thing; that marriage was not what he wanted, not any more.

She waited, sick with dismay, for him to demur just as she had when he proposed.

At least he was honest with her; unequivocally, brutally honest.

'You were right in the first place, Allegra. Marriage isn't for us. Nor do I think we have any need for children. The world's too crowded already. We both have other outlets for our creative urges . . . other chances of being remembered after we're dead.'

'But you told me you wanted children.'

'I've had time to think about it more carefully. I've changed my mind. The forces that encourage people to reproduce themselves are very powerful. But I think we are

429

both too intelligent to allow them to direct our lives. If pets would be a nuisance to us, so would children . . . even more so.'

She didn't argue with him. It would have been as pointless as her mother's arguments with her in the days when Allegra hadn't wanted any commitments or responsibilities.

She said lightly, masking her pain, 'Perhaps you're right. It was just an idea. Allegra Risconti sounds better than Allegra Lomax. But as long as we're happy together, what's the difference, as they say.'

But there was a difference. It kept her awake long after he had made love to her and was sleeping with his head on her pillow. She couldn't understand why, when he seemed to be passionately in love with her still, and determined to have no more separations, he no longer wished to be her husband and the father of her children.

It didn't make sense.

Next morning Allegra spent fifteen minutes on the telephone to London. Liz Shakerley, known professionally as Lady Elizabeth Anson, sister of North's colleague Patrick Lichfield and herself the pre-eminent organizer of English society festivities, said she would be delighted to help with such an exciting and romantic celebration.

'She'll deal with everything . . . food, flowers, music . . . the lot,' Allegra told Jane.

Mavis Osgood was present when Lord Carlyon and his new wife came to the kitchen during the morning tea break to explain that the dance would be a triple celebration and the cleaners and other members of their families were invited to help, wearing dresses and livery of the staff of earlier eras.

'They're a lovely couple,' said Mavis, telling Tark about the announcement. 'He's a bit like Paul Newman, when he was younger. He's got the same bright blue eyes, but he's a lot taller, with dark hair. They was both wearing jeans and sweaters, ever so casual. His was navy blue. Hers was camel with a cable-stitch front. When they was leaving the kitchen, they stopped and spoke to me.'

'Big deal!'

Ignoring her son's sarcastic comment, she went on, 'He knew who I was. He said, "You're Mrs Osgood," and I said, "Yes" – clean forgetting to call him your Lordship like Mrs Bailey told me. Then she smiled and asked me how long I'd been working there. We had quite a nice conversation.'

'So what? They're no bloody better than us. They've got more money, that's all. What they going to pay for this lark? If it's at night, it should be overtime rates.'

'I don't know. They didn't say nothing about paying. It'll be like going to a party. We shan't be dancing and that, but we'll get lovely eats and drinks. It'll make a nice night out.'

'I'm not effing well dressing up to work for nothing for that lot of stuck-up bleeders,' Tark said with a surly expression.

'You watch your tongue, my son. I've told you before. I won't have that dirty talk here. If you don't want to go, you needn't. Nobody's forcing you. I thought you'd be glad of the chance to look round for yourself.'

This was a point he had overlooked.

'Yeah, that might make it worth it,' he agreed, after some moments' thought. 'Specially as you don't seem to be making a job of it.'

'It's inches too tight in the waist and there's no way it can be altered,' Jane said regretfully, later that day.

She was in her bedroom, trying on the dress in which Flora Carlyon had danced at her first ball.

Behind Jane, also reflected in the long looking glass, Allegra was holding the unfastened dress together to give an approximate idea of how it would look if the dozens of tiny hooks were fastened in their silk loops.

The ball dress, designed by Lucile, was made of pale-green satin embroidered with swirls of silver beads, with angel sleeves of silvery gauze. With it Flora had worn a diamond and emerald dog collar in the style set by the Queen, with a diamond aigrette holding pale-green osprey feathers in her blackberry-silk hair.

It was over eighty years since the night when London society had been dazzled by Flora's beauty, but the dress had been carefully preserved inside an enveloping cotton cover, with long tapes sewn to the inside of the waistline to prevent the weight of the bead-encrusted train from dragging on the décolleté bodice with its gauzy sleeves. In later life Flora had liked to look at the dresses of her youth, reliving the memories they conjured. Almost everything she had ever worn had been carefully preserved in bags and boxes neatly labelled by her maid.

Her shoe closets had made Jane gasp. Not dozens of pairs but hundreds were arranged side by side on the racks in the specially built cupboards lined with camphorwood to discourage moths. Primrose silk with velvet bows, bronze glacé kid with ribbon rosettes, dove-grey suede with cut-steel buckles, black satin with glittering paste buckles, red satin exquisitely beaded and lined with gold kid . . . all hand-made and every pair kept on satin or velvet-covered shoe trees. Some of the earliest shoes, made of Genoese velvet by Yantorny, a master shoemaker in Paris in the early 1900s, were stored on cherrywood lasts fitted with gilt rings on the ankle-height tops. Another cupboard contained shoes from the twenties by Pinet, all with jewelled heels.

'Maybe if I bought a waist-cinch the dress would fasten,' said Jane, longing to wear it. 'Why don't I call up Harrods and ask them to send a selection?'

'Try one of Flora's corsets,' suggested Allegra. 'There are at least a dozen from this period to choose from, all with the little pads they pinned under their arms and on their hips to accentuate the smallness of their waists.'

'Okay . . . why not?' Jane agreed.

'You'll have to hold your breath, or at least only breathe from the top of your lungs,' said her sister-in-law when she had returned with an Edwardian corset and was starting to thread the long silk laces, starting at the waist.

Before Allegra started to pull, Jane gripped a bedpost to steady herself, expanding her rib cage to make her waist as small as possible. The front of the corset was fitted with a busk to help mould her body into the fashionable swan bend of the period.

'Ideally your top half should look as if it's a step ahead of your bottom half,' Allegra told her. 'Edwardians didn't separate their breasts as we do. They wore them in one big pouter-pigeon mass. I hope these laces aren't suffering from silk-fatigue because there's going to be a lot of strain on them at first. Breathe in . . . hold it . . .'

As Jane obeyed, North walked through from his bedroom.

'What goes on?'

'What does it look like? Don't stand there. Come and help,' instructed his sister.

With his aid, the corset, made of still-strong white coutil, was laced as tightly as possible.

'How does it feel? Can you breathe?' Allegra asked when it was done.

'It feels fine,' Jane said untruthfully. 'Measure my waist now, Allegra, will you please?'

They had already measured the waist of the dress. Her sister-in-law whipped a tape round the narrowest part of the swan bend.

'Triumph! Four inches off,' she announced.

'That's wonderful. Are you sure?'

'Certain. It will fit perfectly. Try it on again. See for yourself.'

'I will, but I don't want anyone but you to see me in it till the night of the dance. Off you go, North.'

'If you insist, but give me a call when you've finished preening and I'll come and let you out of that thing,' he said, eyeing the corset and the curves of her bottom revealed by micro-briefs under tights.

When he had left the room, Allegra grinned. 'Judging by that lustful look, North has just discovered he's madly turned on by tight lacing. Shall I go and find some black silk stockings and frilly garters so that you can drive him really insane?'

Jane laughed and blushed and shook her head. She was still wearing a bra which she took off before trying on the dress properly.

'It looks stunning,' was Allegra's verdict when all the hooks had been fastened. 'But are you in agony?'

'A little bit,' Jane admitted. 'But I guess I'll get used to it. I'll have to have some dress rehearsals to learn to handle this train. What are you planning to wear?'

Before Allegra could answer, there was a rat-a-tat on the communicating door.

'How much longer are you going to be?' North demanded from the ante-room.

'Don't come in yet. We're not ready,' Jane called out in a flutter.

'He is,' Allegra said grinning.

'Quickly, lock that door, Allegra. I don't want him bursting in before I'm out of this dress. I'll lock the other one.' Jane scooped up her train and hurried to secure the outer door.

It proved a wise precaution as, some time before her sister-in-law had finished undoing all the hooks, North turned the handle and would have come in had the door not been locked.

'Hold on: we shan't be much longer,' Allegra called out, shaking with laughter at the impatient rattling of the knob.

A few minutes later Jane was able to step out of the dress, instinctively covering her almost bare breasts with her wrists whilst Allegra draped it carefully over her arm.

'See you later. Have fun,' she said on her way out.

Foreseeing that her pantyhose were likely to be summarily whipped off by North once she let him in, Jane peeled them down her slim legs, still lightly tanned from the summer. The corset made bending difficult. She wondered how women had managed to eat rich seven-course dinners with their stomachs so tightly compressed. The front upper edge of the corset formed a sort of shelf for her breasts, pushing them together and upwards, the milk-chocolate-coloured tips resting on the lace-trimmed edge of the taut coutil.

Padding barefoot to the door, she turned the key. North shot through and re-locked it. For a moment he leaned against it, devouring her with hot blue eyes.

'Christ! I could name my price for a picture of you in that. *Penthouse* would give me an open cheque,' he said huskily.

Jane turned and strolled away, deliberately giving her bottom a provocative waggle. The next instant he had grabbed her waist and whipped her round into his arms, his mouth coming down hard on hers.

The power of his tall strong body still reduced her to jelly every time he held her like this. She opened her lips, her fingers fanning on the warm solid wall of his chest while his hands skied slowly down the smooth piste of coutil until they came to bare flesh and the edge of her panties. She was standing on tiptoe. He pushed the briefs downwards until, below the firm swell of her buttocks, they slithered to her heels and she kicked them away. His long fingers caressed her behind. He pulled her closer, grinding his hardness against her.

He had come through the door like a leopard let out of a cage. She thought he might take her quickly, pulling her down on to the floor where they stood. But although she was prepared for him to become more perfunctory as her body lost its novelty for him, it hadn't started yet, and didn't now.

Breaking off the long kiss, he swung her up in his arms and carried her to a day-bed piled with lace-covered pillows, designed for the afternoon rests of a more leisured era. After lowering her on to it, he straightened and began rapidly stripping off his clothes.

Jane swung her feet back to the floor and reached out to inch down, carefully, his straining zipper while he tackled his shirt buttons. He let her open his pants, but when she bent closer he drew back, out of her reach.

'I'm too close to boiling point already.'

Naked, he knelt down in front of her, pushing between her legs, dropping soft kisses on the high swell of her breasts.

'When I was a schoolboy, Granny Flora had boxes of bon-bons sent from a shop in Paris. The pralines and marrons glacés were wrapped in gold and silver paper, and the fondants had crimped paper cups. Like this.' He curved the corset's lace edging around the points of her breasts. 'I didn't like coffee creams . . . then.'

As he dipped his dark head, Jane closed her eyes. A convulsive shiver ran through her as his warm mouth enclosed the sensitive tissue and the flick of his tongue sent frissons of exquisite feeling coursing through her body.

She gave a long sigh of pleasure as he pushed her back on to the pillows, his lips still sealed to her breast, his fingertips playing teasing scales up and down the insides of her thighs.

Each time it gets better, she thought, before her mind ceased to function and her senses took over, turning her into a wild, wanton, primitive creature who gasped and groaned and begged him to enter her now, *now* . . . never mind about the corset.

'Now you know what Mrs Patrick Campbell meant by "the hurly-burly of the chaise-longue",' said North.

It was over. He was sitting up with Jane perched on his knees, her back to him, while he loosened the laces.

She was still slightly disoriented. The name and the quotation took a few seconds to register.

When they did, she said, 'It was fun, but I think I prefer the "deep, deep peace of the double bed".'

As the constricting pressure of the corset slackened and North saw the weals left by the whale-bones, he was horrified.

'You must have been in agony, silly girl. Why the hell didn't you say so?'

'Because I wasn't in pain. It just looks that way,' she said, attempting to rise.

Catching her by the hips, he pulled her back on to his lap. 'Those marks look as sore as a schoolboy's backside after a thrashing. Don't try to tell me they don't hurt. I don't believe it. I know all about suffering to be beautiful, but this is ridiculous.' As he spoke, he was gently smoothing the flesh at her waist where the corset had been at its tightest. 'To be trussed up like that for the dance would be insanity.'

'Your great-grandmother survived it.'

'Her waist must have been smaller than yours. She couldn't have danced and eaten with her middle crushed in like this. She'd have passed out.'

'Oh, nonsense, North. You're making a fuss about nothing.'

'You're not going to wear it, Jane. I won't allow it.'

She looked at him over her shoulder, more amused than outraged. 'You won't *allow* it?' she echoed, raising her eyebrows.

'That's right. I won't allow it. If you haven't more sense than to torture yourself –'

'I have a great deal of sense,' she interrupted crisply. 'If I choose to wear a tight corset for one special evening, that's my decision. Your great-grandfather may have been able to give his wife orders, North, but you can't tell me what to do. I'm amazed you should say "allow" to me.' She continued on her way to the bathroom.

When she came out, wrapping a thin silk robe round her, she was appalled to see him gripping the corset with clenched fists, trying to rip it apart. But, old as it was, the reinforced fabric was as difficult to tear as a telephone book.

'Stop it . . . you mustn't destroy it. It's irreplaceable,' she cried, rushing to save it from destruction.

'The damned thing's as tough as a strait-jacket,' he said angrily, marching towards the dressing table.

Having failed to tear it, in spite of his considerable strength, he meant to cut it, she realized.

Her eyes sparkling with anger, she said, 'That corset is a museum piece. Only a vandal would destroy it.'

'Then give me your word you won't wear it.'

'Certainly not! I shall wear whatever I choose.'

'Oh you will, will you?' he snapped. 'Well, if that's how you feel, I'll bloody well cancel the dance.'

For a moment they glared at each other, lovers changed into adversaries.

Then the blaze died out of North's eyes. 'But I can't do that, can I?' he said in a bitter tone. 'It isn't my dance to cancel. I'm not picking up the bills. You are.'

He dropped the corset on the dressing stool and, leaving his clothes where they lay, went back to his bedroom.

Jane sank down on the day-bed where only a short time before she had lain in his arms. She leaned down to pick up the shirt he had dropped on the floor and buried her face in it, wanting to weep.

But only for a few minutes. Common sense told her this was no time for tears, no time for self-pity. It was her fault they had quarrelled. His motive for laying down the law had been concern for her well-being. She should have been glad that he minded about the red marks, not flared at him like a feminist. In fact he was right: the corset *was* too tight to wear at a dance that Allegra expected to go on all night, ending with breakfast next morning.

Jane rose and collected his other clothes and his shoes. She carried them through the ante-room to tap on his bedroom door. There was no response. Either he was ignoring her or he was in his bathroom.

As soon as she opened the door she could hear that he was having a shower. She sat down to wait, rehearsing what she would say. The more she thought about it, the more she regretted mishandling the situation. At least it had brought to the surface his resentment of his position as the husband of a rich woman. They would have to talk about that. It couldn't be left to fester under the surface of their relationship.

When North came out of the bathroom, wearing a white terry robe and towelling his hair, he looked surprised to see her.

'I'm sorry I lost my temper,' he said abruptly. He turned in the direction of the drinks table. 'I'm going to have a whisky. Anything for you?'

'Gin, please – not too much.' As he opened the ice tub, she said, 'I'm the one who should apologize, North. I made you angry. You were right. I can't wear that corset for hours on end. I don't know why I had to be obstinate about it. It

438

wasn't a very nice way to behave, especially not right after making love.'

He had filled a tall glass with ice. Adding gin, followed by tonic, he said, 'Were you faking? I can't believe you can have enjoyed it, trussed up like that.'

'I *never* fake,' she said vehemently. 'I wouldn't on principle anyway, but I don't need to. You always make sure it's good for me.' As he brought her the drink, she stood up. 'Shall we kiss and be friends again?'

After a moment's hesitation he bent his tall head to touch her cheek with his lips. But Jane wasn't having that. She slipped both arms round his waist and hugged him, making him exclaim, 'Watch it! Your drink is spilling.'

She looked up into his eyes. 'Believe me, I know how lucky I am to be married to a good lover. From what I read and hear, they're not a dime a dozen.'

He leaned past her to put down the glass. Then he reached back to feel for her wrists and break her embrace. That he brushed a kiss on each of her hands before dropping it didn't disguise the fact that he wanted to be out of her arms.

As he went back to fix his own drink she sat down, hurt by the rebuff underlying their rapprochement.

But when he sat down in the chair on the other side of the hearth rug, he cheered her a little by saying, 'Women who admit to being wrong aren't a dime a dozen either. I don't know much about these things, but surely if you took the dress to Bellville-Sassoon in London, or even Anna Belinda in Oxford, they could match the material and put in a piece at the back where it wouldn't show much?'

'You're probably right. I'll ask Allegra about it. Let's not worry about that right now. There's something more important we should discuss.'

'What's that?'

'The way you feel about my contribution to our partnership. It wasn't my idea to have a dance, North, and I'd prefer it were cancelled rather than have you annoyed. The invitations aren't done yet. It can be put off very easily. I shouldn't enjoy myself knowing you were unhappy about it.'

For what seemed a long time he studied the liquor in his glass, swirling it round the tumbler. Then with a sudden movement he tossed about half of it down his throat.

'I was shooting my mouth off. Pay no attention.'

'But that's what marriage is about . . . having someone pay attention to your comfort,' she said quietly. 'I don't want you ever to be uncomfortable, in any sense, on my account. I know you were speaking in anger and that sometimes, when people are angry, they say things they don't mean. But other times they blurt out truths they wouldn't say in cold blood.' She paused.

'If you'd prefer not to use the money my father made for anything but repairs and improvements to the house, that's all right by me. We have to have some social life, but it doesn't have to be on a grand scale for me. I mean that sincerely.'

He looked at her then, long and hard. She wished she could guess what was in his mind. With another of his abrupt movements, he sprang from his chair to stand with his back to the unlit log fire.

'To insist that you live at the level I can afford would be unfair,' he said. 'I admit I find my position difficult. But no doubt I'll get used to it. As for the dance, obviously Allegra and Sarah are looking forward to it. As you are, or were – before I went off at half-cock.'

'Yes, I was,' she agreed. 'We had a very quiet wedding which suited us but must have been disappointing for your friends who'd have liked to be there. The dance will make up for that.'

'With the advantage that they won't be expected to fork out for presents,' he said dryly.

It seemed the matter was settled. The dance was on.

When Jane told her sister-in-law she wouldn't be able to wear the Edwardian ball dress, Allegra said, 'There's still one possibility . . . one person who could alter it without ruining it.'

Ten days later they flew to Paris, to visit Francois Lesage, present head of the house of Lesage, embroiderers to the *haute couture*.

With them went the satin ball dress, carefully packed in layers of acid-free tissue paper. Having seen photographs of it, taken by North, Monsieur Lesage had agreed to copy the original beading so that only an expert examination would reveal that the dress had been altered at the waist.

It seemed that matching the silver beads applied in Lucile's workrooms soon after the turn of the century was going to be no problem. The house of Lesage dated back to the twenties when it had been launched on an ocean of beads acquired from Michonet, embroiderer to Napoleon III. Since then millions more spangles and bugles had been added from other sources. It wasn't unusual for a *couture* dress to have 200,000 beads and sequins applied to it, all stitched on by hand by Lesage's forty embroideresses.

Jane had a second reason for going to Paris. She wanted to look up Marie-Simone and deliver, in person, an invitation to the dance. She couldn't understand why the Frenchwoman never wrote now, nor was she ever at home when Jane tried to telephone her.

When Risconti heard the girls were going to Paris, he decided to join them. Whereupon, to Jane's delight, North said he would come as well. It was Risconti's idea to use a private charter service operating from an airport not far from Longwarden rather than fly by scheduled service from London.

The weather was cold that week and Allegra wore a jacket of golden Russian sable with a large Cossack hat to match. Both had belonged to her great-grandmother. Underneath the jacket she was wearing an Ungaro silk blouse and trousers tucked into long tan boots. She cut more of a dash than Jane who was dressed in a grey cashmere coat of severely plain cut over a black sweater dress.

As their flight path was in that direction, North asked the pilot to fly over Longwarden. He wanted to see it from the air.

* * *

Warmly clad in an ancient guernsey, faded to the colour of a cobble by years of sun and rain, Pen set down her wheelbarrow and paused in the morning's labours to watch the small aeroplane passing overhead.

She had been invited to join the expedition to Paris, as had Sarah. Her niece had the BBC coming today, to film her for a programme about riding. Pen had declined on the grounds of being far too busy, her real reason being that she would have enjoyed it only if Ashford had been included.

She waved. As the aircraft disappeared, she bent to pick up the barrow handles and trundled on her way. She was conscious of being foolishly depressed. Not at missing, by her own choice, the day in Paris; nor because winter was coming.

As long as the weather wasn't too appalling, she enjoyed the months when 'the masts and rigging of creation' were laid bare. Any day now the wine-red stems of *Salix daphnoides* would begin to swarm with fat grey velvet mice, and continue to please her eye until May. The Algerian iris, *I. unguicularis*, was another winter delight, flowering in every shade from palest lilac to imperial purple even when snow was on the ground.

Nor was it overwork which made her feel listless, although in October she had the tiring task of storing the apple and pear crops, and this month she had to store the submersible pumps and re-plant some of the fruit cages. She couldn't remember when she had last felt so down. Probably not since Edward was alive.

It had nothing to do with Allegra's presence in the house, except in so far as her daughter's liaison and her son's marriage were reminders of all Pen had missed in her own life.

The chief cause of her mood, as she well knew, was that since Jane's arrival Pen had seen little of her butler. He had spent one afternoon helping her store the pears, but since then she had scarcely seen him, except at meals.

She knew, because Sarah had told her, that he seemed to be taking an interest in Nick Dean. They had been to the theatre in Melchester together, more than once. It was

442

awful to feel jealous of the boy. His presence had been a godsend while Sammy was in hospital and later at a convalescent home suggested by his surgeon. Yet jealous she was. How could she help it when she so longed to be the one Ashford took to Melchester with him?

If only she had the confidence to say, 'Are you and Nick going to the theatre this week? Would you mind if I joined you? It's a play I'd particularly like to see.'

But even if he agreed, and he couldn't very well not, it wouldn't be the same as going to the theatre alone with him. If she could rope Sarah in to make up a foursome it would be better; two young people, two older people. But that wouldn't really work either because North would be annoyed with her for throwing Sarah and Nick together.

In the back of the taxi taking her to Marie-Simone's address in the old 7th arrondissement of Paris, Jane wondered if North was right and it was a waste of time to call on someone whose telephone had rung unanswered the night before and again this morning.

He had volunteered to come with her, but she had refused the offer, saying, 'No, if I should catch her in, I'd rather see her alone the first time after so long. If she's not there, maybe there'll be a concierge who will know why she never seems to be there. It could be she's moved since I had the last letter from her.'

'Without telling you? Not very friendly,' North remarked.

She sensed that, although she had told him about Marie-Simone and how close they had been, he still visualized her as the stereotype rich man's mistress: sexy, mercenary, not very bright.

The taxi dropped Jane outside a large building with a tall gated archway through which, at one time, carriages would have entered an internal courtyard. An elderly man in a black apron had been sweeping the flagstones and now was resting on his besom, watching her. When she approached him and said she had a note to deliver to Mademoiselle Polignac, he directed her to the first floor.

When Jane had pressed Marie-Simone's doorbell three

times without result, it was obvious she had come on a wild-goose chase. She was about to go down when a girl came out of the apartment across the landing. She had a small boy by the hand and Jane deduced she must be a nanny or an *au pair*.

Smiling at her, she said, in French, 'Can you tell me if the lady who occupies this apartment is away for some time, mademoiselle?'

'I've been here six months but I've never seen her, madame,' the girl answered.

'Do you mean she has gone away for good?'

'I don't think so. She comes back to pick up her letters. But I heard she went into a . . . *clinique*, and since then she hasn't lived here.'

The news that Marie-Simone had been ill without Jane knowing it was disquieting enough, but something in the girl's manner as she mentioned the nursing home sharpened Jane's anxiety.

'She was sick? I had no idea. Do you know which *clinique*?' Then, as the girl shook her head, 'Perhaps the old man down below will know where she's living now.'

The girl gave a doubtful shrug. 'I shouldn't think so. If he does, he might not tell you. He's a sour old beast, that one. It was he who told everyone . . .' The girl blushed, looking uncomfortable. 'It may not have been true. He and his wife are terrible gossips. They say nasty things about everyone.'

'What did they say about Mademoiselle Polignac?'

Sarah had felt excited before the BBC television crew arrived. By the time they left she was thankful to see them depart. Not because she hadn't liked them, but because it had been so tedious repeating an action over and over again until it had been shot to the producer's satisfaction.

The day before, she had been to see Sammy at the convalescent home. The point of his going there from the hospital instead of returning to Longwarden had not been to spare her the extra responsibility of looking after him until he was fully recovered. It had been to ensure that he was too closely supervised to be able to hit the bottle again. The surgeon had told her that the rate at which the Irishman must have been drinking for months beforehand had greatly increased the risks of his operation and would make his recovery slower than that of a moderate drinker.

'The hard stuff retards normal healing. He needs thoroughly drying out. His liver can't take that sort of hammering indefinitely,' he had warned her.

She had expected to find Sammy itching to leave the nursing home. To her surprise he seemed to like it there. They had talked in his room, where his tea – and a cup for his visitor – had been brought by a plump little woman, one of the non-nursing staff, whom he'd introduced as Mrs Slane, the widow of a flat-racing jockey.

'So he has someone congenial to chat to and he isn't as bored and restive as I thought he would be,' Sarah told Nick, on her return.

Nick *was* restive. She could tell he didn't like the weather and the prospect of it worsening. In his two years in Fuerteventura he had become used to the sun.

After the television people had gone he pointed out an advertisement in the Situations Wanted column of that week's *Horse and Hound*.

'Mm . . . she sounds good,' said Sarah, after reading the ad he had ringed. 'But Sammy would be awfully hurt if I engaged someone in his absence. He'll expect to be there when I interview his successor. He thinks he's a better judge of character than I am, and he may be right.'

'You're a fool if you don't at least ring this girl. By the time he comes back, she'll have been snapped up . . . if she hasn't already been.'

He marched off, leaving Sarah biting her lip. What she had *not* told him, or Sammy, or anyone, was that shortly after Burghley she had received two good offers of sponsorship. Either of which she ought to have jumped at, overjoyed. Instead she had stalled, playing for time. In spite of all the evidence that Nick was not going to stay and was never going to fall in love with her, she hadn't quite given up hope.

She felt she still had one chance to jolt him out of his apparent indifference to her. Everything hinged on the dance . . . the night of the dance.

'I wish we were staying overnight,' said Allegra, shedding her parcels, when she arrived at the rendezvous.

'We are,' Risconti informed her. 'We are sleeping here' – they were in the bar at the Ritz Hotel – 'and dining at Lasserre. I thought you might want some more time for your Christmas shopping . . . but perhaps you've finished it already,' he added, straight-faced.

Her beautiful eyes gleamed with laughter, the dark lashes contrasting with the long golden guard hairs of the sable hat. She pulled it off, tossed it aside and put her hands on his shoulders.

'I could shop every day for a year here. What a blissful surprise. You'll get your reward on Christmas morning. I've found you what Jane would call the most darling stocking-filler,' she said, kissing him on both cheeks.

'I'm hoping to get my reward before that,' he murmured into her ear as he helped her to take off her furs. 'What would you like to drink?'

'A champagne cocktail, please. Did you find your friend, Jane?'

Jane shook her head. 'A neighbour told me she was away at present. Did you tell Pen we were going to be away overnight, Andro?'

'No, but I told Ashford we shouldn't be back until tomorrow afternoon. If you're wishing you had brought a nightdress, North and I have also been shopping. You will both have something to wear if the hotel should catch fire tonight.'

Jane had her own reason for being glad to have more time in the city. She had not confided her dilemma to the two men before Allegra's arrival. If North knew what she had been told, he might take the view that she ought not to have anything more to do with her father's mistress.

When they went up to the suite they found two bottles of Bollinger on ice in the sitting room between the two bedrooms. They might be a compliment to an internationally-known artist, or it might be that someone remembered that North's grandparents and great-grandparents had always stayed in the Place Vendôme when in Paris.

Allegra was impatient to see the nightdress Risconti had chosen for her. Jane pretended to be equally eager to see North's choice. When she did, in spite of the anxiety weighing on her, she was genuinely pleased.

Risconti had bought Allegra a pair of brilliant green pyjamas, the silk imitating the swirls of malachite, a stone she loved and collected. For Jane, North had selected a peach-coloured crêpe-de-chine dressing gown, cut like a man's, with a silk-fringed sash. But there was nothing mannish about the peach satin teddy which went with it.

'Our table is booked for eight, which gives us plenty of time to shower and relax,' said Risconti, interrupting the girls' exclamations of pleasure. 'As we're going to be spending the evening together, I hope you won't think Allegra and me unsociable if we drink one of these bottles in private.'

'An excellent idea,' agreed North, picking up the other ice bucket.

Jane forced a smile in response to Allegra's wink as they followed the men in opposite directions. She would have welcomed privacy to think out her problem, but privacy to make love was the last thing she felt like.

As they entered the bedroom, papered with pale-blue moiré silk with a gilded corona supporting the draperies at the head of the bed, she debated pleading a headache.

'Is that glum face because you are going to be obliged to sleep with me all night?' North asked, suddenly glancing at her when she had thought he was intent on opening the champagne.

'Not at all! I'm a little tired from racketing around all day. I didn't intend to look glum. I was thinking how pretty this room is.' She hung her coat in the closet. 'Do you suppose there's a special reason for staying overnight? Are they going to announce their engagement at dinner?'

'I doubt it. I don't think they'll marry unless my sister gets broody, which doesn't seem at all likely.'

'She's madly in love with Andro. Women in love do get broody. They long to produce a combination of themselves and the man they love.'

'Do they? How do you know?' he asked, bringing her a glass of champagne.

'It's a well-known phenomenon.'

'Unsupported by genetics, thank God. I should hate to have turned out a combination of my parents. Not that it would have been possible. One can't be a tyrant *and* a doormat.'

Jane stepped out of her low-heeled black walking shoes. 'Is it okay if I have first turn in the bathroom? As we're not in a hurry, I'll take a long lazy tub. It will pep me up.'

He began to loosen his tie. She had wondered, this morning, why he had put on a suit when usually he dressed very casually. Obviously he had been privy to Andro's plan.

'You don't think a rest on the bed might be more effective?'

Ignoring the glint in his eyes, she shook her head. 'I can't wait to get up to my neck in hot water.'

Undressing in the bathroom, she felt guilty about not wanting to go to bed with him, especially here in Paris, traditionally the city of lovers. If only she could explain: confide her perturbation and ask his advice on what she should do.

Even after she had slipped him a generous pourboire, the janitor at the apartments had only confirmed the information she had already been given. The old man had no forwarding address. Marie-Simone picked up her mail in person; there was no way to contact her if she chose to ignore Jane's note appealing to her to get in touch as soon as possible.

One thing her travels with her father had taught her was that hall porters in top-class European hotels were men who were rarely stumped by any question, or any request, however extraordinary. Perhaps, while North was having his shower, she would slip downstairs and ask the porter to find out the name of some reliable investigators. Tomorrow, supposedly shopping, she could instruct them to keep a watch on the apartments until Marie-Simone showed up. They could then follow her back to wherever she was living.

'Did it seem to you that there was a certain tension in the atmosphere tonight?' asked Allegra some hours later, after she and Risconti had retired to their room for the second time.

'Between North and Jane, do you mean? No, I didn't notice anything. Why should there be tension between them?'

'Why indeed? But it was there. I'm surprised you didn't sense it. All was sweetness and light this morning on the way over, and I didn't pick up any hostile vibes when we met in the bar. So they must have had a fight before dinner. How odd. We didn't, did we?' she reminded him.

Risconti took her face between his hands. He seemed to be memorizing every detail of her features.

After a while, when she thought he had forgotten what they had been talking about, he said, 'If they did have a fight, I hope they are making it up now. If they knew that tomorrow our plane was going to crash into the Channel, they wouldn't waste tonight on stupid quarrels ... or sleeping.'

'What a macabre thought,' she said, with a shiver. 'I suppose you're right. If everyone knew in advance how long they had, people with only a short time to live wouldn't waste time on anything trivial. But could we stand living with the knowledge of exactly when it was going to happen?'

'Some people do ... if they're incurably ill, they have to.'

'Yes, and it must be ghastly. I hope it never happens to me. I'd rather go out like my father. Crash, bang, wallop ... all over. Why did you bring up this nasty morbid subject?' She put her arms round him. 'I want my mind taken off it or I shan't be able to sleep.'

'You'll sleep,' he murmured against her lips.

*   *   *

449

When Jane walked into the bedroom in her new dressing gown, North jumped up from the sofa. Barely glancing at her, he disappeared into the bathroom.

She knew he was angry. She had sensed his displeasure all evening, although he had put on a show of being relaxed and good-humoured. So had she. It had been a great strain. She felt exhausted. Also irritated.

Okay, so he had wanted to make love before dinner. She hadn't. Was that a good enough reason to work himself into a foul mood?

She took off the robe and climbed into bed. The last time they had slept in an hotel had been on their wedding night, three months ago. She remembered how eagerly she had looked forward to that night. Tonight, exhausted by a worrying day, all she wanted to do was to sleep.

When North came out of the bathroom, Jane was in bed with her eyes closed. Asleep or shamming?

He walked round to her side of the bed and looked down at her for several minutes. She hadn't switched off the silk-shaded lamp and it shed a soft diffused glow over her half-covered body. She was wearing the thing he had bought her which resembled the sexy loose-legged cami-knickers women had worn in the thirties. One of the thin ribbon straps had slipped off the curve of her shoulder. Her skin had a more subtle sheen than the lace-edged satin shaped to the curves of her breasts. Her hair, her eye-lids, her lips all invited his touch. He wanted her . . . had wanted her for hours, all the time they had been in the restaurant.

She ought not to be sleeping. (He was sure now she *was* asleep.) She ought to be in his arms, arching and writhing with the uninhibited sensuality underlying the calm self-possession of her manner in public, and even in private, except when they were in bed together.

This afternoon, for the first time since they were married, she hadn't come to him with her usual willingness. Tonight, when they got back, she had shot into the bathroom like a rabbit into a burrow.

450

Earlier he had accepted that she was tired after running around Paris, and also disappointed at not finding her father's French popsie at home. (In North's view that was a connection best left to die a natural death.) The tiredness should have worn off while she was soaking in the bath. But when he had gone to refill her glass, he had found the bathroom door locked. Half an hour later she had emerged, dressed, freshly made up, ready to go out.

He had sometimes seen other guys getting those 'I'm not in the mood' signals but had never been, or expected to be, on the receiving end himself. Nor had he ever found other men's wives anything but eager, so why the hell was his own wife suddenly reluctant?

He had a good mind to wake her up and ask her . . . make her want him . . . make her beg for it.

As he bent towards her, intending to peel the satin away from one tender breast and start to arouse her in both senses, suddenly he changed his mind. To hell with it: let her sleep. Clearly he wasn't going to, not with his present hard-on. But there were other ways of dealing with that.

He switched off the lamp. He was still clothed up to the waist. Moving quietly about the room, he put on his shirt and the coat of his suit, leaving his shirt collar open and covering it with a dark silk-lined cashmere scarf.

Shrugging on his tweed coat, he crossed the sitting room, and a few moments later was stepping out of the lift on the ground floor.

The night porter was mildly surprised to see the tall English lord dressed to go out. The porter had worked at the Ritz for thirty years, many times taking home tales which had astonished his wife until, like him, she became inured to the strange things that went on in a great hotel, especially during the night hours.

As North walked up to the desk, the porter inclined his head. 'Yes, milord?' he said politely.

Jane woke up, terribly thirsty. It wasn't until she had trouble finding the switch that she remembered where she was. It must be drinking more wine than usual at dinner which

451

made her feel desperate for water. But could she find her way to the bathroom without putting on the light? She didn't think so. Staggering around in the dark seemed a more likely way to wake North than turning on the lamp. With luck he would be lying with his back to it.

Thirty seconds later, having carefully turned back the bedclothes and swung her feet to the carpet, she discovered her husband wasn't there to be disturbed. Maybe he had gone to the bathroom ahead of her. But no, the door was ajar and the light wasn't on in there. Where else could he be at half-past one in the morning? In the sitting room?

She looked. He wasn't there either.

Puzzlement having only temporarily superseded thirst, next she went to the bathroom and gulped down two glasses of water. Then she refilled the glass and drank the third one more slowly, her mind grappling with the enigma of where he could be if not in the suite.

Could the hotel still have a bar open at this hour? No, it couldn't. If he'd wanted to carry on drinking, he would have had to call room service. Or go out on the town to the kind of bar that stayed open through the small hours. Paris had plenty of those, many of them right around the corner in the Champs Élysées.

She remembered the way he had brushed past when she came out of the bathroom in her nightclothes. If he'd been annoyed with her then, he must have been even madder when he found she had fallen asleep waiting for him to come to bed.

Absent-mindedly, out of habit, because it was what usually followed the act of getting up, she brushed her teeth and combed her hair. She knew she couldn't go back to sleep; not with the thought in her mind that North might not be in the bar.

He had spent time in Paris before. He knew people here. He might still have the telephone numbers of girls who had let him make love to them; and who would again.

Jane paced the bedroom, her arms folded under her breasts. The thought of North in bed with a former girl-friend made her frantically angry. Even worse was the

452

thought that he might have gone out and got smashed and picked up a girl he didn't know. A lot of men did.

Restlessly striding back and forth, she knew that if North had done either it might be the end of their marriage. It was only now, contemplating the possibility that her husband, at this very moment, was lying on top of another woman, that she realized how it would revolt her to touch him or have him touch her if he had been with anyone else.

Maybe that was old-fashioned. Maybe she was out of step. But it was the way she felt and she wasn't going to compromise her standards.

He came back at five minutes past two.

She was sitting down, facing the door, when he opened it and paused on the threshold, palpably disconcerted to find her there, waiting for him.

He came in and closed the door. 'Why are you out of bed?' he asked, somewhat brusquely.

'If you'd woken and found me missing, would you have gone back to sleep?' she inquired with a calm which belied her feelings.

'I went for a walk.'

'At this hour of night?'

'Why not? I needed some exercise after a large meal. It wasn't raining when I went out.'

As he moved into the room, passing one of the gilded wall lights, she saw that his hair was wet, as was his face. His tweed coat must also be soaked but it didn't show.

'You might have been mugged.'

He shrugged. 'Unlikely in well-lit areas. I didn't go near the Bois.'

'You could have left me a note on the telephone pad. It's unnerving to wake up and find someone's disappeared.'

He gave her a blazing blue glare. 'I know . . . it happens to me *every* night, if you remember.'

She knew then with absolute certainty that he hadn't been with another woman. Sex would have released pent-up temper, but it was still there inside him, ticking away like a time bomb.

453

'If you were so bloody worried, you should have called the night porter and asked if he'd seen me,' he snapped. 'I didn't think you'd wake up, but I left a message with him.'

'Don't swear at me, North. I don't like it,' she told him crisply, knowing that in his present mood it would exasperate him.

In three strides he was at the sofa, seizing her wrists, pulling her on to her feet.

'And I don't like you beginning to act and sound like an American boss-woman,' he informed her grimly. 'From now on you'll stay with me *all* night. Is that understood?'

His anger was oddly exciting. She felt driven to exacerbate it . . . to see how far she could go before his temper exploded.

She gave a negligent shrug. 'If you insist.'

Under the taut beard-shadowed skin, North's jaw muscles knotted with rage, barely contained. 'Damn right I insist! I've had enough of that nonsense. You'll be there when I wake up or you'll feel my hand on your backside. ' He let go of one of her wrists and gave her a quick spank.

She yelped, her own temper kindling. As before, when he had ordered her not to wear the corset, the feminist in her was outraged. But at a deeper level, among the race memories and the instincts to survive and to couple, a more primitive being responded to the dominant male exerting his age-old authority.

The sting of her husband's hand on one side of her bottom was the first time, to her knowledge, she had ever been physically punished – and this not for something she had done, for something she might do.

The modern woman was furious. Having one hand free, she attempted to give North a vigorous wallop in return. But her palm never reached his cheek, although the attempt changed his punitive scowl to a grin. Why her desire to retaliate should restore his good humour was something she couldn't fathom. Having her wrist recaptured and both arms pinioned behind her did nothing to soothe her own anger.

'Let me go!' she raged at him, struggling.

'When you've calmed down. Women in a temper tend to throw things,' he said, obviously entertained by her futile efforts to free herself.

'I am *not* in a temper and I've never thrown anything at anyone . . . although I understand now why people do,' she added vengefully, her eyes bright with angry frustration at being so easily held captive by this great grinning brute.

Realizing she was only amusing him more by continuing to resist, unwillingly she surrendered to his superior strength. 'You may be a peer, but you're no gentleman, that's for sure,' she told him cuttingly.

North laughed. 'Never claimed to be. I'm the one who's been deceived. I had no idea you could be such a little hell-cat. Trying to slap your husband's face . . . tut tut . . . what would Miss Manners have to say about that?'

At dinner Jane and Allegra had been talking about Judith Martin, the *Washington Post* journalist more widely known as Miss Manners, the high priestess of American etiquette.

'I know she wouldn't think much of a man using force against a woman,' she retorted.

He didn't need two hands to hold her. His fingers were long, her wrists slender. He took them both in one hand, moving his other hand up to the top of her head. Tilting it backwards, he put his lips to her throat, running them slowly, slowly down the side of her neck from her ear to the collar of her robe.

Jane held herself rigid, willing herself to be unresponsive. It was impossible.

She remained impassive as long as she could, keeping her lips closed and still when he covered them with his. But after a very few moments the warmth and softness of his mouth undermined her resolution, particularly now that his fingers were caressing the nape of her neck and his other hand was no longer clamping her wrists together but gently stroking the place he had hurt.

With a groan at her inability to hold out when he laid determined siege to her, she let herself relax.

455

A few minutes later he picked her up and carried her to the bed.

Flying back to England next day, Jane wondered how long it would be before the French detective agency would be able to send her news of Marie-Simone's whereabouts.

Fortunately it hadn't been difficult to go off on her own this morning. They had all gone their separate ways, meeting for lunch at which Andro had given Allegra a blackamoor's-head pin, the face enamelled, the turban jewelled and a miniature ruby earring dangling from the left ear.

Suddenly, the way he looked at Allegra, the endearments he used, all the evidence of his love for her, made Jane ache to inspire the same feelings in North.

Also on her mind, as the aircraft headed for the Channel, was the hope that she might have conceived during last night's wild love-making.

Over the sea between France and England, she remembered a maxim of the Duc de la Rochefoucauld. *The intellect is always fooled by the heart.*

How could she have fooled herself for so long? She hadn't married North for any other reason than because she was in love with him – had been in love all along, from the moment of turning around on the lawn at Winterbrook and seeing him for the first time.

PART FOUR: Winter

DECEMBER

Foreseeing that if she invited him to the dance as her partner Nick might refuse, Sarah enlisted Jane's help.

'If you ask him, he can't say no.'

By now it was clear to Jane that Sarah was in love with Nick and, if he were not present, the dance would be ruined for her. Although North might disapprove, Jane felt no possible harm could come from Nick being there as a guest rather than a helper. She had talked to him often and with increasing approval. Perhaps he wasn't a suitable husband for Sarah, but as her first love he seemed ideally qualified.

'Certainly I'll ask him. Leave it to me.'

'Thank you. And may I tell Rob and Emily they can come and choose something to wear?'

'I see no reason why not, but I think you should ask North or your aunt about that.'

Jane filled in an invitation card with *Cabo Caballero Legionario Nicholas Dean*. Later she took it to the stables.

When Nick read it, a slight flush tinged his now paling tan. 'It's very kind of you to invite me, Lady Carlyon, but –'

'No buts, Nick. I insist. Apart from the fact that we want to see you in uniform, and this is the perfect opportunity, I'm worried we may have a surplus of girls. That would be a disaster. For a dance to be a success, it has to be the other way round. So I won't take no for an answer. You *have* to be there,' she said laughingly.

'But I can't dance . . . not waltzes and things.'

'You won't need to. We're having two bands and the music will be a mixture of ballroom and disco . . . something

457

for everyone. You can do this, I'm sure. Who can't?' For a moment or two she went into a disco routine.

Somewhat reluctantly, he nodded.

'Fine. That's settled. You'll be there. How could you think of missing it? It's going to be a very special night.'

'Are you busy, Penelope?'

Pen smiled at her daughter-in-law who, having tapped on the door of her sitting room, was peering round the jamb with her dark eyebrows raised inquiringly.

'Not in the least. I'm being deplorably idle. Come and bestir me,' she invited.

Jane was carrying a large cardboard box of the kind in which, when Pen was a girl, shops had used to pack expensive dresses.

'I've found something perfect for you to wear at the dance,' Jane announced, her grey eyes alight.

'But my dear I've already decided to be an Edwardian cook in a print dress and cap and apron.'

'That won't do at all,' Jane told her firmly. 'You must wear something much more glamorous than a print dress. I've found the ideal thing.'

She sank to her knees on the rug in front of Pen's chair and began untying the string which secured the lid of the box.

Pen found that looking at Jane gave her the same pleasure as gazing at a perfect flower. It wasn't often she had the opportunity to study her face at close quarters, but while Jane was intent on loosening a knot, she could scrutinize and admire the long silky sweep of her eyelashes, the flawless texture of her skin and the lovely shape of her lips.

'I'm not a glamorous person,' she said as the string came undone. 'Slinky dresses and revealing necklines are not my style. I should look wrong and feel uncomfortable.'

'I know that,' Jane nodded. 'Slinky's not you at all. This is . . . how can I describe it? Elegant, maybe? No, I don't know the right word. But I do know you'll look stunning in it. So you will at least try it on, won't you? – Just to please me?'

'I'll try it on, certainly,' said Pen, curious to see how Jane saw her.

She watched Jane carefully unpacking whatever she had unearthed in her search of the attics.

Its colour was the first thing to emerge; the deep dark amethyst of black grapes or purple irises. The material was soft and matt but, as Jane lifted it up, soft gleams and glints caught the light.

'I'll hold it up against me to show you the style, but it was made for someone taller.' With supple grace she stood up and shook out the dress.

It was about fifty years old, a relic of the thirties.

'You see it's not a low front,' said Jane. 'A high round neckline like this would need a short string of pearls or maybe, as you have a long neck, a three-strand choker. What do you think? D'you like it?'

'Mm, I do rather,' said Pen.

'It's so beautifully finished it has to be French *haute couture* made specially for someone in your family. The name on the label is Molyneux. May I come and help you get into it?'

They went through the connecting door to Pen's bedroom where she took off her shirt and skirt, and her daughter-in-law gathered the dress into a ring to put over her head.

'It's lined with silk crêpe de chine which has such a lovely feel against your skin, don't you think?' said Jane as Pen's head emerged and together they eased the dress downwards. 'The chiffon is mounted on silk net to give it more body, and the sequins are stitched to the net inside the chiffon so you get just a misty shimmer, not what Allegra calls "Arabian nights glitter" when the sequins overlap.'

Cut close to the body from neck to mid-thigh where it flared from a series of pointed godets, the dress might have been made for Pen's long, narrow-hipped figure. The short sleeves were layered from the shoulder, the edges being pointed to echo the peaks of the godets.

'The hem is trailing a little. It won't when you're wearing high heels. The length will be fine,' said Jane, busy with the fastenings at the back of the neck. 'There: now take a look at yourself.'

Pen picked up the skirt and moved to her long looking glass. Her head looked the same as always; unmade-up face, greying hair. But from the neck down she was clothed in the ineffable chic of a period she had always been drawn to.

'You don't think short sleeves are too young?' she asked, looking doubtfully at them. Being unlined, they were semi-transparent.

'Not at all. You have nice slim arms . . . and a lovely back, which is spoilt by the strap of your bra. Wait a moment. I'll fix it.'

Jane came close behind her and unclipped the back of her bra. 'I'll tuck the ends out of sight and then you can see how it should look.'

It wasn't until she turned away from the glass and peered over her shoulder that Pen discovered the dress was backless. The tops of her shoulders were covered but her back was exposed to the waist.

'I can't wear this – not at my age,' she protested, aware of a sharp disappointment that Ashford would never see her gliding downstairs in a swirl of blackberry-dark chiffon.

'Don't be silly. Age has nothing to do with it. It's what sort of shape she's in that dictates what a woman can wear. You're still as slim as a model. This dress wasn't made for a young girl. It's too sophisticated for anyone under thirty-five. Here, take a look through your hand mirror. That's no old lady's back you've got there,' Jane told her, laughing.

Pen carefully appraised her rear view. It was true her back hadn't changed as much as some parts of her. The skin was unblemished, the spine straight with no sign of dowager's hump.

Her gaze moved upwards. She sighed. It was no use having a young back if one's head failed to match it.

'It doesn't look right with my hair, Jane,' she decided regretfully. 'Perhaps, if it had been black, the back could have been filled in. But this colour could never be matched.'

'No, no, that would ruin it . . . and your hair will be different for the dance.'

'I don't want to dye it, if that's what you're going to suggest.'

'I'm not; but I do think the style needs a little alteration. Instead of having it scraped back and pinned up high on your head, the dress needs a softer chignon, lower down, at your nape. The way the Duchess of Windsor used to wear hers when she was Mrs Wallis Simpson. You must have seen pictures of her with a centre parting and soft waves. If you'll sit down I'll show you how it would look.'

Pen submitted to sitting on the stool in front of her dressing table while Jane's quick deft fingers unfastened her bun. It was flattering to have so much thought given to the details of her appearance.

'Your hair is in excellent condition. I guess that's from *not* being coloured or permed or anything, and always being rinsed in rain water.' Jane put the hairpins in the silver pin-tray.

Pen wasn't a woman who spent time gazing at herself and repining the ravages of time. But when her ageing face and Jane's young one were reflected together, she couldn't help feeling a pang at the comparison.

'You see how the centre parting emphasizes the fact that your face is a perfect oval?' Jane said, holding Pen's hair in a coil at the nape of her neck with the sides brushed forward to cover all but the lobes of her ears. 'Do say you like it, Penelope, because it looks great as well as being right for the dress.'

'Yes, I do like it,' Pen agreed, surprised at how much it improved her. 'But how shall I get it to stay there? I can't stick pins in my neck.'

'I'm not sure how it's done, but my hairdresser will know. You'll have to go to London to choose some evening shoes. We'll fix an appointment for him to do a try-out. On the day of the dance I'll have him come here and give us all wonderful hairdos. Do you have any amethyst earrings? Pearls would be fine, but amethysts would be better.'

'I have some pearl drops which belonged to my mother.

461

But, Jane, I haven't decided to wear this dress yet. I still think it's –'

'You can't *not* wear it,' Jane cut in, smiling at her. 'It might have been made for you – truly. You'll look what North calls a knock-out.'

'You are good for my morale. What with my model's figure and my perfect oval face, I'm beginning to feel quite a beauty,' Pen said, with a shaky laugh.

Although she was trying to make light of it, inwardly she was deeply touched and felt a lump in her throat. This was the affectionate support she had wanted to receive from, and give to, her daughter. But somehow relations between them had always been upsettingly destructive. Failed by her own mother, she had in turn failed Allegra and given up hope of achieving the close bond she knew existed between some mothers and daughters. To feel it springing up now, between herself and this girl whose arrival she had so dreaded, moved her almost to tears.

The last time people had danced in the Grand Saloon at Longwarden had been at a Hunt Ball in 1970. Before that there had been a dance for Ranulf Lomax's coming of age in 1961, and a party for Caspar Carlyon's eightieth birthday in 1953. North's twenty-first birthday, coming after his father's death, had not been celebrated. For fifteen years the seventeenth-century verdure tapestries in the Saloon had been hidden behind their protective curtains, while the carpets in the three smaller drawing rooms lay beneath druggets, being only occasionally inspected for moth larvae and carpet beetle.

For three weeks beforehand all the cleaners, including a number of extra helpers recruited after Mavis Osgood, worked full time to prepare the house for the fancy-dress ball.

It had been a surprise to Mavis to find that none of the cleaning agents recommended on television were used at Longwarden. Paintwork was washed with warm water and something called Synperonic N; floors were polished with mops wrapped in old woollen cloths impregnated with a mixture of paraffin and malt vinegar; furniture was dusted frequently and sometimes buffed with a chamois leather but polished only once a year and then with beeswax soaked in turpentine, not the aerosol spray polish she used in her home.

And woe betide the cleaner found with a dirty duster, or putting even a spotless duster near the chests of drawers inlaid with tortoiseshell and brass. They had to be left untouched for Mr Ashford to deal with. He was ever so particular.

All the chairs in the most posh rooms had what were called case covers on them. They were something like loose covers, only a lot looser, and they had been made to protect the proper upholstery from light and dust when, long ago, the house was closed up while the family spent the Season in London or went shooting in Scotland.

In the old days the case covers had been laundered at regular intervals. But it was many years since the house had been properly cared for and not only had the case covers gathered much dust but the chairs beneath them were dusty. Mavis had vacuum-cleaned some of them, and what a performance it was with Mr Ashford insisting that a special sort of fine nylon mesh had to be placed over the upholstery and the suction applied very gently.

That was just one of his rules. But, to give him his due, he didn't only give orders and go round making sure they were obeyed. He worked as hard as any of them. Often, when everyone else was finished for the day, he would still be on top of the indoor scaffold, cleaning a fancy ceiling by brushing out the mouldings with a hogshair fitch and catching the dust with a small suction cleaner.

Mrs Armitage reckoned he was working sixteen hours a day, what with his regular duties and the extra work for the ball.

Tark wasn't interested in hearing what a hard-working bugger the butler was; but he pricked up his ears when his mother mentioned a silver vault. However the existence of the vault wasn't a lot of use if she didn't know exactly where it was or how much silver was stored in it.

'Can't you play up to him . . . make like you fancy him
. . . get him to show you?' he suggested. 'The silver'll have
to be cleaned, won't it? You could offer to stay late an' help
him.'

'I'm there all day now,' said Mavis. 'I'm not used to
working long hours. It makes my feet ache.'

Nevertheless, while she was putting in her rollers at
bedtime, she thought over Tarquin's suggestion. She
wouldn't have to pretend to fancy Mr Ashford. She *did*
fancy him. When he said, 'Good morning, Mrs Osgood,'
and smiled at her, she felt exactly the same as she had years
ago in Benidorm when Paco Lopez had flashed white teeth
and called her *señorita*.

With his dark hair, going grey at the sides, and his dark
brown eyes, Mr Ashford could pass for a Spaniard . . . one
of the blue-blooded Dons she had read about in her Mills
& Boon books.

Perhaps I will offer to stay late, she thought, spreading
a net over the helmet of rollers. They say he's got a lovely
car. If it were raining heavy one night, he might offer to
run me home. I could ask him in for a drink . . . if Tarquin
weren't in.

Instinct told her that Mr Ashford and her son were
unlikely to take to each other.

The day before she and Pen went to London together, Jane
told her mother-in-law there was so much to be done she
thought they should stay overnight, returning the following
afternoon.

She had already asked Allegra if they might use the
apartment at Carlyon House, and had also spoken to North.

'I'd like to spend two days in London, alone with your
mother. Would you mind if we did that?'

He looked surprised but shrugged and said, 'Go ahead.'

While the rest of the household was preoccupied with
the ball, North was doing a tour of inspection with an
architect who specialized in the restoration and maintenance of ancient buildings.

So it was with overnight cases on the back seat of Jane's

new car that the two women set out early, arriving in central London in the middle of the morning.

When they had unpacked and made coffee, Jane produced a notebook. 'Now this is the plan. First Maud Frizon for your shoes and, if we can't find any there, the other shoe shops in Bond Street. After that we'll have a light lunch before I take you to my hairdresser. When I'm sure he knows what to do, I'll go off and do some more shopping. I thought we could meet for tea at Fortnum & Mason and then have a browse in Hatchards before coming back here. Is that all right with you?'

'Perfectly.'

Pen could remember her mother announcing similar plans, although they had never included browsing in bookshops, nor had her reaction been the pleasant anticipation, even excitement, she was experiencing now, in the company of her daughter-in-law.

The day being both dry and bright, they decided to stretch their legs and walk as far as Maud Frizon. It was not far, cutting across the heart of Mayfair.

'I should have liked to see London in the days when the whole of this area was residential and these were all elegant town houses instead of mostly offices,' Jane said as they crossed the north corner of Berkeley Square. 'I always loved coming to London. Maybe I felt in my bones that one day I should live in this country as an Englishman's wife.'

Pen glanced sideways at her daughter-in-law who was stepping out briskly in polished black slip-on walking shoes, wearing a pale beige raincoat with a long black and beige silk scarf tied in a bow at the left side of her neck. With her shiny long bob swinging in time with her stride and one gloved hand holding the strap of her simple but expensive shoulder bag, she looked much more like a well-heeled American tourist than an adoptive Englishwoman.

'I have a feeling that "the American Countess", as you will probably be known to future generations, will have as strong an impact on the Lomax family as the so-called Chinese Countess,' said Pen. 'None of the English wives has ever had very much influence on their husbands and children, but North's great-grandmother was a very forceful character although she never seemed domineering. As Allegra says in her book, Flora was a determined feminist but she concealed it behind a gentle feminine manner. It always seemed to be her husband who was the author or backer of the reforms she believed in. Rather than lending her own weight to the suffragette movement, she persuaded him to support them in the House of Lords and elsewhere, which he probably wouldn't have done, left to himself. He adored her and could never say no to her, and she thought he was a god.'

'Obviously she was a very indulgent, amusing great-grandmother. From what Allegra and North have told me about her, I can see why they liked her so much. Did you like her, Penelope?'

'No one could fail to like Flora. She was charm personified, and it wasn't a superficial charm. I've never known anyone who took more trouble to please her family and friends. After she moved to London which, although she would never admit it, I know she did largely for my benefit, she would often send me snippets from newspapers and magazines, articles about gardening which she knew would interest me. When the furnace serving the orangery was turned off, to cheer me up she conceived the idea of the butterfly garden. Now all sorts of people have them, including Prince Charles. But it was Flora who inspired the one at Longwarden and who called it the butterfly ballroom. The idea was typical of her. Her mind was as lovely as her face.'

'She sounds almost too good to be true. Didn't she have any failings? Most people do.'

'Perhaps she did when she was young, but not by the time I knew her. She said to me once that she had been very lucky to have love, good health and beautiful surroundings nearly all her long life.'

'But only two children: that must have been a disappointment.'

'It was. The Lomaxes have never been a prolific family. They haven't had difficulty in producing sons, as some

466

families do, but they've seldom had more than two children and quite often only one, which has made the succession a bit uncertain at times. Do you like children?'

'Not if they're brats,' said Jane, smiling, as they turned into Bond Street. 'But I'm sure I shall like my own.' She slipped a hand into the crook of her mother-in-law's elbow and gave her arm a light squeeze. 'You'll be the first to know when I'm pregnant, which I hope will be soon.'

Pen flushed. 'I had no intention of prying, Jane. When you decide to have children is entirely a matter for you and North to agree . . . nothing to do with me. I should hate you to think I was hinting that you ought to start a baby soon. Nothing was further –'

'I know that, Penelope. To be honest, before I arrived, I did wonder if we might have a problem getting along with each other. The relationship between a man's wife and his mother is notoriously difficult. But in no time at all I could tell it was going to be just fine between us. You're the least interfering person.'

'I don't get on with Allegra at all,' Pen said sadly.

'That's a different situation. You may be mother and daughter but it doesn't necessarily make you the same kind of person. I think you and I are quite alike in many ways. You're crazy about your garden and I've fallen in love with the house. Allegra is basically a career girl, even if it's taken her a while to find her métier. Have we time for a browse in Asprey's? No, we'd better leave that till tomorrow. Today we should concentrate on shoes to go with our dresses.'

The shoes at Maud Frizon were, in Pen's opinion, outrageously expensive. They cost more than a good-sized young tree.

'I'm afraid they're not comfortable,' she said truthfully. 'I've always had most awkward feet.'

Jane saw nothing she liked there. They left the shop to look elsewhere.

They had looked in several shop windows when, at the corner of Burlington Gardens, they came to the Ferragamo shop and, at the same moment, both spotted the perfect shoe for the Molyneux dress.

467

Set on a Louis heel, it was made of soft grape-dark suede with a small fan-shaped tongue of pleated grosgrain. Beside it lay a suede pochette with the same pleating hiding the clasp.

It was many years since Pen had seen something irresistible in a London shop window. Long ago, when the children were little, before Edward had reduced her allowance, she had delighted in buying Swiss-made jerseys for North and hand-smocked dresses for Allegra. But the last time she could remember wanting something for herself was far back in her teens when there had been a blue velvet dress she had longed for with the same intense yearning she felt at this moment.

The dress hadn't met with her mother's approval. The suede shoes were equally unattainable. Anything with Salvatore Ferragamo stamped in gold on the pale-grey insole must be at least as expensive as the shoes at Maud Frizon, and probably more so.

'We needn't look any further. They might have been made for your dress,' Jane said jubilantly.

Ignoring her mother-in-law's half-hearted protests, she swept Pen inside the shop.

They had the shoes in her size. They fitted perfectly.

'And they'll look even better with pale-grey pantyhose or stockings,' said Jane.

Pen walked about the thick carpet for a few moments, then sat down and slipped the shoes off.

'They are nice . . . but how much are they?' she asked the saleswoman.

Jane stopped the assistant replying by saying, in a hurry, 'They're going to be my Christmas present. I've been wondering what I could give you and, as I discovered the dress, what could be more appropriate than the shoes and bag to go with it?' She saw Pen was going to protest. 'Please, Penelope – don't refuse. It would give me so much pleasure.'

'It's terribly generous of you, my dear, but I really don't think –' Pen began.

'*Please!*' Jane repeated, in a tone of entreaty. Regardless of the hovering assistant, she clasped one of Pen's hands between hers and said, her grey eyes appealing, 'It means a great deal to me. I know however hard I look I shan't find anything you like more than these shoes. Let me give them to you – with my love.'

Taking the older woman's silence for assent, she gave the assistant a smiling nod and opened her bag to take out her cheque book.

Pen was overcome by emotion; the same emotion she had felt the night Jane had helped her to try on the dress and told her she would look a knock-out. This time her feelings were harder to control. To her horror, her eyes brimmed with tears and the only way to prevent them overflowing was to close her eyelids and fumble blindly for a handkerchief.

On the point of rising from her seat to follow the assistant to the other end of the showroom, Jane saw with dismay the quivering of Penelope's lips and the bright drop which squeezed between her lids.

For a terrible moment she thought that, intending to give love and pleasure, she had given profound offence.

As Pen strove to regain self-control, she heard Jane say, in a low voice, 'Don't be upset, please. I wouldn't offend you for the world.'

Offend me?

Pen opened her eyes and saw through a blur of tears the lovely young face gazing anxiously at her.

'Dear Jane . . . you could never offend me,' she told her, in a husky croak. 'Forgive me for being such a fool. I'm so . . . overwhelmed by your wonderful warmth and generosity. I'll be all right in a minute.' She dabbed her eyes with her handkerchief and blew her nose.

Jane patted her on the knee. 'You stay here while I ask them to hold the parcel till later. There's no sense in carrying it around all day.'

Grateful for her tact, and even more thankful that the shop wasn't full of people covertly observing her lapse, Pen took out the enamelled compact which had been in her bag for years. It still contained the original cake of pinkish compressed powder, now rubbed away at the centre. She patted the puff on her nose and under her eyes.

By the time Jane came back she was sufficiently recovered to say, in a cheerful manner, 'One advantage of not wearing mascara is no awful black smears if one makes a fool of oneself.'

Outside the shop Jane slipped her arm through her mother-in-law's in an affectionate gesture. Setting a strolling pace, she said, 'I'll let you into a secret. I don't have a stiff upper lip. I cry for the silliest reasons. So that makes two of us. But I do wear mascara,' she added. 'Why don't you? Are you allergic to eye make-up?'

'Not that I know of. I suppose most women, as they get older, wear either more or less make-up and I'm in the latter group. It doesn't seem necessary for the kind of life I lead.'

'Not for gardening – no,' Jane agreed. 'But I think it is for the dance. A touch of soft lilac shadow and a little brown mascara. Not black. That would look hard. Let's go to Fenwick's and browse in their make-up department. I'll give you moral support if they try the hard sell.'

'Now we're going to give you a thirties look, aren't we, Lady Carlyon? A centre parting, soft waves over the temples and a loose coil at the back.' Peter, the hairdresser, began to comb her hair, assessing its length and thickness. 'Who has been cutting your hair?'

'I have.'

'Ah, all is explained . . . very naughty,' he told her, in roguish reproof. 'Even with hair this length, worn in a chignon, a good cut every six weeks is an absolute *must*. You've been chopping this with your nail scissors, haven't you? Never mind: there's no lasting harm done and it's in super condition. You must be eating all the right things. Lot's of lovely fresh veggies from your own kitchen garden, I expect. I'm a total believer in "We are what we eat" – aren't you?'

Before she could answer, he tipped her head gently forward and for a few moments she was enclosed in a tent of damp hair while he studied the way it grew at the back

470

of her neck. Another tilt of her head and a few deft strokes with the comb swept the hair from her face and established a centre parting.

'Right: now I'm going to take off about three inches, but don't panic. You'll still have plenty to pin back.'

He straightened and started to cut.

When Elliott Lincoln had advised Allegra to postpone her biography of the field marshal in favour of a book about Risconti, she had been worried about her English publishers' reaction. Fortunately neither Claudia nor Ellen had objected to the change of plan.

Elliott, who was coming to England for the dance, was keeping in frequent telephone contact with Allegra. On hearing that Risconti was painting at Longwarden, his newest idea was that North should contribute to the book. He wanted her brother to photograph Risconti at work on the portraits of his wife and sister, and also to photograph both sitters while they were posing. Elliott thought it would be interesting to show the difference between an artist's vision and a top photographer's vision of two beautiful women.

North's objection, that he wasn't a portrait photographer, the American publisher had dismissed as less important than his international reputation and his relationship to Risconti's subjects.

'Your brother's involvement will broaden the book's appeal and make it even more saleable,' he had told Allegra during one of their long transatlantic conversations. 'With a portrait of the present Countess of Carlyon on the front cover, and your portrait on the back, the book will sell to everyone who bought *Travels*.'

'As the book is about Andro, surely *he* should be on the front cover?' she had pointed out, a touch indignantly.

'Maybe we can get round that by using a photograph of him working on the portrait of your sister-in-law,' had been Elliott's answer.

Allegra's view of the biography was as a serious study of an important twentieth-century portraitist. She didn't want it to become a catchpenny best-seller aimed at a market more interested in an American-born countess than in the development of Risconti's art. However she thought it politic not to express that opinion on the telephone but to wait until Elliott came over.

While Pen was having her hair cut, Allegra was sitting to Risconti and at the same time taping his conversation with North, who was taking photographs.

They were in the old day nursery, scene of her earliest memories, which Risconti had chosen as his temporary studio.

He had given a great deal of thought to what she should wear and how she should be posed. Finally he had settled on the Fortuny dress, with a black and gold lacquer screen placed behind a small Regency sofa. The setting and dress were formal. The pose was not. She was sitting in a characteristic position, one foot on the floor, the other tucked up beside her while she leaned on the armrest, a hand supporting her chin.

Risconti liked to talk while he was painting. By now Allegra had recorded a much fuller account of his life than the facts she had heard for the first time at Sybille's dinner party. Several tapes were already in transcript, waiting for her to rearrange incidents remembered at random into their chronological order. Before that could be done, she would have to organize interviews with other people whose opinions about him were pertinent. Meanwhile she was trying to extract his views on Life and Art. At the moment her brother was doing the job for her by discussing the effect on art of the development of photography.

As she listened to the two men talking, Allegra noticed that when Risconti looked away from his easel to study some part of her, he had a trick of turning his head slightly to one side. She wondered why she had never noticed it before. Usually she was observant of mannerisms but this habit of his had escaped her.

At the time it seemed insignificant.

'I almost didn't recognize you. It's incredible what a difference those little curly bangs make,' were Jane's first words

472

when Pen joined her at a corner table at Fortnum & Mason's Fountain restaurant.

'Bangs? Oh ... the fringe. You don't think it looks ridiculous?' asked Pen.

'I think it's a touch of genius on Peter's part,' Jane told her seriously. 'Why didn't I see that bangs were the finishing touch? It's a transformation, Penelope. Aren't you pleased with it yourself?'

Pen took off her gloves. 'I'm not sure. I should hate to look like mutton dressed as lamb.'

Jane gave an emphatic shake of the head. 'You don't, I promise you. You'll soon get accustomed to the new look. It suits you perfectly ... and not just for the dance. For every day. Did you watch how he set the bangs so that you can do them yourself?'

'I watched, but I rather doubt that I can achieve the same effect.'

After tea they went to the Ladies where Jane insisted on Pen using one of the two new lipsticks she had persuaded her to buy earlier.

That it did make a difference was proved when they arrived at Hatchard's in Piccadilly. A personable man of about her own age was leaving the bookshop as they arrived. As he held open the door, it wasn't at Jane that he looked but at her companion – and with what, Pen realized, startled, had used to be called 'a glad eye'.

'Thank you.' She entered the shop with her colour rising from his admiring scrutiny.

'Don't think I missed that look,' said Jane. 'If you were on your own, he'd come back and pick you up – in the nicest possible way, of course.'

'What nonsense, Jane,' said Pen, laughing. 'I expect he's the type of man who leers at dozens of women.'

'Penelope, that's just not true. He was nice ... and he thought you looked nice. Which you do. You're very attractive. Maybe you weren't as a girl but you are now. Believe it. Enjoy it. Anyone else with your looks would.'

* * *

Between visits to the convalescent home, Sarah telephoned Sammy every other day, always late in the afternoon in order not to interrupt his supper or a TV programme. At one time contemptuous of television, since his operation he had become an addict.

She had been expecting to bring him home a few days before the ball. When she mentioned it he said, 'I'm after changing my mind, child. I'll not be coming back yet awhile.'

'Why not, Sammy?'

A pause. 'I've been invited to stay with a friend for a week or two. I think it'll do me good. She's a very good cook and she has a nice little bungalow, close to the sea. You remember I introduced you the last time you came down.'

'You mean Mrs Slane?' said Sarah.

'Yes, I'm going to spend Christmas with Eileen. The fact is . . . to tell you the truth . . . we're thinking of getting married.'

'You're what?' Sarah cried, aghast.

She couldn't believe it. Not Sammy, the life-long bachelor who, while clearly not homosexual, had never seemed interested in women. A gelding, North had once called him, when Allegra had pondered Sammy's sex life.

'The thing is she's lonely,' he said. 'And so am I . . . or I will be when I retire. There's no sense in me staying at Longwarden if I'm no use there. I'd be better off keeping Eileen company. Nothing's settled yet, you understand? But we've talked it over and we both feel it's worth a trial run. If it works out, we'll make it official.'

'I – I don't know what to say, Sammy. It's . . . it's such a surprise,' Sarah stammered.

'It's a surprise to me, too. But there you are, you live and learn. I never met a woman like Eileen when I was younger or I might have been married before now.'

For a week before the ball, the Grand Staircase was out of bounds to everyone except Mr Woolacombe, a metalwork conservator, and his assistants.

To remind everyone that they must use the other

staircases, dustsheets were rigged at the head and foot of the main stairs and the work of removing the tarnish from the silver balustrade was carried on out of sight. Only Jane saw it in progress, having persuaded North not to look until it was finished.

'It's an unfortunate fact that even in the days when houses such as Longwarden had a large staff to keep them in order, a great deal of harm was done to the metals by over-zealous cleaning and polishing, Lady Carlyon,' said Mr Woolacombe. 'The plate powder used by butlers in the old days and certain present-day patent cleaners have done incalculable damage,' he told her, shaking his head. 'Only last month I saw what might have been a particularly fine engraved steel chimney surround largely ruined by the ill-advised use of wire wool and sandpaper. And the number of ormolu mounts and fine pieces of silver-gilt and Sheffield plate which have been spoiled by injudicious polishing is legion. I do urge the utmost caution if Lord Carlyon's splendid heritage is to be preserved for posterity.'

Jane suspected that part of his anxiety was because she was an American.

'Don't worry, Mr Woolacombe. I have no intention of over-restoring Longwarden,' she assured him. 'Nothing will be done without expert advice.'

'You are fortunate in having a butler who appears to take a serious interest in conservation. He tells me he banned the use of brass polish and feather dusters some time ago.'

She nodded. 'I must admit I hadn't realized feather dusters were dangerous because they can't be washed, and broken feathers may scratch things.'

'A well-informed person in charge of the domestic staff is half the battle,' said the conservator. 'The trouble is many of the good ladies on whom the day-to-day upkeep of historic houses depends nowadays have been indoctrinated into thinking the hard shine produced by abrasives superior to the natural patina of age. Handles and finger-plates on doors are particularly subject to the results of that misguided attitude, I find. You could do a great deal towards preserving possessions, Lady Carlyon, merely by insisting that clean cotton gloves are worn at all times. Being touched by bare hands tarnishes metals and is indeed deleterious to most surfaces,' he added sombrely.

'I'll bear that in mind, Mr Woolacombe. Tell me: when the balustrades have been cleaned and lacquered, how long will it be before they need further attention?'

'It's difficult to be precise, but certainly not for some years ... provided they aren't fingered, or dusted too frequently. A light brushing no more than two or three times a year is the desideratum.'

Another expert who was in the house at the same time was the man who had come to attend to the chandeliers. Unlike the spare, solemn Mr Woolacombe, he was a chirpy little Londoner who listened to what he still called 'the wireless' while he was busy dismantling the cascades of Waterford crystal.

Whenever Jane went to see how he was getting on, he would turn off his radio and launch into fascinating tales of chandeliers he had known.

It was not Mr Chirk's first visit to the house. Now several years past the official age for retirement, he had been coming to Longwarden since he was a youthful apprentice to the firm he had eventually taken over.

'My son's in charge now,' he told her, the first time they chatted. 'I don't do as much as I used. But seeing as this job was urgent and I've been coming here, off and on, for fifty years near as, I said I'd handle it. To tell you the truth, taking it easy don't suit me. Give me a job like this and I'm as happy as Larry. But I'm not so keen on the ones we mostly get these days.'

'What sort of jobs are they, Mr Chirk?'

'Well, y'see m'Lady' – he was simultaneously more respectful and more friendly than Mr Woolacombe – 'there's not a lot of people can afford a fine chandelier in England now. Where you come from they can – oh yes. There's plenty of money – big bucks, as they call it – over there. But here there's not so much call for a fine antique chandelier except from Arabs and pop stars, and usually they only buy them because they're expensive, not because they appreciate the finer points. To my mind an old chandelier only looks right in a setting like this. But most of the people who can pay for them go and hang them on ceilings too low, or put a French chandelier in a room with all English furniture. To my eye, that never looks right.'

Another time, while he was using a hair-dryer to make sure no moisture was left on the glass drops and metal hooks before he reassembled them, he said to her, 'The old Indian maharajahs, they were the boys for buying chandeliers. Very fond of anything made of glass they was. Glass tables, glass chairs . . . you name it, they had it. Back in old Queen Victoria's time, there was an English firm called Osler and a French firm called Baccarat and between them they supplied the world. Hundreds, probably thousands, of beautiful chandeliers was packed up in boxes and sent to India for the maharajahs' palaces.'

His hands gloved to prevent fingermarks blurring the brilliance of the crystal, he held up a loop of drops for a final inspection.

'For the Indian market, there was chandeliers what would have made this one here look like a bauble on a Christmas tree,' he told her. 'Fifty feet tall, over twenty feet in diameter and the best part of four hundred lights . . . how about that? They had to hoist an elephant up to the ceiling to see if it would take the weight. And I'll tell you somethink else most people don't know –' He leaned closer, lowering his voice. '– a lot of them big chandeliers never seen daylight. They was never unpacked. Years later, after we pulled out of India, the British I mean, everythink changed. The old days was over for everyone, including the maharajahs. It was around that time that some dealers with connections in India was able to pick up some marvellous stuff, dirt cheap. There was works of art worth thousands being chucked out with the rubbish. I know for a fact that several big chandeliers was broken up and re-made into two or three smaller ones. How do I know? Because it was Bert

Chirk what did the job. All the posh Bond Street dealers used to come to me when they had a problem with a chandelier.'

'I hope there's no danger of one of these chandeliers crashing down during the ball,' said Jane, peering up at the ceiling fixture.

Although fragile as spun sugar in appearance, the Waterford chandeliers needed thick chains to support their great weight.

'Don't you worry about that, m'Lady. Checking they're safe is all part of the service. And I've had the muslin bags washed so they'll be clean to put on after the ball. Mind you, if there's smoking in here, you'd be surprised what a nasty film of nicotine there'll be on these afterwards ... and on them handsome mirrors,' Mr Chirk added, with an admiring glance at the large rococo pier glasses on the walls between the row of tall windows, each one topped by a festoon blind of red silk.

After careful cleaning with methylated spirits, the thin glass in the ornate gilt frames had more sparkle than before but was still misty with age. Jane liked old looking glasses. Sometimes, gazing at a reflection in one of the many mirrors to be found all over the house, she half-expected to see the room behind her not only reversed but peopled with shadowy figures from the past. She longed to be able to press a button in the frame and tune in to what had been happening on a day of her choice. All those centuries of family life would make far more interesting viewing than contemporary television. It gave her a comfortable feeling to be part of that long chain of people whose portraits and possessions were all around.

She wondered where North would decide to hang her portrait when it was finished. Even if he wanted it there, it would be too large to replace the de Laszlo of Flora Carlyon in his bedroom.

Since Paris he hadn't slept there but had been sharing Jane's bed. She was glad he had put his foot down and ended that rather silly charade she had started. But she didn't delude herself that spending their nights together was a significant advance towards the deeply loving relationship of her daydreams.

There had been no news from France yet. Worrying about Marie-Simone was another cloud in her sky.

When Pen had come back from London with her new hairstyle, she hadn't expected any reaction from her two gardening henchmen. Even after years of working together, they would have thought it impertinent to remark on her appearance.

Their apparent failure to notice any change had been predictable. But she had thought Ashford would venture a compliment, and been dashed when he didn't. He *must* have noticed. Perhaps he didn't like the new style ... thought it unbecoming or, worse, too girlish for her.

He was working terribly hard. However, even on the go for up to eighteen hours a day, he seemed to thrive on the extra effort.

'Have you had *any* leisure this week, Mr Ashford?' she asked, finding him attending to the fire when she entered the library before dinner.

He straightened, removing the household gloves with which he handled the logs and putting them back, out of sight, in a corner of the large square basket.

'It does one good to be fully extended sometimes, m'Lady.'

'But not over-extended. I suspect that you haven't sat down, except to swallow your meals, since you got up this morning.'

She longed to add, 'Sit down now. Have a glass of sherry with me. It's ages since we talked.'

If North and Jane had been out that night, she would have risked it. But they might come in at any moment and anyway she knew Ashford would refuse.

'I haven't done much sitting down, but I had a short walk this afternoon which was equally refreshing,' he answered. 'May I get you something to drink, m'Lady?'

As he came towards her from the drinks table, she said,

'I used to dread dances when I was young, but I find I'm looking forward to this one.'

'I'm sure it will be a most enjoyable occasion for everyone, m'Lady.' His manner was at its most formal. It was hard to believe they had ever spent an hour alone, breathing summer night scents, talking, at ease with each other.

She took the glass from the salver. 'Thank you.'

She wondered what he would do when she asked him to dance . . . insisted he dance with her.

On the morning of the ball Sarah worked in the stables as usual. The familiar routines helped to calm her excitement.

She had lost count of the times she had tried on her dress. Jane was the only person who knew what she was going to wear because Sarah had asked her advice on what to do with her hair. Should she have it cut short in a neo-twenties shingle?

Jane had said, 'No, keep your braid and have it threaded with ribbons to match the dress. I'll find some when I'm in London. It would be a crime to cut your hair. My hairdresser is coming to put mine up for me. He can do yours too.'

Jane had not only found ribbons for her, but a pair of silver kid sandals imported from Italy and two pairs of pale azure tights so gossamer sheer they had to be put on with gloves.

'That's all you must wear underneath,' she told Sarah. 'A bra will show through the chiffon above the beading and you don't need one anyway. I always thought overlapping sequins were tacky, but this dress is lovely. You'll look a dream in it, Sarah.'

Would Nick think so? Sarah wondered, as she brushed out Chestnut's flaxen tail.

The Haflinger was beginning to look as a fit pony should, with a sheen on his coat and his small ears pricked and alert. In spite of what he had suffered at the hands of some callous human, he had never attempted to retaliate by kicking or biting. He seemed grateful to be in good hands and she was becoming very fond of him. So was Jane. She had suggested having the old governess-cart spruced up and learning to drive it.

The main staircase was no longer hidden by dustsheets and Ken Turner and his assistants were putting the finishing touches to a decorative scheme of magical beauty when Sarah went in for lunch.

In the hall a giant spruce had been sprayed with artificial hoar frost, hung with a thousand shimmering icicles and wired with a myriad pinpoint lights. Festoons of frosted greenery, looped between bunches of silver baubles, garlanded the galleries above.

When she peeped into the Great Saloon, she was stunned by the transformation. Extravagantly beautiful swags of silvery-green poppy heads, artichokes, pine cones and leaves draped the doors, the tops of the paintings, the gilded pilasters and the dais put up for the band. When the chandeliers were alight, it would look even more beautiful.

At North's insistence, that afternoon his mother, wife, sister and cousin were all sent to their bedrooms to rest, if possible to sleep.

'*Try!*' he said firmly, when Sarah objected. 'You're going to be up most of the night, if not all night. A couple of hours' sleep now will stop you fading tomorrow morning.'

He made sure Jane obeyed his orders by going upstairs with her and making love to her. She went to sleep in his arms, waking later to find he had gone. Knowing she could rely on him to wake her in good time, and that downstairs everything was under control, she turned over and drifted back to sleep.

North spent much of the afternoon taking photographs of his house. It was like a once-exquisite woman who, after years of letting herself go, had suddenly made a great effort to revive her neglected looks and shine as a beauty again.

The pleasure it gave him to see the silver balustrades restored almost to their original splendour surprised him. He walked up and down the staircase several times,

481

admiring the design from different angles, regretting the places where tarnish had bitten deeply into the silver, leaving irremovable signs of the years of his father's custody when everything had been sacrificed to the stables and the kennels.

Only now, seeing the house as it looked today, with much still to be done but a start made, did he realize how deeply it had pained him to watch Longwarden falling apart.

Wandering into the Saloon, he found Risconti sitting astride one of the gilt chairs round the dance floor. With swift, assured strokes he was drawing the instruments already arranged on the dais.

Looking up from the spiral-bound block on which he was working, he said, 'My Christmas present to you, North. A sketch book of one day in the history of a great English house.' He flipped over the pages to show a collection of drawings begun early that morning. 'The idea came to me when you showed me the photographs you took for *A Day in the Life of Australia* the other night. I thought in addition to your own record of the festivities' – with a nod at North's camera – 'I would contribute a point of view.'

'Nothing could please me more. I take it you and Allegra are planning to come back for Christmas rather than staying on in New York after the opening of Mrs Vreeland's *Costumes of Royal India* exhibition?'

'With your permission, yes; that's what we'd like to do.'

'We'd like it too. Jane and Allegra get on extremely well and you and I have a lot in common. I hope you'll regard this house as somewhere you're welcome to stay any time it suits you.'

Risconti inclined his head. 'Thank you.' After a slight pause, he added, 'You don't think Lady Carlyon is disturbed by the . . . informality of our relationship?'

North gave the question a few moments' thought before he answered. 'Belonging to a conventional generation, she may wish you would make it official; or by now she may take the view that as long as Allegra is happy, that's all that matters. I shouldn't have thought my mother's opinion was of much importance to either of you. Or mine,' he added dryly, suspecting it was really his view the other man had been canvassing.

'No, that is true . . . to an extent,' Risconti agreed. 'But when one has received kindness and hospitality, one doesn't wish to give offence.' He made a doodle on the edge of the page. 'I am serious about your sister. Most serious. But there are reasons why it is better for us to continue as we are. I hope you will take my word for it.'

'Of course. It's entirely your business. If Allegra were Sarah's age that would be different. Your intentions would be my concern. But my sister is a grown-up woman who can manage her own life. And you're a very nice guy whom we all enjoy having among us,' North added sincerely.

He gave the Italian a friendly pat on the shoulder and went away to look at the preparations for the buffet supper which was to be served at eleven.

He was puzzled by Risconti's apparent unease about his continuing liaison with Allegra. Was *she* putting pressure on him? It didn't seem likely. But if she had come to the point of wanting a husband in preference to a lover, why was Risconti reluctant? Did he, knowing her history, as he must, think she might yet lose interest in him? Or had he some reason of his own for preferring the status quo?

Not much concerned by a matter which he felt to be outside his province, yet his curiosity a little kindled by a strangeness in Risconti's manner, North pondered it for a short time and then forgot about it.

When Sarah walked down the Grand Staircase on the high slender heels of her new silver sandals, she was trembling with nervous excitement. Even the night before Burghley she hadn't been as keyed up as this. But at Burghley, if she and Beddo had put up a poor performance, they could have tried again next year.

With Nick, who might soon go away, she had only this one opportunity to make him see her with new eyes.

It was the first time in her memory that the cavernous hearth in the hall had been filled with burning logs, their warm light contrasting with the snow-forest glitter of the huge spruce, its boughs pervading the air with a resinous scent which to her was the essence of Christmas.

When she paused at the foot of the stairs the hall was deserted although she could hear the hum of voices from other parts of the ground floor as the caterers and other helpers completed their preparations.

Then, from the Music Room which tonight was serving as an ante-room to the ballroom, a tall man in a scarlet tunic with a high gold-braided collar came strolling into the hall with a glass of champagne in his hand.

For an instant she didn't know him. It was as if her great-grandfather had come back to life; except that as far as she knew he had never served in the army, nor had he worn a moustache.

'North!' she exclaimed, as she pierced her cousin's disguise.

He had been surveying the tree. As he turned in her direction, she was pleased to see that he also was momentarily taken aback.

She stepped forward and twirled to make the loose strands of beads fly out from the hem of her dress and continue to swing back and forth as she came to a standstill.

'How do I look?'

For a moment he didn't answer. She realized that for the first time he was seeing her as someone other than his horsey little cousin Sarah.

'Like the girl who inspired the song "Gentlemen Prefer Blondes",' he said, with a grin. 'No, seriously, you look ravishing.'

'You look very splendid yourself. It's a magnificent moustache. It's amazing how much it changes you.'

He lifted a finger to stroke the luxuriant growth fanning out from below his nose to beyond the sides of his mouth.

'It's not only this. I've had my hair cut as well. If you look at the portraits of the period, they had much shorter hair when Tom Lomax was in the Scots Guards.'

'Who was Tom? I can't place him?'

'A distant cousin who would have inherited the place if Great-grandfather hadn't married. He served in the Boer

War and then he went out to Australia, leaving all his uniform here. I hope I'm not going to find the collar uncomfortable.'

'It's a good thing you have a long neck,' said Sarah, admiring the still lustrous gold-thread embroidery ornamenting the collar which came close to North's forceful chin. 'You'll have to be careful about eating. Not to get food on your moustache, I mean. Has Jane seen it?'

'Not yet. I've been barred from her room. She wants to make a grand entrance. Have this.' He handed her the untouched glass of champagne. 'I'll go and get another.'

In spite of his initial objection to anything larger than a dance for two hundred, the guest list had expanded far beyond that. Very soon four hundred and fifty people would be converging on Longwarden.

A gossip columnist for one of the tabloid newspapers, who had somehow got wind of the occasion, had implied, in his usual snide way, that it would be a night of unbridled upper-class extravagance. Sarah hoped that none of the stringers who supplied him with information had infiltrated the guest list as partners of people invited to bring someone with them.

The only authorized observer would be Mrs Betty Kenward who, under her pseudonym Jennifer, wrote a social diary for *Harpers & Queen*. A life-long devotee of racing, Mrs Kenward was a close friend of the widow of a baronet who lived a few miles away. They were coming to the ball together.

As she waited for North to come back, Sarah wondered how long it would be before she saw Nick. For her the night would begin with the first glimpse of that distinctive olive-green uniform in the line of guests waiting to be received first by her aunt, then by Jane and North and finally by Allegra and herself.

Allegra smoothed navy-blue tights on to her long legs and stood up to pull the waistband over her hips. She had locked Risconti out of her bedroom knowing, if they dressed together, they wouldn't be ready on time. It amused him to paint designs on her breasts with her cosmetics, and dark tights and high heels drove him wild. But tonight she mustn't be late going downstairs. It would annoy North and disappoint Jane if she failed to be there on time to receive the first guests with them.

Knowing that Jane and Sarah – and even her mother, for God's sake! – were all cutting a dash, although she had seen only Jane's dress, Allegra had decided for once to be a low-key presence. There had been a time when it would have given her a kick to scandalize all the fuddy-duddies by appearing in nothing but cami-knickers and shiny thirties silk stockings. Those exhibitionist days were over now.

I'm almost one of the Establishment, she thought with a grin, as she slipped her dress over her head.

It was made of printed silk georgette, patterned with copper beech leaves and their navy-blue shadows on a taupe ground. It had sheer close-fitting sleeves which ended in points on the backs of her hands and a handkerchief-pointed short skirt cut on the cross from a low-slung waistline. It must have belonged to Diana, her grandmother, who might have worn it at cocktail parties or perhaps, with a shady straw hat, at garden parties or Ascot.

On Allegra's long body it was shorter than it would have been on Diana, showing her navy-blue knees. Rejecting the cliché of a long string of amber beads, she had decided to wear only her dark-blue cloisonné earrings.

There was a knock at the door. She opened it to find Risconti standing in the corridor in cricket flannels and a striped blazer.

In the line of guests waiting to be announced, Nick stood behind a man in a Fair Isle pullover and plus-fours with a woman in a calf-length tennis dress carrying an old-fashioned racquet with Slazenger written on it. Behind him was another couple – an incongruous partnership of a dog-collared parson and a lace-capped parlour maid.

None of them asked what he was. They chatted to the people next to them but ignored him, making him doubly conscious of being on his own in an alien milieu. He had said he would come and he was here, but he didn't have to stay. Except that if he left too soon Sarah might come looking for him. If she wasn't too busy dancing with guys her family approved of, he thought unhappily.

The line moved forward. He could hear Mr Ashford announcing the names of the people ahead.

'Sir John and Lady Saxmundham ... Mr and Mrs Hugo Gargrave ... Miss Lavinia Shanklin and Mr Colin Chalfont ...'

Looking over the heads of the people in front of him, Nick was close enough to see the old Countess shaking hands and smiling, then his Lordship's tall figure with the young Countess beyond him. If Sarah was there as well, she was out of his line of vision.

'Cabo Caballero Legionario Nicholas Dean.'

To Nick's surprise, Mr Ashford announced him as if he were still a serving legionnaire. Suddenly conscious that among all these people in costume for a single night, he was in a uniform he had worn for two years and might wear again, he drew himself more erect to shake hands with his hostess.

He felt that her smile was mechanical and didn't blame her. It must be as tiring as hell, shaking hands with hundreds of guests most of whom, including himself, she might not even recognize.

The Earl did know who he was and didn't look best pleased to see him. But his wife was.

'Nick, you look great. You'll dance with me later, won't you?'

The spontaneous warmth of her welcome brought a curious lump to his throat. In her low-cut dress with her hair up and jewels sparkling in her ears and around her throat, she was the most beautiful woman he had ever seen.

Holding her hand, he bowed and raised it to his lips.

'*A sus pies, Condesa,*' he said huskily.

When, out of the corner of her eye, Sarah saw Nick kissing Jane's hand, looking more like a dashing young colonel than a *cabo*, her heart seemed almost to stop beating.

The uniform, which looked well even on a coat hanger, looked even better filled by a pair of broad shoulders and belted around a lean waist. Under the tunic he wore a lighter green shirt, the collar unbuttoned to show a coloured cravat.

She heard Allegra say, 'Hello, Nick. Have a look round for a cricketer. There's only one here at the moment. If you can find him in the crush, keep him company until we can join you, would you?'

He nodded and moved on to Sarah.

Idiotically, she found herself saying, 'I'm glad you could come,' a singularly inept choice from her stock of welcoming phrases.

Nick said nothing. His hand closed over hers. For a hopeful moment she thought he might kiss her fingers as gallantly as he had Jane's. But all she received was a rather painfully strong clasp. Then he was gone, leaving her disappointed that he hadn't shown any reaction to the way she looked.

Tark Osgood's task at the ball was to direct arriving cars into orderly rows in the paddock nearest to the house. From there, in case of rain, an awning-covered walk led guests to the east front entrance which allowed them to leave coats and furs in the care of cloakroom attendants, of whom his mother was one, before arriving in the Great Hall.

Like the other young men delegated to help with the parking, Tark was wearing his ordinary clothes covered by a shepherd's smock. This, being a pale linen colour, made him clearly visible in the light of headlamps.

Fortified by some beers beforehand, and with the prospect of a free booze-up later, he performed his duties efficiently, even to the extent of opening doors for any birds who looked as if they might give him a worthwhile leg-show when they got out.

For a time the cars arrived non-stop. Then the flow petered out. He and the others decided to pack the job in and get inside, out of the cold.

Hot snacks, coffee and beer were awaiting them in the

room which had once been the servants' hall. He spent a short time eating, drinking and chatting to the other blokes.

Then he detached himself from the group telling bawdy stories and set out for a look round the place.

'Thank God that's over,' murmured Allegra, with feeling, when the stream of arrivals had ceased and they were free to perform their duties as hostesses in a less wearing way than endlessly shaking hands. 'What I need is some more pop. Ashford, you're an angel of mercy' – this as she found that the butler, with his usual omniscience, was at her elbow with a tray of champagne.

'Have a glass yourself, Ashford. You must be parched after all that announcing,' said North.

'Thank you, m'Lord. Perhaps later.' The butler, wearing tails and a stiff winged collar, moved away.

'If his tie were white instead of black, he'd look like a guest; *more* distinguished than some of them,' Allegra said thoughtfully. 'Let's go and see if your legionnaire and my cricketer have found each other, Sarah.'

When the others were out of earshot, North said to Jane, 'Did you invite Nick Dean to come as a guest?'

'Yes I did. Did you hear him say "*A sus pies*" when he kissed my hand? That's the old-fashioned Spanish way of greeting a married woman. It means "At your feet". Wasn't that gallant?'

North looked unimpressed. 'No doubt you meant well, but it wasn't a sensible thing to do.'

'Why not?'

Keeping his voice at a level which wouldn't be overheard, he said, 'It may cause resentment among the other staff. Why should he be a guest when they're not?'

At any other time, she would have responded with spirit to his damping attitude. In the present circumstances her only desire was to remove the look of displeasure from his eyes. 'Shouldn't we start the dancing?' she suggested.

It had been arranged that the first band on duty that night would play background music until North and Jane appeared in the Saloon to open the ball with a waltz. For those who preferred fewer lights and more decibels than the ballroom would offer, a room at the other end of the house had been converted into a strobe-lit disco.

Without telling anyone else, Jane had asked the band leader to play 'A Man and a Woman'. Would North remember their first dance together at the tercentenary ball in Boston last spring?

As he gave her his arm and they made their way to the ballroom, her face was serene and smiling, showing no hint of her inner tension.

In the hush that fell over the ballroom after a roll on the drums, the band leader stepped to the microphone. Himself an old Etonian, he said, 'My lords, ladies and gentlemen, the Earl and Countess of Carlyon will open the dancing.'

All eyes turned to the couple framed in the double doorway at the end opposite the dais.

Sarah heard an elderly voice behind her say, 'Damned pretty gel, don't y'think? Likes hunting, I hear. Rides well.'

She thought 'pretty' an insipid word to apply to Jane's lovely face at any time and especially the way she looked tonight. With her black hair piled high on her head and make-up so subtle as to be invisible, she was every inch as beautiful as Flora Carlyon.

Watching the graceful sweep of Jane's skirt as her cousin took his wife in his arms and they glided on to the floor, Sarah experienced a pang of envy for the state of knowing one was loved. While everyone else continued to watch the Carlyons circle the floor, she flickered a longing glance at the sternly-set profile of her love standing beside her.

In his bachelor days, North had made many romantic and extravagant gestures in his pursuit of women.

Once, at the Hyde Park Hotel, discussing the psychology of women with a friend who was less successful with them, he had noticed a trio of women having lunch at a table by the windows overlooking Rotten Row. With the bravura induced by a stiff gin before lunch and a bottle of Weingut Annaberg with it, he had claimed that, without saying a word, he could launch an affair with the prettiest one, although he had never seen her before nor she him.

Urged by his sceptical friend to substantiate this assertion, he had risen, removed a perfect half-open rose from a lavish arrangement nearby, wiped the stem on his napkin and crossed the room to present it to her, without speaking.

'It may take her a week but she'll call me,' he had said confidently, on returning to his own table.

Two days later he had picked up the telephone to hear a female voice say, 'Lord Carlyon? This is Susan Crane. You gave me a rose at lunch on Tuesday. I've been wondering . . . have we met before?'

For several months afterwards they had spent many pleasant afternoons in bed together.

Now that phase of his life was over, possibly for good. Other women were unnecessary while his bride was an eager partner. Yet while he couldn't fault her performance in bed, their relationship was curiously unsatisfying. He had never known a girl to be as detached as Jane was. In the past they had been too prone to fall in love with him. His wife showed no signs of becoming emotional and possessive.

Earlier this evening, knowing from experience that women responded to sentimental gestures, he had asked the band to play 'A Man and a Woman' for the first dance of the evening. As, slowly, they circled the Saloon, Jane gave no indication that the music had any special significance for her. He felt she was gazing up at him only because it was expected of her and she wanted to create the impression of being the perfect wife for him. As, in almost every way, she was – beautiful, intelligent, passionate and rich. What more could any man want?

As Risconti and Allegra moved on to the floor and other people followed suit, Nick turned to Sarah.

'I can't ask you to dance. I don't know how to do this.'

Two glasses of champagne had given her the confidence to take him firmly by the hand and lead him on to the floor.

'All you have to do is shuffle in time to the music. Don't chicken out, legionnaire. I can follow you.'

Nick saw that to pull away would make them both look more foolish than if he attempted to dance. He put an arm loosely round her and took a few hesitant steps, looking down at her almost bare feet, afraid of treading on them.

'Don't look down. Hold me closer, Nick. It's like riding and I'm the horse. If we're close I can follow your aids much more easily. Like this –' She pressed herself against him.

At the touch of her slim, soft body, he felt a jolt of desire. Oblivious of everything but the need to control it, he only returned to awareness of his surroundings when she said, 'There: you see how easy it is? – If you have a natural sense of rhythm.'

Or a hard-on like the Eiffel Tower in front of two hundred people, he thought, with a flash of humour. For Christ's sake, Sarah, you must know what it does to a guy when you snuggle against him like that.

But, looking into her blue eyes, he was certain she had no idea. The dress which clung to the curves of her beautiful breasts, and the make-up she had on tonight, didn't change her essential innocence. He felt sure she had never been kissed. He wanted to be the one to teach those full, dewy lips the pleasure of kissing.

Aware of Nick's erection, the first positive evidence that he wasn't indifferent to her, Sarah followed his uncertain steps in a haze of happiness.

Claudia Dunbar was wearing a great-aunt's 1928 dance frock, oyster satin with a skirt which was short at the front and longer at the back.

She said to Allegra, 'What is Elliott Lincoln wearing? If I see him I'll introduce myself.'

'He isn't here. He telephoned yesterday to say he couldn't make it.'

'Oh, what a pity. Why not?'

'One of his children was knocked off her bike by a car. She's not seriously injured. A broken wrist and bruises. But naturally he wouldn't come away while she's in hospital.'

'Must be horrible, being separated from your children if you are a fond father,' said Claudia.

The band began another number. Ben, who had been talking to Risconti, turned to Allegra. 'Shall we try this?'

'You've been monopolizing our hostess for quite long enough, Giles. May I have the pleasure, Penelope?'

The Lord-Lieutenant of the County loomed over her, a huge man of six feet five in a frock coat with silk facings which must have belonged to somebody equally massive.

'You're looking most attractive tonight,' he told her, as they launched into a quick-step, his large hand hot on her bare back.

'Thank you, Geoffrey. You look very debonair yourself. Who was the original owner of your coat?'

'My father, matter of fact. I was the last of the brood and he was quite long in the tooth by the time I arrived. Sybil's wearing a twenties Guider's uniform. Rather hot for a dance, I said, but she didn't agree. She still has her naval uniform, you know. Can't get into it now of course. You don't seem to have that problem. Still as slim as you were as a bride, eh?' He squeezed her waist.

Pen had a shrewd idea that until tonight he had considered her skinny. She said, 'Gardening helps. Digging and so on. What do you think of my American daughter-in-law? Isn't she lovely?'

'Beautiful girl. A real charmer. North's a damned lucky chap. Everyone's saying what a fine-looking couple they make. I was having a word with your niece and her partner a moment ago. Interesting chap.'

Pen went on making appropriate replies to his practised small talk. She wished he were shorter. His shoulders were obscuring her view.

She was supported in her duty of dancing with all the old men by the hope of catching glimpses of Ashford. She had said a silent *Hear! Hear!* when Allegra had remarked on his distinguished appearance. Pen felt sure that most people present, if they hadn't given their names to him when they arrived, would have thought he was dressed up as a butler and was actually a man of authority; a surgeon perhaps, or a conductor, even a don. His face, his bearing, everything about him suggested a man of influence. She longed for the time to pass quickly, bringing her nearer to the moment, some time after the supper interval, when she would feel his arm round her.

Twin buffet tables, decorated with ivy and golden-stamened Christmas roses, stretched the length of the Gold Drawing Room from the door at one end to the door at the other.

Silver dishes of fillet of beef with pink peppercorns, sliced terrine of salmon and turbot, little pots of baked shrimps with caviar-butter sauce, ravioli stuffed with truffles, pâté of hare with walnuts, roast duck served with cranberry sauce; these were some of Jane's choices from the possibilities put forward by Liz Shakerley who, for an additional fee of £50 an hour, was herself keeping an eye on the imaginative feast created by her organization.

Nick and Sarah had supper with Rob and Emily Wareham. He was dressed as a butcher in a striped apron and straw boater, she in one of the long print dresses worn by Longwarden housemaids in the morning before World War One. They had brought Matthew with them, in his Moses basket. He was sleeping soundly in Mrs Armitage's sitting room.

'These figs stuffed with Parma ham are heaven,' said Emily, pretending to be intent on the good things to eat while keeping an interested eye on Nick's reactions to Sarah.

That he wanted her, there was no doubt. He sat, scarcely touching his supper, his eyes roving hungrily over her face and figure except when she looked at him. Then he'd eat a mouthful of food, his feelings masked.

Do be careful, Sarah, she thought, anxiously conscious of the younger girl's lack of experience in dealing with any young men, let alone a tough nut like this one. His manners were not uncouth, largely because he had spent so much time with Sarah when they were younger. But the more Emily studied him, the more uneasy she felt. There was something alien about him, and the uniform underlined it. Rob was a big burly man but he looked, and was, of a mild, gentle disposition. Nick looked neither. He had an engaging smile. But his face in repose was harder than it should be at twenty.

Later, when supper was over, and they were in a group which included several well-known eventing riders, Rob asked Lucinda Green to dance with him. With Sarah already spoken for by David Green, Lucinda's Australian husband, Nick turned to Emily.

'I'm not much of a dancer,' he warned her.

As it was now after midnight the others decided to have a look at the disco.

'Would you mind if I took a quick peep at Matthew en route, Nick?' Emily asked.

He came with her to the room where the baby was asleep.

Presently, as they approached the entrance to the disco where a temporary tent-like lobby had been erected to help baffle the noise from within, they became aware of a fracas going on outside.

Tark Osgood, noticeably unsteady on his feet, was trying to persuade a young girl to dance with him and refusing to take no for an answer.

The girl looked flustered and nervous. The boy with her looked indignant but unable to handle the situation. He was not more than seventeen and his dinner jacket emphasized his immaturity.

'Oh, lord,' murmured Emily worriedly.

'I think I'd better deal with this. You sit down here for a minute.' Nick pointed out an empty chair.

'Nick, wait – shall I get Rob to help you?'

He shook his head. 'The less fuss the better.'

Hoping he knew what he was doing, she watched him go up to Tark who was looming over the girl, insisting she dance with him.

When Nick tapped him on the shoulder, he looked

around and took a step back to maintain his uncertain balance.

By now an embarrassed silence had fallen on everyone near enough to have noticed what was happening.

Emily heard Nick say quietly, 'You're off limits here, chum. I should get back to your own party.'

'Mind your own fucking business. Piss off!' Tark told him loudly.

Emily saw Nick's jaw clench and heard a gasp of disgust from one of the older people there. Then Tark grabbed the front of Nick's tunic with one hand and made a fist with the other.

'You heard me, cunt. If you don't want this in your gob –'

The rest was lost in a yelp of surprise.

By the seemingly effortless expedient of putting both thumbs into the palm grasping his tunic, and twisting Tark's wrist with the sideways swing of his own body, Nick turned him from a loud-mouthed aggressor into a deflated bully whose threat changed into a plea of 'Hang on, mate. You're breaking my arm.'

'I'll break them both, and your legs, if you don't keep quiet and behave.'

Nick's voice was still low and calm. With Tark's elbow somehow anchored under his armpit, he marched him away.

'I shan't be long,' he said to Emily, as he passed.

Shortly afterwards, the curtains screening the doors to the disco parted and her husband and the others emerged.

'Hello, darling. What's happened to Nick?' Rob asked.

'He had to get rid of that horrible Osgood youth who was in here rather pie-eyed and pestering a girl.' Emily described what had happened.

'Sounds like a long armlock,' said Rob, when she had told them the manner in which Nick had led Tark away. 'Lucky he happened along. We're going back to the ballroom. It's pretty deafening in there. I'm getting too old to stand it for more than ten minutes.'

Emily went with the others, meeting Nick on the way. He was visibly embarrassed when their comments revealed

496

she had given a graphic and, he seemed to feel, over-dramatic account of his handling of the incident.

Although full of admiration for him, and pleased by the others' commendations, Sarah had something else on her mind. At the first chance, she drew him aside.

'I'm going to the yard. If Tark has been wandering around in places where he shouldn't be, he may have been to the stables and unsettled the horses. I know it's not likely, but he never stops smoking and I'd rather be safe than sorry.'

'You'll get cold out there in that thin dress. I'll go and check. There's no need for you to.'

She shook her head. 'I'd be glad if you'd come with me, but I want to go myself. I'll get a coat from the flower room.'

The room with two deep stone sinks where the flowers were arranged was also a storage place for garden hats, wellington boots, creels and waders, game and cartridge bags, and an assortment of warm or waterproof clothing.

Sarah borrowed a long knitted coat which belonged to her aunt.

'I should put on some rubber boots,' Nick advised, from the doorway. 'Those silver things are pretty but they aren't much protection.'

'If you put on boots as well, we can walk round the house and see how it looks all lit up,' Sarah suggested.

'Mm, a spot of fresh air wouldn't be a bad idea.'

He found a pair of boots to fit him and a hip-length quilted waistcoat to wear over his tunic.

After finding the stables as quiet as they should be at that time of night, they passed under the arch and walked down towards the ha-ha.

'A fine night,' said Nick, looking up at the starry sky.

Sarah murmured agreement. The grass was soggy with dew. Without socks her feet were cold in the boots, but she would rather be out here, chilly and alone with him, than warm and surrounded by people.

They came to a spot from which they could see the south and west fronts of Longwarden and all the principal rooms,

497

their tall windows blazing with light, those curtains which had been closed when the guests arrived now drawn back and some windows opened to reduce the heat generated by so many people.

'It looks beautiful, doesn't it?' Sarah was awed by the splendour of the great house *en fête*.

They could hear the music from the ballroom and see the dancers in motion. In spite of some cars departing, the ball was still in full swing.

For a long time she stood entranced by an aspect of the house she had never seen before and might never see again. Although perhaps now, with Jane's vast fortune at their disposal, North and Jane would often give dances.

She shivered, making Nick say, 'You're cold. Here, put this on.' He stripped off the quilted waistcoat and bundled her into it, like someone dressing a child. 'We must go back. You could get a chill, getting hot dancing and then . . .' His scolding tailed off as he fastened the topmost button and looked at her uplifted face.

He took her cold face in hands which were warm and strong and very gentle, as if he were handling a piece of delicate porcelain. His fingertips stroked her temples.

Then he said hoarsely, 'Oh, Sarah . . .' and she closed her eyes.

In the ballroom Jane was dancing with a man with twine tied below the knees of his corduroy trousers and a moleskin waistcoat over his collarless shirt. He had told her he was meant to be a farm labourer of fifty years earlier and now he was talking at length about the farming of those days.

She was trying to look interested, but her mind was on North who hadn't danced with her again since the ball began, or even thrown her a smile as he passed her with the other partners.

She knew he was expected to dance with as many women as possible. But considering his usual disregard for the conventions, she felt it wasn't only duty which was keeping him away from her. He was annoyed about something. The only reason she could think of was her having asked Nick to the ball – which didn't seem much of a reason for ignoring your wife at what was supposed to be, in part, a celebration of your marriage to her, she thought unhappily.

She could see him now, the realistic black moustache emphasizing the smiling sensuality of his mouth as he inclined his head to listen to the talkative woman in his arms.

Only a few hours ago we were in bed together. Now I might not exist for all the notice he's taking of me, Jane thought, with a lump in her throat and tears threatening. Then she felt angry with herself for allowing him to upset her. That was where her mother-in-law had gone wrong, chiefly with Allegra but to some extent with her son. Pen longed for their good opinion but was too uncertain of herself, too humble, ever to win it. Allegra and North were strong people with no time for weakness. Jane knew if she showed him how easily he could hurt her, she didn't stand a chance of holding him. She had to make him uncertain of his power to hold her and that, right now, meant behaving as if she had been too busy enjoying herself to notice his neglect.

With an effort of will, she began to pay close attention to her partner's conversation.

Sarah had her arms round his neck when Nick came to his senses and wrenched his mouth from the soft lips which had parted so willingly under the pressure of his.

His hands searched for and found her wrists and broke her loving embrace.

'We must go back,' he said roughly.

Hardly knowing what he was doing, his body on fire with longing, he began to stride back to the house, pulling her after him.

Floundering over the sodden grass in loose wellingtons, her feet numb, her mind in a whirl from the impact of her first kiss, Sarah thought they were on their way to the archway room, there to continue kissing in warmth and privacy.

That this wasn't Nick's intention became clear to her only when he passed the door to the stairway and made to re-enter the house by the way they had left it.

When she saw his face in the light of the scullery passage, it began to dawn on her that his reaction to kissing her wasn't the same as hers. He was actually scowling.

Partly from being out of breath and partly from confusion, she didn't ask what was the matter but followed him back to the flower room.

'My feet are freezing.' She sat down to put on her sandals.

He wiped his palms, damp from the wet boots, on the roller towel by the sinks. Then he rubbed them briskly together and came to crouch down beside her and massage her feet.

'You must have marvellous circulation. Your hands are like toast,' she told him.

His hair had grown out of the convict-crop he had had when he first came back. He still kept it unfashionably short but he had a well-shaped skull and somehow it suited him. She wanted to put out her hand and stroke the thick brown bay hair with the endearing tuft sticking up at the crown, but she wasn't sure he would like it.

'Nick . . . are you cross?' she asked uncertainly.

'With myself, yes,' he answered shortly.

'Why?'

'I shouldn't have kissed you.' He finished kneading her feet and moved away to put on his shoes.

'Why not?'

'Put on your sandals. The others will be wondering where we've got to.'

'We haven't been gone very long. Only about twenty minutes. Anyway why shouldn't we go off on our own if we feel like it?'

'It's partly your party. You're not supposed to disappear.'

'I've talked to everyone who was on my list and a lot of people who weren't. I've done my share of the hostessing. Nick, that's dodging the question. *Why* shouldn't you have kissed me? Don't say because you used to work here and are helping out now. Why should it stop us kissing if we want to? You wanted to and so did I.'

He said gruffly, 'Okay, we both wanted it – but for different reasons. You're still a kid, Sarah. You want to kiss and hold hands and that's about all you want. I can't stop there. I'm used to . . . sleeping with girls. I don't want a big romance. I want sex . . . free and easy . . . no strings. That's the way soldiers are.' His mouth twisted. 'It's because someone like me got involved with a girl like you that I'm around.'

She wanted to say, 'I love you. I want to sleep with you. I want to spend every day and night of my life with you.'

But without knowing if he loved her, she couldn't expose her own feelings. In the moments before he kissed her, she had felt sure he did love her. He had touched her so tenderly, spoken her name with such longing.

Now, when he talked in this tone, she wasn't sure any more. He sounded hard, brutal almost.

That there had been other girls wasn't upsetting. She had never expected that he would be like her, a virgin. It was only by a combination of loving him since she was sixteen and being too involved with the horses to have time for anything else that she still had no experience. The wounding thing was not that there had been girls in his life, but that he should still prefer those casual sexual encounters to the heart-and-soul love she could give him.

Nick saw by her stricken face how much he had hurt her. He had a mad impulse to snatch her back into his arms and tell her it was a lie; he didn't want anyone but her.

But he had already spent hours trying to see some way round the obstacles which lay between them. If he had been an Australian, like David Green, and if he could ride well enough to excel at eventing, there might have been hope that, one day, her family would accept him.

As he didn't have an overseas accent but a local one, and he didn't want to spend his life riding and schooling horses, he hadn't a hope of being accepted. There was just no way his life and hers could mesh.

With this in mind, he fought down the dangerous impulse

and forced himself to say harshly, 'So let's do ourselves a favour and forget it happened, okay?'

In silence, perilously close to tears, she followed him out of the room.

When they reached the Great Hall, she managed to control her voice long enough to say formally, 'Would you excuse me, Nick? I'm going up to tidy my hair.'

He watched her go up the wide staircase, the low cut of her dress showing a vee of creamy bare back, the sequins and bugles shimmering with every movement of her hips, her legs as slim and graceful as a dancer's as she moved swiftly upwards on the high silver heels.

She looked poised and sophisticated, but he had a gut-wrenching feeling that when she was safely in her room she would burst into tears.

If he could have followed his instinct, he would have taken the stairs three at a time and caught up with her. But it was the instinct to kiss her which had got them into this mess of deliberate lies on his side and hurt feelings on hers. For her sake, he hoped those feelings were only the girlish crush her cousin had warned him about. As soon as a new groom was found, he would leave and she would get over it.

He would have liked to believe he would get over loving her. He knew he wouldn't. One kiss on a winter night was going to haunt him for ever.

Pen, who still remembered vividly the time when no one had wanted to dance with her, now found herself in the contrary predicament. Men who had known her for years and never taken the smallest interest in her were suddenly vying for her attention, actually flirting with her, some of them in a jocular way, some more suggestively.

They were all, she realized, rather drunk. She herself had been drinking more than usual to give herself courage. Having always believed she had no head for alcohol, it had surprised her to find that the third glass of champagne had no more effect than the first, except to make her a great deal more cheerful and relaxed than she ever remembered feeling before. Perhaps she was one of those people of whom it was said they were born several drinks under par. If how she felt now was par for the generality of human beings, it seemed a great pity she hadn't discovered it before.

Life begins at fifty, she thought, with a giggle which luckily coincided with the end of a shaggy-dog story her partner had been telling for at least five minutes.

'Thought that would amuse you,' he twinkled at her, his eyeballs a network of red veins. 'My wife has absolutely no sense of humour, y'know. Given up telling her jokes. Given up the other thing too,' he added, in a confidential murmur. 'Separate bedrooms and all that. Damned unfair on a man who's still fit and virile, but there you are. Some women are like that. Nothing to be done about it . . . unless one meets someone else in a similar situation . . . lonely . . . looking for affection.'

As Pen took in the implication, the music came to an end. He released her right hand but kept his arm round her.

'What about finding a quiet corner where we can talk? Shall we play truant for half an hour?' His hand was exploring her hips.

Pen felt kindly disposed towards everyone, even lecherous old bores whose wives understandably spurned their revolting attentions. In a mood of goodwill to all men, she searched for a polite excuse which wouldn't offend him.

Before she found one, a voice said, 'Excuse me, m'Lady. I have a message for Sir Robert.'

'A message? What message?' Sir Robert snapped, looking annoyed by the butler's interruption.

'From Lady Frome,' Ashford told him. 'She would like to go home. She's waiting for you in the Great Hall, sir.'

'Go home? The night's still young. No intention of going home yet,' Sir Robert said, gazing at Pen.

'I think Lady Frome may be feeling unwell, sir.'

'You had better go and see,' said Pen.

'Oh, very well . . . but *I* shan't be leaving. I'll be back in a few minutes. Don't go away, m'dear.' With a leer at her and a glance of dislike at Ashford, the bearer of bad tidings, he shambled away.

There was no one else near to hear the butler say quietly, 'Amazing he can still stand up considering what he's drunk this evening. I would have rescued you earlier if I'd seen him being a nuisance.'

'Rescued me? Do you mean you made up that message? His wife *isn't* waiting for him?'

He gave her a bland look. 'I merely anticipated Lady Frome's reaction when she sees the signs that Sir Robert's blood pressure must be perilously high. You did want to be relieved of his presence, didn't you, m'Lady?'

'Oh, yes – very much. I'm delighted. You appeared at exactly the right moment.' Exactly came out slightly slurred. She wondered if he'd noticed. 'Now you can do something else for me.'

'Certainly, m'Lady.'

She thought he looked faintly perturbed, as if he sensed that his unflappability was about to be tested.

She smiled at him. 'Dance with me.'

His expression remained unchanged. For some seconds they stared at each other until he said calmly, 'I think not. May I get you some coffee?'

'No, thank you. I want to dance.' She stepped closer, placing her left hand lightly on his shoulder, her other hand raised for him to hold. 'With you, Mr Ashford.'

As she spoke, to her surprise first one and then all three chandeliers were switched off, leaving the ballroom lit by a subdued greenish glow from spotlights concealed among banks of plants. The effect was to transform the Saloon into an underwater cavern with large clusters of shimmering fish up near the roof and great glistering strands of golden seaweed climbing the walls.

'I didn't know this was going to happen. Did you?' Looking up made her sway. She clutched his shoulder for support.

A hand at her waist, he steadied her. Then the music began and his arm went round her and they were dancing.

*   *   *

Jane was dancing with Risconti. Over his shoulder she caught sight of her mother-in-law's backless dress. Seen from behind Pen could have been thirty. Even from the front, now that she was lightly made up she looked years younger than her age. It wasn't surprising all the older men wanted to dance with her.

Jane did a double-take as she saw who was partnering Pen now. She was even more startled when they turned and she saw the entranced expression on her mother-in-law's face.

Oh my goodness! If North sees this he'll go crazy, she thought, torn between dismay and amusement. They look amazingly good together. Allegra is right: Ashford's a dishy guy when you really look at him.

Risconti turned his head to see what was holding her attention. If he was surprised by what he saw, he didn't say so.

'Until tonight I hadn't noticed the likeness between Allegra and her mother,' he remarked. 'The difference in their colouring and the way they dress obscures the similarities between them. Tonight they are more easily seen . . . although I don't think Allegra would be pleased to be told they are alike in some ways,' he added dryly.

'You're right. I hadn't noticed it either, but now that you've pointed it out I can see there is a resemblance, especially at certain angles,' Jane agreed. 'But they're totally different as people, aren't they? Not at all alike in temperament.'

'I'm not sure. Perhaps Lady Carlyon's character is hidden in the same way that her figure is usually concealed by the clothes she wears for her work,' he said thoughtfully. 'Take what she's doing at this moment. Is it usual for English countesses to dance with their butlers? I don't think so.'

'I believe it used to be a tradition at servants' balls in the old days,' said Jane.

'It may be that Lady Carlyon has had more alcohol than usual and is letting her hair down,' Risconti suggested. 'She may seem old to you, but she isn't too old to want a lover. A discreet affair with the butler would be good for her ... for them both. If I can persuade Allegra and you can persuade your husband not to interfere. You wouldn't disapprove yourself, would you?'

'Not for moral reasons,' said Jane. 'I'd be glad of anything that would make Penelope happier. She had a miserable marriage, I've been told. But I'd also hate to lose Mr Ashford, either because he left voluntarily or North made him leave. How else could it end? North doesn't approve of Nick as a boyfriend for Sarah. Can you imagine his reaction to his mother having an affair with his butler?'

'Yes, I can,' said Risconti, amused. 'There would be a mega-ton explosion of disapproval from North and Allegra. They don't see their mother as a woman who needs to be loved before it's too late.'

'*Dum vivimus, vivamus*,' she murmured. 'It's the family motto. It means "While we're alive, let's live to the full".'

'I came across something similar the other day. *Carpe diem, quam minibus credula postero*. "Seize today; put as little trust as you can in tomorrow." It's the way everyone should live, but not many people do ... unless they've been told time is running out for them.'

North was looking for his cousin, to dance with her. She wasn't in the ballroom or the disco. She wasn't with the eventing crowd.

'Have you seen Sarah?' he asked Emily Wareham.

'She and Nick went to check the horses. Perhaps they haven't come back yet.'

Perhaps they won't, he thought grimly, remembering all the dances at which he and girls whose names he could barely remember had slipped away from the public rooms.

At the time it had seemed part and parcel of every country-house jump-up. Reefing yards of taffeta or net so that the girl could reappear without looking unduly crumpled had been one of his skills. He had no doubt that numerous couples had been, were now or would be similarly engaged here tonight. As far as he was concerned they could screw where they liked as long as it wasn't on his bed. But he took a different view when the couple were Nick Dean and Sarah.

He couldn't deny that Dean looked good in his uniform – the type of upstanding young soldier guaranteed to touch the hearts of old ladies and impressionable girls. Jane thought him harmless. North didn't. He knew more about young men's urges than she did, and the way Sarah looked tonight . . .

He walked briskly through the house, hoping he would be in time to break it up before Dean fucked her.

Light beaming down from the uncurtained half-moon window of the archway room confirmed his conviction that they were up there together. That the light was on might be a good or bad sign.

He went swiftly up the circular stairs and rapped on the door at the top. At first there was silence from within, then a soft thud he recognized as stockinged feet hitting the floor.

A moment or two later the door was opened by Nick. He had removed his tunic and his shirt was open to the waist, showing a muscular chest. For a moment they stared at each other, the antagonism between them palpable.

'If you're looking for Sarah, she's not here.' He swung the door wider, showing the cover still on the bed, but rumpled, and a bottle of Spanish brandy on the table beside it. 'The last time I saw her she was going to her room to fix her face.'

'I see. I take it you aren't coming back to the dance?'

Nick shook his head. 'I've had enough of mixing with my betters for one night,' he said sarcastically.

He was not drunk, but he'd had enough to break down normal restraints, North realized. Something must have happened between them for him to be here on his own, knocking back Fundador. Perhaps he had started something but Sarah had backed off. She might have more sense than North had given her credit for.

'You can tell Sarah I'll look after the horses tomorrow.

507

She can have a lie-in,' Nick added, his tone only marginally less hostile.

North nodded. 'I'll do that. Goodnight.'

Pen opened her eyes in a room she didn't recognize. It seemed to be a small sitting room. She was lying on a sofa, her head and shoulders supported by cushions, her body covered from foot to chin by a motoring rug.

Where was she? How had she got here? Why was she feeling like death?

The last thing she could remember was dancing . . . dancing with Ashford. After that, nothing. A blank. A total black-out.

I must have passed out, she thought, appalled. Where? In the ballroom? How frightful!

For some time she lay still, trying to penetrate the black fog of nothingness between her last rather blurred memory of the dimly lit ballroom and waking up here in what she now took to be her butler's sitting room. Presumably one of the two doors she could see led to his bedroom with the bathroom leading off that.

Thinking of the bathroom made her realize she wanted to pee. That must be why she had woken. What time was it? Where was Ashford? In bed in the inner room?

Putting off the rug, very gingerly she sat up and lowered her unshod feet to the floor. Her shoes, placed neatly together, were beside the leg of the sofa.

Looking round for a clock she saw heavy dark red moreen curtains drawn across the window. A tray with a coffee pot on it and two cups had been left on a low table. One cup had been used, one hadn't. What did that signify?

An old country-made longcase standing in the corner behind the sofa showed a quarter to four. The dance must still be going on. In fifteen minutes' time the helpers would be serving breakfast to revive those with flagging energy and sober up the inebriated – one of them the host's mother.

I had no idea she was a dipso . . . as bad as her husband, he was often half plastered . . . nothing more disgusting than a drunken woman . . .

She could imagine the comments; and the eagerness with which those who had not been witnesses to her disgrace would be apprised by those who had. By now everyone would know. How could she face them?

Thankful to find she wasn't unsteady on her feet, nor was her dress impossibly creased, she stepped into her shoes. Her bag, containing a comb, lipstick and an aerosol flacon of *Magie Noire* which Jane had given her, was nowhere to be seen. She had a hazy recollection of leaving it somewhere in the Music Room, hidden behind some flowers to be retrieved when necessary.

Both bedroom and bathroom were as immaculately neat as she would have expected his living quarters to be. Peering at her reflection in the handbasin mirror, she was surprised to find that she looked comparatively normal. She certainly didn't feel it. Her head wasn't aching but she felt indescribably ghastly, worse than after a bad bout of flu. Taking care not to let any part of her skirt fall in the water, she used the lavatory.

A cake of green soap, a nail-brush and, hanging from the shower taps, a face-cloth and a loofah strap were the only belongings on view. But there was a medicine cabinet at one side of the mirror and although reluctant to open it, she had to find a comb.

Neatly arranged on the shelves were the things she had expected to see: a safety razor, a toothbrush in a tumbler, dental floss, shampoo, Bandaids. Also a silver-capped bottle half-full of liquid the colour of Jane's ball dress. Pen took it out and looked at the label. It was after-shave lotion. *Eau Sauvage* by Dior. It must be this she had smelt while they were dancing, not cheek to cheek but closer than they had ever been before – or ever would be again, after what had happened. How he must despise her: a woman of her age, getting blotto.

On the bottom shelf of the cupboard was a man's black-backed hairbrush, upturned, with a horn comb stuck in the bristles. As she used it to tidy her hair, she knew that although she shrank from facing everyone, she had to do it. Not to be seen again would only make matters worse.

However much she cringed inwardly, she must brave it out as best she could.

After all it wasn't a crime to drink too much, unless one were driving a car. It was just a stupid undignified thing to do; a lapse of which most of the men present, and quite a number of the women, had doubtless been guilty before her.

Longing to creep up to her room, there to lock the door and crawl into bed, Pen put the comb back in place and returned to the sitting room. She was folding the rug and mustering the courage to return to the dance when the door opened and Ashford came in, looking surprised to see her up.

'When am I going to see you again?' asked Barney, Claudia Dunbar's younger brother and one of the extra men organized by Allegra.

'I don't know,' said Sarah. 'I'm busy with my horses most of the time.'

'But not *all* the time, surely? Your cousin has a flat in town doesn't she? You aren't stuck for somewhere to stay if you want to spend a night in London?'

'Yes, she does . . . but I don't very often. I rather loathe London actually.'

He was nice but there was no point in agreeing to meet him. She had only been dancing with Barney because Nick wasn't there.

After rushing up to her room, intending to cry her eyes out, she had realized she couldn't. As one of the people for whom the dance was being given, she had a duty to stay, no matter how unhappy she was.

Later on, with a searching look which suggested he knew they had had a row of some sort, North had given her the message that Nick had turned in early and would attend to the horses if she overslept.

Since then, having danced with Barney more than anyone else, giving him grounds to believe he had made a hit with her, she must now make it clear that he hadn't.

'You see I'm a country mouse and you're obviously a

town mouse and we shouldn't normally meet,' she began.

'Ah, but I happen to have a country mouse grandmother who lives not far from here and is always pressing me to stay. In fact I'm spending the night there. Claudia and Ben have to go back to London, but I'm putting up with Granny. So how about lunch tomorrow?'

'Good morning, m'Lady. I thought you would wish to be woken in time to join the others for breakfast.' Ashford balanced a small tray on one hand while closing the door with the other.

'Good morning,' Pen answered, feeling her face turning red as it had in her youth on the all too frequent occasions when, as now, she had wanted to sink through the floor and never reappear.

He put down the tray which carried a glass of bright orange liquid, a small teapot, milk and one cup and saucer.

'I expect your nap has refreshed you, but you might care to try a glass of vitamin C. It's a very good pick-me-up after a late night, I find. I've put in four one-gram tablets, the dose I give myself sometimes.' He picked up the other tray. 'I'll take this back to the pantry. Not being accustomed to staying up into the small hours, you had fallen asleep by the time I had made it. I thought it best not to disturb you. Among such a large number of guests, I don't think your absence has been noticed.'

As he turned to leave, she said impulsively, 'Mr Ashford . . . don't go.'

He paused, looking calmly at her, no hint of censure in his face. But what was he thinking?

As she strove to find words of apology, he said, 'I believe I know what you want to tell me, m'Lady.'

'Do you?' she said doubtfully.

'Some hours ago you did me the honour of dancing with me. I then had what might be considered the presumption to suggest we had coffee here . . . one of the few quiet places in the house at the time. But you can rely on me to realize that the licence allowable on a special occasion doesn't extend beyond that occasion.'

'No, Mr Ashford, that wasn't what I was going to say. I was going to ... to thank you for looking after me. If you would do one more thing ... I think I left a small envelope bag – it matches these shoes – behind the flowers in the Music Room. If you can find it, would you retrieve it for me, please? I'd like to repair my lipstick before I emerge.'

'Certainly.'

When he had gone, she sipped the vitamin drink. Clearly a direct apology would have embarrassed him. He'd been at pains to pretend it had been fatigue not champagne which had laid her out. Obviously he had brought her here because it was the best way to get her out of sight quickly before she keeled over. He had spoken of being presumptuous, but she knew he would never have suggested having coffee in his sitting room except as an expedient in an awkward situation.

When Tark regained consciousness, nine hours after passing out at Longwarden, he found his mother enraged by the humiliation of having him brought home unconscious after making a drunken exhibition of himself.

'If you're going to take to the booze like your dad, you can find somewhere else to live,' she told him angrily. 'When they came and said you was dead drunk, I was that embarrassed I didn't know where to put myself. And that weren't all, let me tell you. They say you was using bad language outside the disco and they had to get that young fellow what works for Miss Sarah to make you behave yourself.'

Tark was feeling extremely unwell. His mother's voice was like a pneumatic drill boring through his sensitive skull. When he could stand it no more, he yelled at her to shut up and leave him alone. She did, slamming the door of the front room where he was lying on the couch with a bang which lanced every nerve in his hungover body.

It was the following day before he began to feel normal, by which time Mrs Osgood had treated him to repeated accounts of his misdemeanours. He could remember having a good snout round the place, and he had a hazy recollection of being made to look foolish by some bastard in a fancy uniform. This, it turned out, had been the bloke Sharon had been chatting up in the pub one night.

With his evening classes finished until the following term, Nick was again at a loose end.

Mr Ashford was taking advantage of the lull after the ball to have a few quiet evenings before Christmas. Unlike the butler, Nick wasn't much of a reader, nor did he care for television. In summer he would have been able to go for long evening walks, but at this time of year it was dark by four-thirty. For want of an alternative, he went down to the Longwarden Arms.

As she had on a previous occasion, Sharon Cook came in and chatted him up. This time she wasn't followed by Tark.

For a combination of reasons he was staying indoors for a few nights. There was some good stuff on telly. He still wasn't feeling too sharp. He wasn't in the mood for mickey-taking. More importantly, he was skint. He couldn't afford to go out until later in the week. The mood she was in, it was no use asking the old cow to loan him a few quid. Nor could he nick some from her bag. She made sure she kept it by her. He had his work cut out to get her to bring him a packet of fags from the shop.

With Tark out of the way for a bit, Sharon had three nights in succession to work on Nick Dean and get him interested. She had found him attractive before. Now, after what she had heard about him being a guest at the ball and getting the better of Tark, he was even more desirable. With Nick as her boyfriend, she could tell Tark to get stuffed. She had only kept on going with him because there was nobody better around.

For two nights she made little headway, although he did buy her a drink when his own glass was empty. But she had to do all the talking. He listened but he didn't say much.

On the third night she wore her red sweater dress with black lace tights and white boots, and the red plastic spiral earrings she'd bought off a stall in Melchester market the Saturday before. She had washed her hair and spent an hour on her make-up and she knew she looked good. Her mother was out baby-sitting for Sharon's sister and wouldn't be back until late. Sharon had been able to borrow her mother's three-quarter-length black suede coat. It had a white fur collar which went with her boots. She would just have to take a chance that none of Mum's mates saw her in it and told on her.

Nick didn't seem to like the pub much. Even when the fellers tried to be friendly, they didn't get no change out of him. He was a loner, was Nick. Always had been. Always would be. Except maybe with the right girl.

As she tittuped down to the Arms on the stiletto heels of her white plastic boots, ignoring the whistles and shouts of ''Allo, Big Tits' from that cheeky young Bobby Botley and his mates, Sharon's mind was on weddings. If she could get something going with Nick Dean, it wasn't impossible she could be married at Easter. And if Nick was getting married most likely he'd get given his own place on Lord Carlyon's estate. There were two empty boarded-up lodge houses besides the one at the main gate where Ted Rivington lived. Done up, they could be okay.

Nick was there before her, standing at the quiet end of the bar with a half-empty pint glass of lager in front of him and a moody look on his face. He was ever so strange for his age. Didn't smoke. Didn't play the machines. Wasn't interested in football or motorbikes. He didn't even talk about his job or have a moan about the people who employed him. You couldn't call him good company. Yet somehow he turned her on just by the way he stood there, his clean jeans as tight as a sausage-skin over his muscular bum.

'Hallo, Nick. Mind if I join you?' She smiled and opened her coat, displaying the reason for her nickname among the lads of the village.

'Oh . . . hallo, Sharon.'

Sharon was pleased when he asked, 'Same as last night?' and ordered for her.

She climbed on a stool, her short skirt riding even higher over her black lace thighs. Opening her bag, she rummaged in the clutter of make-up, gum, mints and tissues for her cigarettes and lighter.

'Not long to Christmas now. Done all your shopping?' she asked, as she lit up.

'Haven't much to do,' he answered. 'What about you?'

'I've just got my dad's present left. Men are ever so difficult to shop for. Got any suggestions?'

Given an opening like that, most fellers would have snapped back a sexy answer, but he missed his chance.

'What does he do in his spare time? Gardening? Angling?'

'He used to belong to a fishing club but he's given it up. He don't do much in the garden and he's got all the tools he needs for that. It's a problem to know what to give him.'

The barmaid brought her drink and Nick paid for it. Sharon wondered how much he earned.

'Thanks, Nick. Cheers.' She picked up the glass. She was wearing her new stick-on nails, painted to match her dress.

'Cheers.' He sounded as if he was thinking about something else.

After a few minutes more of trying to get him to talk to her, she began to feel a bit peeved that he hadn't said anything nice about the way she looked. Even Tark took a bit of notice, or had, at the beginning.

At that moment Nick drained his glass and put it back on the bar. He looked at his watch. 'I must go.'

In an instant her feeling of pique changed to panic that he was leaving.

'I haven't bought you a drink yet. Have another beer.'

'Not right now, thanks all the same, Sharon.'

'Why've you got to rush off? Is there something good on the telly? You can watch it up mine if you like. Mum's out and so is my dad. We'll have the house to ourselves. We can take some drinks and crisps back with us.'

Most of the fellers she knew would have jumped at the chance to get her alone on the front-room couch with her parents out of the way. Mr and Mrs Cook didn't like Tark and wouldn't have him in the house. But they wouldn't mind Nick being there. Since the night of the fancy-dress ball, it had been all round the village that Nick Dean had been present, not as a car-park attendant, but dressed up, ever so smart, and dancing with Sarah Lomax, Lady Allegra and even the new Lady Carlyon.

'It's nice of you, Sharon, but no thanks. There's nothing I specially want to' see on TV. You can buy me a drink some other time. See you.' With a smile and a nod he left her, saying a general goodnight to the other customers.

For a few moments after he had gone, Sharon couldn't believe he had turned down her invitation. Bloody cheek. Bloody nerve, she thought angrily. Dancing with those stuck-up gits must have gone to his head.

Soon afterwards two girls she knew came in and joined her, their admiring comments on her outfit balm to her rage and pain. But she brooded about Nick's treatment on the way home and her humiliation was exacerbated when her father came in, having spent the evening playing darts at the Angel, and mentioned seeing Nick in the snug.

Sharon went up to bed, seething. She couldn't sleep for the thought of Nick looking at his watch, pretending he had a reason for leaving when all the time he'd only been going down the street to the Angel to get away from her. She had taken some rotten treatment from fellers in her time, but never more rotten than that. She buried her face in the pillow, weeping with anger and disappointment.

In the morning the pillowcase was smeared with the make-up she hadn't bothered to remove before flopping into bed. Her eyelids felt swollen and sore.

'Sh-a-a-ron! You'll be late for work again,' her mother screamed up the stairs.

'I'll be down in a minute,' she bawled back, with a muttered 'Nagging old cow,' as she pushed back the continental quilt.

It was a quiet morning at the supermarket. In the intervals between customers, she sat slumped on her stool at the check-out, chewing gum and thinking what a lousy lot of sods the male sex were, not only Nick but Tark and all the other fellers she'd ever had anything to do with.

Gradually, a way to retaliate began to form in her mind. It was such an easy method of getting her own back for the slight she had suffered last night that she ought to have thought of it straight off.

If it worked, and she felt sure it would, it would take Mr High and Mighty Nick Dean down a peg or two.

Jane was giving Risconti what he thought would be the final sitting for her portrait. That evening he and Allegra were flying to New York, returning on Christmas Eve.

After a five-minute break to walk round the room and stretch herself, she had just resumed her position when Ashford appeared.

'I'm sorry to disturb you, sir,' he said to Risconti, 'but Lady Carlyon is wanted on the telephone. It's a long-distance call, m'Lady. From Paris. Rather than keep the caller waiting while I fetched you, I suggested she rang back after a five-minute interval.'

At the mention of Paris, Jane had leapt from her chair. '*She?* Did she give her name?'

'Yes, m'Lady. Mademoiselle Polignac.'

Marie-Simone. At last.

Tark had come out of seclusion to cash his social security cheque.

There was almost no lunch-hour trade at the supermarket. The manager always went home, leaving one of the girls on duty. Today it was Sharon's turn. When he had nothing better to do, Tark sometimes kept her company and at present he wanted to find out, in a roundabout way, how much face he had lost from the incident at the fancy-dress do.

'Hello, stranger. You feeling better?' Sharon asked, warmly concerned, when he lounged through the IN door.

'I int been ill. I were skint. Couldn't go nowhere till my cheque come.'

517

'You could have had a loan off me,' Sharon said untruthfully. Although Tark was a free spender, when he had it, she felt you could kiss goodbye to anything he borrowed. 'Everyone thought you was staying indoors cos you'd got two big shiners or lost your front teeth or something . . . after that punch-up with Nick Dean.'

Tark's olive skin turned the colour of pickled beetroot. 'Who told you all that shit?'

'I heard people talking about it as they come through the check-out. I'd have come to see how you was, but I thought your Mum might shut the door in my face. I know she don't like me.'

'She don't like none of my birds. Never has. What else d'you hear?'

'Nothing much. Except that my Dad said Nick was in the Angel last night, swanking about how he'd roughed you up. He's been coming down to the pubs regular, every night since the dance. I seen him when I was in the Arms with Mandy and Doreen. If I was you and been made to look a right berk, I'd catch him when he'd had a skinful on his way home. Even things up, like.'

Tark helped himself to a choc bar from the display by the till. 'Yeah, I might do that,' he muttered, tearing the wrapper. 'That bleeder's too big for his boots.'

Sharon watched him bite into the bar and wondered which of the two would win if they did have a fight. At the rate she had seen Nick drinking, he wouldn't be even half-pissed by closing time. He was taller than Tark but not as burly. She thought the outcome would be that both would take a bad bashing before either would give in. Serve 'em right, she thought coldly. Serve Nick right for making her feel small. Serve Tark right for all the times he had fucked her quickly and roughly, like her feelings didn't matter as long as he got his kicks.

'He thinks he's so tough cos he's been in the army abroad. I don't reckon he's that strong,' she said. 'I bet you could beat him easy. If you followed him on your bike and caught up with him in Ice Lane, no one wouldn't see what happened, would they? And he int going to report nothing,

518

not after all his swanking about what he did to you. He'll lie low and keep his gob shut.'

Tark wasn't going to admit Sharon's idea was a good one. He had already given hours of thought to how to get even, but it had seemed impossible.

'Mandy and Doreen were going on last night about how they wouldn't want to go with you no more if they was me,' Sharon went on.

'They'd be lucky. I wouldn't give those two scrubbers a fuck if they paid me,' he sneered. 'I don't know what they're on about. So I got stoned. So what?'

'It weren't that they was meaning,' she told him. 'It was you being shown up by Nick Dean, like he was the tough guy and you didn't dare stand up to him.'

Tark flushed a dark red. 'I'll show them who's the tough guy around here. I'll beat that prick to a pulp,' he said viciously.

Grabbing a handful of choc bars and thrusting them inside his jacket, he stamped off to charge through the OUT door, his black eyebrows knitted with fury.

Sharon watched him march out of sight, the forward thrust of his head, his hunched shoulders and heavy tread all signs of pent-up aggression bursting to be released.

She swung gently on her stool, admiring her artificial nails which were twice as long as her own nails. She felt a pleasant sense of power. The only disappointment was that, having set up the contest, she wouldn't be able to watch it.

As lunch in the dining room at Longwarden came to an end, North said, 'By the way, a guy I met on the *Day in the Life of Australia* assignment telephoned this morning. He wanted me to have dinner with him in London but I've invited him here. He seems to be at a loose end for Christmas. I may ask him to stay with us.' He looked at Jane. 'Depending on whether you like him, darling.'

Sometimes, in public, he called her that.

'If you do, I'm sure I shall,' she answered. 'What a coincidence. I had a call this morning from my friend Marie-Simone. I hope you don't mind, Penelope – I know

519

'I should have asked you first – I *did* invite her to come here for Christmas.'

'My dear child, you don't have to ask my permission. This is your house now,' said Pen. It seemed an apposite moment to add, 'In the New Year I shall be moving into the dairies. As I get old and rheumaticky, it will suit me better to live on one floor.'

'Oh, but that's absurd,' Jane exclaimed. 'There's plenty of room for us all here. More than enough.'

'I know there is, but I like the idea of having my own establishment. I've never had a place of my own. I shall enjoy making the dairies into a granny cottage. You've no objection, have you, North?'

'I think it's an excellent idea, Mama.'

Sarah wanted to bring the conversation back to the subject of Christmas guests. 'Sammy is going to spend Christmas with Mrs Slane,' she told them. 'I don't think he'll ever come back here, except to visit us. Jane, I may ask Nick to eat with us on Christmas Day, mayn't I?'

Knowing it wouldn't please North but her sympathies being with Sarah, Jane said, 'Of course you may. Where else would he eat at Christmas?'

'We could put him next to Colonel Bassenthwaite. He won't have heard the colonel's reminiscences before,' said Pen. 'He might even find them interesting.'

'Who is Colonel Bassenthwaite?' asked Jane.

'One of several boring old fogeys whose presence at lunch on Christmas Day is our contribution to peace on earth and goodwill to all men,' North informed her, with an edge in his voice which she knew related to her giving permission to Sarah, without consulting him.

'You may not want to continue the custom,' said Pen, 'but for some years I've made a point of asking two or three elderly people to lunch and tea. It started one year when North and Allegra were abroad for Christmas. Rather than sit here alone, I asked my old fogeys to join me. They're what used to be called distressed gentlefolk, although their distress is mental rather than financial. They're desperately lonely, poor old things. They don't fit among the old-age pensioners who belong to Longwarden Social Club and have parties and outings arranged for them. Colonel Bassenthwaite *is* a bore, as North says, but he did serve his country in two world wars and I feel he shouldn't be left to spend Christmas by himself.'

'No, that would be terrible,' Jane agreed. 'Certainly we'll continue to have them here. That's what Christmas is all about . . . kindness. I'm sure North feels that way too, at heart.'

She glanced at her husband, wondering if he had a heart. In four months of marriage she hadn't seen much evidence of it.

Since the dance there had been a perceptible constraint in his manner towards her whenever they were alone. Clearly he was still annoyed with her for asking Nick to the ball. Now she had fuelled his anger by agreeing to Sarah's request to have Nick join the Christmas house party.

North might also be annoyed at having Marie-Simone added to the guest list without his consent. Jane herself was worried that she might have acted rashly in view of what had befallen Marie-Simone. The Frenchwoman had sounded fine on the telephone. Just the same as ever. But she wasn't the same. She couldn't be. And what if the strain of being among a group of strangers caused her to have a relapse?

In the evening they had coffee in the library but at lunch it was served at the table. Jane had many things she wanted to do that afternoon, but she remained in her chair when the two other women left the room.

'Some more coffee for you?' she asked North.

He was drumming a devil's tattoo on the mellow sheen of the table. He answered her question with a silent shake of the head.

'You're angry, aren't you?' she said quietly.

At that he looked coldly at her. 'Should I be pleased at having my wishes ignored? Don't pretend you don't know what I mean.'

'I know what you mean but I still think you're being alarmist. What possible harm can come from having Nick

521

share our Christmas? He and Sarah work together every day. And Nick's what, in America, is called a category X person.'

'What the hell is that?'

'It's what you are, believe it or not,' she said, smiling at him. 'An earl who wanted out of his hereditary rôle and made himself into an outstanding photographer. X people are refugees from the regular social classes. They make their own place in the world ... like Rob and Emily Wareham who were both born upper-middle class but have chosen to be category X.'

After a pause, he said, 'If Nick had established himself in some useful country craft and he and Sarah were several years older, I shouldn't object to your throwing them together out of working hours. As things are, I think it's madness. But you already knew my views and chose to ignore them.'

She couldn't deny it. She had. It was the guilty feeling that perhaps, in supporting Sarah, she had been disloyal to him which made her flare up and retort, 'You do have a tongue in your head. You could have intervened. You sat there saying nothing at all.'

'Obviously we have different ideas about what you would call being "supportive",' he said sarcastically. 'Would you have liked it if I had over-ridden you? No, you wouldn't – and with good reason. If not on each other, who can we rely on?'

At that moment the butler came in to clear the table.

'Oh ... I'm sorry, m'Lord. I'll come back later.'

'It's all right, Ashford. Carry on. We've finished here.'

North rose and strode out of the room.

'Mrs Armitage and I will be playing cards later. Care to join us, Nick?' the butler asked him, when he went into the house for his evening meal.

He was about to accept when the cook said, 'I should think rummy would bore him. Poker is what soldiers play, isn't it?'

Although privately he didn't think Mrs Armitage had

much hope with Mr Ashford, receiving strong vibes that *she* didn't want him to join them, Nick changed his answer to, 'No, thanks. I'm going out.'

As he had the night before, he stayed in the Angel until closing time. The snug had a cheerful fire and he chatted to an old bloke who had enlisted as an under-age private in 1914 and managed to survive four years of stinking hell in the trenches.

The old man, who wasn't too steady on his feet, was fetched by his grandson some time before the pub closed. For the rest of the evening Nick sat by himself, thinking about the two Christmases he had spent in the Legion and wondering how his former *compañeros* were getting on.

He hankered for army life and a better climate, yet he couldn't tear himself away from the day-to-day contact with Sarah, frustrating and hopeless as it was. He knew that if he went away, when he came back she would be engaged or married to someone suitable. It was inevitable.

He was still thinking about her as he left the pub and turned in the direction of the triangular green which marked the junction of three roads – the main road which had been an A road before the building of the by-pass, the B road which passed the main gates of the estate, and a minor road leading across country to a smaller village a few miles away.

Tonight, in the lay-by in front of the bus shelter, a group of youths, some on motorbikes, were chatting up two or three girls. Walking along the pavement on the far side of the green, Nick might not have noticed them but for a sudden burst of bawdy laughter which made him glance in their direction.

Seeing the Spanish-looking rider among them reminded him of the incident at the ball. If the Osgood lout had recognized him, Nick wouldn't have been surprised to have some obscene insult bawled after him. But Osgood had been pretty drunk and wouldn't have more than a hazy memory of someone in uniform sorting him out.

A few moments later two of the bikers started their engines and, after much revving, zoomed off along the major road. Nick could hear the fading drone of their machines for some time as he walked along the minor road, the metallic ring of his footsteps the only sound in an otherwise silent night.

For a quarter of a mile the road had houses on either side, with street lamps lighting the single pavement. When these came to an end, the dark moonless night made it necessary for Nick to use his torch.

Near the corner of Ice Lane a car passed him, going in the direction of the village. As the sound of its motor diminished, he heard again the concerted roar of several motorbikes. They were coming from the village, but he didn't think anything about it except to wish the country was as quiet as it had been last night when he walked back.

When he was fifty yards down the lane, which was bordered on one side by a long stretch of thick blackthorn and bramble hedge and on the other by the high wall surrounding the estate, he heard the bikes reducing speed. It was only when the lane was suddenly illumined by the beams of more than one powerful headlamp that he realized they were following him.

In the library at Longwarden, Jane took advantage of a pause in the men's conversation to stand up and say, 'If you'll excuse me, John, I'm going to bed now. Sarah and I are hunting tomorrow so we need lots of sleep. But I'm sure you and North will want to go on talking for hours yet.'

As she spoke, both men had risen, but only John Brodick, their guest, was looking at her warmly. When she flicked a glance at her husband, his blue eyes were arctic.

He was at the door, ready to open it for her, by the time she had finished saying goodnight to the whippet-thin Scots photo-journalist whose friendly manner and fund of amusing anecdotes had made the evening pass pleasantly in spite of her keen awareness of North's displeasure.

'Goodnight.' She knew it was only because his friend might be watching that North bent to peck her cheek.

Going upstairs, she wished she hadn't arranged to hunt

tomorrow and could have afforded to stay awake, reading, until he came up. But it might be two or three hours before the men finished talking and by then he would be tired and not in the mood for a reconciliation.

The long yellow beams of the bikers' headlamps lit up Ice Lane.

Nick had flicked off his torch. His elongated shadow moved in rhythm with his stride. The bikers were some way behind him, cruising at his walking pace. He continued to walk briskly on because he had no option. The hedge on his left was impenetrable. The wall on his right was too high for him to stand any chance of taking a running leap and heaving himself over the top.

Some distance further along, the wall was broken by a tall spike-topped gate put there for the use of foresters and rarely used now, judging by the nettles he had noticed growing round it. Given a little time he could negotiate those spikes, but there wouldn't be time. If he got as far as the gate and made a dash for it, they'd catch up on their bikes in seconds, clawing him down before he was halfway up it.

He was trapped. There was nothing he could do but continue walking, tensed for the moment when, with a surge of power, they ended their cat-and-mouse crawl and surrounded him.

He wasn't sure but he thought there were three of them; Osgood on his bloody great Honda and a couple of sidekicks on smaller bikes. Three against one; and they might be armed with chains, studded belts, God knows what.

They must be as thick as boards if they thought they could beat him up and get away with it. They wouldn't: that much was certain. What wasn't certain was how much they would damage him. He didn't mind being knocked about. Being roughed up was nothing new for him. But these stupid clods, who had probably had to get high on something to get up the nerve to go for him, were capable of overdoing it and leaving him bloody-near dead. If he lay out all night, too bashed up to crawl as far as the road where there was a chance of a car passing, by morning he might have had it.

His only defences were his fists, not even gloved, and his feet. He owned two pairs of jodhpur boots, one for riding and one for walking. The heels of the walking boots were strengthened with pieces of steel to prevent them wearing down quickly. At least one of his assailants was going to feel the impact of that steel. If Osgood had come on his own, even armed with a flick, Nick would have expected to beat him in one-to-one combat. But with three – Christ! Not three. There were five of them. He'd just seen two more up ahead.

So that he wouldn't see them as he turned into the lane, they had turned off their lights while they waited. But now the chrome on their machines glinted in the light from behind him. They must be the pair who had peeled off from the group at the bus shelter. That meant the attack was premeditated. They had planned when and where to get him *before* he walked past the bus stop.

Not for the first time in his life, Nick was scared, and scared shitless. *A mi la Legión!* The yell for help that, had he been in this situation in the back streets of Puerto del Rosario, would have brought *legionarios* swarming out of every bar within earshot, was no use to him here.

Knowing that the chance of a car using the lane at this hour could be written off, he cursed himself for coming this way. The bikers ahead had dismounted and were standing shoulder to shoulder. No longer wearing crash helmets, now, like terrorists, they had their faces concealed by hoods with eye-holes cut in them.

As he went on walking, he saw they had taken up their positions close to the forestry gate. Why they had chosen that particular spot became clear as he got nearer. The gate, or rather the pair of gates, consisted of straight upright bars, each topped by a business-like spike, and four cross-pieces. The nettles had been stamped down and cords and straps had been attached to the cross-pieces in positions which made it clear what they were there for.

To lash someone to the gate.

Jesus! These kooks aren't just going to beat me up. This is some crazy caper they've seen in a film or a horror comic, Nick thought, sweating. He knew the stuff of this pack of pin-heads' fantasies: everything from ritual garrotting to gang rape. He didn't fancy being picked out to play a victim.

With a sudden deep-throated vroom the big Honda passed him, its rider hooded like the others but more for effect than to hide his identity.

He stopped level with the gates, dismounted and had the bike propped by the time Nick came to a standstill, a few yards from him.

Determined not to give the bastards the sastifaction of seeing he was frightened, Nick reverted to the vernacular of the village. 'What's this lark all about then? A right lot of charlies you'll look if the panda car comes round this way, which it usually does, this time of night.'

'No it don't, and you fucking know it. It don't never come this way at night. Nor don't anyone else . . . 'cept you, cunt,' was Tark's retort.

He laughed and the others laughed with him. They began to close in. The hoods hiding all but their eyes, which glittered through the holes in the cloth, gave them the air of menace of the Ku Klux Klan or the fanatical killers who hi-jacked aircraft.

Nick reminded himself that inside the hoods were the faces of easily-led morons who, with a bit of fast talking, he might be able to scare off.

'I dunno what you've got in mind, but whatever it is I'd forget it. Maybe you could get away with mugging old ladies around London, Osgood, but you lay a finger on me and you'll cop it . . . the lot of you. Old Lacock'd enjoy putting you lot inside for a spell. The fuzz'll be banging on your doors before you're out of bed tomorrow. You won't get away with any rough stuff round here.'

Whatever the others were thinking, their leader was undeterred.

'I reckon we'll chance that,' he said. 'Time we've finished with you, mate, you won't be laying no complaints. He won't want everyone to know he int got no balls, will he, fellers?' He nudged the one standing near him. 'I think he'll want to keep his *trap* shut, don't you?'

'Yeah . . . I reckon you're right there, Tarky. That's good, that is . . . keep his trap shut . . . hahaha!' The youth gave a goofy laugh.

After a moment's pause it set off the others. All four of them brayed with laughter.

Obviously Tark's remarks had a double meaning but Nick didn't cotton on until after Tark had moved back to his bike and taken something from the saddlebag. Rejoining the four around Nick, he held it up for him to see.

It was a gin of the kind used by poachers and keepers before such traps were made illegal. At present unset, its sharp teeth were locked together.

Nick felt panic knotting his guts as he looked at the vicious trap and understood their guffaws.

Was it an empty threat? A bluff to break his nerve? Or were they all so high that castrating him with that thing seemed a feasible retaliation for the grievance Tark had against him?

There was a moment's tense silence in which Nick found his terror gone, replaced by a murderous rage at being victimized by a gang none of whom would stand up to him singly.

A killing hate boiling inside him, he was about to attack when the deafening double-boom of a shotgun fired from both barrels made everyone jump and startled a nervous yelp out of one of the youths.

Nick, accustomed to close gunfire and other explosions during his Legion service, was the first to recover from the surprise of a gun being fired over their heads. Knowing the shots must have come from inside the gate, he sprang to one side, removing himself from between the shooter and the bikers.

'I never like wasting cartridges. The next one will be for you, Osgood,' Ted Rivington's voice said grimly. 'Drop that trap, get on your bike and be off with you . . . the lot of you. If you're not out of sight by the time I've counted

528

to ten, some of you'll be going home by ambulance.' He had already re-loaded and was aiming the gun at Tark's legs.

For a moment they stared at him, transfixed by shock and alarm.

He began slowly to count. 'One . . . two . . . three . . .'

What followed reminded Nick – although not until later – of the films he had seen of fighter pilots running to board their Spitfires during the Battle of Britain.

Tark was the last to turn tail. As his cohort scuttled to their bikes, he flung down the gin trap and spat a mouthful of obscenities at the keeper before turning away.

'Not so fast, Osgood,' said Nick. 'You're a big man with that lot behind you. Let's see what you're made of now it's just you and me.'

He was squaring up for a fight when his foster father said sharply, 'That's enough of that. Let him go. He'll get his deserts . . . but not from you.'

Nick glared at him. 'Why the hell not? If you hadn't turned up, he was going to use that bloody trap on me.'

'Well I turned up, so let it rest. You've a witness to what he threatened. Leave it to Sergeant Lacock to deal with him,' answered Rivington.

During this exchange Tark had backed off and sprung on the Honda. Seconds later he was following the others, the five engines revved to a roar as loud as the boom of the shotgun a few moments earlier.

As the disappearing light of the headlamps left the gateway in darkness, Nick was torn between relief that the ordeal was over and frustrated rage at letting Osgood get away.

As the leading bikers reached the mouth of the lane and the noise began to diminish, he said, 'Lucky for me you were around.'

'I've been on the watch for a poacher this last couple of nights. There's been a lot of birds taken this month. I'm not having that. I'll get him.'

Rivington switched on a torch. 'Pick up that trap and take those ropes and straps down. They'll be wanted as evidence. Then come over to this side. You'll have had to climb worse in the army, I'm sure.'

As he dealt with the straps, Nick said, 'I shan't be reporting this. I don't think they'll try it twice and I don't want to be involved in a court case. I'll be leaving soon . . . after Christmas.'

'You're not taking over from Sammy O'Brien then?' the keeper asked, his shotgun broken and held in the crook of his arm.

'No.'

Although Ted had rescued him from a nasty situation, Nick didn't feel in his debt. He had taken too many pastings ever to be on good terms with him. Or to confide his plans to him.

Making easy work of the gate, he landed on the other side. 'Right: I'll be off. Thanks for your help,' he said shortly, flicking on his own torch before setting off along the ride.

'In future I'd keep to the road if I was you,' advised his foster father. 'G'night.'

Jane woke up the following morning to find no ruffled dark head on the pillow next to hers. She was alone.

Had North used the other bedroom from a wish not to disturb her? She doubted that. Knowing his capacity for late hours – he had survived the ball better than anyone – and the fillip he would have got from a long session of shop-talk with an admired colleague, she felt sure that, in normal circumstances, he would have come up to bed in the mood for sex. Wanting her, he wouldn't have hesitated to wake her, confident that she would sleep all the more soundly afterwards. Which would have been true. If he had come in and made love to her, she would have slept a great deal better.

The fact that he hadn't, suggested that even John Brodick's good company had failed to soothe his annoyance with her.

With Christmas so close and Marie-Simone flying in tomorrow, a serious rift with her husband was terrible, thought Jane. But how was she to repair it? She couldn't tell Sarah that Nick was *persona non grata*. That would ruin Sarah's Christmas. All she could do was apologize, which she would have done yesterday afternoon, had there been an opportunity.

I can't go hunting with this on my mind, she thought, climbing out of bed.

In Flora's bathroom – as Jane still thought of it – she brushed her teeth and washed her face. On second thoughts she took off her nightdress and used the old-fashioned French bidet, one of the first to be brought to England, North had told her. Then she brushed her hair, the straight and the curly, sprayed both lightly with *jardins de bagatelle*, and wrapped herself in a towel.

When she opened the door on the far side of the ante-room, all she could see of him was a hummock in the middle of the wide four-poster. Stepping softly to the left side of the bed, she let the towel fall to the floor and, naked, slipped under the duvet.

Her weight settling on the mattress didn't disturb him although usually he was a light sleeper. For a few minutes she lay with her hands between her thighs, making sure they were warm before she touched him. When she was satisfied they were, she snuggled close behind him, sliding one arm round his waist and pressing soft kisses on his shoulder-blades.

Within seconds he was awake. He didn't move, but she sensed he was conscious. Caressing his back with her breasts, she slid her hand down past his belly. His reaction when she touched him was gratifyingly vigorous. Feeling him spring to life against her palm, she felt they were more than halfway to being on good terms again.

The next moment North grabbed her hand and pulled it away. 'Did you have to wake me? I was sound asleep after a late night,' he said brusquely, shifting away from her.

Still in bed, but not asleep, North heard in the distance the clatter of hooves on gravel. That would be the girls setting out for the meet. It must be later than he'd thought.

531

Not that he had to worry about neglecting his guest. John was undoubtedly feeling equally bloody. What in hell's name had possessed them to polish off the bottle of Ballantine's twelve-year-old whisky which John had had in his suitcase, on top of the wine they had drunk at dinner? It was years since he had mixed grape and grain, with the unpleasant results he was suffering from now. As if a godawful hangover wasn't enough to contend with, he had been a sod to Jane.

For fifteen seconds after opening his eyes and finding her wrapped snugly round him, he had felt all right . . . better than all right, his cock coming smartly to attention as it always did when she held it.

As soon as he was properly awake, he had realized he had a ferocious headache and a taste in his mouth like the stableyard drain. But she wasn't to know that. He shouldn't have snarled at her, sending her back to her room as if he'd been angry with her rather than with himself.

After a shower and a shave he felt marginally better, but not much. He went along to his friend's room, found him still sleeping it off and didn't disturb him.

Downstairs North encountered Ashford who would by now have removed the empty Ballantine's bottle.

'Black coffee and dry toast, m'Lord?' he inquired, poker-faced.

North nodded, which made him wince. His head needed to be kept still. He said, 'I'll have it in the study.'

In the study there was a portrait of his father presented to the eighth Earl by members of the Hunt when he had been Master for twenty years. North had been meaning to replace it with something more to his taste, but he hadn't got around to it yet. As he sat down at the desk, the belligerent high-coloured face of his male parent caught his eye.

Edward Carlyon's death had not been the only fatality in the history of the Carlyon Hunt. There had been several, and many serious injuries. North thought of Jane riding a corn-fed horse and not giving it her full attention. Sarah claimed that horses reacted to people's moods before they put a foot in the stirrup; and they didn't react well to riders who were nervous, distracted or upset.

'D'you happen to know where the meet is being held this morning, Ashford?' he asked, when his coffee arrived.

'At the Dog and Duck at Longwarden St Michael, m'Lord,' said his butler, referring to one of the outlying hamlets.

'Ring through to the stables and ask Nick to bring my car round, would you? If Mr Brodick comes down while I'm out, tell him I shan't be gone long. I'm only going to see hounds move off and then I'm coming back.'

'Very good, m'Lord.'

'Isn't that North over there?'

Sarah pointed her hunting crop at a tall dark-haired man standing at the edge of the common where, having arrived at the meet with time in hand, she and Jane had been leading the horses on foot.

'Yes, it is. What's he doing here?' Jane said perplexedly. 'Can something be the matter?'

'Can't imagine what,' said Sarah. 'Let's go and find out.'

They remounted.

North, wearing a raccoon anorak he had brought out the week before when the weather turned colder, had parked his car away from the public house where the Hunt and the onlookers were congregated.

'I'd like a word with Jane in private,' he said, as the girls rode up to him.

'Okay.' Sarah moved off, bending forward to murmur in Bedouin Star's ear.

'Is anything wrong?' Jane asked, looking down at her husband.

He nodded, his dark brows contracted.

Impatient to know what calamity had brought him in search of her, she said, 'What is it? What's happened? An accident?'

'No, no – nothing like that. I was . . . unkind to you this morning. I wanted to apologize.'

She was taken aback. Contrition wasn't a state of mind

533

she had thought he would know about. To put himself out by coming here, to say he was sorry, didn't seem like her autocratic husband.

'I'm sorry too,' she told him. 'I was wrong yesterday. There's nothing to be done about it now, but I promise I won't do it again . . . go against you, I mean.'

The Hunt had begun to move off in the other direction. They could see Sarah hanging back, looking over her shoulder.

North put his hand on Jane's knee. 'You'd better go. Take care of yourself. If the weather turns foul, come home. You don't want a chill for Christmas.'

'What'll you and John do?'

'Not much. Relax by the fire.' He stepped back to let her go.

Jane wanted to jump off Peking and be given a hug. But she stayed in the saddle and said, 'Don't eat all the crumpets, will you? Save some for us.'

On her way to catch up with the others, she felt immensely relieved by the knowledge that now they were on good terms again.

But presently, waiting while hounds were drawing the first covert, the thought came into her mind that perhaps his reason for coming had not been simply to make amends for this morning. Perhaps he had suddenly felt that it wasn't politic to have spats with her. He could survive without her but Longwarden couldn't.

It was an unpalatable notion and one she tried to ignore. But it kept creeping back into her mind and wouldn't be dismissed.

Driving back, his head still aching abominably, North knew he had been a fool to imagine Jane might have been seriously upset by being sent packing this morning.

Clearly, until reminded, she had forgotten the incident and, seeing him, had at once concluded there must have been an accident.

The way she had fled from his bedroom, he thought she had rushed off to cry. No such thing. No one could have

534

looked more composed and carefree than his wife, once relieved of the fear that something was wrong at Long-warden. Mounted on the well-behaved hunter, her black hair confined by a net, her ivory skin tinged with colour by the sharp morning air, she had plainly had nothing on her mind but a good day's sport.

The way she had responded to his apology with instant expressions of regret for her part in yesterday's rift had struck him as palpable lipservice. Argumentative yesterday; this morning, enjoying her rôle as the sporting Countess, she had been too conciliatory to be convincing.

Most of the women at the meet had heavy thighs better suited to old-fashioned jodhpurs or habits. His cousin and his wife were among the few who looked good in their skin-tight breeches. The entire male field, except for a few who were past it, was going to look at Jane's legs and imagine themselves locked between them. He knew what a randy bunch they were: hunting people of both sexes. If he went off to the Antarctic for several weeks after Christ-mas, and she continued to hunt, he wouldn't mind betting more than one of those bastards would have a determined crack at her. He doubted if they would get far; she would miss having sex but she'd think twice before doing anything to jeopardize the position which meant so much to her. Even so he didn't like the idea of their trying, or of Jane being tempted to see if they were better at it than he was.

The only way to be sure she didn't get up to any mischief if he were away for some time was to get her pregnant. That was something else beginning to worry him. He'd always taken it for granted that when he was ready for an heir it would happen immediately, no problem. Apart from when Jane had the curse and one or two other ex-ceptions, they had fucked at least once every day since they were married. Nothing had happened. Was it his fault?

Christ! That would be ironic: marrying an heiress to keep the place going, only to find he couldn't beget a son to inherit it. But he didn't have serious doubts about his ability to procreate. It was just a little surprising nothing had happened yet, but early days to start worrying.

Twenty-four hours later, Jane was on her way to meet Marie-Simone at Heathrow. North had volunteered to drive her but she had declined the offer, not only because he already had a house guest to look after, but because she wanted some time alone with her friend. Also she was excited and nervous. Having to concentrate on driving would be better for her than being a passenger.

After the first fifteen miles the rest of the journey was on the South Wales–London motorway which passed right by the airport. Not many hours after she had picked up Marie-Simone, Allegra and Andro would be flying in, bringing the stocking stuffers she had asked her sister-in-law to buy for her.

Jane had had a Christmas stocking every year of her life until the Christmas after her father's death. No one at Longwarden had had a stocking for years, it seemed. She planned to revive the custom. In her closet was hidden a stocking for everyone who would be sleeping at the house on Christmas Eve. Some, like those for the cook and the butler, contained only two or three things besides the traditional tangerines and nuts. Chocolates, toilet water and a scarf for Mrs Armitage; crystallized ginger, shower gel and a book token for Ashford. North's stocking was the best: filled with many small presents that she hoped would amuse and please him when he opened them in bed on Christmas morning.

At Heathrow an elegant blonde accompanied by a porter wheeling a trolley piled with baggage emerged into the main concourse.

'*Jane!*'

As Jane recognized the woman who had for long held the second place in her affections, Marie-Simone darted towards her and leaned over the barrier to hug and kiss her.

After embracing Jane warmly, she drew back and said, in French, 'Oh, how I've missed you . . . my dear Jane.'

'I've missed you too.' Jane's voice was unsteady. Suddenly her eyes were brimming with tears of happiness. Much about Marie-Simone had changed since their last sight of each other, but not the essential warmth of her personality. She could see that Marie-Simone felt equally emotional. Her hazel eyes shimmered as she also blinked away tears.

For a few minutes they gazed at each other in silence, swept by a wealth of memories, most of them happy, some of them profoundly sad. Inevitably, the sight of each other conjured up the presence of the man they had both loved.

They looked at each other, remembering seven Christmases spent in different parts of the world, sometimes in hotel suites, sometimes in rented houses, but always feeling at home because home, in those years, was wherever John Graham had happened to be.

Had they been meeting in Paris, where men embraced each other and family reunions were often an occasion for tears of joy, Jane wouldn't have cared if her eyes had overflowed. Mindful that this was Britain where being emotional in public was considered bad form, she pulled herself together, saying brightly, 'You've changed your hairstyle. It looks great.'

'You also have changed,' said Marie-Simone, studying her. 'It's more subtle than a new hairstyle. I can't tell immediately what the difference is, but I see it. Perhaps it's that you've fallen in love. I'm full of curiosity about your husband. I never expected you to marry an Englishman.'

'He wanted to come with me to meet you but I wouldn't let him. I wanted you all to myself for a while,' Jane explained.

Marie-Simone switched to English. 'Wait a moment, I'll come round to your side.' With a smile at her patient porter, she headed for the opening in the barrier.

She was wearing a bronze leather trench coat, tightly cinched at the waist, which Jane thought she remembered seeing in a magazine preview, last summer, of this winter's shape-hugging Paris collections. Her hair, a wild wavy mane when they said goodbye, was now a sleek polished bob, shorter than Jane's. With a black cashmere turtle-neck sweater showing at the top of the coat and black ski-pants tucked into short boots, Marie-Simone was still very much *à la page*, as the French said of people in line with current fashion.

Admiring the supple trench which she was almost sure was by Azzedine Alaïa, Jane wondered if it had been a present from a man or if Marie-Simone had bought it for herself.

She had continued to sculpt all the time she was living with them and had bought her own clothes, only allowing Jane's father to give her extravagant presents at Christmas, on her birthday and, at his insistence, on the anniversary of their meeting. She had been dependent on him only in the sense that they had lived and travelled in a style she couldn't have afforded on her own. But she had accepted nothing that she hadn't returned many times over in her passion for him and her loving kindness to his daughter.

Jane waited for her to lead her porter through the crowd awaiting the next flight. When they joined her, she raised an eyebrow at the cases and boxes stacked on the trolley.

'How long are you staying? Six months?' she asked jokingly, but with a tinge of disquiet underlying her raillery. It was North's reaction to Marie-Simone that worried her. She had the feeling they might not take to each other.

'Most of it is for you and your new family,' said Marie-Simone. 'I haven't brought many clothes as it's a short visit.'

Jane felt ashamed of worrying that her friend might outstay her welcome. 'Seriously, I was hoping you'd stay for New Year. England virtually closes down for ten days, they tell me. Is it the same in France?'

'For some people, yes. But I'm in the middle of an important commission. I mustn't desert it for too long.'

'What kind of commission?' asked Jane, as they followed the porter in the direction of the parking lot.

Although, before joining forces with the Grahams, Marie-Simone had specialized in heads of children and adolescents, later, after successfully sculpting her lover's craggy features, she had turned her talent to portrait busts of successful men – a breed with whom her association with John had brought her into frequent contact. Boardrooms in many countries had a bronze bust of the chairman signed with her distinctive monogram.

'A new departure for me . . . a group for the grounds of one of our finest *châteaux*,' Marie-Simone explained. 'The owner has three lovely daughters, aged between thirteen and nineteen. He wants me to sculpt them for his garden. I hope it will lead to other commissions from the *haut monde*, although strictly by word of mouth. Since Mitterrand's wealth tax, *le gratin*' – using a more slangy expression for the French upper crust – 'is terrified of being seen to spend money on anything. It's reached the point when women daren't even wear their new designer dresses except at private parties where there's no danger of being photographed. Everything of value is taxable once it's been spotted by government spies.'

'Don't mention it to North. He dreads that happening here, and in many ways it already is.'

'So one hears. The rich are resented and life is made difficult for them. I prefer the American attitude. They admire millionaires. Being rich is a goal, not a crime.'

Jane didn't correct her impression that North was a rich man. Perhaps, later on, she might confide the nature of her marriage. Or she might not. Her sense of loyalty made her reluctant to discuss North with anyone, even someone as close as Marie-Simone had once been.

'It's so good to see you again,' she said affectionately. 'I hated being out of touch with you. I was so relieved when you called me.'

The Frenchwoman nodded. 'It was a mistake to lose touch. I realize that now. Later, when we've time to talk privately, I'll try to explain what happened.'

In fact it was when they had left outer London behind and were on the Berkshire stretch of the motorway that she confirmed Jane's conjectures.

'No matter what life throws at you – and most of us go through a bad patch sooner or later – never believe that anything out of a bottle will help you survive,' she said suddenly. 'Large bottles of booze . . . little bottles of pills . . . they don't help at all. They make everything worse.'

Jane took her eyes off the road to glance inquiringly at her. She saw Marie-Simone flush.

'I hate to have to admit this to you, but for a while last summer I was in a clinic for addicts. I needed professional help to get me off several kinds of pills and a couple of bottles of wine a day . . . sometimes more.'

Jane took a hand off the wheel and reached for her friend's hand. 'I should have come over and found out why you weren't writing. I should have been there to help.'

Marie-Simone squeezed her fingers. 'You couldn't have helped and I'm glad you didn't see me when I was like that. I was such a miserable wreck . . . soaked in wine and self-pity. You see what I didn't know, until it was explained to me, is that sometimes when people lose the person they love, instead of feeling sad, they feel angry at being deserted. I felt that . . . angry and cheated.'

'Cheated?' said Jane, with a puzzled look.

'Not financially. Your father was generous to me. I need never work unless I want to. But I felt I had wasted years of my life with nothing to show for it. No marriage. No children. No future. It seemed to me then – in that terrible deep black depression – that John had taken my best years and given me nothing in return; except the means to be miserable in comfort. I can see now how stupid it was to feel that way. But you know I come from a bourgeois background . . . generations of respectable, provincial wives . . . and there are times when I see my life through their eyes. They wouldn't approve of it.'

Jane pulled into a lay-by and switched off the engine. Turning sideways in her seat, she said, 'I can't bear to think of you going through all this by yourself. I feel terrible about it. I thought the most likely reason you had stopped writing was because you'd met someone else and wanted to start fresh.'

'No, there's been no one else. That's part of the problem. Seven years with John has spoiled me for ordinary men . . .

540

and although I'm not young any more, the rest of my life is a long time.'

It crossed Jane's mind that, had he been free, Andro Risconti would have been good for Marie-Simone. From what she knew of them both, in some ways they seemed better matched than he and Allegra.

'But other people have worse problems,' the French-woman went on. 'I don't allow myself to brood about the future now. I live each day as it comes, and today I'm very happy because we're together again.' She leaned over to take Jane's face between her hands. 'We were like sisters, weren't we? To lose John and then to be parted from you, by my own choice . . . I must have been mad.'

'I was mad to agree. I should have made you stay in America, or gone to France with you.' Jane lifted her hands to cover the other woman's, holding them against her cheeks.

She could see now that, although disguised by Marie-Simone's skilful make-up, there were many lines which hadn't been there before. But she was still attractive. Her addiction hadn't had time permanently to ruin her looks.

Presently, when the car was in motion again, it struck her that Marie-Simone's remark about living each day as it came was reminiscent of the attitude Alcoholics Anonymous were said to urge on their members.

'Can you drink at all now?' she asked. 'Will Christmas be a difficult time for you?'

'I don't think so. I'm not sure whether I shall be able to drink again . . . one day. For the present I'm staying on the wagon. I tell people I've had jaundice. It stops them pressing drinks on me. I shan't be able to tell if the 1944 Armagnac I've brought for your husband is as good as I was told it is. What is he like? You've told me so little about him.'

'You'll see for yourself very soon.'

Good King Wenceslas looked out,
On the Feast of Stephen;
When the snow lay round about
Deep and crisp and even . . .

The youngest members of the carol-singing party from the village ignored their conductor, the headmistress of Longwarden primary school, their round eyes darting in wonder from the towering glitter-branched spruce to the silver staircase where some of their audience were sitting.

Allegra and Risconti were only just back. They had arrived five minutes before the singers, who now formed a crescent-shaped group in the centre of the Great Hall.

> *Hither, page, and stand by me,*
> *If thou know'st it, telling,*
> *Yonder peasant, who is he?*
> *Where and what his dwelling?*

While everyone else was watching the singers, Sarah was looking at Nick. He was standing with Mrs Armitage and Ashford, deliberately aligning himself with the staff rather than coming over to sit on the stairs with her.

He was wearing his green combat sweater, the cotton patches emphasizing the breadth of his shoulders as he stood, like a soldier at ease, feet apart, his hands behind his back. It was difficult to take her eyes off him. Although they worked together, there were few opportunities to study him closely.

She had a panicky feeling that once Christmas was over he would go. He knew that at this time of year she could, at a pinch, manage the stables single-handed. So the next few days were her last chance to make him change his mind about leaving. There must be a way. There had to be.

> *In his master's steps he trod*
> *Where the snow lay dinted*

Marie-Simone was standing beside her fellow guest, whose first name had given her a pang when they met. But the world was full of men called John. It was one of the minor hurts she had to learn to live with.

This John seemed an intelligent person, with whom she could make conversation without any effort, but until a few minutes ago she had been more interested in studying her host, the husband of her darling Jane.

Then his sister had arrived home and, with her, a man, a foreigner like herself, at whom she had taken one look and known that she had to sculpt that extraordinary head.

There had barely been time for him to be introduced before the arrival of the carol singers. What his relationship was with the sister had yet to be made clear. Not a close one, she hoped. Because, as he had kissed her hand, she had felt a curious sensation which she remembered very clearly from the only other time it had happened to her. The tightness in the chest, the strange sense of recognizing a stranger, the awareness of an uncommonly powerful sexual attraction; these were all the things she had felt when Jane's father had walked into her studio to commission a bust of his daughter.

Alessandro Risconti. The name rang in her mind like a bell. Suddenly, after months of feeling like a zombie, she was alive again.

> *Therefore Christian men be sure*
> *Wealth and rank possessing,*
> *Ye who now do bless the poor*
> *Shall yourselves find blessing.*

'Happy Christmas everyone.' Jane walked into the kitchen and found Nick and Sarah there, drinking hot chocolate after their labours in the stables.

'And a very happy Christmas to you, m'Lady, and thank you very much for the stocking I found tied to my door handle when I went to bed last night. The scarf will go lovely with my new coat,' said Mrs Armitage.

When the two young people and Ashford had also thanked her for their stockings, Sarah said, 'But no one made one for you. How unfair. We'll make sure you aren't left out next year.'

'I wasn't this year. I woke up to find Mère Noël had brought me a stocking stuffed with goodies from Paris.'

Marie-Simone had given it to North to hide.

Christmas Day had begun with the two of them sitting up in bed, scattering the quilt with pretty wrappings and coloured ribbons, and seeing who could make a praline from Fouquet last longest, like a couple of six-year-olds.

Except that a scarlet foil box which Jane had extracted from her stocking had contained a diaphanous bra and G-string which North had made her model for him. Whereupon they had spent half an hour playing grown-up games, leaving themselves short of time to shower and dress before breakfast.

Allegra looked down the lunch table and noticed Risconti in animated conversation with Jane's French friend. She herself was seated between John Brodick, whom she liked, and Colonel Bassenthwaite who drove her insane with boredom.

Today he was going to be hoist with his own petard. The instant he mentioned India, she had him.

The moment came while they were eating a sorbet before the arrival of the Christmas pudding. Jane's idea this, thought Allegra.

'When I was a junior subaltern in India in thirty-two,' the colonel began.

'Ah . . . India!' Allegra exclaimed. 'Colonel, you *would* have enjoyed the show I've just seen in New York. *Costumes of Royal India* . . . absolutely out of this world. Did you know there was one maharajah who was six feet nine inches tall? They showed one of his coats. Silk, lined with hand-made paper for warmth. I had always thought a turban was a turban, but apparently not. It can tell one what a man does, where he lives, even whether he's married. I'm sure you knew that, but I didn't.'

She paused but not long enough for the colonel to utter. 'But what you probably didn't know is that sometimes the knots in courtesans' skirts were so complicated that only they could undo them. Three *hundred* yards of cotton in one skirt . . . imagine it.'

For a full five minutes it amused her to keep him

suspended in unwilling silence while she poured the details of Diana Vreeland's exhibition into his reluctant ear.

After the Queen's speech and tea by the fire in the library, Pen drove her three lame ducks home. She disliked getting rid of them but North and Allegra would have vetoed the suggestion that they should be asked to stay longer. It wasn't as if they were being sent back to cheerless discomfort. None was without the means to live comfortably. It was only companionship they lacked. As they chatted, she had the impression they had all had enough excitement to make them quite happy to spend the rest of the day by their own firesides, watching television.

When she returned to the house, she didn't go back to the library. Sarah and Nick would, she guessed, be busy in the stables at this hour, and the other six young people would be more at ease without someone of her generation present. Although even Allegra had gone out of her way to be affable today, Pen couldn't but be aware that they formed a congenial group from which she was debarred not only by age.

They had all been about the world. Five of them had achieved fame – the Frenchwoman was a distinguished sculptress it seemed – and Jane, although she had had no career as such, had grown up under the influence of a remarkable man and, by virtue of the immense fortune at her disposal, was on equal terms with the others.

Pen had noticed at dinner last night that, without any intention of excluding her from their conversation, they couldn't avoid referring to places, people and matters outside her ken. They had made her more than ever aware how narrow her own life had been. Until Jane's arrival, Pen had spent most of the present decade buried in the country and none of the subjects on which she could speak with authority were of interest to anyone but an equally dedicated gardener.

When she entered her sitting room, the first thing she noticed was a parcel. Wrapped in striped paper the colour of holly berries and leaves, it was neatly fastened with transparent Sellotape but had no card attached to it.

There being no impatient children to consider, it had been decided to make the opening of parcels part of the programme for the evening. They were stacked round the base of the Christmas tree in the library, waiting to be ceremoniously handed out by North when everyone assembled for pre-dinner drinks. This parcel must be a special surprise Jane had planned for her: although all Jane's other presents were done up in a recognizable way and adorned with ribbon rosettes and ringlets in the American manner.

Childishly excited, Pen carefully unstuck the Sellotape so that she could unwrap the paper without spoiling it. If it had been tied with string she would have unpicked the knots, however difficult. It was a book: an expensive book on the great gardens of France which she had longed to buy the day she and Jane went to Hatchard's. Jane must have noticed her interest in it. How typically observant and kind of her. Had she inscribed it? No, she hadn't.

Filled with the special pleasure of receiving a gift which was exactly what she wanted, Pen put a match to the fire and sat down to enjoy this unexpected treat.

She had been there about half an hour when someone knocked at the door.

'Come in.'

'Am I disturbing you?'

At the sight of her daughter-in-law, a smile of great warmth lit Pen's face.

'Not a bit, you sweet girl. I found your lovely surprise waiting for me when I came up. It's the most gorgeous book . . .' She put it aside and rose to give Jane a hug.

'Not *my* surprise, Penelope. All mine are downstairs by the tree.'

'Really? How odd. I felt sure it was yours because you were with me when I first saw it.'

'I was? Oh, that time in Hatchard's.' Jane picked up the book. After a glance at the jacket she, like Pen, looked for an inscription. 'If I had known you wanted it, I should have bought it. Could it be from Allegra? A special private peace offering for all the times she got in your hair in the past?

She did say this morning she had simplified her Christmas shopping by deciding to give everyone on her present-list a book or a book token this year. Or this could be' – she paused, giving Pen a thoughtful look – 'a present from Mr Ashford.'

Pen's immediate surprise was followed by a thrust of excitement. Was it possible?

'It's very expensive,' she said doubtfully. 'The price has been removed from this copy, but I was appalled when I saw what it cost in Hatchard's. Allegra might not consider it an extravagance but I'm sure Mr Ashford would.'

'Not necessarily. He seems to have no one else to give presents to. Why don't you say you found it in your room and ask him if he knows anything about it?' Jane suggested. 'He may have felt it wouldn't be correct to put his gift with the others, or even that you might be embarrassed at receiving one from him. So he put it here, where no one else need know about it.' She glanced at her watch. 'It's time I was starting to change. I'll see you later.'

A few minutes after Jane had left the room, Pen followed her. Avoiding the main staircase, she used the stairs at the end of the west corridor which led down to a hall near the billiard room.

She found Ashford laying the round table in the Red Parlour, Jane's chosen setting for a light Christmas Night supper after the opening of the presents.

The door was open and he was preoccupied with the precise alignment of the silver when she paused on the threshold.

She said, 'This has been a very busy day for you, Mr Ashford.'

He looked up. 'Good evening, m'Lady. I'm sorry . . . I didn't see you there.'

She advanced into the room. 'You were concentrating on the table. What strong nerves you have. I should have jumped a foot if you had caught me unawares. Have you had *any* time off today? I suspect that you haven't.'

'Not a great deal, but that doesn't matter,' he answered, continuing to move round the table, taking the pieces of silver from a shallow baize-lined basket held against his left hip. 'Last year there was very little to do with only yourself and Miss Sarah at home. But this year has been more in keeping with the traditions of Christmas. I know Mrs Armitage has enjoyed the cooking involved and I've been glad to play my part. The year before last I was alone with General Pembroke who was bed-ridden. It wasn't a cheerful occasion.'

'This has been the most festive Christmas we've had here since the last time old Lady Carlyon came down. The following spring she died, and we all felt bereft. She was one of those people whose deaths, to use my son's phrase, leave "a hole in one's heart".'

As she spoke, she remembered that he had lost someone much closer and dearer than a great-grandmother. As he went about his work today, had he been thinking of past Christmases when his wife was alive? Did he still mourn her?

Hastily changing the subject, she said, 'I don't remember seeing this cloth before, or these plates.'

The white table cloth was of a semi-transparent material like organdie with an appliquéd design round the hem and in the centre. It was laid over a longer pink cloth under which she could feel a thick felt protecting the fine patina of the Regency table.

'The cloth comes from what Lady Carlyon calls her marriage chests. I believe she bought it in Hong Kong. The plates are part of a dinner service she found locked away in a cupboard. They were very dusty and she insisted on washing every piece by hand herself. The gilding could be damaged in the dishwasher.'

'They are lovely,' said Pen, picking one up to study the intricate pink and gold border. 'But does that mean you will be washing them by hand after supper? It will take hours.'

She wondered if he would be shocked if she offered to help him. For herself, she could think of no happier way to end the evening than drying dishes with him. On this one day of the year, if no other, surely it should be possible to put aside artificial barriers and behave as fellow human beings? He had been busy all day ensuring their comfort and pleasure. Why shouldn't she offer him a helping hand?

As she hesitated, Ashford said, 'If you don't mind my saying so, shouldn't you be changing, m'Lady?'

Was that a gentle snub?

'Yes – yes, I know I should. Actually I came down to ask if you knew anything about a parcel I found in my sitting room. It's a most beautiful book – one I was tempted to buy when I was in London – but there's nothing to indicate who put it there.'

He had finished arranging the silver. Putting aside the basket, he said, 'I did, Lady Carlyon. I hope you won't think it an impertinence, but I wanted to show my appreciation of your many kindnesses during the time I've worked here. I also saw the book in London and felt it was one which might interest you.'

'Interest is an understatement. I can't tell you how hard it was to resist it . . . and how delighted I am to have it now,' she told him warmly. 'But what I've done to deserve it, I can't imagine. I'm not aware of any kindnesses.'

'Probably not, but I am very much aware of them.' He paused. 'There've been many occasions when we've talked as . . . equals. You may not understand how much that has meant to me, but it's meant a great deal.'

She saw something in his face which brought her love for him welling to the surface, making her long to declare it.

Instead, she said quietly, 'No, I don't understand it, Mr Ashford. As far as I am concerned, we *are* equals. I regard you as a friend . . . one of the few friends I have. I'm glad you value our talks because I do, too – very much.'

At that he looked at her with so much warmth in his eyes she was almost certain he loved her. She held her breath, willing him to say it.

But he didn't and the moment passed. With a pang of despair, she knew that he never would. Not while she was a peeress and he was a butler.

She said, 'I hope you'll sign the book for me. Why didn't you before you wrapped it?'

549

'It seemed very possible you might be given a copy by one of your family. In which case you can change mine for something else. Hatchards are very good about that sort of thing.'

Pen said, and felt herself flushing, 'I shouldn't dream of changing your copy. I'll leave it on the table in my room and I hope, as soon as you have a few minutes to spare, you'll inscribe it for me.'

In the tackroom, Sarah was saying, 'But you *must* . . . otherwise I'll be the odd one out.'

At lunch, Nick hadn't sat down with the guests but had worked with Ashford to help serve the meal. Now he was trying to opt out of tonight's supper party.

'You must come, Nick,' she repeated. 'Jane is expecting you to help North hand out the presents, and after supper there'll be dancing. Who am I going to dance with if you're not there?' Her lips trembled suddenly. She turned away to hide the tears of disappointment which sprang to her eyes.

'Oh, for Christ's sake, Sarah! How *can* I come?' he said brusquely. 'I haven't a suit, for one thing.'

Assisting the butler at lunch, he had worn clothes borrowed from Ashford and succeeded in looking every inch the well-trained footman.

'Nor has Andro. I don't think he owns one. It won't be a formal party. You can wear your new sweater . . . unless you don't like it.'

Before morning stables Sarah had given Nick a parcel containing a fawn cashmere swater. It had cost more than she could afford but she had economized on her other presents.

'Of course I like it. It's great. I just don't want to look out of place . . . as well as feeling it,' he added.

She turned back to face him, her eyes still unnaturally bright. 'You won't look it *or* feel it. John Brodick particularly wants to talk to you about the Legion. He's interested in doing a photo-feature on it.'

'Who's going to help Mr Ashford? He'll be single-handed

tonight. I wouldn't feel right, sitting down with him waiting on me.'

'He won't be waiting on anyone this evening. It's a cold supper and everything will be put out for us to help ourselves.'

Nick scowled at the toes of his boots before shooting a quick glance at her under his eyebrows.

'All right – I'll come,' he said gruffly.

Pen was the last to arrive for the present-giving ceremony. The others were grouped round the fire, drinking champagne, when she entered the library.

All the men rose when they saw her, and her son said, 'We were on the point of sending up a search party, Mama.'

'I'm sorry I'm late.'

'It doesn't matter.' North gave her a glass of champagne.

He was looking magnificent in a smoking jacket of dark ruby velvet with a ribbed silk collar and frogging on the front and cuffs. She hadn't seen him wearing it before but guessed it had been made for his great-grandfather, a man of the same splendid build whose clothes North did sometimes wear.

She took the glass, her hand trembling slightly because she had dressed in a hurry and was now, for a moment or two, the centre of attention, an experience she had always disliked.

'Come and sit here, Lady Carlyon,' said Risconti, inviting her to take the chair in which he had been sitting.

'Thank you, but where will you sit?'

'Next to you when I've fetched another chair.' He moved away to pick up a claw-and-ball stool which he placed beside her. 'Allegra tells me some of the decorations on this tree date from the nineteenth century.'

'A few, yes; and some are Edwardian and some from the period between the two world wars. Although the nurseries here were never full of children, the estate workers had large families and there were parties for them and for the village children.'

Suddenly realizing that everyone had stopped talking and

was looking expectantly at North who was waiting for her to stop, she finished speaking in an abashed undertone.

He smiled at her. 'As my mother has been telling Andro, the decorations on the tree date from the Christmases of my great-grandfather's childhood and possibly earlier. We do know that, as a small boy, he bought the glass bird of paradise which has now lost most of its tail. My grandmother, Diana, brought the angel at the top back from Italy. This year the tree has some new ornaments. They come from the many parts of the world where Jane spent Christmas while she was growing up.'

He paused to glance round the circle of attentive faces, the authoritative thrust of his jaw emphasized by the wing collar of his dress shirt.

'My great-grandfather was born in eighteen-seventy-three. This afternoon I worked out that it's likely to be about the year twenty-seventy before *my* great-grandson has a bride to celebrate Christmas with him. Whether Longwarden will still be surviving then as a private house depends on a number of factors, some outside our control. My wife and I hope it will; and that the Christmas traditions we've inherited, and others we shall introduce such as tonight's supper party in the Red Parlour, will continue long after our time to be enjoyed by our descendants and their close friends. Now I know you're all eager to find out what Father Christmas has brought you so, as his official deputy, with Nick as my assistant, I'll start handing out the parcels.'

From the high ledge of the great carved stone chimneypiece surrounding the cavernous hearth where a huge log was burning, he took down two red velvet hats trimmed with yellowing white fur, one of which he handed to Nick.

Fitting the other on his own head and adjusting the pompon at the end of the point, he said, 'I think the first person to open a parcel should be the youngest of us. Ah, yes, here's something for her. Would you hand this to Sarah, please, Nick?'

Watching Sarah smile up at Nick as he placed a large cube-shaped parcel wrapped in gold foil and tied with emerald ribbon on her lap, Jane was grateful to North for dropping, if only for this one night, his opposition to Nick being treated as 'family'.

It had made her even happier to hear him say 'my wife and I' and to be given the feeling that, already, she had contributed something more personal than her father's wealth to the life and customs of this great house.

Risconti's present to Allegra was a necklace of linked antique cameos. As it happened, Jane had seen it before in a jeweller's in Conduit Street where she had been looking for presents. The jeweller had told her the necklace cost twenty-six thousand pounds. Even for a successful painter, it seemed an extravagant gesture.

Watching Risconti fasten the clasp at the back of Allegra's long neck confirmed for Marie-Simone that the Italian was the lover of the tall, striking English girl as well as the subject of her next book, which was all Jane had told her about them. She should have guessed it, but sitting beside her at lunch he had been so attentive and charming that she had hoped otherwise.

Twenty-four hours of hope: now back to despair, or the edge of it. Being invited to come here for Christmas – the worst time of year for anyone alone – had seemed a godsend. At lunch, seeing Allegra sitting next to John Brodick and finding herself placed beside the grey-haired Italian, Marie-Simone had felt her luck changing at last. A fellow artist, the right age, not married, widely travelled; they had seemed to have everything in common. Now it was plain to see he belonged to Jane's sister-in-law. I hope she deserves him, she thought. Suddenly she felt very tired. If only she could slip away from all these happy, animated people and retire to her room with a bottle of champagne, instead of being forced to sip Perrier and pretend to be enjoying herself.

When all the presents round the tree had been distributed, two remained; the largest and the smallest. The largest had been brought into the library on the strong, rubber-wheeled platform used to transport large logs and other heavy objects from one part of the house to the other.

The object resting on it now had been wrapped in green crêpe paper so that only its general shape was visible and that gave little clue to what it might be.

'Before we come to the mystery object, here's something at the other extreme,' said North, producing a very small package from the pocket of his smoking jacket. 'I was asked to take charge of this because it's so small it might have got lost or squashed among all the other parcels. I wonder if, when it's opened, it will prove the truth of the well-known saying.'

Holding up the tiny package, no larger than the tag attached to it, he looked slowly from face to face, prolonging the expectancy.

'The card says: *From A to A*. It's for you, Andro.'

Everyone watched Risconti removing the wrappings from a small shagreen box of the size to contain a pair of cuff links or a set of dress studs. But it was a small piece of ivory which he took out and held between finger and thumb. After studying it for a few moments, he looked across at Allegra. Putting the fingertips of his other hand to his lips, he threw her a kiss.

'What is it?' asked John Brodick, with a mystified expression.

'It's a netsuke,' Risconti told him. 'A toggle to fasten the cords attaching a pouch to traditional Japanese dress. I've been collecting them for some time and Allegra has found a very beautiful one for me. Can you see? – It's a frog on a roof tile. Proving conclusively that the best presents do come in the smallest parcels, North,' he added, with a grin.

'Not necessarily. I have an idea the mystery object may be someone's heart's desire. Before we find out, I think we all need a refill.'

'It could be a leg-pull,' said Sarah, as North and Nick went round with more champagne.

She was pleased with all her presents, especially *The Noble Horse*, a very expensive book from North and Jane, but a little disappointed with a bottle of *Miss Dior* from Nick. A less expensive but more personal and lasting gift would have made her happier.

'I think it has to be for Jane,' said Allegra, having noticed that her sister-in-law had yet to receive a major present from her husband.

North took an envelope out of his other pocket. He handed it to his mother.

'For me?' she exclaimed. 'Are you sure?'

'See for yourself,' he suggested.

Pen opened the unsealed envelope and drew out a card. Reading the message, she felt a lump in her throat. She looked at her daughter-in-law. 'Oh, my dear . . .'

Jane smiled at her. 'I hope you're going to like it.'

'Come on, Mama. Put an end to the suspense. Get the wrappings off,' said North.

Pen's instinctive aversion to damage in any form made her hesitate to tear the green paper.

'Shall Nick and I do it for you?' her son suggested.

In a matter of seconds the two men had ripped it away, revealing a pastoral idyll carved in old weathered stone: two nymphs, one dozing on a grassy bank after filling a basket with apples, the second dandling a chubby naked infant. The figures were carved with extraordinary skill, the girl's hair, the folds of their draperies and the plump curves of the child's body all conveying tactile softness in spite of the hard unyielding medium from which they were fashioned.

Pen reacted with an indrawn breath and a look of stunned disbelief.

It was Marie-Simone who, sitting forward, exclaimed, 'That's Falconet.' She looked inquiringly at Jane. 'Can it be an original?'

It was Pen who answered her. 'It's the missing Falconet. *The Apple Pickers*. I can hardly believe it. That it's here . . . that it's mine.'

Her excitement and delight overcoming her normal shyness, she held out her arms to her daughter-in-law who at once jumped up to exchange an affectionate hug.

'The *missing* Falconet . . . what's the story?' asked John Brodick, ever the journalist.

'We shall have to ask Jane,' said Pen. 'All I know is that several years ago a man from Crowther's came here to look

555

at some things we were thinking of selling. Crowther is a firm specializing in architectural antiques . . . gates, pillars, statues and on on. He told me about two superb groups by Falconet which had recently been rediscovered. There should have been three but only two had come to light. I remember the others were called *The Chase* and *Fishing*. He showed me photographs of them. Their last recorded owner was the Grand Duchess Anastasia of Russia who had them in her garden at the Villa D'Eze between Nice and Monte Carlo. I imagine they're now in America.'

'I don't know. They may be,' said Jane. 'This one was advertised there. Alison Blakewell saw it in *Town & Country* and called me about it. North and I felt sure you'd like it, Penelope. We thought it would make a pretty centrepiece for your private garden at the dairies . . . if you're still determined to move there.'

The others rose from their chairs to circle the group and admire it from all sides.

'Who is this Falconet?' Brodick asked Marie-Simone. 'It looks eighteenth-century to me.'

'It is. Look . . . you can see his mark and the date on the base.' She pointed out the letters *F.F.*ˣ and *1780*. 'Before he carved this he was in Russia for twelve years working on a monument to Peter the Great for the Empress Catherine. Then he came back to Paris. This may have been his last work before he was paralysed. There's a figure called *Lady Bathing* in the Louvre. I remember drawing it as a student.'

'You say he was paralysed?' said Risconti, who had also been listening to her.

She nodded. 'Can you imagine a more cruel fate for an artist? He was paralysed in 1783 when he was sixty-seven and he didn't die until he was seventy-five. Eight years of misery for him, poor man. I should think he would rather have been dead than incapable of working. I know I should . . . wouldn't you?'

Risconti nodded and moved away, his manner suggesting he didn't wish to dwell on such matters on Christmas night.

'If Falconet has stuff in the Louvre, this thing must be worth a hell of a lot of money, isn't it?' Brodick murmured in an undertone.

'It's an important piece. I've no idea of its value but, as you say, a lot of money.'

Over his shoulder she noticed Risconti helping himself to some more champagne. He drinks too much, she thought, remembering how often his glass had been replenished at lunch. I wonder why?

After supper, the rugs were rolled back to make a space for dancing.

With an inward sigh Pen foresaw that all these mannerly young men were going to feel it their duty to ask her to dance. The only man in whose arms she wanted to be wasn't here. She wondered how North would react if she suggested fetching his butler to be her partner. But she knew Ashford wouldn't come even if she dared to ask him.

He had danced with her once because he had realized she was tipsy and might make a scene if he refused. He wouldn't dance with her tonight. He had made it clear before dinner that, however little importance she attached to their stations, there were marks he would not overstep.

'I'm going to say goodnight, my dears,' she announced, starting to gather up her presents.

'You can't go to bed early tonight, Mama,' said North. 'It's no good pretending you can't dance. We all saw you and Rupert Wymondham giving a good imitation of Astaire and Rogers. Have another drink and let your hair down.'

She liked it when he teased her. Smiling, she shook her head. 'Not tonight. I want to go up and listen to my new record.' Risconti had given her a recording of Yehudi Menuhin playing Elgar's violin concerto. 'And although you may sleep late tomorrow,' she went on, 'I shall be out before breakfast, deciding where to put my beautiful nymphs. I can't tell you what joy it will give me to design a garden for them. Goodnight, Jane darling.'

Kissing the cheeks of her family, and having her hand kissed by Risconti, Nick and North's Scots friend, she left them to continue the party.

Once the heavy mahogany door of the library had been closed behind her and she had turned into the corridor leading towards the main staircase, the house had the special stillness of all ancient buildings in which many generations have lived out their lives and left some essence of the past vibrating in the atmosphere.

Her own footsteps making no sound on a pathway of worn Persian rugs, Pen felt that at any moment she might hear the soft frou-four of sweeping Edwardian evening dresses and catch a faint echo of the conversation and laughter as the pampered women attending a long-ago house party made their way upstairs to be undressed by their maids.

She had listened so often to Flora Carlyon's tales of her first years at Longwarden, when the house had been run by a retinue of servants, that those times seemed almost as real as her own very different era.

Now, thanks to her daughter-in-law, the house was to have a renaissance. How strange that a half-Chinese girl and an American girl, admittedly one with a cosmopolitan upbringing, should both be so much better suited to being mistress of Longwarden than the thoroughly English girl who had come between them, thought Pen.

When she reached her sitting room, she found the fire still alight. It had been replenished within the past hour. A tray with everything necessary for her to make tea or hot chocolate had been placed by her chair.

He must have guessed she would come upstairs earlier than the others, not because she was tired or ready for bed but needing to relax in her own way after a day of being sociable.

Her eye fell on the book she had left on the large table, closed. Now it was open at the fly-leaf. She hurried to read several lines of handwriting.

'Men in their generations are like the leaves of the trees. The wind blows and one year's leaves are scattered on the

558

ground; but the trees burst into bud and put on fresh ones when the spring comes round.'

The quotation, which she didn't recognize, was followed by his initials *P.J.A.*

She took the book to her chair and sat down to re-read the words inscribed in his clear, neat hand. At first she was disappointed because they were so impersonal. But what else had she expected? A declaration of love?

She put a match to the spirit stove under the kettle. Waiting for the water to boil, she began to think that perhaps the inscription was less impersonal than it had seemed at first. If nothing else, it revealed how in tune their minds were. In a more poetic form, the words he had written crystallized her amorphous thoughts about the past, present and future as she was coming upstairs.

He must have been thinking similar thoughts and, from his well-stocked mind, had plucked a quotation which, now she had studied it, couldn't be bettered as an inscription in a book about gardens given to a passionate gardener.

When she had made the tea, Pen put on her new record. As the concerto began, before the soloist's entry, she debated using the house telephone to ask Ashford if he would like to hear the recording with her. But although it had been a day of leisure for her, he had been busy since early morning and, told by North not to wait up, might now be sleeping. She felt she couldn't risk disturbing him. How inconsiderate he would think her if she roused him from a deep sleep; especially when *he* had been so thoughtful of her comfort.

As the exquisite sound of a fine violin played by a virtuoso filled the sitting room, she was reminded of something she had read in Menuhin's life story when, years ago, North had returned from America with the newly-published autobiography in his baggage as a present for her.

Leaving the fireside, she crossed the room to her bookcase and searched the shelves for *Unfinished Journey*. Like herself, Menuhin had married too young and suffered considerable misery before finding the perfect partner in his long happy second marriage.

The page Pen wanted to find gave part of a letter of advice from the American writer Willa Cather to the young Menuhin. Advising him on the kind of girl he should marry, the distinguished authoress had written '. . . real love is not so much admiration as it is the drive to help and make life easy for the other person.'

Had it been merely as a conscientious butler, performing all and more than the duties expected of him, that Ashford had kept the fire going and left the tray by her chair? Or had it been an act of loving concern for her comfort, the 'drive to make life easy for the other person'?

How would she ever know?

At one o'clock in the morning there were six people left in the library. Nick had been the first to leave. As Jane wasn't going to the Boxing Day meet because of her guests, Sarah had persuaded him to go with her. He had said goodnight before midnight and Sarah a short time later.

When Jane noticed Marie-Simone clenching her teeth on a yawn, she claimed to be tired herself and the two of them rose to depart, leaving Allegra and the men discussing the Channel tunnel.

'I shan't be long,' said North, escorting them to the door.

Jane was pleased when he kissed the Frenchwoman's cheek. 'Goodnight, Marie-Simone. I'm very glad you could come. It's made all the difference to Jane's first Christmas at Longwarden to have you here with her.'

Presently, having seen her friend to her room and bade her an affectionate goodnight, Jane went to her own room. She was glad North had spoken warmly to Marie-Simone. On her own behalf she couldn't help being disappointed that he hadn't marked the occasion with one special present. Knowing he would be annoyed if she bought him anything conspicuously expensive, she had given him a gorgeous hand-made Paisley silk dressing gown from D. L. Lord in the Burlington Arcade. He had given her several nice small presents, but nothing which would be a permanent memento of today. Not that she was likely to forget her first Christmas as his wife, but it would have been nice to receive some romantic and sentimental trifle to add to her very special treasures.

What I really wanted was a love token, she thought wistfully. Maybe next year . . .

It wasn't until she undressed and been to the bathroom to take off her make-up that she caught sight of something which hadn't been in the bedroom earlier that evening.

Hurrying to investigate, she found the most ravishing jewel lying on her pillow. Recognizably of the same Art Nouveau period as her mermaid engagement ring, its sweeping golden curves framed the head and shoulders of a pensive girl whose outstretched hand clasped a flower set with emeralds and diamonds. Behind her, fragile and transparent as a dragonfly's wings, was a panel of *plique à jour* enamel of unimaginably delicate craftsmanship. An amethyst flanked by diamonds sparkled above her head and a large shining amethyst drop dangled below her. When she picked up the lovely thing, Jane discovered it was a brooch which could also be worn as a pendant, having two small rings at the back through which a chain could be threaded. It was marked *Vever, Paris*.

She was sitting at the dressing-table, the brooch on the palm of her hand, admiring the fine modelling of the girl's features and fingers, moulded and carved from honey-coloured *pâte de verre*, when her husband walked in.

Her smile radiant, she said, 'I found your surprise. I love it. It's the most beautiful brooch I've ever seen.'

He came to her side. 'Glad you like it.'

'I adore it. Thank you, North.' Impulsively she caught one of his hands and pressed her lips to the back of it.

For an instant his face seemed to soften but then, his tone almost curt, he said, 'I didn't buy it, you know. It was left to me by my great-grandmother . . . one of her favourite pieces from the many my great-grandfather gave her. I'm sorry if that disappoints you, but I haven't the means to buy you jewels of this order. It was very diplomatic of you to include me in the present you gave my mother, but rather pointless. Everyone must be aware that I couldn't have paid a tenth part of whatever it cost you.'

'Oh, North' – she put the brooch aside and pulled him down to sit beside her on the long stool – 'what does it matter where the money originated? It's *ours* now, to share, to enjoy, to make other people happy. I don't care whether you bought the brooch or had it left to you. What matters is that you gave it to me ... wanting to please me ... wanting to make *me* happy. That's the only important thing.'

She raised her arms and slid them round his neck. 'Another thing that made me happy was your being so sweet to Marie-Simone tonight. She's had a bad time since my father died.' She leaned closer, touching her lips to the dent in the centre of his chin. 'Are you tired? I'm not. I'm turned on by this wonderful jacket.' She smoothed her hands over the silky nap of the velvet, enjoying the soft surface texture and, underneath it, the broad hard shoulders.

When he didn't immediately respond, she leaned back and looked into his eyes. What she read there wasn't desire; she couldn't be sure what it was.

'But it's late and perhaps you're tired.' She began to draw away.

'Don't be a fool,' he said roughly, pulling her back to him. 'I've been waiting for this all evening.' He tilted her head back and kissed her.

It wasn't the kiss she wanted, tender and loving. He took her mouth fiercely, possessively, almost, it seemed to her, angrily. Her mind resisted the force she felt burning in him; her body was quickly reduced to a shuddering surrender.

The day after Boxing Day, leaving Angela Dunster, a horse-mad teenager who often helped out during the holidays, in charge of the stables, Sarah and Nick drove to the south coast to visit Sammy.

It was amazing to see the change Eileen Slane had wrought in him. He looked in much better health and even several years younger, dressed in new smarter clothes, with his hair no longer smarmed down with pomade in the habit acquired in boyhood.

To Sarah the most extraordinary change was that he

didn't seem to miss Longwarden or the horses at all. In Mrs Slane's ultra-neat bungalow with its picture windows looking out on small, well-kept front and back gardens, and beyond them the roofs and TV aerials of rows of almost identical bungalows, he seemed to be perfectly at home. Television, shopping trips to the supermarket, whist drives and bingo at a social club for senior citizens – all the things Sarah would have thought would be anathema to him – seemed to divert and delight him.

'Can it last, do you think?' she asked Nick, as they set out for home.

'Why not? He's never been looked after so well in his life. She's a great cook, she does all his laundry, waits on him hand and foot . . . he's living like a king compared with his set-up before.'

'I know, but it's so suburban . . . so genteel. Little mats under every flower pot, dozens of terrible ornaments, plastic flowers in his bedroom . . . it just isn't Sammy.'

'He likes it. He's happy,' said Nick. 'He's a hell of a sight more comfortable than he ever was at Longwarden. That's important to people when they get old. You might hate living like that. So would I. But they don't. Eileen likes all those ornaments. They're souvenirs of places she went with her husband. She told me about them while he was showing you his room. I can't honestly see how the things she's got on her mantelpiece are any worse than some of the stuff at Longwarden. All those pictures of dead birds and hares aren't everyone's cup of tea, you know.'

He was driving. He glanced sideways at her. 'Another thing you don't take into account, Sarah, is that Sammy didn't choose to spend his life with horses. He was pushed into it, same as I was. People like you and your cousins choose what to do with your lives. Most people don't. They have to take whatever's going. It's only when they retire they do as they like for a few years. By then it's too late for a lot of things.'

Sarah murmured agreement. She wanted to get off this subject now. It seemed to be leading towards another discussion of Nick's future. He hadn't said so outright, but she knew he hadn't enjoyed hunting with her yesterday.

It had been no problem to find him the necessary kit. Hunting clothes of every description, including swallow-tail coats, white leather breeches and the protective silk aprons worn before mounting in her grandparents' day, were still stored away in cupboards near the brushing room where a special valet had once done nothing but keep them immaculate.

In a black coat, buff breeches and black boots, Nick had looked very smart. But even though she had found one which fitted him well, he had jibbed at the top hat which was *de rigueur* with the Carlyon for all men excepting farmers and the Prince of Wales.

'I feel a twit in this,' he had complained, unconvinced by her reassurances that he didn't look one.

Although he rode very much better than most of the members and, unlike some, knew better than to ride too close to hounds or ignore the field master's order to hold hard, at every check she had sensed his unease.

Twice, during longish waits, she had introduced him to people as 'My friend Nick Dean'. He had answered when he was spoken to, but mainly in monosyllables and with a marked air of reserve. How could he expect people to be friendly when he himself was so unforthcoming?

After an unpromising start, it had turned out a very good hunt with a mixed pack tearing across a marvellous line of country but eventually losing the fox when he got to ground. As an attempt to make Nick share her enjoyment, it had been a failure – a disaster. Hacking home through a heavy shower, his coat collar turned up, rain dripping from the brim of the detested silk hat, he had hardly spoken. His expression had said it all.

When they had come back to Longwarden to find the Christmas house party included a Frenchwoman, close to Risconti's age and also an artist, Allegra's immediate reaction had been pleasure. She had looked forward to having some interesting conversations with Marie-Simone on her own account.

However, in the days after Christmas, Allegra began to feel that Marie-Simone might be exaggerating her interest in Longwarden's works of art. Wrapped up against the cold in unused, unheated rooms, she and Risconti spent hours studying paintings which had hung unregarded for generations, or bent over portfolios of drawings and early prints discovered in the library.

At first Allegra was amused by their enthusiasm and happy to leave them to it while she chatted to Jane and John Brodick. It wasn't until he left to celebrate Hogmanay with friends in Scotland that she realized just how much time the two artists were spending together. When they were alone, she discovered, they spoke Italian, switching at once to English when someone else joined them, but preferring to rattle away in Risconti's native tongue when *à deux*. Marie-Simone spoke it fluently, with all the accompanying gestures and graphic facial expressions. At first sight, in spite of her chic clothes, Allegra had thought her passé. That judgement, she realized now, had been mistaken. With dismay, she recognized the stirrings of jealousy, an emotion she had always despised in others and never expected to experience herself.

Marie-Simone had allowed Jane to persuade her to stay for New Year. She knew it would have been wiser to leave immediately after Christmas.

Or would it?

Life was so uncertain. Didn't wisdom lie in seizing every chance of happiness, however brief? Was it wrong to enjoy a few more days in the company of a man she could have loved if he hadn't been already committed? What harm could it do, except to intensify her loneliness when she returned to France?

Time, which had dragged so interminably slowly since John Graham's death, now began to race towards the year's end. She couldn't prolong her visit much beyond the first of January.

The more time she spent with Risconti, the more clearly

she saw that in spite of his success and his liaison with the beautiful Lady Allegra – whom Jane liked but Marie-Simone didn't – he wasn't a happy man.

JANUARY

For Jane, Allegra and Sarah, the New Year began with hugs, kisses and good wishes in the Warehams' crowded cottage where many of the thirty guests had had to sit on cushions on the floor to eat the buffet supper Emily had spent two days preparing after returning from a Christmas visit to her family.

Although Risconti had kissed her first, Allegra wasn't pleased to see him turn from her to Marie-Simone. Even though the kisses they exchanged were only on each other's cheeks, she felt sure the Frenchwoman would have preferred a mouth kiss. Perhaps he would also have liked it.

Sarah made sure she was near Nick at midnight. Fortified by plenty of Warehams' plonk, she said, 'Happy New Year', and reached up to kiss him on the lips.

For a few seconds his arms closed round her and she felt his instinctive response, quickly repressed.

Mavis Osgood opened her front door, found Police Sergeant Lacock on the doorstep and turned hot and cold with terror.

It was less than half an hour since she had climbed down from the bus, laden with carrier bags, after a day at the Sales. Her first thought was that she must have been spotted by one of the store detectives, followed to Melchester bus station and reported to Longwarden police station.

'Oh my Gawd!' she moaned, clutching her chest.

''Afternoon, Mrs Osgood. I'd like a word with your son, please.'

'M – my son?' she echoed hoarsely.

'If it's convenient,' he said politely.

She began to realize her mistake. It wasn't her he was after, it was Tarquin. Relief swept her like a hot flush.

Resenting the scare he had given her, she said, 'I don't know as it is. He's upstairs. He might be asleep. He woke up poorly this morning.'

'Had a skinful last night, did he? He should be feeling better by this time of day. I shan't keep him long.'

'What's it about?'

'You'll hear that in a moment. I'd like you to be present when I talk to him.'

'You'd better come through.' The longer she kept him on the doorstep, the more chance there was of someone noticing him there and spreading the word round the village that Tarquin was in trouble with the fuzz, as he called them.

Her opinion of Sergeant Lacock didn't prompt her to usher him into her front room, or to invite him to sit down, or to offer him tea. She showed him into the back room and left him standing while she hurried upstairs.

Tarquin was lying on his bed, chewing gum and reading a comic. He hadn't heard the voice of their visitor because he was plugged into his trannie, his body jerking to the rhythm of the rock music blasting his eardrums.

In response to his mother's urgent signals, he removed the ear-piece. 'Wha's up?'

'What you bin up to, Tarquin? I've got Sergeant Lacock downstairs. Says he wants to have a word with you.'

For a moment he looked uneasy. Then he shrugged. 'I int done nothing. Tell him to piss off.'

'He's not going to leave till he's seen you. You'd better come down and find out what it's about.'

'Bloody hell . . . int there no peace?' Reluctantly, he sat up and swung his feet to the floor.

'Wha's all this about then?' he demanded truculently, as he entered the back room.

Sergeant Lacock gave him a look of marked distaste before saying to Mavis, 'I should sit down, Mrs Osgood. What I have to say may come as a shock to you.'

Mavis sank into a chair. In her most refined voice, determined not to let him guess that inwardly she was quaking, she said, 'Just what is my boy supposed to have done wrong, Sergeant?'

'What makes you think he's done wrong, Mrs Osgood?' Sergeant Lacock asked blandly. 'Been in trouble before, has he? Where you lived before you came here?'

'He's never been in trouble nowhere. He's always been a good boy.'

'I've heard that a few hundred times,' the policeman said dryly. 'Usually in court. You ever been in court, Osgood?'

'If it's any of your effing business – no, I int,' was Tark's sullen retort.

He received a cold stare. 'I'd advise you to keep a civil tongue in your head, m'lad. It's come to my ears that you've been a party to an incident which, if charges were to be laid, could get you into serious trouble.'

The policeman produced a notebook and flicked over several pages till he came to the one he wanted. 'According to my information, on the Friday of the week before Christmas, shortly after closing time, you and some of your mates was engaged in following a young man out of the village with the intention of committing an assault. Fortunately for all concerned, you were prevented from doing so and no harm took place. What have you to say to that?'

'It's a fu . . . bloody lie. We wasn't intending no harm. It was just a bit of a lark, like. Weren't our fault if the silly sod got the wind up. We never laid a finger on him.'

'Who? Who are you talking about?' Mavis insisted.

'Young Dean who's employed as a groom by Miss Sarah Lomax,' said the sergeant. 'But it wasn't him reported this matter to us. He prefers to forget the incident, which is lucky for you, Osgood. We were told what happened by Mr Rivington. If he hadn't happened to be nearby, guarding his birds, and scared you lot off with his shotgun, there's little doubt in my mind that you'd now be charged with causing grievous bodily harm. I'm here to warn you that Longwarden isn't like London where you might get away with threatening behaviour and violence. We're not used

568

to that around here and we're not going to have it. One more step out of line and we'll be down on you like a ton of bricks. Do I make myself clear?'

Tark lit a cigarette and filled his lungs with smoke. He exhaled, turning his head and ejecting a stream of smoke sideways, his expression making it clear where he would have liked to direct it.

'Is that all you gotter say?' he asked insolently.

'That's all – for the present,' the sergeant replied, glaring at him. He turned to Mavis. 'If you want your son to keep out of trouble, Mrs Osgood, I advise you to take this matter very seriously. It's lack of parental control at the root of most of the cases we have to deal with. It may be too late in this case,' he continued, with another stern glance at Tark. 'But I should be failing in my duty if I hadn't spoken to you and the parents of the other lads. We know all the participants,' he concluded grimly. 'I'll see myself out. Good afternoon.'

When the front door had closed behind him, Mavis began to cry.

'As if I hadn't had enough trouble in my life,' she moaned, dabbing her eyes with a tissue. 'There'll be talk, you can be sure of that. You can't do nothing around here without someone noticing. I've been ever so good to you, Tarquin. You've never wanted for nothing. It's not right to worry me like this . . . bringing the police round.'

'So what? Who bloody cares? For Christ's sake stop that row, Mum,' Tark said disgustedly. 'There wouldn't have been no trouble if that old sod Rivington hadn't of interfered. You would have had something to blub about if he'd blown my head off, like he threatened. He ought to be locked up, mad bastard, before he does someone an injury.'

'That may be, but what about your lot trying to do Nick Dean an injury?'

'Serve him right, stuck-up bleeder. The girls what think he's a hero should have seen him that night. Scared shitless he was. Pissed hisself I shouldn't wonder.'

'I've told you before, I won't have that dirty talk, Tarquin.'

'So what you going to do about it then? Put me over your knee and give me a spanking?' he jeered. 'I've taken enough crap for one day. Don't you start nagging.'

The rude retort enraged Mavis. It occurred to her, for the first time, that her son was becoming a nuisance, just the way Ron had.

Her plump hands, so deft at whisking goods out of sight, clenched as she answered tartly, 'I'll tell you what I can do about it. You can find yourself somewhere else to live. You're not staying in this house, Tarquin, if you're going to cause trouble.'

The fierce look in her eyes surprised him. She sounded as if she meant it.

'Cool it, Mum. Don't get upset. Have another cuppa tea. That must be cold by now, innit?'

In an effort to calm her down he took her cup to the sink, disposed of the cooling tea and poured a fresh cupful for her. She was a stupid old cow but she had her uses. For what a bit of smarm cost, it was worth keeping on the right side of her.

'I'll have a drop of whisky in it. I've been all of a shake ever since I opened the door,' said his mother.

As he went to fetch the Johnny Walker from the mirror-lined cocktail cabinet in the front room, Mavis felt pleased with the effect of her ultimatum. She had spoken in temper, using the only threat she could think of in the heat of the moment. But presently, sipping the laced tea after Tarquin had gone back upstairs, she began to consider, calmly, whether her son, like Ron, wasn't becoming more trouble than he was worth.

For two or three days after Marie-Simone's return to Paris, Risconti seemed restless and moody. Allegra pretended not to notice. She didn't want to believe he was missing another woman, but what else could be upsetting him?

One night she woke up to find herself alone in the bed. She put on her robe and went in search of him.

She found him downstairs in the library, drinking cognac at two in the morning.

'What are you doing down here?' he asked, almost angrily.

'Looking for you. Shall I go away?'

He gave her a long brooding stare which filled her with apprehension that she was about to be told he had fallen out of love with her. It happened. It had happened to her countless times.

He shook his head. 'No . . . come here.' He beckoned her to join him.

When she sat down some distance from him, he moved up and put an arm round her.

'I don't like England in January. I want to go somewhere warmer. Will you come with me?'

She felt almost sick with relief. 'Need you ask? Where shall we go?'

'An American woman I painted some time ago has a house in Barbados she said I was welcome to use whenever it was empty. Tomorrow I'll call her and ask if it's free at the moment. If it is, we could go right away.'

'I don't know why I didn't think of it myself. An escape to the sun will be lovely.'

She tucked her feet up beside her and covered them with her robe. 'All my summer clothes are at the flat but it won't take long to sort them out. We could be there by the weekend.'

'If the house is available and we can get a flight, I want to be there tomorrow night. You can buy what you need when we arrive.'

All the clocks in the room began to strike the half-hour. Risconti said, 'It's still yesterday in Chicago. I'll try to get Alice now. The number's in my book upstairs.'

He drained the glass and stood up, pulling her with him.

In the sixth Earl of Carlyon's time there had sometimes been as many as a hundred horses at Longwarden, with forty strappers to groom them. In those days of unimaginable affluence, when in winter one footman spent all day tending the fires and none of the family or their guests would have thought of throwing on a log or drawing the curtains when dusk fell, the sixth Earl had added a large indoor school to the stable block where his horses could be exercised in bad weather.

It was there, shortly after her cousin and Andro Risconti had come to say goodbye to Sarah before driving to Heathrow, that Nick had a heavy fall.

Sarah was riding Beddo at the other end of the school and even he hadn't liked the sudden shattering bang when an aircraft broke the sound barrier. Nick was taking Jane's younger hunter, Minerva, round the jumping course, trying to correct her tendency to rush her fences. Sarah didn't see exactly what happened, but the bang must have spooked Minerva into aborting her take-off and pitching Nick over her head.

As he crashed to the ground and lay sprawled on his back, every fatal or disabling accident she had ever witnessed or heard of flashed through her mind in the moments it took to cover the distance between them and spring from the saddle.

'Nick ... Nick ...' she exclaimed, in terror, flinging herself to her knees beside his spread-eagled body. 'Please God ... oh, *please* ...' she prayed, aloud, bending over him.

He opened his eyes. 'Only ... winded,' he said, in a faint voice.

'Are you sure? Don't move. Lie quite still.' She was terrified his violent impact with the ground might have injured his back.

Neither his arms nor his legs looked as if they were broken, but his spine had taken a terrible jarring. She laid a hand on his right thigh. 'Can you feel my hand?'

He was struggling to get his breath back. He nodded, and nodded again when she put a light pressure on the other leg.

'I'm ... okay ... don't ... worry,' he gasped.

But it wasn't until he had heaved himself into a sitting position and then, with her help, managed to clamber to his feet, that she believed him.

As he stood with his arm on her shoulders, still groggy from having the air bashed out of his lungs, she looked up at him. 'For a minute I thought you were dead. Oh, Nick . . .' She burst into tears, hiding her face against his chest.

He put both arms round her. 'For Pete's sake, there's no need to howl. I'm fine. It's Minerva you should be fussing over. Talk about panic!' He cuddled her, patting her back. 'Hey, come on now . . . why all the fuss? I've come a cropper before and you haven't boo-hooed all over me.'

'Y-you could have b-broken your back,' she mumbled, shaking with reaction.

'Not a chance. I was born to be hanged . . . so Ted used to tell me,' Nick said cheerfully. His hand stroked her hair and his voice was deeper and softer as he said, 'There's nothing to cry about, *chica* . . . I'm not hurt . . . hush now . . . hush darling . . .'

Even without the endearment there was no mistaking the tenderness in his tone. Almost at once her tears ceased. Her breathing steadied. After a moment or two she lifted her head, raising her wet face to his.

'You called me *darling*,' she whispered, her eyelashes spiky from weeping but her blue eyes shining with joy.

Nick scowled. 'Well . . . I'm fond of you, dope . . . don't like you crying,' he said gruffly.

He released her and would have stepped back but Sarah flung her arms around him, locking her hands behind his back.

'You love me!' she exclaimed triumphantly. 'I'm sure of it now . . . I'm not going to let you go until you admit it . . . until you kiss me again.'

'For God's sake, Sarah . . .' he growled, looking so angry and embarrassed that, for an instant, she wondered if her instinct was wrong and it was only fondness he felt.

Then his arms wrapped her tightly to him and he groaned as if holding her close was a mixture of pleasure and pain.

'This is wrong . . . this is crazy,' he muttered.

But he did as she wanted. He kissed her.

*   *   *

573

In the house, North was asking Jane, 'Would you like to go to Barbados with Allegra and Andro while I'm away on my trip?'

After her experience of a New England winter, Jane didn't feel intimidated by anything the weather here could produce. She wanted to know her new home at all seasons of the year and was quite looking forward to seeing the park enveloped in snow.

'If you had been free, it might have been fun to make up a foursome, but I don't think three is a good number,' she answered. 'I'm happy to stay here while you're on your expedition. Maybe I'll spend a little time in France with Marie-Simone . . . take her skiing perhaps.'

Also she was planning, while he was away, to make intensive efforts to recruit staff, and to take expert advice on having a swimming pool built in the orangery. There seemed to be nowhere outside where a large pool wouldn't spoil some part of Pen's garden and to put it inside the orangery would make it usable all year.

'I should have got to hell out of it after the dance. I knew bloody well this would happen if I hung around,' Nick said grimly. 'I should have left before Christmas.'

They were still in each other's arms, standing where he had fallen.

'But you didn't. In your heart of hearts you wanted this to happen,' Sarah murmured happily.

'If your cousin could see me now, he'd kick me out faster and harder than I fell off Minerva,' said Nick. 'And I wouldn't blame him. He warned me to keep my hands off you.'

'North warned you? When? I didn't know that.'

'Ages ago . . . soon after I got back here. He told me to watch my step with you. I told him I would. I more or less gave him my word.' As he spoke his arms dropped to his sides and he would have ended their embrace had Sarah, her arms round his neck, not refused to release him. He put his hands up to grasp her wrists, trying to disengage her hold but unable to do so without using enough force

574

to hurt her. 'Come on, Sarah: let me go. If we go on standing like this, someone is going to see us.'

'What if they do? We're not doing anything wrong. North had no right to forbid you to touch me. I've never heard such old-fashioned nonsense. I'm not a minor. I make my own decisions.'

'You know he was right. There's no possible future for us.'

'He may not think so. I do. I've loved you a long time, Nick . . . since before you went away. All the time you were gone, I missed you terribly. I know you didn't miss me. Not then. But you would now . . . wouldn't you?'

He ignored the question, saying bleakly, 'You missed me because you weren't going around with any other guys. The way you feel now . . . you'll get over it. You'll have to. We both will. No way are we ever going to get your family's approval. As soon as they know, I'll be told to pack and get out. They won't have me here five minutes once they find out.'

Sarah thought: We could marry without their approval. They would have to accept a *fait accompli*.

But she knew he would never agree to a hole-and-corner wedding.

'I think you're wrong,' she told him. 'Why should they be so against us loving each other?'

'You know why,' he answered, with a trace of impatience. 'They'll say it's because we're too young. But even if we were older, it wouldn't change their real objection. I'm working-class . . . a working-class bastard . . . that's what it boils down to.'

'Oh, Nick, I could *shake* you at times,' she exclaimed, in exasperation. 'Working-class . . . what does it mean? Not what it used to. *Everyone* works hard now. Even socially "working-class" is meaningless. Class is an out-of-date concept. It's what people are in themselves which matters today . . . whether they're bright or dim, generous or selfish, amusing or dull . . . all those things. By those standards you score brilliantly. How many other local boys would have had the initiative and guts to go off and join a foreign army? They're the qualities which matter; not who your parents were or how they lived their lives.'

'It isn't only my background your family are going to object to . . . it's the fact that I haven't any kind of future lined up.'

'You're forgetting something. Like you, I haven't really got a family,' Sarah reminded him. 'My father is dead. Goodness knows what's happened to my mother. Wherever she is, obviously she isn't the slightest bit interested in me. As for the others . . . if Uncle Edward were alive he might disapprove, but Aunt Pen won't. She's had too many rows with Allegra to want to start lecturing me. Even North isn't seriously interested in what I do. He was probably only warning you not to make a pass at me. Our loving each other is different.'

Nick had never seen her so lit up. Since the night of the dance, when he had slammed her down, he had been aware of her misery and hated himself for causing it. Now she was glowing with happiness and he had caused that too. It was hard to resist the appeal in her eyes, or the temptation of her soft parted lips.

Was it possible she was right and, together, they could overcome all the obstacles between them?

An hour before touch-down Allegra went to the lavatory and changed her sweater for a short-sleeved cotton shirt lent her by Jane because there hadn't been time to pick up any of her own cool clothes. She also peeled off her tights and pinned up her hair.

When she said goodbye to the cabin crew and stepped from the aircraft into the starry night, the damp heat made her thankful for bare arms and legs and no hair on the nape of her neck.

The baggage began to come through. Customs clearance was quick. Soon they were in a taxi on the last lap of the journey.

A few miles from the airport, the driver turned off the main highway and they followed a country road winding between fields of tall sugar cane. Near the top of a hill two massive stone gateposts appeared in the beam of the headlights. The taxi swung through them and followed a sloping drive lined by trees and shrubs.

'By the way, the house is called Paradise,' said Risconti.

The house was lit by moonlight and starshine when she saw it for the first time. She would never forget it.

'Hello, Nick. Come in,' said Emily.

He ducked his head under the low lintel of the cottage door.

'I went to Melchester this morning. I bought this for Matthew.' He offered her a parcel.

She led him to the other room where her son was sitting on the floor banging a plastic flower pot with a wooden spoon, surrounded by other bits of harmless household equipment.

Nick said, 'He won't be able to work it. Perhaps it's not right for his age. You may have to keep it for later.' He went down on his haunches and joggled one of the child's bare feet. 'Hi there, Matthew old buddy. How're you doing?'

Emily was always rather touched by Nick's behaviour with the baby. Rob, in spite of his size, had the look of a man who would be good with small children. Nick didn't. Even out of uniform he looked like a soldier on leave from a crack regiment; toughened and tempered by discipline and strenuous training. There was even something slightly dangerous-looking about him. It surprised her that he could be so gentle with her infant son.

The toy which had caught Nick's fancy was a furry clockwork caterpillar which humped its way across the floor, rolling its eyes as it moved. It segments were covered with bright-yellow soft nylon bristles. Matthew was fascinated. He pursued it on hands and knees but wasn't quite sure he wanted to touch it.

'What can I offer you, Nick? Coffee? A beer?' Emily asked, when the caterpillar had been re-wound several times.

'A beer, please.'

When she returned from the kitchen, he had put the toy back in its box and was sitting in an armchair giving Matthew a canter on one of his long muscular legs.

'What took you to town?' she asked. 'Did Sarah go with you?'

'No, I went alone. I felt like a change of scene for a few hours. I get a bit restless at Longwarden.'

'You're not really a village person, are you?'

'No, I'm not . . . which complicates things.' He paused. 'As if they weren't complicated enough already,' he added, lifting Matthew from his leg to the floor.

It seemed to be a cue for her to say, 'Oh, are they? In what way?'

'I'm in love with Sarah,' he said quietly.

'And she's in love with you.'

Emily's statement seemed to startle him. 'How did you know? Has she talked to you?'

'Not a word. I guessed. And why not, half the girls in the village have their eye on you, I shouldn't wonder.'

To her amusement, he flushed, embarrassed by the implication. He was tough, but he wasn't conceited, she thought approvingly.

'If Sarah was one of them there'd be no problem,' he said broodingly. 'We'd get married and I'd take her with me. But she doesn't want to leave England. Everything that matters to her is here.'

Emily found nothing to say. She was beginning to realize that, having confided in her, he was going to ask for advice.

'I understand that,' Nick went on. 'But what she doesn't understand is that I don't fit in, and never will. I'm not their class; that's the long and the short of it. They're thoroughbreds. I'm not. God knows what you'd call me. But it's not good enough for Sarah. I know that even if she doesn't.'

It was Emily's turn to feel embarrassed. She agreed with him but she didn't want to say so.

At that moment, to her relief, Rob entered the room. 'Hello, Nick. How are you?'

Before Nick could reply, Emily said, 'Have you time for

a beer and a chat? Nick has something on his mind.' She turned to him. 'You don't mind Rob knowing, do you? Actually we have discussed the possibility that you and Sarah were in love.'

'Has it been that obvious?'

'Probably not to everyone. Perhaps we recognized the signs having been in the same state ourselves not so long ago.'

'How does Sarah feel about it?' Rob said, looking at Nick. 'Have you asked her?'

'She wants me to join forces with her, but I'm not keen on the idea. I was pushed into being a groom. I'll never be an outstanding rider . . . a top eventer. I'm lousy at dressage. It bores me. Sarah wants us to be a husband and wife partnership like the Greens and Mark Phillips and Princess Anne. But David Green is an Aussie and Mark was an officer with a middle-class background.' Nick turned to Emily. 'I bet your parents wouldn't have let you marry a blacksmith if he hadn't been to a public school and had the right kind of accent.'

'I'm sure they'd have been more unhappy if I'd wanted to marry someone with the right accent, as you put it, but none of the really vital qualities, such as kindness and a sense of responsibility,' she answered.

'That's absolutely right,' Rob agreed. 'But the main thing in your case, Nick, is that there's no way it will work if you two don't want the same life . . . or not at this moment. I feel Sarah's too young, and too involved in eventing, to have any other commitments. So are you. You're not twenty-one yet. Go off and see some more of the world. She'll still be around when you get back.'

'Time won't make any difference,' Nick said heavily. 'Even if I made some money – which isn't likely – around here I'm always going to be the illegitimate son of a gamekeeper's sister-in-law.'

'Only in the eyes of the older, more narrow-minded people,' Emily said firmly. 'What Rob says is more important. Marriage never works out for people with different objectives. However much I loved him, it would have been crazy to marry if I'd wanted a London life. You said earlier that you were restless . . . in need of a change of scene. You're a born adventurer, Nick. You've never had strong family ties – quite the reverse if half the stories about Ted Rivington are true.'

Nick said, 'I don't know what the hell to do for the best. What do you think, Rob?'

'I'm not sure advice is worth much. We all have to make our own decisions,' Rob replied thoughtfully. 'I've already told you, more or less, what I think. I know it's damned hard to wait when you want something or somebody, but you and Sarah do have an awful lot against you and not very much going for you. The only thing in your favour is that hers isn't a conventional family. That makes them slightly less likely to throw up their hands in horror at Sarah wanting to marry you. But she's too young, Nick. That's the crunch.'

After a pause, he went on, 'Why don't you go to North, tell him the way you feel about her, but say you realize it's not on – or not until you're both older. In the meantime, if I were you, I'd re-join the Spanish Legion. You speak the language now. You won't be starting at the bottom. A soldier's life seems to suit you.'

'It does . . . or it did,' Nick agreed. 'But I don't know that it will now . . . the way I feel about her.'

Hearing Ashford speaking to Jane about his projected holiday made Pen start to consider going away herself. Not for a holiday as such, but in the hope that far from familiar surroundings she would be able to view her dilemma with more detachment. The problem was where to go.

In spring or summer a motoring tour of Scotland or southern Ireland would have appealed to her. In mid-winter the risk of bad weather was too great.

Expense was another consideration. She couldn't afford a long flight to the exotic places where people of unlimited means sought the winter sun. Somewhere cheap with a mild, dry climate and good walking was what she had in mind.

When a travel agent in Melchester suggested a package holiday in Spain, Pen studied the brochures he gave her and came to the conclusion that neither Marbella nor Benidorm was a place where she could feel at ease.

She still hadn't made up her mind where to go on the day she went to London for her annual dental check and, at Jane's firm urging, to have her hair cut again by Peter.

Between these appointments she went to the Marble Arch branch of Marks & Spencer to buy thermal underwear and thick tights. She was waiting in line to pay for the things she had chosen when a woman whose face seemed familiar joined the short queue. After eyeing each other uncertainly, they both realized at the same moment where they had last met.

'It's Penelope, isn't it?' said the other woman. 'I'm sure you can't possibly recognize me, but I was Helen Sedgefield. We were at school together.'

Pen nodded. 'Your parents lived in the Far East and you used to fly out there for holidays.'

'How clever of you to remember, considering it's well over thirty years ago and I'm now a grandmother. Are you?' Helen asked, smiling.

In the years since their schooldays, her hair had turned prematurely white but it had remained thick and curly and her bright hazel eyes and cheerful expression were the same as when she had been deputy head girl.

'Not yet, but I may be quite soon. Are you here on a visit?' Pen asked. She seemed to remember reading in the old girls' section of the school magazine that Helen had married out East.

'No, we live in England now. Since my husband's retirement, home is a cottage in Kent where at long last I have a garden I shan't have to leave behind as I have with so many gardens when Jack's job forced us to move every few years.'

'I'm a gardener too, but my life has been just the opposite. I've lived in the same place for over thirty years,' Pen told her. 'I've been a widow for some time.'

'Could we lunch together?' Helen suggested. 'I've discovered a rather nice place just across the road.'

'I'd be delighted to join you,' Pen agreed readily.

It was to the Selfridge's Hotel, tucked unobtrusively behind the great department store, that Helen took Pen. Within fifteen minutes of meeting they were comfortably settled on a banquette in the restaurant.

'This really is an unexpected pleasure,' said Helen. 'I don't often come up to London, but Jack had to come today and I thought I'd come with him. We're meeting for tea at the Over-Seas League. By the way, my married name is Wimborne. What's yours?'

'Carlyon.'

'Now . . . what to have? Last time I had the low-calorie salad and a glass of white wine. I think I'll stick to that.'

'I'll have the same. Tell me about your garden, Helen. What sort of soil are you on?'

Their mutual interest in gardening launched them on a conversation which revealed that Helen's husband had worked for one of the international petroleum companies. It was clear that, unlike Pen, she had never had cause to regret her marriage.

Pen said as little as she could about her own married life and was also evasive about her children, choosing not to disclose that they had both achieved fame. Fortunately, if Helen knew of North as a photographer, she didn't connect his name with Pen's and had no idea that the garden in which her school-friend toiled was many times larger than her own and had been, at its zenith, one of the finest in England.

They had finished their salads and were having coffee when Pen remarked, 'You're very brown. Have you been re-visiting Singapore?'

The other woman shook her head. 'We've just spent two weeks in Spain. We have a tiny village house there which we use quite a lot in the winter. Jack would like to live there all the time but he knows I prefer it here, so we compromise.'

She paused, her expression clouding.

'Usually we go to Spain early in January and stay there till the end of February. But this year we had hardly arrived before Jack developed a health problem which we felt should be checked at once. That's why he's in London today . . . to have some more tests. Even if the trouble isn't serious – which I'm praying it may not be – we shan't be going back to Spain. My eldest daughter is expecting her third child soon and she needs me to look after the others while she's in hospital.'

'I'm so sorry about your husband. How very worrying for you.'

Helen nodded. 'It is. That's why I came with him to-day – because I couldn't stand staying at home. I knew I shouldn't be able to settle to anything. He wouldn't let me go to Guy's with him, but at least I shall know how he got on sooner than if I'd stayed behind. I didn't intend to unload my troubles on you, Penelope. Probably you've been through something like this yourself and have no wish to be reminded of it.'

'My husband was killed in an accident. It was very sudden . . . and I can't pretend I was heart-broken,' Pen confided impulsively. 'We were hopelessly incompatible. Not like you and your husband.'

'What a shame,' Helen said sympathetically. 'Yes, we've been very happy. Whatever happens, I shall have that to hang on to – thirty years of wonderful happiness.' Her voice broke and she bowed her head, her hands tightly gripping the paper napkin on her lap.

Pen saw that to pat her arm or to speak to her could undo Helen's effort to regain command of herself.

Catching the eye of their waitress, she said, 'May we have two more coffees, please, and also two glasses of brandy.'

Helen blew her nose and discreetly dabbed at her eyes. 'Dear me, what a lapse from the iron self-control enjoined on us by Miss Darrington,' she murmured, striving for lightness and referring to their former head mistress. 'I hope brandy won't go to my head. A salad isn't very good

583

blotting paper. Still I expect they'll be very small brandies, not like the lavish measures they give one in Spanish restaurants.'

'Where is your Spanish house?' Pen asked. 'Is it on the coast?'

'No, no – it's several miles inland. We prefer to stay clear of the tourist areas. Sant Jeroni has attracted some foreigners, but only the more discriminating ones. If ever you want a quiet holiday with nothing much to do but go for long walks through the vineyards or up stony mule-tracks, you must borrow our little house. We often lend it to friends when we don't want to use it ourselves. It doesn't have a swimming pool or any garden to speak of. There's a tiny courtyard at the back where I grow a vine and geraniums which Maria, our neighbour, waters for me when I'm not there.'

'It sounds delightful,' said Pen. 'How do you get there? Can you fly or do you drive?'

'We fly – either to Alicante or Valencia. Sant Jeroni is more or less midway between them and they both have cheap charter flights. We take a taxi from the airport and hire a small car when we arrive. Out of season, it's not expensive.'

The girl reappeared with their coffees and brandies.

Pen said, 'What an extraordinary chance that I should meet you today. I've been looking for somewhere to go for a quiet holiday. A travel agent did suggest Spain as the best place for a cheap winter holiday, but all the resorts in the brochures look terribly off-putting.'

'Most of them are,' Helen agreed. 'But I'm sure you'd adore Sant Jeroni. The local people are dears, as friendly and helpful as can be, and you'd be perfectly safe on your own there.'

'Could I manage . . . speaking no Spanish?'

'Yes, yes – no problem. You'd need to mug up a few basic civilities such as *buenos dias* and *muchas gracias*. But with supermarkets and sign language, anyone can manage in Spain nowadays. When do you want to go?'

Pen told her the dates she had in mind, adding, 'But I

couldn't *borrow* your house, Helen. You must let me rent it from you at the going rate.'

'I wouldn't hear of it, my dear. I must warn you it's very basic. So don't go expecting luxury or you'll be disappointed. I'll give you my telephone number,' Helen continued, opening her bag. 'As soon as you've fixed up your flight, I'll write a note to Maria, telling her when to expect you. She'll open the shutters and make up the bed. If you're arriving late on Saturday, she'll make sure the fridge is stocked with all the essentials.'

Later, as they were leaving, she said, 'I can't tell you how much I've enjoyed this unexpected reunion. Although we were never close friends at school, I always liked you. Later in the year, I hope you'll come and see my garden.'

'I should love to. Helen, it's not important for me to have my hair done today. Shall we spend an hour or two window-shopping together? I can easily ring up and cancel my appointment.'

'It's sweet of you, but no – please don't. I'll be all right, I assure you.'

Hurrying south towards Berkeley Square, Pen's sympathy for the other woman's anxiety was mixed with nervous excitement at the thought of going on holiday by herself. By the time she arrived for her appointment, she had decided not to mention the matter to her family until the arrangements were *fait accompli*.

In one of the deserted store rooms in the old kitchen wing at Longwarden, Tark was settling down for a long wait. He had his small trannie to help pass the time, a sleeping bag and a half-bottle of whisky to keep out the cold, and a whole sliced white loaf spread with marge and sandwiched with tinned luncheon meat to stave off hunger.

Getting himself inside the house had been no sweat. Chalky had said it'd be dead easy, and it had been. Now all he had to do was to sit tight until it was time to go and pick up some samples for Chalky to show his mates, the professionals who'd come and turn the place over proper, once he'd proved it was worth it.

After that he'd come back to kip down until, some time tomorrow morning, he was able to scarper. That could be the tricky bit. If he did run into anyone on the way out, he'd say the same as he'd planned to if he'd been seen coming in: that he was looking for his mother.

He grinned to himself. At this very moment the stupid old cow was running around with a duster in his fucking Lordship's front rooms while he, Tark, was sat here, out the back, waiting his chance to nick a pocketful of the gold boxes that they had lying around on tables.

There hadn't been nothing handy for nicking when he'd had a snout round at the dance. Later on, when he'd said to his mother they didn't seem to have no silver cigarette boxes nor nothing, considering the money they'd got, she'd told him that everything like that had been put away and locked up, in case anyone got in what hadn't been invited. In the normal way, according to her, they had silver photograph frames and stuff worth hundreds of quid lying around all over the place. But the old berk in charge, Mr Ashford, would notice in a minute if anything went missing, she had added.

Tark thought she'd only said that because she hadn't the nerve to nick nothing herself. Funny that. She'd walk out of a shop with anything that took her fancy, cool as a bloody cucumber.

Tomorrow he was going to London. The sooner he passed the stuff over to Chalky, the better he'd like it.

Chalky was a mate from Tark's London days. His mum was a scrubber and the bloke what knocked her up must've been a nig-nog because although Chalky's skin wasn't much darker than Tark's, he had frizzy hair, thick lips and yellow eyeballs.

Chalky and her lived in a room in Notting Hill, near the Portobello Market. As a kid he'd spent most of his time hanging around the market, on the look-out for Yanks with wallets in their back pockets, or Yanks' wives putting their handbags down while they looked at something they wanted to buy. On Saturday mornings, when the market was swarming with tourists hoping to pick up a bargain, sometimes

Chalky had struck lucky and got something for nothing. He had told Tark there wasn't many bargains let go on the antique stalls. The dealers was too fly for that.

Among the dealers was some what didn't ask questions if they was offered something they reckoned would fetch a good price off a rich Yank. That was what Chalky'd do with the stuff Tark picked up tonight; flog it to some of the dealers who knew fucking well that anything Chalky was selling had to be nicked, but who didn't give a shit about that, long as they made their bit.

Course Chalky would take his cut, and a bloody good cut it was, Tark thought grudgingly. But as well as flogging the stuff, he was going to show it to some pros and set up a deal with them. Tark, who wasn't born yesterday, hadn't let on exactly where he was living now. If Chalky and them knew that, they could make a bloody good guess where the house was what didn't have no burglar alarms, nor any dogs worth worrying about.

For that information, they'd have to pay him, and not peanuts either. Chalky had said that most big houses in the country, like this one Tark knew of, was so well-equipped with electronic eyes and alarms what alerted the local fuzz that the odds against getting in and out was too high to make it worth trying. But this place of Tark's sounded easy.

The room he had chosen to hide out in was as far as possible from the main passage connecting the stableyard with the main part of the house. The chances of anyone finding him in here were nil. Judging by the dust and the cobwebs, it was years since anyone had been in here.

This particular room had the advantage of a large wooden table, something warmer to lie on than the cold, stone-flagged floor; and the floor had a drain in it where he could have a piss without making his hiding place stink. If he needed a crap later on, he'd go in the room next door – unless he could hang on and do it right in the middle of one of his Lordship's carpets, he thought, with a smothered guffaw. That'd give the old butler a shock, finding a pile of shit on a carpet tomorrow morning.

Thinking about the night of the dance rekindled his hatred of Nick. What would be good would be if, when they they found some stuff missing, they thought that bleeder had taken it. Yeah, that would be great, that would. He could swear blind he hadn't, but how could he prove it? There wouldn't be none of Tark's dabs to show who *had* done the job. Chalky had warned him to wear gloves and not to touch nothing with bare hands.

From sadistic thoughts about Nick and what he would like to do to him, Tark's mind turned to thoughts of Sarah.

He had seen her briefly that night, tarted up, looking a treat in a dress that showed she had bigger tits than he'd thought. Thinking about her slim body in the slinky blue dress, and the way her legs looked with high heels, gave him a hard-on. He lay down on the outspread bed roll, unzipped his black leather trousers and imagined Sarah astride him.

Late that night Nick packed his kitbag. Then he sat down to write a letter of farewell to Sarah.

It was no use trying to say goodbye to her in person. She would only beg him to stay and he might not be able to stand firm. If she cried, he hadn't a hope.

This way was the best. No arguments. No tears. No last kisses. In the morning when he didn't appear at the usual time, she'd come up and find him gone and the letter left on the bed. By this time tomorrow night he'd be far away from Longwarden.

Explaining his reasons for leaving, trying to make her understand that he didn't want to desert her, but he had to, there was no other way, was ten times harder than writing an ordinary letter.

Even after several false starts and scrunched sheets of paper, his final attempt didn't really satisfy him. He knew how much it would hurt her to read it from the way it hurt him to write it. Hurt like hell. But Rob's advice had been sound: the longer he delayed making the break, the worst it would be for them both.

The letter written and sealed, he set his alarm clock to

wake him at four in the morning. He needed a few hours' rest before setting out.

When he lay down, his preparations completed, it was long past his usual bedtime. He was tired but not sleepy. In the hope of dulling his mind and stopping him thinking, he got up and drank a strong slug of Fundador, the Spanish brandy which had been one of Sarah's Christmas presents.

She was such a sweet, thoughtful girl. They could have been so bloody happy if she hadn't been who she was, or he had been someone like Rob. Even then it might not have worked out. She was so bound up with eventing. Competing at Badminton in April was all-important to her. Except in so far as it affected the horses' training programme, she didn't care if the weather between now and then was unremittingly cold, wet and miserable. He did. Day after day of grey skies and drizzle depressed him. There were places where winter wasn't like this, or only for a day or two at a time. But when he was out of this climate and back in uniform somewhere, would he miss her as much and more than he'd missed the camaraderie of the barracks while he was over here?

Oh Christ, this is hopeless, he thought. I must get some sleep if I'm going to leave here at four.

Another pull at the bottle failed as an effective opiate. His mind went over and over the reasons why he must leave, without convincing his heart he could face a future away from her.

Sarah sat up and switched on her light, unable to sleep. Her mind was too full of Nick and a disturbing intuition that, even though he had finally admitted to loving her, her hold on him was still uncomfortably tenuous.

Apart from the strong pull of Spain and his life in the army, he was deeply, obstinately convinced he wasn't good enough for her. None of her passionate arguments had succeeded in shaking that conviction. She felt sure his attitude had its roots in the years of being relentlessly abused and denigrated by Ted Rivington. Most people in Nick's age group weren't oppressed by feelings of inferiority, whatever their origins. Nor, it was clear, was he when he was abroad. It was only here, at Longwarden, that he seemed preternaturally conscious of his unfortunate start in life.

All day in Sarah's mind the belief had been growing that, if only he would make love to her, Nick would see everything differently. So far, however, instead of being eager to get her into bed, he seemed determined to avoid any situation which could lead to it. Today, if she hadn't taken the initiative, they wouldn't even have kissed. Both times it had been he who had pulled away, stopping short of the uncontrollable kisses she would have welcomed.

But if I went to him now . . . if he woke up and I was there, sitting on his bed . . .

The memory of how he had looked that first morning, sleeping, made her shiver with longing to be locked in his arms.

The more she thought about it, the more she convinced herself the time had come to take a bolder initiative.

Leaving the warmth under the duvet, she grabbed her quilted dressing gown and stepped into sheepskin slippers. This, her former bedroom, now in use again, was not one of those with a bathroom, but it did have a washbasin, concealed by a screen, in one corner.

Sarah brushed her teeth, combed her hair and sprayed it with toilet water. She decided that her brushed cotton nightshirt wasn't exactly a turn-on. Her summer clothes were stored here, including a pretty nightdress of see-through blue voile.

As she put her keys in the pocket of her dressing gown and flicked on her torch before turning off the room lights, she was trembling, partly from cold and partly from nerves.

When the time came to make a move, Tark found himself unwilling to leave the security of his hide-out. He took a last lung-filling pull on his fag, held with finger and thumb, before flicking it to join the other dead butts scattered all over the floor.

The air in the room was thick with the stale exhalation

of hours of chain smoking. After relieving himself over the drain, he put the neck of the now more than half-empty bottle to his lips and tilted his head back. The final swig made him feel better, bringing the alcohol in his system to a level at which the dark unfamiliar corridors of the huge house seemed less spooky than they had moments earlier. After pulling on the gloves, he flexed his thick fingers and rotated his shoulder joints, movements he associated with big powerful blokes, afraid of nothing.

'Right, matey. Here we go then.'

Remembering how, on the night of Nick's homecoming, they had alerted Mr Ashford to their presence in the kitchen, Sarah switched on no lights as she flitted through the great silent house, only the beam of her torch showing her the way.

As she turned the last corner and entered the long bare passage leading to the stableyard, someone else with a torch was coming towards her. Thinking it was Nick, she stopped short and reached for the switches close to the corner. As two bulbs illumined the passage, she froze in astonishment. It wasn't Nick. It was Mrs Osgood's nasty son who stood there, equally transfixed, his full pink mouth hanging open.

She was the first to recover. 'How did you get in here?'

Although it was often left unlocked during the day, at night the door at the far end was locked with two different keys. She had a pair. So did Nick. There was also at least one spare set on the butler's large key ring.

Tark looked like a frightened horse in the instant before its bolts. Then he seemed to take hold of himself.

'Now don't go screaming the house down. I int going to hurt you. If you wait a tick, I can explain.'

Sarah hadn't thought of screaming. Surprise, not fear, had been her immediate reaction. It wasn't like finding herself face to face with a stranger whose presence would cause instant panic.

'I think you'd better,' she said sternly.

'Well . . . it's like this,' he began, moving towards her.

591

'I – I had a row with me Mum, see, and she locked me out. There weren't nowhere else I could go. I couldn't sleep rough, not this weather. So I thought I'd come here, like. I didn't mean no harm – honest.'

Sarah's instinctive reactions all had to do with horses rather than people. The important, the vital thing with horses, if their behaviour was threatening, was never to show fear or anger and certainly not to turn tail. Calm, quiet-voiced reassurance was what was required in most cases.

With this principle deeply ingrained, she didn't back away as he approached her. But neither was she reassured by his explanation. It sounded a story made up on the spur of the moment.

'I see. But how did you get in?'

'Through a window what was open.' He gave a jerk of the head at the warren of passages and rooms leading off the passage where they were. 'I was going to kip in the stables, along of the horses, but I thought that might upset 'em. Then I noticed the window bin left open.'

That confirmed he was lying. All the ground-floor windows in this part of the building were protected on the outside by heavy iron bars. There was no possibility he could have entered by a window.

'Where are you going now?' she asked.

'I was looking round for a toilet. Where was you going?'

'One of the horses is sick. I have to check he's all right. You can come with me, if you like. There's a lavatory in the yard you can use.'

As she spoke she stepped past him, heading for the outside door. Once she had it unlocked she would be safe. At the moment she wasn't. The fact that he was wearing gloves made it clear he was up to no good. If he realized she knew it, he'd clap one of those gloved hands over her mouth before she could raise the alarm. What he might do after that, God only knew. Anything was possible. Badly scared amateur burglars had been known to kill before now.

592

For a moment it seemed she was going to get away with it. He let her walk half a dozen paces before he caught up and grasped her arm.

'You got perfume on, int you?'

Forced to a standstill, she gave him a baffled look. She had forgotten the scent she had sprayed on her hair.

'You're not going to see no horse. You're sneaking out to where he sleeps . . . that bugger Dean. You're having it off with him, int you?'

He leaned towards her, making Sarah recoil from his nicotine and whisky breath.

'Let me go,' she said angrily, wrenching away.

Both were mistakes: the involuntary shrinking and the attempt to break free. He grabbed her roughly with both hands.

'If he's going to get a fuck, how about something for me?' He hauled her against him and kissed her.

At first it was only his hot lips she had to endure and they were horrible enough. Then his great thrusting tongue forced its way into her mouth, making her choke with revulsion. She struggled violently, and she was a fit girl with the strong shoulders and arms of all eventers. But her muscles were useless against his half-drunken brute force. Attempting to fight him was futile. Her resistance seemed to excite him. If he was going to rape her, there wasn't a thing she could do.

When she tried going limp, at least it made him break off the long sickening kiss.

He grinned at her. 'That's more like it. Get a feel of this then.' Gripping her wrist, he forced her hand down between their bodies, pressing it against the hard bulge inside his trousers.

'Please . . . let me go,' she pleaded. 'I've got the keys to that door. You can leave. I won't tell anyone.'

'Not much you wouldn't . . . bitch.' His leer had become a black scowl. 'You've messed me up proper, you know that? You and your sodding boyfriend.' With sudden terrifying violence, he rammed her hard against the wall, holding her there with his leg pushed between her thighs while he fumbled with the buttons of her dressing gown until, becoming impatient, he ripped it open, exposing her thinly veiled breasts.

She was preparing to scream, even if no one would hear because they were all far away and soundly asleep, when the sound of his heavy breathing was joined by a sharper noise; the scrape and snap of a key being used. Seconds later it was repeated. As the yard door was pushed open and Nick appeared, she began to sob with relief.

It took Nick less than two seconds to take in what had been happening. At the same time Tark let go of Sarah and stepped away from her.

Pulling the front of her dressing gown together, shivering with cold and shock, she watched them advance on each other. Tark had his back to her now. She couldn't see his expression, only Nick's. It was demoniacal. He looked ready to kill.

What happened as soon as they reached each other was swift, brutal and decisive. Tark made a grab at Nick's chest, at the same time ducking his head. Whatever the outcome should have been, it didn't come off. Faster than a snake striking, Nick brought one knee driving upwards into Tark's groin.

With an agonized howl he collapsed and fell to the floor where he lay, doubled up, moaning.

Nick drew his foot back and kicked him hard in the buttocks. 'You filthy sod. I'm going to take you apart.' He reached down and grabbed a handful of Tark's curly hair, savagely jerking his head up, making him shriek with fresh agony.

'No, Nick – you mustn't. Stop it!' Sarah ran towards them, knowing she must intervene or Tark would be beaten senseless. Even after his assault on her, she couldn't stand by and watch Nick inflict more punishment.

'Please . . . please . . . I can't bear it.' She seized his arm, almost afraid he would turn on her.

He gave her a strange blank look. 'He would have raped you.'

'I know, but he didn't . . . and I can't take any more.'

The message seemed to get through. He nodded. 'I'll throw him out. Be back in a minute.'

Heaving Tark to his feet, he lugged him, still bent and stumbling, towards the door.

Shuddering now, badly shaken up, Sarah tried to get a grip on herself. She rubbed her hand over her mouth, trying to erase the imprint of slobbering lips. Her whole body felt soiled and degraded by the close contact with Tark's.

The short-lived but vicious fight had been like a second assault; she had never seen two men go for each other before. In her world such things didn't happen. What she had seen in Nick's face had been almost as frightening as the lust in Tark's.

Nick came back, looking himself. Still angry but sanely so, not out of his mind with blind, uncontrollable rage.

'Are you all right? Stupid question. How could you be after that?' He put his arms round her. Gently.

He must have been drinking as well. For an instant the smell of liquor and his tall, powerful maleness made her flinch from being touched.

'It's all right. He's gone. You're safe now. I'm here. Just take it easy.'

He spoke as he would to Tatty if something upset her, and with the same effect. After the brief recoil, Sarah slumped gratefully against him, his strength a shield, not a threat.

'Oh, Nick, it was awful . . . horrible. Thank God you came.'

'Jesus, yes! If I hadn't . . .' He drew her more closely into the shelter of his arms. 'I came in to fetch my combat sweater. I'd left it in the airing cupboard. If it hadn't been for that . . .' She felt his body clench at the thought of what would have happened but for his intervention. 'What were you doing down here at this time of night? How did he get in the house?'

She had buried her face against his shoulder. With a slight shake of the head, she said, 'I don't know . . . how he got in. I was coming to see you. Oh, I'm so cold . . . so freezing.'

'You'd better come up to the room. I'll make you a hot drink.' His arm round her waist, he led her towards the door.

The only light in the yard came from the lantern beside the door to his staircase. Most of the yard was in darkness or deep shadow. While Nick was locking the door to the passage behind them, they both heard a sound which made Sarah jump and clutch at him. It hadn't been a horse noise.

'I thought you said he'd gone,' she breathed.

'Easy, girl.' Nick's warm hand covered her cold shaking fingers for a moment before he took a torch from the pocket of his padded waistcoat.

He flashed it towards the inky darkness of the archway. Tark was there, leaning forward, a puddle of vomit on the bricks at his feet. He was still holding his crotch and supporting himself with a hand on the wall.

Nick strode towards him. Sarah hung back.

'I thought I told you to get the hell out of here.'

Tark let go of the wall to screen his eyes from the strong beam shining directly at them.

'You'll get yours, fucker . . . you wait. I'll get you . . . I'll get you for this.' He retched, but nothing came up.

'Try it,' Nick told him coldly. 'You got off lightly this time. Next time you come at me, shit, you'll get the works and no messing. Now beat it. I won't tell you a third time.'

He transferred the torch to his left hand and, fist clenched, moved menacingly forward.

Tark reeled away through the arch, muttering a stream of venomous filth, much of it unknown to Sarah.

'Come on: let's get you warm.' Nick bundled her up the staircase.

Reaching the tiny landing, she said, 'I think I'm going to be sick too,' and hurried through to the lavatory. Although she wasn't normally squeamish, the sight of Tark throwing up had made her own stomach uneasy.

Crouching beside the pan, she heard Nick moving about in the other room. The closing of the cupboard door made

596

it sound as if he had been putting things away, although she had never known him to be anything but tidy.

The queasy feeling passed off. She washed her face and rinsed out her mouth. Feeling less defiled but still perished, she rejoined him. The electric radiator was beginning to raise the temperature and the electric kettle had already boiled.

'You'd better have a tot of this as well,' he said, pouring brandy.

'My feet feel like lumps of ice. Have you some socks I can borrow? Better still, I could sit in your bed and put the electric blanket on . . . unless it's on already?'

'No, but that's a good idea. Put it on full,' he suggested.

Snugly ensconced in the familiar bed, warming her fingers round a hot mug of tea, the brandy gleaming like a topaz on the night table, Sarah began to feel better.

'What about the police?' she said. 'Ought we to call them tonight or will tomorrow do? You saw he was wearing gloves? That could only be because he intended to steal things.'

Nick sat on the edge of the bed, level with her feet. 'Tell me exactly what happened . . . where you were when you first saw him.'

She described her first sight of Tark and all that had followed up to the moment when Nick had opened the door. He listened without interrupting, but his jaw knotted with muscle when she spoke of being kissed. At the end he was silent, frowning thoughtfully down at the threadbare oriental rug overlying the fitted sisal matting.

Finally he said, 'I don't think we should tell the police. It sounds to me as if he was on his way in, not on his way out. If that's so, the less said the better.'

'You mean let him get away with it? – Apart from what you did to him?' When he nodded, she added, 'But why, Nick?'

He raised his eyes to her face. 'In my book what he did to you . . . what he intended to do . . . is a hell of a lot worse than pinching stuff. But if you tell the police about that, they're going to start asking questions. What you were doing in your nightclothes in that passage at that time of night will be the first thing they'll ask. Your cousin or his wife will be there when they question you. Bound to be. What are they going to think?'

'I see what you mean. I hadn't thought about that.' After a short pause, she went on, 'I could tell them what I told Tark . . . that I was going to a sick horse.'

'He didn't believe you. Nor would they. If one of the horses had been sick, I'd have been looking after it. Or if you had come down here at night for that reason, you'd have dressed first. Anyway none of the horses are sick. Your family know that even if the police don't.'

'Mm, you're right,' she conceded. 'Anyway I'm hopeless at lying. I don't think I could to the police. But how can I keep it from North that Tark broke into the house? I have to tell him *that*, Nick. I can't not.'

He was silent, thinking about it. Watching his preoccupied face, Sarah began to realize that part of the purpose of her midnight excursion had been achieved already. She was in his bed. Now all she had to do was to persuade him to join her.

'Are you warming up now?' he asked.

'Yes, I'm feeling much better. But the other pillows would be nice. Then I could lean back.'

For reading in bed, the divan was equipped with four pillows, all with piped covers to disguise them as cushions by day. Nick fetched them and piled them behind her.

'Thank you. That's much more comfortable. Don't go away.' She caught hold of his sweater and made him sit down nearer to her than before. 'You don't mind if I stay for a bit, do you? If I go back to my own room I shall only lie awake thinking about what happened.'

'All right . . . for a bit,' he agreed.

He hadn't pursued the matter of why she had been coming to see him. Probably he guessed the reason – what *other* reason could there be? – and thought it best not to question her.

'Do you know what I should have minded most if he *had* raped me?' she asked quietly.

'Don't think about it, Sarah. Try to forget it,' he said, frowning.

'Tomorrow I will. Tonight it's fresh in my mind. It's better to talk about it, Nick.' She slipped her hand into his. 'What I should have minded most would have been that drunken beast having something I was keeping for you. Does it seem silly to you that I've never wanted to make love with anyone except you?'

His fingers tightened on hers. 'No, it doesn't seem silly. It seems very nice,' he said gruffly.

He lifted her hand to his lips, pressing them against the back of it. She felt sure, as he bent his head, she saw tears filling his eyes. Nick moved to tears because she had kept herself for him? What a strange man he was. So brutal not long ago, but always so gentle with her. When he went on nuzzling her hand, keeping his head down, she knew she hadn't imagined it.

'I'm getting a bit too warm now.' Pulling her dressing gown off the shoulder furthest from him, she managed to wriggle her arm out of the loose sleeve and pull the robe round behind her. It was automatic for Nick to help her remove it completely. Then he saw the pink tips of her breasts through the transparent voile and astonished her again by flushing a much deeper pink. As if he had never been close to a half-naked female before.

'Christ! No wonder you were frozen,' he said, quickly looking away. 'Anyone would be in that thing.'

'I thought you slept without anything on.'

'I do, but I don't run around in the raw. Not in January. Would you like some more tea?'

She recognized it as a pretext to move away and took counter-action by once more holding his hand. 'No, but there's something I should like.'

Nick didn't answer. Perhaps he sensed what was coming.

'The best way to help me forget that revolting kiss in the passage would be for you to kiss me. Please, Nick.' She leaned towards him, putting her free hand to the back of his neck and gently stroking his nape with the tips of her fingers.

'For God's sake, Sarah –' He sprang up, trying to tug his hand free.

She refused to let go, clinging to it with both hands. 'At least hold me close for a minute. Or are you put off me now? – Now that he's pawed me?'

'You know bloody well it's not that,' he retorted vehemently. 'I want to kiss you . . . to hold you . . . but I know if I start I may not be able to stop.'

She said softly, 'Why must you stop? I want to go all the way. I love you, Nick. I want you to take me . . . tonight. *Please* . . . is it so much to ask?'

For a moment, as she looked longingly up at him, she thought he was going to hold out. Then, with a stifled groan, he sank down and gathered her close.

'If he had hurt you, I would have killed him,' he whispered, before he kissed her.

She surfaced from a deep sleep, remembering at once that something wonderful had happened.

At first she thought it was autumn and she was at the George at Stamford, the morning after winning the gold at Burghley. Then the confusion cleared and she knew it was winter and last night she had gone to sleep with Nick's arms round her and their legs tangled together, as snug as two puppies in a basket.

Some time in the night he had got up. She remembered feeling a draught and murmuring, 'Where are you going?'

'Only to have a pee.' He had tucked the duvet round her shoulders and she had drifted back to sleep. She also had a vague memory of feeling him kiss her cheek. Perhaps that had been when he came back to bed.

Now it was morning. Still dark and probably unpleasantly cold outside the cosy nest of the down-filled quilt. Where was he?

Not in the bed. It was far too narrow for two people to be able to lie in it without touching, especially when one of them was his size. Perhaps he was up. What time was it?

Turning on the lamp on the night table, she saw that it was two minutes before her usual getting-up time. Nearly always her body-clock woke her shortly before the clock would have done, although after such a disturbed night it wouldn't have been surprising if for once they had both overslept. Where was he?

There were no sounds coming from the shower room. Beginning to be rather puzzled by his absence, she sat up, pulling the duvet with her, a smile of satisfaction curving her lips at the sight of her flimsy nightie lying discarded on the rug.

Then she caught sight of the envelope on the wide window ledge: an envelope with *Sarah* written on it in Nick's hand.

As she leaned forward to reach for it, it wasn't the cold air on her naked back but a premonition which made her shiver. The envelope was lightly sealed. Putting her thumb under the flap, she hesitated; knowing in her bones that her world was about to fall apart.

Sarah heard George Burton's milk truck drive into the stableyard at its usual time while she was quartering Berber. It startled both her and the horse when the milkman suddenly appeared at the door of Berber's box. 'Morning, Miss Sarah. Can't get in this morning. Door's locked.'

'Oh . . . sorry, so it is.' She spoke soothingly to Berber, wondering if George would notice she had been weeping.

Had it not been for the noise made by the horses when she and Nick failed to appear at the usual time, she would still be lying in the archway room, crying her eyes out. But even when the sky caved in, the horses still needed attention. Luckily she always kept a change of working clothes in the stables. She hadn't had to trek back to her room in the house and lose even more time before hurrying to make a start on twice as many chores as usual.

'I – I came round the house instead of through it this morning. And I left the keys in my other jeans. I'll have to run up and get Nick's. I won't be a minute,' she said.

Nick's letter was on the unmade bed where she had left it when impatient whinnies and the noise of a bucket being

601

overturned had reminded her she couldn't go on crying all day. The sight of it made her lips quiver but she managed to blink back fresh tears.

'Shan't be sorry to have a cuppa tea. Shakes you up, seeing a bad accident before you've had breakfast,' said the milkman, waiting for her by the door at the foot of the staircase.

'An accident?' Sarah repeated, without interest.

'Mind you, the way that kid rode his bike, it was on the cards he wouldn't never make old bones. Still, asking for it or not, it's a shame a young bloke his age . . . smashed to pieces.' He grimaced. 'Proper nasty it was. I didn't see him myself. They'd covered him up when I got there. But even the coppers looked as if it'd turned their stomachs, and they're used to that kind of thing.'

Absorbed in her own disaster, the last thing Sarah wanted to hear was the details of a fatal accident.

As she hurried to unlock the door for him, the milkman said, 'His mother works up here, don't she? Or did, until this happened. You won't be seeing her again for some time, I shouldn't think. What a shock for her, when they tell her. Her only son. Dead as mutton. What a terrible shock.'

As the import of this sank in, Sarah slowed down and stopped. 'You mean it's Mrs Osgood's son who's been killed?'

'That's right – Tark Osgood.'

Mavis Osgood had seen Tarquin's visit to London as an ideal opportunity to arrange a visit from Rita, a contact she had made in London who disposed of the goods for which Mavis had no personal use.

She had thought getting rid of her surplus might be a problem after they moved to the country, but it turned out that Rita had a lot of suppliers in the provinces. Some she visited frequently; others, including Mavis, at longer intervals. It was some months since her last call.

Rita arrived very early. She drove a small plain van with nothing about it to attract attention, and she herself, when at work, was a plain, plump, middle-aged woman with a forgettable face.

She preferred it when her clients had a driveway inside the garden so that she could back up the van and load the goods unobtrusively from the back door or the garage. In Mavis's case this wasn't possible. The van had to be parked in the street and a number of large cardboard cartons taken in and out of the house in full view of passers-by and inquisitive neighbours. This was the reason Rita made a pick-up only when Mavis was starting to run out of storage space.

On arrival she brought in the cartons and had a cup of coffee and a chat. Then the two women got down to business.

Melchester-born PC Keith Stock had started his career in the Metropolitan Force because he thought London offered more varied and interesting police work than the constabulary of his native county.

He hadn't bargained for meeting and becoming engaged to a girl who not only didn't want to be parted from her mother but also was dead against Keith staying in London where he might be involved in a riot. Madly in love, he had yielded to Carol's persuasion to apply for a vacancy at Longwarden.

On his first morning on duty at Longwarden, PC Stock was the passenger in a panda car when it was directed to go to the scene of an accident reported by a cowman moving his herd along a back road near Lord Carlyon's place.

In several years in the London force, PC Stock had never had to deal with a more gruesome accident than the one which had caused the death of a local ton-up boy called Tarquin Osgood. Later he was told by Sergeant Lacock to accompany him on the equally unwelcome errand of informing the deceased's widowed mother.

'It's good riddance to bad rubbish. That's the fact of the matter,' said the sergeant, on their way there. He told PC Stock about his recent visit to the house.

'How d'you think she'll take it, Sergeant?' asked the constable.

'Hard to say. May be hysterical. May take it quietly. Never can tell, in my experience. It's at times like this we could do with a WPC. They're better at breaking bad news, especially in cases where there's no husband.'

Outside the Osgoods' house was a dark green Ford van with a London registration number. When PC Stock pointed this out, Sergeant Lacock paid scant attention, being in the process of bracing himself for one of the most painful duties of his occupation.

When Mavis came to the door he didn't expect her to look pleased to see him.

'What's it this time?' she asked, with a snap. 'My boy's not here today. If you want to see him, you'll have to come back another time.'

She would have shut the door in their faces but the sergeant said quickly, 'It's you we want a word with, Mrs Osgood.'

'Me? What am I supposed to have done?'

'If we could come inside for a minute . . .'

'It isn't convenient,' she said shortly. 'I'm entertaining a friend. You can state your business without coming in, I'm sure.'

'I'm afraid we have some bad news. There's been an accident. Your son –'

'Oh, my God! Is he hurt bad? Where is he? Where did it happen?' She no longer peered round the door but let it swing fully open, both hands clutching her chest.

'It happened just outside the village.'

'What? But he went up to London. I wasn't expecting him back until late tonight. What was he doing near here?' she asked in bewilderment.

The two policemen exchanged glances. Already there were features of the accident which puzzled them. To these she had added another.

'That I can't say, Mrs Osgood. Before we go any further I think you ought to sit down. Perhaps your friend could put the kettle on.' He made to step inside the hall.

'No . . . no, I've told you . . . you can't.' Her voice had risen a pitch. 'How bad is it? Where have they taken him? If he's in Melchester hospital, I'll get my friend to run me there.'

'He's been taken to Melchester – yes, but not to the hospital. I'm very sorry to have to tell you your son didn't survive the accident. It would have been very quick. He wouldn't have suffered, Mrs Osgood.'

In view of her nervy manner, Constable Stock expected her reaction to be a loud scream or a flood of tears. It was neither. Her eyeballs rolled up in their sockets and she started to sag slowly sideways.

They caught her before she fell. 'Not the front room. That'll be cold. Through the back where it's warm,' said the sergeant.

A radio was on in the back room. The table was spread with what, a month earlier, would have looked like an unusually large array of Christmas presents waiting to be wrapped. Standing with her back to the door when PC Stock opened it, a woman was packing things into a large cardboard box.

Without looking round, she said, 'I can take as many of these electric curling brushes as you can get for me, Mavis. They're more in demand than heated rollers these days.'

She glanced over her shoulder and saw the two policemen heaving Mrs Osgood's limp weight through the door and on to the couch. Her jaw dropped. She looked aghast.

'Hello, Rita,' said PC Stock. 'Fancy seeing you here.' He turned to the sergeant. 'The last time Rita and I met, she'd been booked on suspicion of receiving. We couldn't make it stick, unfortunately.' He surveyed the goods on the table. 'I think we might this time, don't you?'

While she finished the chores, Sarah had done some intensive thinking about all the implications of the milkman's news.

If Tark had been killed, no one need ever know he had been in the house last night. That was one worry removed. But it was a trivial anxiety compared with what had replaced it: the fear that somehow Nick was involved in Tark's death.

She saw now that she should have guessed Nick was planning to leave. Why else would it have been necessary for him to retrieve his sweater from the airing cupboard at that hour of night? Equally obvious, in retrospect, was that what he had been putting out of sight while she was in the loo, feeling sick, had been his already-packed baggage. If only she had been more alert, instead of shocked and upset by Tark's attack on her, she would have seen all the signs that Nick was ready to move out.

What tortured her more than his preparations to leave without telling her, except by means of the letter to be read after he had gone, was that the events of the night hadn't changed his mind. Was it possible that by making him make love to her she had actually reinforced his decision to leave Longwarden?

If it were not so, why had he followed his plan through?

It was unbearable to think that what, for her, had been a night of supreme happiness, had not been enough to delay him even for a day.

But since the milkman's arrival, her pain, her despair, her failure to understand how he could have loved her and left her, all those emotions were nothing compared with the heart-freezing fear that he had had something to do with Tark's fatal accident.

Now, as she passed the spot where less than twelve hours ago the dead youth had terrorized her, she wasn't thinking of that ordeal but of Tark's threat to 'get' Nick, and of the words Nick had whispered. *If he had hurt you, I would have killed him.*

Was that what had happened while she was peacefully sleeping? Had Tark still been lurking somewhere near the house when Nick had set out on his journey? Had they had a second fight? Had Nick lost control and killed him? And then somehow made it look as if Tark had died in an accident?

It was a possibility almost too horrible to contemplate, but she couldn't dismiss it from her mind. And she knew that if Nick *had* killed Tark, it didn't affect her love for him.

> *Love is not love*
> *Which alters when it alteration finds.*

The words of a Shakespearian sonnet, committed to memory at school but imperfectly understood, came back to her now as she realized that nothing Nick might have done or could ever do would alter her love for him. It had long been and always would be an 'ever-fixèd mark' in her life.

'Where's Nick?' asked Mrs Armitage, when Sarah arrived at the kitchen on her own.

Sarah had planned her reply to this question. For the time being it was better if no one knew he had gone for good.

'He's going to be away for a few days. Last night he had a call from a man who was in the Legion with him. They're meeting in London. Nick left first thing this morning. That's why I'm late for breakfast. I had more to do than usual.'

The explanation was accepted without comment. Mrs Armitage was dying to discuss the shocking news brought by George Burton.

'Young Lady C has gone down to the village to see if there's anything she can do for poor Mrs Osgood,' she told Sarah. 'I do feel sorry for that woman. She idolized her son, even if nobody else had a good word for him. It's enough to give her a nervous breakdown.'

But for the news about Tark, Sarah would have avoided having lunch with the others. She wasn't hungry. All she wanted was to be alone with her misery.

However, because it was important to glean every detail she could about the accident, she wanted to hear about Jane's call on Mrs Osgood.

She had forgotten that her aunt's eldest brother, Sir Geoffrey Standish, would have arrived during the morning to spend a few days at Longwarden. Also Jane had some news for them of a sufficiently astounding nature to ensure that she was the centre of attention.

'You're not going to believe this at first,' Jane told them, unfolding her napkin. She had asked the butler to remain in the room because what she had to tell was of equal interest to him. 'When the police went to tell Mrs Osgood the news about her son, they found a dealer in stolen goods at the house. That little woman, who looks so ordinary and respectable, is a professional shoplifter. When she heard about Tarquin, she fainted. After she'd revived she admitted everything, first to the police and later on to me. She's been stealing things all her life. She feels she was driven to it by parents who wouldn't give her things other girls had. Then by a very mean husband and recently by her son who bullied her into stealing for him.'

'Sounds to me like the usual sob story petty criminals invariably trot out when they're caught,' said Sir Geoffrey. 'Have the police found anything from this house among her loot?'

Jane shook her head. 'I don't think so. The stores in Melchester are where she did most of her stealing. Nothing has disappeared while she's been working here, has it?' she asked the butler.

'No, m'Lady. Had it done so, I should have reported it.'

'Would you have noticed necessarily?' said Pen. 'We've a lot of bits and pieces lying around . . . snuffboxes . . . étuis and so forth.'

'That is so, m'Lady. Nevertheless I can assure you nothing has been missing since Mrs Osgood was engaged. When I myself first came to Longwarden and found there was no room-by-room inventory of the many small valuables in them, I thought it advisable to make one. The last complete check was made before the ball in November when everything pocketable was put in safe-keeping. Apart from the periodic checks I make, I'm confident the rest of the cleaning staff would be quick to report the absence of any object, however small. In Mrs Osgood's first week here, she was frequently taken to task by her colleagues for not replacing an object precisely where she had found it.

Mrs Ashman and Mrs Bailey are especially particular about that.'

'Good. In that case you won't have to waste time appearing in court to give evidence. If she's been systematically shoplifting all her life, let's hope she gets a stiff sentence,' Sir Geoffrey said sternly.

'I don't think a woman who's just lost her only son would be likely to get a stiff sentence,' said his sister. 'She'll be put on probation, I imagine.'

Sarah said, 'How was he killed? What happened? Do they know?'

'I asked about that,' said Jane. 'Not in Mrs Osgood's hearing, naturally. There was no other vehicle involved, as far as they know. But I gather the boy had been dead for some time before the police got there. They won't be able to say exactly when the accident happened until after the autopsy. Whatever Mrs Osgood has done, you have to feel sorry for anyone who has to identify her son after a horrible accident.'

'When will the inquest be?' asked Sarah.

'I don't know,' said Jane. 'Nobody mentioned that. Where would the inquest be held? In Melchester?'

'Longwarden inquests are held in the back room at the Arms,' said her mother-in-law. 'The coroner for this side of the county is our local solicitor. He'll probably arrange the inquest as soon as the post mortem's been done.'

That evening, after her last look at the horses, Sarah went up to the archway room. It seemed impossible so much could have changed in such a short time. Yesterday at this hour she had been a virgin, Tark had been alive and Nick had been here, although preparing to leave.

She was wondering how she was going to endure the agony of waiting for the inquest to reveal whether there had been any suspicious circumstances attaching to Tark's fatal accident, when the sound of footsteps on the staircase made her catch her breath.

Had he come back? For an instant her heart leapt with mingled joy and anxiety. More than anything in the world she wanted him to return to her, but not at the risk of being arrested for manslaughter, or worse.

Almost at once she realized that the footsteps, although male, were not his. With North now in Antarctica for the south polar summer, the only men in the house were Geoffrey Standish and Mr Ashford. As she opened the door, the butler came into view.

He said, 'I was going to look for you in the stables but I saw the light on up here. A few minutes ago, I had a telephone call from Nick.'

'Why didn't you put him through to the tackroom or here?'

'There wasn't time. It was a very brief call. As soon as I answered the telephone he said he was calling from abroad and would be cut off very soon. He asked me to tell you he'd be writing to you, and he asked if you were all right. I said you were, to the best of my knowledge. He started to say something else but we were disconnected.'

'What was it he started to say?'

'I caught the words "Keep an eye . . ." which I assume was going to be a request for me to keep an eye on you. I think you were probably aware that when he left here Nick was going rather further than London, weren't you, Miss Sarah?'

She nodded. 'But how did you know I knew?'

'It was a guess. Your normally excellent appetite seems to have deserted you today and you haven't looked quite yourself.'

'Did you know Nick was going away? Had he told you?'

'I knew it was in his mind . . . had been for some time. Not that he had decided.'

'Did he ask your advice? Did you encourage him to go?' she asked, with sudden bitterness.

'It's some time since we discussed the subject. The only matter on which he consulted me was whether I thought he'd do better to re-join the Spanish Legion or try a spell in the French one. He never asked my advice on anything of a more personal nature . . . although I did suspect that the problem of his future was more complex than he let on. I liked Nick very much. I sometimes wished he were my son.'

Suddenly the need at least to confide her love, if nothing else, was overwhelming.

'I wanted to be his girl . . . eventually his wife,' she said, with a break in her voice. 'Oh, Mr Ashford, what am I going to do? I love him so much and Nick said he loved me. How could he leave me? How *could* he?' Her face crumpled like a child's and tears began pouring down her cheeks.

Somehow she found herself weeping all over the chest of the butler's off-duty sweater while he patted her back and murmured, 'Poor child . . . poor little Sarah,' as if he were *her* father.

'I've never seen such gorgeous hibiscus, Elizabeth,' said Allegra, coming downstairs to find the Barbadian house-keeper tucking the flowers into a cascade of pale-green hops on the hall table.

The gardens at Paradise were full of hibiscus bushes, the colours of their flowers ranging from dark pink and palest lemon to white, salmon pink, vermilion and soft apricot. Every morning Isaiah, the gardener, Elizabeth's husband, cut fresh blossoms to replace those which had wilted during the night. Compared with the hibiscus which grew in the warmer parts of Europe, the flowers here were huge. In the large airy rooms shaded by a wide verandah which encircled the entire house, their colours seemed to glow even more vividly than in the bright light outdoors.

Indoors, the flowers and Elizabeth herself, with her burnished dark skin and wiry black hair, gave an exotic spice to the blending of furniture made from Barbadian mahogany but copied from designs in fashion in England in the late eighteenth century and the modern American chintzes of the curtains and slip-covers.

'And you arrange them beautifully,' Allegra added, paus-ing to watch the housekeeper completing the spectacular display on the Sheraton-style half-moon table facing the open front door. From the door and the portico outside, a long vista of rolling cane fields could be seen through a break in the trees which bordered the grounds.

'Thank you, ma'am,' said Elizabeth, beaming.

With a diaphanous sarong over her bikini, Allegra was on her way to have her pre-breakfast swim in the large Roman pool concealed from the rest of the garden by high walls of coral stone over which flowering creepers had swiftly flung swags of colour.

The American banker and his wife who were the present owners of Paradise had introduced modern amenities, such as the pool, with the greatest discretion. None of their improvements detracted from the eighteenth-century elegance of the house and its gardens.

Originally, Paradise had been the centre of a sugar estate covering a thousand acres. The sugar lands had been sold off about eighty years ago when the family who had built the place had died out. Three hectares of woods, lawns and meandering paths set on the crest of a hill nine hundred feet above sea level were what remained. The temperature at Paradise was always five degrees cooler than in the hot streets of Bridgetown, the island's small capital, or down on the fashionable west coast.

Allegra had swum twenty lengths and was floating in the shimmering water, gazing at the cloudless morning sky, when Risconti pushed open the arched wrought-iron gate in the wall.

He had been soundly asleep when she had slipped out of bed without disturbing him. Perhaps it was the climate which made him sleep longer and more heavily here than he had in England or America. Although, as the bedroom was air-conditioned, she couldn't see why his sleep pattern should have altered. Unless it was that, instead of drinking wine, he was having rum punches before, with and after dinner.

Allegra's father had been a heavy drinker who probably would have succumbed to cirrhosis of the liver if he hadn't broken his neck, while the only evidence of his whisky consumption was a network of spider veins on his nose and cheeks. North, in his twenties, had drunk much more than he did now; and even in her old age Flora Carlyon had continued the habit, inculcated by her husband, of drinking a bottle of vintage champagne every day.

Allegra herself had consumed large quantities of liquor in her wilder years but had felt less need of it recently. One rum punch before dinner, one or two glasses of white wine with the meal and perhaps a liqueur with her coffee was the most she wanted to drink now. However from the night of their arrival she had begun to notice that Risconti was drinking more. Not that it showed in his behaviour or in his sexual performance, which was as ardent as ever.

'Good morning. Why didn't you wake me?' He came to the edge of the pool. He was wearing a white terry robe and blue canvas espadrilles.

She swam to where he was standing, smiling down at her.

'You might have been having a wonderful dream.'

'I only have wonderful dreams when we're apart. When we're together, nothing my subconscious can devise is as good as the reality of being with you.'

'That's a very pretty speech so early in the morning.'

He dived into the pool. When he surfaced, close beside her, he said, 'A pretty speech implies flattery. Everything I say to you comes from my heart.' He put his arms round her and kissed her.

With her arms round his neck, they sank. She had never liked boisterous water games and playful duckings. But held close by him she felt no urge to break free. She held her breath, knowing he would bring her to the surface before she needed more air.

Later they had breakfast on the verandah.

'I can understand why the people who built this estate called it Paradise,' said Allegra. 'Although perhaps it wasn't as beautiful then as it is now.'

From where she was sitting, two pillars wreathed in crimson bougainvillaea framed a view which included a fine old mahogany at the boundary of the garden and, in the middle distance among the cane fields, a line of towering cabbage palms, their straight slender trunks crowned with feathery bunches of leaves.

'I think today we should do some more exploring,' said Risconti, as he finished his paw-paw. 'We've been here a week and we've only been outside the gates a couple of times.'

'I've been entirely happy inside the gates.'

'So have I.' He reached for her hand. 'If there is a life after this one, which I don't believe, it has nothing to offer me which I lack here. I should be very happy to spend the next twenty years at Paradise . . . alone with you.' He curled her hand round his face and pressed his lips to her palm.

'Oh, darling . . . I feel the same,' she told him huskily.

Although for the rest of the meal their conversation was of a more mundane nature, Allegra was left with a feeling which grew on her during the day: that, without saying anything about it, she should stop taking the pill with the hope that before they left here she would have conceived his child. Presented with a *fait accompli*, she felt sure he would change his mind about marriage.

The first time she saw the wild east coast of the island was on a day of high winds which rippled the surface of the cane and made the giant casuarinas, known in Barbados as mile trees, sweep the sky with their lacy branches.

Risconti was renting a bright-yellow mini-moke with a striped awning and, the day before, he had taken her to bathe from an uncrowded crescent beach shared by one small hotel and a few attractive private houses, including Bellerive, the home of Claudette Colbert, on the safe Caribbean coast.

After spending the morning swimming in calm aquamarine water with only a small fringe of foam where it lapped the powdered coral beach, they had lunched in the open-air water's-edge dining room of the Cobblers Cove hotel before driving back to Paradise to spend a passionate hour in the shuttered coolness of their bedroom.

They had been told by a couple at the next table at Cobblers Cove that the east coast was like a different country from the Caribbean side of the island where the tourists were concentrated. Swimming on the Atlantic side was taboo because of surf and undercurrents.

'Paradise isn't the only house with a romantic name,' said Allegra, as they set out in the moke. 'I've been studying the old map on the landing. There's a Moonshine Hall in St George's parish and a Lion Castle in St Thomas's. Sweet Vale . . . Lemon Arbour . . . Content . . . the whole island abounds with lovely names. I wonder if all the people who built the great houses have been written up already, or if some fascinating character has escaped the biographers' net?'

'I doubt it. If one has, you won't be here long enough to do anything about it.'

His tone was a trifle curt, making her wonder if, despite his avowed support for her writing career, deep down he resented the claims it made on her.

'Perhaps we'll come back every winter. I can't think of anywhere better to escape from the miseries of January and February in London and New York.'

He didn't answer. When she glanced at him, his face had an oddly set look, unlike his normal expression.

'What's the matter, darling? Why are you frowning?'

'Was I? It's nothing . . . just a slight headache.'

It was on the tip of her tongue to say, 'I'm not surprised after the rum you drank last night,' but she thought better of it.

'I've some paracetamols in my bag if you'd like one.'

'No, thanks. A walk by the sea will soon blow it away.'

Her first sight of the long lonely beach running for miles down the east coast, washed by huge breakers sweeping in from almost three thousand miles of ocean between this dot-on-the-map island and the vast continent of Africa, was from Cherry Tree Hill.

Risconti stopped the moke and they climbed out to spend some time watching the endless succession of waves rising, curling and breaking into layers of white foam off which the strong wind was whipping veil upon veil of spindrift. Seen from their vantage point, it was a magnificent sight.

When they reached sea level she saw the surf at close

quarters; torrents of water roaring in from unimaginable distances battered the beaches with a noise and a force frightening in its relentless savagery.

All along the shore there were notices warning visitors of the danger.

'Can you imagine anyone but a lunatic attempting to swim in that turmoil,' she said, with a shiver. 'Even a strong swimmer wouldn't stand a chance out there.'

Risconti cupped his hand behind his ear to signal he hadn't heard her above the thunder of the sea.

'I said nobody but a suicidal maniac would set foot in that maelstrom,' she shouted, her hair blowing about her face like the mops at the top of the cabbage palms.

He nodded, turning away, his own short grey curls remaining comparatively neat.

Allegra hesitated a moment before following him. She had tramped windswept beaches before, but never with surf as high as these gigantic combers which came surging towards her like ravenous beasts.

She felt a strong urge to run after him and yell, 'I don't like it here. It's *too* wild. Can't we go somewhere else?'

Normally Sarah seldom bothered even to skim the local morning newspaper, but the day after the inquest she was the first person in the house to read the report of it.

DRINK AND BLACK ICE KILLED LONGWARDEN MOTOR-CYCLIST was the headline which jumped out at her.

What the coroner had actually said, and this was quoted verbatim towards the end of the report, was that in the absence of witnesses of the accident, the reason Tarquin Osgood's motorcycle had left the road must remain a matter for speculation. The most likely explanation was that, returning home in the early hours of an exceptionally cold morning with patches of black ice on several roads in the locality, he had hit such a patch and, under the influence of the alcohol found in his bloodstream, had been unable to correct the resultant skid. Another possibility was that he had swerved to avoid running over an animal which had crossed his path.

More likely to vent some of his rage against Nick by killing it, thought Sarah, as she read that.

Another aspect of the tragedy which must remain unexplained, the report continued, was why Osgood had been approaching his home by way of a minor road which was not on the direct route from London, his intended destination when he had last been seen by his mother the previous day. Nor would it ever be known why he had returned to Longwarden considerably sooner than planned. Nevertheless the coroner was satisfied that no other vehicle had been involved and that the principal cause of the accident was the amount of alcohol consumed by the deceased – a warning to other young men in charge of powerful motorcycles.

Had it not been for one piece of evidence among the findings of the police surgeon who had performed the post mortem, Sarah would have finished reading the report with a great weight removed from her mind.

Most of the burden had been lifted. No suspicion of foul play had been mentioned. What continued to trouble her was the time of the accident. She had hoped to learn that Tark had died at an hour when it would have been impossible for Nick to be implicated because he had been with her.

In fact the multiple injuries from which Tark had died instantaneously had occurred within a two-hour period when she had been soundly asleep and Nick *could* have been involved.

FEBRUARY

Pen's flight to Alicante landed in mid-afternoon. She had brought only one small suitcase and a capacious flight bag, both lent to her by Jane, an experienced air traveller to whose advice she had listened attentively. Outside the glass doors of the terminal, so Helen had told her, she would find a taxi to take her to Sant Jeroni.

Following her friend's instructions, she showed the driver the address of the Wimbornes' house and, in carefully rehearsed Spanish, asked him to write down the fare. As it was not above the amount she had been told was reasonable, she surrendered her case and settled herself in the back seat.

'Oh, and *por la autopista, por favor*,' she remembered to ask, as he started the engine.

'*Si, si, señora.*'

The way through Alicante ran alongside a marina crowded with pleasure craft. On the other side of the road was an avenue of tall date palms. It had been cold and grey in London but here it was sunny, warm enough for old men to be sitting about without overcoats.

By the *autopista*, Helen had told her, the drive to the village would take something over an hour. Once past the tollbooths the driver put his foot down. Soon they were speeding through a hinterland of barren, greyish-brown hills.

The scenery increased in interest as they moved north. The bare low hills merged with higher, more rugged *sierras*, none with snow on their summits like the immense Pyrenees at whose peaks she had looked down with wonder earlier in the afternoon, but still an impressive sight to someone unaccustomed to mountains.

At last they turned off the *autopista* and she opened her bag to give the driver a note with which to pay the toll. Soon they were travelling along a less smoothly-surfaced road which wound its way inland and gave Pen her first delighted sight of an orange grove, bringing back lines of poetry learned long ago at school – *He hangs in shades the orange bright, like golden lamps in a green night.*

Dominated, from a distance, by the tower of the church, the village of Sant Jeroni seemed to consist of one narrow street leading to and past a small square.

Here the driver slowed down to ask a woman to direct him to the address on Pen's slip of paper.

'*Ah, la casa de los Ingleses.*' She bent to peer at his passenger and gave Pen a smiling nod before explaining to him where the house of the English people was to be found.

The village was larger than it seemed at first sight. Beyond the square, streets sloping upwards led off the main thoroughfare. As they turned a corner, Pen had an impression of narrow pavements, adjoining houses, mostly whitewashed, with bars protecting the windows and stout doors, one or two open to give mysterious glimpses of dark interiors.

Two more corners had to be turned before the taxi came to a standstill outside a house whose door had an unusual brass knocker in the form of a woman's hand.

That the brass was polished and gleaming must be thanks to Maria, who was Helen's neighbour and caretaker. No sooner had the taxi stopped than the door of the house was opened and a small, plump woman, wearing a jumper and cardigan with an apron over her skirt, appeared on the threshold.

Most of her words of welcome went over Pen's head, but the friendliness of her manner was unmistakable, as was her watchful eye as Pen paid and tipped the driver. Before he had driven away, she had ushered Pen into the house.

Compared with the large lofty rooms to which she was accustomed, the Wimbornes' house was a doll's house. Immediately inside the door was an area which, originally, must have been the equivalent of the front room in the houses in Longwarden village.

Now it formed part of a larger living area with two steps leading down to a lower level at the rear. In this part of the room a tall window and glazed doors admitted considerably more light than the small, barred windows on either side of the front door.

'This is charming,' Pen said aloud, as she looked about her.

The inside of the house had been colour-washed a pale shade of terracotta. The floor of old, worn clay tiles was spread with several cream rugs. The curtains were of natural linen, as were the squabs and cushions on the cane sofa and chairs. To this simple basic décor Helen had added a congruent mixture of Spanish and English finishing touches. The painted ceramic candle-holders on the walls were obviously of local origin, but the flatback Staffordshire figures on the ledge above the hearth, where a wood fire was burning, must at one time have stood on an English cottage chimney-ledge.

'*Es muy bonita . . . si?*' said Maria, watching her reaction.

'*Si . . . muy bonita,*' Pen agreed, nodding emphatically.

She went to look out of the door and saw a small, high-walled patio which, like the house, was on two levels. Before she could study it in detail, Maria took her by the arm to show her the tiny kitchen.

Overriding Pen's protests that one of the two small bedrooms would be perfectly adequate for her, Helen had insisted she must use the largest bedroom because it was lighter and sunnier than those facing the street. What she had not told Pen, leaving it to come as a surprise, was that the back bedroom had a small *mirador* built on top of the kitchen and giving a breath-taking view of the valley to the south of the village and the mountains surrounding it.

'Oh, Maria, what a darling house. I'm going to be so happy here,' Pen said, in English, hoping her tone would convey the pleasure she was unable to express in Spanish.

Evidently it did. Maria nodded and beamed, and then indicated in sign language that while Pen unpacked her case she would prepare a hot drink.

It didn't take long to unpack and dispose her belongings in the comfortable bedroom and tiny bathroom. When she went down the winding stairs, expecting a cup of coffee, she found a pot of tea waiting for her with two sticky-looking pastries.

For her meal later on, the Spanish woman had bought a pork chop to be accompanied by a salad which she had already prepared, and a large potato, scrubbed and wrapped in foil. This, she demonstrated, was to be baked on the hearth in the living room.

For dessert there was a basket of tangerines, some with fresh leaves attached to their stems. As for wine, there was *blanco* in the refrigerator or *tinto* on top.

Finally, before returning to her own home, Maria did a graphic mime to explain that if Pen had any difficulty help was at hand next door.

'*Muchas gracias, Maria.*'

'*De nada, señora. 'Dios.*'

The Spanish woman departed, leaving Pen to sit down by the fire, aware of a curious feeling that she hadn't left home but had come home.

As the afternoon light slowly faded into dusk and she drank a third cup of the slightly peculiar-tasting tea, she knew only one thing was missing – or rather one person.

Had the chair on the far side of the fire been occupied by P. J. Ashford, she would have been more than content. She would have been happier than she had ever been in her life.

Pen arrived in Sant Jeroni on a Thursday. On Saturday afternoon she was basking in the sun on the terrace outside the living room when she heard the rap of the door knocker.

The woman standing in the street wasn't Spanish. She had been a blonde whose hair, now largely grey, was brushed smoothly back from her forehead and held by an Alice band, navy-blue to match her guernsey. With it she wore clean, sun-faded jeans and white training shoes. Her face was a mesh of lines but her body was slim and youthful.

'Mrs Carlyon? I'm Lucilla Bolton . . . a friend of the Wimbornes.'

'How do you do? Do come in,' Pen invited, standing aside.

'Thank you. How are you finding Spain? It's your first visit here I believe?'

'Yes . . . and it's love at first sight,' Pen answered, closing the door.

Mrs Bolton laughed. 'Far be it from me to disillusion you, but you are rather lucky to be in this village with a treasure like Maria next door. We live nearer the coast which unfortunately is sadly changed since we bought our house twenty years ago. There were very few foreigners here then and life was altogether nicer. We still like it, but there are a number of problems which didn't exist when we arrived.'

Pen said, 'I was sitting outside, drinking wine. May I offer you a glass?'

'May I have water instead? I love wine, but for people who live here it's all too easy to drink it from morning to night. When one's on holiday, why not? For everyday living, I find it better to stick to the old Far East rule of no alcohol before sundown.'

Following Pen to the kitchen, she went on, 'Helen mentioned your visit in her last letter to me. She said you would be on your own here and I wondered if you'd care to come to a party we're having tomorrow? It's a lunch-time affair. One o'clock until whenever it breaks up.'

'How very kind of you. Thank you, I should be delighted.'

'Are you renting a car while you're here? If not, you can come by taxi and someone will give you a lift back.'

'I thought of having a car for my second week. For the first week I'm happy exploring the valley on foot.'

'In that case the number to ring for a taxi is in Helen's list of instructions for people who borrow the house. Do you speak Spanish or would you like me to make the call for you?'

'Please, if you would. At the moment my Spanish is limited to about twenty words.'

'I didn't know if, like Jack and Helen, you had spent time in South America and picked it up there.' As Pen shook her head, Mrs Bolton went on, 'What a relief it was to hear that the trouble which made the Wimbornes cut short their post-Christmas visit has turned out to be less serious than Helen feared. I was so worried for her, poor dear.'

'Yes, although I don't know him, I was also very glad, for her sake, when she told me it wasn't cancer.'

'You haven't met Jack?' Mrs Bolton said, looking surprised.

As they moved on to the terrace, Pen explained her meeting with Helen after more than a thirty-year interval.

After some conversation, Lucilla Bolton made the call to the taxi company.

'If it turns up late, as it may, don't panic,' she advised. 'I've invited people for one but I know from experience that some won't show up until three.'

'What should I wear?' Pen asked her.

'Anything you like. If it's fine we shall be on the terrace which is a sun-trap like this one. Goodbye. I'll look forward to seeing you again tomorrow.'

The taxi to take Pen to Lucilla Bolton's lunch party was only ten minutes late.

She had spent the morning sitting in the sun, debating what to wear. Thanks to her daughter-in-law, she had with her what Jane called a capsule wardrobe intended to cover every contingency.

Jane was a great maker of lists and her method of packing for a trip was first to list all the activities in which she was likely to engage. For Pen's holiday she had listed walking, sunbathing, sightseeing and finally, making Pen laugh and shake her head, 'dinner date with attractive stranger'.

Having completed the list – refusing to cross out the last item on it – Jane had then insisted on emptying Pen's wardrobe and drawers so that every article of clothing and decoration was immediately visible.

'Otherwise you tend to forget things you haven't worn in a long time,' she had explained to her mother-in-law.

Her theory had proved to be correct. A number of things Pen had forgotten she possessed – some cloisonné beads, a silk scarf and even a blouse – had come to light.

Jane had an inspired eye for things which would go together. She had seen permutations of garments which would never have occurred to Pen whose thoughts about clothes were still conditioned by her mother's arbitrary rules.

It was one of Jane's unconventional combinations she had decided to wear for the party. After all she was going

623

to meet people who didn't know her and therefore wouldn't be surprised whatever she wore. If what she had on wasn't the customary rig for a Costa Blanca lunch party, what did it matter? She wasn't even going as herself but under the semi-alias of Mrs Carlyon. It gave her a strange sense of freedom from all the restraints which had governed her life in the past. She felt a different person.

The Boltons' house was on the seaward side of the *autopista* in a region where the vines grew on creamy-coloured soil, not the rich red earth of the vineyards around Sant Jeroni. Fortunately Mrs Bolton had jotted down some directions in English and Spanish as the house wasn't easy to find, being at the end of a rough track with other tracks branching off it.

Cars of several nationalities were already parked in the forecourt when the taxi arrived. A tall man with a drink in his hand watched it draw up and came forward to open the passenger door.

'You must be Mrs Carlyon. I'm Robin Bolton. At present I'm on duty as a parking attendant.'

'How do you do, Mr Bolton. It's most kind of you and your wife to include me in the festivities.' She turned to her driver. '*Cuanto es?*'

Having paid the fare and thanked him, she turned to her host. 'Your house looks as if it might have been a farm at one time.'

'It was. The centre block is the original *finca* and these wings on either side were added by us to accommodate Lucilla's mother and our four children and their offspring when they come for holidays. By the way you'll find most people here are very informal and tend to use first names on sight. Do call me Robin.'

'I'm Pen . . . short for Penelope.'

'I see some more people approaching, so if you don't mind I won't leave my post at the moment. If you go through that door and turn right and then left, through the drawing room, you'll see the terrace beyond it. You'll find my wife there and she'll give you a libation and introduce you to people. I shall hope for a chat with you later, Pen.'

Amused by the gallantry of this last remark which she felt she would not have received in her other persona, Pen followed his instructions.

It was immediately obvious from the appointments in the white-raftered drawing room that the Boltons had spent a considerable time in the East. Two large washed-silk Chinese carpets covered the floor, their pale fondant colours being repeated in the cushions on the white chairs and sofas. The rusticity of the rough-plastered, white-washed walls and crude beams supporting the roof were in strikingly effective contrast to the sophistication of a life-size golden buddha seated in the lotus position, and a collection of jade birds.

As she passed through the room, Pen caught a brief glimpse of herself in a large gilded looking glass and wondered what Allegra would think if she could see her conservative mother arriving at a party in a dark purple shirt unbuttoned to show the fuschia-pink tee-shirt beneath it, both tucked into cream cotton jeans she had bought for their cheapness and intended only for gardening.

To these Jane had added a lilac scarf of her own for Pen to pull through the loops and wear as a belt, and a 'ruby' brooch. This had been a present from North who, as a small boy, had bought it for sixpence from the white-elephant stall at the village fête. It was one of her dearest keep-sakes, but she had never thought of wearing it in public until Jane had pounced on it as a fun accent for the purple shirt.

About twenty people were standing about, chatting and laughing, on the sunlit terrace surrounding a sparklingly blue Roman swimming pool when Pen paused in the shade of the verandah outside the drawing room.

Well, this is the best chance you'll get to try being a fun person for a change, she told herself silently, a moment before she stepped out into the sunshine.

'Hello . . . your taxi was on time.' Her hostess came to shake hands, her blue eyes noting Pen's clothes. She was wearing a long loose striped garment embellished with vivid ribbons. 'What would you like to drink? There's *sangria* . . .

not, I promise you, the lethal brew some people inflict on their guests. Or there's straight wine or gin-and-whatever.'

Pen had already drunk two glasses of white wine that morning. She asked for a third.

'Are you an artist, Mrs Carlyon?' Lucilla asked, leading her towards an outdoor bar in the charge of a young Spaniard. '*Un vino blanco, por favor, Paco.*'

'What makes you ask?' Pen enquired.

'The colours you're wearing. They suggest an artistic flair.'

It was on the tip of Pen's tongue to explain that the flair was not hers but she changed her mind. She knew Jane wouldn't mind her taking the credit.

'I'm glad you like them,' she said. 'I was admiring your caftan. Is it a caftan?'

'No, it's Mexican actually. A present from one of my sons. Now come and meet some of the other people who live here.'

Her hostess swept her towards the nearest group of guests and, having introduced them, went away to welcome the people whose cars had been approaching when Pen entered the house.

In the next forty-five minutes they were followed by many others until about fifty people were present. Nursing her fourth glass of wine, counting the two she had had at home, Pen wondered how long it would be before they ate something more sustaining than the olives, almonds and thin slices of sausage which were being handed round by two Spanish girls.

'These almonds are from the Boltons' own trees,' the woman beside her told her. 'Lucilla is very domesticated. She has a Spanish daily whose family come and help at parties, but she does all the cooking herself and the food here is always delicious, isn't it George?'

Her husband agreed that it was. 'The Kilmartins have just arrived,' he said, looking in the direction of the verandah which Pen had been told was known locally as a *naya*. 'It's unusual for them to be latecomers. Who's the chap with them, I wonder?'

His wife turned to look. 'Oh, that must be Colonel Somebody who was Tom's CO. The last time I met Marguerite she said he was coming to stay with them.'

Pen glanced at the people she was talking about and was transfixed. One of the men was a sandy-haired Scot whose nationality she would have guessed even if she hadn't heard his surname. The other – the man she had just heard described as the colonel who had been his commanding officer – was her butler.

At Longwarden, where it was an hour earlier than in Spain, Jane was alone in the library, reading the Sunday papers. Sarah had taken a day off to visit Sammy, leaving the new groom, Kate Hastings, in charge of the stables.

She seemed a very capable girl, if rather uncommunicative. So far in several attempts to chat to her, Jane had failed to penetrate her reserve. But if she hadn't much to say for herself, she had abundant energy. When not busy with the horses, she was redecorating Sammy's cottage. Jane had asked her to lunch today but Kate had refused, saying she had too much to do and would prefer to knock up a meal at the cottage when she felt hungry. Not a girl to kowtow or mince her words, Jane had thought with amusement, after her invitation had been politely but firmly rejected.

Had North been at home today, his long frame would have been stretched on the opposite sofa while he read Auberon Waugh, Peregrine Worsthorne and other columnists whose opinions interested him. About this time he would ask her what she'd like to drink before lunch. Today, with both her husband and Mr Ashford away, she had to fix a drink for herself. As it wasn't unusual for her to ask for a soft drink, it wouldn't have surprised North to see her fixing tonic on the rocks. But in fact there was a special reason why she wasn't having gin or vodka. Her period was overdue. If it stayed that way, it would be a long time before she drank alcohol again.

*   *   *

The shock of seeing Ashford standing within a few yards of her was so great that for a time Pen was mentally and physically paralysed.

Around her the party continued as if nothing had happened, but for her time came to a standstill. The chatter and laughter were muted, and the people around her disappeared. Only one person remained: the tall, dark-eyed man who had been in her thoughts every hour of every day since they had said goodbye.

Was it him? How could it be? Who else could it be? A twin brother? He had told her he had no brothers. It was him . . . it must be. But what was he doing here, in the guise of a former colonel? And why, when he learned where she was going, hadn't he told her he would also be in Spain?

'Do you know the Kilmartins, Mrs Carlyon?'

Pen came out of her trance and realized the woman beside her had asked her a question she hadn't heard.

'I'm sorry . . . I was miles away.'

'I asked if you knew the Kilmartins.'

'No . . . no, I don't. I – I was staring because the man with them reminded me of someone.'

As she offered this explanation for an aberration which had clearly been noticed by her companions, Pen dragged her gaze away from the familiar face now several shades browner than when she had last seen him.

Would he be equally stunned when he spotted her? Had he realized it was not impossible they might run into each other while staying in the same part of Spain? If they were introduced – not inevitable at a party of this size – how would he react? If they weren't, would he seek her out? Or pretend not to know her?

A fresh flurry of surmise made it hard for her to pay attention to some information about the Kilmartins.

'Hello, Tom. Still taking your daily dip?'

The man called George – Pen hadn't caught his surname – raised his voice to attract the Scotsman's attention. Their hostess had disappeared, probably to expedite the meal now the last of her guests had arrived.

'Hello, George. Yes, we're still swimming. Hello, Vera, how are you?'

The Scot and his wife shook hands with George and Vera but didn't kiss them, Pen noticed.

'This is Mrs Carlyon who's staying in Sant Jeroni,' said Vera.

'This is our house guest Piers Ashford,' said Mrs Kilmartin. 'Mr and Mrs Bramshaw used to live in Malta, Piers.'

Pen watched him shake hands with Vera Bramshaw. Then he turned to her and their eyes met for the first time, although he must have looked at her while Vera was introducing her to his friends.

'How do you do, Mrs Carlyon?'

As if they were strangers, he smiled, clasped her hand for a moment and turned to George Bramshaw.

No one could have guessed from his manner that he and Pen had lived under the same roof for almost two years.

The buffet lunch set out in Lucilla Bolton's dining room was as delicious a feast as Vera Bramshaw had forecast.

But as Pen filled her plate with a selection from the wide range of appetizing dishes, she was no longer conscious of the hunger she had felt earlier, only of the man who was standing behind her in the lineup.

After Robin Bolton's announcement that luncheon was ready, the groups on the terrace had begun to merge in a leisurely flow towards the dining room. In the course of this movement Pen had become separated from the Kilmartins and the Bramshaws and had fallen into conversation with a Dutch girl she had talked to earlier.

The girl was in front of her now, still chatting in fluent English but making little sense to Pen whose wits were totally befuddled by the presence behind her of Colonel Piers Ashford.

Was it by chance or design that he was there? She hoped it was by design.

At last the Dutch girl paused for breath and Pen seized the opportunity to say – as she might have done if they had been strangers – 'Is this your first visit to Spain, *Colonel* Ashford?'

As she spoke she glanced up at his face but only for an instant before returning her gaze to the buffet table. Even that fleeting glance was enough to set her pulses racing.

'No, I know Spain quite well,' he answered. 'Although it's a number of years since I was last here and a good deal has changed in the meantime. How do you like Sant Jeroni? The main street is very narrow, I seem to remember.'

'Much too narrow for modern motor traffic and not nearly as attractive as the side streets and back streets. I'm in a tiny house not far from the church. Although it is a thoroughfare very few cars actually use it. My first impressions of Spain have all been delightful.'

He said, 'Unfortunately Benidorm and Marbella have given Spain a bad image in the minds of people who haven't been here or, if they have, have only seen the ruination of the coastline and none of the magnificent scenery of the inland areas.'

'The scenery surrounding my village is splendid,' she told him. 'And the valley itself, with the almond orchards in blossom, is lovely. It's hard to believe that it's February and northern Europe is freezing.'

They had come to the end of the table where the napkins and silver were set out. By this time, Pen was pleased to see, the Dutch girl was deep in conversation with the woman in front of her. When their glasses had been replenished by the girls who had served the appetizers, the two of them moved off together.

Outside the room Pen paused and looked around. The long *naya* was furnished with groups of low tables and chairs, most of which had already been taken. Other people were finding places to sit in the multi-arched building at one end of the pool. She had been told it was an old *riu-rau* built for the storage of carts and crops and now used as a pool pavilion.

As she hesitated, he said, 'Shall we stake a claim to that arbour, Mrs Carlyon?'

He was holding both plate and wine glass in one hand

by having the foot of the glass on the rim of the plate and keeping it there with his thumb, leaving his other hand free to gesture in the direction of an arch with bougainvillaea trained over it and a stone seat beneath.

The seat wasn't wide enough for more than two people to share it. It was at a little distance from the flat-topped parapet at the edge of the terrace which had also had cushions spread along it.

'*Salud.*' Her companion raised his glass of red wine and gave her an enigmatic look before he drank.

'Salud.'

'The Boltons can't have been pleased when their fine view was marred by that excrescence,' he remarked, with a nod in the direction of a distant but unsightly rash of white villas on the hillside to the south.

'I'm sure they were horrified.' Unable to contain her impatience a moment longer, Pen burst out, 'Why didn't you tell me you were coming to Spain? I almost fainted with shock when I saw you arriving.'

'I'm sorry. It must have startled you. I thought it very unlikely our paths would cross here,' he told her.

'Now that they have, don't you think I deserve some explanation? What on earth are you doing as a butler if you were a colonel in the army . . . Mr Kilmartin's commanding officer?'

'Who told you that?'

'Mrs Bramshaw. She was told by Mrs Kilmartin.'

He frowned. 'It's a pity Marguerite didn't keep my past to herself. However, to answer your question, an ex-officer cuts very little ice in civilian life. Having no qualifications to fit me for equivalent positions outside the army, I had to adjust my life to my limited skills.'

'But surely you must have a pension?'

'Yes, but at fifty-five and in good health I'm not ready to be put out to grass. The old nursery maxim that the devil makes work for idle hands is nowhere more clearly exemplified than among the foreign community in this part of Spain. No end of people take to the bottle for want of a more useful occupation.'

'Quite a number of butlers have become alcoholics,' Pen pointed out. 'I can't believe that it's necessary for a man with your background to squander his gifts waiting on us.'

'I derive a good deal of pleasure from waiting on you and your family, *Mrs* Carlyon,' he replied, with the same slight emphasis she had given to his rank while they were at the buffet table. 'And as an officer's principal attribute – at least in the army of my youth – was held to be the power of leadership, I still exercise that in the command of my cleaning squad.'

He laughed, but it made her heart bleed to hear him speak so light-heartedly of what she felt sure must, at first, have been a humiliating come-down.

'Do your friends know what you are doing now?'

'Yes – and disapprove. The Kilmartins are rather conventional, especially Marguerite. I can be quite sure she won't talk about my present occupation,' he said dryly. 'She refuses to accept that my new career suits me very well.'

'If they know won't they quickly realize that I'm part of the family you work for? My name . . . and the fact that we're sitting together so soon after being introduced . . . they can hardly fail to put two and two together.'

'I haven't gone into details about my employers and I don't think they have any idea who owns Longwarden. As for our sitting together, there's nothing very remarkable about a man on his own attaching himself to a woman also on her own – particularly if she happens to be by far the most striking person present. Would it be impertinent to ask why you're incognita?'

Flushing with pleasure at his compliment, Pen explained how it had come about.

'But while we are here I would rather you used my first name and I shall use yours,' she went on. 'In fact I think we should try to forget about England and our everyday lives and behave as if we are strangers who have happened to meet on holiday. Don't you agree?'

He gave her a thoughtful look and she wondered why he seemed doubtful.

'I'm not using my full name here. My grandfather used

to call me Pen ... and sometimes Penny Dreadful,' she said, with a smile. 'I've always hated Penelope. So while I'm in Spain I'm Pen.'

As they talked, Pen was aware of a number of speculative glances being cast in their direction; and aware of the pleasure it gave her to be eating her lunch beside this supremely attractive and distinguished man.

'May I get you some more? I don't think you tried the very good fish mousse,' said Piers, after their host had strolled round urging everyone to have second helpings.

Pen handed over her plate and watched him return to the dining room. She noticed other women eyeing him as he passed and wasn't surprised that, among all the jowls and paunches of this largely elderly society, his lean waist and still clear-cut jawline should attract wistful looks from women whose husbands had let their bodies deteriorate.

I have no right to be critical. I was letting myself go until Jane took me in hand, thought Pen. She and Piers have changed my life. But for her, he would never have noticed me as a woman, although even now I don't *know* that he finds me attractive. He may just have been being polite when he said I looked striking.

Finding the Boltons' garden more appealing than the majority of its occupants, she let her gaze wander appreciatively from the still, sky-reflecting pool to the orange trees, laden with fruit, growing from square gaps in the old hand-made clay tiles with which the terrace was paved.

Turning to look through the arch at the lower garden, her eye was caught by the bare-branched beauty of a fig tree and by large clumps of plants with spire-shaped bright coral flowers.

'Would you like some more wine, Pen?'

After being lost in thought, she turned to find Piers had returned, accompanied by one of the Spanish girls who was carrying two jugs of wine.

'Yes, I should ... *gracias, señorita.*'

'What do you think of the garden?' he asked her, as he sat down.

'I was thinking what fun it would be to have a winter house here and design a Mediterranean garden.'

'Really? I shouldn't have thought you would ever be tempted to leave your garden in England.'

'But it isn't *my* garden in the way a garden here would be. Now that North has a wife I feel it would be a good thing if I weren't around all the time. However as I can't possibly afford to buy or build a house here, it's only an idle pipe dream,' she said, with a shrug. 'Mm . . . this fish thing is brilliant, as my daughter would say.'

'Until I saw you today, I hadn't realized how strong a resemblance there is.'

'Between me and Allegra? You can't be serious!' she exclaimed. 'We couldn't be less alike.'

'So I thought at one time. Today, dressed as you are and looking more relaxed, the likeness is striking.'

'It's a good thing she can't hear you say so. She would be appalled,' said Pen. 'As you can't fail to have noticed, my daughter and I are not *en rapport*.'

'Perhaps that will change now that you've started to strike out and be more assertive.'

When she looked up, he added quickly, 'I'm sorry . . . I shouldn't have said that. These unusual circumstances made me forget for a moment that I have no right to speak so frankly.'

She said, in a low voice, 'You have every right, Piers. Surely you know that for months I've regarded you as a friend. Sammy used to say what he liked to Sarah. Why shouldn't you to me?'

'Sammy enjoyed the privileges of long service. He had known her since she was a child.'

'But he wasn't the bulwark that you are. To have someone one feels one can turn to in any contingency is a very . . . comforting sensation.'

'Thank you. I'm glad you have felt that. I –' He broke off and rose to his feet as their hostess approached. 'We've been agreeing that your fish mousse is ambrosial, Mrs Bolton.'

'Lucilla,' she corrected him. 'Thank you. Most people

634

seem to enjoy it. But I didn't come to break up your conversation; merely to say the puddings are on the table and I hope you'll do justice to them. Neither of you two people can claim to have any weight problems.'

'I'm sure we should if we came to your parties frequently.'

'Not if you interspersed them with strenuous climbs. I hear Tom and Marguerite took you up Bernia yesterday.'

He nodded. 'Tomorrow we're going on another hill walk they know of. I wonder if you'd like to join us?' he said to Pen.

She was overjoyed that he wanted her company, but she said, 'It's kind of you to suggest it but your friends may prefer to have you to themselves.'

'On the contrary, having already spent a week listening to Tom and me reminiscing, I'm sure Marguerite must be sick of it.'

Lucilla had drifted away to speak to some other guests. Now another woman came over and, addressing Pen, said in an American accent, 'Hi! I'm Kathy Myers. Lucilla says you're an artist. So am I. Have you come to live here?'

By the time Pen had cleared up this misunderstanding, Piers was talking to someone else. As happened at parties, they were drawn away from each other. Pen received the impression that newcomers to the area were always eagerly seized on by those who had been here some time and were perhaps bored with familiar faces.

By four there was still no sign of the party breaking up and she had no desire to leave while Piers was still here. Even to see him from a distance made her absurdly happy.

'We haven't talked at all yet.' Suddenly Marguerite Kilmartin was at her elbow, smiling at her. 'You're staying in Sant Jeroni, I think Vera said. You have friends there?'

'A school-friend who has a house there. But she isn't here at the moment. I'm under the wing of her very nice Spanish neighbour.'

'So you're on your own?'

'Yes.'

'In that case why don't you join us for supper this evening? It will only be a light snack after the feast we've had here, but I always feel that a lunch-time party leaves a certain sense of anti-climax, and particularly for someone living alone.'

'How kind of you. Thank you,' said Pen. 'There's one slight problem. I haven't hired a car yet. I came by taxi and Lucilla encouraged me to think I could easily get a lift back. But it may be that from where you live Sant Jeroni is rather far.'

'No problem. Tom can run you home in ten minutes.'

'In that case I'd be delighted to come to supper. You and your husband are keen windsurfers I hear.'

'We took it up last year. We're regarded by most people here as madly athletic but that's mainly because so many of them are inactive. What are your interests?'

'Gardening and music,' said Pen. 'Listening to music. I don't play an instrument. I took piano lessons as a child, but it wasn't my forte.'

'Piers is very keen on music. When his wife was alive he usually arranged his leaves to coincide with music festivals at places like Salzburg and Bayreuth. Camilla had given up a musical career to marry him. She had a beautiful soprano voice. They were the happiest of couples and it was a tragedy when she died so young. Only just into her forties. But that was eight years ago and I think he's got over it now.'

Pen was silent, her heart wrenched with pity for him and for his wife, if she had known she was dying and would leave him in lonely misery.

'They were planning to live here in Spain,' Marguerite went on. 'It was they who inspired us to buy a house in the sun for when Tom's service career was over. But of course when Camilla died it wrecked all those plans and poor Piers couldn't bear to come here. For a long time we only saw him if we were in London and he came up to have lunch with us. Tom is hoping that from now on we shall see more of him. They have always been very good friends and I was fond of Camilla. It's unusually fortunate when husbands *and* wives get on well, don't you think?'

'I'm sure you're right,' Pen agreed.

'They had no children unfortunately. I feel that would have helped. We have three. Two sons and a daughter. Have you children?'

'One son and one daughter, and a very dear niece who is virtually a daughter as she lost her parents as a small child and has lived with us ever since.'

Pen sensed that the other woman was wondering if 'us' referred to an absent husband and was curious about her marital status. She said, 'I'm a widow.'

'Are you thinking of coming to live here or is it purely a holiday?'

'Purely a holiday, although having been here a few days I can quite see why people do live here. The climate is wonderful, isn't it?'

At this point they were joined by the two men. Tom Kilmartin said to his wife, 'It's getting on for five. I think we should make a move, darling.' He looked at Pen. 'Has my wife persuaded you to take pot luck with us?'

The warmth had gone out of the day and the light was beginning to fade when the Kilmartins' small Spanish car drew up in front of their house, giving Pen her first close-up of a modern Spanish villa. This one was similar in style to those which, erected *en masse*, had despoiled the view to the south from the Boltons' *finca*.

Tom and Marguerite's house was also part of a development of more or less identical buildings, all with Roman-tiled roofs, white walls, arched *nayas* and shutters painted a colour most aptly described by Allegra's favourite expletive.

The garden was tidily kept but uninspired in its planting, with no trees other than the pines which had once covered the area and still formed copses on vacant plots. A purple bougainvillaea, a colour which Pen liked less than the crimson, apricot and white climbers in Lucilla's garden, overhung the arches of the *naya*.

Inside it was to be seen that Marguerite wasn't a woman with a natural flair for decoration. There were one or two good pieces of probably inherited furniture, but compared with the cosy charm of the cottage in Sant Jeroni, the sitting room here, with its white walls and heavy dark furniture, had a stark and comfortless air. A hideous red and black rug and unlined red repp curtains seemed only to accentuate the scullery-chill of the walls.

Lucilla's house had been full of potted azaleas and cyclamen as well as many green plants and baskets of wild bell-heather. Here there were no flowers at all, which to Pen was as strange as a room with no books or paintings.

She found herself wondering if she could make friends with a woman who could live with unlined red curtains and not even one African violet or spray of fruit blossom.

All the happiness she had felt earlier, the feeling that it must be fate which had brought her and Piers together, was suddenly pierced by doubt.

If life had taught her anything, it was that some communion of interests was essential to a close relationship between a man and a woman; and an early sign of future disharmony was being bored by the other one's friends. She had had no close friends for Edward to dislike, and had been too ignorant to realize that being daunted by his horsey intimates should have been a warning.

The Kilmartins seemed to be Piers' closest friends. When his wife was alive they had formed a congenial quartet. But Pen had an uneasy feeling that only a superficial amity was possible between herself and Marguerite. Possibly the feeling was mutual. The other woman might not take to her.

Somehow it seemed a bad augury.

Sarah had come to dread Sunday. On Sunday there was no post, no chance of the promised letter from Nick arriving. It was only the hope of a letter which kept her going, the expectation that today might, at last, be the day she heard from him.

Where is he? Why doesn't he write? she thought despairingly, driving home from her visit to Sammy.

As had Mr Ashford, the night she had admitted her love for Nick, Sammy seemed to feel that going away had been the right thing for Nick to do. But of course neither of them knew that he had been, briefly, her lover.

Halfway back to Longwarden she passed the lay-by and the rubbish container in which, on the outward journey, she had disposed of a disgustingly grubby sleeping bag, a transistor radio and an almost empty half-bottle of whisky, once the property of Tark Osgood.

Sarah had found his belongings about a week after his death. By then she had come to the conclusion that he must have entered the house by the yard door when it was unlocked during the day. A search of the disused rooms in the kitchen block had confirmed this theory. She had swept up the cigarette ends and put them in a dustbin. Disposing of the sleeping bag and the radio had presented more of a problem. To attempt to burn them in the garden incinerator was too risky. It seemed wiser to wait until her aunt's car was at her disposal and dump them somewhere far away.

It was starting to sleet, the flakes melting on contact with the windscreen. Determined not to think of Nick, which still made her cry when she was alone, she wondered how her aunt was getting on in Spain.

'If you don't mind my using the car, I'll run Pen back to her house, Tom,' said Piers, rising to his feet. 'If we're going to make an early start tomorrow, it might be as well to have a reasonably early night.'

'I agree. Are you sure you can find your way?' the other man asked.

'Yes, I know Sant Jeroni.'

'I had better lend Pen a shawl. It will be chilly outside.' Marguerite beckoned Pen to follow her.

It could scarcely be chillier outside than it was in the Kilmartins' bedroom, thought Pen, repressing a shiver as she entered another white room also with a marble floor, the colour of uncooked liver.

They slept in twin beds, she noticed. Perhaps strenuous days on surfboards, horseback and hard courts did not make for amorous nights.

The thought surprised her. Perhaps there is something of Allegra in me, she thought, remembering Piers' remark at the party.

'Would you like to use the bathroom?' Marguerite opened a door leading out of the bedroom and switched on some lights. 'I'll leave the shawl on the bed,' she added.

The bathroom had a grey marble floor and blue and white ceramic tiles from floor to ceiling. It reminded Pen of a butcher's cold-room. She was glad she wasn't staying in this house. It had obviously cost much more than the Wimbornes' pied-à-terre, but she knew that if she had found herself here on her first night in Spain, she would have been tempted to fly back to England next day.

The shawl Marguerite had put out for her was made of thick strands of white nylon and Pen could imagine Allegra's reaction to it. However it had been a thoughtful gesture to offer it to her and she drew it about her shoulders before returning to the sitting room.

'Thank you so much for having me. It's been a most enjoyable evening and I'm looking forward to tomorrow,' she said, shaking hands with the Kilmartins.

Some minutes later, when the car was on the main road, she said to Piers, 'You seem to have no qualms about driving on the "wrong" side. I expect you've done it before. I wonder how I shall get on when I hire a car next week?'

'As an experienced driver I'm sure you'll manage very well. Are you planning to go far afield?'

'Not very far but I feel I should do some exploring. Is Valencia worth seeing?'

'It has an interesting art gallery but it's not a city I like. Alicante is more attractive. I think you'd do better to potter about in this area. Perhaps we could spend a day or two pottering together.'

This time she didn't demur. 'I'd like that very much.'

'You must have a *paella* while you're here. I know a place where they do quite a good one. If the weather stays hot we can eat it outside, by the sea.'

The journey to Sant Jeroni took considerably more than ten minutes but it wasn't quite half-past ten when they passed the *plaza*.

'Would you like to come in and see what a village house is like?' she asked him. 'But perhaps you already have.'

'I've been inside one or two empty ones. I'd be most interested to see what your friend has done with her place.'

They left the car by the church, where there was more space, and walked down the narrow street. There was a full moon and the night had turned cold, making her glad of the white wrap.

They were a few yards from the house when the door opened and out stepped Maria.

'*Ah, señora . . .*' She launched into a flow of rapid Spanish.

The only word Pen understood was *estufa* from which she deduced that Maria had lit the gas stove. This was confirmed by Piers who said, 'She has been in to light the fire for you.'

'*Gracias, Maria.*' Pen introduced him. '*Mi amigo Señor Ashford . . . Señora Lopez.*'

They shook hands and chatted in Spanish. His didn't sound rusty to Pen. It seemed very fluent, the language accentuating the deep, pleasant timbre of his voice.

As well as lighting the stove which showed a welcoming glow, Maria had switched on some lamps. The contrast between the visual warmth and tranquillity of this room and the harsh colours and hard surfaces of the one they had left was, to Pen's eyes, most marked.

Piers must have shared her reaction. He said, 'This is delightful. I think Tom and Marguerite made a mistake buying into an *urbanización*. It was all done in rather a rush, under pressure from a smooth-talking agent. I myself don't care for their house, although perhaps I shouldn't say so when I'm enjoying their hospitality.'

She said, 'It's a matter of taste, but I do think these russet clay tiles make a pleasanter flooring than marble. I suppose marble is cool in summer. Would you like coffee or a drink before you drive back?'

'How about coffee *and* a drink?' he suggested, smiling.

'Why not? I'll make the coffee if you'll deal with the drinks.'

Presently, when they were settled in chairs close to the *estufa*, their conversation was interrupted by the telephone.

Pen had already received calls from Jane and Helen, both of them anxious to know if she was all right. She wondered who was calling now.

'Mother?' Allegra's distinctive voice came over the line as clearly as if she were calling from London to Long-warden. 'How are you getting on?'

'Splendidly, thank you. How nice of you to inquire,' said Pen, guessing it was at Jane's urging that Allegra had rung up. 'I've just come back from a party . . . my second party today. I've been out to luncheon and supper.'

'Heavens! You are living it up. Is the village a hotbed of Brits making mad whoopee?'

'There are some more English people and other foreigners here, but I haven't met them yet. The luncheon was at an old farmhouse owned by some friends of the Wimbornes and there I met some other people who invited me to have supper with them.' A spirit of devilment entered Pen. 'I've just been brought home by a fellow guest who is having a nightcap with me. Could we chat a little later? I doubt if I shall go to bed much before midnight.'

'I only wanted to say hello.' Allegra's surprise was audible. 'I'm glad you're having a good time. Who's with you? Male or female?'

Echoing a retort her daughter had once snapped at her, but using a friendlier tone, Pen said, 'If you must know, a very charming English colonel with whom I feel sure I'm quite safe.' She laughed and gave Piers a wink. 'Goodnight, Allegra. Thank you for calling, darling.'

As she replaced the receiver, after waiting to hear Allegra's startled 'Goodbye', Pen realized it was a long time since she had last called her darling, or felt on equal terms with her. Tonight, all at once, she did.

'That will give her something to think about. Wouldn't she be amazed if she knew who the colonel was?' she said, picking up the glass of brandy Piers had poured for her.

His amusement was tinged with disquiet. 'And perhaps disturbed,' he said seriously. 'If I hadn't already decided to give up my post at Longwarden, I shouldn't be here with you now, Pen. You must realize – I certainly do – that we can't be informal here and revert to formality in England.'

'You've decided to leave!' she said blankly, the laughter in her eyes extinguished. 'But I thought you were happy at Longwarden . . . or, if not happy, content.'

Piers gave her a long, grave look. 'I stopped being happy nine years ago, when I was told my wife had a terminal illness,' he said quietly. 'I loved Camilla very much. Watching her die was very hard, but being without her was worse. The future seemed . . . empty and pointless. I had two more years of service before I retired. That kept me going for a bit. I don't know what I'd have done, possibly taken to this' – tapping the glass he was holding – 'if the job with General Pembroke hadn't come up. When you and your son interviewed me, I tried to give the impression I had been employed as his batman. In fact I was helping the old boy to write his memoirs. He was lonely and I was lonely and between us we strung the job out and made it last longer than necessary. It was just about finished when he died.'

Pen's eyes had filled with tears when he spoke of Camilla. Although she herself had never known married happiness, she had often imagined it. She couldn't bear to think of this man, whom she loved, enduring the long-drawn anguish of his wife's fatal illness and then being left on his own, with no children to comfort him and his military career soon to end.

Not wanting him to notice her emotional reaction, she avoided looking at him by playing with the end of the scarf she was wearing as a belt.

'I still didn't know what the hell to do with my life,' he went on, after a pause. 'It was the general's sister, a rather eccentric character who used to descend on him sometimes, who saw your advertisement in *The Times* and put the idea of becoming a butler up to me. It was one of her teases. She considered her brother a stuffed shirt and she thought I was too conventional and self-important to be anything but shocked by her suggestion. I suppose that was my first reaction. But thinking it over I realized that polishing silver and so on in a quiet country household would suit me as well as what I'd been doing for the general. As indeed it has – until recently.'

Her fingers stopped twisting the scarf. She gave him a questioning look. He was staring at her intently but, as so often in the past, she couldn't divine the thoughts behind his inscrutable gaze.

'Until recently?' she prompted, with a sudden tightness in her chest.

Piers leaned forward in his chair. 'You feel your life has to change now that your son has a wife. It's equally clear to me that my rôle must change this year. There will be more entertaining, more living-in staff, more need for a professional butler rather than a competent amateur. I liked it the way it was when I first came to Longwarden. I don't want to be in charge of a larger household. As soon as I get back to England, I shall ask your son to find a replacement for me.'

'I see,' said Pen, striving to mask her acute disappointment.

For a heart-stopping moment she had thought his answer was going to be something quite different from this matter-of-fact explanation of why the post no longer suited him.

'What will you do?' she asked dully. 'Where will you go?'

'That I've yet to decide, but it will be somewhere abroad. Six years ago, when I left the army, I invested the money intended for our retirement house in a deferred income account. The account matures later this year. It will be tax free if I'm living out of England.'

The tears which had sprung to her eyes a few minutes earlier threatened to well again. No doubt it was the unaccustomed amount of wine she had drunk which had brought her emotions close to the surface. First pity, and now self-pity.

'We shall miss you,' she said, carefully controlling her voice. 'Especially Sarah and I. But now that I know the truth, I'm surprised you've stayed with us so long. We always felt – all of us – there was something mysterious about you. Now all is explained, as they say.'

'Not quite. There is one other thing I haven't told you, but I think it must keep for another night. It's time I was on my way. I don't want Tom and Marguerite to think we have lost our way, or crashed their car,' he said, rising.

She went with him to the door. 'Thank you for bringing me home.'

'It was a pleasure . . . m'Lady.' A smile curled his mouth.

She found it a strain to smile back. 'Goodnight.' She offered her hand. 'I'll be ready at ten o'clock.'

'Goodnight.' To her surprise, he lifted her hand and brushed his lips over her knuckles.

A moment later he had gone, pulling the door to behind him. She turned the key and listened to his footsteps receding in the direction of the church.

When they came in she had forgotten to go upstairs and switch on the electric blanket. Going up to repair this omission, she found that Maria had done it. The bed was already warm.

Returning to the sitting room, she collected the cups and glasses and took them through to the kitchen. Before turning off the *estufa*, she plumped the cushions of her chair but left his as they were.

What had he meant by saying there was one thing he had to explain to her? It was impossible to sleep while her mind was full of uncertainty. Like a love-lorn girl, she thought over every word of their conversation at the party and at the Kilmartins' house.

They would now be peacefully sleeping in their twin beds and no doubt Piers was asleep, also in a single bed. They would hardly be likely to have a double bed in their visitors' room if they didn't sleep in one themselves.

Now, thinking of him in bed, she was filled with envy for Camilla who, if her life had been short, had lived to the full while it lasted.

I stopped being happy nine years ago, when I was told my wife had a terminal illness.

They were the happiest of couples. It was a tragedy when she died . . . only just into her forties. But that was eight years ago and I think he's got over it now.

645

I would trade the rest of my life for one year of happiness with him, Pen thought restlessly.

The next day would have been perfect – had she and Piers been alone.

It took them almost three hours to climb the steep, stony track which led up, through a wooded gully, to a deserted farm on a lonely plateau and, from there, to a higher point with spectacular views.

The two men were carrying rucksacks containing a picnic lunch which the four of them shared when they reached the summit of the climb, an outcrop of crags which the Kilmartins called Wuthering Heights.

From this pinnacle, several thousand feet above sea level, they could look down and see the sparse traffic on the winding ribbon of the *autopista* and, beyond it, the outline of the coast and the glittering sea. In the opposite direction, inland, lay range after range of mountains, as far as the eye could see.

Pen would have liked to contemplate the views in silence but the Kilmartins kept up an almost non-stop conversation which, for her if not for Piers, detracted from the remoteness and isolation of this place.

North had lent her a camera with which to record her holiday. What she wanted to capture was the sun-burned face of Piers so that, whatever happened, she would have photographs of him; but instead of the close-ups she would have liked to take, she could only snap him in a group with the others.

The walk down took rather less time but was in a way more tiring because it was easier to lose one's footing on loose stones.

By the time they arrived at the car, she was tired. When Marguerite suggested having dinner at a restaurant, and asked her to join them, Pen said, 'Thank you, but if you don't mind I think I'll have a light supper and an early night.'

'Oh, dear, have we worn you out?'

'Not at all. I've enjoyed it. But exercise and fresh air do

make one sleepy and I should hate to nod off in public. I usually do keep earlier hours than most people.' She almost said, 'Don't I?' to Piers, but managed to change it to, 'Both going to bed and getting up in the morning.'

He said, speaking to Marguerite who was sitting in front with her husband but had not yet fastened her seat-belt and had twisted round to face Pen, 'I know I'm included in the invitation to the party tomorrow, but two parties in three days is heavy party-going for me. Would you mind if I opted out? I'd like to show Pen the *barrio medieval* in Benisa and one or two other local places of interest – that's if you have no other plans for tomorrow?' he added, turning to Pen.

Before she could answer, Marguerite said, 'I think that's a splendid idea. I know you're not mad about parties, Piers.'

'Will you spend the day with me, Pen?' Piers asked.

She smiled and nodded. 'With pleasure. Sightseeing will be much more enjoyable with a Spanish-speaking guide.'

'Good. I'll organize a car and pick you up about ten.'

'Use this car,' said his friend. 'Some people near us are also going to the party. They won't mind running us there and back. No sense in hiring a car when you can have this one for nothing.'

On the outskirts of Sant Jeroni Pen felt she ought to ask them in for a cup of tea.

It was Piers who declined the invitation with a firm, 'Some other time. I think what you ought to do is hop into a hot bath. It will help to reduce any stiffness you may feel tomorrow. I'm going to do the same, if I may, Marguerite?'

At Pen's request they dropped her in the main street because she wanted to do some shopping. The shops in Sant Jeroni closed between one and four-thirty but were open again until seven and sometimes later.

As the car drew away from the spot where Tom had stopped to let her out, Piers turned to look through the rear window and raise a hand in farewell.

Pen waved back. She felt very happy at the thought of a day on their own. It made her feel like a girl looking forward to her first date, which perhaps was silly at fifty, but that was the way she felt.

Tomorrow she could remind him about whatever it was he hadn't told her last night.

Before Piers arrived to take her out the next day, Pen had her hair washed and set at the village *peluquería*. Fortunately this was not one of Lola's busy times and she did Pen's hair almost as well as Peter and for a fraction of the price.

When Pen returned to the house, Maria was flicking dust from the black-painted *rejas* barring her ground-floor window with an implement made from strips of chamois leather attached to a short stick.

'*La señora es muy elegante,*' she said approvingly.

Pen laughed. '*Gracias.*' She unlocked her door and hurried upstairs to change.

She wasn't quite ready when she heard the rap of the knocker. Going through to one of the small front bedrooms, she leaned out of the window. 'Good morning. It isn't locked. Walk in. I'll be down in a moment.'

As she had no idea what sort of restaurant they would be lunching at – the open-air place by the sea or somewhere more formal – she had decided to wear the purple silk shirt with a tweed skirt and cashmere shawl. The skirt was part of a suit which had been made for her by the late Michael Donnellan, an Irishman who, years before, had been one of London's leading couturiers with stars such as Claudette Colbert and Vivien Leigh and most of the English aristocracy among his clientele. Flora had gone to him for her country clothes. The suit to which Pen's skirt belonged had been a present from her. Jane had seen that although the jacket was dated, the pleated skirt was a classic which could be worn for ever.

'I hope I'm suitably dressed,' she said, coming down the stairs to find Piers looking out of the window at the little patio.

He turned, his dark gaze sweeping from her newly-set hair to the chestnut sheen of her English walking shoes. He himself was wearing one of the nicest tweed sports

648

coats she had ever seen with a Viyella shirt, the collar unbuttoned to show a Paisley silk scarf.

'You always look right,' he told her. 'How are you feeling this morning? Any stiffness?'

Pen had felt some twinges in the backs of her calves but she wasn't going to admit to them and make herself sound infirm.

With less than perfect truth, she said cheerfully, 'I feel fine. If I lived here I'd soon be skipping up tracks like a mountain goat. May I offer you a cup of coffee before we set out, or is it too soon after breakfast?'

'I'd like coffee, thank you. May I take a closer look at your patio?'

'By all means. We'll have coffee out there.'

She went to the kitchen to fill and switch on the kettle, and then to watch him through the window as he studied the back of the house.

Unlike other men of his age who sometimes neglected to wash their hair as often as they should, Piers seemed to wash his every day. It always looked clean and springy. He was greyer than he had been the first time they met; but he was the same physical type as Edward's terrifying grandfather who had been in his seventies but still with a thick head of hair, at the time of her marriage.

Pen could remember clearly the ordeal of meeting the old Earl. He had not liked his eldest grandson, who was also his heir, and he hadn't taken to her, Edward's tongue-tied fiancée.

While she was still within earshot he had said gruffly to Flora, 'Don't think much of his choice. Nothing to say for herself and their daughters will have thick ankles.'

In fact Allegra had excellent legs and Pen's were not as unsightly as he had made her feel they were. As his wife had been one of the great beauties of the Edwardian era, with a figure to match her lovely face, very few other women had come up to his exacting standards.

Looking at Piers, sensing that he, like old Lord Carlyon, would keep his looks all his life, Pen felt a pang of regret that she had missed seeing him as a young man. But if they

649

had met as young people he wouldn't have looked twice at her. She had not been the kind of girl to catch the eye of a dashing subaltern.

She opened the window. 'Where were you in 1953, Piers?'

'Fifty-three? I was in Malaya, as it was then, taking part in the campaign against Communist terrorists under General Templar. Why do you ask?'

This time she answered truthfully. 'I was thinking what a very good-looking young man you must have been.'

He laughed. 'I expect I thought I was God's gift to the opposite sex. Raw second lieutenants are prone to have a high opinion of themselves, as are young men in general. Although Nick seemed an exception to that rule. I wonder if Sarah has heard from him yet?' He disappeared through the french windows and, a few moments later, joined her in the kitchen. 'Where were you in 1953? Still at school, I imagine.'

'No, I was married.' She busied herself with spooning instant coffee into cups. 'I'm sure you must know about my marriage. It wasn't a success.'

'I've always discouraged Mrs Armitage and others from telling me that sort of thing; but, yes – I have grasped that it wasn't a happy marriage.'

'Edward didn't want to marry anyone. As he was obliged to, he looked at the current crop of debs and picked out the one most likely to produce sons. I had three older brothers and five uncles. As for me . . . I did what I was pressed to do. I had very little backbone. It never occurred to me to tell *my* mother to get lost,' she said, with a rueful shrug. 'And the strange thing is that when my daughter rebelled against my ideas, I was angry with her. I didn't realize how much better my life would have been if I had rebelled.'

'Our generation didn't. You weren't the only one. If I had my life over again I shouldn't have gone in the army.'

'Really? What would you have done?'

'Something with my hands. A thing I enjoyed at school was throwing pots, but no one would have taken me

650

seriously if I'd said I wanted to become a potter or a stonemason. It would have been regarded as a waste of my expensive education to become a craftsman. Only a handful of my contemporaries did anything eccentric. But their children are far less malleable. Neither of Tom's sons has followed him into the army.'

He picked up an earthenware bowl she had left on the worktop, a country utensil with beauty in its simplicity. 'I still sometimes feel an urge to try making things like this.'

'Why don't you?' said Pen. 'What is to stop you? You could be a famous potter like Bernard Leach.'

He smiled. 'I rather doubt that, but you're right, there's nothing to stop me buying a wheel and a kiln when I've decided where to settle.'

She remembered that the other night he had said there was something he had yet to tell her. She wondered whether to remind him. Although she was curious to know what it was, she was also afraid that when she had found out she might wish she hadn't.

Piers carried the tray to the patio for her. She followed with a basket of *mandarinas*. They sat in the sun, peeling the succulent fruit and breaking them into segments, each one tasting like a distillation of the golden warmth which had brought them to ripeness.

'Mm . . . this sun is heavenly,' said Pen, closing her eyes and lifting her face to it. 'It said on the news from England this morning that they're having freezing fog in many parts of the country. Aren't we lucky to be here?'

When he didn't reply she opened her eyes. He was watching her.

Ignoring her remark, as if he hadn't heard it, he said, 'Is there anything you have always wanted to do which you could do now?'

She said slowly, 'Not in the sense I think you mean. I've always wanted to be happy. When I'm at work in the garden, I am happily occupied. To be happy when one's not working is something different. One can't achieve that by oneself. That kind of happiness has to be shared with someone else.'

651

'Have you never thought of trying again – marriage, I mean?'

The spontaneous reply was, 'Not until recently,' but she was afraid of saying anything which could reveal how she felt before she had stronger evidence of his feelings. Wanting to believe something, could, she knew, warp people's judgement. She wanted desperately to believe he was taking her out today because he had grown to care for her. But his motive might be closer to pity than love. He might merely feel sorry for her: a lonely woman on her own.

It was no less truthful but more cautious to answer, 'I have thought about it. The fact that my parents weren't happy and that Edward and I were incompatible hasn't turned me against marriage.'

Piers glanced at his watch. 'I think, if you've finished your coffee, we should continue this conversation in the car. After I've shown you Benisa, it's about an hour's run to the place where I thought we'd have lunch.'

The town of Benisa where they spent much of the morning was not a place which would have tempted her to stop had she driven through on her own. But off the unprepossessing main thoroughfare lay a *plaza* of greater charm and winding streets of the old quarter where there were some fine buildings and picturesque corners to photograph.

The next phase of their day out together took them through a region of citrus orchards where the branches were bowed with the weight of oranges and grapefruit and some had begun to fall on the rich red soil.

Their destination was a village smaller and more remote than Sant Jeroni. A cluster of houses surrounding a simple church, with the ruins of an ancient *castillo* perched on a nearby crag, the place had a small dark bar which didn't immediately strike her as worth the drive from Benisa.

Behind the bar an unshaven middle-aged man was reading a paper. In front of it the floor was littered with cigarette ends and sugar wrappers. Three or four Formica tables and chairs and two slot machines, one for music and the other a Star Wars game, completed the appointments.

In spite of his unkempt appearance, the proprietor's manner was civil. After an exchange of pleasantries, he called out 'Amparo!' and a stout woman in a pinafore came through from the back of the premises.

A few minutes later they were being ushered on to a terrace with a view of the surrounding mountains, the citrus orchards and, some miles away, the Mediterranean.

'Now I see why you brought me here,' said Pen.

'And not only for the view. The señora is a good cook. Nothing fancy, but everything fresh and cooked in oil from her brother's trees.'

As Amparo prepared the table, wiping the top and then spreading a white paper cloth which she fixed at the corners with plastic clips, she told him what there was to eat.

'There's not a choice here,' he explained. 'Today she has lamb chops with artichokes, mushrooms and *patatas fritas*. I hope that's all right for you.'

'It sounds delicious.'

Each time she bustled out, Amparo looked hard at Piers as if something about him puzzled her. When, after a longer interval, she appeared with the *entremeses*, the Spanish equivalent of hors d'oeuvres, and gave him another searching look, her plump face suddenly lit up.

'*Ah, me acuerdo!*' she exclaimed.

Pen understood only snatches of the rapid-fire Spanish which followed. But, aided by the many gestures which accompanied Amparo's words, and by her own intuition, she followed enough to understand that Piers's last visit to the restaurant had been many years ago, when he had had no grey hair – here Amparo pointed to his temples – and when his wife – what a beautiful voice! – had sung like an angel.

It was impossible to judge his reaction to being reminded that the last time he had sat on this terrace Camilla Ashford had been with him. As if he could ever forget, Pen thought miserably.

'Amparo!'

She was called away, leaving Pen with the feeling they

were no longer à *deux* but had been joined by the unseen presence of the woman he had loved and lost.

Perhaps she is always with him. Perhaps, if *he* ever considers marrying again, it will be only for companionship, not for a full relationship with a woman who means as much to him as Camilla did.

That isn't enough for me. I want to be loved as deeply as he loved her, Pen thought, with an ache in her throat.

He offered her the spoon and fork provided for helping themselves to the large dish of *entremeses*.

'I don't know how much, if any, of that you understood?'

'It doesn't matter. You don't have to translate everything for me. This looks like Parma ham,' she said, offering him a loophole.

'Here it's called *jamón serrano*, mountain ham.'

While he helped himself to the selection of smoked meats, quartered hard-boiled eggs, anchovies and black olives, Pen sipped the strong red wine and stared at the distant sea, from here a pale silvery-blue.

Piers finished filling his plate. He picked up his glass. She expected him to say *Salud* as he had at the Boltons' party and again at the picnic yesterday. Instead he held the glass to the light and thoughtfully studied the deep brilliant colour.

'Amparo remembers me; but only because on one occasion when we came here I persuaded my wife to sing. She was to have been an opera singer. But we met and there was no way our careers could be made to combine. So she gave up hers. I've often wondered if I was wrong to accept that sacrifice . . . if she would have got more out of life as a singer than as a soldier's wife. She always seemed happy, but it can't have been much fun living in army quarters and hobnobbing with women with whom she had little in common.'

Pen said quietly, 'I shouldn't think an operatic career is fun all the time. Draughty dressing rooms . . . rivalries . . . temperamental scenes . . .'

'Oh, yes, there would have been drawbacks, there always are. But it must be hard for a woman to submerge herself

654

in a marriage – particularly one without children – when she could have been someone outstanding in her own right. I took it for granted at the time, but I've often thought about it since.'

She picked up her fork and began to toy with the food. She had been hungry when they sat down. Now she had lost her appetite. In her mind's eye she could see clearly that other day, long ago, when he had sat here in the sun with a different woman.

Trying to ease his mind on one score, she said hesitantly, 'Perhaps you've been brainwashed a little by all the propaganda put out by the women's libbers. When I was young – when your wife was – most girls still thought of love as the be-all and end-all. If you loved your wife very much and she loved you, I'm sure she never regretted giving up her career. Given the choice between fame and happiness, most women, even now, would settle for happiness.'

He nodded. 'Perhaps you're right. Anyway what's done is done and nothing can change it. I don't spend much time in the past. For a long time I wouldn't come here, to this part of Spain. I felt it would be too painful. It isn't. Not any more. I knew as soon as I arrived that it was going to be all right. And now you are here, and –' He stopped short. 'If we don't get a move on, the chops will be cooked before we've finished eating this.'

As they drove back to Sant Jeroni, Pen was silent, her mind full of Piers's unfinished remark and the warm look in his eyes as he had begun it.

Although after lunch they had lingered, drinking a second jug of wine and discussing many different subjects, he had said nothing else to confirm and increase her euphoria. Even so she was *almost* certain now that her hopes and longings were about to be realized – perhaps not yet, but quite soon.

The patio was in shadow when they entered the house.

'We can have tea on the *mirador* which I haven't shown you yet,' she said.

When the tray was ready, she led him upstairs and

through the bedroom to the *mirador*, still in the gentle sunlight of late afternoon.

Looking at her view of the valley, Piers said, 'It's a pity, from a scenic point of view, that the rivers have all been dammed, leaving only dry river beds. Even without any water, this is a marvellous outlook.' He surveyed it for a few minutes and then turned to look at her. 'Where would you like to go this evening? The others aren't expecting me back until late. There's a restaurant at Moraira which has a Michelin star.'

'I don't think I could manage another large meal,' she answered, handing him a cup of tea. 'If it wouldn't be boring for you, I'd be happy to light a fire and have a lap supper here. I've some goat's-milk cheese called *cabrales*, recommended by Helen, and plenty of fresh bread and fruit. Would that be enough for you?'

'I can think of nothing I'd like more.'

By half-past five the sun had begun to sink towards the rim of the mountains and the warmth was going out of the day.

'I'll go down and get a fire going,' said Pen, standing up.

'I'll do it for you.'

She shook her head. 'You're on holiday. In this house, I shall wait on you.'

'Let's do it together.'

She smiled. 'If you insist.' Turning away for a last look at the valley in the sunset glow, she said, 'I do wish this cottage were mine.'

She heard the other chair creak as he rose from it. A brown hand fell on her shoulder.

'I've been wishing *you* were mine,' he said in a low voice, as she turned to look at him.

'D'you want ride on one of them buggers?'

The strident Yorkshire voice made Allegra, who was lying face down on a towel on the beach at the Sandy Lane Hotel, raise herself on her elbows to see who had disturbed her doze.

A few yards away a man and his son were watching the

656

jet-ski machines zooming back and forth across the bay. The man was the cooked-lobster colour of a newcomer from a northern climate who, white as a grub on arrival, has spent far too long in the sun and will pass a painful night. A beer belly overhung the band of his shorts. There was a tattoo on his forearm.

Nearby, sitting on one of the sunbeds provided by the hotel was his lobster-coloured wife, her overweight body uncomfortably stuffed into a shiny stretch-satin strapless bathing suit with reinforced cups. On her tightly permed hair was a straw hat with raffia flowers round the crown. She was rummaging in a beach bag with *Barbados* stitched in pink raffia, framed by pink and yellow daisies, on the side.

Producing a bottle of sun cream, she began to anoint her fat arms, obviously unaware that her hot flesh was begging for shade. She had a kind placid face which reminded Allegra of one of the cleaners at Longwarden. But Mrs Bailey, much of whose worldly wisdom derived from the pages of *Woman's Weekly*, would have known better than to expose her unaccustomed skin to this powerful sun for hours on end.

Catching Allegra's eye, the woman gave a shy smile. Allegra smiled back. She would have liked to go over and say, 'If I were you I'd stay out of the sun until tomorrow. One has to be awfully careful for the first week here.'

But one couldn't give advice to strangers. She might take it in good part but her husband would probably swing round and tell Allegra to mind her own bloody business.

Leaving Risconti at Paradise where he was starting a portrait of a very old man from the village, Allegra had come to the hotel because she was curious to see if it were still as delightful as her great-grandmother's description of it.

After her husband's death, Flora Carlyon had spent several years trying to ease her loneliness by travelling. She had first come to Barbados as a guest at Heron Bay, the most spectacular mansion to be built on the island since Sam Lord's castle in 1826.

Heron Bay, a Palladian design carried out in great blocks of coral stone, had been built after World War Two by Ronald Tree, a banker, Member of Parliament and the heir to an American fortune. His wife Marietta had been one of the Boston Peabodys and Flora's daughter, Rose, had married into another great Boston family.

In the days when Flora had stayed with the Trees, only a small élite circle had enjoyed the delights of wintering in Barbados. In the sixties, the Sandy Lane Estate, a British rival to the American Mill Reef Club on the more northerly island of Antigua, had been developed; and also the Sandy Lane Hotel where Flora had watched the young of her privileged milieu dancing under the stars on the circular floor between the two curving staircases which Allegra could see as she rose and shook out her towel.

After pulling an airy sun dress over her now-dry bikini and picking up her leather-soled thongs, she gave the woman in the hat a friendly nod before going to dabble her sandy feet in one of the small stone pools provided for that purpose.

Although the man with the loud voice might think that what he was paying an exorbitant rate for was the same exclusive preserve from which his father and grandfather had been rigorously debarred, she had seen at a glance that it wasn't. The elegant architecture remained and perhaps the one hundred and fifteen bedrooms were furnished with the same taste as the original sixty-odd rooms, some of which Flora had been shown before the place opened its doors.

But none of the guests she had seen bore the distinguishing marks of the *galère* who had made Sandy Lane what it was in the sixties. The only person she encountered who did have breeding and style was a tall, chic Barbadian girl who was working in one of the hotel's expensive boutiques where Allegra browsed before driving back to Paradise.

When she told Risconti about the man with the belly, he said, 'If you don't like people like that, what are you doing with me?'

'Darling, there's no comparison. That toothless old boy

you're painting is descended from generations of slaves but he has *far* better manners than "D'you want ride on them buggers?" It's all a question of intelligence.'

She walked into his arms. 'Did you miss me? No – you were too busy painting. There's a poem by Kahlil Gibran I've always thought a perfect description of the perfect relationship. It's the one about "spaces in your togetherness". Have you ever read it?'

Risconti shook his head. 'Can you remember it?'

Often punished during her schooldays by being made to learn poetry, Allegra had developed an excellent memory and still learned by heart anything she liked.

She put her arms round his neck. Resting her cheek on his shoulder, she began to speak the poem.

> *'Love one another, but let there be spaces in your togetherness*
> *And let the winds of heaven dance between you.*
> *Love one another but make not a bond of love:*
> *Let it rather be a moving sea between the shores of your*
>   *souls.*
> *Fill each other's cup but drink not from one cup.*
> *Give one another of your bread but eat not from the same*
>   *loaf.*
> *Sing and dance together and be joyous, but let each one of*
>   *you be alone,*
> *Even as the strings of a lute are alone though they quiver*
>   *with the same music.*
> *Give your hearts, but not into each other's keeping.*
> *For only the hand of Life can contain your hearts.*
> *And stand together yet not too near together:*
> *For the pillars of the temple stand apart,*
> *And the oak tree and the cypress grow not in each other's*
>   *shadow.'*

She raised her head and looked into his eyes. 'Isn't that beautiful? Isn't that how love should be?'

Any of the Englishmen she had known would have been embarrassed by having a love poem recited to them. Andro wasn't ashamed of his deepest emotions. She saw that he was very much moved.

'Yes . . . that is how love should be,' he agreed huskily.

Then, to her surprise and concern, he began to weep, burying his face in her neck, clutching her painfully close to his heaving chest.

Pen opened her eyes and knew, without knowing why, this wasn't the right time of day to be waking up.

For one thing the lamps on either side of the bed were alight. It was possible she could have fallen asleep while reading and left one lamp on. But not both. Also the curtains were drawn and she always opened the curtains before climbing into bed.

Her puzzlement was increased by her third discovery – that she wasn't wearing pyjamas. Under the sheet and the light warmth of the Wimbornes' duvet she was naked. Then, in a lightning flash of clear, startling recollection, she remembered the reason for all these puzzling circumstances. It wasn't morning. It was evening. When she had fallen asleep she had been lying in Piers's arms after making love. Even more unbelievable, she had enjoyed it, had welcomed him into her body and, when it was over, clung to him, weeping with relief because for the first time in her life she had understood why men and women found pleasure in the strange act of love.

Where was he now? Downstairs? Gone? What time was it?

Raising her head to look at the clock on the night table, she found it was half-past seven, more than two hours since the moment on the *mirador* when he had turned her towards him, searching her upturned face before taking it between his hands and softly kissing her mouth.

Remembering that first gentle kiss and the other more passionate kisses which had followed it, she felt her insides churn with rekindled excitement.

The sound of footsteps on the tiled staircase made her suddenly shy of facing him. She closed her eyes, feigning sleep, trying to breathe quietly and evenly while her heart was pounding with excitement.

Inside the bedroom his footsteps were muffled by the carpet. She heard some slight sounds which might be something being placed on the night table, then a movement of the mattress indicating he had sat down on the side of the bed and was probably watching her.

She felt a kiss on her forehead, another on her cheek and then a third on her mouth. Reassured, she opened her eyes. He wouldn't have kissed her so tenderly if he had been disappointed in her.

'I was only half asleep. Have you been up long?'

'Long enough to find out there was no champagne in the house and to buy a bottle and chill it. You were sound asleep when I left you,' he said caressingly.

She blushed. 'Didn't you sleep?'

She had thought it was men who were exhausted by sex, not women.

'For a short time.' Piers turned his attention to the bottle of champagne, unfastening the wire mesh securing the cork before easing it out so slowly that only a wisp of vapour escaped as it left the green neck.

Pen sat up, pulling the down quilt with her and tucking it modestly round her. Whatever had happened in this room while the sun was setting and night falling, and she was faintly shocked by some of the things she remembered, she wasn't yet ready to sit with bared breasts in front of him. Besides, although he had switched on the electric radiator, it didn't make the room warm by comparison with the snug warmth of nestling under the quilt. She wondered if he were warm enough in his shirt sleeves.

'There's a sweater belonging to Helen's husband you could put on,' she suggested. 'They leave quite a lot of clothes here. She said I was welcome to borrow whatever I needed.'

'I'm not cold. Are you, my love?'

The endearment, spoken so naturally, as if they had long been lovers, touched her to the heart.

'A little. Could you bring me my shawl? I think I left it downstairs.'

'I've already brought it up with me.' He draped it round

her bare shoulders and arranged the pillows more comfortably behind her.

'Better?'

'Lovely, thank you.'

She wanted to call him 'darling' as she had when they were making love, but she was still ridiculously shy of him. How was it possible to be shy after all the things they had done together? Yet it was. She couldn't look at his mouth without remembering, vividly, how and where those firm lips had caressed her; and how she had writhed with pleasure, all inhibitions put to flight by his skill.

He gave her a glass of champagne.

'To us,' he said, touching glasses. 'I never thought we should be together like this, but we are and I'm very happy. I hope you are too.'

'I didn't know it was possible to be so happy. Thank you, Piers,' she said humbly. 'You don't know what you've done for me. I always thought there was something lacking in me because I never . . . wanted a man the way other women seem to. It was wonderful. Thank you.'

She reached for his free hand and pressed a soft kiss of gratitude on the back of it.

His fingers tightened round hers. They touched glasses again and drank the pale bubbling wine.

'I should like to stay here with you for the rest of my stay, but how do you feel about that?' he asked. 'I think Tom and Marguerite are under the impression that I took one look at the party and fell for you lock, stock and barrel. I shall have to explain that we've misled them a little. In the circumstances, I'm sure they'd understand if I left them and moved in with you. But you may prefer not to advertise our relationship until we've made it official. You are going to marry me, aren't you, Pen?'

'If you're sure that's what *you* want.'

'I was never more certain of anything; but it's going to cause a lot of raised eyebrows, you know . . . Lady Carlyon marrying her butler.'

'If you were really a butler, I suppose it would. At our

662

age ... what does it matter, as long as we are happy together?'

'*I* don't think it matters at all, but your family may have reservations.'

'North won't care a jot. He's caused many a scandal, as has Allegra. As for Jane, she doesn't approve of the English class system – or the American one.' A thought struck her. 'Piers, these party walls aren't nearly as thick as the outsides of the houses. I wonder if Maria has heard us talking up here and wonders why you're in my bedroom? She's one person who *would* be shocked if you moved in with me,' she went on, lowering her voice. 'For the Wimbornes' sake, I shouldn't like her to think they have friends who are immoral, by Sant Jeroni standards.'

'I expect the village has its share of adultery and other venial sins, but I take your point,' he agreed, speaking more quietly. 'In that case why don't you dress and come down by the fire which should be well ablaze now. I'll go and start the supper.'

He rose from the bed and refilled their glasses. His dark eyes glinting, he said, 'After the unexpectedly strenuous end to our outing, I thought I'd have a steak for supper. I bought a big one. Would you like to share it with me?'

Pen smiled and shook her head. He blew her a kiss and left the bedroom. For a while she remained where she was, leisurely sipping the wine and savouring the most wonderful feeling of well-being she had ever experienced.

Pondering the immediate future, she had two ideas which made her throw aside the quilt and scramble out of bed. Helen's Moorish looking glass, set in a frame of pierced metal, reflected a tousled head and eyes alight with happiness. As she brushed her hair, she thought fleetingly of the pale face and reddened eyelids which had looked back at her after her first night with Edward.

How was it possible for two men to perform the same basic act so differently? she wondered. Then she remembered that Edward and his younger brother had been utterly different as horsemen; the one free with whip, spurs and shouts, the other despising such aids and treating his horses with kindness and infinite patience, as did his daughter.

Perhaps that was why Allegra had never stuck to one man until she met Andro Risconti, thought Pen, as she dabbed *Arpège* behind her ears and on her wrists.

Perhaps all the men in her daughter's life had been disappointing lovers and she, being of a generation of women who didn't have to take on trust a man's understanding of their needs, had continued searching for one who wasn't. The idea that Allegra's acerbity – recently much less in evidence than it had been at one time – might have stemmed from the frustration and disillusionment which had marred Pen's life was something she had never considered before.

'To ring up Longwarden and ask if I can have another week off – yes, that's an excellent idea,' said Piers, grating Manchego cheese to put in her omelette. 'I can't move in here and I'm not sure about the wisdom of moving to an hotel. Thinking it over, Pen, I believe it might be wise for us to err on the side of discretion until we're married. I'm not suggesting an embargo on making love, merely that we shouldn't spend our nights together until we have everyone's blessing.'

'In that case I have another suggestion,' she said. 'Why don't we fly home tomorrow, get married by special licence in the chapel at Longwarden, and come back here for our honeymoon? By this time next week we could be Colonel and Mrs Ashford.'

She made the suggestion jokingly, although with an element of seriousness. Evidently Piers took it seriously. She watched him thinking it over while he went on preparing the supper and she leaned against the worktop, sipping champagne.

'It's tempting – but no, I think not,' he answered, at length. 'We should give your family more warning of our intentions, including my intention to give notice. If I ring up about that and tomorrow we both write letters explaining the situation in full, they'll have time to accept the idea before we reappear. They aren't to know that our feelings towards each other have been growing for a long time. I don't think either of us has given much sign of it. Certainly *I* didn't receive any unequivocal signals, and I was on the alert for them,' he said dryly.

'I thought I made myself plain when I asked you to dance with me.'

'I'd have liked to believe your behaviour that night, but I felt it was probably largely the result of this stuff,' he told her, draining his glass.

She refilled it for him. 'It did have something to do with it because I shouldn't have had the courage to ask you if I hadn't been mildly tiddly. But I didn't mean to overdo it.' She blushed at the memory.

He put an arm round her waist and drew her against him. 'You were enchanting,' he murmured. 'I wanted to dance with you for the rest of the night.'

Pen leaned against him, resting her head on his houlder. 'So did I,' she said, with a sigh. '. . . *over the hills and far away she danced with Pigling Bland*. Did you have that story read to you when you were little?' She looked up at him. 'Why did I have to wait so long to find you? All these years we could have been happy . . . Ah, no! I'm sorry, my love. I forgot for a moment: you *were* happy.'

'And am now to be happy again. God knows what I've done to deserve it.'

They had supper in front of a fire of gnarled *algarrobo* logs and olive branches. Afterwards they shared a second bottle of champagne, sitting side by side on the sofa with Pen's legs tucked up beside her and his arm round her shoulders.

'Darling, there's something I must say to you,' Pen said, breaking a silence of several minutes while they watched the wood flame and sputter on its bed of ash.

'That sounds portentous.'

'It is quite important.'

'Say away then.'

She swung her legs to the floor and turned to face him. The firelight gave his sun-burned face a Red Indian tint.

665

She indulged in the pleasure of touching one of the fans of crisp silver hair above his ears.

'It's about Camilla. I don't want you ever to feel that I might be jealous of her or of the happiness you had with her, and that you must try not to mention her. That would be absurd and wrong. If I had loved Edward I shouldn't want to forget him or feel I must never refer to him. For people of our age, everyone we have loved – whether wife, husband, child or friend – is part of the fabric of our life. We can't snip them out and forget them. So, please, when you remember a joke you shared with her, don't stop yourself smiling. Or if we're somewhere you visited with her, or if you hear music she sang, and it makes you sad, don't think I would resent it. I could never resent anything which has made you the man you are – the man I love.'

Having made this, for her, long speech, she wished she hadn't. Years of being made to feel foolish, first by Edward and then by Allegra, had damaged her confidence to an extent which could not be repaired quickly, even by the morale-boosters of the past few hours.

It was with considerable relief that she felt Piers's arms go round her and heard him say thickly, 'Pen, you are such a treasure. How many women in the world would have said that and meant it? My God! I'm a lucky man. First Camilla and now you.'

As they hugged, their cheeks pressed together, she became aware that his was damp.

He had been touched to tears, she realized, with wonder and joy.

In the time of his hero, Lord Wellington, nicknamed the Iron Duke, strong men had wept without shame when their feelings were deeply engaged.

But Piers was the first modern man she had known to shed tears. The proof of his sensitive core made her love for him quicken. She clung to him, filled with tenderness. Here, at last, was her ideal. A strong man who could cry, when moved; a man, accustomed to command, who had so little false pride that he could also take orders.

'I love you.'

The words broke from them at the same moment.

The next thing Pen was aware of was being swept up in his arms and carried back to the bedroom.

'Did I hurt you before?' he asked her softly, as they lay under the quilt.

'Hurt me? Oh, Piers, you wouldn't know how to hurt a woman. But it was like the first time for me . . . the way the first time should be,' she murmured gratefully.

Later, with great reluctance, he left her to return to his hosts' house. Carefully setting the guard in front of the dying fire, Pen went back to bed, but not to sleep.

For more than an hour she sat up composing a letter to explain to her son and daughter-in-law what had happened. Although she had told Piers that North would take the news in his stride, doubts about his reaction were beginning to creep in.

It was true, as she had said in the kitchen earlier, that North and Allegra had provided much fodder for Nigel Dempster and other gossip columnists. However that was some time ago. North was now a reformed character with a lovely wife to whom he seemed likely to be as faithful as his great-grandfather had been to Flora.

Allegra, too, appeared to have been diverted from the ruinous course of her earlier twenties, thank God. Whether her relationship with Andro would eventually lead to marriage was difficult to predict, but at least it was no flash in the pan like all her other amours.

Like religious converts and recovered addicts, reformed characters tended to go to extremes, Pen had noticed. Far from receiving her news, as she hoped they would, with surprise followed by a shrug, it might be that her children would think it their duty to oppose her remarriage. If they couldn't actually stop her, they could put pressure on Piers, making him have second thoughts.

His feeling that he and she shouldn't stay together until they were married showed there was a strong streak of conventionality in his make-up. Both North and Allegra had the shrewdness and ruthlessness to recognize that facet of his character and play on it. If they chose, they were capable of making him feel that, regardless of his distinguished military career, he was known in the village and to their friends as a butler and therefore to marry their mother must cause embarrassment.

As she finished her letter to them, Pen wasn't sure how they would react. The more she thought about it, the less sanguine she became.

'What did the Kilmartins say when you told them about us? Were they flabbergasted?' she asked, when Piers arrived the next morning.

'More by your real identity as my employer than by the news of our sudden engagement, as it were. They had already decided it was love at first sight and something to be encouraged. I'm afraid I couldn't get out of our having dinner with them tonight. But at least we shall have all day alone together.'

He took her in his arms and kissed her, lightly at first but then with increasing ardour until at last he raised his head to ask, 'Is the woman next door likely to burst in on us?'

'She's gone out for the day . . . to see her sister in Altea. Why?' she teased him.

'You know why.'

He grabbed her hand and hurried her, breathless and laughing, up the narrow staircase.

She had left the bedroom window wide open and sunlight was pouring over the neatly-made bed. With the quilt and the pillows flung in a heap on the floor, lying on the taut fitted undersheet was almost like making love in the open air.

'We're being watched,' Piers murmured lazily, when they were lying at peace, her head on his shoulder, her eyes closed against the bright light.

Pen sat up in a panic, looking for something to cover herself.

'Only by a black cat . . . the soul of discretion,' he said, chuckling.

'What a beast you are,' she told him fondly, lying down again but this time propped on her elbows close to his side, smiling into his eyes.

The word discretion had reminded her of her misgivings late last night. Her smile faded.

Piers distracted her by running his fingertips lightly up the long undulating curve of her back from buttock to shoulder. 'I can't believe this,' he said. 'You make me feel like a boy again. Do you realize that making love three times in about eighteen hours is a signal achievement for a man of my age – especially after a long time without sex.'

'You aren't old. Your body isn't old . . . it's strong and beautiful.'

A cloud, obscuring the sun, caused an instantaneous drop in the temperature.

He turned his head to the window. 'I hope it isn't clouding over. I was planning a picnic lunch. Not involving a trek like the one with Tom and Marguerite. I'm conserving my strength for better things,' he said, as they rose from the bed.

The cloud was an isolated one which, when it passed, left the sky clear. They dressed and went down to have coffee. Pen showed him her letter to North and Jane.

'Do you think it's all right?' she asked, as he finished reading it.

'Couldn't be better. Which reminds me I must make that telephone call. May I use the one here? Public telephones in Spain are inclined to gulp money and cut one off in mid-sentence.'

'Yes, do, but I don't know if you'll catch either of them in at this time of day. North may not be there yet. He was due back the day before yesterday, but he may have been delayed.'

At his suggestion, she listened in on the bedroom extension while he made his call to Longwarden.

It was answered almost immediately by a brisk male 'Hello?'

'Good morning, m'Lord. This is Ashford, speaking from

abroad. With your permission, I should like to extend my time here by an extra week. I realize this must cause some inconvenience but circumstances have arisen which make an extension of leave a matter of importance to me.'

'Are you in some kind of trouble, Ashford? Anything I can do to help?'

'Thank you, m'Lord, but no – I'm not in trouble. It's a personal matter, too complex to explain on the telephone. You will be receiving a letter soon, but I felt I should telephone immediately.'

There was a few seconds' pause before North said, 'Knowing you, I'm sure your reason is a good one. Yes, take whatever time you need; a week or longer if necessary. So far as I know my wife has no plans she can't handle without you in the immediate future.'

'I'm relieved to hear it, m'Lord, but I have to tell you that as soon as you and Lady Carlyon can find a suitable replacement, I should like to leave Longwarden. The circumstances I've mentioned make it desirable for me to retire from your service at the earliest possible date.'

'Good God! That is a shock. What the hell is going on? Where are you, Ashford?'

'That will be explained in the letter, m'Lord. You should receive it in a few days. Goodbye, m'Lord.'

There was a crackle in Pen's ear as Piers cut the connection.

'It was nice of him to think of your welfare before his own convenience,' she said, when she joined him downstairs.

'It didn't surprise me. He's your son, my dearest.'

'And your future son-in-law, even if he doesn't know it yet.'

'Yes . . . all being well,' he agreed, reviving her unexpressed fears that having given her happiness the capricious gods might decide to snatch it away from her.

'Where are we going today?' she asked presently, as they left Sant Jeroni behind them, en route for the picnic.

'To a tumbledown farmhouse I discovered years ago when this old boy on his mule was a more common sight than it is today,' Piers answered.

A bend in the road had brought into view a countryman riding a blinkered mule, with a liver-coloured Spanish hound following behind.

Pen was firmly determined not to let herself worry about future difficulties. She was going to concentrate on the pleasures of the present and let *mañana* take care of itself.

'A lot of these little houses dotted about the countryside seem to be closed up,' she remarked, as they passed a whitewashed cottage which, like most of its fellows, had a date palm growing outside it.

'They're *casitas* belonging to town-dwellers who come at weekends and in the hot summer months,' he explained. 'Probably the present owners' parents or grandparents lived in them and off the land. There's a drift from the land now. Coming back to Spain after several years' absence, it's very noticeable how many of the dry-stone walls of the terraces, which were in good repair when I was last here, are now being allowed to fall down. A lot of the older walls are supposed to have been built by the Moors, centuries ago.'

The last part of the way to the farmhouse was along a rutted dirt track descending into a valley where, long ago, the slopes had been terraced for cultivation but were now a mixture of tilled earth and tended trees and areas falling into wilderness.

It was a peaceful place with no sign of human habitation until the track turned a corner marked by an ancient olive tree. There, ahead, was the farm, larger than Pen had expected and built of large weathered cream rocks, lichen-speckled Roman tiles forming a roof with half a dozen different pitches as if the house had been built one room at a time over a period of many years.

The track ended behind the building which stood on more than one level with most of its windows overlooking the valley and blank walls facing the yard formed by two long *riu-rau* built at right angles to each other. Here, two tall date palms had been planted a long time ago. There was also a fig tree, bare-branched now but looking as if it would bear baskets of delicious fruit later in the year.

The door to the farm had as its uneven lintel the twisted

trunk of an olive tree. The door itself was very old, studded with massive nails.

'The owner leaves the key concealed in the ivy,' said Piers, producing a key of medieval size from among the leaves surrounding the doorway.

'How did you discover that?'

'When the wind blows you can see it. There was nothing inside the house the first time I came here. It's been deserted for years. You needn't have qualms about trespassing.'

Inside, the farm was dark, small windows admitting thin shafts of sunlight when Piers opened the shutters. But a door on the valley side of the building led, by stone steps, down to a sunny patio which instantly she could see as a leafy alfresco dining room with honeysuckle and other sweet-scented climbers twining up the stone walls in place of the rampant ivy.

'I'm amazed that no one has bought it. None of the foreigners, I mean,' she said, as they ate their lunch.

'It's rather off the beaten track. It would be expensive to bring electricity and a telephone here, and it would take a great deal of work to make it habitable and comfortable by northern European standards.'

'Yes, one sees that,' Pen agreed. 'But it has such tremendous possibilities. If I had money – which I haven't – I should buy this place like a shot, assuming it's for sale. I could make it into a dream house.' She gave him a smiling look. 'Before I fell in love with you, the secret light of my life was a vicomte called Charles de Noailles who was one of France's great gardeners. As well as his garden at Fontainebleau, he had a place in the south, a Mediterranean garden. If this farm were mine, I should follow his precepts and create the most beautiful garden on the Costa Blanca,' she said dreamily.

'I'm sure that's well within your scope, but don't you think you'd miss England? A lot of expatriate wives are not altogether happy here, Marguerite tells me,' said Piers. 'The men like it, but the women miss seeing their grandchildren regularly, among other things.'

672

'Grandchildren must matter more to women who have no consuming passions,' she answered. 'I have two now – you and gardening. I should have thought, if one had a nice house in the sun, one's children and their offspring might descend on one rather more often than one really wanted. I must say I love Spain. I'm sure I could live here happily.'

They were sitting on small folding chairs which Piers had produced from the boot, with a camp table, and set up by a large mimosa which would soon be in flower.

'I've always loved mimosa,' she went on, admiring its feathery branches. 'I wonder how old this one is? It must have been planted by the last farmer's wife. I can't see him bothering with anything purely ornamental, can you? But she may have been more artistic.'

'I planted the tree,' said Piers.

She stared at him. '*You* did?'

'Twelve years ago . . . when I bought the place. The farm is mine. I came out here first thing this morning and put the key on the nail hidden under the ivy. I didn't tell you it was my house because I didn't want to influence your reaction.'

'You bought it for Camilla,' she said, in a low voice.

He nodded. 'Several times I've intended to sell it. It cost a song but would fetch a good price now, even without power and water, except what collects in the *cisterna*. I don't know why I've kept putting off getting rid of it. I suppose because I've loved the place since the first time I saw it. Occasionally I've debated living here on my own.'

'It's too large for one person,' said Pen. 'It needs at least two to share it, with others coming and going.'

Their chairs were placed together. She laid her hand on his forearm and gently squeezed it. 'Between us, we could make this a perfect place for two people, both with rural inclinations, to live. But I have no income, Piers, or even any goods and chattels worth speaking of. Have you any furniture? I suppose not if you always lived in houses provided by the army.'

'I've a few bits and pieces in storage, probably none of

them suitable for a Spanish farmhouse. Financially we'd have no problems. D'you remember my telling you about an investment I made when I left the army? Those funds will be more than enough to put the house in good order and furnish it decently. Also, of course, I have a pretty good pension. But even without money worries setting up home in what is at the moment a semi-ruin is going to mean a lot of hard work.'

He covered her hand which was still resting on his arm. 'Are you sure you want to take on such a mammoth project? Mightn't it be wiser to look round for a property in better repair with an existing garden you can gradually alter?'

'Wiser perhaps, but not as much fun or as satisfying as starting from scratch,' she answered. 'We're not young, but neither are we old. We're fit and active. A challenge will do us good.'

Discussing their future home kept her mind happily occupied for the rest of the afternoon and while she was having a shower and changing to spend the evening with the Kilmartins.

They were about to set out when the telephone rang. Pen picked up the receiver. 'Hello?'

'Penelope? It's Jane. How's the holiday going? I called Allegra just now and she said you seemed to be having a wild time down there. Who's this dishy colonel you're dating? Or is he one among many?'

Her daughter-in-law's voice, a welcome sound the first evening when she had telephoned to check that Pen had arrived safely and was comfortable, this time was a reminder that her family's reaction to her plans was still unknown.

But in reply to Jane's teasing inquiry, she answered lightly, 'But of course. You didn't think, after all the trouble you took to smarten me up, that I'd be spending my evenings with a good book, did you? Tonight I'm having dinner with a dashing ex-major.'

'Good for you. I'm glad to hear it. How's the weather? It has to be better than what we've been having here. Maybe North and I should join you, now Sarah has Kate to keep her company. Or would that cramp your style?' Jane asked, laughing.

Pen also laughed. 'Come by all means, as long as you don't mind occupying twin beds. I'm using the Wimbornes' bed which has an electric blanket. None of the other beds has, and although the days are very warm the temperature does drop at night.'

'By the way, this morning North had a very strange call from Ashford. He didn't say where he was – somewhere abroad – but he called to ask if he could prolong his trip and to warn us he wants to leave. Isn't that a blow? Did he give you any hint that he was thinking of leaving?'

Pen said, with perfect truth, 'No, none at all. But I'm sure you can easily replace him.'

'Yes, maybe so, but I like him. I don't want to lose him. When he comes back I'll try and persuade him to change his mind.'

It made Pen feel uncomfortable to continue a conversation which, when her mother-in-law's letter reached them, Jane would realize had been disingenuous.

She said, 'I must go now, my dear. We're an hour later here. Thank you for calling. Give my love to North.'

'Do I gather there's a possibility they may come down?' asked Piers, when she had rung off.

'No, no – she was only joking. When she told me about your telephone call to North it made me feel horribly two-faced. I wonder how long it will take for my letter to get there?'

At Paradise, Allegra was lying on a sunbed by the pool, wishing their time in Barbados wasn't running out.

She would have been happy to stay another month had the house been available. But it wasn't. Some other friends of the owners were coming to stay in it shortly. She had made inquiries about alternative accommodation, but everywhere nice was fully booked and to rent somewhere crummy would be too much of a come-down after this heavenly place.

Her reluctance to leave surprised her. Now that she had

completed the first draft of the book and had no work to occupy her, she ought to be looking forward to taking it back to London and hearing what Claudia thought of it. There was also the imminent wedding of one of her oldest friends to look forward to. She didn't want to miss that.

At the same time she wouldn't have minded lying around, lotus-eating, until England started to warm up after the second-coldest February of the century.

Andro wasn't lotus-eating. He was painting like a mad thing – dashing off brilliant sketch-portraits of people in the village. Today he was painting an old man whose grin revealed a mouthful of pointed stumps, the result of cane-chewing in his youth. Present-day Barbadian youths had superb teeth and fine, athletic bodies which they carried with straight spines and a jaunty gait.

Allegra thought Andro was working too hard. After sleeping heavily when they first came, now he seemed reluctant to go to bed at all – except to make love. To her relief he was drinking less, but he was also less relaxed.

He had done so much work that, yesterday, they had had to go to Cave Shepherd, the Bridgetown department store, to buy an extra suitcase for all the canvases and sketch books. After finding it tiring at first, he seemed to have adjusted to the climate and be possessed by exceptional energy.

In the days following the first visit to the *finca*, Pen and Piers spent much of their time there. They measured the rooms and made a plan of the farm and its outbuildings. They spent hours discussing how best to modernize the place while retaining its essential character.

As they couldn't continue to borrow the Kilmartins' car for their comings and goings, Piers hired one. On Saturday – only six days after their meeting at the party, although it seemed longer – he drove her to various garden centres where Pen was disappointed by the range of Mediterranean plants on sale.

As for the urns and garden ornaments displayed at the roadside *cerámicas*, they were almost all hideous. She began to foresee that it wasn't going to be easy to create a Spanish garden to compare with the legendary gardens of the French Riviera. She wasn't daunted. The more problems and obstacles there were, the more satisfaction it would give her to overcome them.

For lunch he took her to the place by the sea where he ordered a *paella* for two and they explored the rocky fore-shore while it was being prepared for them.

The vivid saffron-stained rice, mixed with pieces of chicken and squid, and ornamented with pink prawns and slices of lemon, made a good, filling meal which tasted all the better for being eaten out of doors.

Afterwards they drove back to Sant Jeroni for what Piers, smiling, called a siesta.

The broad shaft of sunlight which, early in the morning, shone on the scrolled cane headboard of the Wimbornes' bed, had by late afternoon moved its focus to the opposite side of the bedroom where stood one of Helen's most interesting pieces of Spanish country furniture. This was a pine chest of drawers with a bombé front and brass handles, a sturdy piece with smooth-running drawers.

Lying in bed after making love, Pen wondered, not for the first time, where the carpenter who had made it had seen the more handsome piece of furniture which must have inspired it.

Piers was asleep.

The night before, they and the Kilmartins and another couple had dined at a small inland restaurant run by a Spanish couple. She cooked and he, once a member of a well-known singing group, waited at table and later brought out his guitar and sang to the diners.

It had been one in the morning when Piers brought her home, longing to spend the rest of the night with her but resolutely determined not to. It must have been nearly two before he had gone to bed. Therefore it wasn't surprising that after eating paella, drinking wine and making love, he had fallen into a deep sleep.

She turned quietly on to her side and lay watching his

sleeping face, her heart full of love and gratitude for the change he had made to her life. She was learning so much about being a woman from him.

Until recently she had believed – and she wondered how many women of her generation were equally ignorant – that making love was something a man did to a woman; he being the active and she the passive partner. Piers was beginning to teach her that this was not how it should be, and to show her how she could please him.

Looking back, she could see that even if Edward had made love to her with greater finesse, it might have disgusted her more than his inept assaults on her body. She hadn't been physically attracted to him and could never have stroked and kissed his heavy, white, hairy body with the enjoyment it gave her to caress every part of Piers.

I wish I were thirty, thought Pen. I wish I could give him children.

Presently, moving with stealth in order not to disturb him, she slipped out of bed and put on her blue wool dressing gown before creeping downstairs to make China tea.

She was waiting for the kettle to boil when someone rapped the brass knocker on the front door. Thinking it must be Maria, Pen went to answer the summons.

When she opened the door, she was momentarily paralysed to find her son and her daughter-in-law standing outside.

'Surprise . . . surprise!' Jane said, beaming, reaching out to hug her.

'My dears . . . how lovely to see you,' Pen exclaimed faintly, submitting to her embrace.

'We've come for a few days in the sun,' Jane explained. 'But don't worry: we're not going to crowd you. North has booked a room at the *parador* in Jávea.'

North bent to kiss Pen's cheek. 'Hello, Mama. How are you? Have we disturbed your *siesta*?'

'I wasn't asleep. I was making tea when you knocked.' She had not yet recovered from the shock of seeing them and was still rooted to the threshold.

'Are you going to offer us a cup?' he asked, when she made no move to invite them in.

Pen pulled herself together and stepped back to let them enter.

'I'm sorry . . . it's the surprise. You're the last people I expected to find on my doorstep. How did you get here? By taxi?'

'No, I hired a car at the airport,' said North, helping his wife to take off her coat.

'How clever of you to find me.'

'Not very. We had your address and this isn't *my* first time in Spain,' he said, with a quizzical look.

Jane was looking around her. 'What a pretty house.'

Pen wondered if the sound of the knocker and their voices had woken Piers. What an awkward situation! Was it possible her letter had reached them already and they had set out post haste, hoping to dissuade her from what they saw as middle-aged madness?

'Have you received my letter?' she asked. 'I didn't think it would have arrived yet.'

'It hasn't,' said her son. 'Why were you writing to us?'

'I had some news to tell you.'

'So have we – wonderful news!' Jane's eyes glowed with excitement. 'That's partly why we came. I wanted to tell you in person. I'm going to have a baby.'

At this Pen forgot for a moment the embarrassing predicament in which their arrival had placed her.

'My dearest child, I'm so pleased. That is the best possible news.' She put her arms round her daughter-in-law and kissed her again, on both cheeks. 'This calls for champagne, not tea.'

Jane shook her head. 'Not for me. I've decided to cut out alcohol while I'm pregnant. I'll drink the tea while you and North drink the bubbly.'

'Jane, if you wouldn't mind making the tea, North can be opening the champagne while I dress,' said Pen.

She showed them the kitchen.

'You said you had news for us,' Jane reminded her, as Pen gave her son one of the half-dozen bottles of Cordoniu which Piers had brought into the house when he called for her that morning.

'Yes . . . but it can keep for a minute. I shan't be long.' Pen escaped and shot up the stairs.

She found Piers sitting up in bed, dipping into the book of short stories she had left on the night table.

'You have visitors, I gather,' he said, in a whisper, as she sat down close to him.

Clearly the sound of voices from below had been too muted for him to recognize them.

She nodded and rolled her eyes. 'You'll never guess who,' she whispered. 'North and Jane have turned up.'

Anticipating his reaction, she put a cautionary finger to her lips as she told him, and his startled '*What!*' wasn't loud enough to be heard by the two downstairs.

His sudden change from relaxed ease to a bolt upright posture and a look of appalled dismay was so strongly reminiscent of a scene in a French farce that Pen's consternation was abruptly transmuted into hysterical mirth.

'Be sure your sins will find you out – how right Nanny was,' she whispered, before collapsing against him and shaking with muffled laughter.

His arms enclosed her. She could tell by a movement of his chest that like her he couldn't help seeing the farcical element.

'Are they intending to stay here?' he asked, his lips close to her ear.

She lifted her face from his shoulder. 'No, thank goodness. That would have sunk us. They've booked a room in Jávea. You'll have to lie low until I can get rid of them. Tonight we can have dinner with them and explain the situation. I don't think at this stage it will help for them to discover we've been going to bed together. I think it would shock them.'

He looked at her doubtfully for a moment or two. Understanding his nature, she sensed he didn't like the idea of lurking up here while she coped on her own below.

'It's the only way, darling,' she whispered.

'I suppose you're right, but I don't like being underhand.'

'Discretion is the better part of valour,' said Pen, *sotto voce*, quoting another piece of nanny lore. 'Our private life isn't their business.'

She rose and dressed quickly, conscious that Piers was watching her and he wasn't happy with his clandestine part in the unexpected domestic drama.

When she was ready, she gave him a kiss and whispered, 'I'll let you know as soon as the coast is clear.'

Amusement bubbled again and burst out in a stifled giggle. She saw an unwilling grin curl the corners of his mouth. But when, at the door, she turned to blow him another kiss, the frown had returned.

Perhaps it was only because her conscience pricked her, not for doing anything wrong but for being a party to deception, that Pen felt they looked at her oddly when she joined them in the sitting room.

'When should the baby arrive, Jane?' she asked, striving to sound natural.

'Towards the end of October.'

North was standing by the open french windows. Having watched Pen come down the stairs, he had turned to look at the patio. Now his gaze returned to her face.

'We're not the only visitors you've had today, Mama.'

'Er . . . no, you aren't,' she agreed, wondering how he knew.

'Was it the dishy colonel or the dashing major who left his jacket in the courtyard?' asked Jane, smiling at her. 'Or have you added another beau to your string since we talked?'

'Oh! It was the colonel,' she said, with a rather forced laugh. 'It was he who brought me all that champagne this morning. Tonight he's expecting me to dine with him. In the circumstances, I'm sure he won't mind if I bring you two with me.'

'This sounds as if it could be the start of something big,' said her daughter-in-law, with gentle raillery.

Pen seized the opportunity. 'It is. That was my news. The colonel has asked me to marry him and I've accepted. So we have two things to celebrate. Your baby and my engagement.'

North looked aghast. 'You can't be serious. Good God, you've only been down here just over a week.'

It was a natural reaction. Pen, although inwardly nervous, maintained an air of calm.

'We met three days after I arrived . . . but not for the first time. I've known him and liked him for much longer. I haven't gone out of my mind, North. There's no need to look so alarmed. This is no mad holiday romance, if that's what you're thinking. It's a considered decision by two mature people who have a great deal in common.'

Jane, from whom Pen had expected a warmer response than from her son, was looking puzzled and doubtful. 'Well . . . this is a surprise. Who is he? Have I met him?'

Before Pen could answer, North said, with angry impatience, 'If you think I'm going to stand by and allow you to make another disastrous marriage, you can think again. Hasn't experience taught you anything? That self-important old fool is just as selfish as Father. His first wife hardly dared say boo to a goose. Do you think he won't bully you? Of course he will.'

When it dawned on her who he was talking about, Pen began to laugh.

'Not Colonel Bassenthwaite, North,' she managed to gasp, between spasms of mirth.

'Are you out of your mind?' Jane exclaimed, looking at him in amazement. '*Would* your mother marry that horrible old man with his yellow moustache and little piggy eyes?'

He cast a baffled look at Pen, who was still convulsed, before saying, 'She doesn't know any other colonels.'

From above came the sound of a door closing with a sharp click, followed by footsteps descending the stairs. Her laughter instantly stilled, Pen saw her son and his wife exchange puzzled glances before looking to see who was about to join them.

Had it been North's irate outburst which had brought Piers down, she wondered. How would North react to this?

In the stunned silence as he came into full view, Piers looked first at her. She read in his eyes the message that he had heard her son's raised voice and preferred to be at her side in any altercation.

As he looked at the others, she said, 'This is Colonel Ashford, formerly Commanding Officer of the 14th Lancers.'

She was watching her son as she made the formal introduction. This time, perhaps because the second shock was blunted by the first, his reaction was slower to show.

It was Jane who exclaimed excitedly, 'I knew it! I knew this could happen when I saw you dancing together. I'm so thrilled that –'

'Will you be quiet, please, Jane.'

North's icy command cut off the eager outburst. She looked like a crestfallen child.

He continued quietly, but in a manner which reminded Pen strongly of his great-grandfather's chilling authority, 'I realize that how you choose to behave is your affair, Mother, but I think I'm entitled to ask you' – he turned a freezing blue gaze on the older man – 'for some explanation of your part in this . . . bombshell.'

'Certainly,' Piers agreed equably. 'A letter explaining the situation is on its way to you now. The simple facts are that for a long time your mother and I have felt a growing rapport, although neither of us was entirely sure of the other's feelings. While I was employed as your butler, I felt nothing could come of it. I intended to leave Longwarden without revealing my love for her. When we met here, I changed my mind. It seemed foolish to throw away the chance to start a new life together. I have a house here in Spain which your mother likes, and the means to support her in comfort. We've decided that although it may cause some temporary embarrassment if the press get hold of the story, that is less important than our future happiness. Naturally we should like to have your approval. But, as you've just acknowledged, at our age we are answerable only to ourselves. You have my assurance that your mother's welfare will always be my primary object.'

As he said this, he reached for her hand and raised it to his lips.

His declaration of love, and the unequivocal firmness with which he had made it clear that he meant to marry her, with or without her son's blessing, brought tears of happiness to Pen's eyes.

Jane's eyes were brimming, too, as she came and seized Pen's other hand, saying throatily, 'Dearest Penelope, I'm so very happy for you. Congratulations, Colonel Ashford. For what it's worth, you both have my warmest blessing.'

'Thank you, Jane darling.'

'Thank you, Lady Carlyon.'

The two women looked at North, wanting him to be part of this happy occasion. But although his expression was not as cold as before, it was clear he could not accept this turn of events as readily as Jane did.

'I think Jane and I should check in at the *parador* and meet you later,' he said, in a reserved manner.

'We can check in later,' said his wife. 'Right now we should be drinking to *my* good news which Colonel Ashford doesn't know yet.' She beamed at him. 'I'm pregnant. Isn't that great?'

'Terrific . . . very exciting. We must certainly drink to that . . . if nothing else,' he added, with a somewhat quizzical glance at her husband.

For a moment longer North's face had the same expression of guarded disapproval Pen remembered from years ago when Edward had introduced her to his autocratic grandfather.

Then, suddenly, her son's face relaxed. 'I suppose I'm in no position to object to this sudden engagement after announcing my own marriage on the strength of a much shorter acquaintance,' he said dryly. 'As I don't share Jane's prescience, it will take me time to adjust to the fact that my butler is about to become my stepfather, but meanwhile I wish you both well.'

Taking his mother by the shoulders, he kissed her on both cheeks before offering his hand to Piers.

'Though why I should be expected to congratulate you for not only depriving me of your services but those of my irreplacable head gardener, I don't know,' he said pleasantly.

The few days that North and Jane spent with them were a time of perfect happiness for Pen.

Relieved of the worry that her son might oppose her marriage, she basked in the pleasure of being with three of the people dearest to her. Perhaps now that being loved by Piers had given her confidence, she might in future enjoy a better relationship with her daughter.

Jane pooh-poohed North's concern that long walks up and down mule tracks might be too strenuous for her.

'Walking is fine,' she insisted. 'Plenty of gentle exercise is good for me.'

It was on one of the walks that she said to Pen, 'Isn't it nice that, after a few sticky moments at the beginning, my husband and your almost-husband are getting along well? Now that Piers can be himself, as it were, he and North have a lot in common. I'm sure now they're going to be good friends.'

'I think you're right. They certainly have more in common than North ever did with his father. They were poles apart in every way. I always felt sad about that; but relieved that my son didn't take after my husband,' Pen added candidly. 'Genes are very unpredictable, the way they jump generations. Sarah is almost completely her father's child, but North's looks and much of his character come from his great-grandfather. I wonder whose looks and traits your baby will inherit?'

'Who knows?' Jane propped her foot on a convenient rock to re-tie a loose shoelace. The action made her hair swing forward in a dark silky curtain which emphasized the delicate lines of her profile.

'What an exciting year it's going to be,' she said, as she straightened. 'Your wedding next month. A place in the British Olympic equestrian team for Sarah if she does well at Badminton in April. Our baby in the autumn, and possibly a second wedding if Allegra and Andro go

685

on being as happy together as they seem to be at the moment.'

Only hours before their flight back to London, Risconti suddenly decided to put off his own departure for the two or three days it would take him to paint a picture of the house as a present for its owners.

'You'll enjoy your friend's wedding just as much without me there,' he said, when Allegra objected to this eleventh-hour change of plan. 'I don't much like that kind of occasion, but you'll know everyone there and can have a good time on your own.'

By this time the cases were packed and Allegra was in that state of last-day fidgets she had always disliked at the end of holidays. She had no wish to prolong it for several more days and felt he ought to have thought of his idea sooner. It was inconvenient for her because now she wouldn't have him to talk to on the long flight back, and inconvenient for Elizabeth who needed a few days' grace to prepare the house for its next occupants.

Risconti dismissed the first argument by saying that she would undoubtedly spend most of the flight with her nose in a book, whether he was there or not. As for Elizabeth's house-cleaning, he wouldn't interfere with that because he would sleep on a sunbed in the pool-house where he would be perfectly comfortable for a few nights.

Having failed to budge him from this decision, Allegra was still feeling put out when the taxi arrived to take her and most of the luggage to the airport.

'Don't be cross with me, *cara*,' he said. 'I wish I were coming with you but I must stay and do this thing. Don't leave me without a last smile . . . a last kiss.'

He sounded so forlorn that she relented and gave him a loving kiss. 'I hate going without you. If something goes wrong with the aeroplane, there'll be nobody to hold my hand.'

'Nothing will go wrong. Don't be foolish. Goodbye, my darling.'

He held her tightly against him for a moment longer,

then released her and stood aside while she shook hands with Elizabeth and her husband.

As the taxi started down the drive, she twisted round to wave to him through the rear window. But only the two Barbadians were watching the car out of sight. Risconti had disappeared into the house. He had always hated farewells.

The tarmac at Heathrow had the dull sheen of pewter as the flight from Barbados taxied from the runway to the terminal buildings. Unbroken cloud overhead signalled more rain in the offing. Allegra sighed as she peered from the aircraft window.

The consciousness of being becomingly tanned and feeling on top form physically in a city full of pale, wan faces was some compensation for returning to the dismal greyness of London after the bright light and vivid colours to which the weeks in the Caribbean had accustomed her.

Not long after Allegra's arrival at Carlyon House, Jane telephoned to check that Allegra was back and to tell her that she and North had only yesterday returned from visiting her mother-in-law who, incredibly, was engaged to be married.

'The wedding is fixed for next month and you'll never guess who the bridegroom is.'

After they had discussed this astounding development at some length, Jane went on to announce that she was pregnant.

Allegra was warm in her congratulations, but she couldn't help feeling downcast by her sister-in-law's second piece of news. Her period was due tomorrow or the next day and she knew already she wasn't going to miss it as she had hoped. Already her breasts felt tender and part of the reason she had been snappy with Andro about his staying behind had been PMT.

After talking to Jane, she called Claudia and they had a chat. Then she made some coffee and went through the accumulation of mail.

Tired from the flight, depressed by the dashing of her hopes of emulating Jane, she decided a nap was a better idea than dealing with the unpacking. Connecting her answering machine and recording a new OGM that she was back from Barbados but at present catching up sleep, in case Andro decided to call, she undressed and fell into bed.

When she woke up six hours later, having slept for much longer than she expected, the headache had gone but not the disoriented feeling following a long eastbound flight. After some more coffee, she began to unpack.

Near the bottom of her clothes case, sandwiched between two sun dresses, was an envelope. Andro must have put it there when she wasn't looking. It was typical of him to think of hiding a message to cheer her up when she got back without him.

Eagerly she opened the envelope and extracted several sheets of Paradise writing paper. Expecting only a short note, she was surprised he had written at such length.

> My dearest darling girl, my only love
> I want you to brace yourself for a very bad shock. If I had known, last spring, what lay ahead, I would have spared you the pain I know you will feel when you read this – the same pain I feel as I write, knowing that very soon I must say goodbye to you for ever.

Oh, my God! Why? *Why?*

The sheets of paper began to quiver as the horror of what she was reading made her hands shake. She gave low moans of distress.

'*Jesus Christ!*'

The sudden startled exclamation from behind the pages of *The Times* made Jane look up from her letter from Marie-Simone.

When North lowered the newspaper and met her eyes across the breakfast table, she knew instantly that whatever had caused his exclamation had not been merely an act of folly on the part of the government, the unions or some other powerful influence on the state of the nation. Such things often made him fulminate, but now she could see from his expression that whatever he had just read had had a more profound impact that what he called 'the idiocies of our masters'.

'What is it?' she asked anxiously. 'What's happened?'

He folded and re-folded the paper and passed it across to her, tapping a single-column headline.

TRAGIC ENDING TO ARTIST'S CARIBBEAN HOLIDAY

Barbados, Friday
Alessandro Risconti, the Italian-born portrait painter whose sitters include the Princess of Wales and the Prime Minister, Mrs Margaret Thatcher, is missing, presumed drowned, after disappearing on Tuesday while staying in Barbados. He had been on the island for six weeks and was due to leave for London a few days after his disappearance.

Mrs Elizabeth Harris, housekeeper at 'Paradise', a plantation great house now owned by American friends of the artist, was the last person to see him, the day before local police found his rented vehicle near a lonely stretch of Atlantic beach, a part of the coast where tourists are warned not to swim. A bathing towel, beach shoes and a shirt were recovered from the shore, suggesting that Mr Risconti had disregarded the prohibition. Mr Isaiah Harris, gardener at 'Paradise', said he had seen Mr Risconti swimming in the pool and he was a powerful swimmer. 'Perhaps he felt it was a challenge to try his strength against the surf.'

After telling Mrs Harris he was going to bathe, Mr Risconti added that he would be out for dinner and might be late coming back. Mr and Mrs Harris, who live in a cottage in the grounds, did not report him missing until he failed to appear for breakfast the following morning.

'We thought he had gone to one of the safe west-coast beaches. It is a terrible tragedy. He was a very nice man and made himself popular with everyone while he was here,' Mrs Harris told a reporter.

If Mr Risconti survived the heavy surf pounding the beach where his belongings were found, he may have been carried far out to sea. Experts familiar with the coast think his body may not be recovered.

While Jane was reading the report, North had risen from the table to make a telephone call, but by the time she looked up he had replaced the receiver.

'All I can get is that flaming answering machine with a message she must have recorded the day she got back. She can't *still* be sleeping off jet lag.'

'Try calling the caretaker. Get him to go up right away, North. If she's seen this she'll be frantic. We have to contact her quickly. Oh, poor girl . . . poor girl . . .' Her voice cracked. Her eyes filled with tears. She could so easily imagine how she would feel if North had died in such a way. It was enough to send anyone out of their mind.

He did as she suggested. When the caretaker answered, North had no need to announce himself. His distinctive voice was instantly recognizable to anyone who knew him.

'Stanley, I need to speak to Lady Allegra urgently, but she's got her machine on. Would you go up and . . . She's not? How do you know? I see . . . yes . . . yes, a terrible thing to happen . . . they would be, bloody vultures . . . certainly . . . I know I can rely on you . . .'

'What was all that about?' Jane asked impatiently, when at last he rang off.

'She's not there. She's taken the Mini and gone. He has no idea where. He doesn't even know how long it is since she left. The first he heard of all this was early this morning when he had the press on his doorstep. They broke the news about Andro to him. Fortunately Stanley's number isn't in the book so they can't block his line, pestering for information and preventing us from keeping in touch with him. Not that Allegra will go back there once she's found out. She'll know the press will be after her and go to ground somewhere . . . possibly here.'

'But they can't have contacted her already so why isn't she there? Oh . . . I'd forgotten. She's going to a wedding this week. A wedding somewhere in the country. Maybe it's today. She could be on her way now and they'll have to break the news to her. How do we get in touch with them? I don't even remember her friend's name.'

The metallic sound which woke Allegra was the rattle of a pass-key. She didn't recognize the noise or the room where she was lying on a double bed with an orange candlewick counterpane. For the first few moments of consciousness she didn't know where she was or why she was here.

Like innumerable other hotel rooms, this one had a compact bathroom between it and the corridor. The maid who had unlocked the outer door didn't realize the room was occupied until she came round the corner formed by the bathroom wall.

'I'm sorry, miss. I thought you'd gone. Most people have by now.'

On weekdays the majority of the hotel's patrons were reps who checked out after an early breakfast. The maid had never known anyone to be still in their room at eleven o'clock. She took in the rumpled bedspread and the clothed figure and ravaged face of the young woman she had disturbed. This was the last room she had to do and she wanted to get away early today if she could.

'Will you be staying another night, miss?'

'I . . . don't know.' As memory returned, Allegra flinched from the pain which came with it.

'You have to vacate by twelve noon if you're not stopping.'

'Yes . . . all right . . . I'll decide in a minute.'

Allegra dragged herself into a sitting position. To her relief the maid went away. She couldn't cope with people at the moment. She couldn't cope with anything.

There had been a few hours yesterday when she had got enough grip on herself to drive the car out of London and find a place to hide where no one knew her or could get in touch with her. Having arrived and checked in with a semblance of normality, she had fallen apart again. Even undressing and getting into bed had been too much of an effort. She had kicked off her shoes and lain down and not moved again until now, except once in the middle of the night to get up for a pee. Hour after hour she had lain with

691

the lights on, staring at the blank screen of the television, tortured by a mental picture of Andro walking into that terrible surf to end his life before it became intolerable for him.

Hundreds of thousands of people live with blindness, *he had written, in the letter explaining his suicide.* I know I can't. Never to paint, never to see light and colour and form, would be, for me, to live in hell. I couldn't endure it. I'm an artist – or nothing. There's no other way I'm able or wish to earn my living. I know you would willingly support me, but I can't face a future of being dependent on you and in total darkness, perhaps for another thirty years or more. A short life, lived to the full – and these past six weeks with you at Paradise have given me more happiness than most men experience in a lifetime – is better than three score and ten of 'quiet desperation'. I've had it all, as they say; and the best, my dear love, has been our time together. My only regret is that my own stupidity prevented us from having longer with each other.

What intensified her suffering was that he had chosen to drown himself to save her from having her name linked with a suicide. As if it mattered when so much mud was already stuck to her reputation.

It will seem an accident, *he had written, in the four-page farewell, every word of which was now and for ever imprinted in her mind.* You've suffered enough from scandal-mongering. I don't want you to be hounded again on my account.

What courage it must have taken to go into that seething sea, she thought with a shudder. She couldn't bear to think of his body being viciously tossed and tumbled by the great angry breakers, of salt water flooding his lungs, choking him. The worst thought of all was that, when it was too late, he might have regretted his action and struggled frantically to save himself.

She groaned and fell back on the bed, burying her face in the pillow, trying to blot out the horrible images of him being pounded on the rocks, the brown skin she had loved to stroke becoming a bloody mess of lacerations. But there was no escape from the tormenting visions conjured by her imagination.

Someone tapped at the door.

Oh, God, what now? Not the maid again.

She lifted her head and called out, 'I don't want to be disturbed.'

Whoever it was tapped again, more imperatively this time. Cursing, Allegra hauled herself to her feet and went to the door. On the way, a wave of dizziness made her lurch against the wall and bang her elbow.

It wasn't the maid who was standing outside in the corridor but a middle-aged woman in a white blouse and dark skirt.

'I'm sorry to disturb you again, madam, but the maid thought you might be feeling poorly. I'm the assistant manager. Is there anything I can do for you?'

'The maid is mistaken. I'm not ill. There's nothing I want but to be left undisturbed until I decide to check out.'

Allegra closed the door and turned the security lock.

If only I had some sleeping pills, she thought, as she lay down again. Apart from a restless doze for perhaps half an hour before the maid let herself in, she had slept hardly at all since opening the letter. Her head ached. Her eyelids smarted. But her brain wouldn't let her escape into the merciful nothingness of sleep.

She knew the giddy feeling on the way to the door must be caused by not having eaten since the day before yesterday. But she had no desire to eat. The thought of food made her feel sick. If the room had had a refrigerator stocked with drinks, as some hotel rooms did, she might have been able to drink herself into a state of oblivion.

She wondered if the hotel would supply her with a bottle of gin if she asked for it, or if that would be against the rules. No wonder Andro had started to drink more while they were at Paradise. She understood why now. He had been trying to dull the despair of knowing he was going to lose his sight and nothing could be done to save it.

Had it already been in his mind to take his own life? Or had she unwittingly put the idea into his head?

Nobody but a suicidal maniac would set foot in that maelstrom.

To know it was to spare her that he had chosen a violent death, rather than the easier way out of an overdose, was bad enough. To suspect that it might be her careless remark which had made him contemplate suicide made her groan with anguished remorse.

Andro . . . my only love . . . how can I live without you? How can I stand the loneliness . . . the awful emptiness of a world where you don't exist? Why didn't you let me have a baby? Why leave me with nothing but these nightmares of how you died? A child would have been some comfort . . . something of you to make it worth staying alive. Now there's nothing . . . no point . . . no purpose. I might as well have died with you. We could have gone out together . . . not in the sea . . . in bed . . . in each other's arms. Or in the bath with our wrists cut . . . they say that's a painless way. You lie in warm water while the blood seeps out slowly, making you drowsy. It doesn't even make a mess for other people to clear up. All they have to do when it's over is to pull out the plug.

Outside, on the dual carriageway which she had been aimlessly following when the hotel sign caught her eye, an extra-large heavy-goods vehicle rumbled past and the building vibrated.

She lay on her back, staring at a hairline crack in the ceiling above her. She was thinking that she didn't *have* to go on living without him. Nobody had to live if they had the courage to die, and perhaps it wouldn't take much to puncture the veins in her wrists.

She had brought her toilet bag with her. There was a disposable razor in it. Not as good as a razor blade for what she had in mind, but if one could nick one's legs with it sometimes, it should be possible to open a vein only thinly protected by skin.

She wondered how long it would take to become unconscious.

At Longwarden, North had managed to check that the wedding was the following day and not such a distance from London that his sister would have needed to set out before tomorrow morning. He had also found out she had talked to Claudia Dunbar on the day she returned. Otherwise her movements were a mystery.

Jane had managed to keep calm while North was telephoning. Now, when neither of them could think how or where to find Allegra, her control began to give way. She had an intuitive feeling that somehow her sister-in-law already knew what had happened and must be half crazy with grief.

When her insight into Allegra's anguish made her burst into tears herself, North sprang from his chair and came to her.

'Take it easy, Janie. I know it's a ghastly business but you mustn't let it upset you. Think of the baby.'

He bent over her, patting her back, while she buried her face in her hands.

'How can I help being upset?' she sobbed. 'They weren't like us. They were desperately in love with each other. Is that so hard to understand? Even if we don't feel that way, we should be able to grasp what it means to other people. Without him, she won't want to live.'

'You underestimate her. Allegra has plenty of guts. It won't help her to get through this to have you breaking down.'

'Oh, you're an unfeeling bastard,' she burst out, in sudden rage at his failure to understand what love meant to others.

She jumped up and rushed from the room.

Allegra was in the bathroom, staring at her reflection, both bath taps running, when a key turned in the lock of the outer door. To her amazement, a few moments later there was a tap on the bathroom door.

'I've brought you a pot of tea and some hot dry toast, Miss Smith.' It was the voice of the assistant manager speaking through the bathroom door. 'If you're not in your bath yet, I should have a cup of tea first. When you've had a bad night, there's nothing like a cup of tea.'

How had she entered the room with the security lock on, Allegra wondered. Suddenly tea and hot toast sounded irresistible. She turned off the taps and went into the bedroom to find the older woman folding the rumpled bedspread.

'Ah, good, I caught you before you started to undress. Sit down and I'll pour your tea. Even if you're not hungry, try to eat a little toast. You've had nothing since you arrived . . . unless you brought food in with you.'

Allegra shook her head.

'No, I thought not. Sometimes the reps save on their expenses by bringing in a takeaway dinner instead of using the restaurant. Your waste paper basket is empty and there are no crumbs to be seen.' She smiled. 'I'm Mrs Macroom. You look as if you might have a headache so I brought you a couple of tablets. But eat a little something first. I don't believe in taking pills on an empty stomach. Shall I open the window a little? Some fresh air may help.'

Allegra sipped the hot tea and took a small bite of the toast. There was something about Mrs Macroom which reminded her of Nanny Lomax who had nursed her through her childhood illnesses and been the surrogate mother of her own and North's early life.

'How did you get in?' she asked.

'We have to have a gadget which will open the doors even when they're locked. The maids aren't allowed to use it, only the manager and myself. Sometimes people are taken ill and ring for assistance but they're too sick to unlock the door for us. I felt sure you were in trouble so I took a chance that you wouldn't get me the sack if I'd misjudged the situation,' she said, with another smile. 'I don't want to push in where I'm not wanted, my dear, but I've been through bad times myself and we all need someone to turn to, if only a sympathetic stranger.'

'You're very kind. I'm sorry I was rude to you before.'

'You weren't rude. I'll be back in a moment.'

She went out of the room, leaving Allegra sitting by the open window, burning her mouth with gulps of hot tea because she had suddenly acquired a raging thirst. For about eighteen hours she had been shut in a small room with the central heating full on. For longer than that she had had nothing to drink.

No wonder she felt physically ill as well as emotionally pole-axed. She must be starting to dehydrate. She remembered how, in Barbados, at every meal Elizabeth had filled large goblets with iced water and urged them to drink it to replace the fluid they were losing by sweating or, as she had called it, "perspirin".

By the time the assistant manager returned, Allegra had poured herself a second cup of tea and was eating another piece of toast.

'If you don't mind, I'll have my coffee break with you,' said Mrs Macroom. 'I've asked them not to disturb me for a while. I thought it might help you to talk about whatever it is that's happened to you.'

When Allegra was silent, she went on, 'Do your family know where you are? If you've come away without telling anyone, they may be very anxious about you. Shouldn't you let someone know?'

'There's no one to worry about me. I live in a flat in London. I'm often away. I don't always tell my relations when or where I'm going.'

'Won't the people where you work be worried if you don't turn up?'

'I work at home. If I'm gone for a week it won't matter.' Allegra's voice dropped to a mutter. 'There's only one person who would have worried about me, and he . . . he . . .'

Her hand began to shake, slopping tea over the rim of the cup she was holding. Some spilled on her skirt and the carpet as she put it back on the tray and gripped her hands tightly together to stop the violent spasm.

'He's left you?' asked Mrs Macroom.

Allegra closed her eyes. 'No . . . he's dead . . . drowned in the sea. I shall never see him again. *Oh, God . . . I can't bear it!*'

She bent her head over her knees and burst into racking sobs.

She was woken by Mrs Macroom who was sitting on the edge of the bed, gently shaking her arm. The curtains were closed and the room was only dimly lit.

'What time is it?'

'Seven o'clock in the evening. You've had a good long sleep but I want you to wake up now and have a bath and some food. Otherwise it's more than likely you'll wake up hungry in the small hours. I've run a nice warm bath for you, and your skirt has been cleaned and your other clothes washed and pressed.'

'You're being incredibly kind to me.'

'That's what we're meant to be . . . kind to each other. Not to inflict pain and sorrow. Have your bath and get dressed, Miss Smith. I'll come back in half an hour. We'll have a light supper in my room. I live in the hotel.'

Which must mean she is a widow . . . she's been through this awful void and somehow survived it, thought Allegra.

She had no idea for how long she had wept her heart out in the other woman's arms. Mrs Macroom had comforted her like a mother, or how mothers were supposed to love and succour their children in times of disaster. But never in a hundred years could Allegra have cried like that on her own mother's shoulder. It would have embarrassed them both.

As she lay stretched out in the water, the patches where her bikini had prevented the whole of her body from becoming a uniform golden brown were a knife-thrust reminder of how, only days ago, she had lain on the bed at Paradise with Andro pressing warm kisses on the paler triangles.

I must *not* remember, she told herself. One day . . . but not now . . . not yet. I mustn't think about the past . . . or the empty future. I must try to get through one hour . . . one day at a time.

When she had climbed out and dried herself, it was automatic to rummage in the toilet bag for her Rochas deodorant. Having used it, she put it on the glass shelf with the plastic razor left there earlier. Looking at the thin rim of steel, she wondered what would have happened if Mrs Macroom hadn't come in.

Would she have cut her wrists? Now she would never be sure. While she was hesitating, Mrs Macroom had intervened. The critical moment had passed. Since then she had wept. She had slept. It hadn't made her feel better. How could she ever feel better? But at least the impulse to annihilate herself was no longer in her mind.

Mrs Macroom's room was twin-bedded, with one bed removed, making it more spacious than the room Allegra was in.

'As you see, I have different curtains and my own bed-spread. The people who design interiors for hotels are very keen on hot colours. I suppose they're considered more cheerful and welcoming. I find orange and red very trying colours to live with. I prefer a more tranquil scheme,' she explained. 'Fortunately the carpets here are beige. In my last post . . . oh, they were eyesores!'

'You've *made* this room.' Allegra was relieved to find she seemed to have recovered the power of making normal conversation.

'Most of my things are in storage, but I kept a few small pieces out – the stool and the hanging bookshelf – to make myself feel at home. As a young girl, before I met Con, I was a hotel receptionist. After our youngest daughter started school, I went back to work part time. It was just as well I did because after he was killed I needed to work full time. That's a picture taken the summer before the ambush.'

She picked up and handed to Allegra an enlarged and framed snapshot of a burly man leaning on the top bar of a field-gate and turning his head to grin at the camera.

'The ambush?' Allegra repeated questioningly.

'He was in the Ulster Constabulary. The IRA mined the

road which they knew the police van would be using. He and two others were blown up.' She spoke quietly and matter of factly. 'The others were much younger men. One had been married a year and his wife was expecting a baby. The other was newly engaged. At least Con and I had had twenty years together.'

'We had almost a year . . . but a lot of that time we were separated.'

Allegra had thought she was drained of tears, but now her eyes filled again.

Mrs Macroom put the photograph back in its place and pressed her into a chair. 'Don't try to stop yourself crying. A stiff upper lip doesn't help . . . and nor do the bottles of pills they push into people these days. Don't let anyone persuade you to stuff yourself with sedatives. To weep and to grieve is the best thing . . . the natural thing.'

She patted Allegra's shoulder and gave her a couple of tissues from a box by the bed. Then she poured out two glasses of sherry.

'I cried over Con for a long time,' she said, sitting down. 'Now and then, I still do. You never get over losing someone you love. But after a while you accept it. The bad part just has to be lived through as best you can. I decided I wasn't going to be a burden on my children, and I put my mind to getting on is this business. Next year I hope to make manager. A few years of that and I'll have enough money and experience to set up a place of my own.'

Sipping her sherry, she talked on about her plans, her quiet enthusiasm for the life she had built for herself holding Allegra's attention sufficiently strongly to stop her thinking of other things.

While they were eating, and sharing a bottle of wine, Mrs Macroom revealed that she was one of the few women to have been admitted to the Guild of Master Sommeliers.

'I thought a knowledge of wine – which is still unusual among women – would be a useful qualification.'

Although she talked mostly about her experiences in the various hotels where she had worked since returning to England, Allegra sensed that it wasn't because she was a self-centred woman but rather because she knew there was nothing she could ask her guest which might not be hurtful.

Towards the end of the meal, Mrs Macroom said, 'I think when you feel ready to leave here, you shouldn't go back to London for a while. A flat in a big city isn't a good place to be when life is in chaos. It's better to be in the country, in my opinion. It's more soothing to the spirit to be surrounded by natural rather than man-made things. Why not go to Longwarden?'

When her guest looked taken aback by her reference to Longwarden, Mrs Macroom rose from the table. Going to the hanging bookshelf, she took from it a copy of *Travels* which Allegra had failed to notice.

'My elder daughter gave this to me the Christmas before last. I recognized you from the photograph on the back.'

'I registered as Jill Smith because I felt I wanted to . . . hide myself away.'

'Yes, I understand that feeling and you needn't worry I shall let on who you really are, Lady Allegra.'

'Allegra. After seeing me howling my eyes out, anything else would be silly.'

'Would you autograph your book for me? I enjoyed it very much. I've read it again since the first time.'

'Of course . . . with pleasure. May I use your first name?'

'Pamela.'

Allegra found a pen in her bag. She wrote – *To Pamela, for wonderful kindness and understanding which I shall always remember with gratitude*, and added her flourishy signature.

Mrs Macroom looked pleased. 'I'm glad I was in the right place to give a little help. Will you take my advice and go to Longwarden?'

'I don't know that I want to inflict myself on my new sister-in-law. She hasn't been married long. I don't want to cast a blight on her life and my brother's.'

'I shouldn't worry about that. When people are happy it takes a lot to depress them. Do you like her?'

Allegra nodded. 'She's a darling.'

'Then I should go and stay there, if I were you. In a big place like that you can be by yourself most of the time, but they'll be there when you need them. I'll look forward to your next book. By the end of this one I felt as if I'd known your great-grandmother. What a wonderful life she had – although not without its troubles. She was such a beauty when she was young but the picture of her I like best is the last one.' She turned to the final photograph showing Flora Carlyon in her nineties, her white hair drawn into a knot at the back of her head, her fine ivory skin a network of delicate lines. 'There's so much kindness and wisdom in that face – and beauty still, although she was a great age.'

'To my brother and me she was more like a fairy godmother than a great-grandmother. She was one of those people who make every day special. She never spoiled us. We had to sit up straight and behave like angels when we were with her; but she gave us fascinating presents and arranged amazing adventures. North had always wanted to go up in a balloon. She organized that for his tenth birthday and the next year we flew to Paris for her eightieth birthday party – just the three of us.'

For a few moments, as she remembered that happy occasion long ago, a flicker of her former animation lit Allegra's drawn face.

'That would make a nice story for children,' said Mrs Macroom. 'You could call it *Adventures with my Great-Grandmother*. Most children love their grannies but not many have one like yours. A book like that would need drawings, but if you can't draw yourself there must be plenty of artists who would do the pictures for you.'

Her suggestion conjured a memory of the quickly done pen-and-wash drawings Risconti had made of Barbadian children; middle-class schoolgirls in crisp cotton uniform dresses, village boys playing cricket with an improvised bat and wickets. What fun it would have been to collaborate on a book for children with him.

The thought of what they had shared in their short time together, and of all the years of love, laughter and achievement which they had lost, brought fresh tears to her eyes.

As they spilled down her cheeks and she wiped them

702

away with her fingers, she said huskily, 'I'm sorry . . . it's just that . . . the man I loved was an artist. He would have done perfect drawings for me.'

Allegra said goodbye to Pamela Macroom on the third morning after her arrival at the hotel. She felt she was leaving a haven to resume a life which would be empty and dreary for a long time to come. But at least the first shock was over and she had made a friend who had been through the same trauma and rebuilt a life shattered, in her case, by an act of senseless terrorism.

'Perhaps a bit later on, on one of your weekends off, you might like to come and stay at Longwarden,' she suggested, as Mrs Macroom was walking to the car with her.

'Indeed I should. That would be a wonderful treat . . . if your sister-in-law wouldn't mind.'

'When she hears how good you've been to me, I'm sure she'll want to meet you.'

With nothing more to be said but their final goodbyes, Allegra stepped forward and gave the other woman a hug. Not normally demonstrative with her own sex, she felt a surge of affection for this valiant widow whose rather ordinary appearance gave no clue to her resolute character.

I expect if I'd met her while her husband was alive, I should have written her off as a dull housewife, she thought, as she drove away. Possibly she *was* dull then, wrapped up in her husband and children, working part time only to make some extra money. But somewhere inside her there must always have been a strong core. Have I got it in me?

It took her three hours to reach Longwarden. Inevitably, the last part of the journey reminded her of the times she had driven Risconti there. The memory of him sitting beside her, his arm stretched along the back of the driving seat, was painfully clear. She began to wonder if it was a good idea to go there, to sleep in the bed they had shared. But where else was she to go? The flat in London was even more full of memories.

She thought of the tapes he had sent her from America.

703

How would she feel if she re-played them now? Would they intensify the pain or would hearing his voice be a comfort?

She remembered the packet of love letters which had been found in Flora Carlyon's work-bag with the last of the many embroideries she had stitched in the seventy-six years between her arrival at Longwarden as a bride and her death in North's arms, under the flowering empress tree, in her London garden.

At some time in her long widowhood, she must have become afraid the letters would fall to pieces from being read over and over again. To preserve them, she had kept each sheet in a transparent cover so that it could be read without further damage to the fragile paper. The letters must have gone everywhere with her. Several times Allegra had caught a glimpse of one before it was quickly put away. Not until years later had she read them herself.

But if my love-tapes survive me, they won't be read by my descendants, she thought, with a pang. I'll never have children now. I shall have to be content with being an aunt to North's and Jane's children; a spinster aunt who writes books and perhaps keeps a cat for company.

A telephone call from Mrs Macroom had relieved Jane and North of their most acute anxiety. It was also a relief to Jane, when Allegra arrived at Longwarden, that North gave no sign that his sympathy for her was mixed with anger at the worry she had caused him by disappearing.

Until they knew she was safe, they had hoped the news about Risconti would not reach Sant Jeroni where Pen and Piers were prolonging their time there to organize work on their future home. Fortunately word of the tragedy did pass them by until Allegra came home, after which North told Piers what had happened and he broke it to Pen. They would have come back immediately if North hadn't dissuaded them.

'To hurry back would be pointless, Mama,' Jane heard him say to her mother-in-law. 'There's nothing you or any of us can do for Allegra. She wouldn't like it if you altered your plans on her account. You know what she's like. Write to her. That's the best thing.'

One night, almost a week after Allegra's return to Long-warden, when dinner was over North took himself off to his dark-room telling Jane that it might be late before he finished what he was doing and in that case he would sleep in the other bedroom. Since the day she had been goaded into calling him an unfeeling bastard, he had shared her bed but hadn't touched her. She had apologized later for that outburst, but relations between them were strained.

At eleven she put out her light. At half-past she switched it on again. Not feeling like reading, she decided to go downstairs and fetch her needlework, left in the library. She was stitching on a canvas-work cushion, a Christmas present from Marie-Simone.

The great silent house in the small hours didn't make her nervous. She didn't believe in ghosts and, if she had, she wouldn't have been afraid of the wraiths most likely to haunt Longwarden.

Not that those of North's forebears who were of the greatest interest to her had died here. They had gone to the Great Perhaps, as Marie-Simone, borrowing the expression from Rabelais, called it, from other places. So far as she knew, of the many deaths which must have taken place in the ancient house, none had been violent.

Already, although she had been here so short a time, the house held important memories for her: events imprinted on her mind too vividly ever to fade. Her arrival . . . the Christmas ball . . . the Christmas house party . . . the conception of her first child.

As she flitted along the corridors and down the main staircase, switching on lights as she went, the thought of this child – the certainty of its love for her – was one safe, sure thing to cling to on a night like this when the uncertainty of North's love prevented her from sleeping.

She was on her way back to her bedroom, not far from Allegra's door, when she heard a strange noise and paused. The sound was followed by others – muffled moans, each one growing louder. They had to be coming from her sister-in-law's room.

Realizing that Allegra must either have been taken ill or be having a very bad dream, Jane advanced to the door and quietly opened it.

The room was illumined by moonlight. In the bed, thrashing wildly about, her face partly masked by the sheet, Allegra was panting and groaning, engaged in some violent struggle conjured by her subconscious. In her dream she was probably screaming at the top of her voice.

Hurrying to the bedside, Jane felt for the switch on the lamp. As soon as it was alight, she leaned over the bed to free Allegra's mouth and nose from the twisted sheet and shake her gently awake.

'Allegra, wake up . . . you're dreaming . . . wake up now.'

It was several moments before the light and her voice penetrated Allegra's nightmare. Even when her eyes opened, they were still seeing the scene in her mind, not the quiet lamp-lit room.

Her eyes wild, she clutched at Jane's arm with frantic strength. 'You must save him . . . hurry . . . hurry. Don't stand there . . . get help . . . go for help. Don't you understand? He's drowning! You must save him . . . oh, please . . . *please!*'

It was the agonized appeal of a woman frenzied with terror, knowing that her screams and sobs were futile. No help would come.

All at once she sank back, weeping, her mouth turned down like a child's, her beautiful face distorted by grief and misery.

It was the most pitiful sight Jane had ever witnessed; the more so because, for most of the time she had known her, Allegra had been on a crest of success and happiness. To see her brought down like this wrung Jane's heart with pity for her.

What comfort could she give? None: there could be no comfort for a woman whose lover had died in such a terrible way. It must haunt her to the end of her life.

Acting on instinct, doing the only thing she could, she

climbed on the bed, lay down beside her sister-in-law, and put her arms round her.

A long time later, keeping very still because she thought Allegra had fallen into an exhausted doze, Jane was surprised when the older girl suddenly gave a long shuddering sigh and said, 'I'm better now ... hysterics over.' She rolled free from Jane's embrace. 'What time is it?'

Easing her cramped shoulder, Jane looked at the clock on the night table.

'Half-past twelve.'

'Oh, God ... seven hours till morning.' Allegra lay on her back in the centre of the bed, her eyes closed, the lids pink and swollen. 'Why are you up at this hour? Surely I wasn't making enough noise to carry to your room?'

'No, I was passing your door. Would you like me to make you a cup of tea?' She knew Allegra had an electric kettle in her bedroom.

Allegra nodded. 'Yes, please.'

Jane swung her feet to the floor but paused before rising from the bed. 'It would make you feel better to wash your face with warm water and then splash your eyes with cold,' she suggested gently.

By the time the kettle was boiling, Allegra had put on a robe and been to the bathroom. Her face was no longer blotched and streaked with tear-stains, but her eyes were still puffy and she looked tired and wretched.

'Do you have any pills that would help you to sleep?' Jane asked.

Allegra shook her head. 'I don't want to start that. They don't really do any good. They knock you out but make you feel lousy next day.'

Jane took her a cup of tea.

'Thanks. Are you having one?'

There was an unspoken appeal in the other girl's upward glance. Clearly she didn't want to be left alone yet but hesitated to ask Jane to stay with her.

'Yes, I will. I'm not at all sleepy.' Jane filled a cup for herself and settled in a chair. Deliberately, she asked, 'Do these bad dreams happen often, Allegra?'

'Almost every night. I suppose they can't go on for ever. I seem to remember having a lot of nightmares as a child.' She swallowed some tea. 'I have to tell someone the truth. Andro's death wasn't an accident. It was suicide.'

'What?' Jane stared at her incredulously. 'Why would he kill himself?'

'The first time I met him, at a dinner party, he told me his father had gone blind . . . Andro thought from a war injury. Actually his father must have had a condition called familial macular degeneration. It tends to run in families but not necessarily affecting every generation. Last autumn a New York eye specialist told Andro he had it, and that it wasn't curable. It began as a disturbance in one eye, then both were affected. Any object he looked at directly was distorted, although he could still see it clearly if he turned his head sideways. I noticed him doing it, but I didn't realize what it signified. Before long he was going to be totally blind. That, for him, was tantamount to death.'

Allegra had gone back to bed and they had continued talking until, eventually, she dropped off to sleep before Jane left her.

In spite of the hour, she didn't return to her room but went first to see if North was in his great-grandfather's bed. He was, but not deeply asleep. She had only to touch him lightly to wake him.

'What is it? What's the matter?' he demanded, apparently thinking there was some kind of emergency.

'Nothing . . . everything's fine. But I have to talk to you, North.'

'What time is it?'

'It's the middle of the night . . . half-past two. Don't be angry with me for waking you. It's very important. I must tell you right away.'

'What's so important it won't keep till tomorrow? Why are you up at this hour? Are you feeling ill?'

He heaved himself into a sitting position, rubbing a hand over his face. Unusually for him, he was wearing pyjamas although the jacket wasn't buttoned.

'No, I'm fine. I just couldn't sleep. I went downstairs to fetch my canvas-work and, as I was coming back up, I heard noises from Allegra's room. She was crying out . . . very distressed. I rushed in and found her asleep. She was having a terrible nightmare . . . about Andro drowning. After I'd woken her, she was upset for a long time. Maybe an hour. It's going to be years before she gets over it, North.'

He raked a hand through his hair. 'I know. I'm extremely sorry for her. We all are. But you mustn't allow it to upset *you*. Is this why you woke me up? To tell me Allegra had a nightmare?'

'No, of course not. Would I do that? But it does have something to do with what I want to tell you. Allegra's been very controlled. She's kept most of her grief to herself. A while back, when I first woke her, the dream she had had was so vivid it broke down her normal controls. She wept inconsolably, North. It made me cry too. I couldn't help it.'

'You should have called me,' he said, frowning. 'I would have stayed with her.'

'I'm glad it happened,' she told him. 'I'd prefer it hadn't in the sense that I hate to see her so unhappy . . . so lost without him. But some of the things she said made me see how foolishly I'd been acting. Acting . . . that's the operative word. Playing a part. Telling lies . . . or rather *not* telling the truth. Well, I'm finished with that now. From now on I'm going to be honest.'

'Jane, I haven't the foggiest idea what you're talking about. Could you explain it more clearly? What's this part you say you've been playing? What are the lies you've been telling?'

She took a deep breath and looked bravely into his eyes.

'The very first time we met . . . the first hour . . . perhaps the first minute . . . I knew you were someone special. When we danced at the ball, before I even knew you properly, I was in love with you. If you had been solely and simply a photographer – not an earl, not the owner of this house – and if you had asked me to travel with you, living

in tents and grass shacks, I would have gone with you –
gladly. All this time I've been crazy about you. I can't keep
it in any longer. I have to say it. I love you . . . I love
you . . . I love you.'

She burst into tears. Jumping down from the edge of the
high bed where she had perched to talk to him, she ran
across to the anteroom.

North caught up with her as she was fumbling blindly
with the handle.

'Why are you running away?' he demanded, catching
hold of her.

'I . . . didn't mean . . . to make a scene. I meant to . . .
to . . . t-tell you very calmly.' The words came out choked
and disjointed between gasping sobs.

The emotions brought close to the surface by sharing
Allegra's anguish were now overwhelming. She clung to
him, weeping unrestrainedly, her tears spurting on his bare
chest.

He held her close, patting her back. 'Hush, Janie, hush
. . . don't cry. It isn't good for the baby.' He soothed her,
stroking her hair, until the storm of tears slackened.

'I'm sorry,' she murmured, when she could speak coherently. 'I didn't plan to do this. I was just going to tell you
the truth . . . not be hysterical about it. I guess I picked a
bad time . . . being already so sad for Allegra.'

He tilted her face up to his. After a pause, he said quietly,
'Your timing is fine. I've suddenly realized what's the matter
with me . . . why it bothered me when you called me an
unfeeling bastard. You were right, I'm afraid. That's what
I used to be. Not any more. I love you, Jane.'

'North, you don't have to say that. I don't want you
feeling an obligation to love me. That's why I've never
admitted before the way I feel.'

She was shivering with nervous reaction. He scooped
her up in his arms and carried her back to his bed.

Climbing in beside her, folding her in a close hug, he
said, 'I didn't love you at first. I can't deny it. I wanted to
go to bed with you . . . and I wanted your money for
Longwarden. Somewhere along the way that changed. I

suppose I didn't want to admit it, even to myself, because I didn't think you would ever feel the same way. You seemed to delight in throwing out subtle reminders that we had a marriage of convenience. Even when we were in bed together, I never felt your heart was involved.'

'But that's exactly what I thought . . . and it terrified me. I knew sex wouldn't hold you for long . . . not sex by itself. You'd get used to my body and bored with it. Men always do. Unless they love the woman inside the body.'

'I could never be bored with your lovely body,' he told her. 'I've had more pleasure in the time we've been married than in the rest of my life. You make love with such marvellous gusto. But afterwards, every time, I was left with the feeling that I'd been to bed with a whore. Beautiful . . . good at her job . . . but with no more feeling for me than a very expensive, very expert call-girl.'

'Darling! How horrible for you! And all the time you thought that, my heart was *bursting* with love. Sometimes I could scarcely bear it . . . to kiss you, to hold you, but never to *tell* you "I love you". It was so hard not to say "darling" except when we were downstairs, pretending to be a normal couple.'

'You acted the part so well when we were with other people. You'd look at me with soft eyes and a lovely tender sort of smile; but when we were up here, alone, your manner would change completely. You were always cooler . . . more distant . . . keeping me at arm's length.'

'Oh I let you come closer than that,' she said, with a glimmer of a smile.

'You were never unwilling to make love, or – as it appeared – to have sex. I could always excite you,' he agreed. 'But that wasn't much satisfaction except on a purely physical level. I should have known what had hit me when I couldn't wait to get back here after the trip. I found half a dozen reasons for it not being as enjoyable as usual . . . none of them the real one . . . that I missed you.'

'Not nearly as much as I missed you,' she told him, her eyes glowing with happiness. 'What a fool I was not to tell you as soon as you got back, or while we were in Spain. I was so envious of your mother and Piers being openly in love.'

MARCH

By the time they left Spain, Pen and Piers had set in train the first stage of the renovations to Las Golondrinas. They had chosen this name for the farm because of the many swallows' nests built under the eaves of the outbuildings and along the great beams supporting the roof of the seven-arched *naya*.

Tom and Marguerite Kilmartin were among the few people they were inviting to their wedding. Having met North and Jane, the Kilmartins were now privy to Pen's correct style for the short time remaining before she ceased to be a peeress and became Mrs Piers Ashford, a status she knew she would find much more to her liking than her years as the Countess of Carlyon.

'I think we should also invite Helen Wimborne and her husband. Without your friendship with Tom and my school friendship with her, we should never have met at the Boltons' party,' said Pen, when they were discussing the wedding. 'And there's one other person I feel has a right to be there – if she would like to come.'

'Who is that?'

'General Pembroke's sister. But for her you wouldn't have answered our advertisement. I'd never have known you existed. I should have ended my days a weather-beaten old woman who had never had a lover.'

'And I a lonely old bore, harping back to his military career instead of looking ahead and planning the future,' said Piers. 'I don't know about Iris Pembroke. She lives in a village in Italy, has done for years, and she might not want to make the journey. But I'll certainly write and suggest it.'

'I didn't realize she was a spinster.'

'She isn't. Her husband was killed in World War Two. She'd already made her name as an artist and she chose to keep it up, much to her brother's disapproval. I rather fancy she and Allegra would find themselves kindred spirits in spite of the age gap. Miss Pembroke was ahead of her time in her attitudes. In her late thirties she had a child by an Italian whom she liked but didn't wish to marry. Her brother knew nothing about it. She told me after he died. She knew he could never have understood how she could have done such a thing. I think she thought I wouldn't either but was less likely to have apoplexy.'

Two hours before dinner, on the eve of the wedding, Miss Iris Pembroke arrived, driven to Longwarden by Piers who had met her flight at Heathrow.

Miss Pembroke was seventy-five but seemed not to belong to that or any other generation. Clearly she dressed, as Allegra did, in whatever clothes took her fancy, regardless of fashion or any other rules of dress.

The weather continued cold and she had travelled in a prune velvet cloak with a sable lining and a large sable hat which covered her forehead. Her small pointed face and sharp inquisitive eyes made Pen think of a Beatrix Potter mouse.

Having shed her luxurious outer garments, their guest revealed herself as a woman with curly white hair, which she deftly restored to the shape of a dandelion clock, and a slim and still supple figure clad in a brick-pink Breton fisherman's slop caught in at the waist by a belt of Indian silver chains with a large flashing rhinestone brooch pinned in the middle of her bosom. Under the slop was a silk shirt with clean but frayed cuffs, and a scarf of thin silk was wrapped round her neck like a hunting stock. Her lower limbs were concealed by a pair of very full trousers (which North said later were Moroccan) which billowed to below her knees where they met her soft leather boots.

When, after the introductions, Pen suggested she might like to rest in her room, Miss Pembroke said firmly, 'No, thank you. I never rest. I may soon be doing nothing else.

It will take me precisely half an hour to unpack and dress for dinner. What I should like at the moment is a small measure of brandy in a glass of hot water with two or three cloves, if you have them. Piers, would you bring the box, please? It contains my wedding present.'

She turned to Pen. 'If you don't like it, please be frank and I'll suggest other things which may suit you better. I don't buy presents any more. All my life I've been a great collector. A magpie, my brother called me. Now I'm giving my treasures away to save my executors the job after I'm dead. Not that I expect to die for many years yet. If I run true to family form, I should last till nearly ninety, by which time my house will be bare of all but necessities and I shall have had the pleasure of seeing my possessions disposed among people who will appreciate them. A sensible plan, don't you think?'

'Very sensible,' Pen agreed, beginning to warm even more towards this eccentric woman.

Miss Pembroke's present was a set of vermilion lacquer dishes with matching soup bowls. The dishes were plain but the bowls were hand-painted with delicate brush strokes of gold representing leaves of bamboo.

'They are beautiful . . . thank you,' said Pen, holding a dish as light as the pad of a waterlily, with the deep glowing sheen of many, many layers of lacquer.

'I found them in the Marché aux Puces on my first visit to Paris after the war,' said their donor. 'I've been told by an authority on oriental applied arts that they are of very fine workmanship.'

Later, when Iris Pembroke had gone up to change, Pen arranged the red dishes in the room where the other presents were on show. Her first wedding had been an ostentatious occasion directed by her mother with little regard for Pen's wishes. This time she was the arbiter and her decision to display the few presents they had received was to give pleasure to the cleaners and her two older gardeners, all of whom would be present in the chapel tomorrow and who had clubbed together to buy her, on Jane's advice, various household linens.

Pen slept alone as she had every night since returning to Longwarden. She and Piers had come back to find that Jane had already engaged a temporary replacement for him, and Piers's belongings had been moved to one of the visitors' rooms. It would not have been difficult for him to make his way to Pen's room, unbeknown to the rest of the household.

However, eager as they were to be together all the time, they had decided to wait until they were married before spending their nights together.

Inevitably, as she lay in bed on the night before her second marriage, Pen remembered how she had felt in the last hours before her first marriage.

Panic-stricken, she recalled. Racked by eleventh-hour doubts that she was doing the right thing, but equally frightened of the scandal and fuss if she backed out at the last moment.

How different were her feelings now. Not even the tiniest doubt flawed her certainty of the richly fulfilled life ahead of her.

In her room at the end of the corridor, Iris Pembroke was also remembering a wedding far in the past.

Forty-four years ago, in wartime London, she had married one of her brother's junior officers and had been his wife for eight months before he had been killed in action.

Most people, knowing the bare fact, would conclude it had been a tragedy which must have blighted her life. It had been tragic for his parents. They had never recovered from the news of his death. But Iris herself had recognized that a marriage based on physical passion and the urgency of the times must have ended, like so many other war marriages, in the divorce courts.

She had never married again although she had had several lovers including the father of her son. She had known that, for her, happiness lay in independence. If the price of independence was sometimes to be lonely, she must pay it.

As her life had turned out, she hadn't been lonely often. Her work had been her companion; and the thoughts of the world's great writers, on which she could call at any time, had enriched her mind more than the conversation at dinner parties from which, as an unattached woman, she had been excluded.

At the one which had just taken place, by virtue of age and a measure of fame as a painter, she had been placed on the right of Lord Carlyon, a young man of compelling looks and interesting achievements.

She had liked him and found him amusing, but the others had been a dull lot. With the exception of the horsey child who had scarcely opened her mouth all evening, the women had been of a genus very different from Iris's own: women who moulded their lives to a matrix of their husband's choice. She had nothing against them but knew that, in earlier years when she had still been desirable, most had been suspicious of her.

Piers's wife-to-be was a pleasant creature with a redeeming talent for gardening. They seemed destined to be happy.

But it was the red-haired daughter whose book she had read and enjoyed whom Iris had hoped would be present. Strange that she had been missing. When questioned, her brother had said she would be present tomorrow but had offered no explanation for her absence tonight.

Miss Pembroke replaced the spectacles she had removed while she was thinking. The clock on the night table showed it was half-past twelve. She rarely slept before one and then only for a few hours. She needed very little sleep.

She picked up the book she had brought with her, a translation from the Latin of *De Rerum Natura*. She read for some time until she came to a passage which she read twice:

From the heart of the fountain of delight rises a jet of bitterness that tortures us among the very flowers.

She laid the book down on the sheet and looked at her hands, as yet untouched by arthritis but for long the hands of an old woman with prominent veins and liver spots. Sometimes it made her sigh to realize that never again would she go to the fountain of delight, by which he must surely mean love.

Yet it was true now as then, when Lucretius had written his book in the first century before Christ, with love there was always pain, if only the dread of losing it.

Allegra had been unable to face the wedding-eve dinner party and had asked to be excused. She would have liked to go away until the whole thing was over, but she knew it would have hurt her mother, and the letter Pen had written from Spain had been unexpectedly loving and understanding. Allegra felt she owed it to her not to blight her great day by being absent.

Half an hour before the service was due to start, she went to her mother's room to wish her well. Jane was already there in an Anne Klein suit of fine cream wool crêpe with a saucer of black and cream straw tilted over one eyebrow.

'You look marvellous, Mother.' Allegra appraised Pen's wedding dress, her usually critical gaze approving the subtlety of the Missoni knit two-piece inspired by the muted colours of an antique Bargello embroidery. 'Stunning! From Brown's, I presume? Who would have expected to find *you* shopping there?' she added, with a quizzically lifted eyebrow.

'Who indeed?' Pen said, smiling. 'What do you think of my hat?'

She turned to the bed where, on a nest of tissue paper, lay a spiral of velvet matched to the deep plum threads in the silk-knit Italian top and wool-knit skirt of the same pattern. The outfit included a soft bulky mohair jacket.

North came in. 'Time to go down, girls. We mustn't start running behind schedule or Mama and Piers will miss their ferry.'

When his wife and sister had left them, he said, 'We're going to miss you, you know. Very much, Mummy.'

The loving look and the name from his pre-school days, when every week had brought her the obligatory ill-spelt letter beginning *Dearest Mummy* and ending *Lots of love, North*, brought a rush of tears to her eyes.

She blinked them away, exclaiming, 'Don't make me cry, wretched boy. It will ruin my make-up.'

'I expect there'll be lots of wet hankies among the old dears,' he said, meaning the cleaning staff. 'Have you remembered to move your engagement ring over?'

She nodded. Piers had insisted on buying her a beautiful aquamarine ring which was now on her right hand. Her wedding-ring finger was bare. The platinum ring, an empty symbol of eternal love, which Edward had placed there in front of a large congregation in St Margaret's Church, Westminster, and which she had worn for over thirty years until the orange-blossom pattern had worn down to faint indentations, was now in a twist of paper in the waste paper basket. It had no place among her keepsakes.

One of North's first pairs of shoes with a scuffed toe; a chaplet of silk primroses Allegra had worn as the smallest bridesmaid at another fashionable wedding at St Margaret's; these were among her treasures. But Edward had given her nothing, except the wedding ring, which had not been family property. Very soon now she wouldn't even bear his name.

'Look what I found on my breakfast tray this morning,' she said, remembering that North hadn't seen, as Jane had, the exquisitely simple Jean Lassale crystal-faced watch which had been Piers's wedding present to her.

Near the entrance to the chapel, her son offered her his arm and Pen slowed her eager pace. Ahead of her, through the tall double doorway, she could see the great marble altar-piece framing a painting of the Holy Family by Murillo. Normally covered in Victorian crimson velvet, today the altar had on a beautiful modern cloth commissioned by Flora Carlyon and worked by members of The Embroiderers' Guild in gold kid and winking beads on specially woven white tweed.

To the right of the altar stood Piers with his best man, Tom. To the left Sarah waited to take Pen's small suede clutch bag with a bunch of violets attached to it.

At a signal from someone who could see them approaching, the village church organist, up in the chapel's organ gallery, began to play louder chords. In the pews flanking the aisle which was normally bare but today was spread with a long Persian runner, heads turned to see them coming.

As they approached between the open doors, Pen's nose caught the first whiff of the chapel's distinctive odour of cedar wainscoting, this morning mixed with the fresh scents of flowers and greenery.

In the back rows she saw the white head and the bald one of her two faithful henchmen. Nearer the front an eye-stopping gold lamé turban made her wonder for a second where the small maharajah had come from until she realized the head was Miss Pembroke's.

At the step dividing the chancel from the main part of the chapel, where the vicar was waiting, North stepped aside. She gave her bag to her niece who was looking, she noticed, uncharacteristically pale and nervous.

Pen smiled at her and then, more radiantly, at Piers. In an involuntary gesture of love and happiness, they reached for each other's hands.

As the organ stopped playing, from somewhere behind came a loud sniff.

The vicar began the preamble. '*Dearly beloved . . .*'

It had been arranged that as they would be deprived of the usual moments of privacy in the car from church to reception, the bride and groom should have ten minutes' respite in a small room near the State Dining Room.

The first few minutes were spent in each other's arms, after which they noticed that someone had thoughtfully provided a bottle of champagne on ice.

'Musn't have too much of this. I don't want to start our honeymoon by being breathalysed,' said Piers, as he filled the glasses.

Their time alone was almost up when North came in, looking rather less cheerful than the occasion warranted.

'The press have got wind of it, blast them. Flitton has

719

just taken a call from the *Sun*. They wanted to speak to me but he told them I wasn't available and wouldn't be drawn into answering their questions himself. "I am not empowered to answer inquiries about my employer and his family, sir," was what he told them. He seems a reliable chap – almost as good as our last butler,' North added, grinning suddenly before his expression reverted to one of annoyance.

'Thank you, m'Lord,' Piers replied, with a straight face. 'I take it that if my wife and I should fall on hard times and be forced to seek a position as a butler and gardener, you will furnish us with a good reference.'

This made North grin again. Then he glanced at his watch. 'You have half an hour to circulate before we sit down to lunch. I have a nasty suspicion that if there's been a leak to the press, there'll be photographers waiting to snap you on your way out. Probably not only at the main gates but at all of them. How the devil to elude them is beyond me at the moment, but perhaps your military mind will conceive a strategy, Piers.'

'Does it matter if they do catch a glimpse of us as we drive past?' asked Pen, too happy to care if the tabloids did make a nine days' wonder of their marriage.

'It will be more than a glimpse,' North told her dryly. 'Press photographers and photojournalists are ruthless in getting the pictures editors want. They know you won't risk running them down and they'll swarm round the car and take close-ups. The fact that it isn't a mésalliance probably spoils the story from their point of view. But if there happens to be a shortage of sensation this week, they can work up something pretty juicy. They needn't stick to the facts, you know,' he added sardonically, as he opened the connecting door for her to pass through and mingle with the wedding guests.

A few minutes before North was due to ask everyone to take their places at the table, Pen saw him listening intently to something being told him by Piers. As she watched them, both men put their heads back and roared with laughter. Next she saw North beckon Flitton and speak to him confidentially. The new butler – it seemed likely that he would become a permanency – listened and nodded and also showed signs of being amused, although less openly.

What were they plotting, she wondered. Obviously something to do with evading the press.

In order for Pen to have her gardeners on either side of her during luncheon, Jane's table-plan placed bride and groom opposite each other at the centre point of the long table.

It was she, with her inborn skill at getting on with people and knowing how to put them at ease, who had known, without Pen's advice, that the two old countrymen and some of the other helpers would enjoy a meal at the table more than eating and drinking standing up.

On Piers's right and left she had placed Mrs Armitage and Mrs Bailey, the senior cleaner. The rest of the family and their guests from away were spread out among the guests from the village. The luncheon itself had been provided by Party Planners and was being served by some of the outside staff who had first come to Longwarden for the dance.

Chatting to Mr Hazell and Mr Craskett while Piers conversed with the women on either side of him gave Pen little opportunity to satisfy her curiosity about the discreet conference before lunch.

At last she had the chance to lean towards him and ask, 'Why were you and North laughing just before we sat down?'

'I can't explain now but North will, after the toasts.' His dark eyes gleamed with amusement. 'We've cooked up a scheme which I think will prove rather fun.'

With that she had to be content.

'Ladies and gentlemen . . .'

North's height and presence and his resonant voice hushed the babble of voices and made all eyes turn towards him.

'Before I ask you to drink to the health and happiness of the bride and groom, I should like to express our pleasure at having you here to share the first great event of the year at Longwarden. I have reason to believe there may be other memorable celebrations here before the year ends, but none more pleasing to us all than the marriage of my mother who, I think, is quite unaware of how warmly she is regarded by everyone who knows her.'

At this point, to Pen's confusion, there was an outbreak of clapping and murmurs of 'Hear, hear'.

'I'll second that, m'Lord,' Mr Craskett called out.

Not wishing to be outdone, but being shyer than his colleague, Mr Hazell said quietly, 'And I.'

Blushing and smiling, Pen gave each one a hand and, squeezing their rough, calloused fingers and speaking to both, murmured, 'Thank you, my dear friends.'

It was an emotional moment which, while North went on speaking, caused both the old men to fumble for large cotton handkerchiefs and mop a few tears under cover of blowing their noses.

Pen's eyes were bright and her lips quivered for a few moments as North continued, 'In her thirty-odd years at Longwarden, my mother, aided by the two redoubtable helpers who are sitting beside her today, has brought the gardens to a peak of perfection. They are not, like some English gardens, at their best only in summer. Here, thanks to skilful planting, there are things to admire all year round and no season when a walk round the house fails to please the eye and refresh the spirit. That is a singular achievement, particularly when one considers that in my great-grandfather's time the head gardener then, Mr Edgefield, had no fewer than fourteen assistants as well as half a dozen gardeners' boys. All of them working for much longer hours than most people do today.'

Anticipating the murmurs this last remark would call forth, he paused.

'However, as most of you know, my mother is one of the exceptions. She has worked, winter and summer, for hours which our trade union leaders would deplore as sweated labour. As also have Mr Craskett and Mr Hazell, both of whom are officially retired. All three work from choice rather than necessity. It is a labour of love which has kept them hard at it at weekends and on evenings when the rest of us have been relaxing.'

Again he paused, his vivid gaze sweeping his audience before he went on, 'The history of this old house is full of interesting episodes and fluctuations of fortune. Most of us here knew, before my sister's book was published, the romantic story of my great-grandfather's journey to China and how he brought back, as his bride, a beautiful half-Chinese girl whose English grandparents had been in service as a gamekeeper and cook. I believe future generations will consider it equally romantic that the man we now know as Colonel Ashford came to Longwarden to perform the duties of a butler – which he did most efficiently – and met and married my mother who has been, in effect, the head gardener.'

At this there was some more clapping and everyone turned to smile and nod at the bridal couple.

'Unfortunately,' North went on, 'this has already attracted the attention of the press. A few minutes ago I was told that several photographers are waiting to take pictures of them as they leave; and the local police have already been called in to deal with a trespassing journalist who, if he hadn't been intercepted, would by now have been peering at us through the windows.'

'Disgraceful!' said Mr Wimborne, and others agreed.

'I was at a loss to see how to deal with this nuisance,' said North. 'However his tactical training has enabled my stepfather to come up with an imaginative scheme to outwit these intruders on a private occasion. We shall need the help of several of you to put it into action and I'll leave him to explain his plan in a moment. My enjoyable duty now is to ask you to join in a toast to two people who will be greatly missed but who leave with our warmest wishes for their new life together in Spain.'

While North had been finishing his speech, a soft-footed, unobtrusive waiter had been quietly going round the table, replenishing everyone's glass. Now, as chairs were pushed back and the rest of the company stood up, Piers and Pen remained seated, gazing at each other across the table.

When the toast had been drunk and he rose to reply, she felt a glow of pride at his distinguished appearance in a lounge suit of fine grey worsted, with a white carnation in the button-hole.

'My Lord' – there was a twinkle in Piers's eyes as he bowed to his stepson – 'Lady Carlyon, ladies and gentlemen, my wife and I thank you for your good wishes. Although we are both in those rather dull-sounding years known as middle age, I feel sure no young couple could be happier or more excited at the prospect of setting up house together than we are today. We are grateful to my wife's son and daughter-in-law for giving this delightful wedding party for us, and we thank you all for your presents. For the time being, they will remain in safe-keeping here until our farmhouse is ready for occupation. It will then give us very great pleasure to send for your generous gifts and to think of you when we use them. I will only add that my wife's "green fingers" won't be idle in Spain. However her garden there will be very much smaller, which makes me hopeful that she will spend as much time with me as with her beloved plants.'

To laughter and applause he sat down, and Tom rose to speak.

'Ladies and gentlemen, it's time for the bride and groom to cut the cake, after which he will brief us on his plan of campaign. Having served under him for many years, and been involved in a number of hazardous enterprises of his devising, perhaps I should warn you to think twice before volunteering for whatever he has in mind now. But I must say that, although his strategies sometimes seemed to have little chance of coming off, in practice they always did. Like you, I'm extremely curious to hear his latest plan.'

Outside Longwarden's main gates which, during World War Two, had been saved from being melted down for shell and bomb casings because they were masterpieces of craftsmanship by a famous French ironsmith, Tijou, the men from the tabloids smoked, picked their teeth and gossiped.

'Don't think we're going to get much out of this, Terry,' said one photographer to another. 'This old bird, Lord Carlyon's mum, hasn't been in the news since she married his dad, donkey's years ago. Okay, she's been having it off with the butler and now they're making it legal. So what? I don't reckon it's much of a story.'

Terry shrugged. 'I don't either, mate. But short of a bombing, a murder or the rape of an eighty-year-old, it's the best there is. And she is Sarah Lomax's aunt and the mother of that red-haired bitch who was shacked up with – Hello, hello, that hatchet-faced bloke from the lodge is coming out. Maybe he's had the word to open the gates. This could be it, lads.'

At half-past two, as Ted Rivington opened the main gates and the photographers readied themselves, the other gate into the park was also being opened. There, at the east gate, one staff photographer and a couple of freelances were backing their hunch that the former Countess would attempt to leave unobserved by what had once been the tradesmen's entrance to the estate.

There was no possibility of her leaving by the north gate. It had been unused for so long that a large bed of waist-high nettles had grown up around it and only faint traces remained to show there had once been a carriageway from it to the house.

Soon after Rivington, ignoring the waiting men, had pulled back the heavy main gates, a car appeared in the distance. It was the Wimbornes' Rover with a bunch of shiny silver balloons dancing in the air behind it. As it came near them, the newsmen saw it was being driven by a man with white hair. The woman beside him was wearing a gold turban and a garment with a fur collar. The man at the wheel and his companion maintained gracious smiles while the men from the press clustered round their vehicle. But they ignored demands for them to wind down the windows and the car crawled steadily forward until it reached the public road and the driver tooted his horn before increasing speed.

'That wasn't the Countess. She was too old,' said one

photographer, watching them drive away. 'If you ask me those two were decoys.' He went over to Rivington who was standing with folded arms, watching their activities. 'You must know her by sight. Was that her? It wasn't, was it?' Receiving no reply, he said, 'Have a few jars on us in the pub tonight,' and offered him a fiver.

Rivington looked at the note and the man with silent contempt and crossed the drive to resume his stance on the other side.

The photographer glowered at his back and muttered, 'Up yours, Jack.'

A moment later another car came into view.

Outside the east gate, Major Kilmartin was driving away in the organist's car. He was accompanied by one of the cleaning staff wearing a pale blue outfit and the model hat she had bought for her daughter's wedding the summer before. On the seat behind them were two empty suitcases and an old shoe was tied to the back bumper.

'They took pictures of us?' she said. 'Do you think they were fooled?'

The second car to leave by the main gate was Pen's, with Sammy O'Brien at the wheel and Helen Wimborne in the passenger seat.

They were followed, after an interval, by the vicar, no longer wearing his dog-collar, with Mrs Kilmartin.

By this time the Wimbornes' Rover had re-entered the grounds by the east gate, having stopped briefly en route for Miss Pembroke to move to the back seat and Jack Wimborne, by changing his tie and putting on a peaked cap which Jane had remembered seeing in the attics and fetched for him, to appear to be her driver.

'Let us hope we added to their confusion,' said Miss Pembroke, after bowing benignly to the press who had no sooner taken pictures of the first bridal car to leave than another had appeared with a second cleaner in her best hat sitting beside the handyman.

* * *

By the time the caterers' van came down the drive to the main gate, it wasn't necessary for the driver to slow down, lean out of his window and say kindly, 'You're having your legs pulled, mates. If you're waiting for the 'appy couple, you'll be 'ere a long time. They're spending their 'oneymoon 'ere. Straight up. You won't see 'ide nor 'air of 'em for a week or more. I been told by the cook.'

With a sympathetic chuckle at their expressions, he drove on, soon to be followed by a clergyman who peered at them over the tops of his spectacles as he drove past and turned in the opposite direction from that taken by the van.

It was early evening when a British car, which half an hour earlier had been crossing the Channel, swung into the courtyard at the side of the Grand Hotel Clement in a small town near the French coast.

Piers Ashford and his wife unclipped their seat-belts. While he got out, she leaned over the back of the seat to pick up her hat and the plastic bag containing the clerical collar he had worn until they reached Dover.

There hadn't been time to post it back to the vicar before boarding the hovercraft which had brought them to Calais. That would have to be done here in Ardres tomorrow morning, before they set out on the second stage of a leisurely journey to Spain by way of quiet roads and small family-run hotels such as the one where they were about to spend their wedding night.

The Hotel Clement, which had been in the hands of one family since World War One had been recommended by the Wimbornes as a haven of typical old-fashioned French comfort in a quiet and picturesque town. They had often made it their final stopping place when motoring home from Sant Jeroni, and its nearness to Calais had made it ideal as the Ashfords' first stop on the journey south.

The room to which they were shown was at the front of the building, with red velvet curtains and white muslin veiling views of the square which the hotel faced. The double bed Piers had asked for was a high one with carved head- and foot-boards. A sprigged pink paper covered the walls, the dressing table had a top of salami-coloured marble and the gilt wall-lights took the form of bunches of roses. A table flanked by two chairs stood between the windows and a *belle époque* chair, upholstered in red velvet, stood near the *armoire*.

When Pen opened this to hang up her jacket, she found it contained two large square-shaped pillows in fresh cotton cases.

'There's nothing old-fashioned about the bathroom,' said Piers, after looking in it. 'Would you like a bath before dinner, darling?'

She nodded. 'But first I should telephone North and tell him it all went swimmingly. Would you get through for me, Piers, while I unpack my washing things?'

A few minutes later, from the bathroom, she heard him speaking to her son. She returned to the bedroom and perched on the high bed beside him as he said, 'We only arrived a few minutes ago. Yes, a very smooth crossing, thanks. Here's your mother. I'll leave her to tell you about it.'

He handed over the receiver and put his arm round her waist.

'Hello, North. Have the Wimbornes gone home? Not yet? Then you can tell them how much we like their hotel. Yes, it all went like clockwork. As soon as the van driver was certain he wasn't being followed, he let me out of the back and I sat with him until we arrived at the café he had suggested as a rendezvous. We had about ten minutes to wait – just time for a cup of tea – before "Canon" Ashford turned up. I think a dog-collar suits him. It was very sporting of the vicar to lend him the disguise. I thought he might be a spoil-sport but he didn't mind at all, did he? What happened at your end after we had got away?'

While she was listening to North's answer, Piers took her free hand, the third finger encircled now by the classic gold band they had both preferred to any more decorative designs. He pressed his lips to her palm.

Pen was silent a few minutes longer. Then she said, 'Do give them our warmest thanks, won't you? I musn't go on talking now. We both want a bath before dinner and it's an hour later here. Give everyone our love, especially my dear Jane. *Au revoir, mon fils.*'

She rang off and leaned against Piers. 'I was once told I had a good accent. The trouble is I've forgotten almost all the French I once knew. Perhaps it will gradually come back as we wend our way south. I do remember a few words. *Je t'aime . . . mon amour.*'

'When did you learn that? In extra coaching with the French master?'

She laughed. 'No Frenchman under eighty would have been allowed near us.'

He was undoing the silk-covered buttons which fastened her top. She began to loosen his tie.

Looking into his eyes, she said softly, 'It's taken an awfully long time for my dreams of love to come true.'

Sarah tapped on Allegra's door. After a pause, she heard her cousin say, 'Come in.'

Allegra was sitting at the writing table, facing the door, with her typewriter in front of her. Her elbows were on the table, her hands clasped under her chin.

'Am I disturbing you?'

Allegra shook her head. 'I wasn't writing . . . just thinking.' Her tone was listless.

When she rose, leaving the table and crossing the room to the sofa, she moved as if it were an effort to stand up, to walk. The swift step, the restless energy which had been characteristic of her had gone.

She had picked up an empty glass from beside the typewriter. As Sarah stood hesitating close to the door, her cousin refilled the glass from a bottle on the table by the sofa.

'Would you like a drink?' she asked.

There were bottles of tonic and bitter lemon on the table, and an ice tub.

729

'No, thanks.'

Allegra had poured out a good three inches of gin. She dropped in a cube of ice but she didn't top up the glass from one of the smaller bottles.

'Well, come in if you're coming,' she said, with a touch of impatience.

The sharp tone almost made Sarah change her mind. Perhaps it had been a bad idea to confide in her cousin, but who else was there? She couldn't talk to Kate Hastings and Jane, if she knew, would be sure to tell North who would instantly hit the roof – especially when he found out that Nick's promised letter had never come. Sarah had heard nothing from him since the telephone call taken by Piers.

Allegra looked across the room, belatedly realizing that the younger girl looked pinched and worried. 'Did I snap? Didn't mean to. Sorry.' She sat down at one end of the sofa and beckoned, her manner more encouraging.

Impelled by the need to tell someone, Sarah obeyed the gesture. As she sat down, she said, 'I – I don't want to be a nuisance but I need some advice. There's no one else I can ask.'

'I don't know that I'm much of an oracle.' Allegra swirled the gin and the ice cube. 'What's the problem?'

As her cousin raised the glass to her lips, Sarah said baldly, 'I think I'm pregnant.'

In the silence of the first-floor room at the Hotel Clement, the sudden ringing of the bedside telephone jerked Pen out of a deep sleep. Momentarily disoriented, she couldn't think where she was or even what the noise was.

Piers's reactions were quicker but he answered the call with an English 'Hello?' rather than a French one.

As he spoke, it flashed through her mind that it had to be a call from Longwarden, and who there would call them tonight except in an emergency?

Oh, God, not Jane's baby! she prayed, remembering how her daughter-in-law had gone rushing up to the attics to find the chauffeur's hat for John.

An icy fear clenched Pen's insides. She would never forgive herself if the excitements of her wedding day had caused Jane to lose the child she wanted so much.

Piers switched on the light. 'Yes, Madame. Thank you. We'll come down at once.' He replaced the receiver. 'That was the proprietress reminding us that we said we wanted dinner.' He looked at his watch. 'We have half an hour before they take the last orders.'

She gave a soft groan of relief. 'I thought something awful had happened.'

'If we don't get a move on, something awful will happen. We shall go without an excellent dinner.' He had already sprung from the bed and begun to dress. 'If Madame hadn't rung up, we should probably have gone on sleeping until the small hours and woken up famished. I should have set the alarm on my watch but you put all practical thoughts out of my head. Come on, darling, up you get. Wimborne tells me the cheese board here is the finest he's ever come across. We don't want to miss it.'

Hurriedly, still feeling dopey from the abrupt awakening, Pen retrieved the expensive pale-grey suspender tights Jane had seen in Simpson's Christmas catalogue and bought, with ivory silk-satin and écru lace cami-knickers, for Pen's trousseau.

Presently, in the hotel dining room, a mouthful of wine, a piece of light crusty bread and the first spoonful from a small earthenware pot filled with tiny hot mushrooms in a buttery dressing restored her equilibrium.

She didn't tell Piers about the reason for her panic, the more piercing because she herself had lost babies.

After the mushrooms they had rabbit with prunes. Then the cheese trolley arrived, living up to John Wimborne's claims for it. Not only the local cheese from the three little Norman towns of Camembert, Pont-l'Évêque and Livarot, but cheeses from far parts of France; the pear-shaped Auvergne farmhouse cheese tinged with pink garlic called Gaperon, the creamy blue-veined ewe's-milk cheese matured in the caves at Roquefort, and about fifteen others, all in perfect condition.

Finally, when it seemed the attentive waiter would be disappointed if they didn't, they both had a slice of French apple tart with fresh cream, followed by coffee with the golden liqueur of Normandy, Bénédictine.

'After this we must stretch our legs,' she said. 'If we eat like this every night, all the way through France, I shall need a new trousseau by the time we reach Spain. My waistband feels quite tight already.'

'If you do put on a few pounds you'll soon work it off in the garden at Las Golondrinas. But yes, I agree, a stroll round the town would be good for us. I'll go up and get your jacket.'

Although it had modern outskirts, the heart of the town was old, with a large space which looked like a marketplace, surrounded by ancient buildings, as well as the smaller *place* in front of the hotel.

They walked arm in arm, with interlaced fingers, not talking now as they had during dinner but knowing their thoughts were in harmony. She felt that perhaps for both of them the joy of this close companionship was enhanced by their knowledge of loneliness.

Although her life had not been without some sensual pleasures – music, the scent of flowers, the beautiful paintings and objects to be seen in every room at Longwarden and the equally beautiful views to be seen from its windows – it had never included any of the heavenly sensations she had enjoyed in the high carved fruitwood bed a few hours earlier.

How had she lived without them; without this strong, gentle man in whose arms, each time, she learned more of tenderness and passion?

She looked up as he looked down.

'Shall we go back?' He pressed her arm to his side.

'Yes, let's.'

The red velvet curtains had been drawn and the bed turned down on both sides when they re-entered their room. It had a snug, homely air. The big solid bed, built to last generations, seemed to welcome them back.

Piers closed the door and turned the key. As she unfastened her coat, he turned her to face him. His fingers were cold from the night air as he tilted her face up to his, but his mouth was warm on her lips.

AUTHOR'S NOTE

The Individual Gold Medal at the European Championships at Burghley in 1985 was won by Priceless ridden by Virginia Holgate.

Bestselling Women's Fiction

☐ A Better World Than This	Marie Joseph	£2.95
☐ The Stationmaster's Daughter	Pamela Oldfield	£2.95
☐ The Lilac Bus	Maeve Binchy	£2.50
☐ The Golden Urchin	Madeleine Brent	£2.95
☐ The Temptress	Jude Deveraux	£2.95
☐ The Sisters	Pat Booth	£3.50
☐ Erin's Child	Sheelagh Kelly	£3.99
☐ The Ladies of Missalonghi	Colleen McCullough	£2.50
☐ Seven Dials	Claire Rayner	£2.50
☐ The Indiscretion	Diana Stainforth	£3.50
☐ Satisfaction	Rae Lawrence	£3.50

Prices and other details are liable to change

ARROW BOOKS, BOOKSERVICE BY POST, PO BOX 29, DOUGLAS, ISLE OF MAN, BRITISH ISLES

NAME. . . . .

ADDRESS . . . .

. . . .

. . . .

Please enclose a cheque or postal order made out to Arrow Books Ltd. for the amount due and allow the following for postage and packing.

U.K. CUSTOMERS: Please allow 22p per book to a maximum of £3.00.

B.F.P.O. & EIRE: Please allow 22p per book to a maximum of £3.00

OVERSEAS CUSTOMERS: Please allow 22p per book.

Whilst every effort is made to keep prices low it is sometimes necessary to increase cover prices at short notice. Arrow Books reserve the right to show new retail prices on covers which may differ from those previously advertised in the text or elsewhere.